# PARRICIDE

# PARRICIDE

*The second installment of the misdemeanours
of Dr Felix Culpepper*

## Richard Major

IndieBooks

*Parricide:*
*The second installment of the misdemeanours of Dr Felix Culpepper*

*By Richard Major*

*Map by Alick Newman*


*Published by IndieBooks London*

*www.indiebooks.co.uk*


*Set in Minion Pro 12/14*

*Printed by Printondemand-worldwide, Peterborough*
*ISBN: 978-1-908041-63-0*

*© Richard Major 2019*

*For Mary and Geoff,*
*for Josie, Ella and Dylan,*
in loving memory of our time in Andalusia,
where we saw
the mystery of the bulls.

*"Strength" Gallo said. "What do I want with strength, man?*
*The bull weighs half a ton. Let the bull have the strength."*

# THE COLLEGE OF THE BLESSED SAINT WYGEFORTIS IN CAMBRIDGE
## FOUNDED A.D. 1513 BY ADAM WORTHYAL LORD BISHOP OF ST ASAPH

1. Allegorical Fountain
2. Tower of Lethe
3. Erebus
4. Kitchens
5. Senior Combination Room
6. Lodge
7. Antechapel
8. Tower of Acheron
9. Cocytus Court
10. Temple of Priapus

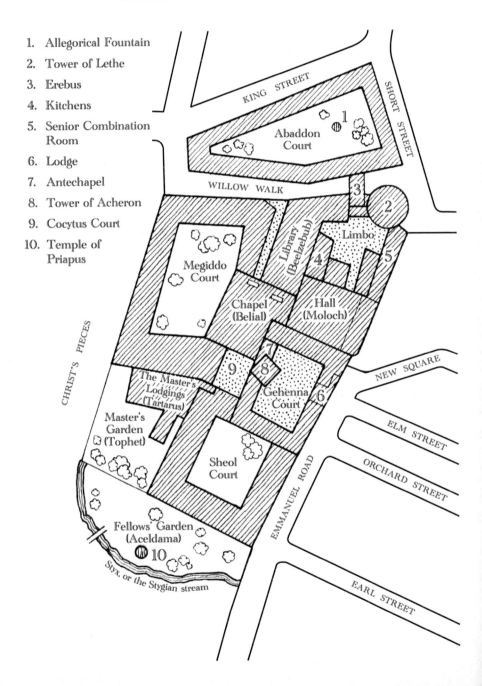

# Contents

# *Prologue:*
# The Grand Orrery

Fireworks. They started going off the moment natural light was doused.

Tonight I came to bed too early. Hours later I'm still sleepless. I lie here with curtains open, staring up into nested infinities.

The sky's unusually black. A disgusting wisp of moon, a waxing crescent, barely visible against pale green effluent, vanished – a suicide-pill three-quarters-dissolved in chartreuese, that was it – vanished at tea-time. Sunset was, as usual, a nothing. But for once our massive sodden solid despair-making East Anglian clouds, their bottoms dimly polluted at night by human lighting, have blown away. My bedroom's as black as (they used to say) a coal-cellar. As black as the obliterating place into which, if I'm lucky, my self-important ideas will shortly, please, be sucked.

Anyway it's as black as the sky, which is black as my room except that it's pierced with so many million stars – pierced with silver stars and also, intermittently, splashed about with ferocious unpredictable colours. Not supernovas. Tonight's Guy Fawkes: the fifth of November in the year of grace (not that it shows) two thousand and thirteen.

Think, man! Think yourself to sleep.

Think of what?

Out there, forty-seven thousand million light-years off, lie the ramparts of the visible universe but *pah!* we're not visiting provincial regions toward the frontier, where there's nothing but tumbling rock, and fire, and grit whistling through void. The nucleus is here, rainy earth, where creatures think (some of us, after a fashion), and invent stories bigger than the universe.

The centre of the earth's Europe, of Europe England: these facts do not require demonstration. The heart of England is her pair of ancient universities: the essence of the country, the perpetually-renewed seed. Thus (baiting the obvious objection) Cambridge is the core of the core of the core. And St

Wygefortis' – vilest, most lurid and corrupt of Houses, uniquely notorious, wonder and despair of Vice-Chancellors, college *sui generis* – is self-evidently pith of the pith of the pith of the pith.

Nor do we need to look far for the focal figure of St Wygy's. It is Dr Felix Culpepper, Tutor and Fellow in Classics, whose voice we are hearing. I.

Embarrassingly, *my* all-pivotal life has *its* pivot *here*: I mean in my bed. Not for the joyful reasons we might hope. This bed has been a sort of void since the spring, when it was quitted by "Abishag" (as the other undergraduates call her): Lady Margot ffontaines-Laigh, only child of the thirteenth Lord Rievaulx; my student, my creature and until March, as was proper, my mistress. The old-fashioned word was hers. After March, all through Easter Term, Abishag was my opponent and scorned me. Then over the summer she was my, as she would no doubt put it, rival. For the last month, nothing. Term resumed early in October, and for these four weeks she's been neither enemy nor friend. She's smiled politely and avoided my teaching. – Of course she's a second-year Classicist now, and as a species second-years are notoriously superior. But have *I* deserved quite such cool oblivion? Didn't I introduce her, contemptible fresher as she was, to the mysteries? I don't mean poems Greek and Latin (though they're not nothing), I mean my other, fatal arts. To be sure, I've been working those arts with her gone; but how vacant they seem!

Thus I lie here in bed alone, feeling the concentric circles turn about me, out as far as the last queasy quasar.


I'd be less haunted by this sensation if, some years ago, the curator of this university's science museum hadn't taken the glass cover off one their greatest treasures, the Grand Orrery, and let me play with it.

An orrery is (like my bed) a model of the universe. Since the universe can't be modelled, it's really a model of the men who designed or commissioned it. The Grand Orrery in our science museum is a serene toy, perfectly unironic, made in palmy Georgian days of etched brass, crystal, ivory and curiously-wrought enamel. Some happy country gentleman, finishing off the madeira in his library after a serene solitary dinner of many courses, would rise, only a little unsteadily, put down his Horace, blow out all the candles but one, and place that one in the middle of his orrery, representing the sun. Then he'd turn a clockwork key and set his ivory moons and planets circling, casting mathematically-perfect shadows on the panelling of his large secure house, and on the gilded leather of his books.

He cherished his orrery because it was reliable. It reliably flooded his mind with rational thoughts, nicely fuddled by wine; with Deist sentiments, vague from lack of prayer; and no doubt with a certain pleasant political smugness. It was simple enough: he could afford such an instrument while his compliant tenantry, sleeping out in the soft explicable showery English night, could not, and did not want one. (*The very Idea, Sir!*) All revolved about the landowner; *revolution* was something he couldn't conceive, I mean revolution of the sort hatching over the Channel. There'd been a perfectly good revolution in England in his grandfather's day, which had got rid of the divine King and the royalist God. Now the king was a dependable appointee, much like a parson, and every squire was sun of his own estate. (*We enjoy, Sir, the Blessing of a most rational, proper Liberty.*) The blessing! Smiling, he blew out his solitary candle and staggered bedward, in familiar darkness.

I sympathise with that squire, I wish I could be him. But I found, left alone in the museum with his orrery, that I couldn't enjoy it. Making the spheres turn seemed nightmarish. And having played with that toy, I can't get it out of my head. I'm the centre, yes, but of *what*? I've no estates, only a bank account and an uncertain empire over certain undergraduates (none of them of Abishag's calibre), some of whom occasionally help me assassinate. I have my College Fellowship, but my fellow Fellows dread me. Beyond College there's a State of sorts, which sometimes uses, always distrusts me. Beyond England there's God. I'm vexed with Him for creating me; I think I might have been allowed to invent Him.

There's story, of course, the story of me. I can always escape into the contemplation of what I've done, the unfinished narrative of astonishing deeds of which I am the hero. But sometimes even *that* is not quite clear. I feel oddly like a stopgap, antagonist not protagonist, someone's creature. Without Margot the tale of me barely chugs along.

So all-in-all I'm worn. My proper self-delight pales; the sun and other stars spin about me less reliably. The exhausting suspicion that I'm not the centripetal mind, the exhausting conviction that I *am*: these jar on each other, they graunch, the gears seize up. My sanity, always a little fragile, wears away – which is why my bed is the centre of my life, even now I go to it in solitude. It holds the innermost circle within my consciousness, the circle of benevolent *unconsciousness*. Isn't a black hole provided at the centre of every galaxy, preserving hygiene by sucking up the broken fragments of worlds? I go to bed to escape myself.

I came early to bed tonight because it's Guy Fawkes.

Every year our undergraduates (although every year they're explicitly forbidden to do so by the Master) burn a guy in Abaddon Court, beside our huge Allegorical Fountain. It's a very old-fashioned guy rigged out in papal vestments, for St Wygy's is an old-fashioned or irredeemable college. We had a filthy time of things during the wars of religion, perfectly mercenary. We hid priests or betrayed them to the castrating, disembowelling knives, as best suited. Later we helped cut off Puritans' ears, we turned Puritan, we ejected Puritans. We elected and deprived infidel Fellows. Nothing remains to us but an antagonism toward all systems, a wistful prejudice in favour of nihilism. The impulse behind burning the pope is thus mainly fiendish. By tradition the St Wygefortis' guy bears the face, not of the reigning pope, but of the reigning Master.

Sir Trotsky Plantagenet has, without at all deserving it, a very good face: a remote-king-carved-in-marble face, with wavy chestnut hair thicker than mine, squared-off Norman temples, commanding eyes, jaw like a bastion. Everything appropriate to his name and inappropriate to his character. He has a thin skin. He resents the burning of the guy, and every fifth of November is fool enough to collect a posse of porters and intervene, just as festivities are turning riotous. Last year Lint, the Head Porter, ended up in the fountain, with a sprained ankle too; the Master himself vanished, and was discovered at dawn reeling about behind the kitchens, drunk as a judge from cheap whisky poured down his throat, face and boxer-shorts blackened by sooty hands, trousers missing, wobbling head crowned with a half-incinerated tiara.

He was enraged and, once his hangover wore off, vengeful. But the Guy Fawkes tumult can't be prosecuted any more than it can be suppressed. The rioters are always discreetly half-naked and masked, and won't testify against each other the next morning when hauled before the authorities.

Sensible adults like me keep carefully out of the way. We lie low, listening to shrieks and shattering panes over in Abaddon, pretending not to hear. ("An unlicensed party, Master, last night? Surely not. I was at work, I noticed nothing.") It's easy enough to picture our students capering about firelight like so many junior demons. Where's the pleasure in watching *that*? We lie low; we have, up high, the irregular gaudy splendour of fireworks. I lie insomniac, and watch those.

Toward eleven I hear the double-doors of my set open and close, open and close, quietly, quickly, without fuss, as if by one well-used to the manœuvre. There's a peaceful soft tread across my sitting-room. A pause. An encouraging suspiration of heavy cloth, coat sliding to rug, rustling papers. Silk dryly crackling over flesh. Clasps unclasped. The door of my bedroom begins to open.

I'm not sophisticated enough to take these developments calmly.

I have enough self-respect to pretend to be calm.

A figure, somehow deeper black than the pitch-black air, moves across the room and stands over me, silent, between window and bed.

There are so many stars I can make out, as negative space or intensified lightlessness, the shape of a naked woman, motionless. Dimensionless. Immense against the constellations. Pegasus looms over her right shoulder, Cygnus defines her left, Cassiopeia crowns her; the Dolphin shows between her legs. Awe keeps me quiet, unless, of course, it's terror.

Then at once there's a bloom of light far huger than any galactic cluster, blasting a quarter of the vault with garish scarlet and emerald. *Ptttth-wack!* A sky-rocket has exploded over Christ's College. My bedroom's lit with incredible disco-glare –

The flash is gone in an instant. But for that instant it's rendered my bed and my own body solid. It's made three-dimensional the curves of my visitor's bare form. It's given her proportion. I open my arms to her finitude, and she descends. My vacancy is allayed. The orrery spins. The epic resumes.

# VOLUME ONE

"The depth closed me round about,
the weeds were wrapped about my head.
I went down to the bottoms of the mountains;
the earth with her bars was about me for ever."
The Lord spake unto the fish, and it vomited.

JONAH

# I. *Prima Materia, a bedroom interlude*

Now that the incorruption of this most fragrant ambergris should be found in the heart of such decay; is this nothing? Bethink thee of that saying of St. Paul in Corinthians, about corruption and incorruption; how that we are sown in dishonor, but raised in glory. And likewise call to mind that saying of Paracelsus about what it is that maketh the best musk. Also forget not the strange fact that of all things of ill-savor, Cologne-water, in its rudimental manufacturing stages, is the worst.

*Moby-Dick*

A bedtime story, eh? A bedtime story .... What a funny thing to want. Can't you just sigh after we've made love, roll over, sleep? ...

Yes yes I *heard* your sigh, Abishag *mio*. Very nice it was too.

I'm sighing too, you know. Inside. So glad to have things back as they were –

What? Yes yes yes yes, *not* as they were. I understand, you made it clear an hour ago. You're back on your "own terms". Not as my "girl", as my "partner." You are henceforth learning the trade. Exactly. But it is just good to have you back on any terms.

I know I never sound like this. But I mean it. It's been so long since spring. Then over summer – your preposterous commune – *ouch!* Pax! *Pax!* – your *remarkable pagan experiment* at Westley Waterless. Your world-defying experiment. Is that all right? ... Settle.

Then for four weeks you smile from a distance, until – why *tonight?* ... Of course, the fireworks. And the usual *fraças* in Abaddon – were you there?

What did you do to the Master this time? …

*What?*

And him such a freshly-minted convert, too! …. Quite, I realise; but still. Poor Sir Trotsky. And as for Seb – he'll go too far one day. He's already –

No, no, I'm not trying to get out of it. I'm concocting a story in my head. Not making things up, I don't need too, just fixing things together…. Partly about Seb, as it happens. *Not* about you of course, you've been wandering off, far from this bed of mine, in peripheral places. Naturally you've had a dull time of things….

Don't sniff so haughtily. I'm not necessarily bored without you, not always. Exciting things happen even in this bed – ah, *there* was a twitch. A fiery glow in your eye, I should think, if I could see anything. But I don't mean that. Adventure orbits about me *even when I'm lying here alone.*

A story, then, an admonitory story. An infernal tale. Let's begin. Don't interrupt and don't snooze until I tell you you can.

Hwæt!

It was, let me see, mid-July. Almost four months ago. Just after your Westley Waterless escapade. You patronisingly kissed my forehead (ridiculous chit) and took yourself off. And I sank back into my book. My damnable damnable *damnable* book. *Culpepper's Quincentenary History of St Wygefortis' College.* O God O God what weariness. It was done, after a fashion, at the beginning of August. It went off to the publisher and I went off to – well, you'll have heard: British Columbia. My loyal minions will have been gossiping. I might tell you the full story later if you're good. Then to the Congo in late July, as you know. To St Andrew's, to Lundy….

But then – here's the thing – *then* I had to come back. Drag myself to College a whole month before term. My devil-publishers had sent back the proofs. Everything, they said, needed to be twitched. They wanted a better index. They required illustrations. Agony. Oh yes it's getting done – my sitting-room's covered with the galleys, don't dare touch them tomorrow. But I died a little with each footnote. And meanwhile I had to endure the other Fellows in summer mode.

Abishag, my Abishag: you cannot conceive the pure hellishness of College toward the end of Long Vac. All the other colleges surrender themselves to conferences, or summer-schools, or tourists. Only Wygy's bolts its gates. Our porters have orders to repel. No Fellow goes away except, usually, me. The others all stay, getting more and more eccentric, madder and madder and madder, more and more themselves. More what dons would be always if you young ones weren't about during term, inhibiting.

By late summer, when I returned to Cambridge from barbaric places, from the Congo and the Celtic fringe, St Wygy's defied description. To picture it you'd need to be Hieronymus Bosch, I can hardly give you an idea –

Yes, yes, that was a flourish. I *am* about to give you an idea.

Let me see.

The bedders were running a brothel from a van parked in Willow Walk, stocked with elderly pseudo-schoolgirls in rusty gym-slips, who apparently needed to punish and be punished. The van produced a smacking of leather almost industrially regular, perfectly audible here when I opened my windows.

How d'y'think I enjoyed that, eh?

The Bursary had turned into a daytime burlesque, Sir Rory and his little friends from the kick-boxing gym performing an endless transvestite floor-show for each other. Sometimes the party burst forth: there'd be a crocodile of degenerates prancing through empty Courts, the Home Bursar himself all floating scarves and mail-armoured breasts – Joan of Arc attending a *matinée* at the Folies Bergère, perhaps. Then back to their month-long orgy.

Or pseudo-orgy. The Master maintained that Rory & Co. were "humbuggery", the look, the clamour, not the thing itself.

Poor Sir Trotsky. Conversion, sobriety and the long summer between them revealed a jadedness, a world-weary chill in the Master that I didn't much like. I regretted last year's ravening despot.

At least Horse-Faced Nikkie hadn't changed. This summer she was bringing taxi-drivers back to her rooms. Either because she has a genuine taste for taxi-drivers or, as she claimed, just because she's researching her next sociological screed. Apparently the republic of learning cries out for graphs of sexual practice, obscene tables, constructivist analyses, critical *apparatus critici*. Either way there'd be a racket most mornings: Nikkie being beaten up when her guest realised she wasn't go to pay him. Nikkie shrieking for the porters.... A fair pleasant noise to wake up to.

And once I was awake, there was no respite. Constant uproar. I'd lie nearly whimpering, trying to smother consciousness in my pillow. This pillow, yes. Perhaps you detect tooth-marks …? Day and night, hurly-burly. Giddy ecstatic human shrieks of flagellation from the white van. Straightforward wholesome roaring and sea-shanties from the drunks. Howls of vivisection – Dymwood the zoology Fellow had set up an informal lab in his rooms, beyond the ken of University regulation. For the amusement of himself and his graduates.

And from every window open to the mildness of September, solitary refined voices. The simple low ceaseless contented murmur, insidious as wave-fall on a quiet coast, of middle-aged dons talking to their imaginary friends.

But d'y'know what the most typical noise of summertime Wygy's *is*? Not howling. *The tearing of paper.* Bizarrely loud it seems, when it goes on all day. Many Fellows are content to sit about the lawns of Sheol Court and Megiddo, in academic undress, tearing the pages out of books written by rivals....

No, it's not "pathetic." It's trying but – d'y'know what a ribosome is? The teensiest possible biological machine. There are ten million ribosomes in each of our ten trillion cells, and all every one of them does is read without ceasing. Not literature, you understand: *manuals.* The genes send out manuals on how to build proteins, the ribosome reads .... Perhaps ribosomes have holidays, perhaps they're allowed breakdowns. Frolicsome seconds when they rip RNA to molecular shreds. Maybe that's what keeps them going, what lets them endure their unspeakable eternal task –

Anyway, that's how our more pitiful dons manage. Actually, it's nice to see so many academic texts being dealt with. The noise irritates but I'm broad-minded enough to see that it's necessary. Even the Widdler can see that, she abandons her usual protectiveness, she hands over her books by the armful –

What? *Why's* she called the Widdler? I admit it's a puerile nickname, even by donnish ... I've remembered. Long ago she was formally introduced to Governing Body by Dr von Spluffe, who as you knows says *weal, wiolent, Wikings* – she's too proud of her wonderful *englische Sprache* to tolerate correction. So Miss Vydler was announced as 'Mizz Widdler, our new Fellow-Librarian, *ja*'; everyone tittered, the name stuck. Poor woman, poor wild woman. Oh yes, she's wild enough. More interesting than you term-time denizens of Wygy's can know. All the Long Vac this scrawny tapestry-clad spinster gives herself over to ecstasies of self-harm. She's too sensible to kill herself at once. It's a matter of fretting her feet with razors, acid-drips on her knees, grating .... Rapture! Rapture! A thousand times over each summer, Hortense Vydler enjoys the weird joy of the suicide, in attenuated, delicious installments. Only a tiger-hunter knows it, perhaps: a hunter who stalks his prey through tropical mountains for weeks, then one breathless blazing afternoon comes across the brute snoozing behind a rock deep in dense ghastly dark-green fronds, snout slobbered with fresh gore – points his rifle behind the stripy ear, shuts eyes that are rolling back in his head in primal blood-lust, pulls the trigger and barely hears the report explode in his skull for the roar of orgasmic consummated hatred – and when he opens his eyes, wet with tears of joy, finds himself at the mountain-foot, the hunt about to begin. D'y' follow? She's gunman and tiger both, there are no words for the frantic intensity of her baiting of herself ....

You're looking scornful. But haven't you glimpsed the Widdler in the last days of term, metamorphosing from a frissy book-tidier into a bacchante? Haven't you seen her snatch up a catalogue card when she thinks no one's about – wet-lipped, white-eyed, dappled with cold sweat – quiver with the gorgeous horror of the deed – and *plunge it back at random?* No? Well you should be ashamed of your self-absorption. It's fascinating. A few weeks into Vac and she's tripping out of the library with folios piled high, pressing them on startled dons, murmuring 'Rip them! Gnash them, so! Make them *feel* it!' She stands by listening while the precious pages tear, head flung back, palms pressed into the rough stone of the Courts 'til they're raw, eyes rolled inward in a crisis of *abhorrence* ....

Sneer as you like, I admire the book-rippers and their supplier. They're following their own bent. I'm more contemptuous of those who need pharmaceuticals to help them on their way. There's always a steady traffic of *them*, mincing and sidling their way to the Dispensary, where Mrs Oathouse conducts such wild experiments with opiates.

Although if you asked me to pick out the worst of summer .... I'd say Sir Trotsky's piety. Even more gruesome than the general depravity, more wanton. A paradox, d'y'think? Or not.

That curious Abyssinian who claims to be rightful prelate of Gondar, exiled by the Derg? The one who cut such a poor figure in your notorious life-sized chess as your Black Bishop? Him. He turned up again, starving, and Sir Trotsky tried to keep him in a hermitage in the Master's Garden. As one might keep a beetle in a matchbox. Of course it was no good. The Home Bursar's conga-line kept sweeping him up into day-long gorging. He found that truffled *confit* was something he could not resist. Eventually he had to be taken off to a sanatorium with Type II diabetes.

By the time he left, the Abyssinian had thoroughly miffed poor Woolly. No Anglican chaplain can be expected to enjoy the rivalry of a narrow-minded ascetic who's poisoning himself, and as a riposte to the friar he installed bronze prayer-wheels in his antechapel to add to the pandæmonium. To add *greatly* –

It was the chanting that most got into my head. Indeed it's a rule of life (have you noticed?) that the spiritually-inclined make a greater worldly ruckus that their worldly friends. Why is that? Why was the worst commotion over the summer *religious*? Amharicised Latin from behind the Master's Lodge, aggressively loud, curiously nasal. Woolly, aggrieved, spinning his drums and chanting *The jewel is in the lotus, The jewel is in the lotus* at the top of *his* voice. From the summit of Acheron descended endless monotonous grunting in Middle Egyptian –

What? Oh, that was Elmo Yoxley and Olga Freke: do you know 'em? Our Tutor in Berberology? Our Egyptology Junior Research Fellow?

Yes yes, the chubby couple. Shortish. Well, *short* then. But not without a certain wormy charm it's generally thought. Ugly you say; I suppose so. Be reasonable, Abishag. Members of creepy disciplines *have* to go with each other, they repel everyone else. Besides, Freke and Yoxley are so obviously fated. So weirdly alike. Such perfectly matched round heads, little round torsos, legs. Like snowmen. They wear each other's clothes, y'know. Go together to the same hairdresser. They're indistinguishable from behind. They're dreadfully in love with each other, can't bear to be in different rooms, often –

*What?* Yes, their affair's "morbid" – *really*, child. *All* love tends to death. You can be, for all your cleverness, dreadfully young.

Listen. Yoxley and Freke, with all their cooing and finger-holding, accomplish very little during term. But this summer they bestirred themselves. Got their hands on a mummified cat – nicked it, that is to say, from the Fitzwilliam Museum. And set about trying to *resuscitate* it. They named it Shishak, after the first pharaoh of the XXII$^{nd}$ or Berber Dynasty, whose loyal subject the cat had apparently been before it put on immortality –

No, *not* revolting. You can be a very harsh young woman, you realise that? *I* found the whole business with Shishak rather touching.

Morbid? Morbid? *Think.* An obsession with civilisations dead thousands of years before Rome began. Naturally that tends to morbidity. And superstition. How not?

Freke and Yoxley lavished incantations over Shiskak night and day. I don't mean they kept up necromancy up without ceasing. Just that their Vigils and Offices were unpredictable – timed, I understand, to coincide with moonrise over the Pyramid of Cheops. Suddenly we'd hear thumping drums from the top of Acheron. Then the great cry from the Egyptian *Book of the Dead*: "A royal offering to Osiris, Foremost of the Westerners, the Great God of the Necropolis…!" This is the *ka*, you understand, begging Osiris to be spared hell. "Westerners" doesn't mean us, it means those who have passed west into the setting sun. In other words, the Dead.

So perhaps it does mean us.

Anyway, I heard the chant so often it stuck in my head.

All this is what you miss if you're not here with me over summer.

"Suffering," you say? Yes, with me, suffering.

Amidst the noise, all this infernal noise, I was heroically wrestling with my footnotes. Therefore I'm the hero of the story.

But I now introduce the *subject*, Eddie Ebbe. Y'know, the chemistry Fellow downstairs from me. With the face of a particularly mournful pug.

You've heard he's away on sabbatical this term? Well, that's a lie.

He wasn't, to be fair, annoying, or not particularly. Poor man, I suppose that's his epitaph: Not Particularly Annoying. He was here throughout the summer, of course, conducting idiot experiments in his rooms. Not too troubling. An occasional *bang!* If I went downstairs and put my head 'round the door, there'd be a wreckage of crucibles and alembics, crystal aludellums and lead retorts, with Ebbe in the midst, solemnly sponging flecks of blood off his midnight-blue velvet robe, eyes big as a night-creature's behind his protective goggles. But with everything else, what's a chemical or even alchemical explosion now and then?

Nothing lasts. All at once, every year, a fortnight out from term, everyone at St Wygy's remembers that you appalling young people will be coming back.

We'll all be on display!

There's frantic cleaning up. No more of the Oathouse's laudanum cocktails for breakfast. No more septuagenarian odalisques bulging out of hockey-kit. We thrust aside our vices and illicit lore, we try to remember *something* about what we'll soon be teaching. The penitent Widdler, moist about the chops, sets about restocking her shelves, looted by the paper-tearers and by herself.

The most shameless Fellows even pile their desks with academic journals, affecting to have spent the summer as the other dons in the Colleges have. As *I* really had this year, worse luck.

Hypocrisy on this scale is a strain. In the last weeks of Long Vac a new agony, a particular sort of distress, settles on St Wygefortis'. College must must drag itself towards respectability before the porters unbolt its gates, and it rejoins the prim, godly world beyond.

This year, as September faded toward October, the only stragglers were Yoxley and Freke.

At first they had tried to shape up like everyone else. They faced facts: their experiment had failed. The *ka* of their embalmed cat remained in the Underworld. They duly smuggled the mummy back to the Fitzwilliam and set about preparing lectures on dust, Nilotic or Mesopotamian as the case may be.

But almost at once, all over College, people began to hear, or thought they heard, low dry vague scratching at windows. Something unknown was trying to get in. As it might be, a cat.

And perhaps there was a stray moggy about. (No doubt most ghost-stories are just unexplained cat-noises exaggerated into narrative.) More likely there was nothing, and communal hysteria conjured up these vague sounds. After all, most of the Fellowship were "going cold turkey." Or in the grip of *delirium tremens*. Or trying to fit into tweed jackets after a summer of wearing lingerie or bear-suits.

But Freke and Yoxley had no doubts. It was Shishak! Their own sweet Shishak, resurrected after all! They should never have lost heart, they should have reflected – they told us on High Table at lunch, babbling with joy – that these return journeys from the Underworld take time. Billions of miles away in the dismal land of Duat, where the sun retires after sunset, their cat had heard them chanting – awoke at last, better late than never – clawed its way out of its linen wrappings – found itself in the basement of the museum – escaped through a grating – crept through Cambridge – to Wygy's – questing for its masters who had been so dogged in reciting their Coptic spells.

So now their idea was first to domesticate the thing to College life. 'We're going to put out saucers!' cried Olga Freke, 'Of milk,' exclaimed Yoxley, 'everywhere!'

No one answered them. Except where Elmo and Olga's globular heads bobbled up and down with glee, High Table resembled a panel of manikins. Sir Trotsky sat in the middle, telling his beads, click-click-click, between courses, and contemplating, perhaps, the Beatific Vision; anyway, he bore a gentle aggravating faraway smile. The other dons sat on either hand, blanched, unwell, motionless, staring, aghast at the prospect of term. Now and then one of them would whinny or twitch as chemical withdrawal bit home. Hardly anyone ate. Chyld the butler, who despite being bent nearly double had spent the Long Vac wantoning in his pantry with *demimondaines* seventy years his junior, leaned his hunchback against the panelled walls, face grey and purple-mottled, shaking so violently that gobs of chianti flew of the decanter he held in both hands, gently sprinkling his thighs.

Mind you, term didn't fill *me* with joy either. It's never much fun pretending to teach the ineducable. And I had *your* snubbing to look forward to. But at least I was capable of speaking, and therefore of annoying. The general silence of High Table nettled me. As did Olga and Elmo's triumphant grins, like pink half-circles painted on balls of snow. 'Saucers of milk!' they cried. 'For our own Shishak!'

So '*Really*,' I said, staring up into the carved ceiling; 'milk. I call that unkind.'

'Unkind?' 'How unkind?' they exclaimed, spherical heads, which barely cleared the board, swivelling toward me, spherical eyes bulging. 'How?', 'How?' When not finishing each other's sentences, Yoxley and Freke generally speak in unison.

'Death's cruel,' I remarked, still ignoring them, still gazing into the heavens, 'they say; but – '.

'What *is* death?' put in Woolly, hoping to smooth away disagreement. The Chaplain hates quarrels, they're full of ideas. 'Is not death, in a special sense, life?'

'Damn fool,' said the Master gruffly, not looking up, 'they're *not* the same. They're *different* points in the one process –'

'Ah, but is not process, *ultimately*, itself another word for point?'

The Master sighed, and I persevered with baiting the happy couple. 'Death's cruel, but the alternative' (at which the Master was pleased to titter quietly, pausing in the midst of the *mysteria dolorosa*), 'the *alternative* may be worse.'

'How do you –', 'Mean?', 'mean?'

I dropped my gaze and pointed a contemptuous finger. 'You two! You had Shishak's mummy to work on, yes? But not, I noticed, the matching canopic jars. Lungs in one jar, isn't that how it goes? Intestines in another? Then stomach, liver?'

'Indeed,' 'Indubitably,' nodding grotesquely and in perfect time. As you'll have noticed, they resemble a heterosexual Tweedledum and Tweedledee.

'Well then, *the innards* won't have heard your spells. They'll have remained with dog-headed Anubis. Or wherever Ancient Egyptian guts went. If kitty comes back to life it may be lithe, but it'll be unnatural and empty.' (A bit like me, you're obviously thinking; cruel child.)

'Ah,' 'Oh,' they exclaimed, and their wee round twin heads sank. It's curious how certain I am they'll never actually marry, never pup. A third being, imperfectly snowman-shaped, would spoil their fearful symmetry.

I felt rather pleased with myself. 'It won't be able to meow, or nibble, or sip. Just prowl. Milk will seem to it a mockery.'

But they were only crestfallen for a moment. 'Cheese!' they cried, as one. 'We'll put out –' 'A pungent –' 'Gorgonzola, in fact!' 'Gorgonzola!' '– chopped.' 'So he can feed on milk –' '*spiritually*', whereat the Master's smile became quite abominably amused. He popped his rosary back into his pocket, almost chuckling, and gestured to Chyld for more wine; Chyld, starting, fell, his decanter shattered, blood –

This is by the by. Gorgonzola is exactly what Freke and Yoxley did. Left porcelain bowls all over College. The weather was unseasonably still, warm, in those final days of the month, as you may remember. The stuff decayed quickly. Whether the dispersing vapour of it spiritually nourished the reanimated feline nostrils, as the twins fervently believed, or not, I cannot say. It certainly modified the atmosphere for the rest of us, those last days of Vac.

St Wygefortis' seemed to ride in a suffocating blue haze, becalmed between September and October, between fading vacation and unborn term. Or even between life and death – the sort of carnage that's frightful enough yet seems an incident in rebirth. College was bathed in the essence of rot, that fecund rot from which forest-floor mushrooms rise, coming forth drenched in pong, alive because so many corpses are abroad, dying because alive –

Ahem.

Naturally Olga and Elmo didn't dare put any gorgonzola near *me*. The second floor of Megiddo Court, staircase IV, remained untainted. They were afraid of my sneering. Quite right too. But their diffidence didn't do me much good. Ebbe was always been easily put-upon, and a particularly heaped-up bowl of blue cheese, soon very brownish, sat by his first-floor rooms. Its perfume rolled up past my door; it reached the top of the stair; and the region just outside Ebbe oak's was dense with the fumes. The spectre of cows that had lactated in the plains of Lombardy six months before.

Maybe the stench is what finally undid him.

For Ebbe was taking the end of summer harder than anyone.

His research is to do with palladium hydride – getting it to absorb hydrogen at high densities. In the very distant hope that someone some day somewhere will get hydrogen atoms to fuse at room temperature. And thus, obviously, release oceans and oceans of cheap energy. Such was Ebbe's official work.

Really he was, is, a sort of neo-alchemist – no, don't *shrug* like that. I have a famous alchemist in my family tree, I have a weakness for alchemy. Anyway, Ebbe's alchemical ideas were subtle, I want to do them justice. Let me see.

He believed there's an occult vein of Paracelsian wisdom lost in the Enlightenment. Arcane wisdom hidden *inside* the usual arcane wisdom of alchemy. For fear of the Inquisition. "Chymical" discoveries so potent the early scientists were frightened into forgetting them – you're still tensing your thigh, see! it's quite rigid. Esoteric knowledge makes you clench. No wonder you can't share in my ….

*Listen.* The overt point of alchemy was – yes yes, to fabricate gold, what a blunt literal mind you have. You're wrong. Gold was only part of their ambition. They proposed to render down the complex muddled substances we see into *prima materia*. The first undifferentiated matter, the origin of everything else. Matter as it emerged from Chaos before God started shaping the worlds – what?

Oh yes I suppose so, *hydrogen*. If you *like*. The name we give a solitary proton. The first, simplest, smallest atom. The one all the other atoms are made *from*. – Y'know, I don't think that's very interesting. Hydrogen indeed. Best, Abishag, if you don't speak. You tiresome tiresome shallow little materialist, you.

*Unlike* you, the alchemists had no end of fine enthralling names for the primal quintessence. They called it *the Philosopher's Stone*, as even you will have heard. But also *Spiritual Blood. Dissolved Refuse. Spittle of the Moon.* They called it *Dung*, and in the same breath *Heart of the Sun*, for it's the source at once of every physical glory, and of all dirt.

No, more than that: *because* it's the lowest possible dimension, the basis, it *must* be base. All corporeality descends to it, as to the grave, to be resurrected – perhaps transformed, perhaps glorified. Moonlight rendered down to spittle so it might become, through humiliation, more superb even than moon, more tangible than silver. Refuse diffused until it is fit for transfiguration.

*Prima materia!* Ebbe grew quite mystical as he discussed it. No, not that, he couldn't *discuss* anything, his English was too feeble. But he used to show me passages in the *Theatrum Chemicum* – the only sort of poetry he could grasp, poor cattle that he was, and his eyes would screw up with rapture behind plastic spectacle-frames as I read it aloud. '*The Spittle of the Moon contains in itself all colours and all potential metals; there is nothing more wonderful in the world, for it begets itself, conceives itself, gives birth to itself*' – and he'd manage to get out 'T-t-t-true.'

Regular alchemy's not so different from regular chemistry. You beetle away in your lab, torturing matter – normal, complex, compromised matter – by physical processes. First you achieve blackening, *melanosis*, then whitening, *leucosis*, *xanthosis*, a yellowing, finally purpling, *iosis* – then you have it.

But Ebbe believed there was a shortcut, a secret high road *within* the secret science. Certain Hermetic philosophers hoped to recover the Adamical tongue, the ur-language of mankind, learned from angels. You knew that? No? Well why should you. They did. Adamical gives us the actual name of a thing, the name Adam conferred. Not some arbitrary linguistic label. And things respond to being called by their true names. They yield themselves. Matter yields its energy, which is almost boundless.

That's what excited Ebbe almost to the point of shrieking aloud. He believed certain alchemical books might contain scraps of Adamical, and with it unspeakable power over minerals – unspeakable power, megajoules and gigajoules of power.

He hoped to recreate some of these very curious experiments. Each summer he stole some foul dusty alchemical quarto from a library and tried to read between the lines. Or from the margins – one of his theories was that secrets were printed with invisible ink for the discovery of adepts....

A funny mixture, Ebbe. In term-time he was exactly the scrawny young oik from Bristol he appeared, a scientist's scientist. Hunched shoulders, filthy white lab-coat. Dreary. Paralytic-shy, too: mad raw nervous hands tearing at the air as he bustled about with his head down, unwashed, friendless, vegan, mildly unhinged – well, you've seen him.

Or have you? Have you looked close enough?

I took a certain macabre interest in Ebbe's face. He had no features to speak of. His hair was so haphazardly hacked about he might have done it himself (though in fact this wasn't so), his immense glasses hid, as they were meant to, whatever he had by way of eyes, and below the plastic rims things dwindled to an "etcetera" and a "and so forth". No chin, just a half-shaved, much-scraped working Adam's apple. Then his T-shirt's frayed edge. It was an suggestive face nonetheless, expressing a whole way of life: not merely wan but clammily grey; not merely untouched by sun, but stained by the unwholesome light of laboratories where florescent tubes make more terrible the yellows and cyans of bubbling flasks. A masturbator's complexion, the squamous epithelium of a near-troglodyte, broken up not by nose or mouth but, here, a light snowfall of dandruff, here a spectacular boil (it reared beneath his left ear). A raw patch of pustular dermatitis added drama to the line of his tiny jawbone, and the dull umber of his forehead was enlivened by a blazon of vermillion eczema.

Beneath that eczema fizzed thoughts both pallid and less pallid. He wasn't just a scientist's scientist. He has it in him to transform. As each summer goes on, he does. The white coat turns into a velvet gown with enormous slit sleeves and matching cap, because that is what Dr Dee wore. He stands almost straight; he ceases to shave, his pimples disappear under the beginnings of a silky beard. By the end of each summer, although he's as taciturn as ever, he looks almost formidable: half-wizard, half-mystagogue.

His rooms metamorphose too. A massive copper-topped bench – I can't think where he gets it – runs the length of his sitting-room, crowded with quaint disquieting equipment. An anthanor, that is a distillation furnace diffusing its heat through ashes of bone. A cucurbit, or flask of sublimation.

An ambix from Averroes' *atelier* in Marrakesh. A notebook kept by a Cathar (before the Cathar was burned) containing the dictated verses of an elemental dæmon in an unknown alphabet. A speculum of obsidian, heaped with ground horn, that had once been used for Aztec sacrifice.

Or so Ebbe said. Who knows? Who knows where he got the parchments that hung over his walls? The chart of the Atlantan mountain of myrrh? The diagrams of the crypt beneath Solomon's Temple, where the gryphons were kept growling in a chryselephantine cage? Who knows how seriously I should take the tall oak stand in the middle the book open, densely annotated by Dr Ebbe using two quills, one of purple ink, one of gold?

This summer Ebbe's book was *Fasciculus Chemicus*, claiming to reveal the *Ingress, Progress, and Egress, of the Secret Hermetick Science.* Of course poor Ebbe's Latin's just as dreadful as you'd expect. Negligible as his English. So he'd come upstairs and, stammering a good deal, standing on one foot then another (I don't want to exaggerate his summertime dignity), manage to get out 'B-b-book.' That is, he wanted me to help untangle the writing he thought he had found hidden within the overt text of *Fasciculus Chemicus* – hidden acrostically, palindromically, steganographically –

Margot, are you asleep? … Well good. But you've gone all still and marmoreal on me. You fill me with suspicions. Do attend. Put your head up here. – Better.

Ebbe brought me these mangled Latin coded tags. We'd expect gibberish. And gibberish is what they largely were. Still, from his semi-hysterical, inarticulate questioning, I picked up what he was trying to find.

Yes, shrug if you like. His nonsense was wearying. And slightly obscene. Like any tedious superstition. Yet it did not merely disgust me, the way the summer delinquency of the rest of College did. I was a moved. Can I explain why?

Ebbe, poor imbecile, was without knowing it a sort of bad poet. A poet who hadn't even heard of poetry. Who'd had a purely scientific and mathematical education. Who'd never been taught the simplest decent English. Who could barely grunt. Who was nonetheless an unconscious æsthete, although everything in his life and training had been ugly – have you noticed, Abishag, how extremely ugly chemistry is? It doesn't have to be. An astronomer will write

> I read the parallax
> of Arcturus,
> in Boötes,
> with a heliometer.

Which is ravishing. A botanist says

> The leaves of the mallow family,
> *Malvaceæ*,
> are lanceolate,
> and ovate,
> and often lobed.

Music! Alone among the sciences, chemistry has resolved to look and sound as ungainly as it can. When chemists speak the words that come out are like this:

> The most cost-effective methodology for tetrahy-
> drofuran fabrication is oxidizating n-butane to
> crude maleic anhydride.

And anyway they hardly ever use words. They speak in formulæ – and have you noticed how *revolting* chemical equations look? No? Well glance at a blackboard some time, and shudder. Their symbols are a libel on the beauty of material substance.

Poor Eddie Ebbe was tortured by ugliness without knowing why. He had no language to express pain, no language to express anything but titration. Thus every summer he allowed himself to go a little mad, and think about hieroglyphic monads, the mystical subsumation of ether, and ouroborotic chrysopœia. He tried to conjure rust and soot into the Spittle of the Moon, from which the worlds were once formed. *Progymnasmata alchemiæ* …. It all sounded lovely, and did no particular harm. It was a bounded madness kept him sane enough to endure the banality of another term. Another term teaching industrial glycerine extraction to boys and girls spotty and dull as himself.

*Summer's lease hath all too short a date.* Suddenly it was late September. Ebbe the æsthete had to lay aside his Renaissance magic and his velvet. He had to get back into a dirty T-shirt with a dirty joke on it, then a dirtier lab-coat. He had to resume professional unseemliness. A term lay before him, of propagating horrid noises and hideous signs. And this end-of-September suddenly seemed to him too awful.

I've blamed those bowls of Gorgonzola for Ebbe's fatal despair. But to be fair, to be chronologically exact: an end did come to *that* business after only three days. On Sunday 29th September.

Every science, no matter how demented, has an empirical side. Even sociology. Even the raising of dead cats. It occurred to Yoxley, after much failed
hunting about for their darling Shishak, after much fruitless chanting of the
*Hymn to Ra* at dawn, to slip once more into the basement of the Fitzwilliam
and see whether the mummy, stowed at the back of a shelf in a dim corner,
might still be in place, still intact.

*It was.*

Which should have put an end to their nonsense.

But of course while science can be empirical, no *scientist* is. They all have
ideas to cling to. Freke persuaded herself, then had no difficulty persuading
Yoxley, that their little treasure was indeed alive, and loved them. Even if its
embalmed flesh still slept in its linen swaddles; its intangible *ka* was abroad,
haunting College. The trick was just bringing the two together.

In short, late that night they burgled the Fitzwilliam a second time. They
brought their darling horror back to Wygy's, into Sheol Court, up staircase II,
and into Elmo Yoxley's rooms. There it was installed, against College regulations, as their pet. Or as the baby they'd never have. They got a small wooden
child's trolley and fixed it on, upright – you'll understand it was tightly
wrapped, a miniaturised version of any Egyptian mummy, with an alarming
grinning feline grin painted over the linen. On Monday, the last day of September, the young lovers appeared with this contraption, and went about the
Courts and corridors of St Wygefortis', gaily pulling it behind them, hoping
to snare the *ka*. 'Here, puss puss puss!'

They had no luck that morning and brought it into lunch, swaddled up
in an acid-free curating-cloth.

At lunch the Master spoke to them sternly in front of us all. We were
rather more alert by now. The worst of the D.T.s had receded; we were close
to grounding ourselves on the shore of normal hateful term-time life; Long
Vac's voyage through death lay behind us. 'Dr Yoxley, Dr Freke: it is just
eight days before our undergraduates return. These eccentricities must cease.'

Up and down High Table most of the dons nodded.

And the twins submitted sadly. 'Very well, Master,' they murmured,
patting poor Shishak on his head as if to say *Back to Anubis with you, darling!*
' We promise we'll be finished before Belshazzar's Feast' – which is another
fine College tradition we don't advertise. On the last free Tuesday of Long
Vac (that is, the next evening) the Fellowship bids farewell to freedom with
one final bacchanalia, at which we drink up all the extravagant wines we
shouldn't be seen drinking during term, and gorge off the Founder's plate.

That might have been that. That should have been that. Unfortunately the trolley carry-on had charmed the Chaplain.

Or perhaps Woolly, still smarting from having to take down his prayer-wheels before the start of term, thought this a fine way of getting his own back on the Master.

Anyway, he piped up from the far end of High Table.

'I find what dear Olga and Elmo are doing, Master, in a special sense, *most meaningful*. Do we not recite in the Creed – that unhappily *confining* text – *credo in carnis resurrectionem*? Is that not what these two young people are doing? Vindicating that doctrine, or should we not say feeling? I should like to *help*.'

The Master looked down his nose. Baptism has not brought out much softness in him; he merely sees everything from a perch in eternity, and is correspondingly even more contemptuous than before. But he could hardly object to an œcumenical prayer service. And so after lunch, and all afternoon, all that balmy afternoon of the thirtieth of September, and well into the night, we could heard the three of them noisily at it in Chapel. They were importuning Osiris in the name of Shishak.

> *Hail to Thee O Mighty God, Thou Lord of Maāti.*
> *Thy name I know,*
> *as too the names of the Forty-Two*
> *keeping ward over sinners*
> *to feed upon their gore on the day*
> *of the estimation of character.*

They chanted in English, for Woolly had argued that dead languages are *excluding*. Olga Freke had improvised a translation from the *Book of the Dead*.

> *Behold, to Thee I come!*
> *I have not consorted with worthless folk.*
> *I have not repulsed the god at his appearances.*
> *I am pure. I am pure. I am pure. I am pure....*

Most of us, as we meandered about College that afternoon, and heard the drone through the Chapel doors, were inclined to titter. But not Ebbe. He'd *shuddered* when he saw the trolley – I noticed him. He'd been blenching and *distrait* at lunch. All day I'd noticed him on our stair with a fatal disorder in his eyes, behind his horrid N.H.S. spectacles.

I think I understood. Ebbe couldn't learn Adamical and animate minerals. Nor could he make hydrogen overflow with fussile energy. He couldn't transform death to life. Neither – to be sure – could Woolley, Yoxley and Freke. But at least *they* were still trying. Theirs was the more resilient lunacy. If all you have is a cultivated delusion, what's left when you find you're undeluded? Maybe that was it.

Or am I overcomplicating? Possibly it had nothing to do with his failure to find Dissolved Refuse, the ur-element. Perhaps it *was* just the nauseous odour of bad cheese. Which certainly lingered about the lower reaches of this staircase. It may suddenly have been more than flesh could endure – at least such shabby flesh as adhered to the bones of Eddie Ebbe.

Vomitting, Margot: let's think about vomitting. Don't you think it's the most extraordinary noise the human body produces? Or even the most wondrous thing the human body *does*? It's *miraculously* loud. I've heard Seb the afternoon after a bender making all Abaddon Court echo.

The next morning I was lying here dozing in this bed – the bed you assume (vain, self-centred creature) to be an eventless void without you in it. A boring, out-of-the-way bed. When it isn't. It remains the vortex of events. Prodigies gravitate to it.

In this case, the event was an immense orchestral gurgling retching choking erupting hullabaloo beneath my floor. From Ebbe's rooms. He gagged and chucked, he puked and hurled and spewed, he struck high notes and bass rumbles, he was at once liquid and metallic. I lay listening for a while. Like everyone is who has to live beside undergraduates, revolting unclean creatures as you are, I'm a connoisseur of regurgitation. This wasn't drink-vomit, nor indigestion, nor stomach 'flu. This was the rich extravagant sonancy of poison.

What did I do, d'y'think? Smiled gently, covered head with pillow, tried to go back to sleep? Yes: that would be in character. But as I say, I've a soft spot for Ebbe. There were selfish reasons too ....

I didn't hurry, mind. I got my dressing-gown on and strolled down the stairs. His door was locked, but that wasn't a difficult: I could kick it in, since there was nobody about on the stair except the Muckhatch. Nothing excites the Muckhatch. O how I miss Bessie Elmsgall, occasionally. *There* was a bedder! *There* was a brooding presence. Whereas Mrs Muckhatch had passed through the infernal carnival of a St Wygy summer vac without any flicker in the dull mineshaft of her eye. Now I simply waved my hand at her, and the indifferent woman floated away. I counted to twenty, then attacked. The door gave way on the fourth kick.

Ebbe was lying face-down in an immense pool of granular sick. He wasn't dead, he wasn't even precisely unconscious, just shattered, twitching, dry-heaving. The empty bottles he'd used were conveniently at hand – they'd rolled against the wainscotting. Three of them. Sodium thiopental *and* pancuronium bromide *and* ketamine.

*Really.*

It is, I admit, a fiddly business poisoning yourself – or, of course, anyone else. It's low art rather than high science, therefore one of the many tasks done more elegantly by amateurs than by professionals. Professionals go about things too cleverly by half, they over-think. Whereas I – .

Consider (if the topic's not to macabre for a girl clearly eight-ninths asleep) the American death-cell. Committees of anatomists and legislators keep refining an already-elaborate recipe. The condemned is easy prey: a half-witted bungler of a petrol-station hold-up, strapped to a gurney, preposterously obese, already groggy with a lifetime of imbecility, television, recreational sedation. What could be simpler? Yet he generally kicks and shrieks for quarter of an hour after his injection, bringing killing into disrepute.

Whereas a disgruntled teenager, emptying without forethought a bottle of paracetamol, manages well enough. Even an idiot – I'm thinking of my sister who did just this –

No I'm *not* discussing Agatha. Certainly not. I never do. My subject's myself, not her. Consider my own great triumphs. They have been entirely offhand – I'm *not* being pompous or immodest, Abishag, despite that half-drowned sneer of yours. Besides, enormous happiness *does* make me pompous, why shouldn't it? I'm making a point. Never over-prepare anything. Improvisation puts you in accord with this improvised universe. Carefulness undoes itself.

That's why Ebbe, a professional with all modern chemistry at his beck, botched his escape. He gave himself thiopental to induce coma, *and* pancuronium to paralyse his lungs, *and* ketamine to produce elation. (Elation! As if life should end like an operetta – final frothy reprise, laughter, descending curtain.) The three naturally got muddled up on the way down and came surging out as vomit.

I knew I could bring this virtual corpse back to life. More, I could I could work a larger miracle and *remake* him. That's the point of my story, which you seem to find so soporific. Eddie is at this moment, because of me, not merely alive but a bandit-hero. As you'll hear if you can keep those eyes open.

First things first. I rifled through Ebbe's alchemical clutter and came across a gold-plated pot with hinged lid called, I believe, an *auroscaphium* – beautiful word, like most of the words in alchemy. Which was of course

Ebbe's problem. Gold-plated, you understand, because gold doesn't react. Its contents can't corrupt, I mean any more than they are already corrupt. I took this auroscaphium and carefully scooped up his sick – not a jolly task, but the glory and obvious necessity of it set off most of the physical –

Why? *Why?* How can you ask, or mumble into your pillow, *Why?*

You want to be my novice? Yet have never considered the value of vomit, I mean the vomit of the well-poisoned? (Or even the clumsily-poisoned?) Shallow-minded child. Pshaw!

You ought to know that such regurgitations are immensely precious. Almost their weight in *etcetera.* Don't you know there are emergency-room nurses who pay off their holiday-cottages by pumping the stomachs of suicides and selling the results?

'Why' indeed! Haven't you heard that if a sperm-whale's unprofessional enough to swallow a giant squid, beak and all, its bile duct excretes a waxy slurry called ambergris over the sharp bits? A blob forms, which the whale vomits up. It floats on the ocean for decades. Air, sun and water transfigure it. Its reek becomes the greatest of perfumes, at once sweet, marine, dark, opulent, earthy, animalistic: ambergris. The little that washes up on beaches sells at a thousand pounds an ounce, considerably more than gold.

That's the one true alchemy. Not the nonsense Ebbe tried on his copper bench, what he did in his tummy. Indeed that's the true power over death and life. Not fusty hymns from *The Book of the Dead.* Vomit is ambergris, vomit is the precious tincture of the cosmos. Vomit is the spittle of the moon.

So here we come to the crux. Because I was grateful to Ebbe, I bothered transfiguring him. That worm's now a lover, a warrior, a *savant,* a grandee. What a glorious progression of events, Abishag, eh?

*Eh?* You *are* asleep! How appalling! What an insult!

But oh God, my dearest, my darling, how *plausible* you look asleep. Lying there sleeping through my splendid talk. Sleeping through the fireworks ....

No; no fireworks. They're finished. It's quiet out. Just blackness and a rising wind. Nasty weather blowing in. It'll be foul tomorrow.

Today! Listen – no, don't listen, you're asleep – but that's midnight sounding from the tower of Little St Mary's. Foul weather *today.*

But not foul in here. Calm in here. All calm. I'm so glad you're back. Even with your sarcasm. And arrogance. And your ambition to be my "apprentice." Which is not going to happen. Although you'll no doubt remember to badger me about it tomorrow. And ask about Ebbe. And ... so forth.

Meanwhile good night my lo – my girl. Good-night. Sleep and gather power. We'll make love when we wake. Late. Very very late.

# II.
# ACNESTIS

Death meets us every where, and is procured by
every instrument, and in all chances, and enters in
at many doors: by violence, and secret influence,
by the aspect of a star, and the stink of a mist, by
the emissions of a cloud, and the meeting of a
vapor, by the fall of a chariot, and the stumbling
at a stone, by a full meal, or an empty stomach, by
watching at the wine, or by watching at prayers,
by the Sun or the Moon, by a heat or a cold, by
sleeplesse nights, or sleeping dayes, by water
frozen into the hardnesse, and sharpnesse of a
dagger, or water thawd into the floods of a river;
by a hair, or a raisin ....

JEREMY TAYLOR,
*The rule and exercises of holy dying*

*very very early, 6th November 2013,*
*Dr Felix Culpepper's bedroom,*
*St Wygefortis' College.*

'Human *foie gras*? I can't believe – . No of course, Your Eminence, I understand, four livers is a lot. All fat men, granted. But – . Yes, Your Eminence,
awkward, extremely – . Quite – . Though it sounds like a put-up job, doesn't
Your Eminence think? A patter of bloody footprints leading straight to a
Prior's – . No, no, but is a Scotch Trappist with a *taste*, even for goose *pâté* – ?
Let alone – . Were it man-haggis, now – . No, I absolutely –. Yes –. Yes, I'll
be on the first 'plane. At once. Good night, Your Eminence. What? Oh, good
*morning.... God.*'

'Well?'

'You're awake?'

'That's a stupid thing for you to say, Felix': a remark she would not have dared make to him before the summer, or indeed before last night.

'It was the Cardinal-Archbishop –'

'*Another* stupid thing.'

'– of the Hebrides.'

'Three – I could hear his incredible accent down the line. A hat trick.' She wouldn't have dared; but this was the next morning, the day after Guy Fawkes, and she was in his bed on her own terms.

'There's been a – well, you heard what there's been. Mass murder. At a monastery deep in the Highlands. The bell rang for Lauds this morning, four Trappists didn't show, afterward they were found in their cells, mutilated.'

'You can't *say* "this morning" at six.' She'd never contradicted him in the ancient times before March. 'It's still pitch black.'

'The Church begins her days hideously early. Lauds was hours ago. The Abbot's quite sensibly dawdling. Officially speaking he doesn't know about the murders yet. Only the Cardinal's been informed, and the Cardinal wants me there before the Abbot has to notice the corpses and call the police.'

'So I' (she said, testing the waters) 'am checking flights and trains? Then I'm making coffee?'

'That's what you're doing. Get me to Skelgourock – to Skelgourock! Of all grievous places in the Untied Kingdom of Gothic Britain and Nothing-Ireland.' He covered his head with a pillow while Abishag sat up to fiddle with her 'phone. 'Skelgourock. God God God. I don't *want* to watch the sun come out of the North Sea from a 'plane. I don't *want* to come to full consciousness in – in *Glasgow* – if Glasgow's how one gets to the Archdiocese of the Hebrides. God. God.'

'Glasgow – that's right.' And '*Courage, mon brave,*' she added half-mockingly, half-commandingly: '*courage.*'

He sat up painfully, dropped rather than swung his legs out of bed, paused tragically. On the best of days, it was a sere whining Felix Culpepper who emerged from sleep. Now it was still far from day, and seemed certain to be a bad day for him when it became day; for all his jauntiness on the 'phone, he was a wreck.

Abishag glanced at him tenderly. 'Poor old fellow. Listen, the first flight to Glasgow's not 'til ten past eight. Gets in at nine-twenty. Train to Bridge of Orchy at eleven. Taxi from there. Car rental in Skelgourock, so we'll be with –'.

'*What?*'

'I said, you'll be with the monks in time for a very late lunch. The ones that are still alive and uneaten.'

'Humph.'

'Forty minutes' drive to Stansted, so you'll want a cab in twenty minutes. No, half an hour. No great hurry.'

'Humph…. Back, then.' His back was always itchy when he woke, and one of Abishag's jobs had always been to scratch it. She resumed this duty this now. 'Yes. Yes. Higher. To the left …. The Cardinal was appallingly breezy, did y' hear him? "Four of 'em 'ovis hand their cheerfuls gouged hout 'orrid with a drum."'

'Yes. What did he mean?'

'*Drum and fife,* knife, *Hovis bread,* dead, *cheerful giver,* liver. Christ, the *bore* of having a retired pearly king as spiritual shepherd of the Highlands and Islands. It doesn't matter on television – you've seen him? –'

'Of course.'

' – the camera adores him, his charm's beyond language, it's a sort of music. And the Highlanders don't mind having a Cockney archbishop because what comes out of his mouth isn't remotely like Sassenach. I'm told his chaplains get used to it. Translate him into Lowland Scots in their heads without noticing. But it's agony for everyone who has to do business with him. The brain bleeds trying to keep up …. Now up and down the spine.'

'What're you supposed to do?'

'Find culprit – evidently the Prior. Add culprit to casualty list. Fake five natural deaths. Then vanish before the gavvers get in the way.'

'Are *gavvers* the police?'

'At a guess. "Keep the chuffin' gavvers ahht of it," pronounced His Eminence, "and I daan't wanna read abaht it in the bleedin' gutterin's neivver."' A tremendous sigh.

'*Guttering tapers,*' murmured Abishag: 'papers,' and he uttered a yet more broken sigh. 'Poor lamb. That's a lot of skulduggery to drop on one man.'

'It is,' said Culpepper, far gone in self-pity. 'It is.'

Abishag surveyed the inside of her mind. Highland rain, gulls, distilleries, Calvinists, shaggy cattle: these all flickered about. But the main image, to her surprise, was of Felix *and herself* merrily dashing across a moor, pursuing a mad fat Trappist brandishing a dripping scalpel. She (a girl well-born and capable, a girl who had no business aspiring to such courses) took a breath. 'Then take me.'

'You?' She stopped scratching. '*Take* you? This isn't a jaunt.'

'I don't want a jaunt. Remember? I'm back as your student. Not just in Latin lit. I want to help you in your real work.' She resumed work on his back.

'Of course when I return I'll tell –'.

'No. Pillow-talk's not enough. I'm tired of being your sounding-board.

And travel-agent.'

'You inspire me –'

'Nor yet your muse. I mean to be your partner…. Even poor dim Watson was taken on field-trips.'

'I don't need a –'.

'Who'll scratch your bare back while you're away?'

'Is that a question?'

'No. I mean, what'll happen to this poor itchy spot *here*, the bit you can't reach yourself? Technically known as the *ac* –'.

'– *nestis*. Yes, yes.' Even in his pitiful new-awakened state, Culpepper was aggressive about his word-hoard. 'Noble term, *acnestis*. It sounds like the name of a tragic heroine. There ought –'

'There ought to be a lost tragedy called *Acnestis*. By Euripides.'

'Seneca.'

'All right, by Seneca.'

'… You make fairly good jokes, my girl. I look forward to getting back to them.'

'But meanwhile, who'll make the necessary jokes for you? How'll you stack your memory? How'll you manage the smell of blood? Who'll deal with the acnestis in your mind?'

There was a little pause. The scratching ceased once more; he lowered his head. 'That was a startling remark. It was virtually intelligent.' He didn't sound altogether pleased. 'Almost worthy.'

She rested her forehead between his shoulder blades and said into his torso, gently and very seriously: 'If I can think your thoughts, bring me along to do what you do.'

'It isn't' – also too soft for mockery – 'just a question of cleverness. It's … a gift,' he offered shyly, 'an art,' and by turning his head away created a distinct region of silence, almost marked out in the air by dotted lines, in which the word *art* reverberated. Then he recalled himself, groaned theatrically, literally shook her off, stood, stretched, and vanished toward the bathroom, growling: 'Make coffee.'

Abishag considered his retreating back: red wheals from her nails, vaccination scar, poignant shoulder-blades. Sighing, she slid from the sheets, got into a dressing-gown, went into the dark pantry, found the kettle by feel, clicked it on, sighed again at the sad noise of water working itself into a state, padded across Culpepper's dark sitting-room, held back a curtain, and peered out.

Only one lamp was lit: enough to show all the other lamps of Megiddo Court smashed. A few burnt-out skyrockets lay here and there, and single female shoe. *What*, she thought, *a revolting hour.* It was hard to recapture the thrill of the evening before with everything so frigid and wet. *Utterly revolting. Not quite pitch black, but nothing, nothing to suggest that this dimness leads any-where.* The Court gave no hint of a future, not even of a bleak sleety November morning. Mere disaster seemed to be overtaking the smoothness of night, a more immediate facet of the disaster overtaking the year. *The darkness rots. It's cankered. Pallor shows like grubby brickwork where the stucco's pealed. God.*

She let the curtain fall, switched on a desk-lamp, and groaned again. Normally Felix's desk was a handsome enough sight: brass lamp and granite bust of Bulwer-Lytton on a silk kilim. But this morning, or pre-morning, it too appeared disastrous. Here, presumably, were the galley-proofs she'd been told not to touch: the College history. Desk, sofa and floor were heaped with a clutter of photocopies, notes on torn paper, books held open with other books, manuscripts from the College archives flung about in a way the Widdler had better not know about, academic journals folded in two and propped against pewter tankards .... These wretched proofs were why Felix had been in College so long, unravelling; why he'd not spent the summer in Egypt or Cuba; why he was still so bored, so boring; why she had to solace his boredom. Or share it. Halve it perhaps. Damn the pages.

She found the 'phone amidst this clobber, dialled the number for taxis while her other hand leafed through the galleys. A title-page, *Culpepper's Quincentenary History of St Wygefortis' College*; no dedication, hm; Chapter One. Petulant scribbles and crossings-out down every margin, far too many for a disciplined writer at the galley stage. She skimmed the opening, fulsome praise of the founder of St Wygefortis', Adam Worthyal, Bishop of St Asaph.

> Worthyal, although a pluralist notorious even
> in that age, was one of the morning stars of the
> English Renaissance....

Felix learned prose from his saurian old father. He likes to call it a neo-Victorian style. The other Fellows have ruder names.

> His Latinity was Ciceronian without –.

'Good morning,' said a voice that didn't mean it.

'So you say. Taxi, please, for two. For Stansted Airport. From the Porter's Lodge, St Wygy's. In twenty minutes .... Thank you.' She hung up, careful-ly replacing the sheets in their proper random places on the chaotic desk. *Writing like that'll do no harm. And the book's going to be chocker with pretty colour pictures. So expensive only other college libraries are going to buy it. Let's not worry about the prose.* The kettle reached its climax, squealed, sighed. She ground the beans small. *How nice it would be to go back to bed. Go back to dreaming about that preserved cat carcase …. No. No. Courage, ma brave. I'm going to Scotland.* Her clothes were where she had dropped them; she got back into them.

The bathroom door flew back. Felix made his re-appearance through billowing back-lit banks of steam in a dressing-gown of padded burgundy silk. (*Like a pantomime-demon rising out of a trapdoor. Coils of sulphurous smoke.*) She handed him, no, he took the coffee from her hand. (*Not sulphurous, though. What pleasing smells English gentlemen generate in the morning. Not gentlemen, dandies. Cologne, shaving soap, shampoo. Leather, sandalwood. Very hot water. Flesh that has never been sick or hungry or even very tired.*)

He handed the mug back to her, emptied, and addressed her. The steam had cleared and he was back in cruelly high spirits. *It's always the same when he wakes. First animal discomfort, then remembered human grief. Then hot water. After water, malignant pomposity. Pomposity's a good sign. It means he can keep going.*

'All right. You think you can learn my trade? I don't think you can. Because first' – his chortle was certainly malicious (*Isn't all teaching malicious? A stylised assault?*) – 'first you have to pass an aptitude test. An exam.'

He rooted in the paper rubble on his sofa, found a book, a dull-brown brick, thrust it into her hands: 'Here's a detective puzzle for you.'

She perched on a spot of leather upholstery clear of papers. He straddled the arm and watched her examine the book, a dusty old edition of Holinshed's *Chronicles*.

'Turn to the red bookmark.' She did; he tapped a finger on the page.

'"*This Iohn Gréene …*"?'

'Yes. Read from there.'

> 'This Iohn Gréene did his errand vnto Brakenberie, knéeling before our ladie in the Tower. Who plainelie answered, that he would neuer put to death the two yoong princes.

It's the Princes in the Tower!'

'Yes. If you're going to be an assassin you have to crack the greatest of all murder mysteries. The worst of all English crimes.'

'*This* is my exam?'

'This is your exam.'

'… Who's John Greene?'

'A nobody. Just one of Richard III's henchmen. Brackenbury, of course, is Constable of the Tower of London. Listen. It's 1483. Young Edward V, twelve years old, has just been deposed by wicked uncle Richard, and locked up in the Tower with his brother, who's nine. By the end of summer the boys have vanished. Everyone assumes the usurper's murdered them. Which is a bit much, even for the Wars of the Roses. Richard's regime starts coming undone. If his nephews were alive he'd parade them, but he doesn't. Obviously because he can't.'

'They *had* been killed.'

'Of course. There'd been – is *nepocide* a word? Either on Richard's explicit orders, or just to please him. To give him what he must certainly desire. Rulers do generally get what they want, they needn't commit themselves to words, it's a matter of nods and sighs. Richard had been careful to sigh whenever the boys were the subject of conversation. As if to say, *How can a man administer England well with family troubles like* this *on his mind?* By late summer, *pouf!* the children had ceased to worry him.'

'So it's just a question of *who* –'.

'Exactly: *who* was actually nepocidal? Because, as you see, Brackenbury wasn't. He wouldn't do it. Turn the page. Here's the official story, the one put about by the Tudors after they'd overthrown Richard. The King (they say) dispatched a smooth young gent named Sir James Tyrrel to the Tower. Tyrrel brough a couple of his heavies, Forrest and Dighton. Here. We're in the Princes' bedroom.'

Abishag read aloud:

> '& suddenlie lapping them vp among the clothes, so to bewrapped them and intangled them, keeping downe by force the fether-bed and pillowes hard vnto their mouths, that within a while, smoothe red and stifled, their breath failing, they gaue vp to God their innocent soules into the ioies of heauen, leauing to the tormentors their bodies dead in the bed.

Brutes.'

Culpepper raised his eyebrows. 'Not a very professional judgment, my dear. Sounds like quite a neat piece of work to me – no shrieking, no unnecessary bruising. Anyway,' proprietorially tapping the page, 'you'll see that once Forrest and Dighton are sure the boys are *thoroughlie dead*, they *burie them at the staire foot, meetlie déepe in the ground, vnder a great heape of stones.*'

'Y – es.'

'And Tyrrel rode *in great hast to king Richard, and shewed him all the maner of the murther.* The King was pleased and said thankee kindly. But then he became upset at – what does it say?'

'Um – oh yes, at

> the burieng in so vile a corner, saieng, that he
> would haue them buried in a better place, bicause
> they were a kings sonnes. Lo the honourable cour-
> age of a king. Whervpon they saie, that a priest
> of sir Robert Brakenberies tooke vp the bodies
> againe, and secretlie interred them in such place,
> as by the occasion of his death, which onelie knew
> it, could neuer since come to light.

That seems plausible enough.'

'Doesn't it? Tyrrel made his peace with the Tudors, but long afterward rebelled. So he, and also Dighton but not Forrest, ended up in the hands of King Harry's torturers. According to the official account, they confessed to the murder, but *whither the bodies were remooued, they could nothing tell.*'

'That seems plausible too.'

'Yes it does. It's *entirely* plausible. Holinshed, no fool, accepted the story. He copied it word-for-word from Thomas More, the Tudor minister for propaganda. Other historians repeated it from Holinshed. They're still repeating it. Because: why? Why is that, Abishag? Because *all professional historians are dribbling morons.*'

'Oh. Really? *Are* they?'

'Of course they are. This is the only thing to do with the Princes' death we know about. We *know* the official account's a lie. It's plausible; it just happens to be untrue.'

'How d' we know that?'

'Because by the merest chance, in the 1670s, when some work was being done in the Tower, two skeletons turned up. Boys aged about twelve and nine. Buried in velvet and silk. D' y' know *where* the workmen found them? At the foot of a stair. Buried deep under a great heap of stones.' Abishag was silent. 'Now look just a bit further down. Next paragraph. Holinshed says that what he's reporting *I haue learned of them that much knew, and little cause had to lie.*'

She considered. 'If –'.

But Culpepper had leaped up, had vanished back into his bedroom. 'That's it,' he called through the open door, distractedly; he was noisily getting dressed. 'You have all you need. Solve it. Maybe the most important homicide in English history. Prove you have the murderous knack and you can come with me to Scotland. Fail,' his voice turned unpleasant, 'and you'll never badger me again about field-trips…. Deal?'

'Deal,' said Abishag, suddenly very tired.

'Well then. You know my methods. Apply them.'

*Innuendo, morbid sensibility, self-display, manslaughter,* thought Abishag; although what she called out was 'I'll try, Felix.'

He always took an age getting dressed, especially when he was also getting disguised. So Abishag replenished her coffee-cup, settled down and shut her eyes, considering.

*His methods…. First point. Felix teaches that writing is the test. Deceiving people going about in the real world is fairly easy. The world's a muddle, hardly anyone pays attention. But to make up a plausible lie on the page, on the white page, with no half-lights to hide it in, with your enemy's eye hanging attentively above, inches off: that's hard. Learn to do that, and you'll be able to deceit whomever you want.*

Coffee.

*In fact (second point) Felix says all great novelists must be killers.* 'Who,' says Felix, 'knowing he can concoct irresistible evidence, plausible incidents, unshakeable alibis, could resist employing *his impunity? If he sheds ink-blood, rare and precious, why not mere blood-blood? If he can create fake people for fun, wouldn't he destroy real people for fun? A novelist undertaking a murder knows he won't get caught. Thus we're all at the mercy of artists. And artists aren't merciful.'* More coffee. 'Note that suppressed chuckle in photos of Henry James. *It's not mock-gravity, it's not intellectual self-regard, it says* "I know something that would make you drop this literary periodical, little lady, and scream and scream until you were ill."'

She could hear him in his bedroom, swearing.

*Third point. Felix says reality has a smell. A grammatically correct sentence can still be vacuous. A story can be witty, plausible, telling, yet dead dead dead in the hand. Why? It just happens not to smell of the world.*

He was, she somehow knew, vexing himself about the choice of socks.

*How do you find a teaspoon of sugar muddled into a crock of coarse flour? Looking won't help, thinking won't help. You spill the lot over the table, look away, roll your fingers through the grains. Your finger-tips – you can't say how – detect the minute rasp of crystal.*

Culpepper was humming opera: the sock crisis must be over.

*Fourth point. Most writers copy from nature, producing the smell at second-hand. But great writers commit pure fraud: they rub their fingers in the air and plasticine forms like sausages; they shape it into an albatross that squawks, that has a bit of webbing missing from an ancient fight, that stinks of lobster-pots.*

He was banging suitcases about.

*Either method can deceive a reader. But it has to be one or the other.... Such are the principles of his doctrine.*

She fixed her mind in the necessary posture of morbid sensibility. That is, she tried to twist her mind into the ugly shape of Felix's. She read through the passage in Holinshed, rolling each word under her finger-tips.

She shut her eyes again. What a scramble of contrivance and nonsense it was. What a fabric of governmental fibs. What a mist.

Yet were things in it that were solid and real, things that jabbed and twitched. The murder itself: the sudden jump, the lapping of the boys in their comforters, their flushed skin. We were seeing that through a living eye; necessarily the murderer's eye.

Brackenbury kneeling before the statuette of Our Lady in the chapel of the Tower, almost weeping with fright, but gasping that he'd rather die himself than kill the royal children: that happened. *I see it because someone saw it.*

What else? The burial is true. It sounds a throw-away remark, but it has the smell of reality. We're there, we *burie them at the staire foot, meetlie déepe in the ground, vnder a great heape of stones.* We are –

But before she could think further she found that Felix had emerged from his bedroom smirking for her to inspect.

'Solved it? Thought not. Well then, you've failed. You stay in Cambridge. If you want to help me, check the index to my horrible book while I'm gone. But don't derange the galleys.'

She was scarcely able to feel resentment, being so amazed. It was his usual unpleasant habit to dress as a clergyman when he went abroad; and he regarded Scotland as extremely abroad. Nonetheless, he must have decided to hide in plain view this time. Or did he want to rub the locals' noses in it? For whatever reason, over his clerical collar-and-vest he wore a loud suit of tweeds, with provocative red stripes and yellow checks; he had on an appalling Tam O'Shanter, not tartan but navy blue; and an immense period-revival Inverness cape. The socks he had noisily debated *were* tartan. He even carried a big brass-tipped walking stick. Hopeless! False from his inception! Abishag, defeated and humiliated, covered her eyes, moaned, averted her gaze – .

## *ii.*

'Guid morn tae ye. Thes is th' Royal Caledonian Hotel in Skelgourock.'

'May I speak to' (a spasm of doubt; was he travelling under a pseudonym? Well then, his fault for not letting her know) 'Dr Felix Culpepper. Please.'

'This is,' said Felix's unhappy voice half a minute later, 'the second morning in a row I've been wrenched awake by the 'phone. I shan't survive a third.'

'... Are those *seagulls* I'm hearing in the background? They're like motorbikes.'

'Yes. Gulls. Very loud gulls. They're abroad but I was asleep, did I say?'

'I've solved it.'

'Solved what?'

'The murder of Edward V. And his brother.'

Two heart-beats. 'You can't have.'

'I have.'

'Yet,' with angry patience, '*you can't have.*'

'I have.'

'You have?' He sounded so troubled he might have smothered the brats himself.

'Yes. Here it is. The murders were nothing to do with Tyrrel. Tyrrel was just –'.

'Wait wait wait. If I have to hear this now, I'm turning on the kettle.... All right, go.'

'Tyrrel was just a minion of Richard's who happened, twenty years later, to get himself beheaded. Once he was dead, it occurred to someone in the government that he'd make a convenient scapegoat. So they put it about that Tyrrel had confessed to killing the Princes.'

'Hm.... This seems thin already. "Someone in the government"?'

'Perhaps More himself. No not More. Because it wasn't a very strong lie. And we know how good you godly bookish fellows are at lying.'

'It's too early. Too early in the morning for remarks of that nature.'

'A frail lie. If Tyrrel had really confessed to regicide, why wasn't he publically tried and executed for *that*? If Dighton confessed to throttling the Princes, why was he released? More himself admits that Dighton *yet walketh on aliue*, and the best More can says is that he's a bad sort and there's *a good possibilitie to bee hanged ere he dye.* Which is pretty feeble.'

' ... Yes.'

'The scenario in More and Holinshed *doesn't quite make sense.* Yet it was as good as the Tudor government could do, because, obviously, the Tudor government had no idea what happened to the Princes. The murderer had concealed himself absolutely. He must have been a clever man.'

'I supp –'.

'Two centuries later the boys' skeletons happen to turn up at the bottom of the stair. So we know the datum about *a priest of sir Robert Brakenberies* moving them *from* the stair simply isn't so.'

'Well –'.

'Yet someone bothered telling that elaborate fib. Someone who knew where the bodies *were*, but wanted to make it clear that the burying was quite *separate* from the killing. That it happened days later. That is was done by someone quite, quite different. Which suggests it was –'.

'You're getting warm,' said Culpepper, who sounded chilled, chilled and worried, making a noisy business of milking his tea. 'But what about this. You can torture a man into inventing anything. Tyrrel knows he's going to be beheaded. When he's being racked, and is invited to confess to killing the Princes, he says, "Sure, sure, nasty little nippers, never cared for Plantagenets of any sort, can I get down now?" "Where are the bodies, then?" He doesn't know and can't just guess – if he does they'll just go and check, there'll be no bones and they'll stretch him some more. So, stretched out there on the rack, he concocts this story about the corpses being moved by somebody else. The situation in the torture-chamber generates the story.' He sounded jollier now, sure of himself. 'Torture-chambers *do* generate stories, they're better than libraries, Red Scares, witch crazes. They're novel factories –'

'That's all very well, Felix. Your theory *works*. It satisfies logic. But mine satisfies logic and imagination. So mine wins.'

'Ah,' said Culpepper, who was thinking *The little minx is mastering me. What am I for, then? What am I?*

'Tyrrel didn't know where the boys were buried. And they *hadn't* been moved. It follows he didn't do it.'

'All right.'

'Who did bury them at the *staire foot*? It's oddly vivid, that *great heape of stones*. Someone not used to menial labour remembered the hours he'd spent heaving rocks back and forth in the night, trying not to make too much clatter. But the bodies are *meetlie déepe*. Whoever is remembering has a sense of propriety. Especially about interments.'

'Now you're massaging the evidence.'

'All eyewitnesses to the crime are, by definition, guilty. Yet Holinshed says he has *learned of them that much knew, and little cause had to lie*. His information comes from someone who's extremely guilty but utterly secure.'

'I admit this tends –'.

'Who told More – who told anyone? – about that solitary or near-solitary scene in the Tower chapel? Constable Brackenbury receives the King's secret messenger, throws himself on his knees before his image of the Undefiled, and cries that, by Our Lady, he'd sooner die than put the brats to death. Who saw *that*? Who caught the messenger's name? Who's our source? Not Brackenbury himself: he was killed with Richard at Bosworth. There must have been someone else, someone naturally in the chapel. Someone used to keeping secrets. Someone the Constable didn't think to send out of the chapel because he belonged there.'

'Some of –'.

'And the murder itself. Despite all doubts and fabrications, the actual moment of killing rings true. We test it in our imagination and we're *there*. Either it happened *or* it was invented by some genius of novel-writing. Adult hands *suddenlie lapping them vp among the clothes,* then *keeping downe by force.*'

'Anyone who's ever strangled anyone might –'.

'And why *suddenly*? Picture it, I mean according to the official version. Toward midnight a lock clicks, the door creaks open. In come two grinning unshaven bruisers with muscular fingers, Forrest and Dighton. The boys aren't innocents, they've grown up in the Wars of the Roses. What do they think's about to happen? Where would their final *surprise* be? No, the killer was someone they trusted. Who was already in the bedroom with them. On the bed beside them.'

'Reading them a bedtime story?'

'Reading them night prayers from his breviary. That's a guess, but it covers the data. The boys are getting pleasantly drowsy when suddenly he grabs up the blankets and throws himself over them. How horribly they writhe – but he has *bewrapped them and intangled them,* he pulls out the feather mattress and crams it *hard vnto their mouths.* His cassock is twisted between his legs – his big illuminated breviary is pressed under his knee – then a page rips apart and it thuds on the flags. He's your sort: such a man of libraries that, even in the throes of infanticide, and regicide, he feels a spasm of grief for his spoiled book. The sound of rent vellum sounds worse to him than the choking of –'

'You're now being nasty for its own –'

'– of a child. One small hand's sticking out into the air, twitching. But that doesn't last long. After a minute he can stand up and pull off the pillows and look at them lying *smoothe red and stifled,* while he gets his breath back. He listens. The Tower is perfectly silent. All he can hear is the rage of God booming at him from outside the universe. He's damned of course, but he's a made man, safe in this world as long as this world lasts. One after the other he lugs the small corpses down the stairs, shovels a decent hole, heaps the stones *meetlie.* By dawn, when he washes his scratched hands and goes to say his Mass, there's nothing to see above ground.'

'This –'.

'The man who stowed the boys, working alone, did the murder alone too. That *priest of sir Robert Brakenberies* who *tooke vp the bodies*: he's the guilty man. I fingered him, just sitting holding your Holinshed in my hand. As you asked.'

Down the line from Scotland she can hear her master breathing unhappily.

'Then off I went to the University library to flesh out my solution. I wanted a name.'

Breathing, breathing.

'Brackenbury, I find, kept three chaplains to serve the Tower and its inmates: a Dean and two canons. Which one was it? The Dean was an elderly Augustinian. A saintly man, to judge from the benefactions in his will. He was dead within the year. One of the canons died, still serving the Tower chapel, in 1492. But the other canon was a young man in Richard's day, not long out of Cambridge. Obscure, peasant-born. No doubt peasant-hardy. Ambitious and clever. Audacious too. I picture him the morning after the crime, walking over to Westminster. Discreetly asking to see the King. Richard liked to be seen talking to priests. It helped the public image of his regime. Where King Edward had been a sybarite, cavorting with whores, his brother was sober and pious. Anyway, the King does receive him alone, and they talk at length –'.

'This is simply made up.'

'Yes it is. But the record's clear. Richard showered this young man with preferment. That very month he was made a prebend of Windsor. And simultaneously given a stall at York Cathedral. He was presented to three, count 'em, *three* rich livings in the West Country of which Richard's own Earldom of Gloucester had the avowson. The income from one of them was, let me see my notes, all of twelve pounds. He'd have had to employ a curate or two, but still, twelve quid in 1485! It must have been nearly all cream.'

'Might we –'.

'Bulk cash had come in from somewhere as well. Just before Christmas he bought the manor of Elkingdon in Hertfordshire outright. The next year he got "a grant of the custody of the temporalities of the bishopric of St. David's."

'Num,' said unhappy Felix, 'num. But might –'.

'Loadsamoney. He was collated Archdeacon of Wiltshire. Then Bosworth happened, Richard was dead. But the Archdeacon was quick to make his peace with the Tudors. After that he was unstoppable.'

'Most clerics made their –'.

'More, writing in 1519, insists that the priest who buried the Princes (More's careful not to name him) *secretelye entered them in such place, as by the occasion of his deathe, whiche onely knew it, could neuer synce come to light*. More doesn't just say that the priest is dead, he clumsily *insists* on it. Anxiously insists. He's writing clumsily because what he's writing is untrue, and lying makes More wretched. The priest in question is not dead. He's not yet sixty. He's a prominent churchman. Absentee Bishop of St Asaph in fact. Filthy rich. He's recently founded a new college in Cambridge.'

'You have –'.

'*Wygefortis*: why did Adam Worthyal choose that name?' Abishag and

Culpepper both thought, a little shyly as one does, of the legend of St Wygefortis: how once-upon-a-time a pagan king had a lovely daughter who was secretly Christian; how she refused her father's order to marry a pagan prince; how she prayed her chastity might be preserved by the disfigurement of her beauty; how overnight she grew a beard; how next morning her father, astonished and enraged, had her crucified.

'St Wygy was all the rage at the time,' said Culpepper, miserably. 'Zany extravagance. Metamorphosis. Weird sex. She appealed to fifteenth century taste.'

'Yes, but that's not why she appealed to Worthyal. He chose that name for his college because Wygefortis, too, was a royal child slain on the orders of a close relation, the king. Adam Worthyal built and endowed this place for her because he hoped she might plead for him in heaven. He put up that embarrassing painting above the altar in chapel, that girl on a cross in a sort of ball-gown with a beard to her waist. He knelt and prayed before it. Hopeless reparation. He could never dare confess, so could never be sacramentally absolved. No priest could be trusted with such an explosive secret. Worthyal had to hug – '.

'This is getting like a women's romance. Who was the schoolgirl you did to death last winter? The one addicted to novelettes? Hope something. She might –'.

'Worthyal had to hug his secret to himself. The infinite solitude of it wearied him. It was too vast. It was too secure. He longed to lighten the weight of his safety, to betray himself a little. It soothed his agony to drop hints now and then, to be indiscreet.'

'We can't possibly –'.

'An up-and-coming politician, Thomas More, was researching his abusive life of Richard III. He approached Worthyal for details. "You were then serving in the Tower, my Lord, were you not? What happened?" Worthyal supplied him. Supplied him recklessly. Intellectual to intellectual. He admitted burying the boys. He very nearly confessed the killing – perhaps hoped More would put two and two together. But More didn't guess. Or did, but covered up what he knew, repeating the official lie. Just as you do, Felix, in your history. You praise Worthyal's career as a Humanist, and never mention what his career was founded on. No one ever accused him. If it hadn't been for that freakish chance discovery of bones in 1674, Worthyal's secret would have lasted 'til the end of the world. It was the part of his mind he could not endure, which no one could touch, which no forgiveness could relieve; it was his acnestis.'

'Now you're just re-treading your cleverness of yesterday.... No no, stop. Stop making things up. This isn't a novel. And stop showing off. You've passed your theory exam. Damn you. Get on a 'plane. Come here and let's see how you manage part II, the practical. You may not find that so congenial.'

'Thank you…. *Thank you!* And seriously, Felix: I'm proud to be your disciple. I want to learn to do what you do. The way you do it.'

'*You may not have to.*'

'How d'y' mean?'

What he said next seemed wrung from him. It wasn't gracious. 'I was only trying to put you off with Holinshed. It wasn't really a test. It mean, it wasn't meant as a soluble problem. I was certain it was too hard for anyone to think through.'

'But *you* solved it.'

'… I didn't. As it happens. I only looked into Holinshed because I was curious. To see if there were traces there of Adam Worthyal's guilt. I already knew he was guilty.'

'You did?'

'Go to the bottom right of my desk. The locked drawer. The combination's 1-9-3-9…. Yes? You'll find a eggshell-blue envelope, sealed…. Got it? Bring it on the 'plane. Sit well away from everyone else. Inside you'll find two sheets. Just photocopies, but do be very very careful with them.'

'I –'.

'When you've read them, lock yourself in the aeroplane lavatory, tear them up, flush. Spread them over hundreds of miles of countryside in tiny bits.'

'How romantic.'

'No. Practical precaution. It's time those papers left my room. They're too dangerous. But you've earned the right to see them before they go. You've done what only one reader of Holinshed has ever done – as far as I know.'

'Not you?'

'No, *not me*. Another. Subtle fellow. Name of Shakespeare. Shakespeare did it, alone of all the children of men. And then there had to come along,' said Culpepper, savagely, hanging up, 'you.'

## *iii.*

Margot ffontaines-Laigh was not very depraved; not if we take into account that she was an aristocrat, an undergraduate of St Wygy's, and the mistress of a habitual homicide. She had only a few unruly habits.

Much the worst was fly agaric. She'd abused the stuff during her pagan period last summer, in Quintember, and still doggedly called it *ambrosia*, the ambrosia of the Olympians. And she still occasionally indulged.

We ask: why?

Answer: she was barely twenty and therefore felt immortal.

Bad answer. Age was incidental. She kept consuming ambrosia in obedience to what she called (to herself, not to him: he was vain enough already) the Culpepperian System.

Felix had taught her that the intellect merely plods unless it have access now and then to visionary quarters of the mind. In his case, visions came through wilful mental slackness. He choose to keep the doors of waking thought swinging back and forth in the breeze. Any passing perversity or dæmon or demon was welcome to his consciousness.

Abishag was made of finer stuff. Her thoughts were naturally crisp, brisk and lucid. She didn't have Culpepper's knack of simply forcing open daylit mind to the night. Therefore, she persuaded herself, she required ambrosia to descend to his level. She had to poison herself out of common-sense, like any shoddy village shaman beyond the Ob, getting himself vatic on reindeer urine.

Agaric is hallucinogenic in sufficient quantities. Abishag had already achieved those quantities. She'd nibbled at her dried mushrooms all night as she sat up over Holinshed, dipping them in a glass of port. By seven she had solved the murder, had spoken to her master by 'phone, had been accepted as executioner's apprentice, had been summoned to Scotland.

Why, then, in the fifteen minutes before leaving for the station, couldn't she have left the dangerous muck alone? Why did she fry her remaining mushrooms, stir them into *pesto alla genovese,* and spread them on toast?

*I deserve to celebrate,* she told herself, *I the first person ever to join the dots.* Also: *There'll be no time for breakfast at Stansted.* Also: *I abhor solitary journeys.* Also: *I abominate Scotland.*

Which was all camouflage. Her motive was fear. She was going north to be initiated into Culpepper's profession, and her conscience was in revolt.

*Hallucinogenic* is a strong word. For Abishag, the virtue or vice of ambrosia was merely that it restored the proper strangeness of things. It peeled back the homogenous sheen that comes from too much clever chatter.

For instance: without her mushrooms she wouldn't have had the odd sensation of being literally a follower of Felix. She was on precisely the same route, first, in her taxi, trundling along the same road; then on the same 'plane, pursuing the same errand. Every instant her sitting body passed through the space his sitting body had occupied twenty-four hours before.

She felt her mind piercing his. *I want to be your disciple,* she'd told him. Now she experienced a violent exaggeration of that wish. She was violating his unity, she was becoming Culpepper. She was thinking as he did. No doubt she would sound like him when it came time to speak. Her eyes grew wide and spectral.

Happily, ten past eight on a wintry Friday morning is not a fashionable time to fly to Glasgow. The 'plane was nearly empty. No one fussed over a girl holding a paperback at arm's length to focus her dilated pupils.

We ask: what paperback? And why was she not reading the photocopied pages, as commanded?

Because that eggshell-blue envelope had, frankly, a baleful look. Now that the moment for opening it was at hand, she wanted to put it off. First a quick glance at something innocuous. She'd brought along her tatty schoolgirl copy of *The Tragedy of King Richard the Third*, scribbled-on and even, she thought, smelling still, a little, of school lunches. *I need*, she told herself, *to understand Felix's joke about Shakespeare.*

She knew the play well, had indeed acted Lady Anne in a school production one summer term long ago, four years back, a fifth of her age.

*Great larks, this play*, she thought, turning the pages, *but how raw! What knockabout! Crouchback's just an ogre from a panto. Spine so twisted he scuttles.* Moll Sargon, the class hearty, had virtually played him as a tarantula; Abishag had loathed their scenes together – Molly's nasty furry pinching tendrils on her cheek, ugh! *Half his body must be one great acnestis.... It's just* matinée *propaganda. How credulous young Will must have been to swallow the official lie* – and she pictured him in his garret, wild-haired, open-shirted, inky fingers grubbing through his Holinshed (that dull-brown brick), wetting his pen, trying out a phrase, snickering over it. *Or perhaps he just wrote whatever it took to keep Bess Tudor happy. Being her lapdog –*

'Injurious jade!'

'What?' she said out loud, then glanced nervously up and down the fuselage. (The stewardess, catching this glance, smiled even more brightly – her smile said *Oh God you're a loony and it's only eight thirty-six in the morning* – and the nearest passenger, a weasely cove of the estate agent type, shook his scalp behind his *Daily Maul*.)

'Thou stigmatical base dissembling drab!'

'What?' she repeated, this time in her head, since she realised the voice (a rapid nasal Midlands voice) also proceeded from inside; emerged, in fact, from her imagined Shakespeare. Although he was entirely altered. The smudged hands were now fashionably white and rested, one on a bust of Tacitus and the other, in a fist, on the silk-draped table before him. He was in an acid-green doublet, artfully slashed, with a sprigged shirt tugged through the slashes. His grizzled head, ruby ear-ringed, was topped with a tapering plumed flowerpot of felt, and rested on an immense lace ruff. He was distinguished, baroque, Jacobean, and in a furious temper.

'D'y' frigging *mind*? Came hence to be patronised?'

'I didn't –'.

'D'y' confound me with aught stupid? You say my demoniac hunchback's most monstrous crude, an impossible bogey. How, then, was he meant?'

'An impossibility?' said Margot, as meekly as she could manage. 'A skit on Holinshed? A *satire*?'

'Arr,' he said, relenting, relaxing into thick Warwickshire, 'aye, a satire. That's the word. Th' art a lass as learnèd as bonny.'

Margot remembered his weakness for witty pretty young noblewomen. She tried to plump up her intellect. This was not easy: the ambrosia fumes were rising, her brainpan was full of glittering smog.

But he'd tossed aside the incredible hat and was talking again. 'My stage-play's a fart in the government's face. Especially about the Princes. I winked so hard my eyelid ached. Take up that ill-printed rag-book. Turn to Act IV, scene iii. Do you see what Richard's saying – ?'

'*Come to me, Tyrrel, Soon at after-supper, and thou shalt tell the process of their death…*. But – sir – he *doesn't* come. We never hear.'

'Y' think I *forgot*?'

Margot made deprecating noises within her head.

'Or that I'm squeamish, who batten on infanticide? What lustique fun I'd had in my *King John*, when *that* king orders the murder of *his* nephew!'

'I remember,' said Margot meekly. 'I understand.' And she did: we don't get to hear what happened from Tyrrel because it didn't happen, couldn't happen; because the received version makes no sense.

It seemed he heard, for he almost smiled. 'Ay. Mere clumsy guesswork. As I hint to my auditors, not that those dull-wits notice, they make me vomit. Audience dull-heavy, heaving-light poet, a pretty figure but let it go – read on, if it please 'ee.'

'Should I – ?'

'Ifee would.' He was perfectly genial now. He was sitting on the carpetted table, swinging his short legs, twirling his hat; he had his arm round Tacitus' neck. She rustled the pages while he continued, airily: '*Of course* it's nonsense, this exhumation by the priest. Tyrrel tells Richard on the evening of the crime that he's seen the boys dead, but –'.

'Yes, here it is:

> The chaplain of the Tower hath buried them;
> But how or in what place I do not know.

Oh,' said Margot, stricken with a thought. 'That's *not* what Holinshed says. He says *Tyrell* did the burying. Did you –'.

'He does. There I dared contradict. I set against the official lie a lie of my own. Goading my dull auditors to use their small wit. Picture *my* tale: Tyrrel and his two thugs do the strangling, then summon the chaplain, who bears the boys away and does the digging himself, while Tyrrel, and Masters Dighton and Forrest with loutish arms and dirty fingers, linger upstairs in the empty bedroom – doing what? Discussing the poetry of Petrarch?'

'No, that's absurd. So did you –'.

'If the Princes were interred the night they died, and it needs be they were, then slayer and burier were one.'

'Oh,' she said in a small voice. 'Did you – ? I mean, Felix *wasn't* joking? You *did* work it out from Holinshed, just like me?'

'The cases are *not* alike,' says the thin voice, turning haughty again; the felt flowerpot was clapped on the bald pate. 'My poor wit is *not* quite as yours. Recall that the skeletons hadn't been found in my day. Nor did I have Master Culpepper giving me broad hints. It was *far* more of an achievement.'

'I'm sorry,' said Margot, trying to leave unformed the thought: *After all I'm only just in my twenties and I'm tired of being bullied by older men.*

'I too,' sniffed the poet, 'was in my twenties when I wrote *Richard the Third.* You overplay your youth now and then.'

Margot abased herself: 'They say you were dazzling from the cradle, sir.'

Once more the poet unbent. She was, after all, confoundedly pretty. 'Frankly, my dear, between ourselves, I was…. Well, from Holinshed I was fairly sure a Tower priest did the deed. I dropped what hints I dared. I certainly make it clear that Tyrrel was innocent – he's laughably-drawn. A character as impossible as his master, as Richard himself. And Brackenbury's obviously innocent, being a uniformed booby, conscientiously a fool. *I may not leave it so: I am bound by oath and I will not reason what is meant hereby, Because I will be guiltless of the meaning –.*'

'Yes yes! Only a policeman would say that. With anyone else it'd count as literal ranting.'

The poet smiled. 'Exactly. You're a credit to your Culpepper. Speaking of whom –'.

Something in his tone frightened her so much she banged her paperback shut, cutting off the voice sharply as switching off a radio.

She considered. *How can I be in pupillage to an assassin if I shy from threats?* Very cautiously she opened the book, and the debonair voice resumed within her head.

'Speaking of Felix: you'll watch out, won't you? Th' craftiest knaves are of clerical disposition. Deep-revolving witty Buckingham and so forth. When

Richard wants to seize the throne, he arranges to be found *with two right reverend fathers, Divinely bent.* That's the milieu of slaughter. You'll remember how Lady Anne – '.

She did; and this time she not only shut the book, she shoved it into her bag, pushed the damnable envelope in with it, and stared fixedly out the window, defying the drug, holding off visions until the dreary seat-belt sign lit up and they could descend through oceans and oceans of white-grey swirl, down through the dirty fog-banks.

Glasgow Airport. Clamour. White-grey walls. Huge windows revealing more white-grey air. Everyone's breath stinking of coffee, the coffee of whisky, the whisky of peat. Out this miasma and onto a trivial train.

A station in the midst of the city. Welcome to Queen Street said one sign, just one might read in London; this impression was spoilt by Fàilte gu Sràid na Banrighinn printed underneath. She was in a strange land, on a bracing frigid platform, doped.

Here was her train, bound to go through the mountains to Fort William. Margot, needing solitude, bought a First Class ticket and found an almost empty carriage, harbouring only two sturdy-looking old ladies with tweed skirts, sensible shoes, hairy jumpers, and long severe intelligent faces turned disapprovingly on her as she groped along into her seat.

Abishag sat for a while leaning her forearms across the table. The mist burned away. She had emerged from the dimness of the South. She was leaving behind the wet, sullen autumn of the South, and penetrating the November of Scandinavia: purple, orange and black, not much green; golden moss; white water, black sky, heather, distant snow; everything lit by sunshine that was low, bright, thin, yellow. She'd gone up and up the long thin island of Great Britain; she was climbing up into the stony part at the top; where the light seems to fall from the sky onto the capping rock. She was vaguely appalled by the severe beauty and the barbarically beautiful names of its little stations. Dalmuir, Dumbarton.

Helensburgh Upper, Gualachulain. It was time. She shook herself properly awake, produced the washed-out-blue envelope, looked about (the sturdy ladies were gossiping in Morningside accents, ignoring her), tore it open, shook out two ordinary sheets of paper; then paused, making herself breathe. The atrocity, whatever it was, was long ago. Long ago. She must be less jumpy.

The first sheet was the photocopy of a piece of manuscript. The black-letter baffled her at first. It looked like so many fence posts, lightly held together by tiny horizontal wires.

After a minute or two she had puzzled it out.

> We Adamme bishope of sainte Asaffe do add unto
> the statutes of our colledge of yᵉ blyssed Wygy-
> fortisse thys moste privie codicill ⸿ yᵉ whyche yᵉ
> master & hee alone is to haue in hys keping &
> hauing once reade we wolle & charge that hee is
> to seale jt up & commend to hym who shalle be
> yᵉ master on ladies daye C years hence & in like
> manner againe for each C years until yᵉ end of yᵉ
> worlde ⸿ yt being to our minde passt yndurrance
> that so grete & grievous a synne { yᵉ which we dare
> not brynge to absolucyon nor mayke suffrage of
> holye masses } should be altogthere hyd from yᵉ
> knowlydg of all men for all tyme & utterlie persys-
> she with ourselffe

'The old problem,' murmured Abishag to herself: 'there's a place in the mind we can't reach ourselves, and can't bear to leave it unscratched by other people.'

> ⸿ to wytte that we being then canon of yᵉ church
> of sainte Peter ad vincula in yᵉ tour of London
> dyd wythe our owne hande slaye yᵉ yonge kynge
> edward yᵉ v. & eke hys brother richard yᵉ duke of
> Yorke sons to our late leige lord edward iv. they
> beinge lodged in that pryzon & that hauing done
> thys blody deede as they were wythe us prayeinge
> yᵉ houres of our ladie

– 'Praying his breviary with the boys! Great God in Heaven! That was an inspired guess of mine' –

> did bear the news of yᵉ same to yᵉ usurping duke
> of Gloster callyng hymselfe kynge richard yᵉ iij.
> & was by that damnabill & most bloodye wyght
> richely requyted wyth both pelf & offices in yᵉ holie
> churche butte by yᵉ offended maiestie of Godde
> most assuredly requyted with burninge perdycyon
> the yᵉ whiche to our myghtie distresse we

– and not a word more. A long blank space stretched to the bottom of the page.

It was queer how cold that large whiteness seemed to Abishag. Worthyal had been a vain hypocritical prelate; anyway it was all a long time ago. Yet she couldn't help seeing him, an old, frightened man, in green velvet gown trimmed with rabbit fur, sitting alone at his desk with a candle, unable to finish writing because hellfire was creeping near. 'Of course I'm making that up – the fur-edged mantle, the flickering candle. A bit woman's romancey, as Felix would say. I wish I could see the real Adam Worthyal.'

She sighed, and turned to the second sheet. This seemed to be a photocopy of a card, about a foot square. The shape was puzzling for a second and then – 'Oh course! It's a packet. A portfolio. The envelope containing Worthyal's confession.' The photocopy looked smudged because the packet must be very battered and dirty. It was covered with diverse writing.

In the middle, a crazily ornate hand:

Ego Ioh. Aglionbius :
Magister Collegii Vvigefortiss

– she recognised the name of the Jacobean Master of St Wygefortis', Aglion-by, an early Puritan –

HANC CONFESSIONEM TURPEM
MEA MANU APERTAM
NUNC DENUO OBSIGNO AD ALIOS CENTUM ANNOS
XXV MARS : MDCXIII.

Which is to say, *Having opened this shameful confession, I direct it be sealed again for a hundred years: 25 March 1613.* Below was what in the photocopy looked like a broken black blob, and was presumably his seal.

'Terse,' she muttered to herself, 'terse but not serene. Something put the wind up our Dr Aglionby.'

At the top left, in graceful letters, was this writing:

> In Submiſsion to the Command of the Founder,
> & in accord with the Precept of my Predeceſsor
> in the Maſterſhip Dʳ Jo: Aglionby, I have this
> Evening (it being Ladyday in the XIIᵗʰ Year of our
> Dread Sovereign ANNE, & of Our Lord the one
> thouſand seven hundred & thirteen) privily
> opened this Packet, & with Sentiments of acute
> Diſmay seal up again a Paper miſchievous in
> Substance, & prone to bring open Scandall upon

this College; Taking Liberty to obſerve that the Pafsion of Self-Accuſation springs not solely from veracious but (perhaps juſt as oft) from fantaſtical Cauſe; & that tho' the Guilt of this unhappy Bᵖ of Sᵗ Asaph appear terrible enough, it is by no means concluſive, his purported Crime having been impoſed on his Memory (for aught we know) by the Terrours of papiſticall Superſtition, working upon a Dispoſition naturally scrupulous & melancholick. *Theophilus Knipe, M.A.*

'Wouldn't it be pretty to think so.'

The nineteenth century had contributed lines in a florid, swoopy hand.

> *25ᵗʰ Mar. 1813* Let this MS. return to its iron casket & livid dust, to sleep another century undisturbed. Ζητεῖν τὴν ἀλήθειαν: yet not beyond measure! The most interesting light the paper throws on the melancholy and romantic mystery of the vanished Princes cannot mitigate the heavy slur it lays upon the origins of St Wygefortis'. We are founded, if we are to credit Bishop Worthyal, upon the most infamous deed of the Middle Ages, and perhaps in our Nation's history! Too horrible. *Josiah Myre.*

The Master in 1913, the famous Broad Churchman Gerald Linden-Bowyers, was modest. He'd contributed (in tiny letters, neater than print) only a pious quotation and a pious hope.

> *"Love took up the glass of Time, and turn'd it in his glowing hands."* I receive this testimony of a crueller age and bequeath it to the perusal, a century hence, of what must surely be a yet purer, kinder, more Christ-like generation. *Avē! moritūrī tē salūtant. G.L.-B.*

Finally, Juicy had made an ugly scribble in ballpoint:

> *25.03.2013* How symptomatic of the false consciousness engendered by the class-warfare of bastard-feudalism! I'm tempted to Out Worthyal

for his abusive act toward minors, my relatives
as it happens. Pragmatically speaking, this might
give College a much-needed boost in tourist
income. But we'd surely lose more than we gained
from sensationalism in the medium- to long-
term. I therefore re-archive this text for another
100 years, by which time scientific socialism will
have rendered all aristocratic violence irrelevant.
*Sir Trotsky Plantagenet, Master.*

Margot was riled. 'Typical. Bloody *bloody* typical. Juicy prides himself on
keeping his trust, *and* sneers at it, *and* breaks it anyway by passing this photocopy on to Felix.' A thought stuck her. 'Presumably with a command to bear
it in mind but *not* quote it in the College history. And not to show anyone
else.' Another grim thought stuck her. 'Particularly not to show *me*. Juicy
probably had *me* in mind. He didn't want Felix sharing this revelation with
his squeeze.' She folded the two sheets. 'And how *possessive* Juicy sounds.
Doesn't let us forget that he's a Plantagenet too, just like the Princes.... The
crime was a family matter. Perhaps all serious bloodshed has to be; who can
take blood seriously if it's not your own blood? ... But what a cheap little
wretch the Master is'; and she began to tear the two sheets into infinitesimal
pieces. Then she began to struggle with the pinched slab of glass at the top of
the window. 'And if it comes to that, how *bloody typical* of Felix. He's handed
a straight-forward confession, then makes a mystery of it. Poses to me as
the great detective. The fathomer of age-old crimes. Unraveller of the worst
crime ever committed in England. *Plonker.*'

She had worked it open. Despite the pale sunshine, the frigid air swiped
spitefully at her fingers. The sturdy old ladies at the far end of the carriage, who
evidently thought even fresh air should be enjoyed in moderation, looked up
to glare. She ignored them, and pushed her fingers through the gap. Bit by
bit she released the filthy paper. The wind whipped it away over the hedges
and copses of Dumbartonshire, nibbling her knuckles with its ice-teeth. She
slammed the glass shut, sat down rubbing her frozen hand, and found Bishop
Worthyal sitting opposite her.

That is: she realised it was, of course, just a vivid imagination, begotten
on her by the magic mushrooms she'd been gorging for a day and a half.
With an effort of mind she could see that there was no one in the seat. But
when she relaxed the stranglehold of reason, the empty air thickened: there
it was again.

She knew it was Worthyal, although it didn't in the least resemble the
famous portrait of the Founder in Hall, hung high above High Table in an im-

mense gilt frame. That painting shows the good bishop as he would no doubt have liked to be remembered: as disciple of Cicero and apostle of Quintilian, heir of Cato, equal of Scipio, editor of Demosthenes, correspondent with Erasmus, ally of Colet: the first man in Cambridge to write good Greek. His face is serene, nobly craggy, cold and querulous. His mitre, cope and crozier are borne with a certain air of detachment; clearly he'd be more comfortable with the bare shoulder and brown robe of a professional pagan philosopher. Pensively, he runs his finger over a thick volume – not a breviary – while off to his left is a romanticised view of St Wygy's, half-finished as it was when he died, and stretching behind him a vaguely Attic, somewhat Frenchified landscape, ending with a white-pillared temple.

Such was the baroque Worthyal Abishag saw every day at lunch and dinner. The figure opposite her on the train was not like that. It was naked, haggard, shrunk to the size of an eight year-old child; it was hunched, clenched and entirely hairless, so that its cranium was like the crown of a decayed fungus. Every bone showed. Its hands were grasped in front of it, resting on the white railway-carriage table, fingers writhing over each other. The nails were missing.

Abishag scarcely noticed all this. Her gaze was absorbed by its terrible enormous eyes, big as a frog's. Then she saw, here and there, triple puncture-marks in its skin, five inches apart, half-healed. And one collar-bone was scorched, like the wing-tips of an overdone roast fowl....

She wasn't sure if it could see her. Anyway, why would it care? Its eyes were consumed by shock: a sudden shock repeated heart-beat after heart-beat for eternity. 'The shock of irreparable guilt,' she murmured to herself: 'that's what that look means. It *exists* in guilt. As salamanders exist in flame. It swims in bubbling pitch of self-knowledge. Oh God, God' – it was unbearable; Abishag shut her eyes against it.

Immediately its crackling voice sounded in her skull. 'Don't be squeamish, child, don't dare shrink. I am your Founder. You drink a toast to me after every College dinner. Before every dinner you recite my gr, my gr, gr' – but here a spasm of particular pain passed through its parchment skin; it seemed it could not manage the word *grace*. It knotted its nailless fingers until Abishag was sure they must break, and it puled; biting off the puling to lean forward and hiss: '*You*. You are a nymph of Wygefortis. *My* College. Our College. Our fountain of pollution. You know they came to me on my deathbed to tell me the first Court was complete. You've heard this story? You know what I growled?'

Name it *Gehenna*.

'Yes, "Name it Gehenna". To warn scholars against the penalty of pride, that's what they pretended to think I meant.' The creature's snigger was entirely ghastly. 'You've kept giving infernal names to the place, haven't you? As you've added Court after Court. Tartarus, Sheol. Building after building, sewer after sewer. Moloch, Cocytus, Acheron – a pretty custom', but the voice flinched at each name, as if each name called to mind a particular pang. 'Don't recoil. I am your Founder. I am your benefactor. You are in me and I am in you. I formed you and you formed me.'

Abishag found herself asking 'How?' without meaning to.

'*How?* What do you think turned me into this? One lapse into infanticide? My two little murders for Richard of the twisted back? One breach of the laws of heav, heav' – but this, apparently, was another impossible word. 'Never. *Hear me*'; for Abishag, growing frightened in ways she did not understand, was trying to shut out the words. 'That poor cripple! What could *he* gain from what I did? He was doomed whatever happened, the realm couldn't endure him. If Richard had let the little Prince live, rebellion would have restored him, restored the true king. Because of my deed, rebellion benefited another usurper. There's been nothing but usurpation ever since. Once stolen, a realm cannot be pure again. It never stops getting stolen.'

Abishag, despairing, opened her eyes. The spectral face was unchanged, full of its own ache, indifferent to her. Its gaze was fathoms away, dragging itself deeper into guilt, fathom by fathom without end. The blackened lips scarcely moved. Without looking at her it kept up its thin whine in her mind. 'Richard – pah. Not him. So whom do you think I served? For whom did I break faith? For whom did I wreck Plantagenet England, bring in a parcel of Welshmen happy to play with dirt? Their Tudor extortions, treason trials, schisms, heresies: that was *my* work. Religion twisted back and forth 'til it broke. And you lot. I founded *you*. I spawned your whole caste.'

Abishag's eyes were wide with a new dismay, for she'd detected a sort of ruddy dimness coming and going over the creature's skin, as if cavernous light and shadow moved on it somewhere else.

Still it would not look at her; but its unspeakable bat-nostrils twitched in her direction and suddenly it cried with revulsion: 'I smell it on you!'

What, what? She made a desperate noise, and the two fine Presbyterian ladies put their heads together to wonder what the world was coming to, what with a drunken young woman, Sassenach of course but *still*, in First Class. First Class!

'The reek!' Sniff, sniff. '*That, that!* I'm never free of it. They show me all to you as you come hither and you all' – he was almost beside itself now – 'you all *stink*. Worse that tar on flesh, worse than halite bubbling in the Lake. *Pecunia non olet!*' it ranted. 'Madness, madness, *olet, olet*, of course it smells – nidorous effluvium, maul at the throat, gauze rasp in my lungs, foulest sore, *you*, you are my perdition ….'

It was perfectly abhorrent to be dreaded by such a thing. 'What smell? Tell me.'

With a hiss it collected itself: 'Fool, fool. The stink of stolen houses, of course, *monasteries. Convents.* England's steeped in the juice of larceny. Blasphemy. Everything given G, G, G – every pious offering for a millennium. Pulled down in an instant by the Tudor tiger, left for you lot. You hyenas.'

My lot. She thought of her family, the Laighs, hungry hard-faced Cheshire squirelings.

'I *nose* it on you, yes, yes. Freebooters under Henry. You fawned on Elizabeth. Didn't you? Minced for James, slaughtered Charles. Absolutism, anarchy, atheism, oligarchy. Your next generation brought in the German simians. Yes.'

Abishag's history-master at her school had High Tory. She'd heard this sort of thing before. He'd enjoyed reproaching her for her family's origins. But that had seemed abstract. Now each sentence was bruising her. She tried to stand up.

'Sit, fool. *Why did I do it?* you ask. Who incited the murder? Why did I smother the boys? I'll tell you. *You* made me do it.'

He screamed suddenly, and covered his eyes so he couldn't see her.

'Who killed the Princes, trollop? *Who killed the Princes in the Tower?* – You killed the Princes.'

Abishag's throttled noise made the two sturdy ladies cluck their tongues and glance at each other.

'You used me to do it. You larcenous generations. You called to me from one of England's possible futures: "Spill the legitimate blood, slay the last rightful king," you cackled in my head, "make us possible, found for us a gangster kingdom." A land of thieves. You were in me, now I am in you. A nation of crooked jumped-up muddy hedge-squires, smirking in ermine. Engendered in a bed with a feather pillow by me, your Founder. Come to daddykins.'

*It's not there, it's not there*, insisted Abishag to herself, squeezing her eyes shut and pressing them with the balls of her hands.

'What if I were forgiven my hundred thieveries? A thousand more crowd in before the words of absolution are done, because I am font of the nation's crimes. Now the icebergs are melting in the north and more suffering lies ahead for you than you have words for, but will it wipe out the guilt? Wipe out the guilt? No. No. The defiling blood I shed lies pooled over the whole land, unrinseable' – and the dread of Worthyal filled Abishag so deeply that with a fierce effort exorcised it. She sent it back to hell.

And slumped back in her chair, exhausted, staring at the perfectly empty chair in front of her, wallowing for a moment in the comfort of her empty brain.

The outer world gradually came back to her.

The station called Arrochar & Tarbet was gone.

The stations called Ardlui, Crianlarich. Upper Tyndrum went by.

Now for Bridge of Orchy.

The Orchy is a swift, babbling, foaming, freezing, rocky mountain stream that rises in the Black Mount Forest, hurries down through two sets of rapids, Witches' Step and The End of Civilisation, washes the gallows-hill of Glenorchy, famous throughout the Highlands, then drops into the fresh frigid waters of Loch Awe. When King George's men were pacifying the Clans by fire and musket, they carried the military road to Fort William over the Orchy at the head of the glen. The bridge is a serious affair, built as a bit of military apparatus to hold down hostile country; there is nothing alluring about its stonework. A hamlet nonetheless grew up on the boggy left bank, and in the palmy final days of Victoria the board of the North British Railway (which must have been staffed with heroes or delusives) built a station there, with a branch-line over the hills to Skelgourock, a town which, defying experience, has always thought of itself as a resort.

The North British Railway built Bridge of Orchy's station in a holiday mood. They provided a miniature gingerbread cottage as waiting-room, no doubt meant to be gay with baskets of petunias. Now, in November, it was bleak as a sentry-box; in any case it was locked. Abishag stood beneath its ornate eaves, watching no one else get off her big serious train, and feeling the whip of Scottish cold, which is not playful or sulky like English cold, but Nordic or Atlantic: it whistles in your ear *I'll kill you if I can, kiill you – kiiill you.*

*Jump back on the train,* chirped a childish voice in her head, *go on to Rannoch.* She had studied the map in the train. *Then Corrour, Tulloch, Roy Bridge, Spean Bridge, Fort William*: they sounded good places to go. She forced herself to stay put, and after a minute the Fort William service lumbered away north.

For a minute there was absolute nothing, and she stood on the platform as on the bleak and silent raked stage of a modern playhouse. Or as in the solitude of death.

To the west a toothy line of black hills pent in the valley; to the right a moor, Allt Coire an Dothaidh, sloped up into the sky. That sky was black and ponderous as the sooty stones at the back of a hearth, but beneath the dark sky the air was curiously bright. There were no birds. This funny autumn weather was the beginning of troubles.

Here at last (but it could only have been a minute or two) was the ridiculous little train with a single carriage, wheezing over the amber-and-violet hill. It pulled up reluctantly to Bridge of Orchy station. Feeling absurd, Margot opened a door and got in.

There were, obviously, no other passengers – no natural passengers of flesh-and-blood. And she saw no one else, only the ticket collector, who merely raised his eyebrows ('From Glasgow indeed!') before hurrying back to the warm engine-room.

A few heart-beats. The little train started going back the way it had come.

Her mind wandered off again. She wouldn't let herself think of Adam Worthyal himself, but she considered his crime. She considered the shock of it.

It had been revealed to her. It had been revealed in confidence five times now, to five different Masters. Juicy had blabbed. Did the other four have honour enough to keep mum? Perhaps. But did it matter if they had or hadn't kept silence? Wouldn't the truth *leak* out of them? College was founded on the perfect crime; once a century its head learned this truth. Wouldn't cynicism and murderousness inevitably seep outward from the Master into the whole organism?

Hadn't Wygefortis' always had an evil reputation? Not for stupidity (that was a recent development), but for duplicity, shamelessness, infidelity? Of course there were some wholesome influences at work; the corrupting knowledge must fade with time, the evil must soften. But in the thirteenth year of each century, corporate guilt was instantly renewed. The sacrifice of royal children was brought back to mind; the College fabric was (as it were) dashed once more with their indelible blood. It had happened in 1613, 1713, 1813, 1913; and the defilement had been renewed just ten months before.

Which brought her back to the present. Abishag had always imagined Culpepper as a man alone, a phenomenon. But what if he was merely the most recent example of a local type?

She entangled herself in quaint, terrible speculations.

Felix had taught her that England's sedate institutions – universities, Church, bar, Parliament – remain sedate because they keep hired cut-throats. They *must*. In this changeful world, changelessness implies endless vigilance, relentless squelching of trouble. There is, there must be, secret counter-revolutionary violence always. 'I'm a white corpuscle,' he'd told her, 'built to devour alien bodies. A social necessity. I preserve health. Please don't fuss.'

Where else would such a corpuscle be at home, except at St Wygy's?

'Have there been others at Wygy's like him?' she put it to herself. 'Before him? Of course there have!'

She opened her eyes (the mushroom vapour was thickening in her brain) and found the carriage thronged with many men, all staring at her. Some lounged against the wall, some perched on tables and the backs of chairs. They were kaleidoscopic. There were men in severe Victorian black with white hard high collars. Men in baggy Restoration waistcoats to the knees. In *louche* Georgian suits of rose and pistachio with white stockings, square Henrician tan and black, ruffs, *jabots*, immense lace collars, Byronic open shirts, frock-coats, shapeless World War tweeds. There was even a psyche-delic T-shirt on a longhair from four decades back. Some had shaggy bird's-nest beards like Lord Salisbury's; triangular beards dyed blue like Raleigh's; furry-sausage moustaches like Kipling's. But all alike wore black gowns on top of their get-up; all had mortarboards perched on their cropped fuzz, or cascading curls, or full-bottomed horse-hair, or Tennysonian coifs.

More insidiously, all of them shone on her the same superior, fatal, insin-uating smile. Felix's smile. She knew (in her half-trance she could even smell) that smile of *bloodguiltiness*.

The goodly Fellowship was welcoming a novice. Nothing could disperse their silent grins. No eye-clenching could make them go away –

It was a discombobulated Abishag who heard the conductor cry 'Skelgou-rock, aw! Skelgourock next!'

She made herself look out of the window. They were cresting a last rough hill; the bonny town lay below, wet and shiny in the rags of November sun, opening before her. The track descended, entering back and forth down steep, slippery streets. The slate roofs made a long lazy curve down to the sea-loch, broken up by pale-green-washed walls, white, pale yellow, by ugly mean grey-brick bungalows here and there, by flashes from shop-windows. Flash! flash! The light was thin, pure, piercing. Fishing boats bobbing on the water continued the palette of the houses; their rigging, intertwining and netting as their masts swayed, baffled Abishag's blinking eye.

Beyond, the shining shook across a stainless-steel sea, sea-smelling and sea-ominous but only a mile across. Then came a line of trees on the lonely empty shore opposite the town; rising abruptly into steep hills, covered with shaven lion-pelt; which along their ridge foamed with rock naked but for lichen. Behind the ridge was a line of craggier hills; behind them, at an angle, proper mountains, already hooded with snow. The other way she could see the loch twisting and widening, and finally a confusion of green, grey and tawny islands, almost blocking out a gleam of the bright-black real, the open Atlantic, thirty miles off.

*Very fine – yet* this *is why Northern places are given to world-hating heresies. Calvin, Ibsen. Airy cleanness-freshness is rather appalling. Headlands and islets hanging over endless ocean. Makes the natives feel the world as a mote, blowing across the infinite clarity. The only good is light, immense empty pallid Northern light – uncreated, immaterial. But matter: matter is evil. The physical universe is beautiful, yet it's a shame it ever happened. The world's founded on a lapse. Like my College. Like my nation. Like my family. It was a crime to create –* and thinking these thoughts, so terrible they're forbidden even in the Pit, she distractedly got coat, hat, bag from the rack, defying the immaterial smirking killers in their silly period costume, descending the final slope to reach her lover.

Down! Down they went through the precipitate streets. Down to the station crouching by a dock. She gazed in wonder at leaping marine glow, flickering through a line of palm trees – not very healthy-looking but palms indeed, kept alive by the Gulf Stream. Even a thicket of rhododendrons! Despite its sky, despite its name, Skelgourock was freakishly Polynesian, was – but the train had stopped, she was bursting through dissolving wratths, emerging onto the tiny empty platform, into the haunted land of Scotland, canny, uncanny; into a heavy, bright, sober, Northern afternoon.

## *iv.*

She knew better than to expect congratulations from Felix. When she saw him, at the wrong end of the platform, staring in the wrong direction, his preposterous hyper-Scotch costume flapping about him, once more a voice urged her to flee. *He's clearly full of himself abstracted to the verge of dementia – his posture betrays him – he's not seen you, he'll not miss you, go.*

She mastered herself and walked toward him. He turned, and although his eyes seemed to fix on a point an inch above her forehead he managed to come out with: 'Ah.'

'Afternoon, Felix.'

'Ah …!' His eyes dropped over her face and ended up beneath her chin. 'Enjoy your trip?'

'Well, yes.' (*But there's a double meaning in that, he can smell agaric on my breath – I poisoned him with it in the summer, his hippocampus must still sometimes ache with it.*) She shook her own head in the cool air. 'On balance.'

'This way, then.' He did not offer to carry her bag, which he probably couldn't see it. They moved along the platform. Step. Step. Step.

'And how,' she said at random, because the frantically-abstracted silence felt so awful, 'is the Case of the Mutilated Monks?'

'Case? Your case? Should I carry – *the case!* Ah. Finished. Really. Some tidying up for me for us to do. Then home. To Cambridge…. How's Cambridge?'

'Typical. The Prior?'

'Prior to what?' He was hopelessly bemused. '*The Prior!* No. Innocent as the driven. Quite otherwise ….'

The air was wonderfully cool. She dashed the last ambrosia smoke from her head, and it occurred to her that she was wrong. Felix wasn't self-absorbed, he was frightened. He was, in fact, in dread *of her.*

She had been miserably afraid, on and off, all day. Now (since it's impossible to be frightening and fearful at the same moment) she cheered up. 'It's bloody good of you to let me come.'

'Ah – well. You earned it,' he murmured shiftily, 'in a way…. Do you like my car?'

They had emerged from the station. A huge hunter-green Armstrong Siddeley was insolently parked directly in front. The afternoon was closing in already. Despite the bight air, the sky was heavy and sooty as the back of a stone fireplace. 'A Whitley 18, 1952. I didn't see the point of renting anything inconspicuous.'

'No, there wouldn't have been much point,' agreed Abishag, who was amused at quite how much attention they were getting from the locals. Three freckled children, in possession of a shopping trolley and a fat grandmother (or mother), were gaping back and froth from the Armstrong Siddeley to Felix in his monstrous cape. A small committee of genteel housewives had formed on the station steps.

Felix seemed to bask in his local notoriety. 'Ah?'

'It's *magnificent.* Only you. Bravo. I'm in awe. As ever.'

At which Felix, who was insatiable of praise, cheered up too. Indeed all in a moment he turned boisterous and emphatic. He smiled, the smile of those who triumph from birth. His disciple was still his disciple, the world still made sense. 'Only *me*, eh? In *awe*? Well, *you* can drive it' – he removed from beneath his windscreen-wiper an official-looking envelope with red lettering, and tossed it behind him; 'that way *I* can use my hands to talk. I need –'

'Oi! oi, *sairrr!*' Culpepper turned drowsily. An infuriated young policeman, six foot six, thin and bent as a drooping bean, with a tussock of scarlet hair and a great many bones in his face, was bearing down on them. Like all policemen he had feet of a deformed bigness, but what Abishag couldn't take her eyes off was his hands – which were inhuman, twice the proper size. 'Ah mean, *Minister.*' But the uniformed youth was taken back only for an instant by Culpepper's clerical kit. These are Covenanting regions. The bright wind of hatred must blow for ever from the Arctic pole to their craggy individual outcrops; they hate any sort of priest, daring to stand between damned soul and damning Creator. 'Even *ye* cannae gang throwin' *tickets* oan th' grin, *whoever* ye *ur!*' He snatched up the ticket and flourished it into Culpepper's faraway face.

'Fair point.' Culpepper took it from him, tore it up – but carelessly, just twice, not the way Abishag had torn up the photocopies – screwed the quarters into a neat ball, dropped it into the policeman's giant palm, and with his other hand squeezed the fingers shut on it. 'Good man.' If he had been tall enough he might have patted his head.

The freckled children enjoyed this immensely. Their mother's mouth swung wide, revealing a chaos of gum. One *hausfrau* laid a hand on another's sleeve.

'*Yoo're* feckin' under –'

But here Culpepper, halting the man with a gesture and raising his voice for the benefit of the urchins, took it upon himself to make a speech. 'Aren't *you* forgetting what *you* are? *I* am a voter. My employees, the politicians, hired you as a sort of bouncer, to shoo away riffraff so I can pursue my happy life without annoyance.' Quite a crowd was gathering. (*A rooster that isn't crowing,* reflected Abishag, *can't be absolutely sure it's a rooster. Also: He grew up without brothers, he thinks bullying's safe.*) 'I,' boomed Culpepper, slapping his caped torso, 'am a taxpayer, I *pay you.* Do what I hired you for. You're a civil servant, a very minor civil servant. Serve! Get out of my way before I get up a riot with these other voters and taxpayers', who'd have applauded if they dared.

Abishag, while mildly admiring the *panache* of this speech, recoiled from its mean-mindedness. For she could see, as Culpepper could see and the spluttering policeman could not, a sergeant deferentially hurrying up behind.

'What's all this, McChesney?' roared the sergeant, and the young constable fairly leapt out his pale skin. 'What's all this?'

'Your ginger gorilla seems to be arresting me, sergeant,' said Felix, who seemed to setting up as the hero of the neighbourhood. 'Would you be kind enough to tell Detective-Inspector Motte that I'm being kicked or raped in a police cell, and shan't be able to join him for this evening's patrol?'

'Not all, sir. Not 't all. Misunderstanding, sir.' He was a most flustered, blustering, breathless, ruddy sergeant. He scowled at McChesney, opened the boot of the Armstrong, remembered the freckly children and scowled at them too, heaved in Abishag's bag, shut the boot, smiled pleadingly at her, opened the passenger door for Culpepper, smiled pleadingly at him. 'Hope the patrol goes well this evening, sir.' Culpepper's smile was just a shade this side of a smirk.

Abishag, shuddering, got into the driver's seat, took the keys from Felix's pert upward palm, and pulled away.

'You enjoyed yourself.' In the rear-view mirror she could see the short sergeant shrieking and hopping beneath McChesney's downturned face. The freckled family had never had such a glorious day.

Culpepper did not deign to look back. He detected Abishag's disdain, and, for once, could not discount it. 'Was I' – he sounded almost sheepish – 'disgusting?'

'Yes. That's the word.'

'… Hmf. Well it's because I'm *disgusted*. This whole business, it just stinks of policemen. *Gavvers* as His Eminence would say. I don't think I *can* be fair to them. Right at this roundabout.'

'Yes, but why rail? We have to have them.'

'Oh yah, yah, given the human condition there *must* be, there will be, whores, therefore pimps, therefore hair-gel, therefore factory-girls working making hair-gel; but you don't want to give yourself to a lifetime of work in a hair-gel factory – left. Do you?'

'You have me there,' sighed Abishag, absently.

'Given the etcetera,' Felix was saying, 'there *will* be plods.'

'Yes,' she said, automatically, far away.

'But no one's *forced* to join the Force. Bear left at that crossing…. And now right at the statue.'

'Of *Burns* of course – yuck.'

'Only sneaks and fusspots,' Felix was saying, 'are going to *choose* police work. And stupid, almost necessarily stupid. Only fools are going to concern themselves spoiling other people's killings rather than producing their own. *Therefore* it's right to treat them as cockroaches.'

'Yes, Felix,' she said dutifully, but her mind pursued its own rambling. There was a grand Edwardian hotel before them, with a winter garden along the loch and a band carousel and a tremendous façade of polychrome brick, clearly built in the heady days when the North British Railway hoped to make Skelgourock grand. 'Um – isn't that the Royal Caledonian Hotel?'

'It is.'

'Aren't we going there?' she asked, with longing. She needed to shower. She needed to wash the after-taint of agaric from her mouth.

'We are not. Not until we've finished.' He glanced at her exhausted face. '*Courage, ma brave*. Just a few things to do. Then back to bed. Just follow this road out of town.'

So they drove out of Skelgourock, twisting along the water's edge and then up, up, and for the next half hour worked their way deeper and deeper into the foresty hills.

'Where are we going?'

'We're looking … for a *plod*.' Culpepper sighed theatrically. 'Y'know, I don't think His Eminence was decently frank with me. These murders are a nasty police-ridden business. Not at all the flamboyant private act I had in mind.'

'Me too,' said Abishag. *I'm here as a novice, a probationer, a trainee. Must defer. Must feed him his lines.* 'I've been picturing *The Name of the Rose*. A spooky mediæval monastery with you stalking about interrogating blood-thirsty grotesques.'

'Ah, but the monks aren't *in* their spooky monastery. They're in their summer Retreat House.'

'But it's November.'

'It is. They're in hiding. Last month the Abbot started to receive threatening e-mails from a radical cell, hitherto unknown. Revolutionary Atheist Direct Action.'

'*What?* …. I can't take that seriously.'

'Neither could the Abbot. But the messages were so persistent and vicious that eventually he contacted –.'

'Ah. The police.'

'Yes, the bloody *police*…. Who *did* take it seriously. A Detective-Inspector came hurtling up from Glasgow. Atrocious fellow. Name of Motte. A troop of coppers thumped all over the monastery with their feet. Eventually they tripped over a small-but-perfectly-formed home-made bomb.'

'Ah…. I still don't believe in the Revolutionary Atheists.'

'Nobody did. Conan Motte concluded it must be a cover for Moslem fanatics. He began to envisage revenge bombings of mosques, race riots, no end of pother, and ordered the monks to move out of public view. To somewhere they could be easily protected.'

'Their Retreat House?'

'Yes. It isn't much. A circle of wooden cabins. Way up in the Forest of Rowardennan. The monks usually go there in August. Otherwise it's used for Sunday School outings –'.

Abishag sucked her teeth. They were surmounting the line of hills that banked in the loch to the west. Beyond the view was almost alpine.

' – spirituality-pottery weekends. Inner healing for survivors of middle-class Scottish boredom. That sort of thing. You couldn't call the atmosphere heady.'

'Poor Felix.'

'The Trappists arrived in these cabins on Sunday afternoon, after Conventual Mass at the monastery. One Abbot, one Prior, one Cellarer, one

Bursar – nineteen other monks.'

'What are they like?' she asked, not entirely attending to the answer. The half-visible sun was dropping behind the ocean islands and she was marvel-ling over the paradox of Northern woods: mossy depths more luminous than open air; sideways tunnels out of the murky world ….

'*Not* grotesques. Rather distinguished. There's no Trappist "vow of si-lence", that's an urban myth. They just avoid chatter. Language isn't wasted. When they do speak they tend to be rather witty. Wittier, anyway, than anyone in the Combination Room at St Wygy's. For the last three days they've been in the woods, not doing much of anything because of the weath-er. The cabins, you understand, are only meant for summer use, and freezing cold. "A punitive teddy-bears' picnic," remarked the Abbot. He's rotund and cheerful, tender with his brothers, rather caustic toward the outside world.'

'But why there? Anyone can get at a cabin.'

'Not these cabins. They're remote and, you'd think, secure. Three miles drive uphill into the woods, the end of a muddy track. All night there've been a dozen solid policemen tripping over tree-roots and puzzling the badgers. Damn them.'

'*I* think gavvers are rather sweet. I imagine the badgers do too.'

'A dozen policeman *and* a Detective-Inspector. Motte's stayed on. "Needed here. Coordinate manœuvres. Keep rubber ducks in row": that's what he sounds like. Very pushy and up-and-coming, Motte. Wants to live forever, too. Macrobiotic diet, whatever that means. No ale or coffee. Goes for ten mile runs every afternoon. "You 'varsity types, sporty? *Mens sana in* whatsit, aye? What's your routine? Run swim run that's me. Colonic irriga-tion mud therapies. Fit as a boy of twenty." And so forth.'

'God.' Down the road twisted, into a sunless glen.

'This appalling person has taken a personal interest in the case. "Hate-threat! Anachronistic. Pluralistic values" – he has the rhetoric pat. Will be Chief Commissioner if he lives. He put himself "personally in charge" of the monks' security. He's assured the Abbot that no militant atheist can possible get though.'

'Nevertheless – '.

'Nevertheless on Wednesday night, or rather at three twenty yesterday morning, one cabin didn't respond to the bell for Lauds. A brother went to investigate. It was awash with blood. All four monks had been killed in their sleep – that is, there was no sign of a *fracas*. Just a neat slash across each throat, and a fairly neat slash down the left flank. Liver, for the removal of …. Rather stylishly, the monk who found the bodies didn't scream or run about. He went quietly back to the main hut, where he helped sing Lauds, then qui-etly murmured his news to the Abbot. Who, *very* stylishly, didn't scream or shout for the police either, but made a discrete 'phone-call to the Cardinal.'

'Who stylishly rang you. Us.'

'Yes. Us. He also rang the Home Secretary.'

'The depressing Martin Littlejohn. Oh dear.'

'Yes. Although Littlejohn grasped the need for discretion too. He made it clear to Motte that I was to be in charge once I arrived. Motte's been bridling, of course. Professional outrage.'

'Bridling? Isn't he at all *suspicious*? I mean, about what you intend to do with the culprit?'

'He's a policeman. Naturally prone not to think things through.'

'Ah. Like Brackenbury. *I will not reason what is meant hereby, Because I will be guiltless of the meaning.*'

'Ah yes. That. Shakespeare.' He visibly forced himself to be gracious and offhand. 'Congratulations. By the way. On puzzling out what happened to Brackenbury's little guests. Good girl.' He sucked his teeth an then said: 'Brilliant stuff.'

'*Felix.*'

'Anyway, in *this* case' – praise, it seemed, was at an end – 'the menu of suspects is pretty tiny. We don't need much imagination.'

'Could no one have sneaked in?'

'I don't think so. Twelve policeman were patrolling quite a small expanse of wood. Hard to see anyone getting in and out unseen.'

'So it absolutely has to be one of the monks.'

'Hm? … Indeed that might have been what troubled the Abbot. Especially when he noticed a bloody footprint on the wooden doorstep of the Prior's cabin.'

'Y – es.'

'An Islamicist massacre of Catholic monks would be bad enough. But if an enclosed community started slaughtering *itself*, the publicity would be unspeakable.

'What's the Prior like?'

'A mystic. Perhaps. Abstracted, emaciated, composed. Given to sudden intense silence in the middle of sentences that might have ended cleverly. I'm not sure he and the Abbot much like each other. But of course the Rule precludes much bitching.'

'Does the Abbot suspect ...?'

'No. Evidently not. He wandered out of breakfast and carefully spilled his cup of Darjeeling over the Prior's doorstep, washing the blood away.'

'But then he told the Cardinal.'

'Yes. But only because he thinks someone is clumsily "framing" the Prior.'

'He didn't mention the footprint to the police?'

'No no, no. No one's told *the police* anything. Indeed they still don't realise that four of the monks they're meant to be guarding are already dead.'

'They *don't?*'

'Oh, it's always easy to keep a copper in the dark. The brothers have been going about their usual business, as far as they can in chilly cabins. Seven Offices a day. They sang Requiem for their brothers, but the coppers are dolts, not to say Presbyterians, they didn't notice what was being sung, didn't draw any conclusions. The hut with the bodies has simply remained shut. This is a mild November as November go up here, but it's still too cold for stink. We have until tomorrow morning at least before there's any need for announcements, ambulances, arrests, journalists ....'

'So they're still *secret* murders?' Margot was rather flabbergasted.

'They are. If I told Motte he'd want to arrest the Prior at once. No, here's a thought: he'd want to lure the Prior into the woods, leap on him, hold him down, pump his stomach. For *foie gras* sandwiches, y'know.'

'Igh.'

'You can't blame Motte, it's the police pathology, this longing to get fingers into living flesh. Stomach pumps, strip-searches, force-feeding, nasal probes, groping about in the anal cavity. All grist to their mill. But I haven't told him, so he's done – nothing.'

'I see. And you?'

'I pottered about asking questions yesterday afternoon. At seven I came up in time to hear the community sing Compline, pull up their hoods, vanish into their huts. Then Motte and I spent the night prowling about the cabins, keeping the monks off each other. While the coppers, further down the hill, prowled about the trees, keeping off ravening Saracens.'

'Brave you.'

'I have a revolver hidden somewhere in here. In this cape. I keep discovering more pockets .... What a long night. Nothing happened of course. The six torches of the six policemen made six beams through the forest all night, crossing and uncrossing. Millions of times. Triangles of light forming, breaking up. It became hypnotic.'

'But no one could have got through?'

'No. I'm sure not. And no one stirred from the huts except for five blameless trips to the loo.' He gestured broadly, and Abishag turned left, up a darkening country lane between stone walls. 'At three they rang the bell for Lauds. Everyone was there except –'

'For the four killed yesterday.'

'Except for them. Yes. During Lauds I glanced in the Prior's cabin. Blank, of course, Trappists don't own property. Just a very empty wooden hut. I couldn't think of anything else to do so I went back to the hotel and read the novel I'd brought. *Anna Karenina*. It's my fourth attempt to finish it. I've such a curious antipathy for Vronksy. A sort of innate lust to stab him and stab. I can't explain it – it's a painful thrill to read of him. But then I get bogged down in those unspeakable meadow-cutting chapters. If Tolstoy listed every blade of grass it would be more tolerable. And shorter. Anyway, I didn't get far. Can't remember any dreams. It seemed about ten minutes before you rang and woke me up again.'

Abishag had never heard anything so listless. 'Should I keep on?' she asked severely. They had driven down the length of the glen, turned, and were snaking up it again. The long Northern light was thinning and thinning, lowering, turning more grey.

'Yes. Over the top of that ridge. Motte, I gather, was at the station this morning, making his greatness weigh upon the local constabulary. I've been meandering around Dumbartonshire in this Jag, looking at the sights. I'm due to meet Motte and his merry men at the Retreat House at seven, to repeat our futile standing-watch.'

'Felix. You're a pitiful old duffer. You've not progressed *at all.*'

"Duffer", it seemed, remained forbidden humour. 'On the contrary,' snapped Culpepper, sitting up smartly in the passenger seat, 'I'm finished, it's *solved.* I'd have tidied up and left for Cambridge if I weren't letting you in for the kill, *ungrateful chit.* Do another U-turn. Let's go back down the lane and try the other side of the valley.'

She put on her humble voice. 'What are we looking for, please?'

'*We* are not looking for anything – *I* am, you tell me, too pitiful, I abdicate. *You* are here to pass your practical exam. *You* are looking for Motte. *This*, he told me, is where he's running this evening. When you find him *you* are going to play the great detective and unmask the culprit to him. *I* am having a snooze. We pitiful old fellows are always taking naps. Tell me how it goes.' Ostentatiously, he rested his eyelids.

'But I've no idea who the murderer is,' exclaimed the girl in a dull, ugly voice.

Culpepper performed one of the sighs that made him so loathed as a tutor, and did not open his eyes. Abishag was suddenly nostalgic for last night. It had been hard work struggling with Holinshed, but she'd prevailed, and there'd been no one jeering at her.

'Please can you explain?' she said, in the smallest tones she could manage.

'First principles,' said the insufferable fellow, still feigning sleep. 'What do murderers like? Privacy. They're naturally shy about their kills. They want them inconspicuous. Do you agree?'

'Um. Yes.'

'Why, then, are there been so many *lurid* killings? Guts festooned from chandeliers? Severed heads tossed into prayer-meetings? Wives doused with petrol while waving at parades out windows? Corpses parcelled out between shopping bags and left in public libraries? Eh? Because *those* murders –'

' – *aren't* murders.'

'Aren't murders. Yes. That is, murder's a side-effect. The only point of a spectacular –'.

' – of a spectacular murder is a spectacular murder case,' said Abishag, breaking back into brilliance. 'Or rather, not even the case –'.

'Stop! I mean, yes, you're right. But look, there he is!' Felix had deigned to open his eyes. 'Do you see? That spidery fellow in the black singlet. Vanishing into that copse. Speed up. No wait. There's a car coming. Pull over. That's right. Let it get out of range.... Right, now. Can you still see him? *Damn.* Lost him. No he must be behind that stand of pines. Honk.... Again. Louder.... Ah, he's seen us. Here he comes.'

## v.

The figure had emerged from the trees. It had seen the car, doubtless the only Armstrong Siddeley in Dumbartonshire, certainly the only one with an Inverness-caped jokester in the passenger-seat. It had waved, and was jogging toward them.

*He doesn't,* thought Abishag, look *fit as a boy of twenty.* His veins were ropes across his forehead, his skinny legs were mottled purple (although naturally he had massive policeman-feet). His scrawny ribs showed and vanished, painfully showed and vanished, under the black athletic vest. But he ran gamely enough. A hunting spider scuttling through the gloaming, fangs out. A fleck of dirt on the unstained black-silver woods. A mote in the mind's eye. A hairy stick of a man, approaching fifty, with a face like an ax. And a leaky brain: even at that range he was manifestly one of those weirdly scrutable persons. '*I can tell he's thinking "What's all this then?"*, reflected Abishag, aghast. *I can guess his* next *thought, too: "Who's the voluptuous girl?" I know his type. You can guess what he'll think next – guess and always be right.*'

Sure enough, when he was close enough to see her at the steering-wheel a thought-bubble positively formed over his head: *Voluptuous redhead. Purpose of?*

He was prurient, too, as people generally are when they set up to be healthy. He eyed her dubiously, as they say in novelettes, he raised an eyebrow, as they say in novelettes. About Detective-Inspector Motte it was impossible not to use *clichés.*

'Turn round,' said Felix to his disciple under his breath, 'and take us to

Gualachulain.' He turned the handle to lower his window in a lordly way, preparing a smile.

The light was dwindling quickly now. Motte trotted up to the window. 'Dr! Culpepper!' he gasped. 'Issues?' Close up, his legs were so thick with fuzz it seemed strange there were two of them and not eight.

'Get in, Inspector, do get in.' Culpepper was terribly genial. 'Delighted to find you at last. This is Lady Margot ffontaines-Laigh.'

'Humph!' gasped Motte, slithering into the back seat. It wasn't a very vivid way of expressing professional outrage, but he was clearly in a dreadful state from running, barely able to breathe, let alone speak. He breathed all over her neck.

'She is my assistant, Inspector.'

'*Humph!*' Another disgusting thought-balloon formed.

Abishag eyed him over her shoulder, wondering at the livid spots across his forehead and shrunken eyes; then released the brake and pulled away. Not only were his legs too hairy to belong to a human, it was apparent, now that the sweat had slicked down the hair, that they were too thin, too tubular, above all too jerky to be a mammal's.

The great car purred off down the darkling road. Abishag drove, and thought and thought. This is what she thought: *An immense spider is coiled in the back seat. I wish I could squash it.*

Felix, oddly enough, simpered. 'I don't know about you, Inspector, but when *I'm* in half-marathon training' (Abishag's eyebrows shot up her forehead) 'my great concern is electrolyte balance.'

'Rehydration. Potassium salts,' Motte managed to say. 'Coconut water.'

'Of course, of course. But what about glucose impurities?'

'Now then.'

'Why don't you try this?' Culpepper produced a clear plastic canister with A Souvenir of Loch Lomond in pink lettering on the lid. 'A special trail mix the S.A.S. is working on. Very hush-hush. Highly reduced osmolarity.' He held it up; the policemen's hand or claw came over to grasp it; his sweat was remarkably pungent. 'Sit back, and while your citrate levels readjust, I want you to listen to what my assis – my colleague – what Lady Margot has to say. She has insights on our case.'

Abishag could *hear* him: *He's thinking "Not according to regulations."*

'Irregular,' said Motte, unimpressively, his mouth full. Abishag contemplated him in the mirror: unable to resist the cutting edge in sports nutrition, he had begun nibbling at shards of nut, shredded stalk, slithers of husk, and what seemed literal dust.

Felix flicked his head at Abishag, who took a deep breath. Motte's front teeth, she was thinking, protruded like a bunny's. But it was the mouth-parts of spiders she kept thinking of. 'I was advancing, Detective-Inspector, an idea. A tentative theory. Someone has luridly threatened to murder a community of monks. Why?' The hills were steeper now. They were winding along a descending road. She could see then not see Loch Etive, grey-silver hugged between grey-green hills; see and not see its dark waters trailing off toward the ocean. Nor were her thoughts quite straight. 'Mightn't sensational murders – some of them – be performed with an eye on the coming investigation? Or newspaper reports of the investigation?'

'Nonsense,' gasped the policemen, sucking and clattering his venom fangs on knobbly dried fruit. 'Poppycock.'

'Why (I've been asking myself) are so many murders *fun*? Why are they so *literary*? That is to say: why do they seem just made for the gutter press? Is it because they *are* made for the gutter press? Why does the classic English murder seem designed to be turned into a paperback? Why are these crimes so entertaining, so adorable? Aren't they *meant* to be adorable? Aren't they committed in such baroque fashion, then concealed with such fragility, so they *can* be delightfully unwrapped?'

'Nonsense.' *Nasty girl* Abishag would hear him thinking. *Nasty*.

'In other words, aren't flamboyant murders usually done by the police?' She glanced in the mirror: Motte seemed to be suffering cramps, perhaps outraged by her theory. Or experimental electrolytes might be disagreeing with him. 'A sincere murderer never wants publicity, a policeman always does. He craves promotion. The best way of getting it is to entertain and dazzle the public.'

'Tripe,' grunted Motte, unsteadily.

Suddenly she felt sorry for him, and annoyed with herself for finding him subhuman. *He's just an ugly copper. A copper out of his depth. And he's appalled. He's thinking, obviously, "This posh bitch's trying to pin it on one my men." He's thinking "Is it one of my men? Is it McChesney?"* There was a flash in her head. *And of course it is McChesney! That's why Felix was so horrible to that poor gangling carroty boy.* She had it in her to feel sorry even for poor generally-put-upon McChesney. *What could he do, with the whole puny world treading on him since he was thirteen and first began to hulk, but raven and slaughter?*

But what she said, coldly enough, turning a hairpin, was this: 'A classic murder, Inspector, is a work of art. In real life as much as in fiction. The policeman's the author. He chooses the victim and the perpetrator. He plants the clues, he fabricates evidence.'

Motte made an indistinct noise. The poor man seemed to be in pain. Was it merely irritation? Or was he writhing at McChesney's blow, feeling betrayed and used by one of his own men? *Better that he hear from me and not Felix.*

They had crossed the rise now, and were dropping down toward a new darkling inlet of the silver-black sea. 'In the end every artist has to commit a crudity. You go down to the cells and produce a blatant confession – why else wear heavy metal-tipped boots? But until that moment of coarseness, the policeman-criminal is an incomparable artist.' She spoke more softly. 'One of your local constables is the criminal, Detective-Inspector. He planted the bomb, and on Wednesday night, when he was meant to be guarding the cabins, he killed four of the monks. And planted the footstep of blood to frame the Prior. He wants a bit of your reflected glory. I'm sorry to have to tell you this. I realise it's a shock and a grief. But you understand about duty. We're heading up to the Retreat House now. You're going to have arrest one of your own men. Consider. You must know which one it is. We will –'.

She stopped, because the atmosphere in the vast old car was becoming disordered. Felix, she realised, had his right hand over his eyes; Motte was dreadfully silent. She glanced back at him.

'Wrong, wrong, wrong,' moaned Culpepper. 'All *wrong.*'

'Felix! He's fallen over.' She braked.

'He has?' said Culpepper, wistfully. 'So soon? Drive on. Gualachulain's what we want.'

'I don't think he can speak!'

'Who was so nearly without language –'

'But he seems to be having trouble breathing. In fact, I don't think he *is* breathing.' Abishag was twisted about. Culpepper was silent. Motte lay with his legs akimbo, in every direction it seemed, lips drawn back from teeth, eyes fixed and pure white, rolled oats and sultanas sprinkled about his head like confetti about a bride. 'Shouldn't we find a hospital?'

'No,' he said with a shuddering sigh. 'That would be a waste.'

'A waste of what?'

'Of the expensive drug I injected into his dried fruit.'

Surprise made the clever child stupid for a second. 'You've killed a Detective-Inspector?'

'Hardly that. He's a mass murderer. Do drive.'

She put the car back in gear and pulled away, speechless for a long minute. '*Motte* is the killer?'

'Of course. *He's* the one with a lust for celebrity. Not some village bobby. That was silly of you…. And snobbish. You're always suspicious of the wrong classes. I blame –'

'Stop! I have to think.' Quarter of a mile went past. 'You're certain?'

'Yes – he'd have been hoping for a knighthood.'

'You're *sure?*'

'Not about the knighthood.'

'But about Motte? Sure enough to have poisoned him?'

'Sure of his guilt? Oh yes.'

'And *this* is my practical initiation?'

'This is your practical initiation.' Half a mile more. 'Good thing you were so clever in the theory exam, you've been dense as mud this evening.' Another half mile. More gently: 'This is part of the job, too. A less interesting aspect, perhaps, than puzzling out documents. But it has to be done.'

She would not be patronised. 'What do you think Motte did with the livers?'

'Chucked them into the wood, I've no doubt. You know what these vegetarians are. Can't distinguish man from mammal, flesh from meat. Satiety from nausea. No, don't even think about *pâté*. The mutilation was just to make the crime more toothsome when it reached the headlines.'

A mile, and she said: 'I don't entirely like violence. Now it comes to it.'

'Oh this isn't violence. I'm rarely violent, you know.' And he quite audibly set about distracting her: 'It's so easy for instance to have a bad person invite me back to his hotel room, get him drunk by spiking his sauv blanc with vodka, strip him, slip him into the hotel swimming pool on the wee hours – he settles peacefully on the bottom of the pool to drown, no coroner has anything to say except some bromides about middle-aged men knowing better that mixing heavy drinking and midnight swimming.'

'Have you often done *that*?' says Abishag in a small voice.

'Scores of times, dear child, hundreds. Most Saturday evenings you'll find me lining pools with delinquents.' They were coming down into Gualachulain, a village at the head of Loch Etive, pent in by sullen peaks that suddenly struck Abishag as looking outlandish, unendurably outlandish: Ben Sgulaird, Ben Starav.

'Be serious.' Stob Coir'an Albannaich.

'I am serious. Seriously, Abishag, *you* decide what to do. This isn't a book-test now, it's real. We literally have a victim on our hands. Where are we going to put him? Where's the absolutely ideal place to secrete him? Not a clever, recondite place, mind. The obvious, utterly reliable place.'

A half minute. '*Not* in the sea.'

'Course not.' They were in the village now. 'Second right. The sea's worthless, everything washes up. I'm wrong, third right. No, the *next* one. Up *this* one. Probably. Can you read the signpost?'

'It's called' (the light was almost gone now) 'um, Cemetery Road. Is that ri – *God*. A cemetery.'

'Yes. Cemeteries are the place…. Oh I admit there are rich possibilities in roadworks. Many a murderee sleeps under a mended sewer. But what I say is: if it's leaked once it'll leak again. Then there'll be a skeleton to surprise the workmen. No: for permanence and snugness, what you want is a busy cemetery at dusk. Going-home time for the mechanical diggers.' The hedges seemed solid as walls now; the lane was narrowing. The air was thickening with shadow. 'Mechanical diggers,' he repeated, with revulsion. 'Lazy buggers, gravediggers. In the play, the sexton's finishing Ophelia's grave a few minutes before the coffin arrives. Nowadays there's no devotion to duty like that. They bring in this huge roaring machine. Which can get down ten foot in a quarter-hour. And since they mean to be sleeping off their booze until eleven, they finish all the graves for the next morning the evening before. Even on a rainy evening like this. Result: subsidence. Muddy blurred edges.'

The graveyard was coming obscurely into view, on a ledge well above the village. Nude cliffs rose above it. Everywhere was calm darkling sea. The sun had recently vanished fuzzily into the dim mass of Ireland.

'Right, we're coming up to the gates. Try to look distraught.'

'I *am*.'

'Yes but you don't *look*. You look rather wonderful. I'd kiss you but that chubby troll would see. Good evening, good *evening*,' he minced to the troll in the sentry box, leaning across Margot to speak out of her window. 'May we go in?'

'Ever sae sorry – Minister. We're closin' in fife minutes.' She had a curious face: intellectual and abstracted eyes, ochre hair like an ogre, a peasant's copious chins, a severe and beautiful black frock. She was impossible to place.

'Is it *really* not possible? We've driven all the way from Edinburgh and it took forever. She needs to see her uncle's grave. It's the tenth anniversary of his death. In Iraq, you know. He was a paratrooper.' Abishag lowered her head so her face couldn't be seen.

'Puir mite. Aw reit, Minister, I'll stent a point. Don't be tay lang abit it, thocht.' One finger marked her place in what appeared, from its severe off-white cover and stern narrow columns of print, to be a high-brow French novel. With another finger she pressed a button; the gates creaked open.

'God,' said Culpepper, once they were out of earshot. 'A smaller cemetery than I thought. I hope we're in luck. *Is* there a fresh one? No. Damn .... Yes! Over there. D' you see? Park as close to it as you can.'

They got out. There was earth heaped up in two big piles, and in between was a narrow oblong, amazingly long and thin and black and final. (The sky was growing blacker above them, as if in imitation. The trees rustled restlessly. Everything smelt of cool water and fresh earth.)

'What did I tell you?' Culpepper had got out of the car and was peering triumphantly over the rim. 'Ten foot if it's an inch. Pure swagger to make a digger go so far down. Waste of diesel. But with the price undertakers charge, I suppose there has to be an air of extravagance to their –'.

'Yes.'

'Though in our line of work we mustn't complain.' He was very breezy. 'No one notices when it's a foot shallower the next morning –'.

'Yes.'

Culpepper glanced about. 'Damn, that sly biddy is peering out the window at us. We have to make this look plausible.' He bobbed down and groped under the front seat. Out came a thick hardcover, gilt lettering catching what light there was. It was *Anna Karenina*: a nice old world edition to match the car, perfectly plausible as a prayer-book. 'Now I'm going to hold it open like this. She won't dare approach a minister mumbling Calvinist prayers. While you open the back door. The one facing away from her. No! – discreetly, discreetly. Don't make a thing of it.' Motte fell out heavily, shoulders on the muddy soil, thin legs draped over the seat, neck awry. 'Now you kneel, that's right, and I'll stand guard over you like this. Good. Pull him a bit forward. That's good. Keep your head down. Be pathetic. Think of poor wee Uncle Iain killed by a sniper in Karbala. Now push him forward. That's right, roll him.' Amazing that such a scrawny man could weigh so much. 'Ready? Over he goes.' Heave. The thud was unspeakable: moist, heavy, irreparable. 'Well done. Do you see how the edges are tapered outward?'

'Yes.'

'That's so the sides don't collapse overnight. They go down at an angle. Which means the coffin doesn't reach the bottom, it always gets wedged. There's a narrow unused hollow beneath it.' She stared down. Were Motte's eyes staring back? No, he'd landed on his side. 'Start pushing in soil. You don't need much, you've covering not burying. Just until there's nothing to see but dirt if anyone glances in…. The headstone's dug out over here. Leaning against the soil. Shall I read it to you?'

'No.'

'It says ANGUS WYNESS JOPP BORN 1933 DIED 2008. I deduce, no I presume, that tomorrow's burial is his widow…. Are we finished?'

'No.'

Culpepper, who was getting fidgetty, trifled with the pages of *Karenina*, sighing. 'I presume, no, remember, that you've read this…. What a plot! Levin dotes on Kitty who's in love with loathsome Vronksy who's in love with Anna who loves, perhaps, her husband; everyone remains wretched for, let's see, 884 pages. Where's the sense? It's a miserable roundabout.'

*What a lot of mud*, Abishag was thinking, *goes up my arm when I shovel with my fingers.*

'The primary charm of literature,' prattled her lover, 'is that it's even easier to kill people than in real life.' *This isn't particularly easy.* 'From Homer to *American Psycho*, what pleasure's more constant than removals?' *It'll be better once his head's covered. It'll be better then.* 'How easy to get rid of Anna 'round page 100! Slip her a dose of consumption. Better still, drop her under a horse, a carriage – we guess from the first that so much fluffy charm is due to be mangled before we're done. So why not squash her at once? Gift-wrap her if you like. Lay on a train wreck in moonlit mountains – burning steel, coals hissing in the snow, wolves loping out of the woods to nose the cooling wreckage. Then everyone else could swivel round and realign their emotions more usefully, Vronksy could have Kitty, Kitty Vronsky – the wretch. I've always felt a peculiar hatred for Vronksy, have I said? I can't think why. As if he were a real person who'd crossed me …. Are we –.'

'Yes.'

'I love you, Margot ffontaines-Laigh. Get back,' he snapped the long novel shut, 'in the Armstrong. No, passenger seat. I'll drive.'

She obeyed, dazed, reflecting *But not like you love yourself. Your hidden self. Which I love too. Which would adore me if you let it. Another miserable roundabout.*

He glanced at her. 'Do try not to muddy the upholstery.'

At the entrance, sticking his head out to speak to the clever old woman, who was waiting to lock the gate behind them, he said: 'A good night to you and thank you so much.'

*He does clerical unction well, painfully well.*

'Aw, Minister.'

'Such a comfort to this young lady. I'm sure that's now she's ready to *move on*… I see you have an interment tomorrow? A sad occasion…. Oh? Well, that is a comfort then. Bless. At what time is it – nine?... *Eight?* Well they do say it's the early bird that – that is, I'll bear you in my heart at eight o'clock. Good *bye*.'

## *vi.*

Margot ffontaines-Laigh is fated to live to a great age. In old age, her memory will be cluttered with many sensations, many professional butcheries. She'll be at ease with them all; with one exception. Occasionally her grandchildren and great-grandchildren will notice her smiling to herself as she relives this or that: the night she fathomed Holinshed, for instance. She'll be happy for them to see her disreputable smile: 'I was remembering a holiday I took around Skelgourock, my darlings, long ago. In the early years of this century.' Nothing about that autumn excursion will dismay her – except the last leg, for then she endured a vision that she couldn't blame on fly agaric. The worst hallucinations show nothing that isn't there. Remembering, she will frown. 'Perhaps Granny killed a man'. 'Don't be a nitwit, *'course* she did; but what happened to give her the pip?', 'Probably it was sex' – children always assume that. But there other physical facts that can leave the mind wounded, of which the gravest, perhaps, is geography.

The sun was gone; they ran up and down hills on the way to the Forest of Rowardennan, naked even of tussock along their ridges, nocturnal in their depths; and Abishag had the bad luck to see the world.

*Here*, she perceived, *mountains march into ocean and drown themselves. Fingers of ocean reach into mountain-tops. That slither of loch: I could almost leap it, yet it's the actual Atlantic, illimitable as the wild black billows off Spitzbergen, the Sargasso Sea.*

*Why does Northern water look so uncanny?*

*It's not the light exactly …. Lightness, yes. It's never like this in the South, where the sky seems frail, a tent of silk held taut immensely high – a mere backdrop for golden fire, coming down in mineral jabs. The Mediterranean's all the heavier for being still and dark. Weight below, brightness above. But here –*

*Here lightness sustains solidity. So that –*

*Luminous sea and sky are one, lit the same way, from an angle so low they're virtually lit from below. Soft radiance blends into the droplets of the damp air. Sea and sky joining underneath the land. So that –*
*These lochs are like gashes in the land revealing the sea. Negative islands. It's so Northern we are upside-down. I'm not at the roof of the world, I'm on the roof. The way children think of Australians hanging down. Like –*

*High mountains on fine days: rock immensities held up by air. Air's heavy, brightness and power are within it. Up here –*

*Radiant air below, behind everything, isn't thin, it's. These hills (how I'd like to be a god, reach down, stroke them) are smudges on a window. Likewise all continents and islands. Nothing more.*

*A topsy-turvy world. Airy heaven beneath. We climb upward into earth to be buried.*

*Not topsy-turvy. We perceive it in these ocean place, but it's*

*how the planet really is, always. A sponge of minerals, best looked
at from below. Bobbing on an infinite nimbus, air, space. Nothingness outweighs the very few things there are.*

Abishag was, in short, reaching the state of mind that afflicts Buddhist
monks in the high Himalaya. They don't mind, it's why they came; but it's
hell for a Westerner, whose mind can only stand upright on matter, even
if it's sacral matter; and Abishag in her dismay found herself calling for aid
to – to –

## *vii.*

to Uncumber. *Uncumber in England, Ontkommer to the Dutch. She was
Débarras in France and Librada in Spain. She was called many things, that
was part of her mystique. No fixed name, no particular country or century.
Eutropia, Reginfledis, Dignefortis, Hulfe. Pure irresponsible legend. But always
"Wygefortis" to me. The girl killed for putting on a beard. Patron of my College.
The College of this man here.* Ora pro nobis. *Ugh.*

Culpepper, who was driving along cheerfully and almost humming,
looked at his mistress askance. He couldn't follow and didn't much like her
mood. 'We are now going, as you've probably guessed, to the Retreat House.
For the final tidying-up. Nothing gruelling. Good fun, in fact.'

'We're going to. I mean I'm going to fire the hut.' Her voice was entirely
flat. She stared straight ahead, at the headlights weaving between the boles of
trees. 'The one with the four bodies in it.'

'Yes. Ah. Well-deduced.'

'The Abbot knows.'

'What's about to happen? He does. At exactly ten he'll sound the alarm.
There's a volunteer fire-brigade in Arrochar, which should arrive about
eleven, by which time there'll only be ash. Four monks suffocated by smoke as
they slept. A tragedy but not a scandal. The police will blame bad wiring. It's
always easy to blame bad wiring. No one will mention threatening e-mails or
bombs. "We'll be the front page of *The Scotsman* tomorrow," said the Abbot,
"but something wee near the sports pages the next day."'

'He sounds nonchalant.'

'Patient. Monastic time's roomier than ours. He's had time to absorb the
shock.'

'There have been, what, a dozen Offices since yesterday before dawn.'
Abishag sounded remote. 'A conventual Mass. And a requiem. Those monks
stepped outside time fourteen times.'

'What? Yes. I suppose. Anyway yesterday the Abbot realised the culprit must be a policeman. That's why he summoned outside help. Me. Us.'

'*Us*': she said the word with some revulsion.

'He *trusted* his brothers, you see. Anyway monks and nuns and priests have usually been in slums and seen the police at work. They don't have any middle-class prejudice. He told me as soon as I arrived it was probably the Detective-Inspector.'

'Yet it took you two days to kill him.'

'I didn't kill Motte.'

'… *What* did you say?'

'Abishag, I can't keep pace with your paradoxes and prevarications. I did not murder Inspector Conan Motte. I gave him an ounce or so of a superior alternative to midazolam. He fell into a deep sleep which he could use, didn't you think he looked haggard? Not conscience, I fear, vegetarianism. Or his preposterous exercises. What's a grown man doing running in circles?' Abishag rather overwhelmingly did not reply. 'I *don't* poison, y'know – any more than I shoot. Direct methods are brutal, no, *Brutalist*, whereas I'm Baroque, a Baroque architect of –'

He broke off impatiently, as if in that horrible over-productive state where a man loses interest in every sentence he can conceivably form before they're done, doubting their good-taste before they exist. This way lies silence, the killing sort of wisdom.

'Midazolam, Abishag. Grasp that. He'll have a delightful rest and awake refreshed tomorrow around noon.' Abishag still said nothing, indeed her silence became more intense; yet Culpepper apparently felt contradicted. 'Very well, I admit it won't be a comfortable waking…. Even so, if he can may persuade himself it's just a nightmare he'll just lie back, waiting for it to end, until he slips off into a longer sleep. Not so bad.' Silence. 'True, if he's gung-ho he'll start diddling upward with fingers. I noticed the soil, loose sandy stuff you showered on him. Unsuffocating, frangible. After an hour's work, or less, he'll hit the solid bottom of Mrs Jopp's coffin. Hm? … Which, I accept, will come as a bit of a shock.' Silence, silence. She was thinking of the weight of soft sand, and of being meetly deep in the ground under a great heap of stones, and of a huge spider she'd trodden on as a girl, a tiny girl, only a toddler but already too scared of seeming afraid to shriek aloud; so that the shriek had had to go inward. 'After all,' he persisted more quietly, 'he did disembowel four sleeping monks.'

Abishag uttered a giant sigh and lay back in the seat of the showy antique car, rushing on through the indifferent Forest of Rowardennan. It was night.

Culpepper, relieved, turned chatty. 'Y'know, there was this Byzantine emperor, Zeno, real name Rousombladadiotes which was no good for politics, you can see why he changed to something snappier. Nonetheless he made the mistake of boring his empress, who had the wonderful name Ariadne. Ariadne got him dead drunk, had the corruptible court physician certify his death, popped him into a sarcophagus. Once evening came and the porphyry chilled, Zeno woke. Started hollering. Kept it up for a couple of days. But Ariadne wouldn't she let anyone near. She'd lined up a new husband, you see. Made him emperor, too.'

Fire flared up in Abishag's eyes, but still she said nothing.

'Then there was the time they dug up Duns Scotus, the Scholastic. The inside of his coffin lid was hideously scratched. So that was the end of his Process – he couldn't be beatified for centuries. He'd betrayed unsaintly absence of self-control.'

Abishag, demonstrating self-control, unclenched her hands and folded them across her thighs.

'So much for Antiquity and the Middle Ages. The golden age began with the Enlightenment. They –'.

'Have you made a study of this?' Her voice was so harsh it was almost unrecognisable. (*What were the names Zeno called Ariadne through the stone lid? Pet names? Things they'd called each other in bed?*)

Culpepper glanced at her uncertainly. 'No, well not really. It's just an idea I like turning over'; an idea buried alive then, in the miry soil of Felix's brain, unable to die or get out. She was being silent again.

Not for long. Being hopelessly clever, therefore curious, she found herself saying, with young contempt in her young voice, coldly: 'You think the Enlightenment was the golden age of premature burial?'

'Let's say of the *dread* of premature burial. Taphophobia,' he added, tentatively, 'it's called taphophobia.'

'I know.' She sounded regretful, and weary beyond her years. 'I know that word.'

'Good …. Perhaps because belief in hell was fading. Man never escapes terror, merely transfers it. Since people no longer feared rising *from* the grave, they feared rising *in* the grave.'

She said nothing. (*How terrible these Northern trees look. Flickering past as we drive. Each one seems designed with a hanging or impalement in mind. One glance and a druid would yearn to decorate those boughs with lopped torsos. Like Christmas baubles.*)

'The human appetite for creepiness,' continued Felix, gaily, 'remains constant, it's just satisfied differently. In the century when Lenin and Hitler and Mao actually *existed*, we didn't need imaginary extravagances. The Gothic went clean out of fashion.'

'So you're a throwback.'

'Hm …?' He studied her taut profile. 'I'd prefer to call myself a "heritage nightmare." A happy reminiscence of the golden age. When vivisepulture – that was their word for it! Wonderful! When vivisepulture wasn't just a phobia. It *seemed* to happen all the time. Just before the Revolution, the Cimetière des Innocents was dug up and moved to the outskirts of Paris; an enormous number of skeletons were found twisted over in their coffins. *Had* they woken? Or did the age's terror *create* that impression? George Washington died begging not to be buried for two or three days, just in case. Three days in the muggy heat of Virginia! Pity his poor slaves. And right through the nineteenth century the exhumed were found with hair torn out, fingernails ripped off, arms broken, flesh gnawed from their hands. Sometimes –'.

(*Felix's such a boy,* reflected Abishag; *he never tires of the* grand guignol *aspect. But come: where's the real discomfort in waking up in a coffin? This: knowing you've been faking it all your life. You thought – no you* thought *you thought – that you were a good infidel, hard-bitten. You believed you believed that all mental suffering was solitary. Your mind, you always said, writhed –* she groped for the idea *– in, yes, in that, in an acnestis. The place that can't be touched. Hideously apart, accessible only to the eye of God, and since there's no eye of God because no God, inaccesible. That was your pose: you were a tortured intellectual, you were Jonah in the whale. You said you've always been there. And now you* are *there and you find, my lovely, that it's a surprise. And you don't like it one little bit. You find* haven't *been tortured yet. That's* now. *A new thing.*)

Following this train of thought caused Abishag to miss a few gruesome specimens from Culpepper's taphophobic collection: '… was in Germany, always an eerie place. But it worried everyone. In America there was a well-subscribed Society for the Prevention of People being Buried Alive – is it still going, d'y' think? Shouldn't you send them a cheque? People bought coffins with bells mounted on top, strings dangling inside. Or with poison pellets that were released when the nails were hammered home, to ensure they were really-and-truly comfortably deceased. What a word that is, de*ceased*! Destopped. Dended…. There's a tomb in Vermont fitted with plate-glass panels, safety panels so to speak, you can stare into the non-eyes of the skull; presumably for a while the skull's friends loyally checked for worms and beetles. My hero, Edgar Allan –'.

'Why are you regurgitating this, exactly? It's done with. I killed him.'

'Are killing him. I know a man, father of someone you know as it happens, who relented at exactly this point. His victim came up and only suffered a week in hospital.'

Up! Her geographical nightmare leapt back, had her by the thoat: *there's airy sky beneath, muddy Earth above – brightness topped with graves – we're born buried, lidded by a crust of impenetrable soil – ascend through life 'til we're at the right pitch to be encased.* She reeled with vertigo; set her teeth.

'Keep driving.'

'I hear. I obey.'

The last of day was done. Some acres of dense black woods went by in their headlights while she, in the manner of a child wiggling a tooth to see how much pain could be borne, considered her deed.

*Fee-fi-fo-fum. Fee-fi-fo-fum. Soon words will be formed where they've never been formed since the creation of the world. In the soil beneath Gualachulain. Out of the ground will come shouts, gurgling shrieks, curses, blasphemies, as Conan Motte expresses the wish he'd never been born. Then, still more earnestly, the wish that the universe had never been made. He'll appoint himself spokesman for the harshest corners of creation and reproach –.*

Culpepper, who kept glancing at her sideways, thought it best to interrupt. 'Congrats. That was part two of the exam, Abishag. The practical.' *Ahem.* 'Which you passed. Flying colours. Welcome to the cool boys' gang.'

'Then I don't think you should call me Abishag.' Her voice had no colour in it at all. 'If I'm your assistant. No longer just your young fluff.'

Culpepper peered at her, trying to gauge her seriousness. 'I'll try to remember. Lady Margot…. Righteous killerette.'

This was what she wanted. Had wanted. Wanted. She was satisfied. Nonetheless *Faugh!* she thought; *I've had enough of the underworld over the last two days. Or overworld or whatever it is. I wish I were done with it.*

For she could feel Mrs Jopp's grave, ten foot deep, tapering sides, muddy rim, sandy loam, digging itself into a patch of her mind she knew she'd never be able to reach. She wouldn't be able to fill it in. She'd always have to watch it from a distance.

## *viii.*

Culpepper parked suddenly. They were high in the hills now, back in the woods, and when he turned off the headlights night rushed in on them, noisier than you'd expect as is the way in a wood. Animals coughed, barked, insulted each other and fled. Trees creaked in the slight breeze, dead leaves crackled. Drowning it all out came the tremendous orchestral approach of six constables in their boots, all with torches, all saying 'Hallo, hallo.'

Felix sighed, also loudly. 'Put your head down. *Margot.* Creep up the hill when the coast's clear.' He got out.

'Oooh. Dr Culpepper,' said the policemen, stabbing their beams in his face, playing them over the car, crossing them in mid-air. Then they said: 'Here you are at last, sir', 'Oh look, Doug, 'It's Dr Culpepper', 'So it is', 'Very quiet up here, sir', 'Nothing happening', and 'Do you have Detector-Inspector Motte with you?' One of the policemen, who was McChesney, hung his bony head, humiliated, saying nothing at all.

'No.' The concern in Culpepper's voice was wonderfully modulated. Abishag, no, no, let's get this right, *Margot*, fatal Margot, crouching under the dashboard of the Armstrong Siddeley. She imagined him shading his eyes, pursing his lip, frowning in a manly way. 'Isn't Motte with you?'

'No sir – we thought he must be with you.'

'Hmm. I hope he's all right. Well *in himself*, if you see what I mean. Such a driven fellow. Highly-strung.' Margot could hear them exchanging glances. A seed was planted that would presumably sprout, even in the meagre dirt of their police brains. 'Well if he's not here, I suppose we'd better get on with our patrol without him. I'll look after this sector.' Off they stomped on their amazingly crunching scraping thudding tread.

Margot counted fifty, then opened the car door and stole up the hill.

Between the trees she glimpsed McChesney's weirdly elevated head, catching his red hair in uncountable little branches, his sad receding bottom, and his hands, dangling almost to his knees, quite impossible, like a yeti's. Despite her fascinated gaze he didn't turn and was soon out of sight.

They were all out of sight. It was easy. She reached the top of the hillock and found Culpepper standing, staring blankly at the stars, his Inverness cape about him like a pyramid of wool.

He too did not glance her way as she went past. A few more steps and she was on the edge of a clearing. A large wooden building was on one side, half a dozen peaceful huts on stilts stood in a circle. The galaxies and constellations might have been hung up there just to light the circle of grass between.

The night was strangely mild. Everything smelt of pine. One of the monks was snoring horribly. Something small on four legs flitted behind her.

Felix was at her elbow, not whispering, just speaking like a man in his sleep. 'We're slightly early. I said the fire would start on the dot of ten. Six minutes. May as well use the time. Will you excuse me?' He got out his 'phone and tapped a long number.

'You're reporting back to your demotic Cardinal? Already?'

'Card'nol, Card'nol, for whatya sayin' Card'nol?' drawled Felix, mock-gangsterly. 'Why give de middle-man a piece of de agshon? Nah, I likes to go straight to de Big Guy.' He listened; tapped in a four-digit code; listened again; tapped six more digits. His face so intense it looked almost innocent. He listened; seemed to reach a human being, who spoke softly. *'Domine ad adjuvandum me festina,'* Felix replied precisely, as if repeating a password. Then more stillness, as if he were being put through. He used the time to take off his idiotic cape, fold it, drop it at his feet, kneel on it, and pull off his Tam O'Shanter. A sleepy voice sounded down the line.

'*Sí, buenas noches, Santo Padre. Estoy en la ermita ....*' Remembering (it would seem) the existence of Margot, he produced a cigarette-lighter, handed it backwards over his shoulder, and, when she took it, pointed to the fourth hut along. '*Sí, Su Santidad, se hace.*' She slipped away and left him.

The fourth hut. She stood in the starlight before it, fingering the lighter and wrestling with herself. The impression of airiness became once again intense: earth was a mote amidst those huge floating spheres; and so forth. Perhaps this illusion, like the rest of her complicated psychological churning, was just her way of deferring guilt (which she may have thought suburban, beneath her).

The present issue was, of course, whether she should look inside first. *No need. He said* this *one*, she told herself; then, in contradiction, *It would be awkward if Felix made a mistake. We don't want to cremate living monks.* The first voice did not give up: *It's his job not to make mistakes. Our job. I'm official now. Look at him.*

She glanced back. She was standing in light that seemed incredibly clear, only just too pale to cast a shadow. He was kneeling in the dimness under the trees; she could make out the sturdy outline of his curly bare head, still bent over the 'phone murmuring fluently in Spanish.

*Such a killingly-competent scholar. A worthy successor to Worthyal.* Somewhere a frantic scurry of owl-prey; a swoop; a triumphant hoot. *Perhaps it's always been like this. There are always comedy policemen like Brackenbury (necessarily stupid, says Felix) who can't manage the necessary murder. And there are always fatal high-brows who can. "Right reverend fathers, divinely bent."*

She found that she had decided. Being a high-brow, the point of her decision was lost, unreachable, invisible, beneath the shifting fog of her inner chit-chat.

She went quietly up the stairs of the hut, the monastic cell. Such starry silence beneath the forest kerfuffle of slaying and being slain! She gently lifted the latch. She stepped in.

She looked.

And shut her eyes.

Then quieted herself, thinking: *Why am I troubled? Gore's the raw material of my new trade. I'm not longer an apprentice. I've washed away my childish nickname. I've exited mere humanity.* She opened her eyes. *Yes. I can bear this. I'm a Wygian. Initiate of a college founded on regicide-infanticide. A college named for an crucified girl. A college fated to harbour Culpepper.*

She made herself examine the four monks. They'd been laid out in clean white habits and black scapulars, with rosaries threaded through their fingers. Otherwise they hadn't been tidied. There were visible slashes across their throats, and their pillows, silver-gilt in that weird stellar light, were still soaked through with what looked black, like negative halos. Their faces were neither peaceful nor tormented. They were simply dead: dead, dead, dead, dead, dead. *Nothing rare about that. Death's a railway, freighting away its millions. Seven thousand an hour, they say. Respectable passengers like Mr and Mrs Jopp, properly paid for. Stowaways like Anna Karenina. And innocents like the Princes. And like you, reverend sirs: smuggled aboard.*

So she came out again into the starlight, carrying one of the blankets. She wrapped this round a stilt of the hut, and peered at her watch. Half a minute left.

*It's good to send them home in their cell. Gift-wrapped. Like a Viking funeral, burning a chieftain in his own longboat.... What stars! ... It's ten. It's time.*

She clicked the lighter, cupping the flame with her other hand. *Blinding gold!* said the dominant, aesthetic part of her mind. *Amazing bright gold! Amidst this infinity of pewter and black!* And she bent to touch it to the blanket.

Yet she hardly saw it. Most of her was far away, feigning to watch what only the eye of God could really see: Conan Motte in his most secret place. She found she could still anticipate the thoughts of that most predictable man. *He'll be waking in twelve hours or so. And his fiercest agony (at first) will be finding he has an itch in that tricky place just between the shoulder-blades.*

# III. Cold Fusion,
# *a second bedroom interlude*

If wee can doe this, *Cupid* is no longer an Archer, his glory ſhall be ours, for wee are the onely loue-gods.

*Much Ado about Nothing*

*the Royal Caledonian Hotel, Skelgourock, Argyllshire;*
*eight in the morning, 7ᵗʰ November 2013,*
*Lady Margot ffontaines-Laigh and Dr Felix Culpepper*
*having just finished making love*

Aн.

*Ah.*

Oh my darling….

What are you *laughing* about?
Oh – the seagulls.
Yes. I told you they were fearful.
Kiss me…. Again.

§

I don't think we can go back to sleep, do you? Not with that endless crawing….

Let's get dressed and go down to breakfast. Breakfast is *immensely serious* at the Royal Caledonian, they'll be shocked if we're too late – not just bacon and beans. Lorne sausage, tattie scones. Fried haggis of course. And mealy pudding which is blood-pudding without the blood, all the most dubious parts of the pig. Oatmeal for Presbyterians. Suet, that's a thing here, not just –

"*I think*, Felix, darlingest darling mine, you may be confusing me with some other young girl."

What?

"Who lies silently and says *Oh!* and *Really*, in a little voice so she won't break up your long monologue. Whereas I'm your fellow, your colleague. We're not going down to breakfast for another half-hour, as it happens. We're going to lie here while you amuse me with a story."

Oh. Oh. Are we? ... A *waking-up* story? Really I don't think I'm authorised to go down – . Very well, very well. Hm. I'm going to tell you about –

"What you're going to tell me about is Dr Ebbe. You were spinning me some yarn about transforming him into a great lover –"

I was too. In Cambridge. Just two evenings ago. Though it seems like another age –

"It was. On."

– and you fell asleep.

"I was tired, you were dull. Now I'm not tired, and I want to hear about Eddie Ebbe and his important vomit. What's the use of sick, professionally speaking? And what did you do with him?"

Really. Really I don't think I can allow this, Ab, Margot old girl. Think of Motte – fumbling away at a coffin. On an empty stomach. He's had nothing since his nuts and raisins at five o'clock yesterday, and must be getting uncomfortably peckish. *He'd* want us to make a decent breakfast, I feel. Then to go into the wholesome open –

All right, all right – *don't tickle!* I abhor tickling....

Ebbe. You were still awake to hear about his botched suicide? Good. On.

Of course lots of our dons do try to top themselves. They too usually fail and are carted away to the Deepdene. But I took it into my head that the Deepdene wasn't going to be Ebbe's fate. Can't say why. S'pose I was charmed by his holiday project. So I made him my holiday project.

Anyway I gave Mrs Muckhatch fifty quid to clean him up and get him into bed. And to fix a bolt on the outside of his bedroom door. And on the sly to repair his outer door, which I'd kicked in. She's astonishing with a screwdriver, muscular hairy fingers but deft.

For the rest of that day, and all the next day, Tuesday, Ebbe lay bolted in his bedroom, in a sort of secret asylum. The imperturbable Muckhatch brought him his meals. And slapped him about when he begged for razor, rope, or more poison.

I, meanwhile, was trying to think what to do with him. Hadn't hit on anything by Tuesday night. Which was the big end-of-Long-Vac dinner. Very rowdy. Wednesday morning was correspondingly quiet. Except I heard distant female yelling – ·

"Yes but you're cheating. This isn't turning into a proper traditional story, it's just brisk notes – something modern and experimental. Don't think we're going down for pig scones until I have what I want. Proper fluent narrative, with prompt explanations."

That, eh?

"Yes. With pretentious flourishes. And literary decoration. Baroque, not classical. Fluminous. Try again."

*Try again,* you say. *Fluent,* you say, *baroque.*

How's this, then?

§

And on the eight day God a touch hungover as Who would not be after knocking off a universe and "resting" afterward when we know there can be rest without conviviality nor conviviality without drink, I for one can't imagine human society beyond drip drip sip sip, nor sane existence without society repellent as humanity is and of course God didn't have humans (yuck) to contend with only martial seraphim whom I picture as celestial Guardsmen, and burning cherubim, who must be like dons but even better, and with these He had "rested" on the seventh day celebrating as one does in proportion so that when it is the whole physico-spiritual reality to rejoice over the wines must have been, oh a Niagara of vintages springing perfect from the divine – why are you scowling?

"Because it's still no good. It's whimsical. And orotund. Again."

Put-upon. Browbeaten. That's how I feel.

I was trying to evoke – to calibrate, as a scientific historian might – the particular atmosphere of Wednesday, October the second. One week before the start of term. That is to say, of a morning thirty-six days ago. The morning after the banquet with which, by ancient tradition the Fellowship regales itself to mark the end of Long Vac.

This tradition goes back to the Founder's time. Bishop Worthyal himself gave the naughty name *Belshazzar's Feast* to a carouse he celebrated with his henchmen when the first croner-stone of College was laid in the mud. In the mud, with an infant, officially "overlaid", beneath, bought for thirty groats from one of the town drabs – that's the story.

"I've never heard that before."

Oh there's a lot you don't know. See what happens if you lie quietly like a good little girl? You know what a distinguished Humanist the Bishop was. It's said he danced torch-lit about the stone, in full pontificals, chanting a Lycaian wolf-hymn of his own composition, in the purest Arcadian – iambic trimeter... I do wish it had survived.

"The baby?"

The *text*. Although the Worthyal didn't forget his Christian obligations to infants. The next morning, while everyone else was groaning and puking, he officiated at the hanging of the drab. The borough magistrates were hardboiled men, and it seems the so-called overlaying had struck them as suspicious.

"Oh."

Naturally the feast became a College tradition, as, indeed, did its crapulous morning-after.

Well, this October we were keeping the five hundredth Belshazzar's Feast. It was correspondingly lavish even by the standards of our abandoned institution. Twice around High Table, widdikins, went our loving-cup. Our loving-cup! Something else that's never on show. A chalice looted from Bridlington Priory at the Dissolution, fitted with silver handles, and engraved down the inside with a startling map of the world to come. The circle of the lustful, then of the gluttons, the avaricious, the wrathful, spiralling right down to triple-mouthed Lucifer in the dregs. Each of us gave the end-of-summer toast: *Finita est ætas et non sum mortuus nec adhuc damnatus*: Summer's over, I'm not dead, I'm not damned yet.

Not that we'd got through summer unscathed. The extravagant scholarship of Nikkie the Sociology Fellow – as she fulsomely explained to the company at large – had earned her gonorrhoea. (You should have seen the look in the Home Bursar's face: he sat beside her and would have the loving-cup just after those long jaws of hers had slobbered into it.) Dymwood the zoologist was absent, in hospital and not expected to make a full recovery: the dormouse he'd been eviscerating had wriggled out from under his hand and leapt at his throat. Who'd have thought such small teeth could gnaw so deep? Chyld the butler was visibly in his final decline, although it's true he's been in it for many years. Yoxley and Freke and Woolly were present, but looked sick – sick, sad, tired and unwashed. They'd been up for the last two nights, trying to raise that three thousand year-old abomination, Shishak; and they'd failed. Eddie Ebbe was missing altogether, of course. I murmured to the Master 'Indisposed', which was a fib rather than an outright lie. 'Bloody weakling,' growled Sir Trotsky, whose newfound *caritas* is quite gone by the ninth glass.

Still. As Long Vacs go, this one had not been so disastrous. We drank deep of the rare Málaga sack that traditionally goes into the Bridlington Cup.

The stars were paling before the last of the wise men of St Wygy's staggered or crawled or were carried to bed.

I want to evoke the peculiar sickly quietness that lay on College the next morning. The undergraduates' rooms were swept and aired, beds made, dust-covers put away, yet still empty, empty, waiting for you detestable young people to show up in six days' time. But each Fellow's set was a sickroom, in which a great brain pulsed with anguish, while a dehydrated body tossed on its unclean linen –

"No. No. I'm not having this either, Felix. Your theme, as I understand it, is the metamorphosis of Ebbe. Into a mighty lover. I can be spared your disgusting drinking-bout, since he wasn't even there. I want a love story."

You do? Oh dear .… You become *formidable* after we've made love, have you noticed. Can you explain? … Let me gather my thoughts.

Here we go.

§

Love, *thou art Absolute sole lord*
Of Life & Death –

an Englishman wrote that, but he was an exile, a convert to what the English then thought of as the Church of Spain, the Church of the Armada. And he wrote it about a Spanish girl. So perhaps Crashaw was making a point about the Spanish temperament, not about people in general, not about love.... I'm so glad I'm not Hispanic. Aren't you? Their notion of love – and hate, and loyalty, and vengeance – is so intense that by comparison we don't feel these things *at all*. Which is rather godlike of us. Don't you think?

"No."

No? Aren't you grateful that English love is so nuanced that it – ? No. Well then.

I awoke about nine on Wednesday morning feeling (to distinguish another nuance) delicately-wrought rather than positively ill. I lay quietly in bed and did experiments with my various physical and mental faculties to see if they were intact. They were.

My bed in St Wygy's, as I've pointed out, to derision, is the centre of the cosmos. Things orbit it. Adventures are drawn in as by a lodestone. So it's not entirely astonishing that as I lay there I began to perceive, amidst the general queasy silence proper to the morning after a Belshazzar's Feast, monotonous yelling.

Yes: female and (as I attended more closely) somehow foreign-sounding yells.

Exercising proper caution, I rose from bed, donned a splendid dressing-gown (the grey brocaded one, since you ask), strolled across my sitting-room, lifted a curtain and pushed open a window.

It was an early October morning of steady, thin, glacial sunshine, white void nearly showing though the threadbare azure. The sun was sailing past dark cloudbanks like a clipper negotiating sandbanks. The breeze was only pretending to be playful. There was a stony edge to it, a malice: it meant to cut the leaves' throats and drop their corpses on the lawn. This was late summer hollowed-out.

Megiddo was as empty as you'd expect. Except that suddenly an exotic, uncouth figure dashed across it, paused, looked up at the rows of blind and empty windows, put back its head, and howled '*¡Sebastián!*'

Looking down, my first impression was of a buttercup-coloured aureole, dazzling in the feeble sunlight. Then, foreshortened by angle, I could make out a flat darkish face, awash with furious emotion. Below that, incredible jutting quiverous rounded breasts – far more than mangoes. Almost water-melons. And below *that*, the unmistakable swell of a belly rich with new life.

'*¡Sebastián!*' she roared again and again, scanning the emptiness of Megiddo Court for a glimpse of his own bright bedraggled hair. '*¿Dónde estás, Sebastián?*'

"Benita! My God!"

Yes, Benita.

"Seb's fling in Mexico!"

No, Margot, not a fling. You should have seen him. For a week he was perfectly besotted.

"Then he left Mexico and came back."

True.

"And when he got back here, he went back to rutting."

Only after a few weeks. For those few weeks in March he pined. You mustn't forget that. It was a type of miracle.

"Bah! Pining for that – creature."

Yes. I remember how nasty you were about her back then. When he showed you a photo.

"The artificial tits! The lemon dye-job!"

Let's be perfectly fair about that shade of yellow. In the Third World the backdrop's monochrome, grit, poured concrete. Violent colours work well enough out there. I admit her hair didn't work in chromatic old England, green to grey as we are, and misty. But on its own terms –

"*The gargantuan bosom!*"

Ah well yes. That's certainly unfortunate. But not Benita's fault. It was her bad luck to be born only grandchild of the second-largest drug lord in the Free and Sovereign State of Sonora. If she'd just been left alone, she'd have been unremarkably plain. It was daddy who insisted on the nose-job, breast-implants, bleach. She told us so in March.

"Huh.... So this freakish thing had come in pursuit."

Freakish? Freakish? She looked splendid enough, standing akimbo on the Megiddo lawn. In black lace mantilla and frock, seven months pregnant, wielding two semi-automatic .50 calibre revolvers fitted with black silencers.

Had I not mentioned the guns? I should've, because they were the main point. She'd obviously burst through the Lodge waving these long scary things, and now two of the under-porters (it was Scurf and Clinker) had crept after her. They were lurking terrified under the chapel wall while see wailed '*¡Sebastián! ¡Sebastián!*'

A bizarre scene. Bizarre, but perhaps not unusual. I wonder how many times over the centuries a pregnant girl has broken into St Wygy's, howling for the man who betrayed her? First nuns under the old dispensation, then laun-dresses' daughters, Girton undergraduates …. Ah well. *Love*, as I was saying,

> *thou art Absolute sole lord*
> OF LIFE *&* DEATH. *To prove the word*

– I had only to listen to Benita's voice. I could tell that it wasn't rage or vio-lated honour that drove her. It was love. Love that made her brave enough to defy her grandfather, Don Anibal, Mayor and boss of Cananea. A drug baron immensely rich, cruel, murderous, affectionate and vengeful. Who affected the manners and dress of a colonial *hidalgo* and was held in terror even by his own desperadoes.

I'd glimpsed him during my short stay in Cananea, quietly riding about by day on a mustang stallion, face invisible under a black sombrero, with half a dozen bodyguards trotting behind. In the evening I'd cautiously observed him sitting in the best café, the one on the empty windy plaza, regally alone, regally erect and still, in a splendid panama and a white three-pieced suit. It must have been cut for him in London. The superb cloth flushed wonder-fully pink-gold as the sun sank before him. All the tables about him were carefully empty; two waiters stood at attention, at the right distance, waiting to replenish his glass of vermouth; that evening's *El Universal*, wonderfully smooth, perhaps ironed, lay flat, untouched on his table. His bodyguards, now black-shirted, black-suited, loitered attentively about the peeling col-onnades. Nothing moved in their master's face, cut in smooth crags as from desert buttes, tinted as it might be by milkless coffee. He looked at nothing and must simply have been meditating on the mystery of his being: of Don Anibal Cofresí y Ramírez de Arellano, himself, narco-seigneur of that whole district, from the serrations atop the sierras on his left, over the pitiless, wa-terless desert floor, all the way to the marches of *los Estados Unidos*.

*With all the poverty here*, he might have been thinking, *how much more in el Norte, beyond that grim walled frontier! What poverty of spirit! What insatiable craving for my wares, for the means to forget* what *they are, and to fantasise about* where! *Really, for all my dreadfulness, I am simply a nurse* –

"You're making this up."

I suppose I am. But Don Anibal did look up, you know. This isn't invention, it's history. He looked up and regarded me gravely, me and Seb, lurking on the other side of the plaza. *Blancos* but not, he must have perceived, gringos. *A nurse who soothes a dying child, who covers its terrible staring eyes with a cool hand. What should it do but sleep?* He smiled at this point, and we slunk away, Seb wanting to try out a beer-hall he had seen earlier that day.

No. I wouldn't think of crossing Don Anibal. And I'm an assassin myself in my own small way.

But Benita had crossed him. First she had her way with Seb, who was too dim to understand the risk. Then, six months later – anticipating your objection, this *is* guesswork – she clambered over the perimeter of the family compound by night. Pregnant as she was. And innocent, monoglot, next-to-illiterate – for Anibal had conservative views about female education. Looking at *you*, my darling, who's to blame him? Ouch.

She'd come all this way, and tracked down Seb, who'd never told her his surname – not that she could conceivably have pronounced it if he had. She loved him, then, *loved him*. An explosive state of affairs.

Here's a grave thought. If she'd arrived six days *later*, or on any morning after that, she'd have found College fully occupied. Not the ghost town it was. She'd have found Seb – nothing could have stopped her – curled up hungover in his room. And she'd have been on him, pistol-mouth to his forehead: "Marry me! *¡Sé mi marido!*" Would be have yielded? Or would he have proved a martyr to promiscuity? I wonder.... Horrid either way.

Anyway, I couldn't let his empty blond head get blown off, and although the situation wasn't really my business –

"It *was* your business. It was your *fault*. You had *no* business taking to America and Mexico the irresistible animal Sebastian Hawick Trocliffe."

Hmpf. I remember you thought so at the time.

"You –"

You thought I should –

" – should have taken me."

– have taken you. Hmpf. Well in any case I decided *this wouldn't do*. So, summoning up my courage (and clearing my throat to make sure my voice wasn't squeaky or rusty), I opened a window, and stuck out my head.

'*Buenos días*, Señorita Cofresí.'

'*¡Señor Félix!*' she cried, not shooting me. She'd scarcely bothered speaking to me in March but now her face, beslobbered with tears, turned bright at the sight of me. I'd been with her belovèd, and now here I was here. I proved the godlike vision real. '*¿Dónde está Sébastian?*'

Spanish, I've always found, is simply a gutter dialect of Latin. Speak Latin with a comic accent and you get by. So now I scrunched up my mouth to form Foreign and called out '*¡Ahí, señorita!*' pointing to the opposite corner of the Court, staircase VII, room 13. '*¡El último piso!*'

"But – those are *Woolly's* rooms …."

Yes. Don't interrupt. She blew me a wonderful kiss and bounded across the grass, black lace flailing behind her, shouting '*¡Mi único amor!*'

Of course I was running a risk with Woolly. But Benita, like most children of professional criminals, was wonderfully pious. And the distinction between a priest and our schismatic, polymorphous chaplain would not dawn on her. My calculation was that she'd probably not shoot him –

"Small loss if she did."

… Yes. And if he *did* stay alive, he'd keep her talking for a long time – Woolly picked up Spanish in the 'Nineties, from those irritating communists, the Liberation Theologians. But, as we know, a straight answer to a simple question is beyond him in any language. *Where is my Sebastian?* By the time he'd drawn out the variations on *Is not everyone everywhere in a special sense?* – not to mention his chaotic views on matrimony – well, I'd have time to do something.

Scurf and Clinker, having idiotically stared after Benita, and then idiotically stared at each other, then at me, turned and dashed for the Master's Lodgings. You know how absolute the rule is about the police never being allowed into Wygy's without the Master's explicit command. We are a realm apart. The porters wanted that command before they found themselves peppered with lead.

Meanwhile I'd picked up my Aztec skull, souvenir of our impregnating jaunt to Mexico. I drummed my fingers on its temples for inspiration. What crafty wicked thoughts had once fizzed back and forth within that smooth bone!

I took it back to bed – that galactic vortex of events. I thought.

§

Short of killing Benita, I didn't see how we could get rid of her without handing over a husband. And I didn't think it right to obliterate Seb. And so …

I got out my laptop, I went online, I visited sleekgeek.com.

Heard of it? No? Good. You shouldn't have. It's a site where scientists announce things to each other. It's sensitive and covert and I shouldn't know about it either, but of course I do.

I logged in as *Dr Edward Ebbe, F.R.S., St Wygefortis' College, Cambridge.* His password was PARACELSIUS, a pitiful pun: he'd told me it as a boast.

It was harder to create prose cramped and illiterate and ill-spelt enough to be Ebbe's than it was to invent the science. But after a few minutes I felt satisfied –

"That is, smug."

– and went to my bath, having posted something like this:

> Conssistant prellim. results show palladium
> hydride cathode supersaturated (>985 own vol.)
> with heavy hydrogen isotrope by repeated sudden
> heating ($\approx$ 95°C) and chilling ($\approx$7°C) produces
> during electrolysis self-susstaining fusion of deu-
> terium with >18.4 mega-electrovolts per fused
> pair of atoms. Full paper pubblished online next
> wk. MEGASCORE. E.E.

I didn't hurry. There was no point searching for breakfast in the Combination Rooms, which had seen heavy revelry last night, and would still be lit-
tered with passed-out dons and worse. I sent Mrs Muckhatch to the kitchens
for coffee and kedgeree – look, are you *sure* you don't want to go downstairs?
I could tell you the rest at breakfast. They have those leathery-looking had-
docks called Arbroath smokies –

"Continue."

I obey, sighing. Around –

"Your gluttony's always been *childish*."

– around quarter to eleven, dressed by now in –

"I cannot care."

Around ten forty-five, wonderfully dressed, I went online to see how the
spot price for Brent Crude was doing.

All was well: oil was taking a nasty ("unexplained") tumble, down from
$109 a barrel to a bit below $102. Someone had clearly been reading sleekgeek.

I printed out a page from that scintillating website, wandered downstairs,
unlocked Ebbe's oak, strolled through his disgustingly messy sitting-room,
unbolted his bedroom. And recoiled. Both because the stench of psychosis
and despair, much worse than the night before – I'd visited before going off
to the banquet – and because he had lunged at me.

Ebbe was too small to be frightening as a fighter, but he bared his teeth,
snarling, and I had to snatch up a wooden chair to ward him off. 'Down, Eddie.'

'Grrr! It's only six days to term!'

I agreed that it was.

Then he suffered a moral collapse and fell to his knees, pawing at mine.
'Six days!' he wailed. 'I can't bear it. Let me have a hundred milligrammes of
pancuronium bromide!'

'A waste, old sport – you don't *need* pancuronium bromide. *Not with
FOCFU coming for you.*'

§

How easy it is, Margot, to cure melancholic madness! The prospect of being killed is intolerable, and entirely drives out the idea, or pose, of wanting to kill yourself. Its terror casts out unreal death-longings in an instant.

In this case I simply read out the message I had posted on sleekgeek. 'You're famous, Ebbe, congrats: nine thousand hits already!' – and the skinny chappie fell to bits. He tumbled to the floor. I put the chair down and sat on it; he rolled to and fro on his carpet, then curled like a fœtus. 'FOCFU!' he wailed: 'FOCFU!'

Do you follow my posting?

"Of course not."

It announced a way to induce fusion of heavy hydrogen atoms on a table-top at room temperature. Or in other words, to produce almost any amount of energy from, say, a vat of seawater. Ebbe was thus the greatest inventor of his age, the ultimate benefactor of mankind – although *not* (here's the rub) a benefactor of the cartel known as Organization of the Petroleum Exporting Countries.

OPEC, as all scientists in Ebbe's field know, runs a Fiduciary Office for Cold Fusion Understanding, or FOCFU. Despite the name, FOCFU is not, you understand, a research department. It's an anonymous black glass tower. In an unvisited corner of the Dutch province of Overijssel, standing all on its own amidst fields and contented chomping cows. Inside are a large number of clever quiet men on the lower floors, reading scientific journals all day long, keeping track of every development that might one day produce cold fusion. *Leucosis* so to speak, *xanthosis*, *iosis*…. And an even larger number of fell quiet men on the upper floors, in tight navy-blue suits and (most of them) well-groomed beards, playing extremely violent video games.

The whole business is tremendously well-funded by OPEC, and money on scale, as you know, produces intense calm. Without: Dutch rain pattering on the black glass. Within: a playful neo-'Fifties feel to the *décor*. Piped music, generally Cool Jazz, never repeating. A company restaurant on the top, with a grey view of cattle and polders, Javanese-Thai fusion. A very clean pool and and very-stylish gymnasium in the basement.

Now and then the clever chaps find cause to speak calmly to the grim chaps. A number of the grim chaps leave the dark glass tower. They fly off somewhere. They return. A scientist whose research has strayed toward prohibited truths – or (even more recklessly) hinted at the existence of FOCFU – has endured a sudden, horrific turn of fate.

A professor's car rolls down a snowy bank in the woods, he's trapped in the wreckage, limbs burned off; pine-martens gnaw his face away before he dies. That's what the papers reported of a solid-state physicist at Uppsala last winter. An improbable mishap? Yes, most improbable. Every scientist in the world knows to read between the lines.

The black glass tower of FOCFU is one of the pillars of our modern world. For *oil must remain above eighty dollars a barrel to preserve the happiness of mankind.* Or at least the portion of mankind that rules Saudi Arabia, Venezuela and Gabon. That's the premise. Grant it, and certain scientists need to be sacrificed. I doubt the scientists in question have the breadth of vision to accept what happens to them. But *we can.* The vigilance of the black tower is moving – no? Just as the Inquisition guarded the Faith against denials that would eventually deliver Christendom into the hands of Lenin and Hitler, so FOCFU protects a planetary economy based on petrol from –

"Yes yes. Get on. Stop trying to be funny."

And don't assume, *little one,* that FOCFU is the only way the republic of learning polices its frontiers. Why even in classics –

"It's sad, you know, when you teacher-types strive to seem ominous. Your inner landscape must be *so* morose."

In any case –

"And how pleased *you* sound at the moment. About your *little hoax.* Hydrogen atoms fusing."

Humph. Little, you say. Mankind gets through 3.8 million barrels of oil an hour. I'd wiped out, let me see, forty million dollars since lifting the silver dish-cover on my kedgeree –

"What about the Cobblemire Prize, then? Doesn't College rely on that? Isn't that funded by oil investments?"

– which wasn't as hot as I like it. No, there's no damage to our Cobblemire revenue because I knew the price would bounce back before nightfall. That's what these commodity speculations are like, they barely touch the real world, they only burn speculators. It had *coolled,* my kedgeree that is, because the Muckhatch had evidently stopped to gossip. Or had been stopped to be gossiped at, she's so oblivious –

"Felix. Please. *Ebbe.*"

Ebbe, yes.

He *didn't* show much breadth of vision when I mentioned FOCFU. He squeaked.

You'll grasp that FOCFU slays very few, a tiny number. Not many more than the Inquisition. It's the rumour of carnage that does the trick. Rumour has a sufficient inhibiting effect on the thousands who need to be kept in line. Rumour keeps them hushed, rumour keeps them from unfortunate advances. Ebbe had never had to worry much about such rumours, his own research being so remote from practical application. And anyway unsuccessful. Now, all at once, he knew himself condemned. He clung blubbering to my shoe.

'I thought,' said I, airily, 'you *wanted* to die.'

At which he simply bayed. I'd already cured him. 'FOCFU! FOCFU!'

'All right,' I told him, not quite patting his head, 'Uncle Felix will get you out of this scrape.'

'They'll chop me up with blowtorches!'

'Yes,' I agreed thoughtfully, 'they do do that. Perhaps you should've thought if you minded blowtorches before posting your message.'

'But I didn't post it!' he bawled, 'I didn't, I didn't!'

'*Didn't* you? Oh. Remarkable..... Well then, when FOCFU's representatives call, just explain there's been a mistake.'

The idea of placating a FOCFU ruffian was so appallingly unreal Ebbe had a sort of convulsion.

When he could speak again: 'FOCFU are everywhere!' True enough. 'They'll be here in days!'

'Perhaps if you slip away –'.

'They have infinite money! They never let anyone escape!' Also the case. 'They'll track me down anywhere.'

'Then unfortunately you'll have to trust me. To get you to *nowhere*.'

He had no other option, poor goblin, and started nodding as if he'd forgotten how to stop. 'I trust you, Felix, I do I do I do.'

I sighed over him. 'Better get your toothbrush,' and he popped into his bathroom.

I gazed about his gruesome rooms, doomed to be smashed up when the thugs arrived from Overijssel. There was really nothing he needed, apart from his toothbrush. Nothing he could properly miss. Except for his alchemical clobber, which was not transportable. I fingered with regret a limbeck, happily quoting to myself

> *What potions haue I drunke of* Syren *teares*
> *Diſtil'd from Lymbecks foule as hell within* ....

But Ebbe had already reappeared, shuddering. In clean white shirt and white lab-coat (without which he no doubt felt naked). And I suppose in his rightful mind. I gently took his toothbrush from his hand, which jerked and quivered, and popped it into his upper coat-pocket. Then steered him out of the rooms he'd never see again, slammed the door behind and –

§

What follows is a bit embarrassing. Bear it in mind should you ever find yourself setting too much store by my professional prowess –

"I won't, Felix. I promise I never will."

Bear in mind that I nearly got Eddie Ebbe killed with slackness.

It was perhaps ninety minutes since cold fusion had been announced to the world. It was inconceivable that even FOCFU could move so quickly. Yet the instant we were out the door I heard a chilly voice, vaguely Nordic, from below, at the bottom of the stair: 'Here is the name-plate, do you not see? EBBE. The first floor.'

There's no reason for a Nordic accent to be scarier than any other. But this voice liquified my bones more than – well, I can't remember. Cold. Cold. Strong and merciless as the sea.

As for Ebbe, he turned to rubber. I put one arm about him and leapt across the landing. At the cupboard or closed nook you'll have noticed, built into the wall opposite his door. It's where Mrs Muckhatch keeps her cleaning stuff, as Mrs Elmsgall did before her. We went clambering in amidst the brooms, buckets, mops. I pulled the door to, just as three heavy unflurried footfalls came up the turn of the stone stairs. One more second, I think, and they'd have seen us. A close call if you like –

"Bungler."

The cupboard was of course dark, and stank of the usual sharp chemical smells. Cheap synthetic lemon and lavender. And of what, I fear, must be Mrs Muckhatch herself.

But it wasn't entirely dark. Its wooden door was old and, as my pupils widened, I saw there were slits between its planks. Although I had to hold up Ebbe, I could lean forward, and get my eye to one of the slits.

Three navy blue suits were before me, three men with neatly-trimmed beards. They weren't hurrying, they simply knocked on Ebbe's door, with the softness of men who do not rely on knocking. No answer. They turned to and fro a little, looking up and down our staircase. One of them, a Finn I thought, wolf eyes in a flat face surrounded by silver hair, glanced at the cupboard. Directly at me, whom of course he couldn't see. Nor hear. I'd stopped breathing. The other two had black hair. One might have been Indian, South Indian, the other Arab. The Arab knocked a second time; then without fuss, for the second time in two days, Ebbe's door was kicked in – more efficiently that I had done it. The three men stepped through. They pulled the broken door behind them; and after half a minute I heard the smashing of computers, the throwing-down of shelves. They were taking the rooms to pieces.

By then I'd slapped Ebbe into alertness, we'd emerged stealthily from our cupboard, like players in a West End farce, we'd dashed down our staircase like burglars, and pelted across the Court like schoolboy truants, and shot up staircase VII, and were about throw open the door to Woolly's rooms – when I pulled Ebbe back.

He really looked too uncouth for what he was about to do. Or rather, for whom he was about to see.

§

"All right then – go on. Tell me…. Felix, go on. I want to know…. You're not getting breakfast 'til you finish."

§

Hm? Oh, all right. But – Benita. I was thinking of Benita. The heroine of this tale.

I was out in the passageway doing what I could with Ebbe. Pulling off his lab-coat, chucking it onto a chair. Removing his shocking glasses and stowing them in my pocket. Naked, his eyes were weirdly big and brown; the lenses had somehow shrunk them. I was roughing up his hair, so wildly cut he might have done it himself. Pushing his shoulders back. Taking his hands and sticking them into his pockets so it wouldn't be instantly apparent that he nibbled his knuckles and gnawed his nails. Begging him, in a whisper, to smile, then telling him to stop – his smile wasn't a pretty sight. 'Think about palladium', I hissed, a brilliant touch. It more-or-less did the trick. I mean he looked rapt and brooding in a way that might have been read as manly.

But at the same time, while I was doing all this to the worthless Ebbe (and not enjoying it), I was listening through the door. To the peerless Benita.

Benita! What verve! She was railing. On and on, and on. Her love-soaked voice fell to a passionate rumble, rose to a fervid trill. Lauding, lamenting, rhapsodising. A thousand variations on the inexhaustible theme *¡Sebastián!* She'd no doubt been at it ever since she'd burst in on Woolly. Not quite two hours before.

'*¡La belleza de mi Sebastián!*' I heard through the door. '*¡La inteligencia! ¡La amabilidad! ¡La bondad! ¡La aristocracia! ¡El valor! ¡La virilidad! El –*'

"Stop. *Inteligencia* indeed. Seb's pretty enough. Probably does his duty in bed. But he has the mind of a backward puppy. And the courage of a worm. This Mexican female was simply mad."

Your cynicism, my darling, your harsh young cynicism! It strikes me as curiously naïve. Try to *think*. Being in love's a phenomenon, a thing in the world. I don't approve either, but it's childish to pretend it doesn't exist. Grant the premise: Seb *is* the Adored. Everything else follows. He *must* be brave, kind, *etcetera*. Observation doesn't come into it. Benita derived his virtues from his infinite loveableness. The way a mathematician calculates from a formula, not looking out the window to check. You follow? Human love's just a strange *fact*. Just as God loves man – another bizarre preference, but once you grant it –

"I don't. No, get *on*. Your job's to *raconteur*, not lecture. Tell me what Woolly made of Benita's gibberish."

He was clearly in agony. I could hear his twisted snuffling groans. He knows what Seb's really like, of course. On the other hand, he's enthralled by nonsense and self-contradiction of every sort. So he was at an *impasse* with himself as well as with her.

I, the love-god, was doing what I could with Ebbe's shirt. It was short-sleeved. Buttoned over his enormous Adam's apple – when I heard Benita suddenly change track.

'*El es mi esposo, Padre. ¿Sí?*' And Woolly had to allow that it a certain sense one could almost hold that Seb was her husband, inasmuch as – . *That* noise could only be her slapping her swollen belly: '*¡Su pequeño está en mí! ¿No?*' Indeed, it would seem that his little one –. '*¡Él es mío! ¿No?*' She almost howled her claim to him. He was hers! '*¡Mío! ¿Sí?*'

At which Woolly tried his usual trick of muddling the universe down to a primal blur.

'*Sí, no, Benita? De verdad, todos Sís son Nos, y Nos Sís, sí? ¿No?*' All noes are really yes, all yeses no. It sounds no sillier in Spanish than in English, but perhaps Northern minds are *inclined* to whimsy: our cold and mist mean we're born half-baffled. Latins are less tolerant. There was a rushing noise as of a young vigorous body rearing up, and I thought it best to swing open Woolly's door and burst in, pushing Ed before me – .

§

Sure enough, the Chaplain was cowering in his armchair and Benita was rearing over him in fury. About to thrash him in the sacred name of reason. A thrashing he's been asking for for fifty years.

At the sound of the door she swung about. Her dark uncomely face was bright with desire, at once dashed. She'd naturally been hoping for, therefore *expecting*, Seb. He *would* break in and sweep her up. Since he was infinitely loveable, that was the sort of magnificent thing he *must* do.

Whereas Edward Ebbe – scrawny, ænemic, carbuncular, foreheady Ebbe – was not the sort of thing Benita had ever conceived of.

Equally, the bottle-blonde pneumaticised granddaughter of a Latin American gangster was nothing *he* had dreamt about in all his born days. Ebbe having been born and bred, if we can call it breeding, in a suburb of Bristol –

"So you've said."

He'd wanted to be an inorganic chemist since he could first crawl. He'd never had a romantic period.

So they just stood and stared at each other, with no idea what to think. No clue about what might happen next. Which is always a good beginning for this sort of thing.

"By *this sort of thing* you mean –"

Silence. – I'd got Woolly to his feet, murmured in his ear. What I said astonished him absolutely: 'Great Anthro-Divine Principle, Culpepper! You can't mean it. Twenty minutes, you say?' I pushed him out his door, shut it after him. Turned.

Margot Margot Margot. What potions have I drunk of siren-tears! I mean to say: what a brilliant, *brilliant* man you're in bed with. Blinding. My artistry extends beyond mere killing, which can after all be done artlessly and often is. My art extends to the only thing more overwhelming than death. To – well, let me recount.

I know you think you're initiate now. But you'll still want to go *Ah* and *Oh*.

'*No eres Sebastián,*' said Benita in a dead pinched voice, not untouched with wonder.

Note that she spoke to Ebbe, insignificant as he was. Not to me. I'd subtly made myself half-visible. Abstracted myself from the room. About which I seemed to float like a useful facilitating Puck, immune from amazement, oblique to desire. Oh Margot: how I amaze myself.

I was murmuring in Ebbe's ear. His grasp on language is so pitiful even her last remark was beyond him. 'She's saying: "You are taller than Sebastian,"' which was true, by an inch or so, now I'd got him to stand straight. '... Well, *answer* her, man.'

'Um. Um. Name's Edward Ebbe. What else …? Embarrassing. Um. Chemistry Fellow, me.'

That's what Ebbe always sounded like. A badly-programmed cardboard box.

'He's saying,' I told her in swift, no-doubt-inaccurate Castilian, 'that he, Eduardo, is the greatest scientist of his generation and can fabricate *sustancia psicoactivas* unknown to lesser men. And is a wonderful lover and moreover intoxicated by your spectacular form.'

Benita's eyes narrowed. She is by no means stupid. But her grandfather, as she'd explained to us in March, carefully kept her from the corruption of gringo television shows. Her command of English was as shaky as Ebbe's command of language in general. 'You are ugly, Eduardo,' she said with sublime frankness, as if to dismiss him from her thoughts, 'and without colour, a thing we despise in Mexico. You are spotty as a leper, and moreover very old, not like Sebastián. Perhaps nearly forty.'

'She is saying you're gloriously white as sierra snows blah blah blah, that all Englishmen look alike anyway, so if you wear a blond wig, as you'll have to do, you can pass as Sebastian. And that you barely look thirty.'

'Thirty-three point four, me,' he said, rather grossly.

'"Fie!" I reported to Benita, "'I am but nine and twenty."'

'¡Y tu mamá también!'

Conversation, such as it was, then snagged. 'Er. Er. Er. I've never. You know. *Spoken*. A girl. What we s'posed to talk *about*?' He rubbed the boil beneath his ear – it was one of his gestures, one of his few characterful notes. Perhaps the feel of it inspired him, for he continuted desperately, boldly: 'Chemistry, miss? Interested? Chemistry?' he asked, gazing into her face pathetically.

'"You err, *señorita*. Doubtless I am unlike any man you have seen. But in England I am accounted a paragon of loveliness. My slender limbs allow positions in the act of love that immerse my belovèd in unspeakable transports. There is between us already, I divine, a mysterious erotic chemistry. Yes, a chemistry."'

'¡María, misericordia! I cannot properly understand, Eduardo, the tumult in my heart. I came hither to find *Sebastián*. *Sebastián* is my love. And yet suddenly, mysteriously –', and so forth and so forth.

She was, obviously, in the grip of a certain odd psychological law: possibilities close to hand are easily repelled; possibilities unspeakable and remote, presented suddenly, stagger us. Unable to criticise what is entirely outlandish, we fall in with it. What else can we do?

"Like Lady Anne and King Richard in the play .... Someone once suggested *we* are like them."

What are you muttering about so darkly? Oh yes. We're like Richard and Anne. I suppose. But what strikes *me* is that we resemble *this* odd couple. Benita and Eduardo.

"What. A. Loathsome. Insulting. *Untruth*."

Tsk. *You're* the moneyed offspring of a delinquent, *I'm* a pedantic St Wygy's don: in the grand scheme of things, there's not much difference. Of course we're incomparably better-looking. And we're much better-born than – was that a cough? I hope this chill Scottish air isn't troubling your lungs. Oh it *was* just a cough? That's as well, I was afraid you were trying to imply something controversial. I am getting hungrier for Arbroath smokies every minute, so let me hurry along Benita's admirable speech, which ended '¡Imposible, pero te amo!' And she turned wet beseeching eyes to me, her faithful translator.

'Mary, mercy!' said I, speaking very quickly. 'Let me spell it out, Eduardo, you crawling insect. This armful of warmth, whose child by Sebastian, Sebastian Hawick Trocliffe the sociology undergraduate, you will acknowledge yours, is the only grandchild of the drug-lord of a lovely little Sonora *pueblo*, and this drug-lord's compound is the only spot on the planet where FOCFU will not be able to find you and work down from your pasty skin to your skeleton with a potato-peeler. So you're going to marry her and spend the rest of your life working in Don Anibal's drug lab in Cananea, where you will gradually learn to speak a human language like a man, and to ride and to shoot. And to make love. Your nervous shuffle will be soothed, you'll stalk like a puma. The sunlight will burn away your skin afflictions. How bad can it be? You'll never meet a student again so your contemptible suicidal impulses will not recur. You'll be pathetically faithful to her and after gramps dies when she's running the narcotics empire you'll inherit his white suits and his big moustaches and his cigar. Your job will be to perform the necessary strutting about on a mustang. The gunbattles you'll witness, the tortures you'll decree and observe, will settle and bake your face. You'll acquire the dreadful heavy unchanging gravity of an Aztec idol. You'll move in a glimmering moony pool of fear, not yours, every-one else's. You'll be a different sort of don and on the whole less unhappy than you'd have been here so I think it's time for you to kneel before this being who is infinitely too good for you. *One* knee, moron. – Speak, damn you! Quick, before I change my mind and kick you to death and save you from FOCFU that way. For it is grotesquely possible she loves you.'

He too was in thrall to the psychological law of ineffable oddity. That is to say, he could think of nothing to do but kneel. His pallid face, flushed with emotion (terror no doubt predominant) looked far less unpleasant than usual. He managed to say 'Should we. Dunno. Marry, or something?' which I rendered '"*¿Eres mi amor eterno?*"'

'*¡Sí!*' exclaimed the future *Señora* Ebbe, pulling him up and planting what was surely his first kiss, an enormous one –

Back to me. I felt unwell. It's all very well working a miracle. But this was the wrong sort of miracle. I mean my *métier*'s death not love, not playing Cupid to physical freaks. I needed the scene to end –

"Yes. Please."

'An immense international organisation, *señorita*, is hunting our Eduardo ….' It would have been a ticklish conversation with anyone esle. But Benita, that child of the Mexican narco-wars, had grown up among people with contracts out on them. Her parents had exited her life *via* a car-bombing, her only brother had been scalded to death in a police-cell. (She'd helped punish the policemen.) Assassination to her was what adultery is in better-conducted families, a familiar complication, to be avoided, or managed. I liked her more and more –.

"I not."

'You can't fly out of England, *señorita*, FOCFU will have men in every airport.'

'*¡No es un problema!*' She wasn't worried, brave girl. Neither was Ebbe, since he followed none of this. He was hanging about her neck. The import of kissing had just dawned through the dim weather of his micro-reality. '*¡No es un problema!*' – and fast, fast, she managed it, sitting on Woolly's sofa amidst the cake-crumbs, Ebbe obliviously kissed her hands and arms. It took her just two 'phone calls.

Her grandfather's associate Luigi was on a yacht in the Channel ('Where should he pick us up?' she asked me, covered the mouthpiece; 'Carrick Roads, western shore'). And she summoned a car of the sort that has tinted windows and asks no questions. ('Where?' 'Willow Walk, behind College, in twenty minutes.')

"Just like that."

Just like that ….There are, it seems to me, two parallel worlds coexisting on this one planet. Normal humanity wanders about, saves up, occasionally flies here and there. Dwellers in the alternative world can afford to go anywhere on whim, and do, but they have to do it very privately. There are no airlines in this alternative world, no streets. Presidents, mobster-kings, film-harlots: they haven't walked into a shop for decades, they can't. And Ebbe had been catapulted out of the normal world. Should we feel sorry for him?

"No."

No. Anyway, we of the normal world sometimes have astonishing things to offer to dwellers in the higher realm. When Benita had hung up, exclaiming with self-satisfaction '*¡Ahí! Lo he arreglado todo,*' I blandly asked 'And wouldn't you like to get married first?'

'Married? When?'

'Now. The College chapel in three minutes. *I* have arranged it all.' I was quite rightly pleased with myself,

'*¡Eres un maestro!*' – you hardly ever say that to me, have you noticed? Yet it's true.

"You miscalculated badly about your friends from Overijssel."

Yes, harsh one. And I didn't forget it as we went through Megiddo Court, through Cocytus, under the tower and into the Antechapel. Ebbe had eyes only for Benita and seemed to have forgotten all danger. But I found myself glancing in every direction, twitching at distant footfall – fortunately it was cold enough to justify shivering.

"Good thing you had lemon-hair to look after you. With those two guns tucked away. No doubt she learned to shoot people before she could walk."

Hush. As it happens we didn't bump into the three FOCFU hooligans.

Wygy's was quiet, quiet, empty; quieter than it is easy to imagine here and now, with those *bloody Scottish gulls* circling and squawking.

"Caw caw! Caw caw!"

Oh you think it *funny*, do you? Well anyway, we got through the hushed, hungover College without trouble.

No, our problems began in the delightful Antechapel, where –

"I don't like the Antechapel. Big and empty and always echoing with farty organ music."

You don't like such music? Well cheer up, I feel like singing.

"You can't sing *in bed* – "

Don't sound aghast. It's short.

"I mean, it's too romantic."

Ho ho, just wait.

"What's that noise?"

Quiet. Limbering up. I'm pulling out the sixteen-foot Bourdon. Hear it? *Phrrraa-um. PhrrraaAAAum.* My evil Great-Uncle Wilfrid the Archdeacon taught me to play –

"So you say."

And this was his favourite hymn, Wilfrid's own setting of words by the great ever-gurgling William Cowper.

> *Hatred and vengeance, my eternal portion,*
> *Scarce can endure delay of execution,*
> *Wait, with impatient readiness, to seize my*
> *Soul in a moment.*

> *Man disavows, and Deity disowns me:*
> *Hell might afford my miseries a shelter;*
> *Therefore hell keeps her ever hungry mouths all*
> *Bolted against me.*

"The punters *liked* this?"

Oh Wilfrid never thought of *them*. But *he* loved having it at Sunday School. And at weddings of course. There's a bit about Abiram, whom the earth swallowed up.

> *Him the vindictive rod of angry justice*
> *Sent quick and howling to the center headlong;*
> *I, fed with judgment, in a fleshly tomb, am*
> *Buried above ground.*

"You're trying to bring up Motte again."

I'm not. Here's a big farty Amen and I'm done. A-ha-ha-*HAAH*-menn-nnnn. Hear the diapason? Rumble rumble rumble.

There. Now we're ready for the most grotesque piece of epic anarchy I've ever survived, and only just:

§

hear, O little one, of the Nuptials of Benita and Dr Ebbe.

"A piece of anarchy? Woolly, then."

Indeed. They met us, grinning, standing by the tall case of spiritual books Woolly installed over summer to block out the Founder's tomb.

"He did? Oh, let me guess: *Death is not affirming.*"

Apparently not. *In a very real sense.* But the books, my darling, the books! Paperback Liberal-Jewish self-help, paperback Tantric sexual meditation, pseudo-Zen guides to weight-lost, the –

"*Can't* we get on? Woolly's waiting for you – no, *they* are. W'd'y'mean by *they?*"

Yoxley and Freke, as well as Woolly – they'd grown very thick with him since they started praying over their damned departed cat. *All spiritualities must draw together for all spirit is one, are they not?* Favourite saying of our belovèd Chaplain.

Who, in the spirit of that saying, looked like nothing on earth. Or like a gaudy laundry-basket. With Franciscan sandals peeking out beneath. His cassock, of course of his usual "non-restrictive" apple-green, was muffled up in the saffron robes of a Theravada school abbot – over that the long black cloak of a Shi'te imam –

"Poor love. It can't have been comfortable."

No. Lots of layers. Some tricky hand-clobber too. The same exacting broadmindedness that required Woolly to accept all non-Christian doctrines – while debunking all Christian ones – required him to clutch in his left fist both a fairly-convincing thyrsus, and a *hu*. A *hu* (since you're looking blank) is the flat wooden sceptre of Shinto. You've seen them.

"Yes. But –"

In his right first was a Wiccan wand of hemlock set with many-coloured crystals. Also a set of sour-toned Sikh temple-bells. With which he vigorously blessed us, *gling-gling*. Topping all was an immense mushroom-shaped *taku-hatsugasa*, the dull-red straw travelling-hat of a Buddhist monk. Designed to cover most of his face so he can't be seen. And cannot himself behold vanity. And indeed only Woolly's broad benevolent smile showed. Somewhat preju-diced by the rattling bone-necklace of an African *nganga*.

"Felix, how –"

*Gling-gling – gling-gling, rattle rattle, gling-gling.* Compared to all *that*, Freke and Yoxley looked very nearly decent. They were, as ever, dressed identically. Cream-coloured suits, white shoes. Olga with hot-pink pussy-bow, Elmo in bow-tie of the same fabric. A bridesmaid and a male bridesmaid. They too had jangling brass fertility-bells and were blessing us like mad.

"But –"

I took the opportunity, under cover of this metallic din, to shut and bolt the Antechapel doors behind us. What wonderful nail-studded oaken doors what they are! Hung in Worthyal's day, as you'll know. Carved with all the manifold sufferings of the damned. They swung portentously, they clunked closed monumentally. They consoled me. I might face – I would face – chaos within. At least we were secure from the world.

Then Woolly's *hu* made –

§

"Stop, listen. It's not *nice,* your knowing all these words. *Takuhatsugasa, nganga, hu.*"

No. But Woolly *will* explain things on High Table. My mind gets polluted with odd words. I can't unknow what I know, I don't have the knack.

"Hm."

Speaking of unknowing: the necklace was a gift from your own young Mr Odingo.

"Get on with your story."

I obey.

§

The *hu* made an indefinite chopping motion. The ringing was raggedly cut off.

'Welcome,' purred Woolly in his fruitiest tones. He can, as you know, sound varied as a Wurlitzer organ when he wants: dark oboe *timbres*, harp-sweeps, tinkling notes, distant gleeful plash of fountains.

"There's always been a woman inside his man's voice. And a child. A booming god – "

Yes, yes, he contains multitudes. It was the waters now. 'Welcome young lovers,' he plashed, 'to the fruition of your joys. In a moment we shall process – in no particular order, of course, all is liberty! – into Belial. (*Belial,* my dears, is what we call our Chapel, such an affirmingly subversive name.) And I have a surprise for you. Our dear dear friends – are we *not* all friends, 'though hitherto unknown to each other after the flesh? Our fiends Olga and Elmo have come to support our little ceremony. They are blessèd!'

'And *we*,' cried the twins, prettily tripping over each other's words, 'have a surprise.' 'For you.' 'Shishak – is to be.' 'Your pageboy!' 'Yes, we *knew* you'd be speechless.' 'With delight. Look!'

They stood aside. There behind them was, sure enough, that blasted mummified animal. With its own big hot-pink ribbon-bow about its neck. It had generously shared its little cart with a matching cushion, and the cushion bore two bluish rings.

'Seal-rings!' gushed the merry twain. 'Scarabs!' '*Faience!*' 'Eighteenth dynasty!' 'Borrowed from the dear old – '. 'The Fitzwilliam! But just –'. 'Just the thing!' 'Shishak's so proud. He was – '*Always.*' '– always such a pious puss.' 'Weren't you Shishak? –' ' – dearheart? Such devotion to the –' ' – the cat-headed –' 'goddess Bast. Bast of the Perfumes.'

"Oomp."

You say. As for Señorita Cofresí – well, I've already indicated the conservatism of her religious views. She didn't follow Yoxley and Frere's words, she may have thought that all clergymen dressed like Woolley in these cold countries. But she caught the drift of Shishak. Anyway she took one look at it and bellowed '¡*Paganismo!*'

Woolly gently expostulated: 'My dear girl – *mi niña – tolerancia, tolerancia.* Oн!'

The 'Oн' was because there'd been a sharp p'*THWID*, and because the cat's smirking head had exploded. Shards of linen, bone, dried flesh burst into the air; formed a momentary sphere, a dirty brown flower; cascaded pattering to the Antechapel's stone flags.

It took me an in-out of breath to grasp that Benita had whipped one of her handguns from under her black frock, and had blown off the embalmed head.

The noise of a silenced pistol is like nothing else on earth. It sounded a second time, p'*THWID* – Benita cried '¡*Obscenidad!*' – the mummy smashed, falling in threads and flakes.

We all stared, gobsmacked, at the smear of filth at our feet. Shishak was gone, shot to pieces. Quite a fate for a cat who lived and died ten centuries B.C.

Thirty centuries ago. Yet despite his long desiccation, Shishak stank. Stank perhaps of mice that had broken into granaries under the unfinished pyramids. Mice he'd sprung on one ancient afternoon, had eaten but not digested when he was ritually throttled at sunset in praise of Bast.

§

Elmo and Olga set up a horrific wail.

Their wail reminded me of women in millennia gone, gone, wailing for Osiris. Osiris murdered, dismembered, scattered – mourned afresh each autumn when the seed was scattered in the black soil of Ægypt. Although Ezekiel – d'y'remember? – drunk with abominations, saw women mourning for Osiris at the very Temple in Jerusalem – the Temple once sacked by Shishak's namesake, the Pharaoh. Sacrilege, holy or unholy sacrilege.... Really I can't account for what odd disordered ideas went tumbling through my head. Nor for the curious way I recalled another dubious woman, a certain ancestress of mine, who used cats, I must tell you some time. Anyway, quite apart from the stink, the mummy fragments looked perfectly insupportable, I'm not sure I can explain why. So utterly dreary, don't you see? And old, and impossible, and *hopeless*. In a cosmos where all things seem doomed to be rendered down to primal stodge before they're reconstructed – God knows why – Shishak alone was irretrievable.

Anyway these thoughts, if you can call them thoughts, occupied me while I disgustedly brushed the feline grit under the bookcase with my shoe;

§

and then came an awkward, uncouth moment.

Ebbe was boggling, turning his foolish head back and forth (to be fair, I still had his spectacles in my pocket); Woolly was clearly on the verge of one of his aggressive tirades against intolerance; Yoxley and Freke, disturbingly identical in grief, clung to each other, throwing back matched spherical heads to keen. I was merely coarsely dumbstruck.

Only the heroine Benita *acted*. – I do wish I could make you like her, she was such a wholesome influence on St Wygy's during her brief time with us. – She waved her smoking guns. '¡*Continuar!*' said she.

Said it so decisively that Woolly, instead of a harangue, looked down her barrels and subsided. 'Most unfortunate. Most non-inclusive, I'd go so far as *unhelpful*. We continue, then, *without* our pageboy. I trust the wise and affirming words –'

*Words!* I knew of old Woolly's promiscuous way with words, and I didn't want to see Benita's reaction to Confucius or Joseph Smith. I'd noticed a discarded eighteenth century Prayer Book on those sad shelves. I fished it out pronto, opened it to the right page, thrust it at him. '*This*, Chaplain.'

Once again he sighed. 'Very well, very well. But listen' – suddenly the old angry Ulster light sprang up in his watery eyes – 'no firearms. *Ni armas, señorita, en la casa de Dios.*'

Benita folded her arms; things looked ugly.

'Chaplain,' I suggested quickly, 'how is Belial the house of God? You always deny He has anything to do with it.'

'Symbolically speaking.'

'But you always say the very *idea* of God is narrow.'

'*That* is what it is a symbol *of*.' And there was for a moment such a fierce jut to his chin, he resembled so uncannily his unbending Covenanting ancestors, that Benita herself growled, relented, and placed both her guns in the bookcase, propped against a New Age encyclopædia.

One of Woolly's virtues, as you'll have noticed, is that he can't hold a grudge, can't even be proud of his rare victories. Perhaps the churning in his skull prevents it. In any case, he simply smiled: smiled sadly at Yoxley and Freke, who wailed the louder, smiled forgivingly at me, smiled patronisingly at Benita and Ebbe, turned and, not without dignity, led us into Belial itself.

§

Thus into Chapel we went.

The dirge of Freke and Yokel continued behind us; then died away into snuffles; into sad double pattering of feet, receding; silence. And so Woolly could begin.

'*Dearly beloved, we are gathered together here in the sight of God –*'.

Here a thought struck Woolly and he paused. 'Or gods,' he added brightly. Another crumpled frown. 'Or goddesses.' He considered wider possibilities. 'Or *not*.' And he sighed. He had reduced sense to purest nonsense and could proceed: '*and in the face of this Congregation, to join together this Man and this Woman*.' Another hesitation while he reviewed possibilities homosexual, inter-special, polygamous, all waiting to be affirmed. But since they did not apply, he let the harshly specific phrase go with a sensitive sigh; '*in holy Matrimony*.' Again the pensive hiatus. 'Or unholy.'

My attention wandered. Woolly's voice, let's admit, is beautiful. When he doesn't overdo it. If you don't attend to the content. He gurgled away beautifully while my eyes roamed over the altar.

The side-altar, that is to say. He doesn't like dealing with the high altar, with that uncompromising altarpiece of St Wygefortis' martyrdom. *This* one he'd rigged out extravagantly over the summer. The top of a polychrome totem-pole from Oregon. Candles beyond number. Plastic flowers of a vaguely Eastern cast. A brass bust of Gandhi balancing a plaster bust of Lenin, with between them a full-length twelve-inch Jim Morrison, in clear plastic, filled with stripes of coloured volcanic sand from some desert, Californian one hopes, but –.

"You bloody *bungler*, Felix –"

I know, I know. I was lulled by that voice, that's my excuse. '*If any man –*

or woman; or, indeed, child, or *infant,* although of course it would be hard –
yet possible; certainly we affirm their perspective ....' Woolley had apparently
tired even himself with his fidgets, and finished in a rush: '*can shew any just
cause why they may not lawfully be joined together let him now speak or else
hereafter for ever hold his peace.*'

'Yes,' said a freezing voice behind us, big and merciless as the sea. 'I am
the just cause.'

The happy couple jumped out of their skins and turned. I scarcely jumped
at all (I like to think) but certainly spun about smartish. Woolly of course
looked up vaguely, blinking from under his immense hat, seeing perhaps
almost nothing in his total chaos of mind.

What the rest of us saw was the tall tinsel-haired young FOCFU agent, the
Finn, with his Arctic face flat as a dinner-plate, and a new-looking Benelli B76
in his hand. Idiot that –

"Bungler that you are. Yoxley and Freke would *obviously* have –"

I'm doing this, thank you.... But t'know, I fear I'm *bound* to grow stupid.
Excess –

"I know."

– excess of suffering breaks a mind, but so does excess of pleasure. Wears
through the fibre. My inner life's a fat mass of happy memories, decades of
delight almost uninterrupted – reading Ovid, nocturnes in Venice, the ice-
wine we have on High Table, canoeing in Greece, truffled duck, orgasms – '

"Shucks."

– pulling down that hideous house in summer, *crushing your plots –*

"Hmph."

– and so forth. And so on. Perhaps I'm doomed to decline. Perhaps –

"Yes."

– perhaps my mismanagement of this infernal wedding was the first fatal
symptom. In any case, I *was* an idiot. I didn't reflect that Freke and Yoxley
would –

"Leave the antechapel door unlocked when they –"

Yes *yes,* they left it open. And the conspicuous sight of them dashing
weeping across the Courts attracted our enemy.

Here he was. And Benita didn't have her guns. Nor was Ebbe any good,
he'd gone back in an instant to being damp terrified clay. While I – .

As for Woolly: he put back his head, which was his only way of seeing
under the brim of his *takuhatsugasa,* lowered his brows, opened his eyes as
wide as they would go, pursed his lips, bit his lower lip, considered the words
of his book, then managed: 'You have, I *see,* a, one hardly likes to say *objection,* so unenabling, so almost objectifying. But a, a *contribution,* sir?'

'My objection,' insisted the frigid voice, 'is Dr Ebbe comes with me instant to take down his pseudo-scientific claims from internet and post retraction. Then we turn this woman to widow if she had married which is thus waste.'

But Woolly, who had pursued his own mental experiences for the last few seconds, continued with agonising tender appeal: 'How can one man, person, ever *object* to another? Are we not –'

'He has,' expounded the incredible Northern killer, 'outraged interests of OPEC. OPEC object.'

'OPEC?' wondered Woolly, doubtless wondering if some Inca god had been neglected in his capacious prayers.

'*Quiet*,' snapped the bride and groom, speaking at once; and '*Quiet*' said I, and even the Finn, all of us exasperated beyond bearing with the priest. It gave us the oddest spasm of friendliness. We were comrades against the illimitable mindlessness of the Chaplain.

Presuming on this, and on the fact that this was clearly a man who liked to explain (as Nordics often are), I ventured to remark, looking carefully into the pointing Benelli: '*How* can you be here? It's less than two hours since Ebbe put up his announcement!'

'Always two helicopters we have on roof of tower, manned, fuelled. Got the word, took off. But four hundred and kilometres from headquarters near Zwolle to where we handed outside.'

'Outside?' I said, looking about, bewildered-sounding.

'Outside Cambridge. Over there,' he snapped, turning to point foolishly, testily, out a Chapel window, north-east, 'on the field beyond *mmp. Mmp. Mmp*' –

I think I'm capturing the noise. He was now speaking into the stone flags, face down, for I'd felled him, smashed him down, with a tremendous swing of the bust of Gandhi.

'*Mmp*,' he said again. My blow had landed on the left side, above his ear, possibly mashing the Broca area, which governs speech. If consciousness is a fiction, as certain dizzy philosophers have suggested, the Broca is where the fiction's shelved. A whole three-volume novel's worth. And I'd torn it up. In the end are no words –

"Get on."

True: it made not the least practical difference. I leaned down to cosh him about the top of the spine. Gandhi's prominent nose broke through the skull with a distinct crunch, and the Finn fell perfectly silent.

I straightened myself. 'Objection over-ruled.' Woolly blinked at me very hard. 'Proceed, Chaplain.' Still he paused. 'The next words are *Edward, wilt thou have this woman ....*'

'But,' said Woolly, who found the formation of negativising propositions (as he would say) particularly taxing, 'there is a man lying here at our feet.

Injured. By, it would seem and I make no judgment on the matter, you.' His head was held as far back as it could be and, in the ruddy shadow of the straw, I could make out two eyes of vacant robin's-egg blue.

'There isn't,' I said firmly. 'A corpse in church? How could there be?'

He shut his eyes in concentration. Down came his brim. A lifetime of denying that various things or Persons were ever present in church had made this particular line of thoughtlessness easy for him, wonderfully easy. You could see his mind slithering down its rails of nullity.

He opened madman eyes, regarding the corpse with his head at a winsome angle. 'Yes. *But.*'

'*No hay hombre muerto*,' said Benita firmly.

Then – clever, clever girl – she looked at her lover. Who opened his mouth as if he were drowning underwater, and got out 'Light.' Gasping: 'Light is a wave as well as a particle, so say you see anything in the – ah, ah – visible spectrum' (oh yes yes, he was coming along nicely, Ebbe) 'it's necessarily wavy so easily mistaken.' It wasn't a very powerful lie but it *was* a lie. We'd make a man of him yet.

'I have heard something of the sort,' said Woolly, rustling the pages of his Prayer Book with his nervous right hand. 'Do not the profoundest insights of science so often' – he tangled the fingers of that hand anarchically in mid-air the better to illustrate his point – '*mesh* – with *spiritual* truths which – which – ?' Unhappily his eye had lit on Gandhi. 'That bust seems,' he said, '*seems*, I say no more than that, to be covered with blood.'

'Impossible, Chaplain. The Mahatma' (I was putting the bust back on the altar, making a meal of tucking it under the artificial jasmine and candles; the scarlet wetness over the blind round spectacles and moustache gleamed) 'was a pacifist.'

'That's true,' murmured Woolly, 'that's very very, and very *beautifully* so.' He was on sounder ground now. Denying the existence of war was frenzy of his own stripe. 'Well since we are all in harmony on the point – and contradiction in the face of *harmony* is so divisive I feel –.'

And he sighed as rent in two by the pressure of absolute benevolence.

'*Edward. Wilt thou have this Woman to thy wedded wife …?*'

§

I slipped away – at any moment a witness less biddable than Woolly might appear in Belial. Before that I needed to make the Finn presentable.

On my way back to my set I sighted both surviving FOCFU men: the Arab lurking by the Lodge so no one could leave College unobserved; the Tamil prowling the Courts, waiting for someone to appear, someone who might lead him to Ebbe. They looked impatient. It was now late in the morning. The emptiness of St Wygy's must have been puzzling. Poor fools, if only they knew, there *is* no morning with us after a Belshazzar's Feast.

I myself lurked behind a coign of Cocytus Court until the Tamil had stalked away into Sheol, then dashed across the grass, up the staircase, past the uninteresting cleaning cupboard that had meant life to me a little while before; into my set. I knelt by my freezer, got out my gin bottle, took a slug.

I knelt again. There, waiting for me in the space behind the space where the gin had been, was Ebbe's auroscaphium, frosted over, its gold dimmed. I cracked it free of the ice and brought it out. It was so cold it burned my fingers. I wrapped it in a towel and shook it hard; kept shaking it as I ventured down the stair (no FOCFU), over the Court, under the tower (still no FOCFU), into Antechapel, and back to the side-altar.

§

Where Woolly was still working his way through the lovely Elizabethan prose, with the Finn lying face-down before him, quite invisible to his eyes of unfaith, oozing a pool of thick gore, brain rather than blood. Benita and Ebbe stood before, being made one. What an auspicious beginning!

"A cold fusion."

Ho ho ho. But you wouldn't attempt such a joke if you'd seen them. Love's so formidable, Margot. A gun of tremendous calibre, loose on its moorings. It can swivel suddenly, and still be immense pointing in a totally different direction. Benita's passion for Seb was unchanged, it was just not for Seb any more. So no, not cold.

"Hm. And Ebbe?"

Well, any strong emotion – in his case, despairing boredom – can be rendered down to terror. Which is the ur-emotion, base and basic. Then resurrected, as the alchemists used to say, as anything else. The lowest state's the gateway to *everything*. In this case, yes, to blazing infatuation. Ebbe stood before Woolly with his mouth open. He loved *señorita* Benita.

And it wasn't just *her* voluptuous appeal. I think he was swept away by the beauty of Cranmer. I've said he was a frustrated poet, so ignorant he couldn't give a name to his own longing. Woolly read

'O God, who by Thy mighty power hast made all things of nothing;
Who also (after other things set in order) didst appoint,
that out of man
(created after Thine own image and similitude)
woman should take her beginning'

– and Ebbe sighed from mere pleasure. The words were so perfectly formed. Also, let's not overlook the charm of Woolly's voice. They filled the whole mind, as music does. There was no space left for criticism, even for detachment. So that when they were complete, when silence comes again, those words abide. Ground of thought in the mind in time to come. They cannot be disbelieved.

"*I* manage to –"

Hush. As the great sacrament proceeded, I stooped. Opened my auroscaphium, now burnished to its proper dim-golden glow. Began to shake shards of frozen spew into the Finn's sticky blackish halo. Ahook and shook 'til the golden vessel was empty. Sighing a little at the waste.

"The waste –"

A shame to squander such precious stuff so soon after acquiring it. Though to be fair, it's only got a shelf-life of a month or so, after which even a police pathologist won't necessarily be taken in. Also, I was spending it in the service of the man who'd provided it. Ebbe giveth and Ebbe taketh away, blessèd be the name –

"Wait wait wait. Vomit – "

*Venomous vomit* is for people like me –

"Us."

– like us the most serendipitous substance. Imagine you suddenly find yourself with a corpse on your hands. As you certainly will in *our* line of work. Especially one that obtained its corpsehood with the aid of a blunt instrument. Just pour out the sick you've carefully kept frozen. As soon as it thaws, all's well. No one will doubt the dear departed drank poison, smashed in his head falling, thus has nothing to do with you or your blunt what's-it. You're home free.

'*He that loveth his wife loveth himself,*' declaimed Woolly, '*for no man ever yet hated his own flesh, but nourisheth and cherisheth it.*' He was working his way doggedly through the whole text, even the harangue at the end, usually skipped, about female obedience: '*Sarah obeyed Abraham, calling him lord; whose daughters ye are as long as ye do well, and are not afraid with any amazement.* There,' said Woolly with a tremendous gasp, shutting the difficult book, 'done.' And it was! 'Not *altogether* affirming, but I suppose in a sense the most *challenging* concepts by their very demand for a greater work of reconciliation to *remove* them call forth –'

"Oh God."

Exactly. I couldn't endure Woolly's prattle, being afraid with amazement. Two impatient hitmen were wandering about College, eager to shed Ebbe's blood, and by extension Mrs Ebbe's and mine – now the thing was done I was frantic to get the Ebbes away, away. I took them by the elbows and pulled.

'Must you be going? Dear Benita, *dear* Edward, is seems but an hour ago that –'

"It *was*."

More or less; but an hour of Woolly's a lot. I pushed the happy couple out, over the Finnish cadaver, past the high altar, into the tiny Chantry where centuries of Masses were ineffectually said for the black soul of our Found- er, out and away, Woolly's voice him calling out to us something about the wedding breakfast fading behind us. The last I heard of him, as I pulled the Chantry door to, was

"So much for him. You took –"

Hold on. About Woolly. I glanced back. The last I saw was this: a parson in a bowl of a hat, faintly smiling. Staring up into his Perpendicular roof. Magnificent! Granite ribs, light and dancing as cobwebs that blow across a sky in a sunny breeze, stone music –

"I've seen Chapel, Felix."

– breaking upward in praise of certain fixed beliefs. He stared up at that and, listen, *blotted it out*. Voided creed, stonework, form. That's what I saw.... I imagine you've not been into Belial since summer? Well, Woolly had those mucky stained-glass removed (*such narrow imagery* he said). He's filled the stone casements with translucent plastic sheets. Bearing religious slogans in Sanskrit. Thus only a dim whitish light poured though onto him, onto his jumble of clerical dress, black, saffron, apple-green, dull-red, brown – and he looked *terrifying*.

"Rubbish."

He did. Woolly, having for so long worshipped nothing-in-particular, has reared above himself – like a balloon-seller with a cloud of diversely colour trailing behind – a deity: Nothing-in-Particular. Formed in his own image, but perhaps more formidable. Certainly the air about him seemed to swim. Nothing was but what is not. The defiled corpse at his feet half-dissolved, became putative. Faded away. Speaking of which –

"Stop asking. No sausages. The gulls aren't letting up and neither are you. We're here in bed until your comedy's done."

It *is* virtually done. The last act of *The Marriage of Eduardo* rushed by so fast, fast fast fast, it burst out of time, turned slapstick –

§

You probably know that Chantry debouches, as old books say, straight into that mossy cobbled alley running behind the Library. Which doesn't have much point except to let light through the Library windows. Illuminating empty chairs.

It comes to a sort of dead-end in the wall that shuts in Willow Walk. Can you picture it? On your left, doorway down into what used to be the coal-cellar for Megiddo Court – now holding gardening tools. On your right a grille opening on the Library basement. Ahead, the wall itself, sixteenth century ragstone, mossy, ivy-hang, with a low wooden kennel built against it, covering the unsightly bricked-over coal-hole. But *beside* the hole –

"Yes yes, the secret postern."

Oh. Undergraduates aren't supposed to know about that.

"Simpleton. Of course we do. You bent down, released the rusty old spring, and popped out into Willow Walk – then what?"

Ahem. Yes. That's what we did.

As always, Willow Walk seemed *baleful*. Stone wall behind. Ahead, clean hard pale Georgian blind brickwork of Abaddon Court. Covered arch of Erebus passing overhead. Dim openings on the world left and right. The Walk's in the world but not, in College but not, outdoors yet tunnel-like –

"Been there. There every day. Was Benita's car waiting?"

It was. Black S.U.V. limousine with black windows. Just the thing for people in the alternative universe. Big enough almost to block Willow Walk.

Beyond it was a don's-wife sort of woman, thoughtfully working her way along on an old-fashioned bicycle with its wicker-basket full of autumn flowers and a baguette. To the right, in the relative dazzle of Short Street, a boy who must just have gone through the Walk had stopped, tapping away at his 'phone.

In the shadowy air beside the car stood the driver. Formidable, shaven-headed, tall and black, in reflective shades, mustard polo-neck and black gabardine car-coat. I deduced a shoulder-holster under that gabardine – he was bodyguard as well as driver, as is the way in the alternative world. He acknowledged Benita by not moving his face at all. No doubt he generally didn't smile.

This fellow seemed to give Ebbe pause. At least Ebbe *did* pause, his nourishing, cherishing hand clasping his wife's. He didn't get straight into the car – which was to have large consequences for a number of people. He paused, you understand, for a second or two, while (I should imagine) his Cambridge life ran through his mind. Saying farewell. That was catastrophically enough.

Fast fast fast. 'There they are!' 'That's them!' cried two simultaneous indistinguishable voices.

It was hardly worth turning to look, 'though I did. *Of course* the postern was open again, *of course* Yoxley and Freke had opened it (they'd changed already into identical mourning-black track-suits), *of course* they were pointing – a single gesture by two stubby right arms – at us. And out from the postern behind them were crawling, of course –

"The two FOCFU goons!"

– who saw us and straightened up, growling.

We'd been betrayed. To be fair to the twins, I'm sure they'd no idea what they were letting us in for. The goons pretended to be bailiffs, perhaps, or divorce lawyer's clerks, hunting down Ebbe for some almost-innocuous purpose. The last thing Dr Freke and Dr Yoxley would have expected is what happened instantly – with dashing vulgar speed: the driver-bodyguard made as to –

"Whip out his gun from under his armpit."

No, from his hip. I was wrong. He was wrong, it was awkwardly placed, it wasn't quite up when the two FOCFU men fired, fast, fast, P'*THWID! WID! WID!* Down he went, chest a giant smear of scarlet over yellow, *thud* on the Cambridge footpath.

That old happy syllogism came into play: violence *doesn't* happen in Cambridge, in England. Violent thuds and clicks can't mean what they might mean. The woman on the bicycle, already turning right into King Street, glanced vaguely back over her right shoulder but didn't stop pedalling – the bodyguard had fallen on our side of the car, you understand, out of sight.

Only Olga and Elmo saw, and for the second time that morning must have felt their dusty world was blowing up. 'No!' 'No!' they cried as one and were off, dashing under Erebus. Past the boy, who was entranced with the business of extirpating alien spacecraft, indifferent to reality this side of his tiny screen. Round the bulk of Lethe Tower and away: 'No, no!' 'No!'

Thus we are left alone with our friends the thugs.

The FOCFU men ignore Benita, who's uttering female whimpers, recoiling, hysterically groping at Ebbe, groping pawing at her own clothes – we know what she's reaching for. They step up to Ebbe and me. We back against the ragstone wall. I feel its soft cold moss under my fingers.

'Which of you,' asks the Arab, calm and quiet as you like, 'is Ebbe?'

'He is!' 'He is!' we both say heroically at once.

The Arab takes Ebbe by the collar, shoves him hard into the stones. The Tamil puts his hand on my chest, pushes me back. Leans forward into my face. Next moment, before the question can be repeated more forcefully –

"P'*THWID,* p'*THWID.*"

Er yes. Exactly that. Faster than fast, Benita shoots them down, p'*THWID.* – Listen, though. The Tamil's face, still pressed into mine, allows me the most extraordinary close-up on the great moment. The moment art and religion can't leave alone.

"You too –"

I, also, if it comes to that. Shocking to see it in pornographic close-up, four inches away. Without distraction, for of course Benita knows her business, there are no wanton blasts of blood. She slips her shots in neatly, straight under each left ear, into the jolly old Broca. – Not that it matters much where they go, being soft-nosed cartridges, built to come to bits at the least resistance. Instead of blasting the Tamil's head off, as with the fragile head of Shishak, the bullet blooms into a score of tiny fragments, bouncing through his brainpan, ricocheting off the inside of his cranium, frothing cortex and brain-stem to a watery softness, the consistency of a winter soup. That is to say, my Tamil's utterly instantly dead. Long dead, in a sense. His soul had snapped all connection with his body, gone to Duat and judgment and the abyss. Somewhere his Finn comrade was already slapping him on the back. Shishak was arching its back against his shin. *And* he was already used to non-existence –

"*And*? You sound like Woolly."

– while his body (*hush*) has still not changed one whit. So gentle is his killing. He stands. Head doesn't jerk at being punctured. Eyes still move, fluttering weirdly. Still breathes, breathes *on me*, still stinks in my living nostrils of betel-leaf and a flashy cologne.

I threw my arms about him – of course he was warm, I could fell his uninterrupted heartbeat. I caught him before he could collapse; and here's the remarkable thing, Ebbe, the unworldly "chymical" donnish Ebbe, had already caught his FOCFU man, the Arab, before *he* could collapse. He was getting the hang.

Swift as thought Benita had opened the boot of the car while we half-pushed, half-slung our killers backward, then let them fall, *bw-la-la-lumpf*, into the boot. She was already nodding at the driver's corpse but her nod was unnecessary: we were already bending to scoop it up, I taking the shoulders, Ebbe the feet. Smoothly it went up, through the air and into the boot, on top of his murderers – all three of them still man-warm.

I hope you're grasping how swift this was, how *blasphemously* swift. It was buffoonery, not proper human comedy. This is why I can't abide guns, which amateurs assume are the natural way of doing what needs to be done. Shooting's *unnatural*, it's weirder than my most ornate schemes. It's inartistic, jumbling all the notes of an symphony into one instant blaring chord. It's surreal, too, depending on the fantastically puny, a thirtieth of an ounce, the length of a fingernail. And someone puts on immortality.

Oh to be in North Korea, eh! Where Kim Jung-un executes his enemies, who are often his kin, with flamethrowers. Or starved dogs, or anti-aircraft artillery. With artillery, Margot! Think of the heartfelt, no-nonsense exuberance of that!

Whereas the very word *shot* is mean, quite appallingly curt. The tempo of handguns is preposterous. Four hundred feet a second, a man gone faster than you can say *A man gone*. Consider, by way of contrast, Detective-Inspector Conan Motte. He dies at a credible pace. At this moment he –

"I will *not* consider Motte."

What's this? A touch of taphophobia?

"A touch of human decency."

Hm. Isn't a bit stand-offish to refuse to think of *him* when he's certainly so thinking intensely about *us*? ... But as you like, we're speaking of timing. Decency! Pah! There were three seconds, perhaps two-and-a-half, from the delicate double *bimf* of Benita's shots to her subdued slamming of the boot. Like all expensive machinery the limousine made quiet sounds: *krrnk*. The boy looked up from his 'phone, glanced back and forth, shrugged, walked on, ignoring our brief knockabout. There can be no shooting in England so there isn't. He was lost in his 'phone, his ker-*pow*, ker-*pow*. Three seconds! It would've taken longer to scrape up a dropped ice-cream.

§

Now, Edward Ebbe: he's the puzzle in all this. Benita and I are, in other different ways, professionals. But he was just a pedantic (and superstitious) chemist. His sound instinct about violence, his speed, his sudden callousness: whence?

Surely, by divine gift. The gods picked him out as assassin. That's my conclusion. I was the gods' instrument. There's no whimsy or arbitrariness in what I did to him.

"It's not, then, your fault?"

I don't mean that, silly child. How could I be concerned about guilt? Does a fish worry about getting splashed? I'm interested in cause. I mean that Ebbe was never *meant* to be an academic. His assault on himself was as *needful* as my act against him. He was destined to be great among the *banditti* since the foundation of the world.

The boot clumped shut and I looked at him. 'Well?' which could have meant anything, but which he took as a referring to the bodies.

'The wife,' he said, speaking carefully, not stuttering at all. He spoke without looking me in the eye, and not without some disgust. 'Says we're being collected. By a yacht. And being landed. At night. Near the mouth of the Rio Grande.' God knows *how* his breasty monoglot told him all that. Sign-language? Telepathy? 'We'll pass Brest. Be off the continental shelf. We'll weigh these. Drop them over.'

'¡*Eso es excelente!*' exclaimed the smiling Benita, who could apparently guess her way in English when it was belovèd forming the barbaric words.

'No, *es nada, mi amada*,' he replied gravely, as if honeymooners were exempt from the curse of Babel; '*es nada*.' It was the most ambitious sentence of his life, I should think. Having next to no English, he could suck up Spanish as his first language.

So I bowed at him, unironically. What else was there to do? He looked at me (in a way reserved for looking at demiurges), and got into the car. I kissed Benita's hand; *she* got into the car; they drove quietly away and I'll never see either of them again. Nor see their litter of children.

"Sure to be hideous."

That's what family plastic surgeons are for…. But I'll think of them often. Whenever academic life strikes me as a dungeon from which no one escapes. Excellent Eduardo!

§

I couldn't face crawling back through the postern. I walked round into Short Street, entered St Wygefortis' College conventionally through the Lodge, went back to my rooms, to my bed, which the Muckhatch had made, lay down, and allowed myself to writhe, kick my legs in the air, swear in Attic Greek, and generally indulge in mild hysterics for half an hour.

Because, you see, of the strain of the morning. Because four unexpected corpses is too many even for me.

This clearly wasn't to be a day for lunch. About three I woke, wandered about, talked through their windows to a couple of dons, all sick-hungover. I found the Widdler, however, enduring the afternoon-after in her own fashion. She was striking a pose at the corner of Cocytus Court, clutching her neck with both hands as in a garrote – she's a woman of clavicles, have you noticed? They're her one good feature. Her frightful mediævalish gowns are meant to show them off. Now long cobwebby hair lay as a faint dew on her long pinched cylinder of ribcage, and her fingers tore at her throat.

Tomorrow she'd be back to term-time librarian mode. She'd be *Miss Vydler, M.A.*, as she signs herself in those reproachful notes to erring borrowers; obviously she corresponds with no one else. But this present frenzy was disquieting. Was she was enjoying her last wild summery moments of self-harm? Or (and the moment I had this idea I knew it was right) was this terror? Had she bumped into OPEC's hatchetmen that morning, looking for Ebbe? And what had they told her?

She pushed me over the edge. She was too much. I went back to my rooms, packed a suitcase, and was sidling out the Lodge when I ran into Trotsky Plantagenet. Into a carping, reproachful, self-pitying Sir Trotsky.

'Good afternoon, Master,' I said furtively, hoping to get past him unconversed. He has a bad habit of waylaying people at the College gates.

But he stayed me. 'No, Culpepper, it's not. Never a good afternoon the day after Belshazzar's Feast. But this year ….' He eyed my suitcase. 'We've had intruders. Or so these idiot porters of ours report – well, I can hardly keep up with their story. A pregnant female with yellow hair. Does that make sense to you? No. Well there's no trace of her so I'd put it down to drink, but the porters also claim there have been a couple of sinister young rogues about in matching blue suits, two of them, or three, or five, perhaps only one – anyway they or he do or does or did exist because he or one of him, of them, drat the English language, had the cheek to commit suicide *in my Chapel*. That is, in Chapel.' The Master's grandiose manner's so natural to him it's barely a fault. Don't you think? He's too puffed-up to sound any other way, as an infant has no choice but to pipe. 'What? Oh yes, no doubt about it; the police forensic team have come and gone, very discreetly I'm glad to say. Poisoned himself, gashed his head falling. No doubt about it at all. Quite frankly *puked up his guts as he lay dying*. So report the police. Loathsome business. Just before term too. Think of the publicity. Happily the Chief Constable has agreed to hush it up (he owes us a favour), and officially he – I mean the dead rogue in the shiny suit – was found over in Christ's Pieces, where he bashed his forehead on a tree. I'm telling you this because you always seem to find things out.' I'm never sure how much the Master guesses what I do. What I am. 'You will be discreet and not gossip, won't you?'

'Of course, Master.' Yet here I am telling you. Poor Sir Trotsky.

'There's more, too. Dr Yoxley and what's-'er-name, the Egyptology J.R.F., Olga Freke, yes. I didn't think they were particularly drunk last night, did you? Well they're both thoroughly gone to pieces today. Bleating, shrieking about that filthy preserved pussy of theirs. I told them it had to go back to the Fitzwilliam, but apparently they disobeyed and now it's been crushed, stood on or some such. They're too berserk and incoherent to follow, jabbering about dead drivers. I thought I'd have to send them off to shriek away the term in the Deepdene. But Mrs Oathouse, bless her, turned up and gave them what I think was horse-tranquiliser. She's a jewel among college nurses, that woman.'

'Yes, Master. Won't horse-pills kill them, though?'

'Shouldn't think so. Anyway, it's only Berberology's loss.'

'True.'

'There's *more*. The Widdler's squeaking about men with guns and Dr Ebbe, *and* Ebbe himself seems to have gone mad. Less of a surprise, of course, *him*, not right in the head at the best of times. He's smashed up his rooms, vanished. Appalling mess, computers thrashed to smithereens, all his papers burned in his fireplace …. I suppose I saw it coming. Officially I'm giving *him* a term's research sabbatical – just had a notice posted in the Lodge.' Which is, of course, keeping FOCFU out of our hair. They can roam the globe, trying to sniff him out, him and the insupportable knowledge he doesn't have. He knows nothing –

"There's spittle of the moon. Ingress and egress of hermetick science. Siren tears."

Well yes, I suppose he does know *that*. Not to mention all he'll acquire in the drug-labs of Cananea. What unthinkable psychotropics he'll concoct!

"To send north of the border. To take the edge off the unspeakable boredom of being in America…."

If you like. But I was telling you what the Master told me. 'We'll get rid of Ebbe quietly toward the end of term,' he declared, 'deprive him of his Fellowship for not reporting to us. And that'll be the end of that. But the awkwardness of it …. Oh. And speaking of awkward. Margot ffontaines-Laigh has asked permission to come Up early. She'll be here from Friday morning.'

'Oh?' I said, although in fact the Home Bursar had told me as much an hour before.

'Yes. Quite frankly she makes me uncomfortable. I can't see why she can't return on Monday evening like everyone else but there it is. And *you're* going away are you?', pointedly.

'Back on Sunday, Master. Important manuscripts to read in the British Museum.' In fact I'd made a 'phone call immediately after talking to the Bursar, inviting myself down to Seb's place in Cornwall.

See what a disruptive effect you have on College life?

"Oh? Am I so disruptive? I can't see why. I came Up on the Friday. I wanted to see you. And there was no one about."

No, no one about.

"I stayed in my rooms – er, writing. Studying."

Glad to hear it. While I was jollying. Seb was, I knew, having a house-party, his foolishly-trusting parents being in Paris. Ollie, Rajiv, Tristan and that Hungarian from Pembroke were there, what's-his-name, Róbert. And of course a bevy of Girtonians and Newnhamians, pleased to go wherever they're invited. But apart from the fun, I needed to speak to Seb alone. Before he came up. About, in fact, *señorita* Benita.

"Oh…. Did he *care*?"

About her? Well no. He's entirely over her. She only beguiled him for a few weeks. Back in March, which for him is another lifetime.

"I thought love was absolute sole lord of life and death."

Perhaps. But it has no authority over *stupidity*, which is a *third* realm…. No, it wasn't that. There's another aspect to the Benita question. Um. I don't think I quite told you that in March, er, over in Mexico, Seb …

"Yes?"

Married her.

"Good God."

That is to say: the two of them formally plighted troth before her old nanny. A Yaqui wisewoman or sorceress. A sort of native priestess. As you'll have gathered, Cananea's a heathenish place. I don't know if the ceremony would stand up in the eyes of a canon lawyer – no use asking Woolly, that disgusting neuter, that refugee from aye-or-nay – obviously Benita had decided it *wouldn't* – but it possibly means that when he's born – her child, I mean, somehow I'm sure it's a boy –

"*Oh.*"

Ebbe'll acknowledge him. Although he'll really be a legitimate Hawick Trocliffe.

They aren't so very distinguished, Hawick Trocliffes, but a couple of them have been generals, and one was royal mistress. And the family possesses an earldom. As a matter of fact old Lord Haggardmere, Seb's great-uncle, seems far too depraved to beget children. Seb's the oldest son. He'll inherit if he lays off the cocaine and lives that long.

§

"… *So.*"

Exactly: *so.*

This, then, was my out-of-bedtime story: from this very bed I heard the bloke in the room below throwing up. And the upshot is that thirty years hence the rightful ninth Earl of Haggardmere – though he won't know that's who he is – will be a bandit-chieftain. Terrorising the dusty badlands of northern Mexico. *Which only goes to show.*

"What? What does it show?"

Not sure. Perhaps that it's always best to *stay* in bed. Even if suggestive and exciting events come your way while you're lying there.

But we're getting up now, aren't we? Breakfast? Then Glasgow airport, then our own boggy, soggy kingdom? Curried stomach-linings. Deep-fried porridge. It's been so long.

What? It can wait *another* half hour? Because? – oh, I see.

Ah.

*Ah.*

Oh my darling….

# IV.
# ZOÖN

Grandees are reserved and incomprehensible, peasants explicit and obvious; the Devil twists them round his little finger just the same.

LAMPEDUSA,
*The Leopard*

## *i.*

*Fog – turbid and oily, dun-yellow as tobacco-smoke – rolls sideways in banks, it swirls upward like floodwater. It's a classic London fog, an epic effluvium, a 'pea-souper' to make us nostalgic for Sherlock Holmes, bustles and hansom cabs. Yet such weather isn't obsolete. Clean Air Acts do nothing about the murky Thames, and London still sometimes gets thoroughly fogged.*

*If the fog were just a bit more foreboding, it would be funny. However, it stops short, it won't go too far. It discomfits us.*

*Ugly and freakish in itself, it creates beauty: three-dimensional shadows, haloed street-lamps. Car headlights weave geometric knots. There are fantastic aural effects too, footsteps echoing from who-knows-how-many streets away, and beneath it all the vague slap of great waters, perhaps the river, perhaps the sewers.*

*Where the miasma thins and tears, we make out a dark streetscape: black railings, white-painted brick, and pillared porches arched with dignified metalwork. We're evidently in the western part of the inner city, looking along a Georgian terrace.*

*Most of the windows are still unlit. It is getting on, perhaps, for seven-thirty on a morning late in autumn. The sun would be up if there were a sun, the sky would be lightening if there were no fog. As it is, the air is drab and formless as the earth. What light there is comes from nowhere in particular: it seems suspended in the droplets.*

*Some long seconds of all this. Before we quite get bored we notice a street-sign –* HARLEY STREET W1 *– and then, dropping our gaze, an approaching taxi (that is, a glistening pitch-black mobile tomb, a glistening tumulus, prowling the streets to engulf the bodies of men. London cabs do* not *stop short. They do overdo it, and are so sinister they look comic).*

*This doomful chariot pulls up outside one of the imposing, sedate façades, and disgorges – that's the word – a prosperous figure of middling height, muffled up in an expensive overcoat with black satin lapels, a Liberty scarf, and an impeccable grey fedora. He's in trim early old age, let's say 62 but extremely well-preserved, of the type Great-and-Good: as handsome as he is affluent, as affluent as clever, smoother than smooth, full of fine opinions. Better in short than you and me.*

*It has obviously taken a lifetime of burnishing in very good schools and colleges and opera-houses and restaurants, in the Inns of Court and the Athenæum, to achieve quite so deep a sheen. He wears his superiority simply. It's a fact, like having two legs; he needn't to think about it, so doesn't.*

*It would be envious slander, nothing more, to call him pompous. His charm sets off his self-satisfaction as efficiently as coffee cancels out cognac (a drink he perhaps overdoes).*

*Between the felt hat and the silk scarf the face is long, weary, powerful, poised, tanned, intelligent and severe. Nobly the cheekbones hold up the bags beneath the eyes, and hold back the cheeks from being jowly. In youth this face was thin and red-cheeked. Now it's blurred rather that pudgy with good living, and still strikes susceptible females of a certain type (nannies, back-bench M.P.s, jurywomen) as godlike. When its owner sets about setting them at their ease they are apt to get flustered, and concede more than they meant.*

*The fog is claustrophobic. The sky rests on the judge's fedora. The footpath beneath his shoes seems barely out-of-doors. He crosses it briskly; behind him the red rear-lights of his taxi pass into an eddy and are lost. He steps up into the portico of Number 6, and stands for an instant alone, marble chessboard below, front door before, glossy black even in this fug, dully gleaming its brass nameplate and brass bell-pull. That is his last independent action, because before he can pull the bell there comes the call of a voice.*

A VOICE *(brightly)*: Hal - llo!

*He glances toward* THE VOICE, *which is to his right. A door has swung inward, the door not of Number 6 but of the next house along. Number 5's portico, separated from his own by a spiked railing, is nearly identical, down to its brass plate; but its appearance has been transformed by that opened door. The interior of 5 seems overwhelmingly vivid, like the stage set of a drawing-room comedy seen from the darkened theatre, or like firelight in a midnight forest; and from that interior a rectangle of yellow electric light, improbably rich and rosy, falls out into the mist in complicated rhomboids and prisms. A bar of it pierces the railing to lie across the gentleman's beauti-fully-polished black brogues (if 'gentleman' is the right word. A gentleman is not quite the same as a grandee, and these shoes look peculiarly grand).*

*In the rectangle of yellow is a nurse-shaped silhouette.*

*As he turns, shading his eyes against the glare, he sees that it is indeed a nurse, a women very young, twenty or so – too young, as he knows from experience, to be much stirred by Greatness-and-Goodness.*

THE NURSE (*yet more brightly*): Hal - llo! Sir Julius MacPharlain? In here, if you would be so kind.
SIR JULIUS (*confusion makes him suddenly look more his age*): What?

*He peers at her in mild bewilderment. Her cap is pinned a touch too jauntily on billows of hair, her white tunic is unprofessionally tight.*

But I – I have an appointment in *here*. At Number 6. With Dr Drake.
THE NURSE (*still brightly*): Archibald Drake, oh yes we know all about *that*. You're due for a blood-test at half-past seven. This is the *annexe* to number 6. Where Dr Drake sees his *extra* special cases.

*MacPharlain doesn't quite like the sound of this.*

Come, Sir Julius – we're waiting for you.

*The way she says this only just stops short of being saucy.*

*He hesitates, half an eye on the shut door in front of him. But Number 6 is so quiet it might almost still be asleep. And the nurse is so very young and splendid. Beneath her fake lower-middle-class whine (the requisite accent for her line of work no doubt, it's a sadly mobbish age) he can tell she's well-bred. She might be the daughter of people with whom G&Gs dine – might almost be herself of his subspecies,* H. sapiens magnus et bonus.

*Besides, in the fog the two houses look much the same. This isn't a ratio-nal reason, but appeals to the imagination. Moreover, there's the authority of her uniform (her uniform!). And finally what, after all – resuming his usual Mount Olympus point-of-view – can it matter, number 5, number 6? The detail's beneath him. All-in-all it seems ridiculous to make a fuss and resist.*

Come *in*, you'll catch your death.

*Instead of shrugging, as a lesser man might have done, he smiles his half-nice
smile, the one for barristers who have accepted a rebuke from the Bench.*

*He comes round the railing and into the open door of 5, which she pulls
behind them.*

*We follow them in.*

*It takes a lot of money for a medical practice to place itself in Harley
Street; once there it takes a lot more money to stop looking like a medical
practice. Number 5 has spent those sums, and resembles a country gentleman's Town house. Indeed it looks more like a gentleman's Town house than
it ever did in the days of George III, when it really was one.*

*The shallow dome of the hall is freshly repainted in dark blue, freshly
fretted with gilt stars. What seems to be a Chippendale sideboard is a Chippendale sideboard. The Sèvres vase, also genuine (and blindingly hideous),
holds as many Israeli orchids as any vase might be expected to hold. The
round marquetry table beneath the dome bears pristine copies of* Tatler *and*
Country Life, *arrayed with untidy aristocratic nonchalance.*

*It's all very well done. We follow* MacPharlain's *evaluating glance.
Meanwhile he's allowing the fragrant young creature to help him out of hat,
coat and scarf.*

Sir Julius (*smiling sourly*): I had no idea Dr Drake's premises were so – large.
The Nurse (*twinkling*): We're *bursting* out in every direction! Now *do* have
a seat.

*And she goes, slightly waggling.*

*She is back.*

The Nurse: The doctor will see you now.

*This too she weights with cheap innuendo. Before* MacPharlain *can decide
whether he's amused or not, she has shown him through a coffered door from
the hall into the doctor's consulting-room, which is simply the library of the
house: an oval room with not one medical thing on display.*

*Huge swags of tasselled curtain, the shade of wheat about to be harvested,
keep out the fog and the dregs of night. One lamp burns on the desk, crim-
son-shaded. A cocktail-cabinet of walnut and bevelled glass is artfully lit so
the bottles glow with a dozen shades, like subdued spirits of jewel. There is one
of those sound systems which have to be entirely black, with speakers the size
of small children. Most imposingly of all, there is almost a full oval of glazed*

*bookcases, covering the walls. Each case is full of leathery gold-stamped sets, and topped with a small bust. Marcus Aurelius says Who are you?, Socrates says Who are you? Virgil, Augustus, Dante, Chaucer and Bacon say the same, and so back to Marcus Aurelius.* THE DOCTOR, *too, lolling in an enormous high-backed Strawberry-Hill-gothick armchair behind the desk, looks sniffy and unimpressed. He does not stir, merely offering* MACPHARLAIN *(who glowers) a bland smile, and making a vague swaggering gesture of welcome with one arm.*

SIR JULIUS *(sharply – he is used to being stood for)*: You're not Dr Drake!
THE DOCTOR: Certainly not. I wouldn't be Drake if you paid me. *I* am young-ish. And handsome. Drake has bad breath. My name's Lubbock.

*A talker, not a doer; old-young, not young-old; suit a trifle too good; accent Oxbridge rather than county. A coarse mop of orange hair. Heavy black plastic spectacle-frames – once again fashionable, although* SIR JULIUS *still associates them with the 1970s, corrupt Yorkshire trade union officials.*

SIR JULIUS: Where's Drake?
THE DOCTOR: Dereck Lubbock, in fact, with a prettifying C to soften the angular K. I'm rather standing in for Drake. As he often has me do.

THE NURSE, *in defiance of medical protocol, indeed of human decency, has not gone away. She has sidled behind* LUBBOCK, *propping herself on the back of his chair.*

SIR JULIUS: You're his junior partner?
THE DOCTOR *(very sniffily indeed)*: Junior, junior? Absolutely not. I am called in, I say. *(Airily)*: I'm a specialist. I specialise.

THE NURSE *winks.* SIR JULIUS *is at a loss.*

THE DOCTOR *(disconcertingly switching on a brisk doctorly manner)*: Do please sit down, Sir Julius.
SIR JULIUS *(sitting, but persevering)*: A specialist in what?
THE DOCTOR: In everything Drake isn't. Gifted man but there are things he can't do. Such a child of the 'Sixties, too feely, not the right bedside manner at all. When he tells patients horrific things he's over-solicitous. Soppy. It upsets them, when their cue is to be Spartan. Of course they cry. Don't they, Evangeline?

THE NURSE *smiles down ambiguously.*

Whereas I, *I* am candid. Very very candid.

*He forms an immense, sleepy, happy smile of his own.*

SIR JULIUS *(with faint bluster)*: Have you got the right man? I'm only here for a blood-test.
THE DOCTOR *(with false gentleness)*: As it happens, you are not here for a blood-test. We've no desire for your blood. For now.
THE NURSE *(musingly)*: I would have enjoyed taking a sample. *(Her lower-middle accent has quite gone away. It's troubling that she speaks to neither of the men, but into the air. No, it's as if she were addressing her remark to Francis Bacon.)*
THE DOCTOR *(reaching over his shoulder to pat her hand)*: No bleeding today. We already know everything about you that we need.

SIR JULIUS' *face is all-too-obviously designed to register noble thoughts and superb emotions. His Resilience-Against-the-Blows-of-Fortune has been much admired in its time.*

SIR JULIUS: My blood sugar's pretty bad, then?
THE DOCTOR *(laughing merrily)*: Not at all. A titch high, perhaps: five point four. But for a man of your age, with the responsibilities of a High Court judge, port-drinking for instance, not to mention emotional pressure – Criminal Bench, isn't it? Pleading eyes looking up at you from the dock, eh? "Not six years, m'Lud, not six, pretty please no won't four do? I promise never to do it again when I get out", but you say "Six years, varlet, without parole – take him away" and he's led down calling on the gods to visit you with grief. It must be a strain, the gods, blood (*He lets this sentence dwindle into a sigh*) ....

*Not only do the Great and Good not have to* do *good, their greatness being existential, they do not even need to* feel *great. That is done* for *them.* MAC-PHARLAIN *exists in a world where his godlikeness is generally acknowledged, and often alluded to. In the company of these clowns, toyed with, talked down to, he is ceasing to know himself.*

LUBBOCK *(returning from his reverie)*: Blood sugar at five point four? – pshaw! Give it not another thought.
THE NURSE *(still communing with the busts of the Worthies)*: We guarantee that it will not kill you. (*Each word is wonderfully clear; she seems to enjoy the*

*sounds of English.*)

THE DOCTOR: While we're at it, here's another piece of good news. You came here for a blood-test. A repeat of last month's test. You have to be fasting and therefore you asked to be seen early. It's no fun rushing about on a misty November morning without breakfast, is it? Well lucky old you, our fast's already over.

THE NURSE (*relishing her popular turns of phrase*): There's ever such a nice working-man's greasy-spoon 'round the corner in Weymouth Mews. Len's Caff. You ought to head off to Len's for a fry-up.

SIR JULIUS: I never take much in the mornings –

*with which a spasm of disgust crosses his courtly face. Over the last few minutes he's been separated from his normal existence, which is too rich and full for chatter. Conversation for* SIR JULIUS *moves on high planes. Except for evidence, he says and hears only what is witty or telling. Now he's been betrayed into saying something inane. (Vulgarly phrased, too!) Once a man's tumbled into mindless small-talk, it's hard to climb back onto the plateau. So when*

THE NURSE *utters another fatuous remark*: Len does wonderful breaded mushrooms

*the universe makes less and less sense to* SIR JULIUS, *which is grievous. He finds himself snapping*: I loathe mushrooms. – I want nothing.

THE DOCTOR: No no no, don't be like that. Think of the workmen. You have to set an example. British phlegm, y'know. "The condemned man ate a hearty breakfast."

SIR JULIUS (*positively frightened now*): The what?

*A slow metamorphosis has begun in* MACPHARLAIN. *He is ceasing to look distinguished.* THE NURSE, *peering into his face, jumps up and, distinctly waggling her hips, fetches a martini glass from the cocktail-cabinet's upper-most shelf – presumably the coldest spot, since the glass comes out clouded with frost.*

*She next produces, from a leather handbag, a plastic canister of the medical sort. This she gives a gay rattle over her right shoulder, pretending it's a cocktail-shaker; opens it; and pours into the glass a mound of pink gelatin capsules much like jelly-beans. Finally she makes a little ceremony of twisting the canister shut.*

THE NURSE: There (*placing the martini glass in front of him*). I think *first* somebody needs a pre-breakfast of diazepam. Take the edge off.

*As it happens, the pink mound reminds* MacPharlain *of the raspberry sundaes he loved greedily as a child. But he shakes his head, irritated.*

The Nurse *(enticingly)*: One little piggy makes you mellow, two little piggies make you tranquil, three is sedated, four zen, five – .
Sir Julius *(protesting)*: Dr Lubbock!
The Doctor *(doctorly)*: Sir Julius.

*Unabashed,* the Nurse *perches on the edge of the desk, pert, chin at an angle, four fingers splayed on each knee.*
    *(Of course her behaviour's outrageous, impossible, fabulous. That's precisely why it can't be laughed off, at least not by* Sir Julius. *Fairy-tales are more overwhelming than realist novels because we can't object: why shouldn't magic beans grow into the clouds? What would you expect them to do? How can you complain? So now* The Nurse, *against every social norm, wets her lips dreamily as her crony purrs:)*

I have to inform you, Sir Julius, that there are unusual things in your blood. Your results were so surprising that for a while we were sure of a false positive. But no. Or that the sample was contaminated – it wasn't. We ran many tests, we sent off for a second opinion. A third. I'm afraid there's no doubt.

*Now* Nursie *seems to be concentrating only on* Sir Julius' *eyes, on his soul; she is savouring the moment. She folds one long fishnetted leg luxuriously over the other, resting all her weight on her left hand.*

Poor Drake! He broke down when the third opinion arrived. Old softy. Should have gone into a more *clinical* branch of medicine, don't you think? Pathology, say. No dreadful wounded eyes to confront, no urge to console. Ah well. I'm afraid, in short, that you have claryosis.
Sir Julius *(blankly)*: What?
The Doctor: Of course it's a surprise for you, a shock, you come here for a simple stab-and-suck and instead I reveal your claryosis, which as we all know is incurable, terminal, horrendous and – .
Sir Julius *(aghast)*: I've never even heard the name.
The Doctor *(brightly)*: As the bishop said of the actress. But I suppose you're right. Claryosis *is* a bit ....
The Nurse *(leaning forward, still lost in MacPharlain's widening eyes)*: Out of the way.

THE DOCTOR: Exactly! If it comes to that, *all* venereal zoönoses are *recherché*. You –

SIR JULIUS: I've never heard that word either.

THE DOCTOR: Very wise. Medical terms get skittish if you attend to them. A zoönose is an ailment that hops from a zoön of one species to another. A zoön – isn't *zoön* a wonderful word? Pure mid-Victorian fustian. *(He's obviously entranced.)* Zoön. Zoön. – I'd love to bring the word back into common circulation. A zoön, Sir Julius, is an organism considered as a microcosmos. Autonomous, possessed of its own form, its own fate –

*and for an instant* THE DOCTOR, *clearly not the gregarious type, shuts his eyes in a bliss of contemplation.* THE NURSE, *perceiving herself shut out, darkens a little, and leans back.* SIR JULIUS *attempts patience.*

Perfect. *Because* alone.

SIR JULIUS *(after waiting a second or two)*: However ….

THE DOCTOR *(reviving)*: However. Yes. Unity is imperfection; diseases bring us together. Usually they only bound from zoön to zoön within species. Cats don't get our influenza, we don't get cat 'flu. But there are things you get – we get, one gets – from a handful of animals. *(Almost chuckling:)* If 'handful' is quite right. 'Armful' really. In the case of claryosis, that is. It's not like leptospirosis, what everyone calls Weil's disease. Weil's disease you catch from cute little *Wind in the Willows* voles, not you I mean, anyone. Well anyone who mucks about in boats on sluggish English rivers. An affliction of Oxbridge undergraduates and Olympic rowers. Not without a certain sleazy glamour. Vole piss or vole cum in the water is full of bacilli that make their way up your punt-pole – wham –

*he mimes the leaping-spider ascent of a bacillus of* leptospirosis.

But that's not your problem, oh no. Nor do you even have brucellosis, which you, one, generally gets from rogering mares. No, *yours* is much more rare, virulent, more precious perhaps. It's a disease endemic in pronghorns. And the *only* vector is genital contact. *Antilocapra americana* –

*He has picked up a medical textbook (*Epidemiology and Symptomatology of Certain Ruminant Zoönoses) *and is idly turning the pages.* THE NURSE, *whose professional manner, such as it was, has entirely peeled away, lolls across the desk to peer over his shoulder, on which she rests excited hands.*

A ruminant out in the Rockies. With "a peculiar musky odour", oh yes, quite.

Not horned, it really has *prongs*. Like barbeque tongs. And they *do* have out-sized eyes, don't they?

*He caresses the pronghorn photograph with his forefinger.*

THE NURSE *(huskily)*: Bedroom eyes.
THE DOCTOR: Bedroom eyes. And "distinct white fur on their rumps": perhaps *that* was the attraction, eh? "A highly developed sense of curiosity", highly developed for a ruminant I presume they mean. Not to be compared with the enormous wayward explorative tastes of man, eh? *Eh?*

NURSIE *ogles the* Antilocapra *over her knuckles, ranged along* THE DOCTOR's *left shoulder.*
    *(It's no use saying that this is a put-up job, that people simply don't act this way. We've seen that idea arise in* MACPHARLAIN's *face and die away, defeated. The world is as it is, and the world for him has shrunk to this evil fairy-tale, this mad circular chamber, this bubble in the fog.)*

Amusing supercilious features, don't you think?

EVANGELINE *does.*

Like a cardinal surprised bathing .... Well of course you must remember all this.

*He idly drops the book to the desk, thud, shutting it with a finger.*

Claryosis is a curse out in Wyoming. In a small way. Lonesome cowboys, you know. But you've not been to the American West, have you? I mean not recently. Nor to Africa? No, well then

*– his curiosity is half-roguish, half-scientific –*

anything you want to tell us, Sir Julius? About recent visits to British wildlife parks? I'll give you a few seconds to rack your memory....

MACPHARLAIN *does nothing of the sort. He's now cowered to the point of not caring about looking cowered; but still has enough self-respect not to want to whimper. He concentrates on not-whimpering.*

Hm? I say "wildlife park" because I've noticed that zoos as such, old-fashioned zoos, rarely inspire such frolics. Zoöns boxed: not sexy. It's parkland beauty that does it. Artificial waterwalks, Georgian façades, nude statues, topiary. Critters roaming about free. Takes people in different ways, who's to say. My wife's forever photographing in our garden, worthless blurry photos – blue tits –

*The blue-tits are one horror too many for* MacPharlain. *He scoops up a pink capsule and bolts it, trying to ignore* The Nurse's *beatific smile of welcome –*

but she sends them to this tit-fancying website, which posts them. "It puts me in touch with nature" she says, ludicrous romantic. Although speaking of romance: birds are kosher, I mean *avian* zoönoses can't be sexually transmitted. Campylobacter, cryptosporidium, they're nasty enough, God knows, but you get them from budgerigar shit. Or badly-cooked chicken tikka masala.
The Nurse *(mock-scandalised)*: Never at Len's, though. Clean as the proverbial, Len.
The Doctor: My point is that in your next life, *if* the same urge strikes, you might want to think about buzzards. Turkeys – ostriches –
The Nurse: Swans. Pay-back for the Trojan War.
The Doctor: Ho-ho! – But we're banging on, aren't I? And you still look winded. Need more time? No clear memory, yet, of your fatal pronghorn tryst? Missed tryst? Pissed? List? Long prong, wrong, bong, song, no? ... No? *(Sighing deeply.)* I see you're not going to tell us.
Sir Julius *(fiercely)*: I have never in all my years so much as looked at a wild –

The Nurse *finds this very funny.* MacPharlain, *who is not used to being laughed at, slithers further down the mountain-slope of self-regard. But*

The Doctor *is wearied, he shuts his eyes, waving the denial away*: Of course you haven't, of course, of course. Well, it doesn't signify. Confession can't affect prognosis. Narrative satisfaction, that's all.
Sir Julius *(nearly shouting)*: I've nothing to confess!
The Doctor *(still with closed eyes)*: Let's say we accept that. You *have* nothing wicked to confess. At least not *vis-à-vis* pronghorns. Venereal contact didn't cause your venereal disease.
Sir Julius *(really shouting now)*: I haven't been near an animal! You're making a factual mistake!
The Doctor *(slumped, supine, in his throne; his hand has somehow taken captive Evangeline's right hand, toying with it)*: No doubt, no doubt. Pretty much everything's a "factual mistake", don't you think? (*The point seeeems*

*both to convince and to bore him.)* Biology's a mistake, an overflow of minerals. Man's a mistake, an over-refinement of monkey. We still have to fit it with what we've got. *Pretend* it makes sense. And this, old thing *(he opens his eyes)*, is how *you* fit in.

MacPharlain *tries to interject but* Lubbock *talks him down.*

Anyway, why whine about facts? Why quibble about *deeds?* You're a Presybterian elder they tell me: isn't everything preordained? Doesn't your God *want* to damn people – as avidly the boring old Christian God wants to save them? Doesn't He *create* them damned? – what's the phrase? My great-uncle was a Calvinist …. Oh yes, "ordaining to dishonour and wrath to the praise of His glorious justice".

MacPharlain *is aghast, gazing at the cold corner of his mind where his creed lies stacked in darkness. He has indeed often rejoiced over the arbitrariness of God's judgements. It rhymes so nicely with his own rulings and sentences. Of course he's never thought of himself, the great-and-good judge Julius, among the reprobate. But according to the doctors of his faith, this is one of their Deity's favourite tricks: lull the damned, lure them into piety, get them comfortable, then – surprise!*
     *Meanwhile* Lubbock*'s thumb is exploring the webbing between* Evangeline*'s fingers. He observes* MacPharlain*'s agon; she watches too, now tummy-down across the desk. Her stiletto heels, offensively long, are folded in a scarlet X over her magnificent haunch.*

The Doctor *speaks now like a guru sitting in a Himalayan cave-mouth:* Come! Can it make any difference? Can any fact matter? Calvin aside, zoön to zoön, do you think *anything* matters? That there's any such thing as *cause?* That there's rhyme or reason to what happens to this organism or that? To me or, in this case, you?

MacPharlain, *with a despairing grab, helps himself to another pink capsule.* The Nurse *suddenly giggles and*

her Patient *says, so rapidly he gulps at the capsule and trips over himself:* How – how long. Would you say. How –
The Nurse: As the actress said to the bishop.
Sir Julius *(blurting it out)*: How long have I got?
The Doctor *(breezily)*: Oh, *that. (He opens his eyes and sits up.)*
The Nurse: You *always* forget to tell them. You old billikins.

THE DOCTOR: Yes I do. And then everyone always asks, in such a snitchy way, too…. Let me think. (*He twirls a pencil about his fingers.*) Weeks…. (*He might be fixing the price of a used car.*) Not more than a fortnight. Possibly a lot less. Hard to know because research on your disease is so sparse. But I glanced at your blood down my microscope last night and fuck my sainted auntie, what a swarm of monstrous littlies! Like Luton airport on a bank holiday Friday. Yes, with your count already so high and … an informed guess? By Sunday, or even tomorrow, look for necrosis in the soft tissues. Thighs, bum. You'll probably notice the smell before you *see* any actual putrefaction, but once the blackness gets started, it devours pink flesh faster than you'd think possible – gobble gobble gobble.

*He snaps his excellent teeth, thrice.*

We'll gouge it out if you like (*he shows how with the pencil*), but it's pretty much impossible to keep up with necrosis. Anyway, pretty soon it gnaws down to the luscious marrow and settles in.

MACPHARLAIN'*s humanity is dropping from him. A little more of this and he'll be mere game at bay, a baited animal.*
*But* THE DOCTOR'*s becoming bouncier. Daylight is beginning to seep between the heavy curtains: perhaps he's a daylight person. He says merrily to Evangeline:*

Dearheart, do you have that photograph of necrotic decay?

*She produces another textbook, open at the page. He recoils.*

God no, don't show it to *me*, you trollop – not so soon after breakfast. Show *him*. No? Well then, put it away, if no one's interested.

*And there's another pause.*
*For the first time in his life* MACPHARLAIN *finds what it is to wring hands: an awkward twisting gesture in his lap. He furiously parts his fingers and slaps them onto his thighs, remembering a little too late what may already astir in those soft tissues.*
*He finds it's time for a third capsule.*

THE NURSE (*impatiently; in a stage-whisper*): Fits.
THE DOCTOR (*fussily*): Yes yes I was coming to that. Putrescence, Sir Julius, is unlikely to annoy you for long. In a week at the outside your first spasms will

have begun. Claryosis goes for the whole nervous system at once, spinal cord, brain, ganglia, so it's hard to medicate. Anyway it's a subtle bugger, resistant to morphine, indeed to all opioids. And as for barbiturates! – don't make me laugh. Barbies just make the pain flare up worse somewhere else. And when I say "worse", you ought to know that even to begin with it's a bit of a … smart. Like rabies, you know. Only more so. Or so they say in the literature, such as it is.

*He turns mock-reverent.*

*Such as it is.* Mankind knows so little, so very very little about claryosis. You, Sir Julius, will soon be more of an authority than the entirety of medical science. – A solemn thought.

THE NURSE (*on her flank now, resting her chin on her hand, her feet in Lubbock's lap*): The horse's mouth.

THE DOCTOR: Speaking of thought. Look out for ghastly depression. It's one of the first symptoms of encephalopathical degeneration –

THE NURSE: He means brain-rot, the wordy darling.

THE DOCTOR: They *say* the depression's the worst symptom. Worse even that the neural torture. By "they" I mean Colorado cowpokes with a weakness for lady pronghorns. Yes, anecdotally,

*– he taps the medical textbook on the desk with his pencil –*

psychotic depression's the roughest aspect of claryosis.... But what do they know? We're talking sturdy mountain-men, used to frostbite, used to having their testicles trodden by stampeding cattle, *not* used to nasty ideas. Since you're an educated fellow I imagine you'll laugh off even the most harrowing melancholy. For you, the hardest part will be physical. Every nerve pinging at the same time –

THE DOCTOR *illustrates his* ping *by flicking thumb with forefinger.* SIR JULIUS *winces, as if flicked in the face, as if instruments of bodily torment were already being applied.*

SIR JULIUS: But what are we going to *do*?

THE DOCTOR: *Do?* Good God, man, haven't you been listening? There's nothing to do. That is to say …. That is to say ….

THE DOCTOR *seems suddenly forget all about* MACPHARLAIN. *He sighs, lost in a delightful vision. He is smug, self-important, at peace.*

THE NURSE *smiles down at her lovely happy man, reaching out to take both his hands in hers.*

That is to say, there's a *great* deal to do. Evie and I are going to be very busy. Aren't we? Very happily busy. Taking *lots* of notes. And photos.

THE NURSE: And videos.

THE DOCTOR: *And* videos. Especially once you're hospitalised. I'll be with you non-stop toward the end, doing tests. Trying out what treatment makes claryosis a bit better, what makes it even worse –

THE NURSE: A *battery* of tests. We call it that for a reason!

THE DOCTOR: We'll have you all to ourselves. And the great thing is, we won't have to worry about ethical review boards. Not us three. Quite beyond their ken. Indeed, physically somewhat disjunct –

THE NURSE *(who finds this irritatingly obscure)*: They put screamers in special wards. Remote sound-proof wards. That's what he means. Held down with straps.

THE DOCTOR *(to avoid misunderstanding)*: Padded leather straps. Kindly meant. So there's no self-strangulation, or tearing out of eyes, or other melodramatic excess.

MACPHARLAIN *scoops up a fourth pink capsule, considers judicially, makes it five.*

*We linger for a moment over the look of the things in his palm. They're a most sinister shade of pink. Not for a moment do we believe they're the mere sedative* EVANGELINE *pretends. In fact, isn't there already something* psychedelic *about* MACPHARLAIN'*s manner? As he swallows them*

THE NURSE *remarks*: Anything goes with a screamer. The ward-sisters keep away. Lazy bitches.

THE DOCTOR: Yes, they'll be grateful to Evie and me. Keeping vigil for them.

THE NURSE: Bring us cups of tea. Set up a big folding bed for us I shouldn't wonder.

THE DOCTOR: So on and so forth. Once we've had all possible fun at your autopsy I'll probably take *(he pauses to snap off the top end of his pencil)* your head. There's a 'fridge out back here –

THE NURSE *(coarsely)*: Muck round with heads 'til kingdom come. Always new tests to do on *heads.*

THE DOCTOR *(balancing the broken fragment on his desk)*: Afterward –

THE NURSE: Bring it out for parties. A conversation piece.

THE DOCTOR: *There's* a thought. So we will!

THE NURSE *(pursuing her unwholesome interest in the bookcase busts)*: If we

took the floppy-cap one down –
THE DOCTOR: Which, my sweet? Oh *him*, Chaucer.
THE NURSE: Yes him. I don't much fancy *him*. We could keep Sir Julius up there instead. Deep-frozen, of course.
THE DOCTOR *(with his eye on Chaucer)*: We could … Afterward – I was saying – I'll be publishing an Important Article in the *Lancet*. (*He smiles winningly at his patient.*) Discretely of course, just an initial for you. I was thinking of J. rather than *M.*, if that's not too intimate?
THE NURSE *(world-weary, raising sophisticated eyebrows)*: Initials! Pah!
THE DOCTOR: Well yes. To be thunderingly frank, discretion won't do much good. Nurses these days, I mean hospital nurses, not like the splendid Evie here –

*He doesn't quite slap her bottom.*

THE NURSE *(simpering)*: Ward-sisters nowadays are so mercenary, Sir Julius, it makes me puke. They *always* sell their interesting cases to the tabloids. And what could be more interesting than a famous judge dying in agony from shagging an antelope? Fame!
THE DOCTOR: Fame! – Infamy! At a guess claryosis isn't even going to *be* "claryosis" in a few years' time. Bit of a mouthful, isn't it? It'll be: MacPharlain's disease!
THE NURSE *(dreamily)*: Your family'll have to change *their* name.
THE DOCTOR: God! *here's* an idea. Say your case really captures the public imagination. People might take to calling *all* bestiality after you. "Zoophilia." "Critter-molestation" as the Yanks say. They're bit of a mouthful too. But "macpharlainery": that has a ring, yes?
THE NURSE *(trying it out, in cod-Welsh accent)*: "Look you those bloody farmers, they're after having macpharlained their sheep again."
THE DOCTOR: "Macpharlaining": infamy everlasting. You'll be up there with the Marquis de Sade and von Sacher-Masoch. That's a consolation, isn't it? *More* than a consolation. Perhaps infamy was the point of existence all along. I can't think what else is. You're alive for an instant – what, sixty-one years?
SIR JULIUS *(compelled, like one of Dante's damned, to answer the most foolish remarks)*: Sixty-two. I'm sixty-two.
THE DOCTOR: For a mere sixty-two years. Trapped within a single zoön at that. Then you shrivel, and die, and turn to dust. But not you. *Your* name lives on for centuries. As a perversion. It lives because it grows in dirt. Whatever nourishes grows in dirt. "Macpharlaining" will be the word for rogering animals until Mandarin finally obliterates English. Even then, I'm told Chinese is quite tolerant of loan-words – .

MacPHARLAIN *(although perhaps only because he has bolted so many capsules) has been getting a grip on himself during these preposterous speculations. He has gathered a ragged dignity about him, like Lear on the heath. He has after all been famous in the world of Law for a courtesy which was a form of menace.*

SIR JULIUS: Have you, Dr Lubbock, no genuine comfort to offer me?
THE DOCTOR: … Well. Hm. There's this, I suppose: pronghorns with claryosis are asymptomatic. Which is to say, the bacterium can't make *them* sick, only *us*. So if (despite your gallant reticence) you *do* cherish tender feelings for a particular *Antilocapra* –

*It's not pain as such, it's the grotesque MacPHARLAIN can't abide. Even the trying bits of his life (an early infidelity by Lady MacPharlain, in Venice, with a local nobleman; a reproof, once, from the Law Lords; a bout of pneumonia from which he convalesced in Cyprus) have been inflicted to him with a certain style. They were great-and-bad misfortunes. They did not interrupt his beautiful trains of thought, his table-talk and soliloquys, which might well have been transcribed into* The London Review of Books *for the edification of the wider readership.*

   *This ugly zaniness is another matter. It does not congrue. He has nothing to say to it. To his own horror, he finds he has leapt up, so woozily his chair crashes backward.*

SIR JULIUS: God damn you, I can't endure this!

*THE DOCTOR and NURSE raise their eyebrows; she swings her legs through the air and sits up on the desk. There's silence for an unendurable second. The two villains wait to see what comes next. But MacPHARLAIN can't imagine what comes next. He finds himself muttering an apology, righting the chair (the clatter of its legs suggests hands that are not quite steady), preparing, clumsily, to subside –*

THE NURSE *(another bad theatrical prompt)*: Lady M!
THE DOCTOR: What? Oh yes. (*And suddenly* he *is ill-at-ease. He starts straightening things on the desk.*) Ahem.

MacPHARLAIN *is trying to make his shaking stop.*

I know it's not quite the usual done thing. Indeed it's a bit outside rules of confidentiality. Strictly speaking. But this is such an important case – my whole career hinges on it – certain norms must be set aside. Beside, I'm sure the Chief Medical Officer for England and Wales will certify that – well claryosis really *is* a sort of public health issue, isn't it? It's a Notifiable Disease in the States, and this is the first times it's been contracted anywhere else.... And there's the moral integrity of Britain's wildlife parks to consider. *Anyway,* soon you'll be incapacitated, so she'll *have* to sign you over to me, alive and dead .... In short –

THE NURSE: I've just been on the 'phone to Lady MacPharlain. Telling her all about it.

SIR JULIUS (*who thought he was beyond surprise*): Good God.

THE NURSE: I *imagined* she'd be forgiving. Being such a strong Presbyterian and all.

MACPHARLAIN *bolts a sixth little piggy.*

But she wasn't. Not the least bit.

THE DOCTOR: Of course you *did* wake her up.

THE NURSE: Yes, Dereck, I did. And it *was* a bit of a shock, Julius' indiscretion with a deer.

SIR JULIUS (*enraged*): Once and for all, I have *never* –

THE NURSE: A *foreign* deer, too. She felt that aspect of the situation, I could tell.

SIR JULIUS (*beside himself*): You had no –

THE DOCTOR (*to* MACPHARLAIN, *but looking down at his clutter of textbooks*): I believe she used some strong expressions.

THE NURSE: *Not* what I think of as Church-of-Scotland language.

THE DOCTOR: Indeed. Indeed.

*He pats his knee.* THE NURSE *slips off the desk into his lap, her arms flung round his neck, her head at an endearing angle, staring into* MACPHARLAIN'*s white clammy face.* MACPHARLAIN *seems to be having trouble keeping her in focus.*

THE NURSE: "Tell him he needn't fucking *think* of coming home." Such were her very words.

THE DOCTOR: Her very words: "Don't come home."

THE NURSE: Then she hung up. Slammed it down.

THE DOCTOR (*off-handedly*): Of course she may soften in time. Especially once she sees you at the convulsive stage, it's always very affecting while it –

THE NURSE (*a throatier stage-whisper this time, right in his ear*): Paralysis!

THE DOCTOR: Heavens, I'm forgetting.

THE NURSE *(wriggling in his lap, getting more comfortable)*: We're all over the shop today, aren't we!

THE DOCTOR: I was going on about convulsions as if *that* were the endgame. Whereas convulsions are really just by way of softening you up. After a few weeks of writhing and kicking, paralysis climbs up your spine. Your screaming perforce comes to an end. Naturally nerve pain continues, and I presume clinical depression. Lady M may drop by and pardon you out of pity. But you'll be perfectly still. A new stage!

THE NURSE *(cheerily)*: More work for little us!

THE DOCTOR: We'll take great care.

THE NURSE: Keep you with us for a *long* time.

THE DOCTOR: Electro-shock, gavage –

THE NURSE: He means putting a rubber tube down you. Spooning in mushed stuff – . Oh!

THE DOCTOR: What is it, O most-scrumptious one?

THE NURSE: Here's an idea: mushed-up *mushrooms*!

THE DOCTOR: Mushrooms, why mushrooms? Oh yes! She's on to something there, Sir Julius. Don't like 'em, you say? Well, it's aversion that really churns up a paralytic.

THE NURSE: You can see it in their eyes. They widen when the tube goes in *anyway*, ever so slightly, but I can tell what they're thinking, and if it's something they don't like ….

THE DOCTOR: We'll investigate all your sensitivities –

THE NURSE: Sudden noise, extremes of temperature, pain stimuli…. *(Another sudden inspiration:)* Smells!

THE DOCTOR: Brilliant! Yes: a bowl of some acrid chemical left sitting by your head. Stirred up whenever we think of it. Make a note of that, Nurse. You clever creature.

THE NURSE, *pleased to have done her bit for the upward march, utters a growl from deep in her throat.*

*(And for the moment we're puzzled. Evangeline and Dereck are simply overdoing it, they're flaunting depravity to the point of campness. Is the glitter in* THE DOCTOR's *eyes excitement, or only amusement?)*

Then there are psychological issues. Who knows how much a terminally paralysed man comprehends? I've quite a subtle experiment planned for you. With convicts…. You've been on the Bench for what, eighteen years? There must be lots of men you've sent down who might be glad of a valedictory interview. You won't be able to flinch, but we'll have you on a brain scan. When one of your felons leans over you, I *think* we'll see the terror neurons in your hippocampus flare up. Neon in Las Vegas.

THE NURSE (*hungrily, lifting her forehead from Dereck's chest*): And if we *can't* find any of your old lags, Julius, well – we'll just jolly well pitch in ourselves.

THE DOCTOR: *Really?* No no, Evie, that would scarcely be professional.

*In refutation* EVIE *twiddles his lower lip.*

Oh all *right*…. You ought to know, Sir Julius, that Evie here (*he pushes aside her finger*) isn't terribly keen on lawyers. Are you, Tittykins? The fact is, I was struck off a few years back. For malpractice, of all things.

THE NURSE: *So* unfair. It made my blood boil, Julsy-wulsy – may I call you that? Why be formal, I ask myself, given what's coming?

THE DOCTOR: Fortunately Drake's a trusting soul and hasn't looked me up. But the *insult*, Juls, the insult. It irks. My hearing before the General Medical Council –

THE NURSE (*darkly*): A travesty.

THE DOCTOR: And it was the prosecuting barrister who did the damage. Such insinuations, such nit-picking.

THE NURSE: Dereck was ever so pleased when Dr Drake called him in. "A lawyer you say? A *judge*? With claryosis? What larks!" Those were his words. "What-ho!"

THE DOCTOR: Yes, it's an ill wind …. Going?

– *for* MACPHARLAIN *has reeled to his feet, this time without toppling his chair.*

  *The noise in his throat is perhaps meant as speech.*

  THE NURSE *rises from* THE DOCTOR's *thighs more languidly. She stretches her young arms high over her head, wrists together, eyes on her patient, uttering a ecstatic feline sigh, pleased as if the two halves of her body were thrusting together all down her spinal cord.*

THE NURSE: Rrrrrr.

THE DOCTOR: Very well, you're going. We're done for the moment. Evie, you sadistic slut –

*this time he really does smack her across her buttocks –*

get a cab for Juls-baby, won't you?

*She minces out, casting a ravenous look over* MACPHARLAIN's *shrunken figure. (Again, does she* mean *to lampoon herself?)*

Remember, Juls, this is *au revoir* not goodbye. A few more days and you'll be with us for good. Don't think of running, mind. We're in London, there are cameras everywhere. The Chief Medical Officer has extraordinary powers in cases of this sort. Turn yourself in as soon as your spasms begin.

*We hear from the front door* THE NURSE *calling*: Taxi!

*She returns with the expensive overcoat and hat but not, interestingly, the Liberty scarf.* MACPHARLAIN *is stricken beyond speech or useful action, and she bundles him roughly into his coat, tweaking his defenceless nose.*

THE DOCTOR *(taking the hat from her hand, clapping it without ceremony, backward, onto MacPharlain's shuddering head)*: All right. *(He twists it straight.)* Off you go.

*We see the front door open. (It's broad morning by now. The fog thins here and there; a shy wintry sunniness is making all the black paintwork shine up and down Harley Street. Terribly glimmers the waiting cab.) Out of Number 5 hobbles* THE BROKEN MAN, *twenty years older, six inches shorter, quite consumed with the jitters.* THE NURSE *is helping him out, none too tenderly. Behind them, a heavy drape is lifted aside with a forefinger:* THE DOCTOR *peers into the street, coolly surveying his handiwork.*

*A surprisingly-youthful* TAXI-DRIVER *jumps out of his cab, opening the back door.* THE NURSE *tumbles* SIR JULIUS *in and closes it on him.*

*We find ourselves on the opposite side of Harley Street, looking through the taxi windows to the façade, listening the while to* MACPHARLAIN'S *raw swift breathing.*

TAXI-DRIVER *(after a pause)*: So where can I take you, sir?

*His accent is puzzlingly polished, but* MACPHARLAIN *is in no state to worry about things like that. He opens his mouth to give, presumably, his home address, only to remember he is under orders not to return. For a moment he knows the worst possible human state, which is to desire nothing at all. His face registers that horror.*

*(We can still see, through the cab, the demonic* NURSE *standing on the foggy footpath, regarding the passion of her patient. Her black fishnet legs look peculiarly vicious against the starched white of her skirt. She wears* MAC-PHARLAIN'S *excellent scarf as if it were, not mere loot, but a legitimate trophy of battle: an enemy battle-flag hung up in a cathedral.)*

MACPHARLAIN *sees her too, scarf, stockings and all. He will* not *fall to pieces before her infernal smile, he will not, he will not. He grits his teeth and plays the man.*

Sir Julius: Anywhere at all. Just drive. A long way.

*Which is what cabbies like to hear. Away the cab goes.*

*But we do not follow it. We come back across Harley Street, leaving the* Nurse *and Number 5 on our right, going straight at the façade of Number 6; we pass through the gauze-curtain window, and in – .*

## *ii.*

*The interior of Number 6 is realistically medical. The waiting-room looks like a doctor's waiting-room, with posters about cholesterol on the walls instead of Correggio drawings; there is no Sèvres and there are no orchids. There is just a desk, with the usual bored handsome* RECEPTIONIST *and the usual computer-screen; and behind her a normal-looking door, leading to the* sanctum sanctorum.

*This door suddenly flies open, and a huge fat man bounds out. This is evidently* Dr Drake: *a droll crimson-faced countryman in a three-piece tweed suit, noisy tweed, with lively stripes of deer-gore amidst noisy daffodil yellow and resonant forest green. He gleams. He has a gleaming watch-chain, gleaming apply-cheeks, gleaming flushed pate. He is so genuinely rural it seems a shame to pen him indoors, in London, especially on a day of dense fog, when even the street seems enclosed.*

*He plays the rustic fool well. His large shrewd blue eyes give the game away, but most people (and nearly all his patients) only notice their shrewdness when it's too late.*

Archie Drake: Martha, my love, Martha, I'm bereft! What happened to my seven-thirty?
Martha (*peering into her screen*): Um Sir Julius er MacPharlain (*she doesn't find this name easy*). Here for a follow-up blood-test.
Drake: God yes, him. Stuffy little fellow from Gray's Inn, blood-sugar at six and a half. Been hitting the brandy I should say. Second-blooding and a telling-off. We'll put him on Number Two regime, won't we? Make life a misery for a month. Then it'll drop below five and all will be well.
Martha: Um.
Drake: That said, I imagine life'll stay pretty bleak in *château* MacPharlain. Fuss-fuss-fuss fuss fuss. Whatever d'y'think a grouchy Presbyterian elder like

*him* is doing with a glorious woman like *that*? Sophy MacPharlain! Course you've never seen her, *she's* never ill. But I meet her now and then. Opera-go-ing. Slender as a huntress. And her bones!

MARTHA *(not facetious; she's properly ingenuous)*: Bones?

DRAKE: Bones, I say. Bones like a Viking chieftainess. Breasts – but where *is* the blighter?

MARTHA *(plaintive)*: I'm sure I don't know, Dr Drake. He's *never* late. But *(she has his records up on the screen now)* he does have to come all the way from Barnes.

*She makes it sound like the Odyssey.*

    *Poor* MARTHA: *although she calls herself a countrywoman, partly to please her boss, she really emerged from a "self-contained" Blair-era "estate" built on the edge of a Lincolnshire village. It was a gated huddle of bungalows the colour of over-milked coffee, tidy as a golf-course, silent as a sanatorium for stroke victims. Thus although genuine countryside bewilders her, the liveliness of London appalls her more, even urban foxes going through rubbish bins. She lies awake at night alone, listening –*

DRAKE: Better ring him up and re-schedule something soon. When's my next? Not 'til eight-fifteen? Then there's time for a quick 'un? Is there, is there? Do say yes, my pretty tyrannous dove.

MARTHA, *who is already dialing, tosses her head with mock-disgust and* THE BIG BOY *bounces away, not back into his own room but out another door which, it is to be presumed, leads to a courtyard or garden, for he's bringing from his breast-pocket a silver cigarette-case and pays no attention as*

MARTHA *says into the 'phone*: Hello?

*At once we are at the other end of the line, where a remarkably tall* HAND-SOME OLD WOMAN *with a long head, prominent bones (indeed) in her cheeks and wrists, a modest string of large pearls, and a cashmere cardigan over her shoulders, is holding a receiver in a room of massively-framed landscapes and leather armchairs.*

LADY MACPHARLAIN: Good day. Sophy MacPharlain speaking.

*'Sophy' is short for Sophonisba. But apart from her name there's no nonsense about* LADY MACPHARLAIN; *certainly not about her tartan, nor her precise speech, untainted with dialect. That is, she has a brisk aristocratic Between-*

*the-Wars voice, nothing of the Lowland Scot. Yet we can tell Sophy takes her Scottishness more seriously than her husband takes his. There's a good amateur watercolour of Loch Lomond over her shoulder, signed SMᵃcP, and a bronze of a bellowing stag, Edwardian work, on a chest of drawers.*

MARTHA: Good morning, Lady MacPharlain. This is Dr Drake's surgery.
LADY MACPHARLAIN: Ah. Is my husband still there?
MARTHA: I'm afraid he hasn't arrived – yet *(she adds hastily, waggling the biro in her fingers, thinking of piles-up on the South Circular, slips on the ice, hits-and-runs at the corner of Wimpole Street, all the menaces. She shudders through the police news each evening, conceives of the capital as one tremendous death-trap. As soon as she's cleared her student loans she's bolting back to her Lincolnshire estate).*
LADY MACPHARLAIN: Oh!
MARTHA: I'm sure he's on the way. But he *was* due at seven-thirty.
LADY MACPHARLAIN: I know he was. And he left in good time. Oh dear. I hope the foolish fellow hasn't come to grief.

*She says this more calmly than we might expect. That's her way. She's a cheerful indomitable old gentlewoman, brought up on the catastrophic history of the Scots. Ancestresses of hers stood just as tall and straight as she stands now to receive bereaving news from Neville's Cross, from Flodden, Pinkie, Culloden and Ypres. Her father was drowned by the Imperial Japanese Navy before she was born, and her first strong memories are of the Blitz. Growing up, Sophy assumed her vocation would be to endure war and famine with panache. Hitherto she's been wasted on the late twentieth and twenty-first centuries.*

MARTHA *(solemnly putting down her pen on her blotter)*: I wonder if you'd ask him to ring us back, Lady MacPharlain? When you see him?

*This last remark is uttered merely out of kindness. Martha's already marked down Sir Julius as a victim of London's terrible foxes.*
    *(We are getting the hang of mind-reading, aren't we? We're construing whole trains of thought from tones and fidgets.)*

LADY MACPHARLAIN: I shall. I'm afraid he left his mobile 'phone here. He's coming back for breakfast, then he's due at the Old Bailey. And later's no good – you need him in the morning, don't you, before he's eaten? Oh dear. What a bore for you.
MARTHA: Not at all, Lady MacPharlain. Goodbye now.

LADY MACPHARLAIN: Goodbye.

*She puts the 'phone down gently and we are left staring directly into her brave intelligent face, which is trying to assess its own anxiety. Or perhaps to gauge what shape it will bear if the time for anxiety is passed: if there really has been a mishap.*

*We behold for a few slow beats of the heart the equivocal features of* SOPHY MACPHARLAIN, *bereft, before we break off and depart.*

## *iii.*

*We leave through the roof. Up we soar, above the MacPharlains' Victorian villa and its Victorian garden, twinkling with frost through the rolling fog enveloping the district – which is (we realise, as we get high enough to make out the southward bend of the river) the Putney end of Barnes.*

*We soar and soar until all misty London lies below us.*

*From an aeroplane the view would be void, a tumbling greyish-whiteness. But somehow we can see through the vapours, even through the earth below. Thus we see London as it really is, super-saturated. For London is not the lower valley of the Thames; it is the Thames' muddy estuary.*

*We behold the river itself as it is, emptying half of watery England into the ocean: fourteen thousands gallons every second. Ceaselessly the father of waters swallows his tributaries: the Darent at Dartford, upriver from the Mardyke at Purfleet, before that the Ingrebourne, the Beam, the Roding, the great Lea, which has itself swallowed the Stort, Beane, Mimram, and Hackney Brook. The Ravensbourne falls into the Thames at Deptford, the Walbrook at Dowgate, the Fleet at Blackfriars. The Tyburn (having washed the spot where Sir Julius' more fortunate predecessors sent people to hang, or be gutted) is engulfed at Pimlico. Above the Tyburn comes the Falconbrook, the Westbourne, Counter's Creek, the Wandle, and finally Beverley Brook, named for its long-extinct beavers. The Beverley flows around the walled edge of Lady MacPharlain's garden. Had she tears to let drop, were this a Jacobean poem, Beverley Brook would receive them.*

*Most of these streams are ignobly embanked, culverted, bricked-over, piped through concrete, or buried. But that makes no difference to them. They were there before Londinium; they will be there when London is again nothing but estuarine bog, here and there sprouting a little grassed-over rubble. The waters flow for millennia. Conduits and the buildings flicker above like a brief grey mist. Trees burst up beside them, break out like fireworks pink-*

green-crimson-nothing pink-green-crimson-nothing, fall and blow away like bubbles. Drainage is forever.

Here is not land with water passing through it, but water with land passing through it, half-dissolved. Take a handful of sand, fling in into a creek, watch it form a shape, spindling and long-limbed as a man; a second or two and he's gone. Such is London, a wetter place than Venice.

The odd thing is, London seems wettest not on days when it's being drenched with rain, when its roads glisten like oilcloth and its gutters run with rivulets; it seems wettest in the fog, when there's merely a fuzz of droplets on every surface. On foggy days water is marking as its own London air as well as London earth. It doesn't need to make a fuss.

London is most obviously a water-town on brumous mornings like this, when the rain has done all it can and pauses. Father Thames, who has long infiltrated all that is solid with his damps, now occupies the atmosphere as well. Ground-clouds fill every empty space. The water-table reaches the roots of the lawns. Three-dimensional wetness stretches far below the soil, far above.

England, sodden south-east England, sweet rain-steeped earth, distills herself down her miry gullet, the Thames, so that even the buildings – grey marble, grey stucco, embedded invisible, almost intangible within the grey cold corrosive steam – strain to dissolve. Moss, soggy plaster, distemper of brick: that's how they masticate themselves. They salivate and escape, holus bolus, down to the sea.

On foggy days London reveals itself as a film between the fearful upper and lower abysses of water, no more solid than the green scum on the face of a pond. Even the people scurrying about on that film are two-thirds water, extenuated here and there to be sure with blood-sugar, alcohol, caffeine, and other consoling liquid poisons.

THE HON MR JUSTICE MACPHARLAIN, KT., whom we saw ingest six pink capsules, at present inhabits a world he never guessed existed. (Although for decades he's seemed so well-informed, lecturing drug-dealers on the appalling nature of their merchandise before gaoling them at well above the sentencing tariff.) He has become both less conscious of the world, and very much more. The brown fog, for instance, is unspeakably tangible to him. It surges against the windows of his taxi, it presses its face on the glass, it gulps and digests what he can see of factories and sewage-works, frailties.

They are driving eastward, into industrial parts of London he has never seen before.

Not that direction matters much. One of the properties of fog is to make travel pointless. Wherever you go you remain just where you were within it. The varying solidities are incidental.

Sir Julius' *inner voice; we hear it murmuring from nowhere in particular:* Nothing's serious that isn't liquid .... How can I never have known that? Liquid's been sucking me back ever since I first pulled out of amniotic waters. Odd I ever thought of factories as solid. Nothing's serious ....

MacPharlain *is not philosophical. Few lawyers are. His mind is systematic in a quite different way. But this morning he has fallen into the set of mind engendered by fogs. Fogs entice us, not to disbelieve that solid objects exist, but that they matter. What is an object, after all, but an eddy, a chance precipitation of vapour? Perhaps, just as solar systems curdle within nebulæ, all objects generate spontaneously in some eternal fog....*

*Today the fog is so sinister we picture the Baskerville Hound bounding out of it, not because the fog might harbour mad dogs, but because the Hound is the fog: incarnates it. Those black flanks flecked with mad sweat are what the atmosphere naturally becomes as it becomes more and more woeful. The Hound's white fangs are indentations of mist.*

*The cab is passing east, and we are sinking swiftly out of the clouds toward it. We plummet through the fearful upper abyss, the undulating ripples of miasma, we drop through haze. We spy our prey, the little glossy beetle, trundling east along the A13. The fog bellies and heaves itself about us, it tears itself into buttocks and cleavages, it parts before our descent –*

*as* Sir Julius' *inner voice forms the words:* Liquid. All liquid. One single immense sluicing motion down into death. That is, into the North Sea. The North Sea opens on the ocean. And no doubt at the edge of the world the ocean cataracts: cataracts down into bottomless waters from which nothing emerges.

*His inner voice is gentler, more uncertain than his speaking voice, less grand. If he managed to address his law-clerks telepathically they would not recognise him.*

They used to tell me the world is round, that space is dry. I never believed them. I don't believe them now – .

## iv.

*And we are with* MacPharlain. *We have passed through the roof of the cab into the back seat.*

*His face, which fills up our sight just as Sophy's did, is oddly like hers, for* the Nairnshire gentry are an inbred lot, and Julius is her cousin as well as her husband. But his features are less firm, much less firm. His lips quiver, his eyes flow.

We're appalled at the scale of MacPharlain collapse. His inner voice had prepared us for something better than this. But such a capable man is not used to being incapacitated; and the fact is, he's not meditating on the fog at all, he's simply worrying about himself.

No: it would be better to say that he's feeling himself, attending hysterically to all the idle twinges that pass through the best-regulated sixty-two year-old body on a wintry morning. For at any moment the lacerating spasms of claryosis may seize on him ...!

> The thing which I greatly feared is come upon me,
> and that which I was afraid of is come unto me.
> I was not in safety, neither had I rest, neither was I quiet;
> yet trouble came.

The most frightful thing that can come on you in this world is fear. No illness weakens a body as fast as horror of illness. When dread of a certain thing has settled on a soul, the dreadful thing can no longer be fled. The only man who can't hope to outrun wolves is a werewolf. MacPharlain appears to be, if not quite a semi-wolf, at least a half-baked animal. The zoönose is consuming him. He's being metamorphosed out of his natural species.

Viewers may be wondering: What is the chemical basis of this change? The answer is: Nothing. Mr Justice MacPharlain is enduring nothing, the most frightful of all drugs. The capsules that looked like pink jelly-beans were in fact pink jelly-beans. The Nurse abused his trust.

MacPharlain, ignorant of such matters, imagines himself heavily sedated. He therefore calibrates his fear as far worse than it is. Nothing, it seems, can blunt his horror.

In short, he's gone to pieces more thoroughly than a less finely-wrought men might have done. It's a relief to turn our gaze from his terrible eyes to the clear young eyes of THE CABBIE, which, as in an arty film, float disembodied in the cab's rear-view mirror.

THE YOUNG CABBIE: You look, sir, in a bad way. If you don't mind me saying so.

MacPharlain is surprised out of himself. He's not used to having his appearance criticised. Nor is he the sort to chatter with taxi-drivers. Apart from anything else, their politics are notorious, far to the Right of anything the Great-and-Good care to discuss. Taxi-drivers, who have a nose, detect this *and hold their tongue when* Sir Julius *is their passenger.*

*Now he glances sharply at the official photograph (a weary brown face in a turban) and at the official name-plate (the driver is apparently called* Pratap Singh). *He pauses for an instant, delivering one of his famous silent snubs; then, frigidly,*

Sir Julius *says* Thank you, Mr Singh, no. A touch of head-cold.

The taxi-driver: Sorry to hear it. I find that hot water and whisky–

Sir Julius *(who is not going to discuss medicine with such a person)*: I have what I need. *(To head off further discussion)*: Where are we going? *(– in a tone that means "Not that it matters.")* Where am I?

The Cabbie: You're in Rainham! *(His eyes, hovering in the mirror, twinkle, for he perceives that* MacPharlain *has never heard of the place.)* Rainham is Dagenham only more so. And Dagenham's the next hellhole to the east. Where I grew up.

*Which doesn't explain his public-school accent. It seems that* MacPharlain*'s fate is to be surrounded, this morning of calamity, by well-born young people slumming in proletarian jobs.*

*Nor, indeed – we can see this thought passing over* Sir Julius' *tortured face – does it explain why Pratap Singh (he glances back at the photograph) has acquired youth, white skin, expensively-cropped light-brown hair, and alert green eyes. "Am I being kidnapped?" But he hardly cares, and*

Sir Julius *grunts.*

Mr Singh, *if it is really he:* And where are we going, you ask? Well, since you're bound nowhere in particular I thought I might as well show you nowhere. Not that you can see it, you have to take my word. Out your window is Rainham Marshes. Welcome the abyss beneath London.

*There's nothing visible out of the window but billows of coffee-tinted murk. We might be at the bottom of an ocean of steam.*

Rainham Marshes: God! Acres and acres of waste. Wet stinking mud. Weeds. Water-voles. Wigeons. Godwits. What London was like before there was London. A nature reserve they call it. Dad says the army used to test their artillery out here. That would have been something. But now it's just bloody wildlife.

*If this last speech strikes you as unnatural, you are astute. Looking over* the Cabbie*'s shoulder, we find a pad of notes resting on his knee. He consults* *them as he speaks (and perhaps that's why his driving is so haphazard, so unprofessional). We read:*

> 7. A Nature Reserve. Firing range.
> "Just wildfire".
> 8. If he starts looking better, say
> "You look in a bad way"

*and a little later on*

> 15. East on the A13 to the New
> Road intersection, double back on
> the A1306. Lie about direction if
> necessary.
> 16. "I grew up in Rainham." <u>Don't</u>
> bother dropping your aitches.
> 17. Marshes: muddy, mediæval,
> primal landscape, "abysm below
> London."
> 18. In Nov.: chiffchaffs, plovers,
> dunlins, wigeons, oystercatch-
> ers. Remember to linger over the
> funny names, epic catalogues dis-
> orientate, they suggest bizarre
> grandeur.
> 19. Mention black-tailed godwits.
> <u>God</u> might make him jump. If it
> does go to item 14. Otherwise:

*We see the taxi-driver bend over these notes, furrowing his brow, skipping items with impatient shakes of his hair.*

> 21. Occasional penduline tits, so-
> ciable lapwings, very rare, thou-
> sands of visitors. Stoats, weasels.
> Pretend to see squashed weasel?
> Weasels are always sinister, they
> remind Upper Middles of cocktail
> cabinets.

Wild life. Why d'we put up with it? Every so often some ijjit sights a penduline tit. Then the birdwatchers arrive by the coachload and make a nuisance of themselves. If you aren't a bird-fancier, there's bugger-all to do in Rainham. I'm talking 'bout the old days, mind, before the bullet-train –

SIR JULIUS *(startled out of self-concern)*: "The old days"? The Chunnel rail link was only, what, 2007.

THE PSEUDO-SINGH, *peering at his notes:*

```
23. HS1 rail link 14/11/07. 30% of
your life back. Why live beyond 25?
```

November '07, six years ago last week. Third of my life, near as. I mean, so far, but I think it'll *end up* being about a third. See what I mean? I don't want a twenty-fifth birthday, what's the point? If you've not got it done in a quarter-century, you're not going to do it, are you?

*He's driving with his right hand, running his left finger down his lines of notes.*

```
27. The mere effusion of thy proper
loins,
Do curse the gout, serpigo, and the
rheum,
For ending thee no sooner.
```

Or it's not worth doing. Everything after twenty-five's just work or suffering. Ache, sickness…. Even in the old days, before I was fifteen, life was crud. Jokes. (*The imposter's slang is unconvincing. His heart's not in it, his mind is elsewhere*). At least the bullet-train's made the difference. Ever been on it?

SIR JULIUS *(stiff but bewildered. He's never endured so much pointless small-talk in his life)*: Yes as it happens, quite often.

THE PURPORTED CABBIE: Then you'll know it goes underground at St Pancras and stays under 'til wham!, it bursts out at Dagenham Dock. We larrikins used to stand on Marsh Way overpass and wait. You hear a whoosh as it comes out of the tunnel-mouth. Count to thirteen and swish! underneath. But at eleven you let go. Too soon, it hits the tracks. Too late and blop! on the train roof. The winner's the one with whose used condom splatters the train windscreen. *(An ugly chuckle.)* All the way to gay Paree with a million little mes spoiling the view. – Or Brussels. Wherever it goes.

SIR JULIUS *(genuinely appalled)*: Good God. You did that?

WHOEVER IT IS: Yeah. Obviously it would've been more fun to drop something big. But if the window smashed the bastards would've stopped the train and come after us.

Sir Julius *is reviving. We can see thoughts forming: "Wish I had this hoo-ligan in the dock"; "Must get away from him"; and "Must find an hotel and think."*

As it was, d'y' know what it would've been really good to drop?
Sir Julius (*trying to retrieve himself*): Please take me to –
The Imposter: Me. The big me. Imagine the look on the driver's face when I splashed onto his glass at –

*a pause while he consults his notes –*

a-hundred-and-forty miles an hour!
Sir Julius: – back to London. Turn round. Real London. Fleming's Hotel in Half Moon Street – .
The untrue Cabbie (*driving straight on, still eastward*): There was this great-great-uncle of mine, Henry Strafford. Just married this American bird, young, gorgeous, rich as anything, a toothpaste heiress if you'd believe it. One afternoon just after the honeymoon he's standing on a platform with a first-class ticket in his hand. Not round here, up at Potter's Bar. As the Cambridge express comes thundering by he suddenly just changes his mind – 'about everything. Tosses his top-hat over his shoulder and hops in front. It took off his head.
MacPharlain (*shocked out of himself*): Your great-great uncle was the fourth Earl of Strafford?
The Youth (*genuinely pleased*): You heard of him, then?

*This is like that twaddle earlier this morning, about Len's fried mushrooms. Once entered on a fatuous conversation, it's hard to find a non-fatuous exit.*

MacPharlain: Lord Strafford's inquest was an early example of a judge getting a jury to return a verdict which everyone knew to be nonsense. "Mis-adventure", when –
The Boy: Ah well, funny lot my family.
MacPharlain: Is the name really Singh?
The Youth (*distractedly; he's busy turning over a page of his notes, rejecting suggestions*): No. It's Vane-Powell.
MacPharlain: Oh.

*A pause.*

```
36. Be absolute for death.
37. Thou'rt by no means valiant;
For thou dost fear the soft and
tender fork
Of a poor worm.
```

VANE-POWELL (*abruptly, improbably, inhumanly*): Why not do what Uncle Henry did? Come on: I can see all there is of you. It's not as if you're noble. You're a muddle of filthy impulses. You're not the least bit brave. You're scared shitless at every little virus and bacillus.

*He's entirely stopped trying to sound like a cabbie. What he sounds like is the angel of death, a proponent of misadventure. He's smooth and callous enough to be an angel.*

*Or so* MACPHARLAIN *seems to think. (We're on the bonnet now, staring though the windscreen, past* THE CABBIE's *bowed schoolboy head, straight into the raddled face of* THE JUDGE.)

VANE-POWELL: Uncle had the right idea. Hold life light as a feather. Only morons care. Be absolute for death. The one bit of suicide that can possibly hurt is the thinking about it. The indecision. Skip that stage and there's no pain. You lose nothing when you let yourself blow away. Suddenly one day let go. Today.

*We're back beside* MACPHARLAIN *is the back seat, watching him watch with final horror* THE BOY's *passionless eyes in their strip of mirror.*

VANE-POWELL: Dive off the bridge knowing you'll never touch ground. The train'll catch you before you dash your foot. Specially on a foggy day like this when nothing really exists. Dissolve like a droplet.

*We lean over the driver's seat and watch his firm young fingers run down these lines –*

```
38. Thou art not thyself;
For thou exist'st on many a thou-
sand grains
That issue out of dust
```

*He produces his paraphrase in a rush:*

What are you, anyway? Nearly-nearly-*nearly* nothing. A million globules lifted out of dirt. A botched job, so small it can't matter it's botched. Not worth fussing over. A boiled egg with the top cut crocked, a limerick with the punch-line missing. Just chuck it. There's a spot of butter on your cuff, what d'y'do? Y'wipe it off.

MacPharlain *is spellbound, sickly, but still resistant. He's trying to re-member the glory of his scarlet robes. The aweful stillness of his court when handing down an exemplary sentence. The splendour of opening nights at Covent Garden. The hush of committee-rooms at the House of Lords. Sophy, embracing naked slender Sophy. His own Greatness-and-Goodness.*

MacPharlain *(croaking)*: *My* life has been –
Vane-Powell: Your *life*? You trying to be funny? Think you're *alive*? Being alive's something you've just heard about. Like winning the pools. 'Spose it does happen now and then. But not to *you*.
MacPharlain *(this is wrung from him)*: I've a *significant* –
Vane-Powell: Thou hast nor youth nor age
But, as it were, an after-dinner's sleep,
Dreaming on both.
MacPharlain: *What?*
Vane-Powell: Getting trollied at lunch, that's existence. I'm saying it's like being curled up on a settee after your sticky pud. Vague pictures in your head, childhood games, the odd fuck, big dinners, getting trollied again. And *that's it.* Count up the things you really remember: it's not five minutes' worth. You're in a six-decade doze and that's all it's ever been. You're trained to blather on but if you were sincere you'd have nothing to tell. So tell *Nothing.* Utter *Nothing.* Come to *Nothing.*

Julius MacPharlain *cannot speak. The fog (so very like Nothing) presses on the cab. They're running along the side of a railway. They're turning beside an overpass.*

Julius *(choking, in final desperation)*: Mr Vane-Powell, stop!
The Messenger: Mr Justice MacPharlain, you stop. It's time. Here's Marsh Way. Here's the bridge. Only I think we're a few seconds early –

*He brakes, consults his watch. There's a vague roar suddenly: a massive train in the mist just beyond them.*

Nope, tell a lie, right on time. Here's the 8:58 coming. We –

THE SO-CALLED CABBIE *turns round for the first time to confront his fare;
but his fare's already absconded, and muttering*: He might have shut the
door! *the* BOY *too jumps out into the misty world; where, despite his apparent
nonchalance, we hear him counting tensely under his breath, as he slams the
door*: Twelve? Eleven? … Eight?

*We're standing beside him in the midst of the fog, which is particularly heavy
here, close to the Marsh and the river as it is. Cars go past, honking angrily
because the taxi's so wantonly parked.*

*MACPHARLAIN's already been swallowed up by the turning vapours.
He might have gone in any direction. He might well be down on the A1306,
hailing a more tractable cab.*

*And the train is almost upon us. We sense some sort of bridge rising
above, with a street-sign visible. Just an ungainly street-sign on a concrete slab
(we're a long way from Harley Street)*: MARSH WAY RM13.

VANE-POWELL *(uncertainly. He really doesn't know what is about to happen)*:
Sept? Six? Cinq? Quatre?

*He cocks an ear, counting down silently now. As we do. From the overpass
come confused noises: onrush of train, varied cries, rising to*

VIOLENT SHOUTS OFF: No! Stop him! Hey! –

*while* A HOWL IN THE MIST *utters a purely animal noise as it (we deduce
from the acoustic) plummets, so that on the stroke of zero comes, astonishingly
loud but otherwise only half-hideous, an oddly-musical nigh-to-delicious al-
most-liquid* scrunch *not unlike a vegetable pressed with a fork –*

## *v.*

*which becomes at once precisely that.*

*Fog and sky have vanished; screaming and yelling too, like a switched-off
television. By normal indoor light we behold a tuber of equivocal species,
trimmed to the approximate shape of a truncheon, cooked to a militaristic
khaki. We see it half-heartedly crushed under the tines of a green-plastic-han-
dled fork, rolled petulantly back and forth across a plate, bumping against
tubers of much the same shape, there grey-pink, here orange-grey. We see it
speared, causing it to bleed pale-green water.*

*Suddenly the fork is – not flung down, that would be extreme, but placed crossly on the frilly table-cloth, and*

A FRETFUL VOICE *says*: No, I'm sorry, I'm just not going to. It's too horrid. *And* I have a policing subcommittee this afternoon, with that vile Melvin Scrubbins laughing at me right through. That's enough suffering for today. I want a proper lunch.

*Pulling back, we find we're in a dining-room decorated in accord with to the canons of petty-bourgeois taste circa 1991. There's a ticking gilt mantel-clock on the mantel beside a plaster bust of Lady Thatcher. The pale upholstery is frenetically flecked with stylised orange poppies. Outside, beyond the gauzy curtains, the fog has no glamour, it's merely a greasy film.*

*The fretful voice belongs to* AN OLD YOUNG MAN *with a driving-instructor look to him, rigged out however in a Jermyn Street suit. He has neatly squeezed the splayed finger-tips of one hand between the finger-tips of the other (a rabbitty gesture), and is scowling through this feeble fretwork at his plate.*

*Beside him, at the head of the table, sits a* FLORAL LADY. *She is at first glance simply a familiar type. Her expression is so very genteel we know she'd describe her jacket as being of "a deep rich blue" and her blouse, which foams at her throat into an elaborate* jabot, *as "handmade satin of a subtle pastel green." Yet she's no fool; or rather has tidily swept life's necessary folly into unimportant corners. Her washed-out eyes rest vigilantly on the elderly boy. Her mouth is pursed into what must be its default setting, a faint, refined, dogged, critical smile. She is wearied by this naughty world but unsoiled, and her dumpy, lavender-impregnated body is of the sort that, never having known grace, never knows tiredness.*

*She has a glass of water in front of her, but no nonsense of boiled vegetables. Her fingers, which repose demurely on the lacy table-cloth, resemble clamps.*

THE FLORAL LADY: Now then, we have talked through this, have we not? (*Although her elocution is painfully precise, her accent is quite frankly Basingstoke. This is her tragedy. Her late husband made his money in garden sculpture too late, circa 1991, for her to enjoy Advantages.*) It is only two weeks to the Party Conference, and we do not want to look taut about our tum when we are on the platform. Now do we?

*We glance down and find this allusion uncalled-for. He's not such a bad specimen of his type. True, he has the broad flat knobbly face of a toad, all inconsolable eye, with a slick of sandy hair quite unrelated to his features, patted down sideways atop his skull, looking exactly like a hairpiece although it is (as yet) real. And it's a large cubic skull to set so heavily on such small* shoulders and, below that, on such a billowing of breasts and buttocks. A galleyful of baroque *putti*, as it may be, was chopped up and stuck together to create him. But he is, strictly speaking, formless rather than positively tubby.

THIS MISUSED YOUNG MAN (*regressing even further under the burden of her unjust slur*): Don't care 'bout being fat. Won't eat boiled turnip, won't.
THE WOMAN (*atrociously patient*): But Martin, it is not a turnip. You are aware of that. It is a lightly-steamed yam. Full of sealed-in goodness. And very low in –
MARTIN: Low in everything. *I'm* low.

*This flash of wit wins him a thin patronising smile. She sets about patting his hand. From his apprehensive face we gather that hand-patting is part of her method.*

Please, Mummsie: I haven't had anything decent to eat for days.

*Her pats manage to be at once tender and hard, or paradoxically hard because soft; just like the billows of her fine blue hair, which is fixed as wire; or like her eyes, pale as orphaned sparrow-eggs spilled from a nest, pale as the hull-slicing edge of an immaculate iceberg. Her cheeks, smelling as they naturally* do *of talcum powder, are so soft they seem to Martin to diffuse into the air, yet so firm they might be plumped each morning with fresh blood.*

HIS MOTHER: Nothing to eat? Now then, that is not quite the truth, is it? Who had fresh hot toast for his breakfast? With a nice scraping of soft dairy butter? And who –
FRETFUL MAN (*vowels turning more Basingstoke by the second, despite his Advantages*): I don't care. This doesn't count as lunch and I'm not having any more of it and that's flat.
HIS MOTHER (*pat, pat, pat*): We are being a silly now. A regular old silly-billy. We have to look nice and trim for the television cameras at the Conference, do we not? Statesmanship Comes at a Cost. (*Sententiously: she's evidently picked this up somewhere.*) We are on a diet for a very very important reason. Can we remember what that reason is?
FRETFUL MAN (*pouting*): No.
HIS MOTHER (*coaxing*): I think we can. *Who* is going to be Prime Minister one day?
FRETFUL MAN (*sulky mumbling*): Don't know.

*The patting slows, it beats time as, in a frightful composite of sweetness and menace,*

HIS MOTHER *enunciates*: Tell. Mummsie. Who. Is. Going. To. Be. Prime. Minister.

*It was in this very tone, long ago, that she was wont to address her late hus-band, who was refusing to take proper advantage of their Advantages. Martin remembers what this voice portends. Yet now* THE WICKED BOY *pouts, and will not speak.*

HIS MOTHER *(through her teeth)*: Tell. Mother. Who.
FRETFUL MAN *(a wild act of rebellion)*: Benjy.

*The patting stops. Her hand rests on his, nails tangible on his skin but as yet unpressed, rather in the manner of a sickle leant against the flank of a veal-calf. She never hurries on to extreme measures unnecessarily. It took her, as Martin knows perfectly well, more than a year to procure her husband's thrombosis, and there were* many *moments during that year when she offered perfectly sincerely* to relent. *Ripeness is all.*

MOTHER: We are being a Naughty now. Mr Benjamin Wedgwood is *not* Napoleonic. He is perhaps all-very-well at the Foreign Office. We may even keep him there when we reach Number 10. But you, my little Marty-warty –
MARTIN: You *promised* me you'd *never* call –
MOTHER: My warty little Martin-bird.
MARTIN: *Mother.*
MOTHER: You, the Right Honourable Martin Littlejohn, M.P., are fated to –

*Their squabble has the tired feel of a set-piece. We surmise that it's fought out every lunchtime, every suppertime. Which is not to say it's symmetrical (no conversation is ever that, there's always protagonist and antagonist); nor even that it's static. There are ups and downs, break-outs, feints, armistice talks, bold salients, grand compromises, midnight barrages, blanket bombings, hopeless last stands, bayonet charges, rallies, timid lunchtimes, counter-rev-olutionary suppers. Events are confused, but as in most wars we can discern a trend. For the last two years, Martin has been winning. Slowly the worm wriggles out from beneath the hoof.*

*Thus it must be a relief for Martin's* MOTHER, *as it certainly is for him, and for us, to break off. As they do; for they have heard a polite interruptant patter at the dining-room door.*

*They glance at each other.* MRS LITTLEJOHN *bites her lush lip on the very point of saying:* Enter!

MARTIN LITTLEJOHN, M.P. (*summoning up his manliest voice, even managing to sound overworked, a put-upon maker-of-events*): Yes? What is it? Come in.

*Enter* A TALL YOUNG WOMAN *with black hair in a shiny spherical bun, fringe cut at a geometric angle, and a severe Chanel suit of navy* bouclé: *as august a civil servant as you might hope to see on a late-autumnal noon. Her face is half-handsome, half heavy with intelligence, and there's a similar mishmash of effect with her chin, which goes on too long and ends up implausibly far from her kissable* retroussé *nose. Is this chin, we ask ourselves, serious or not? But her lipstick, an agitating shade of blue, both chilling and* chic, *is a clever calculation. We're meant to notice this calculation. She's armed totem-wise with an anaconda-skin portfolio, open: a most superior sort of clipboard, fit for a Permanent Under-Secretary at the Home Office, which is exactly what she means to be one day comparatively soon, young as she is, and much as she exults in being, already, P.A. to the Home Secretary.*

*Who rises to his feet and tries to compose himself. No good.*

LITTLEJOHN's *lifelong tragedy is his naked toad-face. We haven't yet remarked what it looks like because there's absolutely nothing to describe. It's altogether commonplace except that it's unusually round, round as a Chinaman's, blank-white as a china plate. Its only office is to hold and display whichever of* THE HOME SECRETARY's *small stock of emotions is being served up.*

*At the moment his emotion is puppy-love. He's tortured by having it, tortured by knowing his mother can see it, tortured by knowing she knows he knows she knows he has what she calls Feelings for this particular (Entirely Unsuitable, as is often pointed out) underling.* "Personal Assistant indeed! Now then, that is *not really* what we have in mind in the least, is it!"

*Martin's even more tortured that his sweet P.A. must herself be able to read his face and measure his Feelings. But what's he to do? His failing, ridiculous in a politician, is yet more ridiculous in a lover. Not that he's that.*

*These agonies pass through him in a flash, during which*

LITTLEJOHN *has managed to say, urbanely enough (for his voice has never been the problem)*: Ah. (*And after a busy pause*): Patricia.
PATRICIA ("*posh enough, in her way*", *as Mrs Littlejohn puts it; with overdone, therefore disturbing diffidence*): Home Secretary. I am sorry –

*The Home Secretary's* MOTHER *coughs primly.*

PATRICIA (*loathing undisguised*): *And* Mrs Littlejohn

*– who sniffs decorously.*

I'm sorry to interrupt your –

PATRICIA *is a performer, a professional hypocrite, doubtless a listener at keyholes. Here she pretends to catch sight of Martin's watery roots for the first time and hesitates, as if searching for a word. The* HOME SECRETARY, *who has risen to his feet, flashes a look of mingled triumph and reproach at his* MOTHER, *whose own closed face blackens.*

PATRICIA: – your … lunch. But Andy thought you needed to know at once. Sir Julius MacPharlain –

*Here, suddenly, the comic veers toward the tragic, for*

THE HOME SECRETARY, *blenching at the name, entirely forgetting the whole yam question, gasps:* Oh, *totters back, and clutches the mantel, his fingers dangerously near the Iron Lady's décolletage.* Oh dear!

*A vulgar Freudian might read things into this gesture, since* LITTLEJOHN *has assumed what he secretly calls (what his mother calls too, if only he knew) his "mummy-face": an infantile expression, eyes agog, cheeks rounded, jaw slack. For his self-awareness has snapped. It seems to his disordered innermost mind that fingers craggy with encrusted rings are descending toward him, into his crib ….*

*In short, he is so perturbed – no, so frightened – that his* MOTHER *and* PATRICIA *stare at him in astonishment.*
PATRICIA *(uncertainly):* A judge. Queen's Bench Division.
HOME SECRETARY *(straightening, with sudden tearful rage):* I know who MacPharlain is – I know all about him.

*He gasps at his own blunder. His mother becomes a little frightened on his behalf.*
*So, curiously, does* PATRICIA. *She doesn't love the Home Secretary – that would be absurd – but she synthesises for him the exasperated affection of a bustling sister for a pathetic older brother.*
*She synthesises this artificial emotion from two feelings which are real, raw, and spread copiously throughout her mind. One is her sole passion: she means to be a Permanent Under-Secretary, to ascend to heights where portfolios are anaconda as a matter of course. The other is merely a sentiment, although sincere as far as it goes: she feels sorry for the dingy little oik.*
*Naturally, the vicarious fears of his two women make* THE HOME

Secretary *more frightened still.*

That is! That is to say! I assure the – room *(he has switched to his cagey House of Commons voice, the manner which never convinces the Opposition benches)* I know nothing whatsoever about this alleged judge nor about the so-called actions which have led to his purported arrest which rightly or –
Patricia *(attempting gentleness)*: Home Secretary. Home Secretary. Mr Justice MacPharlain hasn't been arrested, he's dead. He threw himself under the 8:58 Eurostar service to Brussels.
Home Secretary *(after a pause; trying to control his glee)*: Oh. *(Conversationally)*: Did he? Golly. What a thing to do. *(And he actually giggles.)*

Martin Littlejohn's *scrutability is not merely a freak, it's half the secret of his success. Although like all politicians he lies, he has what poker-players call a "tell." It is a tremendous "tell", his lying is instantly obvious, even to babies. And thus when he* isn't *lying, he has a curious negative authority. That's what makes him useful to the authorities, meaning both the government of England, and his own domestic tyrant.*

*Of course both these authorities have to keep him in the dark about everything they* don't *want divulged. But that's easily managed, not least because Martin is mortally afraid of the dark, and thus eager not to know how much he doesn't know.*

*So now the* Two Women, *for all their antipathy, exchange a shrewd glance of the sort women do exchange about their men.*

Home Secretary *(observing himself observed, and striving, hopelessly as ever, to get himself in order)*: A Brussels train, you say? *(Spluttering in his attempt to repackage his giggles as statesmanlike coughs of dismay.)* Good G – good goodness. *(Clearly The-Lord's-Name-in-Vain is another household prohibition.)* The Eurosceptics are bound to make tasteless comments about that.

*A damp quip. Anaconda-skin trembles in* Patricia's *hands.* Mrs Littlejohn, *aghast, feels for her jabot. To fill the silence*

the Home Secretary *officiously demands:* When will the news come out, Patricia?
Patricia *(stiffly, bewildered, glancing into her incomparable portfolio)*: Formal identification in a few hours, Home Secretary. Of course they'll inform Lady MacPharlain before they release the name.
Home Secretary: We'd better leak it, then. We don't want a thing like this breaking in the evening tabloids, we want it in tomorrow morning's broad-

sheets first – eh, mother? No nasty sensationalism?

*Usually* Mrs Littlejohn *likes nothing more than leaks, deploring them or planning them; and she has trenchant views on the popular press. But just now she won't be drawn. She's too much at sea.*

Oh, Patricia – speaking of sensation – there's no question of – you know. Foul play? Or any such thing?
Patricia *(wondering)*: None, Home Secretary. There were five witnesses. Seven counting babies. He ran along a railway bridge, past two families wheeling prams, and jumped.
Home Secretary: That's grand, that ah is to say, unspeakably terrible. The MacPharlains being such strong Presbyterians.... You'd better draft a statement, Patricia. Most brilliant legal mind of his *etcetera*, upright servant of the whatsit, autumn of his and so forth, giant among, deeply grieved, live forever in. You know the form.

*She does; but not nearly so well as he knows it himself.* Littlejohn *is justly proud of his way with eulogies. He's adept at their special terminology:* "lively" *to mean adulterous,* "colourful" *perverted,* "quiet" *senile,* "sad circumstances" *suicide,* "tragic circumstances" *murder-suicide,* "pleasure-loving" *dipsomaniacal,* "home-loving" *tormented recluse,* "Bohemian tastes" *drug-addict,* "very retired" *in a madhouse. The* Home Secretary *can utter these technical words without archness. Condoling is one of the things he's thought to be good for, and he performs far more than his share of representing the government at Great-and-Good funerals.*

*(It's an added advantage that he's so far beneath the mourners socially. They don't need to include him in conversation, which saves a lot of bother. They know the government knows this, and appreciate its thoughtfulness in their hour of grief.)*

*No doubt* Littlejohn *will be dispatched to Sir Julius' funeral. He drifts off into reverie, picturing the occasion with uncomplicated pleasure: there'll be a photograph in the* Times, *probably, of himself, in the porch of the Temple Church, murmuring gravely with the Lord Chancellor .... So he says, quite cheerfully:*

Do a draft, Patricia, and bring it to my desk for personal touches.
Patricia *(a bit scornful, little-sisterly)*: Nothing about topping himself, then?
Littlejohn: About the Sad Circumstances? Goodness no no no. – Um. Thank you.

PATRICIA *leaves, half-bowing to the* HOME SECRETARY *and, after an inward struggle, daring* not *to nod farewell to his* MOTHER.

*Who watches her go with pursed lips, treasuring up the insult.*

*The door closes gently.*

*Thunderous silence descends on the table.*

*Not since she laid the late Mr Littlejohn in the sandy soil of Basingstoke and brought her boy down the valley of the Thames to enjoy and deploy his Advantages – not, at least, since the terrible evening she caught him kissing the Combwell girl – has* MRS LITTLEJOHN *known such a pitch of downright ingratitude. She sits and fumes.*

*The* HOME SECRETARY *sits and waits, not at ease. After a terrible few seconds he retrieves from the mock-leather holder in his shirt pocket his spectacles. He wears 'aviators', popular in the late 1980s, which might one sad day come into vogue once again. Or rather he wears them when he dares, being often shrilly admonished to take them off. It is held that he looks more Prime Ministerial without, and thus often has to stand, anchoring himself with one flabby hand on the back of his chair, blinking at the forehead or chin of whoever is talking at him. "But I can't see anyone," he often says, and is crushed: "You do not need to see, Martin, they are here to inspect* you. *To admire your Nelson Stare. Fixed, we might say, on the far horizon of tomorrow. Deliberately blind to present trivialities. Hand them over." "But I need them, Mummsie, for the Boxes." "Nonsense. As if your dear old mother didn't do all the reading you need to do for you, bad ungrateful child."*

*Now her bad boy inspects her shyly through his large lenses, and the sight of the contraband goads her into speech.*

MRS LITTLEJOHN: Martin Eric Littlejohn. What. Have. You. Been. Up. To?
HOME SECRETARY: Don't be growly, Mummsie. You wouldn't – if you knew –

*and he shuts his lips like a trap, making his usual finger-tent, peering up through the little gaps at the blank plaster of the ceiling.*

*How well he knows how to tantalise his mother! Besides, he's a professional statesman.*

MRS LITTLEJOHN: Tell. Now.
HOME SECRETARY: Well....

*The essence of statescraft is timing. (Surreptitiously he eyes his steamed vegetables. Four more minutes, keep her preoccupied for four more, just four, and they'll surely be deemed inedible. Even by* her.*)*

Well then. Mother: Sir Julius MacPharlain was a wicked man.

MRS LITTLEJOHN (*all-too-obviously thinking 'But he was knighted by Her Majesty!'*): Impossible, Martin!

*– for she's wise enough to let herself be a nincompoop about trifling things: to be a snob, culturally dense, an addict of glossy magazines. There's so little wit in man, so much inanity, and* MARIGOLD LITTLEJOHN *is an economist of the soul. She conserves her resources to govern England.*

What an idea!

HOME SECRETARY (*spinning it out*): Wicked as wicked ever was. He was leading a double life, triple life. Quadruple. Whatever comes after that. He was accepting, no, *soliciting*, enormous amounts.

MRS LITTLEJOHN: Never!

HOME SECRETARY: Oh don't go pretending to be shocked, Mother, you know *lots* of judges take bribes to free the guilty. Not Sir Julius, though. He had a quite different specialty.

*Dong! Dong! – Big Ben startles us by telling noon. We're surprised, not that the Littlejohns lunch very early, which we might have guessed, but that the tolling is so near, almost overhead. We must be very close indeed to Parliament; perhaps in one those short blind expensive streets off Birdcage Walk. Which comes as a shock, since the décor, ambiance, smell, misled, evoking Woking or Dorking. (Let this be a lesson to you. Class-consciousness is all very well, but it's not infallible.) Dong! Dong! Beneath the stately metallic music* LITTLEJOHN's *thin voice continues, taking his time.*

Carved a niche, to coin a phrase. Invented a whole new crime. He paid an enormous retainer to a certain socialite. A very wild woman. Her job was to find out aggrieved business partners, bored spouses, impatient heirs –

MRS LITTLEJOHN (*airily*): This is mere gossip, Martin. Grown-ups do not believe such things. (*Which has ever been her way of worming details out of him.*) Vague fabrications of the lowest journalism, which you are childish to credit.

HOME SECRETARY: Oh very well then, it was Zoë Moxgrave.

MRS LITTLEJOHN: The Countess of Moxgrave!

*For of course she has back-numbers of* Oi! *magazine heaped in a locked cupboard in what she calls "my boudoir." Marigold knows more about Lady Moxgrave's doings than that merry women knows herself, behazed as she usually is by the coke and the Cristal and the jetlag.*

What – what was this job, exactly?

*She struggles not to sound avid. Every year the Conservative Women's Association (almost all petty middle-class, like herself) have her back to give a speech condemning corrupt metropolitan Society, of which Zoë Moxgrave is the most abandoned "celeb". Later, over the finger-food, MARIGOLD shares in a low voice tidbits of what they all scorn, of what they turn their faces from.*

HOME SECRETARY: This Moxgrave woman knows London. Everyone goes to her parties. *(Which is calculated to sting and does sting. MRS LITTLEJOHN would lie naked in a public ditch to be invited; Zoë Moxgrave wouldn't think of hiring such a frump to sweep up the broken glass the next morning.)* And at these parties she … she draws people aside! And they tell her – everything. You see, Mummsie, Zoë ("Zoë"! *Of a truth the worm is turning*) is so notorious it seems unsporting not to be frank with her.

*Despite these urbane remarks, all quoted from overheard grown-up conversations, MARTIN is busy eyeing the margarine, coagulant in the wrinkles of his veggies. It is becoming an unappetising wax of no particular colour. Surely lunch now stands condemned? No, give it a minute more. Be on the safe side.*

She sows the seed: "Sarah darling, if Robin's being as tiresome as you say, you'd be better off with him behind bars!" And watches Sarah's eyes. Then, if the right darkness shows, the next day one of MacPharlain's clerks sidles up to Sarah, offering to have Robin put away.

MRS LITTLEJOHN *(feebly)*: Impossible – surely. Not in *England.*

HOME SECRETARY: MacPharlain's been doing it for years. Judicial assassination. Like hiring a hitman without the killing. Without a margin for error. He could demand enormous bribes because he *always* got a conviction when he wanted one. Such a way of bullying juries. "Do not allow yourselves to be lead astray by arid concern with vagaries of evidence." "Fraud is a technical matter which you, or indeed the Accused, are incapable of following in detail, so let me assure you –"

MRS LITTLEJOHN *(still incredulous)*: But what did Sir Julius *want* with all these bribes? High court judges earn two hundred and fifteen thousand pounds!

*It's the sort of thing she knows. But she doesn't know everything, and HER SON warms to the unusual pleasure of disillusioning her.*

HOME SECRETARY: Poor Mummsie: you *are* going to be shocked. MacPharlain needed the money for his *kept woman.* He had a *string.* A Congolese with terrifying tribal tattoos in a mews flat in Haringay. They tell me. And two teenaged Finnish twins in Canary Wharf, right up high with a view to

Westminster.... And a Ukrainian grandmother in Swiss Cottage.

*He reports this last horror with a certain wistfulness, for which* Mrs Littlejohn *would normally have taken him up sharply, it being policy for Martin
to Save Himself for when he is Prime Minister and can have the pick of the
biddable daughters of titled backwoodsmen. In the meantime no good will
come even of thinking Dirt. She hasn't forgiven him Miss Combwell. But for
the moment she's too appalled to notice.*

Mrs Littlejohn: Dear heaven, how do we know all this?

*The "we" is good; but it hasn't slid by unnoticed.*

Home Secretary (*enjoying the pronouns*): I know, Mummy, because *my*
police force needed *my* permission to "stake-out" the judge's "love-nests."

*He also enjoys getting away with this jargon, which Mummsie would normally
correct to terms more orchidaceous, more in keeping with public-library culture.*

Photographing his comings and goings. Not for evidence, you understand.
Zoë was already "coöperating", she wore a "wire" for us – we've given her
immunity. And the police could have got all the evidence they wanted by
seizing his computers. The photos were for selling to the *Daily Smell*.

*He pauses to let* his Mother *denounce this disgusting organ. Nothing.*
Happily there's a woman called Wendy in Serious Crime who *isn't* in the pay
of the tabloids. She makes her money leaking Scotland Yard's doings to me.

*Suddenly he surprises himself by giving way to a burst of rancour:*

Don't you think it's unfair, Mummsie? *I'm* the Home Secretary, I pay the
police *anyway*. Why should I have to *bribe* them to tell me what's happening?

Mrs Littlejohn *quite likes her son's rare shows of temper. Her approving
moue makes him expand still further.*

Scandalous, isn't it? Well, Wendy got in touch ever so late last night, a *long*
time after supper, you were already sn –

*– dear goodness, he's nearly said* snoring, *which would have provoked a crisis –*

snoozing. Snoozing nicely. She told me the Yard planned to get their dirty pictures and pounce on Sir Julius within the fortnight.

MRS LITTLEJOHN *(smitten by a terrible thought)*: "Within the fortnight"? Just before the Conference! Everything spoilt! I would have had an awful time at the Conservative Woman. They cannot abide sex scandals.

HOME SECRETARY: No. *Exactly*. It was going to be a nasty surprise for everyone. Except the tabloids of course.

MRS LITTLEJOHN: I wouldn't have been able to wear my cerise twinset!

HOME SECRETARY: Yes. And I can just hear the P.M. saying "Bad business about this crooked judge, Martin. All over the *Smell*. Not running a very tight ship at the Home Office, are we? Come and talk to me if you ever find it too much." I *hate* it when he talks like that. Always waits 'til there's a reporter within earshot, too. I'd have had a beastly Conference, and then afterwards when there was nothing more to say the pundits would have filled up their columns with Speculation. You know I can't sleep when there's Speculation.

THE AGRIPPINA OF HER AGE, *who would normally soothe him, isn't attending. She's too busy calculating.*

MRS LITTLEJOHN: This Wendy female rang you last night at, what was it? Five to ten. And you were back in bed by ten past. *(*MARTIN *does not fail to notice that she's betrayed herself. So Mummsie snores with one eye open, does she? He must be more careful.)* And MacPharlain went under the 8:58 this morning. With five witnesses. Less than twelve hours.... How was it done? Who did it? M.I.6.? The Army?

HOME SECRETARY *(pleased to know something she doesn't)*: Not a bit of it, Mummy. But it's terribly hush and I shouldn't tell anyone, not even you.

MOTHER *glowers – slightly, just enough. She isn't really a gorgon, her glowering is too nicely calibrated for that. She knows when* MARTIN *will buckle.*

*Which he does at once, being the most biddable leader of men, prostrate before public opinion as represented by his mother, or by anyone else; prostrate, indeed, before opinion. He's capable of getting off a train at the wrong stop if everybody else seems to be getting off. Don't sneer, though: this is the other half of the secret of Littlejohn's success. It's what makes him electorally formidable. He's firm as a wet cloth stretched over a mouthing, grimacing face; which is exactly how the democracy likes its politicians. They want to see their own tics and grimaces made visible. No democratic politician can be* craven *enough.*

*In any case,* MARIGOLD *glowers and* MARTIN *buckles:*

Chap we sometimes use. Our secret weapon, if you will. He's in Cambridge of all places. Frightful college too, Mother: Wygy's

*– and he,* MARTIN, *attempts to sneer. His face distorts with the snootiness painstakingly acquired at fifteen, when Advantages swept him sobbing into a boarding school.*

   *Where he was known (complexly, as is the way with school nicknames) as In-Hand Littlejohn, partly because his mama was known to have him in hand.*

MRS LITTLEJOHN (*disbelievingly*): A *university staffer?*
HOME SECRETARY (*carefully*): A Classics don, Mummsie. Named Culpepper. To look at him you'd think he was, you know, one of those debonair dons, a bit bored. I imagine he *is*, most of the time. But he does this sort of job on the side. Works quite alone – I mean, no other proper agents. I think he sometimes brings along students to help out. (*It suddenly strikes Littlejohn how exciting this would be.*) As a treat. An outing!
MRS LITTLEJOHN: (*still astonished*): This academic gentleman did it? But *how?*
HOME SECRETARY: Can't say. But he sounded ever so confident when I 'phoned. "I'm still digesting dinner," he told me, "so it'll have to wait 'til morning. What's MacPharlain up to tomorrow?" Well of course Wendy in Serious Crime knew his schedule: doctor's appointment seven-thirty, conference at the Old Bailey at ten, pronouncing sentence on a tax evasion after lunch – not much suspense *there*, he'd accepted thirty thousand pounds from the fellow's daughters to send the fellow down for twenty years. Anyway, Culpepper didn't want to know more. Cut me off and went back to his port. Ever so suave.
MRS LITTLEJOHN: But did he –
HOME SECRETARY (*presuming on her amazement to assert himself*): No mother. I think that's enough. It's terribly confidential. Besides, it's not a nice topic for just after lunch, is it?
MRS LITTLEJOHN, *who, like any good parent, enjoys seeing her child take independent steps, bows her head in mock submission, murmuring*: No, Martin, I am sure you are correct.
HOME SECRETARY (*rolling his napkin decisively, making as to thrust it into its stainless-steel ring*): There'll be a lot of tidying up, of course. Work, work, work. Scores of MacPharlain's convicts to reprieve, pardon, parole.

*He enjoys hearing himself talk in this fashion. What a shame* PATRICIA *can't hear him.*

Thank G – goodness there won't have to be judicial any reviews. The D.P.P. at the C.P.S. turns beastly when –

MRS LITTLEJOHN (*less submissively*): We do not quite like acronyms, do we? They *sound* like swearing.

MARIGOLD *knows herself to be nice: that is, good not because of anything she does, but by being of-the-good.*

HOME SECRETARY: The Director of Public Prosecutions, mother, hates it when I try to undo the work of the Crown Prosecution Service. "Don't speak to me of Justice," she says in her bossiest voice, "what obtains is Reputation." Then if I persist she *leaks*. Then there are questions in the House: "Is the Home Secretary soft on crime?" And *then* there are Speculations.

MRS LITTLEJOHN *clicks her tongue at another not-nice word.*

But with MacPharlain gone, no one will care. I can have those prisoners let go *on the sly*.

MRS LITTLEJOHN *doesn't enjoy the idea of anyone's leaving prison*: All of them, Martin? Should we not keep a few?

HOME SECRETARY: I don't imagine *any* of MacPharlain's convictions are safe.

MRS LITTLEJOHN (*crisply*): Thoroughly pleasant people, Martin, never fall into the hands of the police in the first place.

HOME SECRETARY (*rising*): That's nonsense, Mother. The police are idle and imbecile, they arrest at random. And the D.P.P. is a ravenous omnivore.

MRS LITTLEJOHN (*reestablishing her authority*): Nice little boys don't say such things

– *at which the* HOME SECRETARY*'s baby-badger features crinkle in the most extraordinary fashion. It's his mummy-face, more or less; but with eyes squinched, left cheek hollowed, chin clenched, and other savage nuances. Anyone but a parent ("Martin tells his mother everything, the poor dear") would be able to read this expression. He's wondering if he dare slip the police an anonymous tip-off about Class A drugs in his mother's mansion flat. Or bomb-making equipment. Or Koranic tracts. Or underage Dirt …. Of course he'd get her out before any real damage was done, broken cheek-bones say. But meanwhile it would be salutary for her to have a taste of police custody. The way she fawns on Chief Constables at Home Office coffee-mornings! Pressing her pineapple cake on them, commiserating with them about unkind journalists! If only he dared ….*

HOME SECRETARY (*putting the happy vision aside*): Well *this* little boy has to go and take Measures. I need to get the Ministry of Justice to start "springing" prisoners. Before the news gets out of a nasty suicide on the Queen's Division bench. I will see you –

*Like any good parent,* MRS LITTLEJOHN *knows how much independence her child is ready for. Marty can commission assassinations now and then if he must (niceness being hereditary, invulnerable to deed even in the second generation). He can even take 'phone calls from ladies in the middle of the night, so long as they're police ladies. He still has to eat, on command.*

MRS LITTLEJOHN: *Not* until you have finished your luncheon.
HOME SECRETARY (*firmly*): My so-called lunch has gone cold.
MRS LITTLEJOHN (*with terrible emphasis*): Sit –
MARTIN: Cold.
MRS LITTLEJOHN (*shutting her eyes, almost whispering*) down –
MARTIN (*less firmly*): Coldish.
MRS LITTLEJOHN: *now.*
MARTIN: *Please,* Mummsie, it's choking me.
MRS LITTLEJOHN (*opening her eyes and deploying the same dire molasses voice she used to announce his father's death fifteen years ago: "Now we two only have each other in the whole wide world"*): Lambikin! *Is it?* Very well. We shall turn your root-vegetables into a nice hot stir-fry. You can look forward to that all afternoon. You will have it on brown rice for supper and eat it all up and say thank you. Yes. But *now* you need to wash down luncheon with your lovely barley-water. You know it keeps you regular.
IN-HAND LITTLEJOHN (*stricken*): Mummsie!

*He tries to rise but she locks eyes with him.*
    *After furious wrestling, her gaze prevails. His eyes drop. He sinks back into his seat.*
    *And she, gaily, from a bottle with a smirking golliwog on the label (she shakes it first, to stir the sediment), pours him a dilute sludge so brown it might have been distilled from the banks of Thames: a dense liquid which gurgles, glugs –*

## vi.

*– which, Cana-wise, begins to clarify as we watch: to shimmer, to glow, to sparkle, bubble, foam, crackle, froth; to become, in fact, a cascade of cham-*

*pagne, tumbling from its dark bottle-mouth into a tall glass flute.*

The champagne flute is etched with a design of capering satyrs, and as the golden tide rises it rounds out a translucent satyr, bringing him to equivocal life. He ceases to be scratches on crystal, but takes on three dimensions, the colours of life: dark-brown devil-hoof tinted by the table-top, chestnut fetlock, shaggy blond thigh, sunburnt chest, amber bearded face turned outward, lively with bubbles, grimacing at us.

Wine pours into a second glass, arousing another half-animal satyr, who chases a half-naked nymph round the curve. She silently shrieks in mock dismay and flees, running after another satyr (we see him in profile, from behind, through the swirling wine); he pursues a second nymph, chiton still in place, who stretches before herself her lovely arms, foreshortened by the bend of the glass, toward the first satyr. She never gains on him, nor quite eludes the second satyr; yet seems content.

Pulling back from these immortals, we realise that we've not just experienced a change of bottle. The glasses sit a different table-top (round; handsome bare walnut). We're in a different room, in fact in a restaurant. We read its name back-to-front in the looking-glass over the bar:

## ꓘUAGLINO'S

Through the plate windows, we watch the pleasing bustle of St James on a misty day. When the double doors open, fog, thick as at breakfast-time, billows in to play tricks with the lighting. But outside it isn't as it was: it seems more brightly lit. Some hours must have passed. The invisible sun must be higher in the invisible sky.

Or perhaps (I don't know) one simply gets a better quality of haze in St James.

It is still, of course, grey. But "grey" covers a score of things: silvered-night, tarnished-silver, near-black like pepper, off-white like salt; the grey of cinders, pewter, shadows, grizzled hair, pearl, lead, mouse-fur, slate, and liver pâté left too long in the fridge. The "grey" view out of this window is as opulent and austere as a black-and-white movie, the sort of movie that makes the eye dread returning to the jarring tedium of outdoor Technicolor.

A third flute fills with champagne. THE WAITER (black clothes, long snowy apron, craggy cheek-bones, silky moustache; a credit to Quaglino's) twists the bottle cunningly. A single drop is libated on the walnut. He crunches the bottle into a zinc bucket on a stand and vanishes.

Three well-kept right hands each reach for a glass.

The three lucky people attached to the hands, sitting together around the table, are (once we get used to the tasteful dimness of the restaurant) familiar.

THE YOUNG WOMAN, *free of her nurse costume, looks like, and is, well-*

*bred, beautiful, witty; she's in sober black satin; there's nothing left of the saucy Evangeline.*

*The* BOY, *in good white shirt and excellent tweed jacket, takes us a moment longer to recognise. But then we notice the green eyes we saw hovering in the taxi mirror.*

*The man, in his mid-thirties, although he's doffed his carroty wig, has changed least. He's certainly the* PURPORTED LUBBOCK: *still in the same suit, still, alas, with a taint of medical manners.*

*They clink and say at once*

THE EX-DOCTOR: Cheers!    THE EX-CABBIE: Bums up!    THE EX-NURSE: *Santé*

*and drink,* THE EX-CABBIE *perhaps a bit much for one mouthful.*

*A pause, while each conspirator glances at the other two faces, and finds himself.*

*The three of them are pleased with themselves, yes: they're merry, they're inclined to be rowdy. So much for surfaces.*

*Like all self-congratulation, their self-congratulation is compounded of different impulses, impulses which are not necessarily idiotic.*

*The two young people are quietly overwhelmed at having taken a human life.* THE EX-NURSE *is too sane to be quite at ease,* THE EX-CABBIE, *a decent youth, hardly knows himself in his new* rôle.

*Even the cold-hearted* EX-DOCTOR *is too fastidious to take such a homicide in his stride.*

*They are at pains to keep these misgivings out of each other's view.*

THE EX-NURSE: Now, listen, Felix: this is official. A declaration by your apprentice.

FELIX: Hm?

THE EX-NURSE: I don't care what jobs you take me on. You can play doctor whenever you like. I'm never again being a drug-popping killer-nursie-pooh. You enjoyed it far too much.

FELIX: You were *very* good.

THE EX-NURSE: Well yes I was.

FELIX *(leering)*: Margot was wonderful, Ollie. Savage.

OLLIE VANE-POWELL: Sorry I missed it. Now as to me. My irresistible –

FELIX: The harrowing symptoms! The way she improvised! Hissing "paralytic stage" – ah!

MARGOT: By the way, *does* claryosis exist? We made it sound plausible.

FELIX: No, I invented it.

MARGOT: Pronghorns sound implausible, yet there they were in that horrible textbook.

FELIX: Exactly.

MARGOT: I don't imagine MacPharlain had ever heard of them. He'd certainly never cast his eyes on one, indecently or otherwise. But he believed. Mere nothings killed him.

OLLIE (*dreamily*): Poetry killed him. I slew a judge with poetry. I lullabied him to death – working, of course (*he bows to* CULPEPPER) from a masterful libretto –

MARGOT: I helped concoct that libretto, boy-child. Anyway, the effective bits were Shakespeare –

*But* OLLIE*'s lost interest: he's staring all about Quaglino's while emptying his glass.*

*The décor's silver and pearl, the lighting so low the air resembles a diffuse ore. Banquettes and round tables recede into obscurity, a mezzanine hangs overhead, the walls are invisible: there's a curious sense of space unbounded, upward as well as outward, in which cutlery twinkles, and glassware. Hazy silhouettes, vague figures in dark clothing, move about in the luminous argent murk, or sit, haloed by their table-lamps. It's impossible anyone can be unhappy in such an atmosphere. Quags is to London what the New Jerusalem is to eternity. Ollie beholds a blessèd multitude which no man can number, gathered out of all kindreds and peoples in every affluent postcode, from Kensington & Chelsea, from Chiswick and Kew, from as far off as Hampstead and Richmond.*

– whereas (*continues Margot, unpleasingly*) *I* thought of the feeding-tube on my own. The horror that pushed him over the edge.

OLLIE (*returning from his survey*): *I* pushed him –

CULPEPPER (*bored at a contest not centred on himself*): Y'know, I'd like to dispatch someone with a feeding-tube. Some fat villain. I'd hold him – *we'd* hold down, pour in thickshakes. Half-an-hour. Ruptures begin. Convulsive gagging, heart failure. Don't think there'd be much evidence. Minimal bruising at the wrists, no one would worry about that. Killed by pure appetite –

OLLIE (*who's very young*): Dr Culpepper, Dr Culpepper! Champers is all very well but I'm painfully hungry.

CULPEPPER: God yes, sorry. Shall we begin with lots of oysters? We can look at menus once the medical emergency's abated.

*He gestures expansively for* THE WAITER, *who comes back, not particularly liking this table.*

MARGOT: Are there any oyster-human zoönoses? I mean, can an oyster give us venereal diseases?

CULPEPPER: Don't think so. Only intestinal ones.

OLLIE: Even if you fuck it?

CULPEPPER: It's probably not that sort of restaurant. (*To* THE WAITER, *whose haggard smile has remained in place*): *Vogliamo ostriche, per favore!*

THE WAITER (*refreshing glasses*): Yes sir. A dozen Colchesters each?

OLLIE: To begin with. God it gives me an appetite, committing murder.

*This is said with bravado, loud enough to be overhead by the departing* WAITER – *who merely raises his eyebrows. It's a remark uttered surprisingly often at Quaglino's.*

*Besides, this waiter has the air of a father confessor. It's a common waiterly look; it explains why, contrariwise, good priests remind us of butlers. Although reoccupied with terrible foreknowledge, a confessor-waiter remains attentive to each of us as we appear huddled beneath him. He perceives the inevitable worst, yet judges us worthy of being fed; he pronounces the formula of absolution, "I will bring it at once, sir" or "madam", as the case may be, and retires. Just as*

THIS WAITER *does now*: Yes, sir

– *and he's gone.*

*But* MARGOT *is only recently enrolled as a professional assassin. It's just two weeks since she buried Motte at Gualachulain. She's not yet* blasé *about the word "murder". She frowns.*

MARGOT: Little one, you've done nothing of the sort. It's not clear you broke any law *at all.*

OLLIE (*mock-pompously*): I operated a hackney-cab without a license.

MARGOT: Trifling. It's Mr Singh who'd be in trouble. For renting out his taxi for – for how much?

CULPEPPER (*his attention on the wine*): Just a hundred and twenty quid. And he'd have taken less. (*He's outlining a nymph with his forefinger.*) "O sir it is a most hateful thing to drive in such weather, you are altogether welcome to it."

OLLIE: Damn Mr Singh. *I* incited a suicide.

MARGOT: I don't imagine that's illegal. Whereas I, *I* pretended to supply 120 milligrammes of a class C drug, to a member of the judiciary, too. Poisoning by placebo. And *Felix* broke into a doctor's surgery, very neatly –

CULPEPPER, *using his non-champagne-holding left hand, mimes the delicate probing of a door-lock with a long cunning implement*

– *very* neatly. We were off the premises again before quarter-past-eight. Still quiet as a crypt.

CULPEPPER: Oh, we were quite safe at Number 5. Their specialty's sex-change, which no one wants to discuss before ten.

*He speaks absently, holding his glass obliquely, looking through the satyr and the wine to the nymph, and through the nymph to* OLLIE. *What would Ollie be like as a girl?*

So it opens late.

*What would* MARGOT *be (he peers at her through his flute, as through a lorgnette) made male?*

I knew we'd not be interrupted.

MARGOT: In short, *we* practised medicine without a license. Which is certainly a crime. *You* just chatted to a passenger over your shoulder.

OLLIE: I was the Pied Piper. Piped him to a cleft in the mountainside. In he danced.

CULPEPPER: Ollie, as we know, is a great artist –

OLLIE *lightens at this.* MARGOT *darkens; makes a superior face, empties her glass; her nymphs go back to being mere scratched lines. She's fond of Ollie, but there are more important things at stake here than friendship. She's secure enough as Felix's mistress, but has only just been made his journeyman, and isn't certain he values her cunning so much more than he values Ollie's.*

OLLIE, *who's a curiously pleasant youth given the circumstances, doesn't care about all that, but enjoys needling Margot.*

FELIX, *who's sometimes curiously unpleasant, is amused by the manœuvres of this conversation.*

CULPEPPER: They're here!

THE WAITER *has returned. He lays three oval silver chargers of glittering crushed ice. On each charger lie a dozen opalescent shells; within each shell is plump glistening grey flesh, not quite still. It's as if the varied hues of the fog have taken solid form.*

OLLIE *is rapacious and, as is proper in a great artist, does not wait to see if Grace will be said.*

THE WAITER *empties the champagne bottle and raises one of his mobile melancholy brows at* CULPEPPER.

CULPEPPER: Oh yes. *Another* of these. And then –
MARGOT: Lobster.
OLLIE (*in the Olympian state that follows one's first bivalve of the day*): The girlie speaks truth.
CULPEPPER: Lobster tortellini for us all. With a bottle of Meursault –
MARGOT: Two.
CULPEPPER: A magnum of your nicest Meursault. And then – other things.

THE WAITER *goes. Once his back is turned, his face begins to work, as he contemplates hours more of serving these noisy people. (This altering face doesn't mean he's a hypocrite. He's two people, waiter and man, and the vocation is greater than the individual, although sometimes merely human weariness shows through.)*

CULPEPPER: It would be wrong for the Home Office, which is lunching us, to console our Post-Traumatic Stress with less than five courses. Don't you think?
OLLIE (*in the Zeus-like state that follows one's third bivalve*): The Fellow and Tutor in Classics utters a true word.
MARGOT: Oysters, pasta, sole, salad, venison.
OLLIE: The second-year classicist utters falsity, five's not enough. Six: we'll need something heavy for pudding. To cancel out the devouring fog....
MARGOT (*fruitily, semi-Scottishly, in imitation of MacPharlain*): "De-*vourr*-ring."
OLLIE (*who's still getting used to the idea of being a great artist*): A pity, on reflection, you pretended to drug 'im. That was a mite gross. Physical, you see –
MARGOT: Not. A placebo –
OLLIE: A physical *absence*. It lacked *finesse*. I did the killing without any physical props. To a poet, the soul –
CULPEPPER: Good God – look at *this*.

*"This" is* A NERVOUS FIGURE, *in perfunctory disguise of shabby hat pulled low and sunglasses, weaving his way through the tables. He's clumsy because he can barely see.*

   *He's not what Quaglino's looks for, even at weekday lunchtimes.* THE WAITER *tries to intercept him – but* CULPEPPER *expansively gestures toward the stray, and* THE WAITER *goes to get another chair, sighing visibly once his back is turned.*

CULPEPPER: Home Secretary!

LITTLEJOHN *makes deprecatory twitches with his finger as if to signal*

"*Quietly, quietly!*", *but it doesn't matter, no other table heeds.*

*Behold on the banquette behind us the* CARDINAL-ARCHBISHOP OF WESTMINSTER, *plotting with* THE CHAIRMAN OF THE FOOTBALL ASSOCIATION. *Behold* GILES SHILSON, *greatest municipal politician of the age, hosting a rowdy party of aldermen on the mezzanine.* ZOË MOXGRAVE *is lunching alone, on baked potato and Vichy water, also with sunglasses on.* KATE BECKINSALE *is solo too, in a back corner, turning the pages of an "original treatment." (We can make out the title,* Worrals of the WAAF; *somehow we know she won't get the part; too old; too old.) None of these people feel any interest in* LITTLEJOHN; *Quags does better than him on its quietest days.*

*Only* CULPEPPER *cares, rising negligently to his feet, removing* LITTLEJOHN's *hat and shades, thrusting them into the* WAITER's *empty hands, saying airily:* Welcome, sir! We know who you are. These, these are my henchmen. Henchchildren. That one's Lady Margot ffontaines-Laigh. This is Master Oliver Vane-Powell.

MARGOT *(with a brilliant smile copied from her grandmother, a great and terrible hostess):* Home Secretary. You look so much handsomer than in the cartoons. *(For "hench" has rankled.)*

OLLIE *is too taken up with his fifth oyster to care about the "Master", and simply beams.*

HOME SECRETARY *(sitting, performing a half-hearted upright finger-wave; he does not often sit with murderers fresh from the kill):* Er. Well done all round. It seems things are. Concluded.

CULPEPPER *smoothly proffers the second champagne bottle, waggling his other hand for another glass. The retreating* WAITER *(attentive to each wearying nuance of human vanity, human indecision and greed) catches this gesture, and deeply nods.*

CULPEPPER: Kind of you to come in person to say so.
HOME SECRETARY *(while miming a motherly 'Oh no' to the wine):* Yes, thank you, it was the least. Also. I wondered. No no, really no wine. Never at lunch, it's not allow – I mean, allowing for the time it's not what I want.
MARGOT *(faux-tenderly; bending her head toward him):* You want to know *how* we did it, don't you?

OLLIE, *whose right hand is dealing with his sixth oyster, taps his chest with his left ring finger to indicate "How* I *did it." No one notices.*

HOME SECRETARY (*dry-mouthed*): If you wouldn't mind.
MARGOT (*more detached*): You want to know how a tough bullying character can, in a couple of hours, be inspired to dispose of himself or indeed herself?

THE HOME SECRETARY *cannot speak; he too leans forward, a wild Orestes-light smoldering in his eyes.*

MARGOT: Who?

*This is so dreadful a question* THE HOME SECRETARY, *after blinking twice, decides he hasn't heard it.*
    *There is no answer, obviously; the question's too terrible to answer, the solution's too appalling to picture. (Although just wait a few more pages.) What's significant is that he understands the question, and therefore has to pretend not to hear. He looks for a moment as if he might cry, and*

CULPEPPER, *coming to the rescue, murmurs*: We can't tell you *how*, I'm afraid. Trade secrets, security matter, professional solidarity, sure you understand. Have you lunched?
HOME SECRETARY (*quickly*): Oh yes

*– but his eyes say, much more noisily, No, no, no.*
    *Poor* LITTLEJOHN! *His statements to the House provoke delight because the Opposition benches know that, even if he remembers to keep his face down and mumble through his order-paper so they can't see his betraying eyes, every lie registers on his forehead, which blushes and pales, blushes and pales.*

Yes. I have.
CULPEPPER (*tempting him*): We're *beginning* with Colchester oysters.
HOME SECRETARY (*eager to think of anything but mothers*): Oysters? (*Suddenly ravished at the sight, at the thought*): Oysters ...! No. That is, I've really had lunch already.

*The way he boggles over* OLLIE *disposing of his eighth makes this claim incredible; even to the straight-forward Ollie.*

OLLIE: They're very good, sir.
HOME SECRETARY: They look – but no, I can't – don't.

*He smiles weakly at Margot, unable to withhold submission from any woman who hurts him. He finds he can't endure her sceptical look and blurts out, candid as a child*:

Shellfish are very much Not-Allowed. Too fattening.
MARGOT: Always? Always-always?

THE HOME SECRETARY, *past shame, nods humbly.*

Then *this* is the day to begin doing what's Not-Allowed.
HOME SECRETARY *(in some pain)*: No – it's a – security matter. If Mummsie finds out – that is *(desperately)* when reporters find out where I've been, and bribes, bribe the staff –

MARGOT *sighs. But presumably she repents of her earlier cruelty, for she turns her blinding smile upward to* THE WAITER *(who's placing a glass flute before* THE TREMBLING MINISTER*), and –*
    *Oh why spell out her gesture? He knows, wretched* WAITER, *he knows. He's heard it all so often, leaning his exhausted face forward to catch evasive particulars, as a priest's forehead leans prone on the grille. He's worn and soon he'll be worn out. He's as corroded as a pipe which for so long has borne humanity's pollutive weakness to the cleansing invincible ocean. But while he lasts he's perfectly shaped for what he must bear. His soul is ideally hollowed, he's subdued to his work.*
THE WAITER *(filling* LITTLEJOHN's *glass, so that more nymphs and satyrs spring to improper life)*: A dozen more for this gentleman, madam?

OUR HERO's *eyes have grown big as poached eggs. If internalised prohibitions are hissing in his ear, he ignores them; even "Mumm" on the label seems not to unnerve him: he says nothing and nearly has the courage to nod.*

MARGOT: Please, yes. And after that, tortellini for him too. But *(she lays her hand on his sleeve)* this is in the way of being a state secret. D'you follow? Should anyone ask –
THE WAITER *(woodenly)*: The Home Secretary enjoyed a single cup of our hydrangea tisane. It clarifies the tract. Very thinning.
THE HOME SECRETARY *murmurs shyly*: Perhaps two. Oh *(clearly he's remembering another house rule)* but they weren't very hot. Hot's bad for one.
THE WAITER: Two cups of lukewarm tisane.
MARGOT *says, wonderfully*: Thank you –

*and the* WAITER *goes, fulfilled.*
    *This is obviously the greatest day of the* HOME SECRETARY's *life.*

*He fills his lungs, lets the air go forth trembling, and, greatly daring, reaches for his bubbly. If only Patricia could see him now!*

*And he pauses. Thoughts of Patricia – and, to be fair, the presence of Margot – remind him of something bad boys told him at school. About champagne and oysters being Stirring. Don't they, to use plain language, incite Urges?*

*He was spanked for kissing Denise Combwell. That was odious. Not once since then has he contemplated the possibility of Dirty Carryings-On. Now he dares. "Might I speak to black-haired black-eyed Patricia? Might I?" Frantic images play across the cinema-screen of his face: pleasure, freedom, his own room. (*MARGOT *watches his face, decipherable as a billboard.) "Might I?" Then, out loud,*

THE HOME SECRETARY *gasps*: Oh!

*– for he's seen what's etched on his glass. As he twirls, it comes to life, like an old-fashioned zoetrope: satyr rushes after nymph rushes after satyr, woozily because the hand that spins them quivers. He sips. And it's as if he's imbibing the Attic frolic, as if he can taste the whole glade: oleander and myrtle, cypress, pine, warm skin, warm earth. For the first time in his life* MARTIN LITTLEJOHN *is approaching rapture.*

*Oblivious to all this,* OLLIE*'s been busily eating, and* CULPEPPER*'s been tapping at his Blackberry.*

CULPEPPER: Fame, children! Our romp has reached the newsfeeds. "EURO-STAR MAKES EMERGENCY STOP IN PURFLEET."
MARGOT: Purfleet? That's a long way east of our bridge, isn't it?.

*The* HOME SECRETARY *replies through wine-wetted lips, peering into his glass, apparently counting the bubbles, awed at the number*: It is.

OLLIE, *who first bibbled at three, for whom champagne is obvious as bathwater, watches him benignly, uncomprehending.*

*The driver (his voice has slowed and gone down an octave. He speaks as might a soul obliged to descend from bliss to earth to address a sinner in a vision)* took a mile to apply his brakes. Startled I suppose. That splash of gore over his vision made – ah!

*For* OLLIE *has made a little noise, shutting his eyes to consume his last Colchester oyster, letting it rest an instant on his outstretched tongue.* LITTLE-

JOHN *watches, watches, his features slackening into his "mummy-face."*

CULPEPPER: So no identification yet?
HOME SECRETARY: Hm? What? (*How avid is the human spirit! Although be-mused with champagne-joy, he's already glancing here and there to see where his own oysters may be; and at the same time thinking "I will speak to Patricia, I will! In the Small Conference Room on corridor IV where Mummsie never comes.")* Identification? No, not for hours. Apparently he's a dreadful mess. Oh!

*– his own Colchesters have arrived.*
    *They seem to him (and his face projects the thought) ravishing-be-cause-obscene, obscene-because-ravishing, ravishing-because-obscene. He's muddling sex and oysters, so luridly that* MARGOT *has to shut her eyes.*

THE WAITER (*with a straight face*): Hydrangea-petal tea, sir.
HOME SECRETARY (*his temples engorged with blood*): Oh …. *Yes please.*

*Unctuously, with sacerdotal dignity,* THE WAITER *lays the silver ice-plate before him.*
    *Distractedly, clumsily, gazing at his molluscs as a teenager might gaze as his girlfriend strips for the first time,*
HOME SECRETARY *murmurs, reverent, concupiscent, confused, and as from far away*: A wonderful. I mean dreadful mess. MacPharlain. Still scraping up. Smashed to little bits, splashed everywhere. Twigs. Underside of the overpass. A baby-carriage –

*And he hesitates, serious as Our Lord might have been at the instant of select-ing Peter; resolves on the podgiest of the twelve; pauses once again; anoints his choice with fiery Tabasco, in imitation of Ollie. Visibly, it wriggles.*
    LITTLEJOHN's *forehead is flushed, his eyes soft with passion, the corners of his mouth loose with desire. He reaches solemnly for his chosen oyster.*

When my own time comes, I'd prefer to go in one piece. Like *this* fellow.
CULPEPPER: Quite. A total zoön

*– but we pay no attention to this feeble remark because suddenly, horrifically, we're witnessing lunch from the oyster's point of view.*
    *We see* LITTLEJOHN's *Brobdingnagian fingers descend on us, not quite steady, and over the scalloped edge of our shell behold his appalling flat planet of a face.*

*This is his first oyster, which is an event in life to be sure. But it's equally the oyster's first Home Secretary, its first person, its first outing beyond the paradise where it has lived, feasted and gloried ever since that primordial afternoon in August 2008, when it fixed itself on sturdy rock near Wivenhoe and reared battlements of nacre.*

*Here is a solitary zoön in which no fault can be found. Within its walls it has lived in ecstatic plenty, knowing neither disease nor want. Never has agonising grit provoked the specious artistry of pearl. Best of all, it has committed no thought, endured no emotion. In silence, interior as well as external, it has performed its epic feats. Has not this single oyster drunk forty thousand gallons of the North Sea? Has it not metamorphosed from male to female and back many times, as the seawater cooled and warmed, wamred and cooled, without any expensive aid from Harley Street? Has it not spilled five hundred million eggs, sperm beyond count?*

*These glories lie behind it. Half a minute ago, in the Quaglino kitchens, it was invaded (or rather, she was invaded; at present it's a she) with a shucking knife. The knife severed her adductor muscle, prised off her vault. Now, slowly, slowly, we see* LITTLEJOHN's *unattractive lips open for – such is our solidarity with the poor oyster – us.*

*His less-than-perfect teeth part. We enter his warm maw, we bounce over his epiglottis. We slither kayak-wise down his gorge, whose hot walls flex and constrict us. Ahead, dimly, like the roar of fatal rapids, we apprehend, a pit of hydrochloric acid, of anguish and obliteration: the stomach.*

*The final sphincter parts. Uttering a silent shriek of despair we're though. "The thing which I greatly feared is come upon me." We plummet.*

*Absolute darkness, not absolute silence. Dull churning of the stomach: ceaseless idiot rumble. Is this our end?*

## *vii.*

*After an incalculable time, a sudden sound. An eructive sound, sending us careering upward, from pitch blackness into dark crimson œsophagus, ascending volcanically. A sound that bursts through the teeth and emerges into – air – daylight. Resurrection! Not, indeed, of the oyster's body, but of its pneumatic essence, its flavour, and some of its chemistry. In short, a burp.*

*The burp has landed us before the common face, now distinctly green, of* MARTIN LITTLEJOHN, M.P.

*Pulling back, we find we're outdoors, in almost a different world. Dimness and stillness are gone. The weather has changed utterly; autumn of mists has given way to autumn of bright wind. Friday's lustrous monochrome is blasted away. A tremendous breeze flings wrecks of cloud back and forth about a pale sky. Even the gaunt sunlight is buffeted, the sun itself seems scarcely fixed in place. Hills are plucked like strings. Trees writhe, each creaking at a different pitch.*

*In the middle of this diverse movement, slumped, propped up by the wind, sways* THE HOME SECRETARY, *in billowing dark suit and black tie, sickly face momentarily distended, as is the way with belches.*

*He suffers, he has suffered; there is no reason for suffering of one sort or another to end. The first oyster of* LITTLEJOHN's *life, which will undoubtedly be his last, represented a crisis. It was an event in Cabinet history.*

*He sinned at lunch on Friday, 22nd November 2013, and was stricken by teatime. (I need hardly say the fault was not with Quaglino's – that is unthinkable – nor the shellfish itself, not even his own mollycoddled innards; it was Littlejohn's jittery conscience that undid him.)*

*Now, on Monday, we can review in his too-legible features all the grisly proceedings of the weekend just ended: pukings, writhings, penitence – too late, too late! – groans, squeaks; whimperings as Friday night stretched into Saturday morning; pathetic daylit "Mummsie make it stop!"; yet more pathetic "I'll never do to again!"; her soft infernal murmur in the still first hours of Sunday "Another now my precious", "Mummsie no, NO" as she kneels on the back of his knees, dawn just advanced enough to show in silhouette the copper nozzle. We can still make out the nozzle, etched in* LITTLEJOHN's *mind, therefore in his face; as we can detect scales on prehistoric reptiles who died, fangs locked in each other's neck, sprawled in soft fossilising mud. We can read too the aweful patience of her voice leaning over him, dabbing with a wet warm cloth, on Sunday noon, with the worst over: "My own little Marty-bird will never ever again forget what his dear Mummsie-wummsie says" – the cloth is wrapped 'round his ear – "about food and drink (drink!)" – it's worked into a noose – "or about anything" – it gets a sharp twist – "will he?" "No, Mummsie!" "And no more nocturnal 'phone calls without Mother present. And as for that uncultured creature you call a Personal Assistant – ."*

*She was comparatively gentle with her boy: only when the spasms abated did she actually start to berate. "Lunch twice in the same day! With wine, too! Foreign wine! Ministers have resigned for less." Since Sunday evening she's been at him almost without pause, while he has said "Yes Mummsie" and "I'm unspeakably sorry" in a smaller, smaller and smaller voice. It's now the midst of Monday morning, and the end is not yet.*

MARIGOLD LITTLEJOHN *stands to the right, a little behind her son. Despite her renewed empire over him, she does not look regal. Just at the moment she looks a proper fright and knows it. Beneath her dowdy overcoat her ambitious, unfortunate black funeral-dress of beaded taffeta is heaving about like an oil-slick on a stormy sea. Her right hand clamps down her fried-egg of a black hat – .*

*But if she's enraged by the wind, she's still more enraged by the burp. She doesn't hold with burping at funerals, at table, even in solitude; doesn't hold with of any unlicensed relief; grieves to think that animals squat unreproved in unregulated forests, where leaves are allowed to lie unswept, where the wind fells trees unfined. Now she gives this erring Minister of the Crown a pitiless quite undisguised jab in the back with two fingers of her left hand. The wretched boy jerks himself upright, covering his undistinguished mouth with well-gnawed fingers.*

*We pull back and see* PATRICIA, *standing sadly to Littlejohn's left (in a much more successful black dress, a heavy serge dolman barely moving in the breeze). Yes, she reflects miserably, observing the jab: Mummsie's got Martin in hand once more. Perhaps for good. Two years of rebel advance in the Littlejohn ménage have been wiped out. Patricia lifts her eyes in despair to the bouncing clouds.*

*There's a black coffin before us, a minister of religion at its foot, and a knot of mourners to one side, most of them long-skulled and tall, evidently MacPharlain kinsmen.*

*The background opens: mossy sobbing angels, off-white crockets and obelisks; family vaults like large kennels, miniature Trojan temples, tiny Gothic cathedrals, pagodas; brickwork colourful and strident as a quilt, yellow, faded crimson, blackened; mottled marble, mossy sandstone; leaves of many clashing shades dancing on the tombs; yew-trees whipping about; everywhere weeds. We're in a municipal cemetery of the High Victorian variety: in fact, Kensal Green.*

*The sky's half-a-dozen sorts of shifting pale blue, washing the scene with half-a-dozen sorts of pale light. The black figures standing around the massive black coffin appear to fix the swirling colours. The coffin itself seems to stop the whole flimsy pastel scene blowing away.*

*Abruptly* THE PRESBYTERIAN MINISTER *says* Amen, *ending his long extemporised prayer, its unconvincing, unconvinced words lost, swept away by the nor'wester.*

*He snaps shut his black book, peers at the coffin, shakes his head a trifle obviously, all too clearly meditating on Presbyterian dogma, on Sentence Passed before the Foundation of the World, on Predestination to Dishonour and Wrath. He shakes hands with* THE WIDOW: *a perfunctory shake, awkwardly making no contact beyond the second knuckle. He nods at the* HOME SECRETARY *even more curtly (for he too heard the burp), turns, and is gone. He has seen things more-or-less decently done and earned his fee.*

*The gracious violence of wind pursues him. Leaves scuttle along the path before him in phalanxes, like truant schoolchildren, like prisoners suddenly freed from gaol for no obvious reason.*

*This is the cheery moment at burials, even the burial of overt suicides, after the clergy push off and before the hovering gravediggers get to work. Humans-as-such are briefly back in charge.*

*In the sudden lightening of mood* LADY MACPHARLAIN's *looks about graciously. Her handsome bony form goes very well in its long black dress and heavy overcoat. Her veil is pinned to ripple sensibly in the breeze; her face is poised, enigmatic as a porcelain mask. She might be enduring the grief that scoops out the mind and leaves a psychic cavity, or she might not.*

*In any case, with the dreary Minister gone, the mourners are all at once her guests. She has suddenly become a hostess, and says to everyone, as they line up to kiss her cheek or hold her hand –*

SOPHY MACPHARLAIN: There's lunch at one at the Reform Club. Won't you come?
THE MOURNERS *(severally)*: Of course, Sophy – and we so very sorry, Thank you, Sophy, We'll talk there, Yes, Yes

*and so saying fade into the labyrinth of Kensal Green Cemetery, grasping hats and scarves against the gusts, dwindling into inconsequentiality, becoming like minute ambling figures at the edges of a tapestry, indistinct between the mossy urns and untidy gesticulating trees – vanishing at last, poignantly, without indignity, as they too are doomed to vanish into death itself, one day.*

*Meanwhile* MARTIN *lingers beside the coffin, wondering about spiritual etiquette toward those one murders. He can't decently pray for MacPharlain, can he? No. But ought he to farewell him secularly, or infernally, lost soul to lost soul? – "So-long then, Julius, sorry about Friday, it hurt me more than it hurt you"? (What with the oyster pangs, and Mummsie's renewed domination, this seems to the Home Secretary no more than the truth.) Or should he –*

*But as usual he doesn't get to decide. His parent fixes him by the elbow and steers him to* THE WIDOW.

SOPHY MACPHARLAIN: Home Secretary. Thank you for your kind words earlier *(and indeed his address at the Temple Church – "sad, sad, unexpected circumstance" – had poured emollescence on waters the Minister had churned by clumsily referring to "Julius, our brother called forth from this world, so suddenly taken from us")*. Will you be joining us at lunch?
LITTLEJOHN: Dear Lady MacPharlain, you are –

MARIGOLD: No. (*She's not even trying to disguise the lie of the land. This ungrateful lamb tried to crush her with his so-called independence. He deserves little consideration.*) You are kind but he must get back to the Home Office – mustn't we? (*giving her son's arm quite a nasty jerk with that hand not clapped to her hat*). Goodbye.

*Unresisting, beyond shame,* MARTIN *waggles his hands and mouths "Sorry"; his wind-blown* PARENT *bears him away into dishonour and wrath. Her face is congealed with unexpended abuse, for she's had the funeral and burial to think of fresh remarks about Friday lunch, about Martin's debauch, his unspeakable West End debauch – unspeakable, unspeakable. She can barely wait until they're out of earshot of the corpse to resume her barracking of this future Prime Minister, through whom she will soon, she hopes, scold the whole kingdom.*

ARCHIE DRAKE *watches the Littlejohns depart, amused, massive, rather imposing in a three-piece black tweed with jolly grey stripe. We're surprised to find him here. Well, he's surprised himself. He isn't the type to play the old family doctor and attend the burial of patients (unless he suspects he killed them). He has the air of a man who has been unexpectedly summoned; which is the case.*

*Indeed he now conducts himself as a privileged person, waiting until the last mourner has departed and* LADY MACPHARLAIN *is left alone with her first husband. Or rather with coffined scraps and smears of him; we can hardly regard these morsels as a body, a consolidated zoön.*

DRAKE *stands obedient, expectant, his swift blue eyes out of place in such a huge animal body. Today their cleverness is unveiled. He's thrown off his usual pose as a bluff yokel.*

SHE, *parodying the bridal gesture without making a thing of it, loosens her veil and lifts it back over her head. Barefaced, she turns to* HIM *and smiles: a perfectly simple, intelligent smile of welcome. And he smiles back.*

*These two are not in the least ridiculous, although well past forty and therefore beyond the usual sympathies of literature.*

HE *offers his arm.* SHE *takes it. Without any foolish prattle they both realise they will marry each other at Whitsun.* THEY *walk off through the dead toward the waiting cars, without glancing back at the box containing the atoms of MacPharlain.*

*Which have, however, not quite been left alone.*

PATRICIA *didn't go back to the Home Office with the Littlejohns because she no longer works there. She has been sacked as Martin's P.A. – that is, exiled to the Department for Culture, Media & Sport. He informed her of her "secondment with immediate effect" in the car on the way to the cemetery, with his mother, sitting beside him in the back seat, interrupting now and then to sharpen his remarks. Patricia watched them go, failed lover, trium-phant enemy, and has been biding her time since then, sheltering behind a massive ivy-choked mausoleum guarded by two sphinxes.*

*Now she emerges and stands over the coffin. A little whirlwind of beech-leaves, gay as nuptial confetti, comes to grief on MacPharlain, strewing his coffin-top with scarlet. Patricia brushes them off with the back of her black-gloved hand.*

THE GRAVEDIGGERS, *off on the horizon so to speak, discreetly hold back. They are used to the appearance of youthful mistresses after the legitimately bereaved have departed.*

*How wrong they are. For all her aggressive hair, dress and lipstick (today battleship-grey),* PATRICIA MAULE *is an amiable person at heart, well brought-up. She ended up in the Civil Service through a series of accidents and maintains a sense of decency. No one else seems to care, but it seems to her that Julius MacPharlain really can't go on his way with nothing but a euphemism from the man who had him killed, and cynical prayers from a cleric convinced that he is damned.*

*So*

PATRICIA *says out loud, vocatively:* Ahem
*– then pauses, shy.*

*(The gravediggers are out of range and besides, the wind blows her words away. But it is to be imagined that the angels on the mossy Victorian tombs are pricking up their stone ears.)*

*Patricia's "preferred mode of expression", as they say in Whitehall, is writing intradepartmental memoranda. That's the only time she feels elo-quent. "But* can *we memorandumise the dead?" she asks herself now, looking a little hopelessly at the coffin. She could write out her talking points, then burn the paper…. "Puerile, puerile," she tells herself; "get a grip."*

*She is after all also famous for chairing* HODBURCS, *Home Office Divi-sional Budget Reconciliation Colloquies, in which despite the name no one is reconciled, and the losing Division usually maintains just this sort of enraged, uncommitted silence.*

*So now, in her best* HODBURC *manner*

PATRICIA *asks:* Are we quorate? Let us *(she drops a hand smartly on Sir Julius' wooden home, as if gravelling him to order)* press on. We have three agendarisations in view, which tend in the opinion of the Chair to focalise. One: there has manifestly been a neo-Mummsian counter-revolution in S. *(that is, the Secretary of State; it's how Littlejohn is referred to at* HODBURCS*).*

This Division queries the viability of internal counter-counter-revolution. Your Chair therefore begins a Section 52 secondment tomorrow at fucking Cult-Meedya-Spor', but that aside it would seems S. owes it to parliamentary sovereignty to be a free man. Yes?

*Whitehall English,* PATRICIA *finds, being so lifeless, eases all the usual embarrassment of addressing the departed. It's perfect for séances. Now she's caught her stride, she can speak to the dead judge with curiously assured fraternity, so slight is the frontier between death and life, so enormous the gulf separating officers of the state from little people.*

*Such as* THE GRAVEDIGGERS, *who are still standing afar off. They're decent chaps who assume the best. They're touched to see the dead man's girlfriend mumbling her farewells.*

It is not for Marigold to make her son P.M. so she can sway England through him. It is for me. Demurs?

MACPHARLAIN *staying mum,*

*this point is carried. The stone angels are mute too, but had they decent feeling, in spite of mossed-over faces and acid-rain pocks, they might well tumble from their perches in horror.*

*Not that Kensal Green hasn't seen rum doings over the years: the steady inward traffic of quarter of a million, with occasional outward body-snatching; Spiritualist carry-on in the day; a little necrophilia and Satanism now and then. Why in 1872, only a few yards off, a lead-lined coffin slipped from the pallbearers' hands and crushed one of the mourners, a rare example of obedience to the precept of letting the dead bury their dead. Now it almost seems that prodigy is to be repeated.*

So minuted. Two: you will know, presupposing that the deceased are "in the loop", how you got here. I do. I listened in on Friday's lunch through the keyhole. "Frightful college, Mother, St Wygefortis', Classics don named Culpepper." I presume this Culpepper, although officially employed, might be "rogue" enough to accept outside commissions made in the name of S. Does the committee concur?

*Patricia has two faces superimposed on each other at the front of her head. There is the bureaucratic one with square jaws, that sets like a bear-trap when contradicted during briefings. And there's the one with a ski-jump nose, the one any right-thinking man wants to kiss. It's never clear which face is moving, the beauty or the gorgon.*

Thank you. Items One and Two seem to your Chair to concentre. Is there any objection to sequitirising? Good, thank you. Our discussion is then conveyed to Three: proceeding, ethical aspect of. The crux, Committee, is this: would Culpepper's fee be governmentally expensible? Is it a legitimate cultural slash media slash sporting outlay?

*– and she actually waits for an answer to this Yes-No question. Silence isn't enough.*

*In a minute she'll be gone and the diggers will get to work. Meanwhile they're happy to wait. The wind is always happy to wait, blowing where it listeth, gambolling many a leaf which cannot enjoy a waltz, being dead. And God knows* MacPharlain's *happy to wait, his days of murderous bad judgment being behind him.*

*Therefore* Patricia Maule *waits, with a look of sedulous patience (on either her whimsical or her earnest face).*

*The watery cold brightness of the day swirls all about her, lonely organism that she is, centred in a waste of eternity and infinity.*

*How does anyone ever decide anything? Most of all, how should Patricia decide, if she really requires a deciding vote to pulse upward to her from the undiscovered country?*

*England's predicament is bad enough; the remedy possibly worse; Patricia has the resolve to carry it off, and the moral strength to refrain. Should she, should she, shouldn't she?*

# VOLUME TWO

A man who thinks a great deal about himself will try to be many-sided. Thinking about himself will lead to trying to be the universe; trying to be the universe will lead to ceasing to be anything. If, on the other hand, a man is sensible enough to think only about the universe; he will think about it in his own individual way. He will keep virgin the secret of God; he will see the grass as no other man can see it, and look at a sun that no man has ever known.

CHESTERTON

# V. Ossifrage:
## *Michaelmas term ends*

'*Deus, qui beatum Nicolaum Pontificem innumeris decorasti miraculis,*' mur-mured Sir Trotsky Plantagenet, cynically, staring out through the mullions of his study, half iced-over. '*Gehennæ incendiis, etcetera, etcetera*' – what was the use? Such language did not connect with realities seen or unseen. It was all very well *saying* "God Who didst adorn the blessed Bishop Nicholas with numberless miracles"; it was all very well asking to be delivered "from the flames of Gehenna" through the saint's intercession. Worthy, sensible words on this Feast of St Nicholas. The fact was, they sounded arch, having for the Master of Wygefortis' College a double meaning.

Today, this 6th December, was also the last day of term. And instead of revering the patron saint of children, here he was watching, with glee, the disappearance of actual children, the children placed under his care. There they went (perdition take them, generally and severally); there they went, out across gusty rainy Cocytus Court, with their suitcases and their trunks. Under the dank bulk of Acheron tower they went, out into dripping Gehenna Court, *Gehennæ incendiis*, through the Lodge and into the world: home, perhaps, or off on skiing trips. Sir Trotsky did not care; so long as it was out, out!

*If only*, he brooded, *if only I could fix in my mind which was worse. Whenever a vacation ends I console myself "Well, at least the worst is over" – the returning undergraduates inhibit the Fellowship's worst impulses. Yet in the last days of every term I find himself saying, as now, "Thank God it's finishing." The student body's my torment, my heart bounds to see them go. Yet in six weeks' time – hypocrite! Hypocrite!*

This Michaelmas now ending had been a term of peculiar nightmare, too, culminating in the scandal of Guy Fawkes night, when he had gone out to sup-press the illegal bonfire *yet again*, and been *once more* overpowered by masked students, who'd forced a spliff between his lips him as he struggled *not for the first time*; and although he remembered nothing and had woken up numb in his own bed, there on the College website was a photograph of himself in a ball-gown of purple and scarlet, perched sidesaddle on a St Bernard dog with its fur dyed a streaky red. On his large forehead someone had written with a mark-er-pen, MYSTERY, BABYLON THE GREAT, THE MOTHER OF HARLOTS AND ABOMINATIONS. This photograph was taken down after a few minutes, but the harm was accomplished. As long as he remained Master of St Wygefortis he would be called, behind his back, The Scarlet Woman.

No, that was optimistic. A worse name would no doubt drive out this one, as "Scarlet Woman" had driven out "Juicy", and before that –.

*Ach! Nothing's fixed in this fallen world. All gets worse – that is, more inau-thentic, oligarchically-hierarchised, sinful.* The Master's former enthusiasm for class-war hashed itself up with his new ideal of promiscuous charity. *Until the revolution of apocalypse.*

Meanwhile, out the undergraduates flowed, past his icy windows and away. St Wygy's, lax in most ways, has remarkably strict laws of residence. Junior members must stay Up until after lunch on the last day of term, must go Down before dinner. Hence this dismal tea-time exodus, thrice a year.

*It resembles*, Sir Trotsky thought to himself (with mild desperation, for it was his duty to go and show himself to the retreating mob, to affect concern, and he was dawdling), *it resembles my idea of fleeing a falling city, hustling refugees, parting of ways, grief. More than the blessèd Day of Judgment.... Is it uncharitable of me to be horrified at the thought of one sacked town, but to pant for the demoli-tion of the cosmos? Perhaps. – Oh dear, I really must go out. No escaping it.*

He gazed down wistfully at his changeless Book of Hours on its carved lec-tern: the sort of book meant not to explain the world, not to improve the world, nor even to solace us for the world, but to replace it. It invited escape. And now, in spite of duty, he stared down at, or into, the present page, the Office for St Nicholas' day, and sighed with pleasure and with longing.

❧

Since the catastrophes of summer, Sir Trotsky had resolved not to be drunk, or at least not much of the time. He was therefore living on the plane of sober sense more than he was used to, and far more than he liked. What a relief, then, to have chanced upon this vast book in the College library, the Worthy-al Book of Hours, miscatalogued, misshelved, perfectly preserved by neglect! The Widdler was ferociously protective of manuscripts, even manuscripts she didn't know she had, so he hadn't dared ask to borrow. He had simply purloined, carrying it back to the Lodgings wrapped in an M.A. gown, rejoic-ing at this new method for annihilating the grey universe.

And after five months his Book of Hours had not let him down.

Every day, often, he would open it and vanish. The staff of the Lodgings, who loathed him, peered round his study-door to find him rapt.

Not that he was lost in prayer. Sir Trotsky, although sincere enough, was no mystic. The intense pleasure he took in his illuminated Hours was simply physical.

Like the laptops to which his students were addicted, the book pretended to be bigger inside than outside – although its outside was bulky enough: a solid-looking quarto, two bronze clasps holding fast leather-bound boards. The leather was grubby with age, heavily filigreed in worn silverleaf, and set with an equivocal agate cameo of Persephone, nude and crowned.

Unclasp. Open. The fly-leaf, soiled and foxed, is signed thrice by the Founder. First, in a tiny fussy boyish gothic hand:

> ego adamm vvorthyalle : clericus :
> collegium petri vulgo peeterhovvse :
> vniuersitas cantabrigiensis : mcccclxxiv

– already, this is unsettling, for in 1474 Worthyal was a lad of thirteen; such a book was an impossibly lavish possession for a poor young clerk, even an ambitious one; he can only have stolen it.

Further down, *adamm archidiacono vvyltes MCDLXXXV*. The writing is now rounder, self-consciously italianate.

Then comes + *Sainte Assaffe* written in gorgeous scarlet ink, although with letters gnarled, askew, tortured; and the name is followed by words from the *Parce mihi*.

> *Lette mee alloone : for mie dayes are nothyngnesse.*
> *VVhat is manne that thov shoold desyre him, & probe himm svdenlye?*
> *VVhy settest thou mee up as thy bullseie*
> > *so that mie beyng encvmbereth itselfe?*
> *Novve j shall sleepe in y^e dust : & thov shalt seeke for mee in y^e mornynge : &*
> *j shall not bee.*

Finally at the bottom we find a reckless note, fortunately never seen by the Widdler or the generations of lazy College librarians before her. It is dated *aeprylle MDXXI*, when the Founder was on his deathbed, and reads: *Thysse booke hadde j in myne hande in y^e tovver of londonn when j slew y^e younge kynge edvvarde & his bruthherre.*

All of which is perfectly loathsome.

But then we turn the appalling fly-leaf and enter glory. In the whole book only one page is damaged, containing the evening Office of Our Lady. Half that leaf is missing, torn out, presumably, in the famous rumpus on the bed when Worthyal saw to the boys. But apart from that one place, we can forget the wicked man. For every page is illuminated, and every page makes us grasp.

Of course the Worthyal Hours speak, as prayer-books must, of grief and sin, forgiveness and solace. But the words hardly seem serious. Within these covers we're already in paradise, so that all such mortal pother lies behind us.

Most of each page is a mass of gold or rose or pale green. There are two-inch margins above and to the side; and the bottom half of each page is given over to riotous decoration. There are life-sized wildflowers rendered so wonderfully it is hard not to try to pick them off their goldleaf background, life-sized butterflies surely about to flutter off into the dim air, singeing it as they passed with burning colour.

Except it is not really a riot, and not just decoration. The miniatures are not even really miniature. The illuminations are serious, as if they have slid into this world from a better one, where such perfect beauty in small things mattered absolutely; so that our eye tries to follow them into the larger realm beyond the edge of the vellum; and the mind almost succeeds.

❧

The Master of St Wygy's, who should have been farewelling his charges, was lost in his big dark book. *Nearly,* he considers, *big enough to be the coffin of a baby. An oblong of processed wood into which a man reborn might perhaps climb to be at peace.*

The black-and-scarlet lettering, *Deus, qui beatum Nicolaum Pontificem* and so forth, is caged in a box to the upper right. To left and below are the bishop's teeming miracles. Here he is going about his diocese (a fairyland of crags, white turrets, waterfalls) alleviating a famine. Here an innkeeper places a stew, *blanquette de veau* more-or-less, before him; but Nicholas, evidently the sort of bishop who lunches in mitre and jewel-encrusted cope, rises in rage, sweeps – .

*Sweeps,* sighs Sir Trotsky. *That's the word. It's hard to think these little pictures are still, that they're marks in coloured ink. They flow into each other so – impossible to resist the illusion of movement – .*

Now Nicholas smashes over the three-legged table with his crozier, storms down to the vaulted cellar. Where a barrel bobs with pickled limbs, very pale. Now the innkeeper rages in the grip of two halberdiers, the bishop's minions lift hands in horror; but three boys rise from the brine, naked and anæmic but apparently in good nick, called back by the saint of children.

Back to life! Sir Trotsky sighs, shuts and clasps his Book of Hours. To work, to work.

❧

He peered into the Court through the wet lozenges of his window. It was a raw cruel day, sodden and lightless.

*Distorting, yes, these old glass panels distort; but just look beyond at the reality!* Slowly as he could he got on his black overcoat, laid across the back of a leather armchair; his black muffler, trilby and gloves. *Here, for instance, are two more scurrying refugees, figures less plausible any painted butterfly, less real surely than the illuminations of my prayer-book. Just dingier, infinitely dingier. The Berberology Tutor and the J.R.F. in Egyptology. Hurrying along in identical furs, each lugging an identical ugly yellow gym-bag. No doubt as eager to avoid me as I'm eager to avoid them. But duty, implacable duty –*

Chyld the butler held open the door for him, shuddering in the cold or simply shaking with decrepitude. *Duty!* The Master stepped into the nasty scouring air.

Cocytus is so small, so cubic, so quaintly bobbly underfoot, so overshadowed by Belial (as Wygians call Chapel) and Acheron (as they call their tower), that it seems more well than court. The sensation of emerging from it, into the relative sanity and spacious of Gehenna, is rather like bursting out of the ground.

The Master so burst, and caught the twins just as they were reaching the Lodge.

'Dr Yoxley! Dr Freke!' he boomed; their nervous little shoulders clenched beneath their coats, they turned, and in fact it was Freke, then Yoxley; he'd confused them from behind – not that it mattered much. 'You're leaving us too?' allowing his voice to become a little dreadful. On the whole he preferred his students gone, but he liked his dons to stay put, where he could keep an eye on them. *It's almost a madhouse in Vac, but at least it's a madhouse in one place.*

'Oh – Master! – we', 'We are!' they said as one, in their trying fashion; then came a twin babble in which Sir Trotsky, half-attentive, caught 'Research,' 'Bishop Auckland,' 'Discovery,' 'Thrill.' (*Bumpitty-bumpitty* all about them went the wheels of undergraduate suitcases over the sopping flagstones.)

'You're doing research at Bishop Auckland this vacation? There is perhaps a Berberological collection at the episcopal palace? I had no notion.' Sir Trotsky's voice was pompous and he knew it. *It's decades of esoteric Marxism, lifting me above the herd; that and knowing myself to be, after all, through bastardy, a Plantagenet. What can I do? Now and then I've the grace to regret how I sound. But not now, not addressing Drs Yoxley and Freke.*

Who babbled further, those freaks, using the agonising method of speaking at once and tripping in and out of each other's thoughts, so that hearing them was like being within a single diseased brain, witnessing electricity hiss and spark along its damaged synapses.

(Meanwhile his charges flowed round and by him through the murk, into the Lodge, forth into the world to dirty it further. He nodded at the comparatively good students, a small minority, Ollie Vane-Powell for instance, and scowled, mildly or severely as seemed proper, at the wastrels, reprobates, criminals.)

The Master was making an effort not to hear Elmo and Olga, so their tale formed luridly in the margin of his own mind without mediation. This seemed to be it:

*In the spring of 1890 the wife of the Examining Chaplain of the Bishop of Durham laid out a shrubbery. Not so terrible? It was though, it was. To begin, she was by all accounts a terrible woman, and manured her guelder roses and snowy mespilus in the most terrible way. For a few months before, at Beni-Hassan in Middle Egypt, an immense pit had been uncovered of mummified cats: tens or hundreds of thousands of them, laid tidily in rows hard together in mass graves, like the human victims of some modern massacre. There were so many cats, rather there was so much cat, capitalism had stepped in, modern England having recently occupied ancient Egypt. Tons of this vile carrion was stuffed into bags and shipped to Liverpool on R.M.S. Pharos, to be auctioned off (it came to £15 7s a ton, or five cats for two farthings, precisely the proverbial rate for sparrows), ground up, and retailed as fertiliser. Leverton & Co. had sold two tons of the stuff to this clerical wife, to Mrs Culpepper –*

'Culpepper!' The Master turned sharply round from condemning or pardoning undergraduates. 'Culpepper, you say.' This was more serious. He was troubled to hear that Yoxley and Freke, despite having got rid of their pet obscenity at the start of term, as he, the Master, had commanded, were still obsessed by cat mummy. But if Felix Culpepper were urging them on –

'Yes, Dr Culpepper told', 'It was his ancestress,' 'He told us about', 'Guilty perhaps,' 'He seemed to feel', 'What happened to Shishak,' 'Family legend that she used cat mummies,' 'Suddenly remembered,' 'We looked it up in 1890 newspapers, all true,' 'Joy –'.

'Yes, but what are you going to *do* in Bishop Auckland? In this parson's garden?'

'Not any more,' 'Sold on,' 'A banker owns it,' 'Ruined,' 'Banker in Florida for Christmas,' 'We'll sneak in,' 'Quiet.'

'But you can't *dig*. It'll be an archæological void. There'll be nothing left after a century in wet English soil.'

'No but,' 'We think' –

'So long,' said a young sunny voice, and Sir Trotsky spun about, outraged, for it was the voice of the most wasted of all College wastrels.

'Mr Hawick Trocliffe!' thundered the Master; 'you absented yourself this morning from your Penal Collections!'

'I wasn't awake,' explained Seb, with his seraphic or animal grin, 'and now I off to St Barts; but merry Christmas all the same, Scarlet Woman!' and once again, as so often in Seb's career, an excess of fury shut the mouth of his enemy until it was too late.

*I'll send him down the first week of next term,* the Master told himself, not for the first time. But meanwhile Seb had sailed through the Lodge and, jumping the queue, into a cab (*en route* to a beach on Saint Barthélemy, where he will hear the surf thud on reef, and the sound will not enter his mind to swill it out).

The archæologists, the Master found, had fled him too. Dimly the idea suggested itself to him: *I, Trotsky Plantagenet, am a tremendous bore people wish to avoid. No, no, not possible….*

Anyway, the flood of Wygians out of College was almost over. He had done his duty. He could return to his study and his illuminated flowers; he could bury himself happily alive in his one great book.

Not yet! There was a hand on him, on his forearm: Dymwood the zoologist, dark-haired Dymwood the vivisector, was pawing at him, and Dymwood's rolling eyes were looking more-or-less into his, rather closer than Sir Trotsky liked, blinking wildly.

The Fellow in Zoology had been released from the Deepdene asylum just a few weeks before. You might think would want to coddle himself body and mind. But he too was dressed for travel, in long padded jacket and mountaineering cap; a back-pack rested against his knee.

'O Master! Master! Master!' The medication that kept Dymwood more-or-less sane made him hopelessly garrulous. Even Woolly was hardly getting a word in on High Table; not that Woolly ever said, or mewked, anything but his one idea, that diverse things were exactly much-of-a-muchness. This one idea was no match for the multitudinous babbling of Dymwood, who was now saying: 'Tibet! I'm off to Tibet! What do you think of that? To Tibet!'

Sir Trotsky was carefully prising Dymwood's splayed fingers off his arm, one by one, and dropping his twitching hand into mid-air. 'I wish you a pleasant –'

'To Tibet! For the ossifrage! What a creature he is – mountain-haunting *Gypaetus barbatus*, you know him? You know him, Master? The great Bearded Vulture?'

'I think –'

'The ossifrage! Hideous-headed, swooping from his lair in desolate heights of the Pyrenees? Or the Hindu Kush, or the plateau of Tibet, or the headwaters of the Blue Nile? It's Tibet I'm going to. For him! Tibet!'

'So –'

'Swoops on wings nine foot wide. Nine foot! Snatches up prey, marmot, not just marmot, rock hyrax, chamois, even ibex, more commonly chamois of course, dropping or battering it over the cliff. Leaves it to decay, to scavengers, because all Mister Ossifrage wants is the broken skeleton.'

*Not* much-of-a-muchness, then, this bird. But could Dymwood possibly

make it to Central Asia and back in his present state? 'Are you sure, Dr Dymwood –'

'Wonderful wonderful Mister Ossifrage! As his name tells us, Master,
Master, as his name tells us. As a fledgling he eats meat but not as an adult, oh
no. He's clever. Lives on bones. Uniquely, uniquely, no one else does, I wish I
could, don't you Master? Master? Because he can, you see, he can, his gastric
acidy is pH1 –¦ fiercer than car batteries. Who is like to the ossifrage, Master?
What things he does!'

This enthusiasm was not like Dymwood; he normally had no attachment
to creatures, merely wanting to hear them scream, if they could scream, or snap
or writhe. Was it simply his drugs? The Master smiled as soothingly as he could.
'So we admire it – him?'

'Yes yes yes yes yes, but we are practical, we have a practical end in view,
don't we, don't we? We mean to get his eggs, that's it, eggs of the Bearded Vulture, and bring them back. That is what we will do this winter. A small breeding
colony up there –' And he thrust a finger at the wet heavy pewter heavens. No,
not the heaven: at the top of squat Lethe tower, on the eastern edge of College.

'The, er, ossifrage is endangered, Dr Dymwood?'

'No! No!' The lunatic nearly snarled, he stamped and waved both arms
about in negation, he turned right about. 'No no *no*. Damn the species, damn
damn damn it. Them, all species, let 'em all go extinct in the wild. *We* mean
to breed an urban race of vultures, don't we? Somewhat miniaturised. Able to
nourish itself just on dogs, on dirty-dirty little little dogs.'

'Dogs?'

'Little dogs don't you hear? Small wheezy dogs carried about by rich selfish
women in mink in Paris. We incubate his eggs, train up his chicks, then the
vultures will be loosed on Paris, on the *Parisiennes*, it will nest on ledges and in
towers, so much for all their little dogs, ha ha! Ha ha then!'

It struck the Master (with a touch of nausea) that Dymwood was a presentable man, by the nightmare standard of dons. *His hair would be a good point,
a darkish mane falling sideways, did he not dye it tarry black. True, his forehead
takes up most of his face, his chin's babyish, his mouth a slit punched through
iron. But his lips' crushed-strawberry shade go well enough with his parchment
skin, and his eyes – glazed to enamel blankness from watching too often too near
the torment of animals – might strike a susceptible woman as pathetic. Yes: overlooking wry-neck and squint, Douglas Dymwood might conceivably have had
some sort of sexual history, that is to say, sexual agony, in his past. Presumably
a Frenchwoman long ago did this to him. For which he means to sprinkle her
city with canine blood. Droplets falling on upturned Parisian faces saying "D'où
vient ce woof-woof?" On gilded domes and the green-and-white striped awnings
of cafés....*

The Master, who was fond of Paris, strove to sound tender. 'You thought up this atrocity to punish someone, Dr Dymwood?'

The snickering was abruptly cut. 'No no, too weird for me, too baroque, yes. It is Felix Culpepper's idea.'

*Culpepper! Again!* All tenderness was gone.

'He told me what to do, he did,' gasped the lunatic with jerky movements, seeing wrath in the Master's face. Fast as he could, Dymwood got his pack on his back, and loped out into Emmanuel Road.

Plantagenet's irritation waxed hot, and he went furiously about his emptying College, trying to walk it off. *Culpepper's making a nuisance of himself! Too many ideas, all bad. A nursery gardener of nasty ideas.* He was in Megiddo now; Culpepper's windows were dark, he could be anywhere. *Enough mischief in hand to furnish a rambling novel. But wastes it, wastes it on his peers.* Abaddon Court. More black empty students' rooms. The freezing damp was getting more intense as the last light failed. *Grows a disgusting notion to seedling-size then passes it to them for nurture. To take out into the world and sow.* Sheol Court. Only the dons' rooms alight: youth washed out. The trees huge, barely visible. *Trouble perpetrated here and there by his little flock, fluttering abroad. At least he sends it outward. 'Course, it may come refluxing back with the new term. It won't do…. But what to do? Didn't he announce he was off himself? To West Africa? Doing best-not-know-what? Well he's finished the College history at last, so good riddance.*

The Master was back in Gehenna now, near the Lodge. *Culpepper gone soon; meanwhile every obstreperous undergraduate gone already. For the life of me I can't decide whether this is even a temporary relief.* He gazed about the court, quite deserted now, almost dark with early December dusk. Its windows were black, heavy with water-logged air – all but one. *Not every one! Not all! I'd forgotten. Damn.*

Lady Margot placed herself above the law, even the law of residence; she came Up and went Down as she pleased. Today she'd airily informed the Bursar – and Sir Rory had nervously passed on the information to the Master – that it was not convenient for her to leave St Wygy's until the evening. Thus her rooms, on the north range of Gehenna, were still lit up, with the warm light of gas-lamps: which was another College regulation outraged.

The Master was in mortal fear of her. *Nothing to do but wait out the evening; then she'll quit the place. And on a larger scale, wait until she stops scaring me. How long, O Lord, how long?*

He stood gingerly under the lamplight in the vicious empty dankness; he stared up, wondering, at her windows.

# VI. Kibobakasi,
## *a third bedroom interlude*

The supreme adventure is not falling in love. The supreme adventure is being born. There we do see something of which we have not dreamed before. Our father and mother do lie in wait and leap out on us, like brigands from a bush. Our uncle is a surprise. Our aunt is a bolt from the blue. When we step into the family, by the act of being born, we do step into a world which is incalculable, into a world which has its own strange laws, into a world that we have not made. In other words, we step into a fairy-tale.

CHESTERTON

Within those lamplit windows was Felix Culpepper, who ought to have been in his own rooms packing. He had in fact come over to say goodbye to Margot and have tea. The two of them had just briskly made love on her floor, below the Rothko pinned to her sloping ceiling, her bed being hopelessly heaped with locked cases, a fur, two hatboxes, and an old-fashioned steamer-trunk already bound with leather straps.

Now they were lying side by side gazing up at her oil.

*In principle* (reflected Culpepper) *love's love, lovers a microcosm. The biblical term's "knowledge": you "know" the woman you make love to, that's that. In practice, surroundings join in. Indeed, the more intense the act, the more the backdrop gets folded into the excitement, pleasure, joy, content. Making love in a copse tells you more about botany than you guessed you could know. You "know" the bark on the trees perhaps more than you "know" your lover. Presumably no one grasps the glory, the horror of flying-machines who hasn't made love in an aeroplane loo – I must try to do this. Just now we've been making love inside an abstract painting. And I'm overwhelmed by what I've just experienced of yellow, of its whites and carnal red.*

Thus Felix. Margot's thoughts were even more remote and self-absorbed. She was to take a late train to Paris, in time for a supper party in *le 16ᵉ ar-rondissement*; then, tomorrow, another train to Munich; finally the sleeper over the Alps to Lake Bled. Above Bled was a rented castle, where there'd be very obsolete furnishing and large fires and slabs of roasted game and red wine and a costumed ball, in the company of young people much like herself only less, less.

Sighing, she rose, smoothed down her skirt and, used a spill to take a flame from her gas-mantle, lit her chafing-lamp; she placed over this her copper kettle with its ivory handle. All this equipment was in various ways taboo, at least in College rooms; as became a scofflaw. The kettle began to hum and rattle; she peered out of her window into Gehenna.

'He's looking up at us.' Her voice was curiously faraway, as if she too were viewing this tawdry muddle of world from within the luminous perfection of Rothko. *Faraway* (thought Culpepper) *but not sad. She's never precisely sad after love. Rather, streamlined: festoons burned away; resolved to her essence, more demanding, more severe.*

'What?' His voice was stupid. 'Looking? Who is?'

'The Scarlet Woman.'

'Oh.'

'The Whore of Babylon.'

'Ah.' Awkwardly he got to his feet, awkwardly re-belted, and struck a pose, bottom balanced against the edge of the steamer-trunk. 'Poor Master.'

He seemed to her a little bewildered. *Perhaps the red stripe in my painting overwhelmed him. He's remembered the oneness of all that pumps blood, all that bleeds. Or at least the alikeness of their suffering. His self-pity's briefly broadened into pity.*

'Why "poor"?'

'He can never decide whether he wants us gone or not – he gets churned up on the last day of term. As do we all.' This was nicely said. The two lovers would not see each other for three weeks. Felix was vaguely "popping over to Africa for a few days," which was eccentric and unexplained. Then, stranger still, he was "spending Christmas with my family in Surrey": his widowed father, husbandless sister, both despised, and six year-old nephew, said to be alarming. He would meet Margot again in the last day of the year in London.

She would have thrown over Bled at a word, and come to help him on his African gig (if it was a gig); but he had rather noisily not said a word.

The water was coming to a boil. 'Africa. Africa.' She'd promised herself she wouldn't ask, but Rothko's candid white had pulled her into itself: why *should* lovers have secrets? 'What are you up to? And *where* exactly are you up to it?'

'Oh – Bomo. Thereabouts.'

'Bomo or thereabout,' repeated Margot gravely, like a child. She was pouring water into a tall Multani teapot. 'No, Felix. While this draws, which takes seven minutes and forty seconds, you're going to explain.' She took her place in the only armchair and pointed to a spot on the floor. 'I want to hear about Africa. At story length.'

'What-what? A story? A story *early in the evening*? Absolutely not.'

'Yes.'

'A story going to sleep's one thing. Even waking, since you insisted. But – not now…. You're trying to hound me out of the real world. Turn me into a mere storymaker.'

'No African story, no lapsong souchong and crumpets,' and here was a set to her face showing she might mean it.

Culpepper considered tea, which was physically important to him: 'Well then.' That Rothko yellow stripe pulled apart *amour-propre*, it broadened a man's fancy. With an eye on the kettle he took a huge breath and said all at once: 'Toward the end of the Miocene a pesky simian living on a savannah near the Great Rift Valley a thousand miles east of where I'll be heaved itself onto its hind legs freeing its front paws for all sorts of violent mischief which was bad enough but as a side-effect his brain, suddenly stuck up into the sky, swelled the way a blister swells. Or a cancer. Instead of just spotting fruit or tracking game it started spotting and tracking *itself*. Hunting itself down. Of course it never caught up with itself, it remained a mystery, but this morbid hopeless chase after itself is what we call consciousness and I'm against it.'

'"A story" is what I said, I think.' She was peering into her tea-pot, giving it its single stir.

'Necessary background, that was necessary background.' But he did subside onto the appointed spot on the floor, cross-leggèd (a little proud that in his thirties he could still do this neatly). 'Consciousness –'

She groaned.

'Consciousness – this story requires a cosmic background, hush – is, moreover, against *itself*. Because, you see, it's boundless. There's no reason for any line of thought to stop. And therefore (by an inevitable confusion) no reason for the thinker to stop. But of course he *does*. Which he can't bear. You don't get morbid animals because they're not conscious, so haven't dreamed of unconsciousness. They –'

'You do remember what "story" *means*, don't you?' She had produced her toasting-fork, fashioned from a Fascist dagger, family war booty, and was turning the first crumpet in the flame.

'Consciousness, fear of death, Agatha, Africa as womb. We're getting there,' although he still wore his not-letting-on face

She stopped toasting, amazed. 'Your sister Agatha? You never talk –'

'Hitherto, no. Hush. They – animals, we're discussing animals – live, then die. The human animal, uniquely diseased, can't see a fish washed up on the banks of a stream without thinking "One day soon I'm going to be washed out of the steam of thinking which will go on without me" – and *that's* what can't be borne. No one minds our species going extinct, or even the planet blowing up. It's individual consciousness, the blister, that can't endure being popped.... Who is it that *defines* mankind as "them who through fear of death are all their lifetime subject to bondage?"'

'I'm not sure,' said Margot, getting down the cups, 'that you're earning lapsong souchong.' Her tea was rare stuff, smoked by a Chinese family in Crewe using green leaves brought in illegally. She produced a pot of honey from a cupboard. 'With your African so-called story.'

'Not mine. Story, to begin with, *about* an African story. No, about an Africa-dwelling story-teller. About my dreadful father's wonderful mother. A story about Lady Culpepper. Brenda. A woman of the twentieth-century as she liked to say. Of almost the whole appalling century. Born in 1912, died on the first of January 2000. Died of the fireworks the evening before as it happens. She was disgusted with the nurses in her home for making such a fuss, and kept explaining to them "It's *not* a new millennium, flighty creatures, that begins *next* year." She wouldn't let them wheel her to the window to watch. "Make me complicit with idiots who can't count? No thank you! To bed! To bed!" The next morning everyone was hungover and when they did take her belated tea-tray she'd ostentatiously tired of waiting and died, a twentieth-century woman still. Making a point, I suppose.'

'I condole. But the story. It needs to *begin*. You have three minutes left.'

'When Granny visited she'd tell the three of us bedtime stories. Or rather the two of us, Agatha was never brave enough to stay. Generally she'd run downstairs and make trouble with Marthe, our *au pair*. A very correct Norwegian, Marthe. Marthe would come and sit in our bedroom to make sure the stories were suitable. They never were, although she rarely dared do anything about it. If they got *too* awful she'd throw her apron over her face and grope her way out of the room.

'Occasionally Gertrude and I would hear, with delight, screaming in the night – I don't mean Agatha, who *always* screamed, I mean Marthe. Marthe thinking through what Granny had told us.

'I, Margot, am not restful.'

'No.'

'My inventions are forged weapons: gas to burn lungs, maces to shatter skulls, bombs to vaporise. But Granny's were far worse. Hers *choked*. They pushed you out of time into the void where there can be no air.

'One Christmas Eve. Let me see, twenty-three years ago. It wasn't a pleasant visit. My father had just found out about mother – incredible he shouldn't have noticed all those years, but then he's dull, in perception as well as in every other way. Suddenly that Christmas the house was full of non-stop shouting: my Grandfather Osbert, trying to bully papa out of divorce, and my mother, trying to play the victim.

'It was the last family Christmas, thank God, that's why it sticks in the mind. Marthe, who was complicit in Mama's adventures, was keeping upstairs as much as she could, annoying us, in case anyone thought to question her. I had gone to the girls' rooms to frighten them. They weren't having it and there was soon a general squabble underway to match the squabble downstairs.

'So it was a relief when the nursery door opened and shut (admitting a gust of adult *fraças* from below), and Granny was with us.

'"A story," we cried, "a story, a story!" just like you keep saying now, only with more justice since it was the correct hour, bed-time. "Tell us about Papa, Granny." – *Oh yes please*. Thank you. Perfect.' There was no question of milk or sugar with her lapsong.

'You're only getting this on trust, feline culprit *mio*,' said Margot. 'I expect more.'

'Noble child. "Tell us about Papa," we said. A curious topic to request because although I, obviously, have always been a fascinating boy, and Gertrude in her gruesome way had her points, and even ridiculous Agatha had a pretty face in those days (if she shut her imbecile eyes), our father was insipid. Remarkably insipid, intensely insipid. A spectacular blank. We'd never really thought about him, as children don't, but now the family was in danger of breaking up Gertrude and I were, for the first time, philosophising about it. Useful thoughts. The fear of Culpeppers is the beginning of wisdom.'

'Felix.'

'Thank you, I'm telling my story in my own way …. We were puzzled. When Brenda was so interesting, and I am and I suppose Gertrude, how could Papa be *so* dreary? To ask for a story about *him* was really to ask about *me*. Granny understood this.

'"Ah yes, poor Winston," she said. "Well, I'll explain, but you have to promise not to tell, he couldn't endure it. Here's how it was. – We'd just arrived in the Northern Frontier District of Kenya, on" – '

'Africa at last.'

'See? You had only to wait. "On transfer from Uganda. Where your grandfather had made a terrible mess of his District. As he always did. Failure was always the secret of Osbert's success. He was so deplorably bad at whatever he did that his superiors couldn't wait to get rid of him. Wouldn't even wait to build a case against him and sack him. They'd just propose his transfer as soon as they could. "Great talent useful elsewhere," that was the usual phrase. The result was, he went ricocheting about the Colonial Service. Since there are a bound to be gaps in the ceiling of every room, his general movement was upward."

"'Does that *always* work?" I asked, perceptively. I was off to boarding school in a few months, you see, and beginning to think ahead.

"'No dear, only in the Church of England and sometimes the Navy. I don't think you can rely on it as a method now the Empire's gone and the Colonial Service's not an option.

"'Oh,'" said I, dashed (although of course I never doubted my own ability).

"'Also, my dears, it helped that dear Osbert's such a biddable, credulous man. The men above generally detested and despised him, but he could never despise them back. He's a born lapdog. Craven, y'know, but entirely sincere in his cravenness. His manly aggressive qualities all go downwards, on the animals he tries to hurt, not to mention on his cheap lovers. But when he looks up he's dazzled, as by tropical sun. He just *can't* credit that any man in authority might be fundamentally mistaken."

"'Golly!'" I said. Granny's burst of annoyance, provoked I suppose by the quarrelling downstairs, opened up important ideas in my attractive head. I have never been loyal to anything since that moment.'

'Ah.'

"Golly!'" I said. "How *silly* of grandpa."

"'Quite. And your grandfather applied this *silly* notion even at national level. When the Munich crisis was resolved he was positively infatuated with the Prime Minister – went round our bungalow crooning with love. Our Ugandan servants thought he was bewitched. A few weeks later, when I gave birth to our first son, he insisted on naming him Neville. Revolting name, and I'm sorry to say your poor Uncle Neville always thought so too. And it was just the same after the war, in the rosy dawn of socialism; my third boy, always my favourite, had to be christened Clement. Another dreadful burden in life.

"'But this story happens in the May of 1940, when Osbert was still in thrall to Mr Chamberlain. Neville had already grown into a plain lumpish baby, and I was taking him for an airing late one afternoon, 'round the garden of our new house in Kenya, with his *ayah*, a nice Gujarati woman from the coast. It was the *most* beautiful afternoon; the loveliest day I ever knew in Africa as I remember it. I suppose that's just hindsight. I was walking slowly, because I was two months pregnant with your father and he gave me terrible morning-sickness, not only in the morning. The flame-trees bent down over me. Of course they didn't, but that's what how the tree looks when you suddenly glance up into: every scarlet calyx seems to be gesturing down.

One never gets over the shock of the fire-coloured tongues of the African tulip-tree. *Immortel Étranger* the ridiculous French call it. The early morning sun soared merrily up, up, and the grass danced and twitched about my ankles as I walked. That was real enough too, it was the lizards bolting, getting away from my patent leather pumps. Boring little Neville was rigged out in a sailor-suit, so we must have been due to go out to dine. I was trying to interest him in the blazing red tree, and abruptly" – that's why I thought of the Miocene and bipedalism. Do you see? It's *always* a mistake to rear. It leads to thought, and human thought's necessarily *anguish*. How much better –'

'*Do* get on. And do you want honey on this?'

'Naturally I do.'

'And more tea?'

'Of course, of course, lots. "Suddenly," said Granny, "Neville did sit up in his *ayah*'s arms. He'd never really done that before. She lifted him, cooing, so he could pluck one of the flowers. *Kibobakasi, Kibobakasi!* she kept saying – that's the Swahili name for the flame-tree. The flowers are full of water, y'know, you can squeeze them like water-guns, grand fun; but they leave a yellow stain on cloth, like the stain of tobacco. Of course Neville, awful little creature, set up a terrible wail at being squirted – yelled and yelled as if he were being eaten. So we had to bring him inside. And ran right into Osbert, who was also, it seemed, in his quieter way, in a shameful panic. He'd been listening to the wireless as he got his evening things on. The Germans had swept into the Low Countries at dawn, France was about to be invaded, and in London the government had fallen. Osbert was nearly beside himself, and when he saw Neville with a great splash across his sailor-suit he took it into his head that it was blood. Blood! We had to get away! We were going to be slaughtered! There was no talking to him. And of course he had a point. With France in the throes Mussolini would be sure to join in, and we were just over the frontier from Abyssinia, which was bursting with Italian troops, many of them ferocious Gallas – they outnumbered us a hundred to one. Osbert said he said he couldn't get the image out of his head of Neville in his sailor-suit, bleeding and twitching, gutted, on a Galla bayonet." ("Dat iss not shuitable for to zay to khildren," interjected Marthe in her incredible random accent; we Culpeppers paid her not the least attention.) "Osbert insisted: Neville and I had to be sent Home. So we got back to my family in Liverpool just in time to be Blitzed." … Blitzed. Blitzed.'

'… Felix? … Felix? You're brooding.'

'I am. I'm thinking about Blitzes. – Let's just *obliterate* the twentieth-century, Margot, let's make it so that in a few generations it'll seem history got chopped off in 1913, and faded back in around 2020, with just a vague hangoverish sense of something bad in the dream-life of our species.... What? No, it's not balmy, it's a Great Idea. Granny, who had to endure it, detested it, and she should know. – And if that's not possible, at least let's undo everything that happened and make it as it was before. Fine buildings shattered from one end of Europe to another, decency, monarchies; nothing left but rubble –'

'People under the rubble.'

'Yes yes, but procreation fixes that. I prefer buildings to people. A century of *ruin*. Loss. Rebuilding worse than ruin. Æsthetic apocalypse –'

'How old you seem to me sometimes. Most of the time, really. You'll remember I was born in 1992 – '

'That just means you evaded Armageddon, using frivolous arithmetical means. A contemptible dodge…. Granny and I were wiser. We rage against the twentieth century. Not that she actually raged. She always had pluck. Her generation didn't complain. All *she* said was: "Nineteen-forty: a spot of bother *generally*, so we couldn't avoid it by being in Liverpool. What a shock of coming into Coburg Dock and seeing *nothing*, the city under black-out. All that bright wealth doused! Still, it felt peaceful enough once I got home. Our house in Falkner Square had an enormous garden, with space for a very fine Anderson Shelter. I returned to find Mama growing marrows on its roof to give it an air of utility, but really the thing was being treated as a glorified tree-house by all the Carrs. It was a family secret that no one much liked our big Georgian house. Pretentious and boring. Of course we'd never say as much before outsiders, we were loyal. But everyone preferred the Shelter. My uncles and cousins adored playing in it, Mabel constructed a mock-triumphal avenue of pot-plants leading to it, and Cyril, the artistic one who had epilepsy and couldn't go to the war, filled in with frescoes." What are you doing? Are there more crumpets?'

'No.' Margot had risen and was carefully unpinning her Rothko. She never travelled without it.

'Ah. "Meanwhile, my dears, your grandfather was having a lovely time too. The Italians were so feeble they didn't really invade Kenya, not to speak of. But his special war-powers meant he could run about doing what he liked, the administration in Nairobi was much too agitated to keep track, and what he liked doing, as it happens, was spending his sunny days with a Mrs Card. A widow in some sense. She had a beautiful white house overlooking Lake Rudolf and went about in gauzy scarves and bleached linen, and a pith helmet of course. Behind her house was a tall hedge of white-flowering silky thorn, surrounding a huge pond, thick with creamy water-lilies, in which she kept her famous collection of albino crocodiles."'

Margot snorted briefly. 'Albino crocodiles.' She was rolling up the canvas and sliding it into a heavy padded lockable steel canister which she'd had specially made.

'Granny didn't rate them either. "Lumpish blinking crocodiles, I'm told. But the dull brutes didn't *have* to be fast, because every dawn Mrs Card would have the legs of a dozen snowy ibises broken by her gardeners, who handed them to her so she could throw them in. For some months she and Osbert fed the crocs together and so forth. My dear sweet lady-friends in Kenya were of course assiduous about keeping me informed of these doings. Dear lady-friends always are. Damn their eyes."

"'Dis iss not shuitable," and it's true that Agatha, who found the topic of adultery terrifying, was sniffling away.

"'Dear Marthe, no criticism of my friends applies to *you*," which offended Marthe so much she got up and left, closing the bedroom door sharply. Gertrude and I giggled, Agatha blubbed for real. Granny didn't deign to notice. "Meanwhile back in Liverpool we were so fond of our Shelter that against all reason we were amazed when one wet night there was a proper raid on Canning, our part of town, and we had to go and *use* it. We sat inside listening to the bangs, looking up as one did although there was only the curved corrugated-iron roof, hung with tapestries by Cyril, and feeling the ground shake. Suddenly there was a gigantic bang, so loud a volcano might have been erupting into Falkner Square. It was a direct hit on the terrace opposite us, which went toppling backward and killed I don't know how many people, scores anyway, sooty bodies were still being brought days later. Meanwhile while the bang was still reverberating, and the soil or mud was pouring into our Shelter – so much for the marrows – and putting out all our lights, and burying us alive, although only up to our hips or thereabouts or so, I went into labour. Our Anderson Shelter had become very like a catacomb and I didn't enjoy the sensation of giving birth into the ground. But my mother did a fine job I thought, heaped up with soil as we were and lightless. Cyril composed a sonnet in his head in praise of us all, and recited it over the child's screams before digging us out with his hands. It was a horribly huge child. When the doctor saw it the next day he said it was so big that if I'd carried it full-term it would probably have killed me, as well as itself of course.... I was under orders from my toad-eating husband to name the child Winston if male; so Winston it was. A miserable cub from the beginning, despite its size. Worse even than Neville. Who never took to Winston. Which was unfair, it was *his fault*. When Neville, naughty boy, had his run-in with the Kibobakasi tree – even before that bomb jolted your father into the world – his *rôle* was set. Winston's note was to be pathos. He was to be moistly sad, clammily sad, all the days of his life."'

'This was *not* suitable.' Margot had propped her Rothko in its steel canister against the wall, and resumed her enthroned posture, fingers judicially upright. 'Poor Agatha.'

'True, she was a wreck by this stage. Under the blankets, hands over ears. But Granny had the bit between her teeth. We had asked and she was going to tell us. "It was that African tree that did it. All of us are as we as we are because of what happened before us. Grandmother Eve rustled the apple-bough and here we all are. Neville, bless him, squirted himself with flower-blood and got me sent home to give birth in a grave...." She drew a great breath and managed to smile. "So that's the answer to your question, my dears, I mean the question you quite rightly didn't ask, about why your darling Papa isn't quite alive. Boom! Doom, doom – !" "Stop, Granny, stop!" shouted Agatha from under the duvet, "Felix make her stop talking about naughty Daddy!" So I said –'.

'I think I can guess.'

'"Why is *Agatha* as she is, Granny? Why's Agatha the way she is?"'

'Yes, that's what I guessed you said.'

'Brenda Culpepper opened her handsome mouth, like an infernal fate, to explain, to decree, to define. At which Agatha's eyes, wide with the horror of having the rest of her life fixed by what her grandmother was about to say, appeared out of the bedclothes.

'"No-no-no! Don't do it to me, Granny, *do it to Felix!* Doom *him!* Tell us a story about why *he's* like he is!"

'"Agatha!" exclaimed Granny, who was not used to be shouted at. But Agatha had already bounded out of bed. She dashed into the dark corridor, which she could never bear to do, and plummetted howling downstairs. Soon we heard her blending her awful noise with the roaring of grandfather, of mother, of Marthe (Marthe been dragged into the fight) and even of earthborn Papa, who was piping up at last.

'The shouting went on all night. So Gertrude said; I slept through it. When we crept downstairs at dawn we found the Tree looked like something on the Western Front, the so-called grown-ups having thrown the wrapped presents at each other before they were done.

'Oh yes, it was a *grand* Christmas. Y'know, after that I always managed to be invited elsewhere by school friends. This will be my first Christmas back with my so-called family or what's left of it.

'I suppose that's what brought these jolly memories to mind.'

'I'm sorry, Felix. Really.... Still: is it worth reminding you exactly what I wanted a story about? What *you* are doing in Africa *next week*. Without me.'

Then Culpepper (who was perhaps more distressed by his reminiscence than he was letting on) made his heinous mistake: 'I've *told* you. Consciousness, fear of death. Blooms. Bomo.' He had no business spelling it out like that. Anyway, he had no business using his tutorial voice, the voice that makes him so hated. It was egregiously rude of him. 'If you don't follow – I don't see how you couldn't – you can read about it in the papers next week. But if you'd really paid attention you'd *know* what I'm going to do.'

Margot is very aristocratic, too much for rage to pale her face or darken it, too much for tremors in the voice. But now, perhaps, the redness of her hair deepened in the mellow gas-light: a symptom Felix understood and feared. 'Oh this was a test was it? Not just a story? Another of your story-tests? I'd understood I was beyond being tested.'

Felix, alarmed, tried to speak.

'No there's no more tea so don't ask.' She rose haughtily and glanced out of her window. 'And the Scarlet Woman's gone, so I can potter down to the Lodge and get my cab. Time to begin my trifling holiday. No, *don't* prattle. If you want to help, carry *that*.' *That* was the Rothko.

Culpepper was trying to get off the floor and say 'It's an *extremely* confidential –' but she wasn't having it; she silenced him with the way she put on her coat, and got a fur cap out of one of the hat-boxes.

'You had better', she settled her cap and regarded herself in her looking-glass, 'say no more if it's a *confidential* mission. A *secret* killing, rather than an obvious one I can chatter about with my little chums.'

'You are my colleague –'

'Then in a collegial spirit, do carry that painting to the Lodge.' She glanced about her set (curiously dim now the painting was gone), turned off the gas, and strode out of the darkened room ahead of him, out and down the stair. She swept across Gehenna, and he only caught up with her as she stepped into the Lodge itself. Margot is very young: too young for her irony to be perfectly cold. Adolescent hurt showed through in her gait. Culpepper felt guilty, a rare uncomfortable sensation for him; he scooped up and trotted in her wake, the Rothko held in both arms, he was and looked confused, hoping to make amends.

Through the sound-proof glass of the Lodge it was clear that Lint was indulging himself as he generally did once the undergrads were gone. He'd assembled his three under-porters in the inner room, and was bollocking them for a term's-worth of errors, smacking a wooden yardstick on a table. Behind the table Clinker and Scurf and Loam cringed, wringing their fingers.

When Lint saw Margot, he left of his inaudible screaming, tossed down his weapon, and came springing out.

'Lady Margot! Still here, then? I though the place was empty!'

'Just going, Lint. Listen: I have such a pile of luggage in my rooms. I don't suppose – ?'

'Scurf! Clinker! No not *you*,' this, savagely, to Loam, who had come popping out as well, 'you wretched snivelling weakling, you lady's maid, *you* go and get Dr Culpepper's parcel if it's not too heavy for your tiny painted fingers. But you two! What are you dawdling for? Gehenna II, set 5 – *on the double*, do you think Lady Margot has all evening?' And he peered at her from under his enormous untrimmed eyebrows, wistfully, ingratiatingly.

Normally Margot detested fawning. But now she gave Lint her most brilliant smile to punish Felix, to show him that she had herself in hand, that her disgust was for him alone. 'Thank you, Lint. And merry Christmas.'

By now poor quivering Loam was handing Felix a sizeable parcel, humbly done up in brown paper, just arrived by registered delivery: 'Er, er, thank you –' muttered Felix distractedly; for Margot, ignoring him, had stepped out of the Lodge into night-fast, frigid Emmanuel Road, and raised her arm.

A taxi pulled up almost at once. Another bedazzling smile: 'Hallo. I want to go to London, to St Pancras. The Eurostar platform. Is that too far for you? Wonderful.' And she made a marvellous gesture, spreading her white-gloved right hand over hat-boxes and suitcase, with which Clinker and Scurf had just arrived, panting. 'And there's more!'

Culpepper had joined her now, although she would not look at him. Penitence was gone from his face: he was clearly thinking that his penalty was getting out of proportion to his offence. And two can play at the game of snubbing a lover. So now he shoved the metal tube rough into the cabby's hands, plonked down his own parcel on the footpath, tore off its accompanying letter, and ostentatiously began to read.

So they stood together side by side, a careful two feet between, competitively not attending to each other, with the pernicious bulk of College's east front behind them, and before them the wilderness of Emmanuel Road, full of what looked like and felt like black ice.

After a second, Culpepper whistled with surprise.

Margot, watching the taxi get loaded up, felt that he had scored a point. and returned service. 'Goodbye then, Dr Culpepper, and a merry Christmas to you as well.'

Even at St Wygefortis' it is not the done thing for dons and their undergraduate mistresses to kiss or grope beside the public road. But this was unlooked-for coldness.

However, he barely noticed or affected not to notice the slight, lost as he was in his amazing letter. 'Hm? Yes, yes…. Trust you'll enjoy your snowy mountains in – Austria, did you say?'

'Slovenia. I realise it's hard to keep geography straight as one ages. But do enjoy your freezing family reunion in – *what's* your father's place in Surrey called? Silly me, I forget things too.'

Normally he hated saying the name, but now he muttered 'The Nitch, Westhumble,' abstracted, unfazed, unashamed.

'With Winston, and Gertrude,' suggested Margot, drawing out the appalling phonemes, 'and thingy.'

'My nephew, yes,' murmured Felix, turning a page of his letter.

'*He* must have a name.'

'... Indeed he has. Shiva Elfchild Harmonious-Moonshadow Culpepper.'

Margot was knocked off her high-horse and couldn't speak for a moment. 'I don't believe you.'

'Gertrude,' said Felix, still transfixed by what he read, 'was .... Hm? Going through an intensely hippie period when he was born. Which has worn off thank God. Now she's just an untribal leftie social worker. Vegan, dishevelled, fat. But six years ago she was a militant Aquarian.... And there he is.'

'What's – he, the boy – like?'

'... Hm?' murmured her lover, lost in is letter. '... Sound enough. Very sound, considering. In fact, dangerous. His unspeakable parent sends him to an unspeakable school decked out as an *ashram* where he's taught Meditation, Global Consciousness and Anti-Racist Mathematics. His hatred for it – and, if it comes to that, for her – *burns always with a hard, gem-like flame*, just as Pater says it should. Naturally he wants to escape to Cambridge and read economics. Meanwhile he's appallingly precocious, surreptitiously reads the *Financial Times*, wrapped hidden inside copies of *Playboy* because she believes all love is liberating. He speculates in commodity derivatives.'

'Oh. How – *old* he sounds.'

'How old *you* would seem to *him* sometimes, all the time really. Just think, when you're a tame middle-aged woman he'll be here, tearing up Wygy's – I've promised him to get him in. I wonder if he'll survive the change. Perhaps helping Albert Culpepper in is a form of nepocide.'

'Albert?'

'More likely he'll want to clear the decks. Avunculicide ....'

'*Albert?*'

'... What? ... He likes to be called that. Only out of earshot of Mater – as he secretly calls her – she insists he call her Gert. Earshot's an elastic concept with my sister, her endless spliffs make her imperceptive.'

'And – Albert?'

'Despises weed. His tipple's Enzian, a gentian schnapps from the Tyrol. Surpassingly bitter. He says it cancels out the filthy lentils and mushroom-bake on which Gertrude subsists. I know all this because he writes to, letters of rather terrible sophistication.... Not like this one. *Golly.*' He'd finished it at last, and was folding it up in wonder.

Margot, mad with curiosity, made herself remember how cross she was with this monster. 'I believe you're now performing what low-brow writers call a hollow laugh.'

'I think I am. Margot, Margot! This parcel here, do you know what it is?

It's my re, our reward for our frolics about Skelgourock.'

'Ah.'

'Here. Read this.'

'As long as it's not too *confidential* – '

Which was a touch below her, a juvenile remark. He contemptuously thrust the letter into her hand.

It was thick paper, beautifully laid, discreetly watermarked with a cardinal's tasselled hat, grandly embossed in silver at the top of the first page. There were six sheets in all, covered with handwriting of a sort Margot thought had died out: proper-rounded "copper plate", very large, ornately swirled and sinuous. The ink was chestnut-coloured.

FROM THE VICAR-GENERAL OF THE HEBRIDES,
THE ARCHEPISCOPAL PALACE,
BREADALBANE STREET,
TOBERMORY,
ISLE OF MULL PA75 6PD

*Eve of St Nicholas,*
MMXIII

*F.L.O.B. Culpepper, esq.,*
*Fellow and Tutor, S. Wygefortis' College,*
*Cambridge* CB1 1XJ

*Dear Dr Culpepper:*

*I am commanded by His Eminence the Cardinal-Arch-bishop of the Hebrides to express his gratitude for your advice and assistance last month in the sad matter of our four deceased Cistercian brothers.*

*He hears from the highest authority in Rome – whom he understands, to his very considerable surprise, you saw fit to contact directly – that satisfaction is general there also. As it is here, apart (His Eminence has come in as I write, and urges me to add) from the <u>most</u> (His Eminence proffers a more pungent adverb) unfortunate detail of the Curia's being involved in such a purely British concern. He remains unclear why this was necessary. (His actual comment is "Why'd the willy City Banker need to go* *bothering the Hangman's?")*

*Wishing to offer a fitting token indicative of his
feelings for you, His Eminence requested the Archivio Seg-
reto Vaticano to look through their holdings, which as you
know are unimaginably vast, for material ("Shirt" was his
word) on the Culpepper family. A few days ago we received
from the Cardinal-Archivist, <u>via</u> the London Nunciature,
the attached box, which has at some point been labelled
THE WAPENTAKE OF WORKSWORTH.*

*His Hebridean Eminence ordered me to examine
the contents, evidently composed in the Dominican
House at Openshaw, on the outskirts of Manchester. The
Openshaw archives came to Rome when that friary was
closed after the War; the author was, it seems, among the
casualties of a German missile. WAPENTAKE was not
catalogued, possibly because it is, in places, indecent, more
probably because it was simply overlooked. It therefore
need not be returned.*

*I have just given a <u>précis</u> of it to His Eminence,
who trusts that you will be as amused as he was. Or rather,
in his own, not untrenchant words, which he commands
me to relay: "A right mucky weep-and-wail for you,
Culpepper, sommat to Brighton-Rock you about your own
pith-and-pin", adding a number of no-doubt-jocular insults which I do not feel it incumbent to retail <u>ad litteram</u>,
concluding: "Tell the little Hampton Wick the wages of sin
is knowledge and of mortal sin self-knowledge, duck his
crowd south."*

*Having unburdened himself of these sentiments
he has gone out again, slamming the door, but would no
doubt wish to bestow his Archipontifical Benediction.
Were the smelly old geezer in a better mood.*

Ave atque vale, doctissime,

*Monsignor Hermenegild Boys-Stones*


'That,' she remarked coolly, handing the letter back, 'is an outrageous
name.'

'Pronounced *bosun*, like the *boatswain* on a ship, I gather – I spoke to
him on the 'phone. But it certainly *looks* like a provocation.'

'And the another provocation?'

'What d'y'mean?'

'Giving you something about your family from the Vatican's Secret Archives. Revealing what will trouble you.'

'Oh, *that*.' Culpepper looked very knowing. 'I'm a little tougher than I look, my dear. And 'though she's very very very old and distinguished – the Organisation Monsignor Hermenegild serves – she occasionally overestimates herself. You know how it is. She remembers Byzantium, she's had Visigoths and Huns at her gates, she's kept her correspondence with Genghis Khan and the Emperor of the Incas and Copernicus. I did some research in the Vatican Archives once. Terribly heady: fifty miles of shelves, absolutely continuous since the twelfth century, lots of it still out-of-bounds.... But even the Church has limits. You can be sure she can't tell me anything worse about Culpeppers than what I already know.'

'You don't know how much you don't know.' Her eye was on her luggage, They didn't seem able to fit everything into the cab. They'd taken it all out and started again. 'Can you?'

'Pshaw. This'll be some stale scandal about Uncle Winfred – and nothing would surprise me about *him*. Or it'll be my, let me see, great-great-great-grandfather, Tancred. Who whiled away long evenings in his Westmorland rectory composing pornography. Very elaborate stuff, full of Greek and Latin, appalling no doubt to the good Dominicans of Openshaw. I, though, am untroubled. Scurf!' he had just appeared with Margot's leather satchel, full of laptops and bottles and passports.

'Yes, sir?'

'Will you pop this brown parcel back in my pigeon-hole? I'll have a look it when I get back.'

'Yes, sir.'

Margot was impressed (which she wanted to hide) at her hateful lover's *sangfroid*. 'Now you're over-estimating *yourself*. You may be laying up a nasty surprise for yourself at the end of vac.'

'Nothing I can't easily bear.'

'"Why is Felix the way he is?"'

'Nonsense. Listen, there *can't* be skeletons in the family closet when the closet's already a charnel house, a loose mass of bones. Open the door, a white avalanche comes clattering out.'

Margot paused. She was still on her dignity. 'Speaking of which. What happened to Mrs Card?'

'Who? Oh she tired of my grandfather soon enough. That's what she said. I wonder whether perhaps Granny didn't write to her and warn her off. Granny had a very firm prose style. Anyway Osbert was chucked and – since it was too shaming to hang about Kenya as Rebecca Card's latest cast-off – had himself transferred to Durban. Where he spent the war bungling the censorship of telegrams. Granny joined him with the two boys and spent the war raising the most magnificent pineapples and limes. Uncle Clement was born there, and in '48 –'

'I congratulate your family on the excellence of its pineapples,' pronounced Lady Margot loftily, staring across Emmanuel Road into blackness, 'but it's Rebecca Card herself who concerns me. As one Culpepper floosie to another.'

'You're not –'

'Did your grandfather see her again?'

Felix dropped his voice and spoke quite seriously. 'Margot, don't be so riled with me. Please don't be riled. I'll tell you exactly what my job is in Africa if you like…. You can even' (but this came too late; and he spoilt it by a tiny pause, a half-second's calculation) 'come with me and help.'

Margot had heard the pause. Clearly he warranted more punishment. 'Do whatever you like in Bomo, Dr Culpepper, or wherever it is,' she said in her clear voice, so that the cabbie and Scurf, trying to heave the steamer-trunk into the boot between them, glanced up. 'Tell me next term if it's interesting enough to turn into one of your chaotic stories. In return, I'll let you see nice snapshots of Slovenia.'

'Mrs Card stayed on beside Lake Rudolf,' said Culpepper, managing not to grind his teeth, 'since you ask, for decades. My grandfather never saw her again as far as I know. But she was a fixture of British Africa, one of the celebrities, everyone told stories about her. She never changed. Generations of pale crocs came and went, generations of gardeners, lovers. At independence her gardeners suddenly tired of generations of beatings. She was found, or the indigestible bits of her were found, bobbing in her celebrated pond, staining the lilies.'

'Ah so that's how she ended up, is it? It's worth knowing.'

'Her albinos,' said Felix, trying to lift the tone of the conversation, to lift it back toward whimsy, 'were slaughtered and bought as a job-lot by the Maharajah of Cooch Bihar. If you're ever in Bengal and no doubt you will be, visit the Maharajah's palace and look for the library he gave his wife. Everything bound in white crocodile skin. He was a Cambridge man – Trinity I think – and he met her when she was at' (Felix's voice was wandering; he could see this story hadn't come out right) 'a secretarial college here.'

'A bridal library. How *lovely!* My one shy modest girlish hope is that I might leave behind so worthy a monument myself. But here's my final suitcase stowed at last. *Thank* you, Clinker.'

But it fact wouldn't quite go in. The cabbie and the two porters started pulling the trunk and the other boxes about, swearing under their breath.

'Margot,' muttered Felix low, fast and serious, grabbing at this last opportunity, 'I'm sorry I wasn't forthcoming above every detail of my African gig.'

'"Every detail"?' She too spoke under her breath, but looking away, at the bicycles passing up and down the frigid street.

'That I just hinted.'

'I don't think we had any actual hints. Just pseudo-African family mythology. Irrelevant. Look, my taxi *is* loaded. Thank you for your trouble, gentlemen!'

Then Felix entirely buckled. 'Margot, you are my full partner. I'll never accept another job without asking you first and I'll tell you everything before I do it.' It was as astonishing surrender. It's hard, rationally speaking, to see why he had to make it. 'You're henceforth half-owner of the firm.'

She did turn to him then, and did smile; and instead of gloating (or being grateful) said, 'I'm glad that's clear!'

'Get that idiotic mountain of bags out of this bloody cab. Stay. Come to Bomo with me on Monday.'

Her smile, under her fur hat, became yet more splendid. 'No. I think you'll enjoy doing *one last one* yourself. – But I'm glad we're sorted out our standing in the firm,' and she almost giggled at how flaunting it sounded. 'We'll do wonderful work together next term.'

Clinker was holding the door open for her; Scurf stood almost at attention, alert despite the dreadful icy air; the cabbie waited to get in. It was an imposing send-off. She let her hand brush Felix's and seated herself in the back of the taxi, looking simply happy, without "edge" or affect, which is after all how young, rich, beautiful people with settled careers should look. She sighed, and leaned back, thinking of what was coming, so that as they drove away her senior partner, standing in the stinging, almost unnatural cold, couldn't see her face. Only her while glove showed, imitating or parodying a royal wave in the window: a fast pale fluttering not unlike the motion sacred ibises may have made as an earlier Culpepper, to please his sinister love, tossed them at sunrise, snapped at the knee, into the waiting pond.

# VII. Quadrillion,
## *a letter*

St Wygefortis' College
Cambridge   CB1 1XJ

*Friday afternoon, 10i14*

Margot <u>mia</u>:
you asked, no let's face facts, you <u>commanded</u> me to
compose an account on my doings in Africa before the
start of Lent Term.

I'm glad you wdn't let me just talk it through over
the New Year, but held out for a written story. Obedient
& loyal as I am, I'm taking this p.m. off from my pitiful
academic "work" to write it: my report to my partner.

But first, here's a covering note to make sure you
that you grasp that despite all the derring-do I'm about to
describe, this was a serious matter for me, a crusade; & my
cause was

DEATH.

Not, even that's not quite frank enough (now that
I'm being 100% frank with you). My cause was

DEATH & AGATHA CULPEPPER.

I am sorry I teased you about Agatha when you
asked, that unfortunate tea-time at the end of term, where
I was going & what I was doing. But I did mean it. Agatha
is why I went to Africa, also why I didn't want you to
come. I went to vindicate (or refute) her ending.

*

*Death: I'm for it, me. Obviously. It's my bread-and-butter,
it's my ho, I pimp for it. I mean, we pimp for it. It's our
firm's professional product.*

*But apart from me, us, there's the cosmos, & the
question of cosmic hygiene. Death's what makes life tolerable – if the Playwright didn't bustle His characters off-stage
so briskly, who'd endure the show? – & as with individuals,
so with the characters in history bks. Even more in family
history. So with empires, species. Even stars. Even the
universe. We like these things not because they're grand
but because they're poignant, because they're frail. At the
back of our minds we never forget the one consoling fact,
extinction. Everything has so brief a rôle it can be fitted
inside a number, here on my paper, here:*

$$10^{15}$$

*– one quadrillion years. That's the solar system come &
gone, <u>whouf</u>.*

*And as with solar systems, so with lobster new-
berg. That was the zenith of lunch today & I punished it
enthusiastically. (Thirds!) But pleasures are only pleasant
because we know they'll end. What a fine solar blaze of
vermillion-gold the lobster made on the College plate; yet
wd I have relished it if I didn't know there was a digestif
waiting in my rooms to <u>cancel it out</u>? No. There's no love
or delight about which I don't think 'Soon death will come
& flush this away <u>thank God</u>.' (You excepted of course.)*

*My colleagues flew to Mrs Oathouse after lunch,
bleating for emetics. Not me. My digestif is a civilised
antidote to all the stodge & fat. Albert alias Moonshadow
Culpepper presented me with a bottle for Christmas. Did
I tell you he drank it? I think I have. I've seen (have you?)
Hades-blue gentians growing wild in the Tyrolean Alps,
dotting the mountain slopes, pooling like puddles fallen
from some infernal sky. Who'd have thought they'd turn
into this clear fierce liquid, bitter as human stomach-juice?*

*Gentians … O my love, have I had too much of*

*Albert's flowery tipple? (I'm finishing a fourth glass as I write.) Is it Enzian that's making me poetic?*

*Now I'm recalling a poem by Lawrence, of all people: reach me a gentian, give me a torch. He calls gentians black lamps from the halls of Dis leading us down the darker & darker stairs, where blue is darkened on blueness. Horrible man, Lawrence, horrible philosophy, ditto writer. But here he was on to something. Reach me a gentian.*

*Is enthusiasm for death morbid? NO! Anyway, much less morbid than the opposite, being anti. As was, for instance (Bailiff! Bring up the witness! Arraign her in the box!) that fanatic, my grotesque sister Agatha.*

*

*Twenty years ago my idiot sibling topped herself with 93 paracetamol tablets. We know the number because the ambulance-wallahs paused to count the empty bottles & subtract the ones the grotesque child had scattered messily about the industrial-carpetting of her bedsit, & later that night it was decided (not by me: my vote, both as brother & taxpayer, was No) that this dosage was low enough to try to save Agatha, if we cd transplant her liver, the only bit of herself she'd managed to kill outright.*

*Which was, if you ask me, merely muffing her exit-stage-left. The medical bother didn't make any difference, no suitable liver turned up during the harrowing 4 days that followed. Each had something wrong with it, too small, too big, the wrong blood-type – 'Ah,' said her surgeon again & again although not in so many words, 'zis foie tiède iz not to mademoiselle's liking? Zen take it avay!' Meanwhile sis's belly swelled as if 10 months pregnant with her own delayed nothingness. A curious knot of engorged veins stood out from the engorged skin of her stomach, called, they told me, caput medusæ, Medusa's head. On the 4th day (13th Mar '94), by now motionless & blue-grey all over, not unlike a statue of slate, she finally caught up with what she always claimed to be fleeing, ever since the day in the nursery when she found a butterfly lying dead on the sill & I explained what was what. 'But I don't want to die!' she screamed (screamed!), & I was spanked.*

*Unjustly. The rejection of death's a disease, but she didn't catch it from me. On the contrary, she, in her going, infected me with some of her corrosive despair. She errs & I'm spanked. Where's the sense in that? The illness grew in her own mind. Inevitably it blasted her into stillness & the halls of Dis. <u>Kaputt agathæ.</u>*

\*

*I'm in a bad mood, despite this smelly booze. I'm meant to be in a bad mood, it's nearly the end of vac, there's no call for dash. Wish you were here.*

*Anyway, your report. I despise pretentious titles, there's no reason I cdn't simply call these pages "What I Did in my Hols." Instead look, I'm titling them "Hapax" and giving them –*

*Damn it, I devoutly despise epigraphs. What are they but prose, which is ephemeral, trying to nip the relative immortality of verse? I'm not one for vernacular poetry at all – for anyone since Prudentius. But we've already had Lawrence, & now I'm thinking of (of all middle-brow & suburban interior decorators of the mind) Dylan Thomas. Imagine choosing such a one to kick things off! A dipsomaniac of low birth & a Welshman. Just goes to show what a bad influence distilled gentian has on a fine mind. Black lamps.*

*All right, another glass of dodgy liqueur finished, off we go –*

# VIII.

# HAPAX

*The force that through the green fuse drives the flower*
*Drives my green age; that blasts the roots of trees*
*Is my destroyer.*

DYLAN THOMAS

*We're agreed about the premise – that the yen for immortality is a sickness, a ravening after what doesn't exist so can't be tasted or even sniffed? It must be that way. Think of the trouble we'd give ourselves if we wondered whether such victuals were on offer somewhere! No, the desire not to die must simply be a distemper of the brain, incurable, generally fatal.*

*So much for the overture. Let's put on the detached expression of clinicians to consider a young Akandan who had it Bad.*

⌒

**A PRODIGY**

João Mbingu was the cleverest boy at the Mission school and the Fathers hoped he might become a priest. He demanded guarantees. He daren't spend his life buried in the honeycomb of the Church if there was any risk of not emerging as a cardinal. He had to be famous; otherwise how would the name Mbingu live forevermore? (They'd christened him *João* at random. The name *Mbingu* he'd plucked out of the air at the age of ten: exactly out of the air, for the word means *heaven* or *sky*.)

The Fathers laughed at him and he left them, stealing from their meagre library that finger-burning, self-obsessed book, Augustine's *Confessions*.

What now? The shortest way to fame is the shedding of blood. João

Mbingu joined the army and learned to fight, attacking rebel camps deep in the hinterland of the Portuguese Cameroons. Then he defected and joined the rebels. He was a cruel but not effective guerrilla, being barely five foot tall and delicate for his height. The Mission had fed him up on white bread and boiled fowl, and in the jungle the soft flesh came off his bones. He was sick all the time; moreover his glasses steamed up, and when he took them off he was nearly blind. He once led, or rather waved, his little squad of rebels out of the bush and across a ragged lawn toward a blockhouse, not being able to see the Portuguese infantrymen and their heavy machine-gun. His men, who were more afraid of him than of the colonial soldiery, obeyed, and were shot to shreds. When João reached rebel headquarters, the only survivor of his troop, he was splattered with their blood, with one lens cracked, and thus acquired a reputation for revolutionary audacity.

He was careful not to do anything to blur that reputation. Indeed, he was careful to do nothing more while the Liberation War lasted. He slipped away from headquarters and lay low in a mountain hamlet, later renamed Joãoville, idle and safe. There were scrawny chickens and a goat in the hamlet's one mud lane; these, and the largest hut, belonged to a foolish lady and her two daughters, who were scared of him with reason. These three women slept in an outhouse. João slept alone all night and into the afternoon in the only bed, of teak and hemp-rope. Between cheek and gun was his only book, *Confissões de Agostinho de Hipona*, until his sweat and the steamy mountain air turned it to pulp. It was fed to the goat. Then João had no books, and found no need of them.

He was not a demanding guest so long as he was obeyed. He liked to hear the women gossip, although they were careful never to mention him. (They led such a cramped life he was grimly amazed they found so much to say to each other – he couldn't let them leave the hamlet, to betray him to the Portuguese or to the rebels.) He liked the sound and smell of their cooking. Finally, he liked to lie and listen to the old lady's short-wave radio, the pride of her existence, powered by a diesel generator. It was nearly thirty years old, but mountain folk know how to make things last. The tiny brass Portuguese arms and the inscription REPÚBLICA PORTUGUESA were nearly worn away, not from political feeling but from endless polishing with rendered-down chicken-fat. Its knobs were shiny, it scarcely crackled except just before thunderstorms, and it could easily pick up stations in Freetown and Dakar. Thus in his idleness João Mbingu taught himself English and French.

More importantly, Mbingu taught himself Mbingu, the particular language of his soul. There were no words in Mbingu for *courage, love* or *justice*; indeed only one passion could be adequately discussed in that language, *due-adoration-of-Mbingu*. Within that passion were many nuances and degrees. He could speak to himself of himself as endlessly, as variously, as luxuriantly, as an ascetic mystic speaks to himself of God.

Like any mystic, he was devoted to his one study but generally contemptuous of learning. His education at the Mission remained a discrete presence within his skull, like a brain tumour, quite separate from his own proper thoughts. He was at once mindless and high-brow, even bookish, inasmuch as books might serve the ceaseless propagation of Mbingu.

What is the point of having a mind? To search out Mbingu. His praise is the object and first duty of the universe, for praise proves his presence, while the non-existence of Mbingu was unthinkable. All knowledge is useless except as a path to the mbinguific vision. A cosmos without Mbingu in it would not be cosmic.

João, he was against death: I mean the only death he could believe, the blotting out of the only life that was real. As for the others …!

This is how I imagine him. His rejection of death was so absolute it devoured the rest of his humanity. He wanted immortality and nothing else, until he vanished into that one desire. There was no angle from which he could be described. What we'd normally call *he* was not just unseen, but invisible, even non-existent. What was real about him was – well, I'm not sure we have a word for it. But I want to show what it was like, or anyway what sort of deeds it contrived to commit.

〰

Mbingu's three-year idyll in the mountains was his true education. The Fathers had not trained, they had merely disquieted him. Now, as his body devoured generation after generation of the scrawny fowl, from time to time assaulting one of the daughters, his mind grew sharp and unique, exploring itself in solitude. *I am*, Mbingu would murmur to himself, *the wisest man in the Portuguese Cameroons. The wisest man in Africa*, and in a way this was no doubt so. He alone had penetrated his own unmapped hinterland, he alone beheld the beasts of which only rumour reaches the coastal trading-post. He was full of desire. He was hobbled by absolutely no illusions.

Yet for all its deftness, Mbingu's mind harboured an unconsciousness pure as the inward dumbness of a ruminant.

A gnu stands gazing vaguely over the savannah at a volcano. In the bony mass beneath its mane is a clump of nerve-endings, where trickles of electricity form the perennial image (we cannot call it an idea) of grass. Likewise in Mbingu's mind, often vacant, the icon on Mbingu was never absent. He was paradoxically both inert and rapt. He was lost in the Name. No university-kennelled intellectual, no scholar-hermit in his stereotypic cave, ever channelled more energy to one purpose.

João Mbingu's gnarled bonobo face, which had not seen a mirror since he left the Fathers, acquired in the mountains a godlike sheen. His milky eyes receded into his fœtal skull and began to appear divinely unmeaning. His lips were neither open nor closed. At first glance he was just one more scrawny clerkish colonial *peon*. The second glance left every viewer disturbed. This (by the way; but it's an important point) is why I'm content to think only of João this morning – why I don't need to think of sister Agatha, who looked like, and was, a dismal self-loathing nobody.

↬

But we're getting ahead of ourselves. There was no one to glance at Mbingu in his mountain hamlet days, except the goat and the three women, who kept their faces down when he looked their way.

In short, he did not have a very martial Liberation War. If it comes to that, the war did not involve much actual warfare for anyone. The Portuguese conscripts spent their time acquiring clap in the dens of Vila São Joaquim, the capital. The revolutionary cadres spent their time punishing villages they suspected of cooperating with the government, and purging each other for errors in Marxist-Leninist metaphysics. Each side thinned itself out nicely without often coming within range of the other.

Then suddenly there was a revolution back in Lisbon. Portugal, announced the new junta, was abandoning her empire, *os Camarões* with all the rest.

The Governor decamped, the army vanished; moving quickly Mbingu managed to reach Vila São Joaquim, which he had never seen, in time for the victory parade. He commandeered a jeep (was he not victor of the immortal Battle of the Bumbuna Blockhouse?) and, slightly in advance of the rest of the Akandan Liberation Army, was driven through the streets standing in the back seat, between two young men who had been postmen until the day before yesterday. They men wore fatigues and sun-glasses and cradled Czechoslovakian assault-rifles they did not know how to fire. They scowled terribly at the crowd and looked heroic. Mbingu did not. Although everything about him was small, his chin and lips were so disproportionately tiny he resembled a perpetually-startled baby animal. His tooth-brush moustache was brief and sad, his palms were unusually pink. Moreover, because he thought it best to keep his round spectacles in the pocket of his safari-suit, he grinned and waved at air, at empty buildings, not being able to make out the people. Who, impressed by such obliterating reserve, by his stiff arrogant bearing (the former postmen were holding his legs so he didn't tumble out of the jeep), thought it best to cheer him to the echo.

When they reached the *Palácio dos Governadores*, a larger building than

Mbingu had ever imagined, they found the gates standing open. He had his two young men bolt them shut, then ordered his driver to knock them down. It was, after all, not Mbingu's jeep.

The inhabitants of São Joaquim had played no part in the revolt and were nervous about the arrival of the guerrillas. They were shop-keepers and house-cleaners. The deliberate smashing of valuable things was for them a new, intoxicating idea. With a roar they lost control of themselves, and began to loot the Palace. They were still rioting about Mbingu's wrecked jeep, and he was still shouting at them about immortal revolution, when his unsmiling comrades arrived.

How they would have enjoyed denouncing his act for some fatal shade of Khrushchevism (on the one hand) or hyper-Maoist anti-revisionism (on the other)! But they could not make themselves heard above the mob. As it was, days passed before Mbingu stopped aching from their fraternal embraces, and this time both his lenses were shattered.


## BOREDOM

Such was the beginning of Mbingu's career in politics, or what passed as politics in the Revolutionary People's Republic of Akanda.

He was extremely good at it, having nothing to weigh down his ascent. His mind was perfectly streamlined. He had no conscience and no political views of any sort, Right or Left. More unusually, for an African statesman, he had no tribal allegiances. He had no father. His mother had been an outcast, a prostitute from far away, from God knows where, speaking nothing but truck-stop Swahili and a little pidgin. She had given him to the kindly Franciscans and wandered away. Mbingu was free of clan, friendship, loyalty, weakness of any sort. He had nothing but himself; or rather, not even a self: nothing but this extraordinary spiritual quest to make his name, an invented name, unforgettable. That quest was the only human thing about him. It was his secret from the world.

Immaculate selfishness buoyed him skyward. He twisted, he swayed back again, he betrayed colleagues and avenged their deaths on their fellow betrayers. He waded through blood and did not relent and shortly after his thirtieth birthday was elected President of Akanda with considerably more than a hundred percent of the ballots. (A number of local commissars decided to take no chances; young Mbingu was known to resent lack of zeal in the revolutionary cause.) He was constantly reëlected until at last he bowed to the popular will and accepted the Presidency-for-Life. When I came across him he had been grinding down his wretched little republic for twenty years.

Poor fellow. In the mountains he'd been a spiritual athlete, training his soul to outrun his fellows. He strove, then fell asleep after lunch and dinner like a tired child. He'd duly outrun them all, and been crowned with olive. Now what?

Vacancy, which made it so easy for Mbingu to rise, robbed him of purpose once he reached the zenith. He found himself empty. The one point of existence was to keep existing, the one object of his rule was to rule. It's a dreary business being an African dictator if all you crave is deathless infamy.

He was perfectly aloof. He wanted nothing *for* the Akandan people, good or bad. He wanted nothing *from* then but nervous obedience now, which he got; and hateful memory forever after. And that, he knew, he could not have. A Douala proverb haunted him: *Take thy hand from stirring the bucket, fool, watch how swiftly the water stills itself.* It's hard to nourish a personality cult if you have no personality. Mbingu suspected that, a few years after he died or was deposed, even the widows of the men he'd slain, even the children he'd maimed, would be muddling him up with the previous dictator, Xanta, the one he had overthrown – or confounding him with whichever dictator came next. He'd lose in time their terror, just as he'd lose the cities, mountains and airports named for himself. Humanity's so old and wicked, one cruelty's so much like another. Infamy's nearly as hard to fix as fame. There's no enormity a tyrant can commit which isn't old hat.

Mbingu was too brilliant to muddle himself. He didn't hide from the hard fact of public forgetfulness. He'd learned desire in the exacting school of St Augustine. *I have formed me for Myself,* he'd tell himself, *and my heart is restless till it finds rest in Me.* A good motto, as long as it lasts. But how could he not be restless, when he knew repose was bound to come to an end?

⤳

Margot: I'm bound to point out that Mbingu had more self-knowledge than you had, back in the spring, when you were so full of yourself. You tried to re-label the months. Mbingu knew that this sort of thing is a mistake, an over-reaching. The calendar's too mundane, too close to the life of the mob, which can never be made to care enough who is oppressing and culling it. Its immortality makes it heartless. Mbingu shook his head sadly when one of his fellow Presidents-for-Life, over in Central Asia, renamed the months after himself, renamed bread after his own mother – and even worse, renamed himself *Türkmenbaşy the Great,* Head of all Turkmen, after his country. That's quite the wrong way round. Xanta had declared himself *Baba-wa-Wakanda,* Father of All Akanadans; the title only made Akanda impatient to obliterate daddy, to forget him.

Mbingu had toyed with getting rid of the made-up name *Akanda*. *The Mbingan Republic of Cameroon*? Or, still more baldly, *Mbingia*? No: wouldn't such names be all-too-obviously extravagances that couldn't last?

The people are water. Mbingu could never brand on them the evil stigma of himself. *My immortality must be global. It must be burned into paper, which lasts. How? Even dreadful Turkmenistan is full of natural gas, which makes it a little interesting to the world. But Akanda's a small place, inherently wretched. There's not one thing here you can't find somewhere else.* Thus he mourned.

⌒

There was one moment of rapturous relief, in 1999. An outraged cable arrived from the Akandan embassy in Washington: *Newsweek* had denounced Mbingu as 'the Butcher of Akanda'!

The international edition of *Newsweek*! Eternity at last!

But when the weekly plane from Lagos arrived at João Mbingu International Airport; when the van went bouncing from the airport, swerving round the gigantic potholes of Avenida Mbingu, the main road of São Joaquim, now Mbinguville; when the triple gates of the Presidential Compound, *ci-devant* the Palace of the Governors, had opened for the van, and closed behind it; when the van been unloaded; when a boy in the Presidential livery (monogrammed here and there *J.M.* in fraying gold thread) had crossed the courtyard with its malfunctioning fountain, and come up the big wooden staircase to the shady loggia where the Perpetual President liked to sit with his fly-whisk, twitching, twitching; when this boy had been patted down by a bodyguard; when he had been allowed to approach His Excellency and place the manilla package on the low marble table; when (at last) Mbingu had torn open the package – well, there had been disappointment, grievous and burning. He'd never known such sudden suffering.

He was not on the cover, he was not in the table of contents. The article about him ('article'!) included no photograph – was a paragraph long – merely filled one box on a page of boxes under the single headline 'AFRICAN OPPRESSORS', noting the enormities of the Mogul of Gabú; the Autocrat of Kuruland, recently overthrown and hacked to pieces; the Bully of Côte d'Ébène, who was a half-hearted amateur not to be mentioned in the same breath; *and himself*. This was not immortality. If anything, *Newsweek* had violated his common individuality, traducing him as a mere specimen of a type.

Beyond endurance! *Since eternal fame is my vocation, it's a sacred matter, and this – this is a sort of blasphemy*. It did not soothe Mbingu to ring his Foreign Minister and shout that the entire staff of the Washington embassy was to be recalled. It did not soothe him to sit devising what he would do to them and their families when they got back.

No. Not enough. He added the Foreign Minister and *his* family to the pile, he contemplated *their* shrieks as the heated iron spike made its appearance – . Still not enough. It would have to be a whole village.

He gestured; the bodyguard approached. '*Traga-me o Coronel Nge.*' The bodyguard scampered away to get the good Colonel, and Mbingu, calmer now, gave way to a certain reasonable self-pity. *It's* always *this way. I'm slighted, and find myself committing atrocities with no particular object in view, just because the idea of being forgotten is so unspeakable. Well, at least for a few busy hours the village of … let me think; yes, Madowum, up in Província do Norte, the Northerners haven't heard from me for a while – will not be able to overlook my existence. Ah, I hear Nge coming up the stair….*

It was easy to recognise Nge's gait, his irregular clatter. Akandan mothers imitate it to frighten their children when they are naughty. The Chief of the Presidential Guard was finely-made as a boy, and very tall, his grandmother having been a Nubian slave in the brave days before the Portuguese put down slavery. But a lifetime of adventure had chopped him about. Nge's back was twisted from a police interrogation during the Xanta regime; he had to advance by loping right-hip first, like a crab; one leg was so short that when he tried to stand straight, as he did now before the present dictator, it dangled above the ground. His right hand, with three fingers lost to a premature grenade, had the tic of tearing the air when it wasn't clutching its gun. A knife-slash across his face had split left cheek and right chin, and these puckered wounds so resembled his thin lips that he seemed to boast an X-shaped double smile. When he was winded, as now, breath leaked out of his left cheek in a moist quiet hiss.

'Madowum, Colonel. Madowum: I understand subversion is rife there,' murmured the President, and a gleam came into Nge's good eye. He raised his claw to his shaved head in salute, and loped away.

Mbingu sighed. He knew his severities, whether politically calculated or, as now, merely therapeutic, did him no good. I mean they got him no closer to a place in history. News of Nge's romp at Madowum would dribble back to the capital. Possibly the Western ambassadors might get to hear. At best, one of them would ask for an audience and be brusque with him – with him, Revolutionary Head of State for life! – threatening to reduce aid.

A memorable crisis? No. Mbingu knew nothing would change. Rich countries would keep giving him money, for the same reason they kept sanctioning him, taking money away: it made them feel better. *They relieve in me a drop of surfeit liquidity. I am their spittoon.* After these humiliating interviews he sometimes felt so glum and pointless he'd have *another* village massacred just to cheer himself up and make a point about national sovereignty.

Meanwhile the puling ambassador would have returned to his air-conditioned embassy to write a report, to be sent to Rome or Lisbon, Paris or London, and filed. Which was scarcely better than absolute oblivion. Decades from now assiduous historians might call it up and read about the Madowum atrocity, but would it leap out at them, would they interpret it as a turning-point in postcolonial history? No. Mbingu would merely earn his place in their indexes as one more despot, one more bad man in Africa.

This was not historical grandeur as young João had glimpsed it, back in his spotless boyhood – before he had ever dreamed there could be such random cruelty as the cruelty of the editors of *Newsweek*. His spirits sank so low it was in his mind to call Nge back and

↩

The revolutionary twentieth century faded into the dubious twenty-first, which wore on a dozen years. Black Africa's *rôle* in history remained slight, and even within Africa Akanda's old-fashioned tyranny was disregarded – or patronised as quaint, a period piece that must soon end and be forgotten. Journalists would say as much. They had no compunction.

*Poor fellow*, Mbingu would murmur to himself, *what does it matter* sub specie æternitatis (he'd learned this dangerous phrase in the Mission) *if our face is on every coin, every postage stamp? That our gilt-framed portrait hangs by law in every house and shop? That prayers are addressed to us by every parish priest too timid for martyrdom? We know it won't last.* Self-pity, once indulged, is as hard to shake off as jealousy. *Our grandeur won't last .... And* even now *we never get to see it.*

This was true. The three previous Presidents of Akanda had all been assassinated; Mbingu had, indeed, helped assassinate them. The first principle of his regime was never to leave the presidential compound. He dwelt within, safe but not at peace, with his three wives, his scores of bodyguards, and his thousands of books. His ministers would come in to him through the triple gates. Sometimes, if *o Presidente perpétua* was irritated, they did not come out that way but with the kitchen scraps, dismembered.

It was not a wholesome way of life. Mbingu had been a sensitive little fellow since his Mission school days. He was, according to his lights, what the Americans call a people person. He needed to get out and about, to meet his subjects; and in solitude he grew bluer and bluer.

His power was unchallenged. Every Akandan with political interests in was dead or in exile. All who remained were eager to stay unnoticed. Even Mbingu's Western donors had grown tired of making a fuss about human rights and simply handed over the money, sighing. In any case his rule was a little milder, his massacres rarer. Nge had to remind his master to make himself feared, and the President would authorise killings with bemused wobbles of the head. His heart was no longer in it.

By 2013 the sawdust had quite dribbled out. For a whole year he scarcely moved. The essential business of Akandan government was left undone: disease and poverty had to do what Nge kept pestering him to do. Mbingu, wearing his gnu-face, waved him away.

*What has brought us to this pass? Did we not see our rightful destiny from afar? Have we not pursued it faithfully all our life? Have we ever slackened in devoiton? Are we not working out our salvation in fear and trembling as the Fathers told us to do? We are not yet sixty and feel used up. If it were safe to retire we'd almost be tempted to give up statesmanship. Oh, hell!*

Thus he communed with himself in his agony.

⌇

As I've said, Margot, Mbingu both was and wasn't intellectual. His mind, like everything else in the universe it was a tool. It existed to serve the one good. But it was a sharp tool. He had a certain seasoned faith in its agility. He believed there might be a way of thinking himself into everlastingness.

Therefore he spent many melancholy hours turning over pages in his library, which was an extensive polyglot affair inherited (looted, if you like) from the last Portuguese governor.

It was in the library that the great change came about, on a certain evening, a year into his great sulk, on the last evening of November.

## INTIMATIONS OF IMMORTALITY

These doings must sound bygone: weary hearsay from Assyria before it fell. In fact we're talking about a night just six weeks ago: 30th November 2013, a little after eleven Akanda time, which as a symbol of her incomparable progress is set three hours ahead of Greenwich, rather than one hour, as with her puny neighbours.

A bit after eleven, then. Mbingu's wives are startled to hear mighty shouts. The noise is all the more disturbing coming from such a slight shy shuffling squinting man as their husband. Is he in pain? They daren't go and find out. His library is sacrosanct. His first wife was one of his earliest victim. They have to wait trembling for what would emerge.

What emerges is a brisk laughing shouting fellow, almost a new Mbingu. He visits all his wives, and in the morning they, being plump illiterates, decide he must have been seized by *ndebunze*, ancestral spirits, who sometimes do return to give their living descendants pep.

In fact he had done what is more marvellous, although it happens all the time all over the world and almost excuses the whole pompous pother of libraries. João Mbingu had found exactly what he wanted to know in a book, and so was saved.

What he'd read about was a certain convention of science. I've no doubt that you, Margot, you learnèd child, were aware of it before you could speak. It was news to him, and his first reaction was a blaze of resentment. *So! the Mission Fathers felt they must withhold such perilous knowledge from us natives!* For a moment he might have slaughtered every missionary in Akanda, had there been any left. The next moment: *By Santo António! And they were* right *to withhold it!* For Mbingu is not incapable of a certain olympian fairness.

⌒

This was Mbingu's revelation: Linnæan binomials are never emended. Scientists have wisely bound themselves to this absolute rule. Once a newly-discovered species has had a name registered with an international body that's it, it can't be re-labelled. Thus there's a blind cave-beetle first identified in 1933, styled *Anophthalmus hitleri* for the new German Chancellor, and still called that because there's no mechanism for tinkering with taxonomy. *Linnæan binomials are never emended*: Mbingu read this and found it the word of life to his soul.

Here, then, was the one true immortality. For however great, statesmen go out of vogue: an ungrateful rabble lynches the man, extirpates his family, smashes his statues, burns his portraits, tears down the street-signs, rechristens his airport. The species named for him, those they cannot touch. The unalterable Latin name is all that matters.

A thousand years hence schoolchildren will be getting Stalin and Putin muddled, they'll have trouble distinguishing Führer from Kaiser. *A. hitleri* will still be lurking in its five humid Balkan caves – or not, since it's being hunted into rarity by neo-Nazis who like to own specimens. Extinction for such a reason is just fame inverted. Earth herself may perish; men, unexterminatable as mosquitoes, will infest other star systems; no one'll remember which blob on the map was Italy, which Spain. Yet the encyclopædia article on the wafer-trapdoor-spider *Aptostichus barackobamai* (with a photo of it leaping through its silk-hinged lid to bite a field-mouse) will be as sure as the entry on the flamingo, or the Emperor penguin.

*Caligula will be rehabilitated one day*, thinks Mbingu, *or not; personally I'm an admirer. What do historians' opinions matter? History doesn't have the last word, lepidopterology does. The Giant Silkworm's everlastingly classified as* Caligula japonica. *Yes!*

It's dawn. He's in bed with his third wife and she, bundle of fat innocence as she is, takes credit for his ecstatic grin. He slaps aside her arms, gets out of bed, straightens his spectacles. *And closer to home, consider dear old Julius Nyerere, a monster just before my time, collectivised Tanzania and impoverished a whole people, died smug.* Mbingu dresses himself in his Field Marshal's uniform. *Nyerere may be vilified as the centuries pass, he may drop from view – but anyway a handsome cichlid named* Haplochromis nyererei *will be swimming around Lake Victoria.*

He's passing through the long corridors of his palace now, paved with marble, speckled with mould, stained with the rainwater which can somehow never be kept out. His staff scuttle out of sight as they hear him coming. *"Lake Victoria!" It commemorates the Great White Mother; in a thousand years it will commemorate someone else. Tanzania's a country Nyerere invented, assuredly it won't be there much longer. But the fish will. The fish will. Yes!* He thought of Mbingia, and sniggered. How tawdry tha project seemed behind his new, more beautiful, more spiritual hope.

He's reached the great ballroom, where, in the years before liberation, the Governors of the *Camarões português* entertained. His own less seemly receptions happen here too. Then it was hung with full-length portraits of all hundred-and-three Governors, stretching back to 1649 when Vila São Joaquim was founded at the mouth of the Rio Bragança. Those paintings are gone now, burned. Each has left a long ghostly rectangle, slightly darker than the pale sun-faded orange walls. In each rectangle hangs, askew, a different framed photograph of Mbingu.

*The friars told us boys about creation* (thinks the living Mbingu, looking lovingly up and down the parallel lines of a-hundred-and-three lifeless Mbingus). *They hinted at the truth.* Nothing ever hangs straight in Africa. The god of Akanda pauses before a portrait lurched right over on its side. His eyes are shut, he adjusts it by feel. Chlunkchlunkchlunkchlunk: he's back in the Mission chapel. Cool darkness, gold slits in black shutters, altar candles glaring more palely, fans going chlunkchlunk overhead, prefects walking up and down to make sure the boys are attending. The wonderful child João is attending, he's boggling, brine pricks his eyes, for one of the Fathers is reading from Genesis: 'Whatsoever' (*whatsoever!*) 'Adam called any living creature henceforth that was its name.' *Was I not dizzy –*

Here the string breaks. The photo shatters noisily on the warped ballroom floor.

Normally this would be a shooting matter. This morning Mbingu opens his eyes and magnanimously smiles, lost in pleasant memory. He turns over the ruined photo with his shoe. Mbingu and Mbingu smile at each other through shards of glass. *Were we not dizzy with delight even then, even then? How right the Mission Fathers were to say no more, to desist from flinging pearls before swine. Swine!* He's musing on the other boys at school, who bullied or ignored him, who nicknamed him *Mbungo*, that is, *tsetse-fly*. He's hunted down every one of them in his years of power. Every one. His smile grows wider. "*Whatsoever Adam called any living creature henceforth that was its name.*" *Adam – but not a word of Linnæus. The friars left it for the greatest of their charges, the greatest of all Akandans, of all Africans, to discover that the sovereignty of Adam is unabated! Even now it belongs to whoever publishes a precise description of a hitherto-unknown species in a peer-reviewed scientific journal.*

*What subtle glory!* How happy Mbingu is. He's reverting to the near-seminarian of half-a-century before. He's working the catch on one of the ballroom's gilded French windows. *How frail* – here the handle breaks in his hand, corrupted by eternal warm dampness; he is amused – *how frail, how abstract it seems. A double-barrelled Latinism affixed to some remote organism by a dingy naturalist. Yet it's momentous as baptism.* Mbingu sighs, pushing open a tall glass window, which flashes violently in the early sun, and steps out onto the rusty balcony. *The creature passes in a twinkling from void, from wordless mindless gristle or fibre, into the universe of thought. It's named, it's reborn. It carries into eternity the name that called it forth.* The balcony creaks beneath his slight weight. The Perpetual President laughs.

An uncanny noise. The sentries before the palace leap out of their sentry-boxes, look up, gasp, spring to attention and stand saluting in the morning glare, amidst the barbed-wire and sandbags. He does not notice them. *Lay not up for yourselves treasures upon earth where moth and rust doth corrupt, and where thieves break through and steal.* He is gazing out benignly over Mbinguville: at the square hulking new grey prison on the ridge, the Mbingu Institute for Scientific Readjustment, built for him by the Chinese. At his dilapidated cathedral, once white. Over his fish-market, which he can smell, corrugated-iron already shaking in the hard metallic light. Over the cubic mud houses of his people, each one grubbily pink-washed by decree. Over what had been the Rio Bragança and is, as the Rio do Presidente, essentially a sluggish sewer, although even here early morning is doing wonders with its brownness. *Lay up for yourselves treasures with the International Botanical Congress, and the International Commission on Zoological Nomenclature.*

His ambition is clear in his head. He despises certain celebrity fossils he read about last night: the trilobite named for Marilyn Monroe, *Norasaphus monroeæ*, because it was hourglass-shaped, *Arcticalymene viciousi* named for Sid Vicious just because. Extinct species, pah! *Moth and rust have already corrupted them. When the whole point is never to be extinct. I need my name bolted forever to what will go on living. Proving by its continued existence that I, Mbingu – that is to say, My Excellency Field Marshal Dr João Sana-na huruma Mbingu, Guide of the Akandan Peoples, Perpetual President of Akanda, Ph.D. (João Mbingu Acad.), esq. – that I too existed.*

Something living and growing, that's the point, something close at hand. And all at once it strikes him: he already knows what his species is to be, he already knows where it is. *Glory glory, hallelujah.* he shouts; and, more surprisingly, *Adolphe de Brûlé!*

This splendid second revelation is almost too much. He raises his arms to the rising sun. If he could pray to anything but himself, he might. His laughter grows so strident passers-by in the dangerous vicinity of the palace gates (once heroically knocked down) glance about, see their President, and take to their heels.

Africa's a distillation of the sun. Only the sun is quite real. Its brightness, intense even at that hour, flashes twin suns from Mbingu's spectacles. It turns the medals and epaulettes of his Field-Marshal's tunic into meteors. It makes his tiny white uneven teeth glare. It fills his mind. It casts a black Mbingu-shaped shadow westward over the walls of the palace, the palace once raised, and long maintained, by the servants of Mbingu's predecessors:

*Suas Majestades Fidelíssimas*
the Kings (*pela graça de Deus*) of Portugal
and of the Algarves of either side of the sea in Africa,
Lords of Guinea
and of the Conquest, Navigation, and Commerce
of Æthiopia, Arabia, Persia, and India,
*etcetera, etcetera,*
*etcetera.*

## LIFE IS EXILE

For centuries Portuguese governors had languished in their palace, staring out to sea, petitioning *Suas Majestades Fidelíssimas* for recall, generally dying of homesickness or blackwater fever before manumission arrived from Lisbon. For centuries slavers and missionaries had worked the coast, sometimes dying of want, or thirst, or drink, or drowning, or being speared, before malaria could get them. Still no European bothered to strike into the interior of what is now Akanda. It was 1861 before the first one tried: a gallant, dejected young royalist with sallow skin and a sparse goatee: the Comte de Brûlé.

No traveller has ever been so unadjectival. Adolphe-Marie-Caton-Louis Brûlé scaled ranges, crossed dunes, forded torrents, penetrated jungles, faced down hostile tribes, shot (out of hand) a number of witch-doctors, overawed slave-traders and hunted elephants, without complaint, without excitement, without affect. He seems to have inhabited a half-lit universe, dark beige on light beige.

It may have been the ruin of the royalist cause that left him so dogged. Perhaps he was simply bred that way. The motto of his house is *Devoir et la persévérance*. They seem always to have been a dour lot. The one exception was a bastard sprig, Étienne Brûlé, who migrated to Québec and thrust himself into the conifery centre of the New World. He became a Huron among the Hurons, and in their company saw what no white had seen before: the vastnesses of Niagara, New York, Susquehanna and the Great Lakes. He was still in his thirties when his brother-Hurons ate him.

Young Adolphe de Brûlé, growing up in the family atmosphere of pre-exhausted goodness, resolved to be an explorer too, like cousin Étienne. The king did not return. Europe was a wilderness of infidelity. Duty, duty and perseverance: why not seek out places God had intended to be wild? It was in this weary spirit that he intruded first on the Rif, then on Guatemala, Burma, finally on the forbidding backcountry of the Portuguese Cameroons.

It's also true that he possessed a sprightly wife who encouraged his expeditions. '*Allez, mon cœur, partez!*' the Comtesse de Brûlé would urge almost as soon as he got back. She was zealous for his fame. Conceivably she wanted him out of Paris. She had literary, bohemian impulses and pictured herself as a widow, keeping an intellectual salon. Which is exactly what she achieved; she was quite grand for a while; we find her, as the aged M$^{me}$ Timoléon d'Amoncourt, tucked away on a page of *Sodome et Gomorrhe*.

Meanwhile Adolphe rivalled in Africa what Étienne had done in America. He was almost certainly the first white man to see, certainly the first to ascend, the steamy overgrown volcano he christened Mont Saint-Louis, later Monte Mbingu. In his dull way Brûlé observed its subdued eruption; he described a dozen undiscovered species of fauna and flora on its slopes, including the spectacular golden Cameroon chimpanzee, *Pan troglodytes mariantoinetti*, now extinct. As he descended the volcano a mangani ape, *G. gorilla burroughsi*, tore his arms with its fangs. He dutifully wrote up his notes (switching to his left hand when his right became fetid and paralysed), packed them up in waterproof cotton for shipment to Europe, then settled down to die in agony far up the Gboko River – that is, the Rio Mbingu – in the village of Gboko, which he marked on his map as Sainte-Orthodoxie. It has since become Fort-Presidente-Mbingu and has a barracks where appalling things are done.

The Comte's last words were 'The discomfort doesn't cease': what a ghastly way to make your bow! '*L'inconfort ne disparaît pas.*' God! Back in the Faubourg Saint-Germain his widow, yawning prodigiously, perhaps murmurming 'Bon Dieu!' now and then, saw his manuscript through the press. *Un Journal d'une expédition à travers les montagnes des Camerouns portugais, et à certains autres lieux* (Paris, 1864, four volumes) remains, a century and a half later, a classic of colourlessness.

～

Yet Brûlé supplanted Augustine as Mbingu's favourite author.

It had to happen. The literature of Akanda was not large in the dark days of Portuguese oppression, and has been even slighter in the glorious epoch of the Revolutionary People's Republic. An Akandan dictator wanting to read about his possessions pretty much has to read Brûlé, who was not just the first but almost the last literate human to describe hills, plateaux and streams which, for added piquancy, are now generally named after the dictator himself.

Mbingu had thoroughly updated the nomenclature in his own copy. Wherever he opened *Un Journal d'une expédition* he'd find pencilled crossings-out all over the page and lots of pencilled *Mbingu*s and *João*s and *Presidente*s in the margins.

But it wasn't just vanity that made Mbingu delight in Brûlé. In his years of wistfulness, and especially in this final year of comatose despair, the President had leant upon the explorer's quixotic spirit. He learned to love that pious drabness. It consoled him. Was not Brûlé's fealty (to *Dieu, honneur, sang* and *roi*) rhe twin of Mbingu's stubborn devotion to Mbingu? The spirit of the aging, Mission-reared tyrant reached yearningly toward the young bigot. *How lonely you were, Comte! How hemmed in by a* canaille *who would not understand! How I admire you, pioneer of my domains, seeker-out of my eponyms!* Turning over the familiar pages of *Un Journal*, Mbingu, solipsist and monster, came as close as he could ever come to fraternity, to humanity, to love.

～

As we'd expect, the Comte was an extremely cautious naturalist. There's only one controverted observation in his whole book. Thus occurs in Chapter XCVIII of volume three, where he mentions seeing on Mont Saint-Louis a curious mountain orchid, deep blue in colour, epiphytic, quadripollinial and sympodial (which means, let's see, it often grows up trees but doesn't kill them, has four blobs of pollen, and – some over-subtle point to do with root growth). This particular flower has never been seen since. To be sure, there's a species rather like it, *Polystachya cooperi*, immortalising an unworthy Mr Cooper: a rare, indeed endangered orchid, growing only in the vicinity of Monte Mbingu. But since *P. cooperi* has cream or greenish-white flowers, botanists have been inclined to disregard Brûlé's sky-blue orchid as a freak of nature, or a mistake.

Or even as a fib. This is view implied in the standard work, McMahon's *Dusky Bloom: Mountain Flora of West Africa*. "As for the blue *Polystachya* purportedly observed by M. de Brûlé, who was, after all, an eccentric, a Frenchman, doubtless given to sensational impressions, we may confidently ...."

*A fib!* What pleasure it gave Mbingu to rip that page out of *Dusky Bloom*. Still, the slur remained, McMahon himself was out of reach, and Mbingu felt a pang whenever he re-read Brûlé's account of the blue flower. *A falsehood by* you, *Comte? Impossible! Calumny! Is it not mortal sin to bear false witness?* Of all the catechism, this was the one prohibition still alive in the darkening mind of João Mbingu.

## TIME OUT

*Now look, Margot. About true testimony and darkening minds. – Let's take a break from the Akandan comedy. The first act's done, predicament, relief. I've something more personal to record if I dare. Do I?*

*Let's approach it this way. I have a soft job: I help expensively-schooled young persons such as you read things that were written to be enjoyed. In Latin, a language which is, all things considered, easy and fun. A soft life. The only people I know with a softer time are those fatuous so-called colleagues of mine who 'teach' literature in the vernacular. (Why not hire adults to help youths* eat*? Sit behind, arms round, lift fork, push jaws up and down, dab lips?)*

*However, there's one gruelling aspect of my line of work: the blank refusal of students to work through long dull paragraphs, in Latin or English. You invariably* skip *– you're almost physically unable to work your way through. Thus I know that if I'm dreary enough in the first few sentences of a paragraph, you'll jump to the next. If the dumpling's inedible, anything is safe inside. Thus I can both relieve grief by writing down the following awkward reminiscence, yet be sure it'll remain unread: clever* clever *Felix Culpepper, who is now talking to himself. Stupid* stupid *Agatha Culpepper, who early on a certain evening 'phoned me. It was a bad moment, not that it was ever a good moment to converse with Agatha, which is to say listen to her monologues about the horror* *(as she called it) of being blotted out and her agony (so she reckoned it) at the meaninglessness of mortal life, callow ideas even for a nineteen year-old, don't you think? Ah but you're only twenty-one yourself, Margot, and not reading this anyway. Of course I might this once have listened to Agatha, that would have been virtuous. I might have hung up on her which would have been at least human; after all, I was then just short of my sixteenth birthday, and might reasonably have repelled sepulchral chatter. Instead I put the 'phone on the sofa, covered it with another heavy sofa cushion, and stole away. I believe I invented this trick. I've often used it to insult callers. Delightful to think of them talking away – wheedling into nothingness – growing at last troubled by my limitless silence – finding it more crushing than any riposte – begging for some answer, bullying, shouting – still I keep mum – they grow enraged – contradicting, accusing themselves – falling silent themselves – breathing, exhausted – slamming down the receiver still unsure if I'm listening divinely detached, amused…. I'd be interesting to know how much wheedling Agatha did before giving up. Perhaps none: perhaps she took her medicine, ninety-six gulps' worth, down the 'phone, the moment I stopped speaking. She was always a noisy gulper, a messy eater, belcher, snorer, farter, stomach-rumbler. We can't tell. She was found by her flatmate, sexy Isabel, in a coma, with her 'phone off the hook. This was just an hour or so after Aggy rang me, and she was still alive, more or less. Isabel, bless her, hung up and called an ambulance, and the police failed to trace Aggy's last call. Naturally I didn't 'fess up then and haven't told anyone since. Yet the episode's been on my mind on and off for twenty years. Aggy was boring God knows even as sisters go, but for once I would have liked to hear her trite arguments for despair, I mean if they really did reach a proper conclusion with the ripping open of six packets of paracetamol. The weakness of eloquent nihilist rants on high table is that the necessary conclusion's never reached, never acted out, although I occasionally give a steak-knife a bit of shove in the direction of the speaker, <u>Come on, prove your case</u>. I'm unconvinced by despairing philosophy, and remain, all things considered, rather cheery in my views. There. That's the incident, no, appalling confession of non-event, purged onto paper. <u>L'inconfort ne</u>*

*disparaît pas* – still, I'm glad I've written it down. I'm
possibly a wicked man but share one noble principle
with Mbingu: even if we skimp our duties to God and
man, our duty to immortal history remains. Since
we're mortal, our most mortal sin is to bear ceaseless
false witness, thus killing truth (which is to say reality)
once we're ourselves dead, unreal, unreadable. It's
heinous not to record the whole truth somewhere.
*There*. Now for one dull sentence to round out this
dumpling-paragraph and make sure you don't try
nibbling through the dough backwards, and so to Act
II. The Comte de Brûlé was so fanatic a monarchist he
wouldn't touch stamps bearing the scandalous words
RÉPUBLIQUE FRANÇAISE, and insisted his wife send
her letters through the Belgian legation, a very slow
process which meant he died without knowing he was
a father at last, the father of a very beautiful son who
died at nearly a hundred leaving scores of descendants.

## A BALL

So far: President Mbingu has discovered that the name of a species is changeless. And: the tidings have fallen on him like a gospel. Then: on his first bright
morning of rebirth he realised what the species must be.

Therefore: he decreed a ball. Every religion has festivals, and Mbingu's
worship of Mbingu was not unsociable just because it was selfish. What, on
this day of days, was no revelry to be ordered? When Mbinguan immortality,
hitherto a matter of faith, had taken scientific shape? Unthinkable!

He swung about from the sunny balcony and strode through the corridors of the presidential palace shouting for secretaries. By noon his cabinet,
his chiefs-of-staff, the editor of the *Correio da Mbinguville*, the harassed Director of the National Bank and all the ambassadors had been summoned to
a birthday celebration for the following evening, the second of December.

&#8253;

President Mbingu had last kept his birthday just two months before. What
of that? One of the privileges of orphanhood is not to know the day. It was a
privilege he did not forgo. His birthday parties were frequent, especially since
he had sunk into paralysing despair. They were his one relief. They pleased

him, although no one else, often ending as they did in abrupt changes of ministers, in rampages by his drunken bodyguard, then summary executions the next morning when the President was crapulous. Mbingu's upbringing at the Mission had not extended to wine-drinking. In any case he was so delicately-made he would have done better to leave it alone.

~

Warily, therefore, before the siesta was over the next afternoon, the shop-keepers of Mbinguville put up their shutters. The President-and-Guide's birthdays, which generally ended in riot, sometimes began that way too. The most cautious took their families away, to spend the night out on the shapeless fringe of Mbinguville, where the shantytowns of immigrants from *Província do Norte* blur into semi-jungle and informal dumps, and the monkeys come down to scavenge behind the tents, picking resentfully at the loose stitches holding together the plastic sheets.

Warily nightfall settled on the city. Of course nightfall is never very tranquil in Mbinguville. Dusk is when headless bodies make their appearance in the Rio do Presidente. Even after days such as this, when it's worked, the electricity fails around sunset. In any case there's a curfew because of the Emergency, which has lasted since independence. But tonight felt different: this was intensified silence, the blackness of a city sacked.

Warily the ambassadors tied their white bow-ties. Many of their wives had developed sudden political head-colds and would all stay in their Residencies with the gates bolted. These women sat on double-beds to watch their husbands pinning on decorations, saying, depending on temperament, '*Ne bois rien!*' or '*Achtung!*' or '¡*Odio estas bolas!*', none of which helped in the least.

Warily, very warily, Ernesto Nge, Commandant of the Presidential Guard, donned in solitude body armour, then a ceremonial uniform tailored to minimise his various deformities. Warily he arranged the silver braid that usually made him feel so expansive. It was a year since Mbingu had commissioned a massacre worth remembering. He been looking at him, at Nge, strangely of late; Nge half believed their ancient partnership was coming to an end. He strapped a second revolver into the concenient hollow left by his badly-healed broken pelvis.

Warily the Bishop of Vila São Joaquim began to recite Vespers, glancing now and then out the bars of his cell, high in the wall of the enormous grey prison, over the stricken stillness of Mbinguville. Or of São Joaquim. Which? That question was precisely why he'd been in solitary confinement for four years. The President generously allowed God to share his own glory in the services of the Church; it was only fair his own name should be embedded in the episcopal title. The Vatican was dragging its feet. So here the Bishop of whatever-it-was sat. Warders passed his *fufu* and rice through the trap without speaking. He received no news. But he could smell trepidation in the air. 'Not *another* birthday?' He shuddered, and went back to uneasy prayers over the darkling city.

⌇

Only the Presidential Compound, which has its own generators, blazed away, like a garish gambling paddle-boat trundling down a lightless river.

Most unwarily, in the depths of the Compound, the President began a bottle of lager and adjusted his colourful turban. It was his fad at present to dress in "native" robes, designed in Paris on principles of speculative *orientalisme*. Two of his wives nervously hung about, trying to shake out the folds of his robe, and being slapped about.

Nonetheless, the great man found himself quite teary with joy, even before the thin beer took hold.

*The only question is where, where: where should I publish my formal description of* Polystachya mbingi? *Not in* Portugaliæ Acta Biologica – *it is too dry.* The American Journal of Botany, *I think, yes.* "A New Species of Epiphytic Orchid in Montane Akanda. João Mbingu Ph.D." – *nothing more, no grand titles. I am simply a citizen of the republic of letters, casting my shining coin of truth into the treasury of learning. I offer it, sneering in passing at the cold scepticism of McMahon's* Dusky Bloom. *I bow.* Plaudite omnes. *Now I can die happy. Except that I can never die.* A few more sips of weak beer and he would be drunk, even before the party began.

In fact the party was already beginning, in a desultory way, in the huge decrepit ballroom. The invitation had said six o'clock; everyone knew better than to turn up before eight; now, at nearly nine, the host had yet to appear, and the flower of Mbinguville Society was restless. The palace servants, scared half out of their skins at having to make a decision, had yielded at last to Society's demands, and started filling glasses. But they daren't bring out the *canapés* without orders, they daren't. Everyone sighed for the master of ceremonies, a flamboyant perfumed creature of mixed Tuareg and Greek descent, engulfed a year ago in the last purge. He would have smoothed over the absence of the birthday boy, he would have got the party going. Without him the social life of the palace was chaotic.

So now the guests milled about in tails and gowns, pinched with famine, while offstage, in a warm pantry, trays of Iranian caviar and tinned *foie gras* lay open to the tropical night air, so that a gorgeous time was had by spores of botulism (*Clostridium beijerinckii*, named for Martinus Beijerinck, a curmudgeonly bacteriologist of yore) and by *Salmonella bongori* (immortalising a lizard from Bongor on the Logone River, in whose gut that strain of salmonella had first been isolated).

The presidential band had yet to rebound from the loss of their bandmaster, shot about the same time as the master of ceremonies. It had struck up *Um segundo sol,* a blaring tune, as soon as the first ambassador shuffled into the ballroom, but the President-and-Guide did not appear to welcome him. Dreading to seem unpatriotic, they therefore repeated the national anthem; and played it again; then again and again and again.

> *A second sun lights up the Bight of Bonny:*
> *Mbingu smiles, and all the world is gay:*
> *Immortal light breaks forth from Africa.*
> *Akandans! Greet the revolutionary day.*

After twenty airings mania began to show in the face of the bandsmen, and of the guests who had to hear.

The only people at ease were young Hūwangdi, Beijing's man in Akanda, and his wife – for he had dared to bring his wife. But then Aisin Gioro Hūwangdi was always at ease in the presidential compound. He was the one diplomat who always had access to the moody President.

What did they discuss? Everyone supposed that Hūwangdi was pressing Mbingu to admit Chinese aid and Chinese advisors, accept dams and roads and bridges, and become a satellite. Which was nonsense. Mbingu had no objection to money as such, but he was canny enough to know the peril of development. How many brother despots had fallen after their people grew maddened by the sight of well-fed foreign workers in luxurious portable cabins! No, he was content to keep revolutionary Akanda torpid with fear and malnutrition.

And as it happens, the Chinese ambassador was of the same mind. He offered nothing. The charm of Hūwangdi was simply Hūwangdi's conversation. His topics were the purity of his own Manchu ancestry, his freedom from the smallest soiling of Han blood; and the prospects of a renewed Celestial Kingdom. 'My House survived Mao, Your Excellency, because it was simply too aristocratic to persecute. With the Bolsheviks exterminating millions of belching yeoman on the charge of being landlords, it would hardly do to arraign a real gentleman. The contrast would have been too telling.' Mbingu would smile urbanely as to a fellow prince. Gutter-born, he was local heir to their Most Faithful Majesties the Kings of Portugal, Lords of Conquest, Navigation, and Commerce. That was the outward sign of his inward divinity. He loved social distinction. 'There are many such Houses left in China. None perhaps quite as well-descended as mine. All Communism did was cleanse the upper orders of dubious elements. Soon we shall be back in the saddle, with some well-born Manchu, I cannot think who, as Son of Heaven, and you may be sure we will not make the same mistakes a second time. It was excessive leniency that tempted the peasantry to stir. But we will reintroduce the pigtail and generally beat them down. *Beat. Them. Down.*' The Chinese ambassador, in short, felt about the Chinese much as the Akandan president felt about Akandans. They were both students of the science of holding down the multitudes. Present despot and future despot spent many hours together in intellectual communion.

That was why Hūwangdi and Madame Hūwangdi could stand now so aloof and so calm, pretending to sip their disgusting cocktails, lost in reverie, thinking how things would be in the Forbidden City. He was receiving with *hauteur* the clumsy kowtow of the visiting Russian Prime Minister. She was redecorating the Hall of Supreme Harmony with a sea-green dado, edged with interlocked dragons of gold ....

'Friggin' *Charlie*,' remarked the American ambassador, gazing sourly at the Hūwangdis. 'Charlie's always got something up his sleeve. That's why I asked for the Af-ree-kaka Bureau, to get away from Charlie. Never been happy round them.'

'Quite,' said Sir Alaistair Knatte, the newly-arrived British ambassador. The Chinese ambassador (although he *did* look disturbingly pleased with himself) was the least of his concerns. Sir Alaistair was the new boy and everyone had been trying to frighten him with stories of local atrocity. They had succeeded. Those hundred-and-two fly-spotted portraits of the President on the ballroom walls, for instance, all garlanded in the national colours – with one mysterious empty space: no one else seemed to mind them. But they struck Sir Alaistair as unspeakably sinister.... Moreover, he was uncomfortable in body as in mind and spirit. The local version of *fufu* (boiled cassava, yams, unripe plantain) rarely agrees with newcomers' insides. It was not agreeing with his. *Why must I be poisoned at lunch on my first full day in Africa? It's incommensurate. I did not ask to be sent here. If only,* he thought for the thousandth time, *if only I had not been so very, very reckless in Dushanbe. And I'd only been sent there as punishment for bad behaviour in Minsk. Why can I never learn caution? What will become of me if I don't? What will they do to me this time if I fall? They're* aren't *any posts worse than Mbinguville except Canberra of course.* He glanced shyly at one of the Senhoras Mbingu, enormous in a peek-a-boo gown designed, it would seem, for an underaged harlot attending her prom in Florida. *No no, I think I can be strong this time.*

A wretched-looking servant, one-eyed, quick with languages, was replenishing their glasses. 'Oh yes, sir. You sir? Yes sir.'

Sir Alaistair rallied. *Traditions of the Service.* 'Um, cheers, Mr, er, Rosen –.'

'Call me Chad. Up yours.' The American ambassador was a tall, tanned, booming squash-player, with a tremendous grin of perfect teeth, and shoulders bursting out of his tail-coat, which he called his tux *de luxe* to distinguish it from black-tie. 'Christ. What are we drinking?'

'Very best brandy alexander,' moaned the waiter. 'Very best Libyan brandy, very best cocoa powder, very best condensed milk.' Sir Alaistair's gut clenched.

'Christ,' repeated the American ambassador. 'Correct me if I'm wrong, but what it looks like, I think this is fair, is raw sewage.'

'They're *your* sanctions, Chad,' remarked the Portuguese ambassador, Adriana, an extraordinarily beautiful young woman of whose violet eyes Sir Alaistair was already afraid. 'You and your Security Council friends *will* keep trying to punish Akanda. Therefore *our* so-called brandy has to be trucked in through the oases. From a distillery in Benghazi.'

'It's not just brandy in those trucks, honeychile. There's guns and oil, and naughty ole things like that,' said Chad, who was making all these moves on her.

'Of course. But since you know Mbingu gets whatever he wants, why keep pushing for more sanctions? It makes no sense.'

'Bite me.'

'*Really*,' said Alaistair under his breath.

Adriana beamed at him lushly for being her knight. Poor fellow, it was always thus. His comb-over was so desperately in need of flattening, his tie of straightening, his shoulders of brushing for dandruff: no self-respecting woman could keep her hands off him. The smile of Chad, who saw two years of siege-work melting away with the arrival of this gaggle-toothed baldy, became exactly like the dentition of a shark.

But before he could say anything, there was a flurry of servants and a ragged fanfare of trumpets from the presidential band. What joy to leave off *Um segundo sol* and break into *Happy birthday to you*! The servants flung themselves against the walls, the guests drew themselves upright, preparing diplomatic smiles, and the Guide of All Akandans appeared, ascending the great staircase on the arms of, indeed held up by, his other two wives.

Knatte was appalled. *A drunken emaciated infant baboon bundled up in beach-towels!* This was much worse than he had been warned.

He was the new boy. But even the oldest lags of the *corps diplomatique* were startled at how far downhill Mbingu had gone since his last birthday party. They couldn't know it was the demoralising effect of immortality. If you are certain your name will live in honour as long as the world lasts, it's hard to bother with self-control. Thus when the President reached the bottom of the staircase, he simply giggled and sagged. His two wives tried to hold him up, but he smacked them away irritably, and ended up sitting or crouching on the top step, head lolling. *Happy birthday* died away. A disastrous quiet settled on the ballroom.

Mbingu's little hand emerged from his lurid robes; rose; travelled through the air, with every eye on it; arranged itself with forefinger outermost; was seen to be pointing toward the one-eyed waiter and his silver tray of drinks. The cocktail glasses began to tinkle together noisily. The man was beside himself. But his President's finger beckoned and, with death in his heart, the wretch stole forward. He bent. Mbingu's hand swayed vaguely back and forth, far too low. The waiter bent lower; still the groping hand could not reach the tray. The waiter looked wildly at the wives, who shrugged their tremendous shoulders. With desperate resolution the man laid his burden on the parquetry of the ballroom floor, just by the President's feet, and, still clutching the edge of the tray as his badge of office and hope of safety, prostrated himself full-length. Mbingu's fingers closed blindly on the stem of a glass.

(The Chinese ambassador and his wife smiled gently at each other. Yes, this ceremony might well find a place in the imperial court etiquette of restoration Peking.)

Her Britannic Majesty's representative, however, decided things had really gone quite far enough. Calling down upon himself the spirit of Raleigh and Nelson, he lifted his glass of creamy brownness to propose a toast. 'Your Excellency: many happy returns!'

He was a new boy. He was not to know. But he shouldn't have said that. The ghastly silence deepened. *Many* implies finitude. Everyone else knew Mbingu's horror of mortality. Adriana bit the luscious pillow of her lower lip, lowering her lovely face and running a finger round the rim of her glass. Chad, coarsely, blew out his cheeks and shook his head. The servants went as pale as they could go. Mbingu, raising his head, scrunching his small eyes through this tiny round frames, considering. No, he would not drink to that. With the ornate formality of the inebriate, he emptied his glass onto the thick hair of the prostrate waiter, then banged it on the back of the waiter's head, briskly and lightly, as one bangs a tuning fork. The glass shattered and a thin meander of blood coursed past the man's ear, mingling with cream and sweat, pooling on the shiny wood.

(Madame Hūwangdi marked the act. There's artistry in the gestures of a tyrant, as in all extreme human action. Brutishness itself can have a certain finesse. A flush of terrible beauty stained her pale high wonderful cheekbones. That, *that* was the way rice-wine would be served in the restored Manchurian court.)

The tension was insupportable now. The Minister of Education, a silly fellow, resolved to ease it. 'May the President live a hundred years!' he called out. Unlike Sir Alaistair he should have known better.

'*Cem anos?*' shrieked little Mbingu, throwing back his chin, reviving from his stupor in an instant. '*Depois?* Then what?'

'A thousand! I mean a thousand! Two!' Too late, too late. Already Nge was slipping out of the shadows, looking for the presidential nod. He got it, and the Minister of Education was removed. It was slickly done; this was far from being the first time. Nge took the cocktail glass from the Minister's hand with his own left hand, at the same time jabbing his mutilated paw, not violently, almost playfully, into the Minister's adam's apple, just enough to silence him for the second it took his men to seize him from behind, heave him into the air, and whisk him away, through the curtains, out of sight, downstairs, into the beyond.

Everyone in the ballroom began talking at once at the top of his voice with the most frantic cheerfulness. Everyone except since Sir Alaistair, who was feeling decidedly poorly. Nobody, everybody made clear to everybody else, had noticed anything wrong. The band launched into *Summertime*. The Hūwangdi put their beautifully-carved heads together to refine still further protocol at the Manchu court. Adriana leapt upon the editor of the *Correio*, clutching his sleeve. Waiters rushed hither and yon. The *canapés* came out, so richly perfumed with cholera no one was hungry enough to touch them. Blessing, the popular South African ambassador, began to rhumba.

'Swell party,' exclaimed Chad, ironically, to no one in particular; he had not noticed the Britisher at his elbow.

'Does that sort of thing often happen?' asked Sir Alaistair in a small voice.

'The rhumba? Every time. Blessing can't hold her drink – but ain't she great? Oh, you mean the Minister. Hell no, not recently. Mbingu's been so bipolar for the last year everything's gone kind-of serene. Something must of bounced him out of it. Now listen up, my friend, a*propos* bouncing. We need to have a short discussion *re* Adriana.'

'Shouldn't we,' murmured Sir Alaistair very quietly indeed, 'knock off the little beast?'

'*Adriana?*'

'No. Mbingu. Shouldn't we eliminate him? We *can't* have this sort of thing going on.'

'Point B, yes we can, because Point A, no we can't,' said Chad in his least friendly voice. He'd endured three years of Akanda and didn't like a Brit just off the 'plane telling him the score, especially if he was also muscling in on the only plausible white poontang east of the Bomo frontier. 'The dude cannot be hit. He never leaves this compound. Notice how he made *us* go through a metal-detector? He's untouchable. Speaking of which –'.

'Could you fellows send in a missile?'

'No can do McGoo,' said Chad. 'The Russkies are still making a stink about our *coup* in Kuruland last month. We've had strict orders from On High. No more sub-Saharan regime change. Not even where there's a doolally president and Charlie waiting to buy things up.'

'I'm sure that if necessary *we –*.'

'"We"? Yeah *sure*, let's have *you guys* do it. *You guys* terminate him without leaving teensy greasy bunny-prints all over the machete. Then I'll be real impressed. Speaking of impressed. I don't much like the way you were working the sympathy vote with Adriana. Y'hear? In a two-bit hellhole like Mbinguville *esprit de corps diplomatique* implies a seniority system, and *I –*'.

Sir Alaistair wasn't listening. He knew all about his allure. He only wished he knew how to turn it off. *If women would leave me alone I'd be head-of-mission in Central Europe by now.* No, his blood was up. He was damned if he wasn't going to liberate Akanda from João Mbingu.

'I'm sorry, Chad, I really don't think this will do. My blood is up. *Measures must be taken.*'

One of Alaistair's ancestors fell in a snowy skirmish in the Crimea, bayonet in hand, volume of Lucretius in his pocket. Alaistair himself, in his day, had stood up to Munton Minor, bully of the Lower Sixth. My swashbuckling grandfather adopted him as *protégé*. It's folly to ignore that resolute flare of Knatte nostril. Munton was guilty of such folly, and earned a split lip; Chad was guilty now, sneering 'Lay it on me, babycakes, you take a whole bunch of *measures* against Mbingu. Turn him down when he invites you to afternoon tea, that'll sting.'

You're not, Margot, quite as foolish as Chad. You've already have recognised Sir Alaistair Knatte as the protagonist of this story, if not its hero – I am its hero; we'll come to me in due course. Meanwhile, you know to keep your eye on Sir Alaistair as he withdraws, aggrieved, to stand apart, sulking if you like, as Achilles was sulking when he strode back to his tent and left the Achæans to be chased like sheep to and fro across the plain of Ilium.

Idly, loudly, to and fro, move the diplomats and statesmen and artists of Mbinguville, flinching a little as the stinking trays of nibbles are borne about untouched. The prawns are blue and seem to glow; the caviar trails a plume of poison dense as the steam of a steam-train. One of the fat First Ladies fascinates an experimental poet from Angola. Adriana chats brightly to the Minister for Sport; Chad, seriously worried about her, nods and nods as the Moroccan *chargé d'affaires* speaks and speaks, but that cunning Talleyrand hears not a word, he's only staying put because he wants Adriana to see his abs side-on. One hundred eighty reps, one-eight-oh frigging reps of belly crunches every frigging morning, have carved six perfectly-formed bunches of sinew from his tummy. They look like hamsters jostling under a blanket; she should be able to check them out through this faggot joke-waistcoat; how come she's not feeling tender passions? 'Pan-African subsidiarity!' exclaims the Moroccan, and Chad nods, flexing. The band is back to *Summertime*; they know so few tunes. 'Haw haw', chortles someone just behind him, 'Haw-haw, haw haw', 'They do not feel it the way we would,' explains Madame Hūwangdi in French, 'Exactly so!'

How lively everyone seems. But Knatte is still apart, silent, watching, con-spiring with himself to shed the President's blood. *They're speaking so loudly so they can't make out that crippled blackguard and his men letting themselves go with the Minister of Education. Oh this is appalling, simply appalling.*

. This is serious. Despite Uncle Alaistair's manners, there's a gentle fa-natic emphaticism about him. which may be what commended him to my grandfather. When he is not terse from indigestion his way of saying *No* is *Oh good heavens never in an age would it occur to me to think anything of the sort.* It's nihilism, of course: nihilism in its wistful English form, but perfectly destructive for all that. In an absurd universe, nothing is more real than the absurd gesture, and nothing is more absurd than violence designed to create order. This is the line of thought that turns gentle bookmen into berserkers. It was what made a hero of his ancestor, Major Ethelred Knatte, the student of Lucretius, who was discovered with his effete moustache freshly waxed and, at his feet in the snow, four Russian serfs in the grey uniform of the Dnieper Regiment, 'chopped up 'orrible,' remarked the sergeant-major who found them, 'and dead as mutton thank the Lord.' An old-fashioned Akan-dan would say that Major Knatte had chosen those serfs to be his slaves in the feasting-hut of his ancestors. Queen Victoria awarded him a posthumous V.C., which was to express the same idea in another way. His descendent has inherited the medal, and sometimes fingers it, meditating. He has inherited the same wistful murderousness.

Meanwhile, Mbingu has cheered up. The gloom of too much laager has been cancelled by a swig of brandy. He has got to his feet. Minions have wheeled in a four-tiered *gateau* of syrupy *fufu*, a surprise gift from his grate-ful people. He has butchered it with an emerald-encrusted sabre, left behind by the last Portuguese governor, kept for birthday cakes, occasionally used on people. Now waiters trot about pressing irregular blocks of iced *fufu* on shrinking guests.

The President is too drunk to give a speech, but not too drunk to think. *Happy birthday to me! My heart is full. Why do I trouble myself over the insults of the late Minister? Death cannot touch me, so it should not alarm me. I have eluded it. All these dear people are doomed to extinction; my name is not.* He looks about. He's at the stage when one longs to unbosom. To whom? Everybody is vehemently making small-talk. Everybody but one: a tall round-shouldered shabby white man, standing alone with clouded eyes;

dangling, across his evening clothes, a cross on a pink and pearl-grey ribbon. Heads of state – even heads like Mbingu, even of states like Akanda – learn to recognise chivalric orders. Here, *here*, is a Knight Commander of the Order of the British Empire. Just what the doctor ordered.

Mbingu gathers himself together, reels through the crowd, which parts smartly, leans on his cake-smeared sabre, and stares up into the face of Sir Alaistair Knatte.

'You're Her Brick, Her Brick, Her Brickange Majee's new 'bass 'dor t' me?'

Knatte, startled from daydreams of tyrannicide, opens his pallid eyes as wide as they can go. The President's eyes, which are red, meander unfocussed, working their way up from Knatte's chest to his forehead. Knatte dazes down, aghast. The two men look utterly unlike. Yet we detect a certain brotherhood. Both have reconciled clerical temperaments with havoc. Both are zealots who believe in nothing. Both are men of blood. It's right for Mbingu to meet his bane in such a one.

Not that Mbingu realises the similarity or the danger. Knatte's just another whitey, an excuse for indiscretion. He drops his voice to a conspiratorial rumble while placing the non-sabre-propped hand, trembling, on Sir Alaistair's outraged elbow. 'I poshess the see, seekra of 'ternal life. Fought I sh' tell y'. Got tell som'un.' And out it spills: Linnæan binomials, Hitler's beetle, the Comte de Brûlé's unconfirmed sighting of a blue *Polystachya* orchid in Mbingu's very own mountains; his vision of finding it again, of making it his own forever. 'My'shelf – I'll nebber, nebber nebber nebber let another man toush 't, nebber. Course.' He should not have said all that. 'Sho I'm shaved, shee?' A deplorable lapse of taste, a perilous lapse of judgement.


## A HANGOVER

Libyan brandy is virulent. It was the third morning before Mbingu's hangover began to subside, and even then it left a gritty residue of pessimism.

*No,* he told himself in this mood of reaction; *no, I cannot expect miracle upon miracle. The eternity of species is revelation enough, I can't wait for Brûlé's damned flower to turn up. If Hitler is content to live on as an Alpine beetle, if Caligula makes do with a Japanese worm, I must be grateful for whatever's going.... Besides it's dangerous to wait. At this moment I'm still mortal. I could die without possessing a species in which to make my eternal abode. It feels as if I am about to die* at once. *Oh father Linnæus* he prayed (no African, Europeanised or not, Franciscan-educated or not, strays far from ancestor-worship): *Father Linnæus, have mercy on me. The ache, the ache.*

Once his head let him, he set to work.

He'd sent orders to all the academic bookshops, and on 7th December scores of scientific journals arrived in Mbinguville on the weekly 'plane from Lisbon. The same boy who'd disappointed him so much back in '99, when he brought the offensive *Newsweek*, the boy Mbingu had then, after a minute's struggle, spared, was now a gangling young man. This gangling young man groaned up the stairs of the presidential loggia with boxes of *Botany, Journal of Avian Biology, Arachnid, Journal of Field Ornithology, Zootaxa, Anals del Jardín Botánico de Madrid, The Auk ....*

What plenty, what plenty! New species, Mbingu found, are announced all the time. Fifty times a day! (*In my father's house are many mansions.*) He was not even the first person to seek everlasting life by this means. He spotted shy, cautiously-worded advertisements in the back pages of some of these journals. Apparently there exists a discreet market in naming biological discoveries – not, of coruse, of *course*, after mere simple millionaires frightened by oblivion – but after "worthy non-profit donors."

*If the Leader of the Akandan Revolution is not a worthy, who is? True, Akanda is profitable: it's yielded immense sums, waiting for me in my Swiss bank. But this just means I'll need to cast about for a university willing to bend the rules in return for a little munificence. That surely won't be difficult, professors being as they are.... Yes, some university department of bacteriology.... Hm, hum, no; not a bacterium. An insect, then? Why not, say,* Scarabæoidea? *Apparently two hundred new species of scarab are discovered each year. Some shiny, handsome. I could easily buy one up.... But to be commemorated to the end of the world by a* dung-beetle! *By coprophagy! By birth, breeding and matrimony performed within droppings! This is worse than obscene, it's ....* He couldn't quite say what it was; there is no word for *comic* in the inner language of Mbingu.

He simply shrugged and turned the page of the *European Journal of Entomology*. He considered wasps. Why not some new-found wasp (*Arachnospila mbingi*, or *Priocnemis mbingi*), passing through its brief incessant generations, world-without-end? Wasps never die out. Yes; but what a lot of wasps lay their eggs in living creatures, to provide the young with meat as they emerge! *What an ill-bred way of outlasting the centuries... My Name is a great thing. It would be improper to bestow the adjective* mbingi *just anywhere; in the half-eaten spider-brain, for instance....* And then the shreds of St Augustine stirred in his own brain. *Indeed might it not be worse than improper – might it not be dangerous? Once the word* mbingi *becomes flesh, that's that. My immortality will be fixed on* this *creature, no other. And wouldn't everlasting life on parasite-wasp or scarab terms be troubling like ... well, the less comfortable sort of eternity?*

He meant the sort of eternity the Fathers had promised to wicked boys who smoked behind the bath-house or neglected their grammar. For half a century Mbingu had kept watch on his mind, never letting that nerve-racking word form. Yet the word was there, hovering behind his thoughts; and without doubt the reality existed too. He dare not risk reaching it on the back of bug.

With a sigh he shut the *Journal of Entomology*. So much for the *classis insecta*.

Discoveries thin out as we move up the pyramid of creation. It would be fine to be a bird, but only five or six new birds arrive *per annum*. Mbingu brooded darkly over *Hylopezus whittakeri* and *Capito fitzpatricki*, the 2012 discoveries, the ones that had just got away. *Damn you, Fitzpatrick; curses upon you Whittaker.*

Each year brings in a scant score of new mammals, mainly of the order *rodentia*. Humph. Humph.

A dilemma, then. Should he be patient, then, and make overtures to an ornithology department? Or shrink from the gamble of waiting, and become instantly a tree-frog? Or a carnivorous plant? Plenty of those. But wouldn't he feel regret as the millennia rolled by, and bugs by the billion dissolved in his pitchers?

〜

A week of this.

Late one a clammy evening – that is, a month ago, on the thirteenth of December – as he sat and mused, wrestling with his own great soul, an e-mail arrived. It was an e-mail addressed to his secret account, known, he believed, only to Nge and to ambassadors. It was an e-mail with a photo attached. He peered, askance, then clicked.

*Dear Perpetual-President and Guide of the Akandan Peoples*, it began (and Mbingu's heart swelled. How rare for foreigners to get his titles just right).

> *I am a naturalist who, trekking overland from the*
> *highlands of Gabú, recently paid a solitary visit to*
> *your fortunate nation, where, even in those remote*
> *mountains, I saw on every hand evidence of your*
> *kindly rule, and of the burgeoning prosperity of*
> *revolutionary Akanda.*

The idiot wriggled in his chair with pleasure. His youngest, fattest wife, who never liked seeing anyone read – such bad, bad sorcery – put her head on an angle to watch Mbingu's face.

> *I spent some days on the flanks of Monte Mbingu,*
> *admiring its natural wonders. Most were de-*

*scribed in the handbooks I had brought with me,
but I confess myself puzzled by an cerulean or
electric-blue orchidaceous epiphyte I spotted one
evening just before departure, hugging a twisted
juniper root in a large lava clearing half-way up
the mountain's north-eastern face. There is nothing like it in McMahon's* Dusky Bloom, *although
it must surely belong amongst the* Polystachyinæ.
*I had no time to make a close observation, and
since I had to be back in Gabú the next day. I have
now returned to my village atop the Manitoban
permafrost, where I serve humbly as a schoolmaster, and thought I might submit the question
to Your Excellency, assured of Your Excellency's
concern for the flourishing arts and sciences of
your country. A photograph is attached, register-
ing the G.P.S. coordinates. Forgive the diffidence
that bids me remain anonymous, and sign myself
merely*

*A CANADIAN MBINGUNIST.*

The photo wasn't quite in focus, but there was no mistaking those jaunty mouse-bonnets, dangling from tangles of curved, thorn-studded stalks. It was like *P. cooperi*, but vividly blue, and somewhat larger.

In the corner the camera had recorded latitude and longitude to five decimal places.

For a few seconds Mbingu's rapture was so huge he wasn't sure he could on living. (His youngest wife wondered this too.)

↪

You will say, Margot, that a baby wouldn't be taken in by so transparent a fraud; that's not psychologically adroit of you. Do grow up. Like great fear, great joy shuts down the intellect. Mbingu was experiencing elated panic. Of course he couldn't *think*.

In any case he was a mystic. Since Heaven had called him in infancy to the pursuit of sempiternal fame, why shouldn't there be, in mellow age, a miraculous realisation of his hope? What was more fitting than for Mbingu to pass from paternal care of Akandans (in his present state of mind he quite forgot what his government was like) to an Akandan paradise? Why shouldn't coincidence arrive to hurry on his apotheosis, wafting from this vale of tears to the sunny flanks of a dormant volcano, to live forevermore as a rare and wonderful orchid?

For he'd always been sure Brûlé, his venerable comrade, had not been lying. He'd been morally certain there *was* a blue tree-orchid on the volcano-side unknown to science. In some mystical sense he'd been certain that he, Field Marshal Dr Mbingu, was destined to rediscover it and name it. Of course he didn't stop to ask himself if the e-mail was plausible.

A minute later he was too anxious to ask. *These tropical mountain orchids flower for just a few weeks. The photograph's dated – ten days ago! No time to lose! Should the bloom be gone – worse than death! I'll taste the coming centuries of oblivion in one moment!* (His wife laid a consoling hand on his knee. He slapped it away.)

His first impulse was to send an expedition to Monte Mbingu the next day. He saw it in his mind: Nge trudging up a trail up the sacred mountain with a well-armed entourage of thousands – spears of sunshine through jungle canopy, racket of birds, monkeys – Nge glances right, left – sights it there, a flash of blue, quadripollinial, epiphytic – plucks it, reverently, obediently – bears the specimen back to the presidential compound. Mbingu waits, heart breaking with happiness – there's a stir, the expedition is returning – the cathedral choir, summoned for the occasion, sings hallelujah – the pesky Bishop, released from prison, blesses, censes the flower – it's instantly set in plastic, mounted in gold – it sits on the presidential desk while he composes the article announcing a new species, *Polystachya mbingi* – thus is fulfilled the divine command breathed over him while he yet lay nameless in his motherless crib – *Thy name shall live for evermore.*

But the impulse collapsed at once. Dare he send Nge to the mountain to bring back a specimen? *What if Nge guesses its significance? What if he seizes it for himself? What if Nge publishes in* American Botany? *Ach!*

At the thought of *Polystachya ngi*, Mbingu's blood turned to wax. His face became wild. He was certainly a madman at this point. How could he imagine Nge noticing a flower, or indeed anything insusceptible to torture? Nevertheless, his wife read horror in his face. She knew books were always bad magic. 'Come in to bed, *bwana*,' is what she said. 'Whatever it is can wait 'til morning.'

For a moment he stared through her as if she were air. This was how he looked at people before he had them taken away. She felt faint.

But nothing of that sort happened. He shook his head again and again and then let himself be led to her bedroom. There she stripped of the terrible stiff gilded uniform; but when it was off he fell backward into bed and turned from her, lying with his eyes open and blank like the sacred ancestors carved from mahogany in her village meeting-hut.

She was a mountain girl, a simpleton, very honest.

## A RECOVERY

João Mbingu was a complex man, very wicked. Wickedness did not make him any more complex, though. It was like the fine crazing over the foundations of an unstable building. At this final crisis, when he had only to reach out his hand (or Nge's half-hand) to the tree to pluck immortal life, parts of him crashed down, and what was left was floppy, babyish. Or worse than babyish – for as Mbingu's master, Augustine, says, babies are cross and perversely greedy for milk; whereas João was greedy only for himself. (His mother has a lot to answer for.) He wanted there to be more and more João, and for João to last forever. So now he had to send for the flower; but dare not send for the flower; so that his only desire was fulfilled and thwarted at once. What was left of him was a slight fraction of a man, less than an infant.

This he lay most of the night, the recluse, the self-worshipper, the one reduced to the size of a bean, immured in many walls within walls, the closest of them very tight. None of his prisoners up in the Chinese-built prison were as thoroughly pent; certainly not the Bishop, who woke himself at midnight to recite Vigils. *Nolíte obduráre corda vestra* he chanted: *harden not your hearts, as in the provocation.* It did him very little good, cocking an ear as he did to the anxious silence of the twice-named city. Something was up. And in fact it was the tyrant whose heart bloomed in the unlit hours. Mbingu came back to life. Of course his body was hale enough, not yet sixty; and he'd lived for this chance all his life. But it was a black miracle nevertheless, which I cannot explain.

〜

His youngest wife woke two hours before sunrise and found sitting up beside her, wearing his spectacles, in shirtsleeves: a bad sign. 'No,' he was saying. 'No no no.' He said it in a voice like a boy's. 'Now. Now. I must do it. And now. Now' – and suddenly he was gone, leaping out of bed, running, which the President had not been seen to do since the Liberation War, down the stair and off – she flung herself at the window to watch – round the kitchen-block. It impossible that he should run but he ran. He had suffered a transformation, and she wondered which god had wrought it. He was pelting round the corner of the palace where the laundry had been before the plumbing failed (now the girls had to carry the Presidential clothes down to the creek and beat them on rocks). There was nothing in that direction but the cobbled square at the back of the Compound, and yet that was the direction he was running.

〜

It had been a stable-yard in the days of the hundred-and-third and last Portuguese governor. His wife was a great rider, but didn't think it fair to bring a decent galloping horse to such a country, so *Sua Excelência o Governador de Camarões Português* laid out a cobbled yard for her, and she solaced herself by trotting about on a local nag she named Ponpon.

On the day they left she'd wanted to shoot Ponpon before the mob got him. Her husband persuaded her this was unnecessary. Thus the poor creature was being clumsily dismembered in the palace stables (how its eyes rolled as its legs came off!) at the very moment young Mbingu was smashing in the front gates.

In colonial times those gates had been wooden. Now they were a formidable business of steel and spikes, cameras and bollards. But Mbingu, a dour student of foreign newspapers, did not rely on them. African rulers can be overthrown on the spur of the moment if a spasm of resistance seizes their people. He never forgot his calling to deny death, and did not want to end up like Ponpon, whose skull was still nailed up above his wrecked stall. Therefore, many years before, he'd discreetly taken flying lessons in Lagos, then turned the stable-yard into a heliport. A small lovely helicopter was always waiting there under a tarpaulin, fuelled and ready, in case Mbingu's luck ran out. It was not big enough for any of his wives; nor did he mean to take Nge with him if the evil day came. He'd fly out alone over the Bight of Bonny, damp-eyed perhaps at the ingratitude of his subjects and the ferocity of fate, but clear-headed. He'd land on the island of São Tomé, where he had a long-standing arrangement with the authorities. Within a day or two he'd be settling into his Algarve villa (already staffed, waiting for him), making 'phone calls to his bankers in Berne.

He'd often imagined the evil day. If by day, he knew to keep the mountains hard to his left and head straight out to sea; if by night, he'd be guided by fire, for Mbinguville would surely be burning. He'd fly high to avoid small-arms fire, unless the Akandan Air Force was already with the rebel, in which case he'd skim the rooftops and take his chances. In any case, in a few minutes he'd be over the ocean.

He'd thought it all through. What he'd never imagined was flying inland, deep into the terrible land of the Akandans. But that is what he was about now in the half-light.

He pulled off the tarpaulin, jumped in, and set the engine whining, faster, faster, louder, higher, higher, faster.

The whole Compound woke. His youngest wife heard it where he'd left her, sobbing in bed. His two older wives heard it, and were wise enough to tremble. Nge heard it unstartled in the tiny bolted room where he spent his solitary nights, and lay staring into the darkness, stroking his aching half-hand, considering. Mbingu's fatuous guards leapt from bed and began running about.

The blades turned, sickly-slow then swifter, thwacking, louder; at once the chopper, cloaking itself in a whirlwind of stable-yard dust, shook upwards into the grey pre-dawn air. It straightened itself and shot off, over the walls of the compound, then low over the low roofs of the city.

Mbinguville was still dark. The electricity never comes on before eight. Now it was raucous with barking – which everywhere reached a *crescendo* cancelled by the racket as the chopper passed, so that all the stray dogs seemed to bark silently. From every hut and shack heads poked out, frightened white eyes stared up.

Over Avenida Mbida the chopper went, past the shuttered burn-out wrecks of Portuguese villas, over the prison where the bishop, breaking off Lauds, shut his eyes, wondering; over the barracks, over what is called Shantytown – although the whole city is really a shantytown – and away. Away, not toward the Atlantic and asylum as everyone would expect, but to the north, to the hinterland.

His kingdom dimly opened before him, banana-plantations, rubber, scraggy stands of cocoa, all going back to bush, for the sanctions were severe and exports were drying up. Crowns of palm-trees bucked and swayed beneath Mbingu like kelp in a heavy tide. The paling stars reeled about him, the peaks of the coastal range to the west were already gilded, the orient sky was reddening.

Who'd believe the wizened little scoundrel could feel such exhilaration? It wasn't just being out of gaol for the first time in a decade. Before him lay unending life. He was flying into paradise.

Only happy men can stop thinking of themselves. A few miles beyond Mbinguville Mbingu was so fascinated by an abandoned hut, with a sprinkling of skeletons, that he swerved and circled. Yes: a collar of tiny bones about a sharpened post. That would be the baby or babies. Five more skeletons, variously sized, about the hut door, two of them small, perhaps female; they would not have died so easily.

This was the "random terror" those fools at the foreign embassies liked to complain about. Which was nonsense. Mbingu understood through meditation and Nge grasped by instinct that terror must never be perfectly random. If it is, everyone thinks *Why not me next? I may as well risk revolt.* There must be a shred of excuse every time. Then people spend their energy not plotting, but collating clues, portents, compiling ever-more-subtle lore about how to avoid the attention of the police.

*What drama*, thought Mbingu, breaking away from the sight, and turning his machine back toward the inner depths of his nation; *what rich complexity and I've brought to so many drab agrarian lives! I wish I could make the ambassadors see it.* He recalled his last, petulant interview with Chad, who'd been expostulating about some killing or other. 'Since there are no limits to the richness of *justiça revolucionária* –', 'Jesus, Mr President –', 'I beg your pardon, Mr Rosensitz?' 'I mean, Jesus, Field Marshal Mr Perpetual President', '*Obrigado*' – .

Yet suddenly he sighed. It would be an exaggeration to say his dinosaur heart had been stirred by the dried-out carnage beneath him. Nonetheless, he was a man of his continent. It made him solemn to think of skeletons lying so long in the light. (The light was thickening now, the heavy dull enormous directionless pre-dawn light of West Africa.) Day after day this brightness would lift itself from the dry soil, always the same, tirelessly, and those bones would appear out of the darkness, each day a little whiter, more desiccated, forever and ever. – Of course the family must have been guilty of enmity against the revolution. They had had to be done away with, and naturally no kinsman would dare bury them, dooming his own family. This was all as it must be. Yet how fearful, how fearful, to lie endlessly uncovered, naked beyond nakedness, under the eye of the sullen sky-god of the tropics!

Who was almost risen now. There was a confusion of greyish aureoles and bars of orange cloud off to the east. Shafts of yellow were grating their way over the tableland below. Presently Mbingu came across a herd of cattle casting westward shadows twice as long as themselves. A cowherd family had raised a tent and lit a fire to cook breakfast. They were breaking curfew, for the regulation extended as far as the railhead at Umbarta. It occurred to Mbingu that for too long he had delegated to Nge the business of African governments. A *Presidente perpétua* should not be above local law enforcement. He opened the helicopter door and, flying with his left hand, swept low, firing with his right: six cartridges pumped out of his Magnum: *P'kow! P'kow!*

It would have taken superhuman luck to kill anyone. Still, he sent the felons scampering into the bush and even wounded one of their beasts. He yodelled in triumph and swept up, away, delirious – over the last villages of the southern plains (they heard him and trembled) – then over the tops of the jungle that hems in the left bank of the great river, Rio Mbingu or Rio Gboko as you prefer.

## MORE INTERRUPTING CHATTER

*So that, Margot, is it. Four weeks ago João Mbingu vanished completely. He's flown out of history into legend.*

*Which is to say: I'm told that Catholic-minded Akandans think he deliberately crashed his helicopter into a thermal vent in the Sahara, reaching his master Satan, who'd summoned him to make report.*

*Those who wear their Catholicism with a difference believe he flew up to the clouds to clouds to copulate with the Thunder Witch, who slew him in disgust because of his pink hands.*

*As they are updated, Portuguese encyclopædias, which take a mild interest in lost colonies, will shrug cynically: Mbingu, João, (1954?–?), Ditador da Akanda – that's how the entry will begin.*

*The C.I.A. frankly hasn't the foggiest. For years to come Africa journalists at a loss for material may pad out their pages with conspiracy theories. No doubt alien-abductionists will develop a view.*

*I, however, know what happened. I know where he was going. You'll understand that I'm guessing at his thoughts, but I'm not guessing his actions, which can be deduced. Curtain up, then. Act III.*


## THE TRAGIC


About the time the sun was well up the President would have crossed the Rio Mbingu. (Let me consider the map; yes.) Then he'd have turned left, flying almost due north along the great serpent of water, turning to burning pewter as the light strengthened. The hills close in here. There are no more farms. The jungle grows thick, stretching away for a hundred miles to the west.

The engine, deafening his ears, would have made his eyes more keen. He'd have seen the early morning steam rising from the tree-tops. Far off in that blue haze was Joãoville, where he'd spent the Liberation War becoming himself –should we say *him self*? Down there was Fort-Président-Mbingu, *né* Sainte-Orthodoxie, where Brûlé speaking drearily now of the King of France, now of his indifferent wife. In the broken mountains south-east was Bumbuna, where Mbingu in his youth had broken the arrogance of Portugal.

And now, due before him, the cone of Monte Mbingu began to fill the sky: brilliant green below, black above, with wisps of cloud about its eroded crater. Muuaji-wa-Mfalme is what the locals call the mountain, *king-slayer*, and although they've forgotten to what legend or prophecy the name alludes, the peak retains a evil reputation. No one goes up. The sloping jungles are nearly pathless. It would madness to think of approaching it even by chopper, except that on the north-eastern face lava has formed irregular shelves.

Mbingu would have circled the mountain carefully, map in hand. There was the escarpment, there the forking canyon, *there* the widest ledge of raw lava, the one the Canadian had named: almost an acre in extent, barely softened by grasses, already at this hour shiny enough to hurt the eyes. It's flat thought, landing is possible. He brought his flying chariot down on its eastern edge, in the shade of trees bordering the rocky waste.

↬

The engine slowed and coughed and died, and the fever left his mind as abruptly as it had come. The gods let him see how improbable his quest really was. The silence of the engine shouted *Fool!* at him. *Fool!* Of course the e-mail was a trap. A Canadian amateur trekking in from Gabù? Nonsense! He'd been lured from the cocoon of his compound to this lonely spot where armed men would be camping, set to ambush him.

Madness to try to take off again – they'd shoot him down – best take cover – he dived from the helicopter – dashed over the abrasive lava – into the surrounding bush – swivelled his gun back and forth – threw self behind tree – stood peering out, waiting on his final destiny.

↬

The north-east platform of the volcano Mbingu is an ugly corner of nature. It's unchanged since the Comte de Brûlé, that most unnatural naturalist, pitched camp. But Brûlé did not notice the ugliness of the site any more than he noticed the tremendousness of the view. His journal entry for *8th mars 1861* records that sunrise was at 06:49, the altitude 3,812 metres; that it was the eve of the *fête des Quarante martyrs de Sébaste*, thus a fast-day, so he would abstain from the haunch of giraffe he'd shot the day before; that visibility was up to sixty kilometres over the northward savannah once the morning mist dissipated, with herds of about forty elephants towards the horizon, and perhaps a hundred zebras – passionless imbecile! The young Count saw all that – the aweful solar thurible burning off the purple veils as it swung high in the hand of its seraph – the infinite tarnished-gold plain studded with acacias to the curving rim of the planet – fleets of regal grey beasts swaying like distant argosies – dappled white-and-black, zebras fleeting across the new faultless morning, the scent – and he didn't write what it was *like* because, being inhuman, he didn't know.

Having failed to notice the planet, Brûlé looked blankly about his dismal campsite. *This north-eastward face of Mont Saint-Louis is marked by an eruption that evidently occurred in the last fifty years, and has left deposits of uneven basaltic fragments at lower altitudes*: which is to say (in human language) that the tortured bellowing of the infernal crater vomited a torrent of red-hot rock along the broken heights of the volcano; when this pooled to a lake, and hardened and eroded, it broke into monstrous boulders of sterile rubble, each of which tumbled in turn, with a crashing that would have been the terror of the countryside for twenty miles about, into the shallow valleys below, shattering into ragged hunks, choking them with arid rubbish.

The ridges themselves are still thickly forested, but between them lie barren ledges, flat enough to camp or land a chopper, and so well drained that they stay parched even during the Rains. It's grubby grey stone of the type architects call clinker, much like the pulverised concrete left over when a factory is demolished. It tears boots, it chokes any growth but occasional tufts of fountain-grass.

There are half a dozen clinker flats wedged into the folds of the volcano, but Mbingu had studied the schoolmaster's email. This was the second clearing, going counter-clockwise. Anyway the coordinates were clear. This precise wasteland was the right place – that is to say, the intended wrong place, the spot he'd been lured to.

⌒

It would be interesting to know how long he lurked behind his tree, heart banging against his thin ribs, feeling the high air thin in his lungs, listening for his murderers, before he could persuade himself there were none.

There was stillness, that is, no human movement. There was noise of every other sort. A tropical montane forest is the loudest place on earth, worse than any city street. Life shrieks at full strength, beginning with the insects (African cicadas beggar belief), stretching up to huge blatant birds and simians. Preuss' monkey does not cease to praise Herr Preuss and his Creator. The rose-ringed parakeet, *Psittacula krameri*, honours forever Herr Doktor Kramer. But Mbingu remembered from his days as an effete guerilla the particular rhythm of humanity. We sound like no other species, and if you listen long enough you detect the human taint through the texture of nature. Here there was none. He was alone, he was not being assassinated.

He was however the victim of an impudent fraud. The greatest man in Akandan history duped by some idle Canadian prankster! Inveigled into roaring away from the palace like a truant! Into running and hiding – it was intolerable and all Manitoba must be burned to stubble.... Impossible. Of course no one had seen him. Still, the shame was not nothing. He'd fly back at once and take it out on his wife, perhaps on all his wives ....

He stepped out of the shadowy bush into the mineral glare of the lava-field, resumed his prescription sunglasses, and strode toward his helicopter. One final contemptuous gaze over the nasty clearing, over ashy-pale stone, green-black of jungle, a flash or two of white (no doubt some vile stinking waxy flower), a glint of blue, whitish late-morning sky behind everything – it was silly how his heart had tripped over itself at that tiny flash of blueness.

Self-respect prompted him to get in and fly away. But no, out of mere or-derliness he supposed he ought to check. Nonchalantly as he could, keeping an eye out despite everything for assassins, he strolled back across the lava flat to the far side. It *did* (he allowed himself one glance at it) look oddly like a blue orchid. Not that it *was*, of course. – There was a visual riot of flowers along this raw edge of jungle, where trees stopped dead at the rim of broken stone, and sun was plentiful. He glared left and right, half expecting a wise old monkey to be watching him, amused by his folly. (*He won't be so amused when my revolver comes out.*) Well then, this must be more-or-less the spot.

God oh God, oh God – *alleluia, vocavit Adam animæ viventis ipsum est nomen eius, alleluia* – all the praiseful words from Mission days came bubbling out of him. For she was there, she was before him, she was at his feet, just as in his vision only infinitely more beautiful, more majestic, above all more blue, a quite incredible colour like nothing else in nature, neon or freshly-cut sapphire. She was undoubtedly what he had hungered for, much like *P. cooperi* but distinctly bigger and – his eyes were swimming, he could scarcely make her out – blue.

No eye had rested on her since those of the blessed Brûlé (*Brûlé! Brûlé! I shall build you a chapel! I shall have the witch-doctors immolate infants!*), and it seemed to Mbingu in the ecstasy of the moment that the little flower itself rejoiced to be seen once more: to meet her master, to receive her proper title after millions of years of namelessness. It seemed almost that she strained toward him, begging to be harvested, so that she might gather him into her own eternity. There was something nuptial in the transport of that moment, something too of the greater festivity of the last day, when one might hope to hear the ultimate acquittal, *Well done, good and faithful, enter into thy rest* – but to whom is it given to pronounce the joyful verdict *on himself*? Who is at once both St Peter at the gate and the justified soul admitted to happiness?

The little President tumbled to his knees at the very edge of the lava wilderness, crying beatifically 'Polystachya! Polystachya mbingi!' and reached forth a single reverent hand to pluck (much as Adam must have reached for the tree *scientiæ boni et mali*), so that his last thought will have been intense tactile surprise: *The stalk is tough and rubbery.* I mean this will have been his last thought if the neurons formed themselves quickly enough. For the root of the dyed rubber flower was a copper wire connected to a workmanlike bomb buried six inches into the soil, composed of two pounds of gelignite in a plastic bag and a simple detonator.

The African bush is the noisiest place on earth, the most *blasé*. Not even in battle does the boom of high explosive make so slight an impression. Clouds of parrots and parakeets burst from the tree-tops and flew back and forth shrieking. But they do as much when a coconut falls: they enjoy panic. Green and red monkeys swarmed up branches gnashing their teeth, for they are naturally belligerent. Once the echo died away everyone lost interest. Five minutes after the blue orchid was picked, you'd never know anything odd had occurred.

There was, it is true, a patch of burned gristle and gut. But jungle absorbs filth, even human filth, easily it absorbs sound. In the African sky scavenger birds wheel eternally, miles from each other; when one sees a morsel and drops, others follow; the rumour of meat spreads for hundreds of miles within minutes. From well over the borders of Akanda they came, from Kuruland and the Federation of Bomo: Rüppell's griffons, evil-faced birds with wizened bodies. The clearing was soon black with their wings. They snapped at each other over such dainties as the near-teetotaller's liver. His larger bones they bore away, perching on acacia boughs to worry them in peace. Before the sun had reached its zenith the griffons were gone, and insects were busy tidying away the crumbs, trampling down the tiny shards of Mbingu's shattered spectacles with their far tinier feet.

**THE ELEGIAC**

St Wygefortis' College
Cambridge   CB1 1XJ

*.... with their far tinier feet. Nothing more. His undoing*
*has merely fattened certain tropical birds & ants.*
*No, let's make a flourish Uncle Alaistair, & say Life*
*has gorged on Death, as it can, as it must – just as human*
*flesh is sustained by the flesh of beasts – because, presum-*
*ably, the two are the same stuff.*
*Other than that, Mbingu has evaporated, leaving*
*nothing. Of course his helicopter's still up there. But I think*
*we can just leave that to the jungle & not give it a thought.*
*Even a helicopter can be digested without a strain on that*
*green gullet. The canopy will already be putting out feelers*
*over the rounded glass of it – stalks & runners. Creepers*
*will have annihilated it within a month. It'll soon be quite*
*invisible from the air – not that anyone's likely to be flying*

*low over that cursed volcano any time soon.*

*And I rather like the thought of that bubble of civilisation (controls & padded seat) going on existing in near-darkness, with the obscene sucking underside of creepers visible through the glass to the absolute nobody within.*

*In short, Godfather, your request is fulfilled. Mbingu's uncanny lust for fame has brought him uncanny oblivion. Gravelessness, datelessness. Witnesslessness. Even monumentlessness – since I hear from the news services that last night the mob pulled down his statue. I hope you got to see that. Perhaps you were there with a bullhorn, organising the romp.*

*Though as I write this, it occurs to me the rogue isn't quite obliterated. There's one manifestation of Mbingu still cumbering the globe. I mean the rubber flower. No scavenger is likely to have carried it away & you know, Uncle, I'm glad. I took far more trouble over the flower than I did over the bomb. The bomb was cobbled together in a couple of minutes, while the sweat dribbled down the back of my neck, & a shimmering lizard played peek-a-boo with me round the trunk of the juniper, & the pilot of my own helicopter wandered about the clearing incuriously, smoking a joint, listening to Miles Davis on his headphones as (he told me) he always did, forming with his hands the angular, jagged shapes of the music, spreading outward rather than pushing forward. And meanwhile I squatted over a shopping-bag of gelignite, twisting the fuse-wire with damp fingers. A rough job.*

*But the flower was a masterpiece. I was almost as proud of it as Mbingu would have been. I ordered it from Bruges, from a secret workshop used by all the world's great botanical gardens. (Did you know, Uncle A., that the most spectacular plants – the roped-off specimens punters come to see – are forever dying, out of spite or embarrassment, so that generally they've been replaced by immortal fakes? The authorities discreetly keep artificial back-ups of everything in reserve. It must save them a fortune in water. Perhaps I shouldn't have told you. I know how much you enjoy the Chelsea Flower Show & it's no part of my plan to spoil your pleasures.) I was very exacting in my specifications: a slightly-larger-than-life-size replica of* Polystrachya cooperi, *dyed chrome blue.*

*They came back to me sniffily:* Monsieur *must be mistaken, such an organism* n'existe pas. Monsieur *must be aware* il n'y a rien qui lui ressemble dans "Mountain Flora" de l'incomparable McMahon.

Monsieur *gave them a rocket down the 'phone. Damn McMahon. Who were* they *to doubt the word of the saintly Comte de Brûlé?*

*Yes, I expect my bogus orchid's still lying in a cranny of those spiny rocks, too large & unappetising for any insect to disturb. The blast will have stripped flesh from the dictator's ex-thumb & ex-forefinger: those charred slithers will pinch, will have fused with, the melted stalk of his eponym.*

*The undeviating, unforgiving, unforgetting eye of the equatorial sun rests on it. But it's so expensively made I don't think the dye will fade. The heaviest monsoon won't wash it from its declivity. It will remain – & this is as close to immortality as biological tissue ever gets.*

*So Mbingu's quest has not wholly failed. I hope this consoles his shade. As long as the world lasts, or rather until the volcano blows up (as is overdue), Akanda will bear –*

*No let's do this with another flourish, Uncle A.*

*– Akanda will wear as a corsage pinned with bone to her breast a unique example, a hapax, of* P. mbingi, *a species in the family* Orchidaceæ *not formally known to science.*

*Your affect'nate godson,*

*Felix*

↝

HER BRITANNIC MAJESTY'S EMBASSY,
RUA BUMBUNA, MBINGUVILLE,
THE REVOLUTIONARY PEOPLE'S REPUBLIC OF AKANDA

*19ᵗʰ December 2013*

*My dear Felix –*
*I have read your very long email over three times, and remain dazed by what you have to tell me.*

*Let me first repay your torrent of news with a few*

*dribbles of my own, since you ask what is happening in*
*Akanda, I mean here in the capital.*

Nothing *has actually happened yet, nothing absolutely*
*of any sort whatsoever.*

*That is to say: it has been chaos since Mbingu vanished,*
*not that it is not more-or-less chaotic at the best of times.*
*Yes, as you say a crowd broke up his equestrian bronze in*
*Praça Mbingu two nights ago. (I most certainly was not*
*there in any sense, Felix. That is an outrageous suggestion.*
*Never in an age would it occur to me to be present at*
*anything of the sort. It is one thing for a diplomat to solicit a*
*tyrannicide, quite another for him to countenance a riot in a*
*host country. The traditions of the Service are flatly against*
*it.) But the police turned up and machine-gunned the rioters*
*before they had quite finished smashing the thing. I believe*
*the horse's metal legs are still standing as far as the hocks – a*
*rather equivocal memorial.*

*Evidently the palace has still not nerved itself to act.*
*I gather they still believe Mbingu may be playing a trick*
*on them by disappearing: testing their loyalty. They quite*
*reasonably dread his coming back breathing vengeance.*
*Officially he is on a 'surprise tour of inspection upcountry',*
*although the Foreign Minister had the ambassadors in this*
*morning to drop hints about 'abscondment'. 'Christ, fellas,*
*suck it up and move on': remark of my American colleague.*
*My Portuguese counterpart has been more helpful, and*
*indeed has asked me over to her Embassy this evening to*
*dine and to discuss the possibilities of a joint European*
*démarche, saying more-or-less what Chad said but more*
*decently. As the curfew is being rigorously enforced and the*
*electricity is almost permanently off, I suppose I shall have to*
*stay over after dinner. I wish I were entirely easy in my mind*
*about* that.

*So you see affairs in Mbinguville are* not *satisfactory.*

*As to what is happening up on the mountain .... I*
*do wish you were a shade less sardonic, Felix, I wish you*
*wouldn't tease me with subdued blasphemies. I owe it to*
*your grandfather, whose* protégé *I was, to remind you about*
*the reality of life and death, although I admit he was sar-*
*donic too, inasmuch as he was anything. Dear Osbert cared*
*so little about existence beyond hunting.*

*I, too, am content, although without your unkind
hilarity, that a single example of Mbingu's orchid remains in
the world. A hapax, as you say. (What uncouth words you
dons seem to need to get by on!) It is pleasing because it is
tragic, tragic because unique, unique because a work of art;
art, being human, shares in our essential sad beauty.*

*For might I remind you that man is the* only *brute that
dies? It's being a* hapax *that makes one seriously mortal and
therefore, perhaps, immortal. In all these fearful millions of
years, amidst the billion men, the quadrillion organisms,
there is only one rare Felix, one unduplicated Brûlé – one
poor Alaistair Knatte (and no doubt one is quite enough).
Our final loss of ourselves, or not, is absolute.*

*But no wild animal is individual. Nothing is lost when
it dies, any more than when I cut my hair, not that I do
very much any more now there is so little to cut. The species
is merely renewed. The self-same zebras Brûlé saw are still
nibbling the same savannah, identical in impulse and habit.
If he did spy a blue* Polystachya *on Mont Saint-Louis (but
I don't think he did, the whole business was a mare's nest
from the beginning) that very flower is still there.*

*And it strikes me too that there was more in Mbingu's
story than clowning. He was attempting a terrible thing: to
storm into eternity. True, Osbert's clerical brother Wilfrid
(a sinister fellow) used to announce with relish that heaven
suffereth violence and that the violent bear it away. But
Mbingu's ambition was more dreadful than that. He
proposed to storm not heaven but nature. He was aiming
not to surmount human mutability, but to plunge below it.*

*Which is a heresy, I admit, and warrants death. Not
that you did much good in killing him, heresy being another
thing immortal of its nature.*

*My dear boy, I do apologise for sounding sententious,
captious and orthodox, as, of course, godfathers are supposed to do, even godfathers who have just nudged their
godsons into drastic courses.*

*Your bewildered,*

> *but grateful and devoted, godfather,*
>
> *Alaistair Knatte*

⮑

'Is the Lord of Ten Thousand Years afflicted with melancholy?' asked Madame Hūwangdi in exquisite Manchu.

Handsome young Hūwangdi gravely shook his head. He was enthroned on their four-poster bed, which they had decked out with red silk hangings on three sides; he wore the double-breasted yellow embroidered robe of the Manchu court; the tiny gold pagoda atop his scarlet hat danced. 'We are merely meditating on the fate of the savage chieftain of this distant land.' This is how the Hūwangdis speak to each other when alone.

'Is it permissible to enquire if the savage chieftain had been allowed to become,' pursued Madame Hūwangdi, with a sumptuous gesture, 'the friend of the Son of Heaven?'

She was sitting in a silk carpet before him, naked but for an immense black square court headdress rising from her stiff coiffure. Her flawless body was like clouded alabaster. The tall copper incense-burners that lit the room made shadows play over it as she spoke, dancing between the wonderful moulding of her bones.

'No, O Chief Consort of the Dragon Throne. His conversation was unenlightened and tedious, and his form uncouth. His ruthlessness, although admirable, was guided by no philosophical precept.' Such was the usual formula for dismissing barbarian kings in more fortunate eras. Thus the Hūwangdis speak to each other, using the imperial tongue, so nearly extinct; their bedside book is von Möllendorff's *Manchu Grammar* of 1892.

'Might, then, the unworthy servant know if the Auspicious Descendent of the Dragon is disconcerted at the vanishing of the vile Mbingu?'

'Not even that, Propitious One. We regret it only because our sympathy was piqued by his over-vaunting ambition. You know he aspired to live forever? He craved apotheosis without leaving the earth; the realm of heaven without God. These were perturbing thoughts. We do not think he would ever have been understood.'

'I greatly fear he is already being forgotten.'

It was the seventh night since Mbingu's dematerialisation; midwinter's night, as it happens, a turning-point without meaning in the limbo of the equatorial regions. That afternoon Nge had at last summoned up courage and announced that he, Ernesto Nge, was bowing to the will of the freedom-loving Akandan people and shouldering the presidency – the former president, that traitor, having fled to his imperialist masters (and was therefore henceforth not be so much as named, on pain of whatever popped into the new president's head). The population of the prisons had changed a bit, many in, some out; the Bishop naturally stayed put. Two of Mbungi's wives had come to sticky ends. The youngest and plumpest had solaced her week of widowhood by taking Nge's hand, what there was of it. For a few hours, in the heat of the day, there'd been gunfire here and there, the presidential guard prevailing over freedom-loathing persons. Now, with nightfall, the guardsmen were at play, rejoicing in their master's elevation. The Hūwangdis could hear distant screams of murder and rapine, floating over the walls of the diplomatic cantonment from the other, less fashionable side of Avenida Mbingu – which had already become Avenida Nge. By the same presidential decree Praça Mbingu had been redesignated Praça Nge, Mbingu Airport Nge Airport, Monte Mbingu Monte Ernesto....

'President Mbingu is being forgotten, yes. And we have no patience to endure this new forgetful tyranny, which must wax in its turn, dwindle, fall and be forgotten. We will demand immediate recall to Peking. It is time we beheld again the lands over which we are fated to hold sway.'

Madame Hūwangdi widened her incomparable eyes and grasped her hands together. 'The packing, the packing!' she moaned, glancing about. This room alone contained two standing vases, Ming, five foot tall, enamelled with peonies and giant goldfish, inclined to scratch if crated in straw – and then there were the copper incense-burners – and even those jade lions, which look so unbreakable, are not ....

Her lord, disregarding these domestic concerns, cast his eyes upward. A *caisson* of gilded mahogany was set into the ceiling above him, worked with a coiled dragon of *vermeil*; from the dragon's jaws hung a cluster of golden balls. Its tongue is a topaz, its glowing right eye is a ruby. Its glowing left eye, which looks more-or-less like a ruby, is actually a camera secreted by M.I.6.

Hūwangdi closed his eyes. 'The thought occurs to us, most lovely wife,' he murmured dreamily, 'that the Mandate of Heaven, while munificent, is never everlasting. The dynasties of the Middle Kingdom have their allotted season and no more: two and half centuries for the Great Qing, before that three for the Ming, one for the Yuan, three for the Song. Each House inevitably falls once it has wearied Heaven.'

'Whatever happens,' she began, a shade less diffidently, 'this time we are *not* using that Dakar moving firm. They – '; but she was being ignored.

'Did not Zheng the First Emperor render himself ridiculous by his pursuit of the elixir of life? It is written that he dispatched six hundred young men and women in ships, to find the nostrum in the hands of a thousand year-old magician on the slopes of the Penglai mountain.' The way his wife breathed now might, in one less finely-wrought, be called a sigh. 'You know our mind, Beauteous One. We mean for the fruit of our bodies to reign felicitously from the Forbidden City as generation succeeds generation. But do we hope for the Hūwangdi era to last forever? No. Thus it occurs to us that the barren Mbingu surpassed us in dynastic pride. Our own aspirations seem by contrast … *petit bourgeois*.'

Then the Empress stopped thinking of packing, and laughed; and elegantly performed the kowtow before her lord. There are no words for the beauty of her compressed breasts and arched spine. The lamps made of each vertebra a separate gem. One of her flanks was tarnished gold, the other vellum. With her face still on the carpet before the Emperor's silver-worked slippers she said formally: 'The Morally-Deficient One craves to be informed if it be the will of the Radiant Highness presently to embrace her.'

And back in Cheltenham, at G.C.H.Q., Pauline, who has heard this before, leaned forward smartly and clicked a switch. The screen went black, and, although the Hūwangdis, urgently wrapped in each other's arms and legs, did not notice, the left eye of the dragon dulled. 'Good *night*, Your Imperial Majesties,' said Pauline, not unkindly '– you *silly* love-birds'; and she set about tidying away her desk clobber, her notebook, her box of tissues, her own copy of von Möllendorff. For Pauline is a nice girl, despite her work, and draws the line at spying on 'any actual goings on if you know what I mean. I mean it's private whoever's doing it innit? And they're sweet young things anyhow, I call it a crying shame they're not where they're meant to be already, I've always had a soft spot for royals, I still have a quiet weep when I think of that Lady Di, oh no *thank* you Mrs Q., I'd love a last cuppa but I really do need to get back home, I've got a nice bit of brisket waiting for my supper and it's early up tomorrow 'cos I'm on Oval Office shift tomorrow yes it's awful innit him holding them secret meetings at oh-two-hundred Eastern Standard what's he thinking of, and what about Michelle I'd like to know, not that they're not a sweet young couple too, oh yes *please*, if you wouldn't mind filing *my* disks too that would be ever so kind, I know it's against regs but my varicoses are killing me proper from all that sitting, you're one in million Mrs Q.' – which just shows the importance of regulations, because Mrs Q. is the former Miss Clinker, sister to our youngish under-porter. (But for God's sake, Margot, don't mention this to him.) In gratitude for my having got her the job at Cheltenham she's in the habit of passing on to me anything particularly luscious.

## THE HEROIC

To me. I am the hero of this story, although mine was a remote, fleeting sort of heroism.

I was only in Akanda for a few hours. It seemed wiser to sleep across the frontier in Bomo, at a decrepit Hilton, with soggy golf-links long abandoned to the pangolins, and a pool in which no one swam but certain leaf-green pythons. At night the palm-civets descended to prey on fruit-bats in the ruinous restaurant garden. On my first evening on those parts I sat with the civets, drinking duty-free Irish whiskey, and contemplating the mystery of João Mbingu.

There are Japanese cattle so expensive they're hand-fed each day, sung to, masturbated, even massaged, all to fit them for the culminating blow. Mbingu's career had been like that: one long preparation for the axe, my axe. I was priest of death, he was sacred victim, sacred because blasphemous, blasphemous because, alone among the brief teeming organisms of this planet, he absolutely declined to die.

The next day, just after lunch which was hateful, my Miles Davis-fancying helicopter-pilot landed on the Hilton fairway, and flew me off over the vague frontier. We were back before dinner, and I departed Bomo after breakfast the next morning. I have never seen, and hope never to see, Mbinguville – or rather ex-Mbinguville, for of course Nge has rechristened it. He modestly didn't name it Vil Nge as we'd expect, but let it go back to being Vila São Joaquim, city of the father of the Mother of God.

My touch on Akanda was very light. No one knew I was about except God, and God's chum and informant Sir Alaistair Knatte. I was at Lisbon airport, changing planes, when I sent Mbingu that assassinating e-mail. I was back in College when MYSTERIOUS DISAPPEARANCE OF WEST AFRICAN DICTATOR appeared on page 4 of the *Daily Telegraph*. The next day the story was on page 2, with an obsolete photograph; the next day page 4 again; then nothing, nothing.

⌒

I brought back nothing from Africa. My hotel in Bomo was no place for souvenirs, ceramic or bronze. Everything in the hotel lobby shop seemed to have been imported from sweatshops in the Far East. No, I forget: I did return with a midwinter tan, a heroic colour which I think made a few of my colleagues jealous.

It was certainly admired by you, you flighty creature, Margot. Oh God! What joy to escape to you after Christmas with my family.

Here's the fantasy that kept me going through the tedium and occasional atrocity of Westhumble in Surrey.

*Far off, a quadrillion miles away, in some frigid bedsit of the world-to-come, Field-Marshal João Mbingu (Ph.D., João Mbingu Acad.) is spending his first post-mortal Christmas in the company of Miss Agatha Culpepper (BStud. [failed], Brunel). How easily I can picture him, my exploded victim! Indeed, how easily I can picture both of them, my two glum victims! Neither looks at the other. They sit untouching on a morose camp-bed, staring up through the skylight, grimy and rain-pocked with their own self-pity, at the everlasting sky, blasted to grey by their own misery; and in flat voices complain, competitively, how horrible it is not to exist.*

Well, with the help of dead Agatha I endured the company of the three surviving Culpeppers, then got away from Westhumble to enjoy the company of a single ffontaines-Laigh. Thank God *your* parents were elsewhere. It was a merry week together, wasn't it, in Regent's Park? And we kept the New Year dramatically. What a sky-rocket it was that ushered out 2013! I wish had time to record it. Anyway, a few days into 2014, on the day you went off to the London Library to pretended to work, I thought I'd better stroll over to Whitehall, look up the Foreign Secretary, and make a clean breast of the Akanda business. (Before you ask: I didn't take you only because you would have upset Benjy. He'll take some getting used to this partnership idea.)

Benjy pretended to be stiff about it at first. 'I mean Culpepper, that's a bit thick don't you think? A bit *ultra vires*. We can't have British subjects blotting-out foreign Heads of State just because they disapprove. Or because some crusty old-friend-of-the-family asks. Even if the crusty friend's a dip. Anyway, not without asking Her Majesty's Government's say-so first. Blotting-out's *our* province. *Honestly*. It could easily have become An Incident.' But Benjy's too boyish to disguise his friendliness for long, or his high spirits. By the time he'd finished his pheasant soup he was saying 'Blew up old Mbingu indeed!' and 'We've been meaning to clear out that sewer for two decades. Ho ho ho!' (We were lunching at the House of Commons, so he didn't keep his voice down. Worse things were being discussed gaily enough at other tables.) 'Very neatly performed, Felix …. And old Ally Knatte put you up to it, did he? Even found out *how* to do it – never thought he had the gumption. Obviously wasted in Africa…. Of course Nge isn't much of an improvement on the *ancien régime* …. What? Oh yes, 'fraid so. If anything Nge's slightly more homicidal than Mbingu. We've had hair-raising reports – a *démarche* just this morning from the Nuncio, apparently Nge sacrificed the Bishop of Vila São Joaquim to the ancestral spirits for New Year. Terribly old-school affair, on the beach at dawn, with a pyre, dancing *ngangas*, the Palace Guard strafing seagulls when they came to scavenge – yes, it surprised us too, Nge's never been considered pious. His new wife apparently egged him on. *Unfortunate*. The Republic of Akanda,' he said, putting on his Cabinet voice, 'still awaits the reign of her philosopher-king…. But the thing is,' relapsing to the manner of the Lower Sixth, 'the thing is, *we've jolly well done our bit*. Just wait 'til I tell the Americans! I think I'll ring Kerry after lunch – Washington must be awake by now. They're always on to us to "show our teeth" yet in Akanda they didn't dare make a move while *we* …. Yes, Knatte has Done Very Well. Grand things in store for him.'

Alas, they weren't. Before Alaistair could be gazetted to a better place, that very evening, back in Akanda, a shocking scene occurred. It was at the new Madame Nge's first reception, marking the election of her husband with 181% of the popular vote. Suddenly, in the midst of a performance of folk-dancing, Adriana the fragrant Portuguese ambassador was seen to adjust the dishevelled knot of the tie of the British ambassador *with a certain air*. And just as suddenly the American ambassador was seen to leap upon his rival, pummelling, kicking and even biting him before he could be dragged off.

The heat, the heat, everyone officially said; the poor fellow's momentarily been taken funny. But it wasn't a momentary thing, of course, it was Uncle's old trouble, which is perennial. Certain flowers fabricate not perfume but the stink of carrion, which is perfectly floral of them since fragrance isn't an ornament, it's the essence of their existence: they pump out whatever it takes to attract the requisite insect. Alaistair Knatte's scent of decay drives women of a certain sort wild. Nothing can ever change that. He's always going to be a liability to the foreign service.

Everything leaks in a place where there's so little to talk about. Within a day details of his latest scandal had got back to the various Western capitals. Diplomacy, which usually proceeds with gigantic slow efficiency, now and then stumbles and is swift.

Adriana has already been recalled in disgrace and dismissed from the Portuguese foreign service (she intends, I hear, to keep a boutique in Coimbra), but Lisbon naturally desired a gesture from us as well. It wasn't entirely the poor girl's fault, after all. A few days ago I had a dispirited e-postcard from Uncle Alaistair, with a tinge of reproach: he's been appointed Cultural Attaché in Canberra, effective immediately. I'm sorry for him, indeed I do feel faintly responsible, but after all *I did my bit*.

⤸

As for Chad Rosensitz, though! He, it seems, is a darling of the gods. Perhaps they relish his abs. He alone escaped the *dégringolade* of Akanda.

You'd think it might count against an ambassador to apply fists and teeth at a diplomatic reception to an opposite number (from a friendly embassy, too). But no: the State Department grandees gathered that Chad had been avenging himself on a rival, on a *successful* rival. They smiled on that. A victim at last! What characterises members of every foreign service is perilous irresistiblility. It's the occupational hazard of diplomats, as drink is visited on poets, impotence on actors, dandruff on academics, *etcetera etcetera*. Sexual ineptitude is a valuable commodity in Chad's profession.

Thus he was not only forgiven, he was immediately recalled and promoted to a cushy desk-job in Washington. He's now almost in his second week of jogging into work tennish, and taking two-hour lunch-breaks in the gym across the road. In the evening he plays the Old Africa Hand at parties in the Virginia suburbs, narrowing his eyes to slits as he describes safaris (experienced on *Animal Planet*) or riots (read about in *Time Magazine*).

M.I.6. has the Virginia suburbs of Washington very well covered, and thus, through the kindness of Mrs Q., I can cite Chad *verbatim*.

'A bunch of Yoruba with sharpened scythes coming down the strip of poop they call a road, hollering and cussing, nothing between them and the goddam embassy gates but you – *that*, my friend, is what puckers your A-hole in Africa.'

As he says this he literally constricts his *gluteus medius* enough to lift and dimple the cheeks of his *panniculus adiposus*. (The necessary signals flash down the subtle neural pathway named Reil's Ribbon. Every clench immortalises Dr Johann Christian Reil of Halle.) And as Chad performs this dimpling, he stands sideways to the most plausible woman in the room so she can appreciate that mighty spasm of muscle through the thin cotton of his dockers.

'Yes ma'm, *of steel*,' is what he's ready to say should she ask: 'four hundred squats, four zero-zero friggin' reps to get 'em this rock-like.'

He's sincere. He believes he squats for her; for her he goes commando ('Cum *man* do: yes ma'm'). But obviously his bottom's his life's work, his bid for immortality, the actualisation of his soul, the artistic uttering-forth of the mystery of individuality which man must achieve before he passes into that greater mystery, death; and Chad's nickname round the office is End-in-Itself. He hideth his soul in the cleft of the rock. 'Four hundred reps every goddam day,' he says to himself as he steps out of the party into the Virginian night (close, dark and still as a tropical tomb), alone. 'Christ, what does it take to hold off old I mean middle age?'

# VOLUME THREE

Imaginary evil is romantic and diverse;
real evil is gloomsome, monotonous, sterile, boring.
Imaginary goodness is boring;
real goodness is always new, marvellous, inebriating.
"Imaginative literature" is thus either boring, or immoral
(or a blend of the two).

SIMONE WEIL

# IX. *Nihil validum, another letter*

ST WYGEFORTIS' COLLEGE
CAMBRIDGE   CB1 1XJ

*Sun evening, 12i14*

*Dymwood's ossifrage has undone the Chaplain, Margot,*
*& I feel hard-done-by. So I'm writing to you <u>again</u>.*
*Try to beam back pity even if you're too busy to write.*
*There's no one here who sympathises with me.*
*When I returned to College a week ago I detected a cold*
*air of reproach, a most unXmassy feeling though after all*
*we were still just within the 12 Days & might have aimed*
*at a little charity. Instead, the human chill in the Senior*
*Combination Room has increased, & the reproach seems*
*centred on me, as if I were ultimate author of these accu-*
*mulating catastrophes.*
*These are notes toward my defence, proving, if*
*only to you, us, that I am <u>not</u>. The blame lies largely with*
*Dymwood, Yoxley & Freke, a little with von Spluffe, most*
*of all with Woolly himself. Not with me & certainly not*
*with the sinless bird.*

**WHY IT WASN'T MY FAULT: A STATEMENT**

Icy snowlessness: don't you think it's the v. worst of England's winter modes? This afternoon, when I sat in my rooms, writing up – for you, as Equal Partner in Assassination – my report of the Akandan affair, the contrast has seemed to me painful. On the one hand, radiant jungly scenes on my paper; on the other, the blasted monochrome out the window. On the one hand my essentially innocent Xmas vac; on the other the unholy doings of my brethren.

*How wickedly unfair to blame me.* While I was still blamelessly in W. Africa, Freke & Yoxley – ancient historians! nothing to do with me! – were in Bishop Auckland, working themselves into a most sinister frenzy.

This is what I've heard. They easily found the location of what had been in my great-great-grandmother's day a dapper Georgian villa, not far from the bps' palace. The villa had long been sold, demolished, built over with unspeakable 1960s flats, which were themselves now condemned & empty. All about was scrubby wasteland, overgrown to the knee, dotted with informal rubbish-dumps.

Yoxley & Freke had seen worse on North African digs. They had a nose for buried foundations, & they made resourceful use of old town plans. After a few hours they'd traced the outlines of the lost parsonage, & by sundown they were sure they'd fixed the site of its mummy-fertilised shrubbery.

Obviously there was no point using trowels. Long ago the last crumb of mummified cat would have melted into wet Northern humus. But what was dissolved physically might be present *metaphysically*, excavatable with the mind. So the idiots thought.

They got out blankets & thermos-flasks & folding-chairs & planted themselves in the midst of it, intertwining chubby indistinguishable figures. They hummed a little of *The Bk of the Dead* under their breaths, wh rose in visible puffs toward the glittering midwinter stars.

& by dawn, when they reeled back to their bed-and-breakfast, they'd made the greatest archæological discovery of their age – of any age. So they persuaded themselves. The ruined shrubbery was awash with vibrations: fizzing, positively fizzing with the *kas* of cats from dozens of separate dynasties.

For the next three weeks they spent every night on-site. Only at night. Quiet & mystery facilitated, they said, their particular sort of research. By day, too thrilled to sleep, they wrote up their notes, planned the great bk that would revolutionise ancient history, & alas sent rapturous emails to their chum Woolly.

Woolly showed these emails to me. The funny young couple said they were beside themselves, they were learning to tell *kas* apart, to tease out single voices from the general ghostly uproar, they were taking down dictation in Middle Ægyptian, rolling back the limits of their discipline in every direction.

For of course cats (especially pharaonic cats) go everywhere, see everything. Every cranny of Near Eastern antiquity was known to these subtle, sacred creatures: from the esoteric lore of the ancient Berbers to the political secrets doings of the court at Thebes & Amarna, at Tanis, Saïs & Alexandria. Cats had been in every tent, throne-room, council-room & bedchamber.

They'd lurked mewling behind pillars that atrocious night when the heretic pharaoh Akhenaten abjured the gods & scattered the priests, screaming at his blasphemy, down the moonsoaked steps of the temple of Amun-Ra. They'd sat smirking beside Rameses' throne when he was baited by the changeling Thutmoses, whom the Hebrew slaves called simply Moses. At Memphis they hissed when the Persian conqueror Cambyses slew the God-Bull Apis with his brazen spear, then ordered roast beef for lunch – although they'd not disdained to chew divine scraps thrown them by that doomed demented emperor. They pawed at the rug when Cleopatra was dumped in a rug before Cæsar's sandals, & from beneath a couch witnessed, purring, the four bare feet of her brisk courtship of Antony. They had even (for Freke & Yoxley were pedants) scampered over the desks of the vizier's clerks, reading all the returns on the grain-tax.

Being mummified could not derange their knowledge, any more than being buried for millennia, roughly disinterred, shipped to Liverpool, ground up as manure, scattered on my gt-gt-grandmother's hydrangea-beds, or even partially absorbed up the stalks of hydrangea which had run to seed & been throttled by decades of weeds.

Obviously this was manic, nothing but hallucination; what would you? It was past reason, it was *love* –

That word. I know what you're thinking. I cannot use this after-all-necessary technical term without having you splutter or sigh. I halt, therefore, to explain & clear myself of soppiness.

A *proportionate* liking for a thing or person is a matter of taste, or even ratiocination. Love's altogether different. It's always vaster than its object: that's its *definition*. Since it's already exorbitant, it can't be proportionate, & there's no reason for it not to increase. Thus love, all things being equal, always devours the lover.

Fortunately things are not generally equal. There are usually distractions, which is how we manage to survive. Universities, for instance, exist to deaden intellectual excitement, to stop it growing into mania & burning up the mind. Yoxley & Freke were disproportionately enraptured by their dusty disciplines, & also disproportionately enraptured with each other, but the atmosphere of Cambridge damps down passion of all sorts, & as long as they stayed within university bounds they were safe, even from that mastering energy of life & death – here of course you roll yr eyes – love.

Was it my fault that their infatuation escaped all bounds this Christmas vac?

Well yes perhaps a little, since it was I who sent them up North to look for my gt-gt-grandmother. I did it, let me see, partly out of guilt for what happened to Shishak. Partly because I wanted their accusing faces out of sight for a while. Partly because I did suddenly remember the old family yarn about her & her sacks of Nilotic mulch.

But it would've been no more than a holiday excursion – Olga & Elmo would have suffered no more than over-excitement, occupational hazard of dons – if their frenzy of *love* had not been corrupted, radicalised, weaponsied. bedlamised, by Woolly.

Woolly: that villain. *My rival* – there's the bitter truth of the matter, Margot. I know I've always played him for laughs. But in fact my antagonist could eliminate by *confounding* almost as well as I can by *elaborating*. I make the admission through my teeth. Woolly's apparatus for invention was nearly as formidable as mine.

Ever since the pubescent William Leigh emerged from the fastnesses of Ulster, he'd torn, unswerving, down the same trajectory. As a boy he'd lubricated his way out of Protestant doctrine with the phrase *In a special sense*. His doctoral thesis, *Credo in Nihilo*, set records, even in theological publishing, for weak sales, but there was a clear focus in its obscurity. Before Woolly had left his seminary he'd learned to sing-song "We just don't know," which remained his favourite saying, his inevitable response to any undergraduate fool enough to ask after faith or morals; after a while his answer to virtually every question. 'Will you pass that jug, Woolly? – is there any cream left in it?' 'We *just. Don't. Know.*'

It wasn't merely that he could shuffle together jarring ideas so thoroughly they could never be sorted out again. He had a cosmic *rôle*, like a man sent with a wet sponge to destroy a fresco. 'In a v. special sense the empty sky *is* starlight, don't you see?' He was never really feeble, he only pretended to dodder, he was a prophet, ignoble bane of the luminous dragon Distinction, blurrer-away of the universe.

Even Woolly, with his mind permanently dishevelled, could recognise love is, & Woolly knew how fatal love is. He had no business going scuttling north to snare Yoxley & Freke, besotted with antiquity & with each other. Unsporting is what I call it.

Dr William Leigh went north by rail on the last day of 2013, armed with a metaphysical weapon which I confess I'd furnished him with myself – oh dear, this does make it sound like the spreading carnage *were* my fault. But I'd not meant him to commit murder with it. To be quite frank, I'd meant it to kill *him*.

The came a breakfast toward the end of Michaelmas when I decided we'd all had enough. It was time for him to go. So I'd murmured: 'Ever heard of *mokujikigyo*, Woolly old thing?'

Dymwood had just been released from the madhouse (prematurely, as was apparent to us all) & was burbling away down one end of high table, noisily, joyously, ceaselessly, banging a silver mustard-pot on the oak for emphasis. I was breakfasting like a gentleman on morels, fried potatoes, Shropshire black ham & curried trout. The chaplain, sitting across from me, was nibbling at dry muesli like a granary rat. I suppose it was this excess of vegetarianism that brought *mokujikigyo* to mind.

'*Mokujikigyo?*' carefully, as if it were the name of yet another Unknown God. 'Well in a certain sense ....'

'Something from the good ole days, Woolly. Japan's centuries of isolation & serenity. Under her prudent beneficent Shoguns. Now & then a monk's passion for stillness would turn – violent. He'd deepen his usual asceticism into an extreme diet called *mokujikigyo*, or "eating a tree."'

'A *tree*.' Woolly's washed-clean white-blue eyes, lambent & tenantless, rolled in their sockets.

'That is: for a 1000 days he'd consume only nuts & seeds, shedding all body-fat. For a 1000 more just roots, bark & pine-needles. Then he'd drink *urushi* tea, infused from the sap of a tree called the toxicodendron. It made him vomit & dry out. And killed off the flora & fauna that sit quietly in all our entrails, waiting. Waiting to gnaw at us once we've matured into corpsedom.'

I'm proud to say that Woolly put down his muesli spoon, shuddering a little. 'Life-denying?' he asked himself.

'Pah. Thoroughly desiccated, with shrunken organs, the monk seats himself smiling in his tomb, in the lotus position, with air-tube & bell. And begins to meditate, chanting a mantra. His brethren brick him in. Each morning thereafter they hear his bell tinkle once. When it falls silent they slide out the tube, seal the hole. Another 1000 days, they open it up. Inside (if things have gone well) is a perfectly preserved cross-legged mummy, needing no further treatment. They carry him straight into a temple to be worshipped as a manifestation of the Buddha. You can find such mummies all over Japan.'

'Elitist?' worried Woolly. It was one of his favourite open-ended words.

'Oh no. Surely no worse than our being academics in the first place? What's our chomping away at books but half-hearted self-mummification?' And, dropping my voice: 'Just look down the table at Miss Vyddler –'

But before I could enlarge on this theme, at the other end of high table

Dymwood's wittering rose to convulsive shrieks & Chyld, at a nod from the Master, approached with the large hypodermic kept on a sideboard for just these occasions. There was a *fraças* (Chyld got kicked off the dais, poor dotard), & by the time Dymwood had been borne off, Woolly had vanished too. I rather assume the seed had fallen on stony ground – that he'd forgotten what I'd told him.

He hadn't, though. Instead he tumbled it together – which is how Woolly's mind worked, I'll be damned if anyone blames me for it – with something quite different, *jeeva samadhi*. Which is (as you'll pretend you already know but don't) the practice of certain Indian gurus who have themselves enclosed alive within tombs which then become the foundation of great temples. The theory is the guru *doesn't* die: he sits there comfortably forever, beyond eating or sleeping. If we looked inside the tomb we'd find him still merrily chanting. No one does look, it wd be rude, he doesn't want his meditation interrupted. A mob quite rightly assaulted a television-crew from Bombay who recently tried to poke a tiny camera through the walls of one of these deathless tombs.

The Hindoo miracle expunges death, the Buddhist discipline quells biological life; *mokujikigyo* & *jeeva samadhi* are *opposite*. But Woolly shook them together into an extravagant myth of his own. To be, by choice, so far *beyond* the usual human fate – to be not dead, like most people, nor dying, like us the minority, but simply *outside* – this seemed to Woolly the ultimate spiritual experiment of the age.

So he bloody well should have tried it *on himself*. That's the point I will stress to the Master if I'm ever asked to explain myself. My mind is an arsenal of deadly imaginings which anyone is welcome to, & which no one has any business *retailing*.

Woolly, the coward, did nothing with my idea for weeks. Note that, *nothing*. Until he got those over-excited emails from the deluded archæologists up in Bp Auckland. Then he became over-excited himself, & went north, knowing perfectly well how to manipulate Elmo & Olga – how to pervert their love both of each other & of the past.

Love, obviously, was his handle.

Perhaps erotic love is always perilously close to the desire to merge, to cease & be lost in the belovèd. And certainly historians are close to wanting to die to the present & pass by intellectual suicide into (how does Prospero put it?) *the dark backward & abyss of time.*

You'll remember that Woolly, too confused to lie, was weirdly persuasive when he chose to assert. A head so empty is a bright canvas, it can be written on in letters of flame. These two youngish Cambridge academics were soon convinced that, by committing a certain abomination, they might escape mortality & finite personhood. They would exist forever as one in the halls of

Bast, amidst undying rivers of gambolling cats, limber & black, tens of thousands strong, dancing about their fat round knees, freed from the terrene curse of speechlessness. Olga & Elmo would spend their numberless centuries interviewing cats from every century of Ægypt, pre-dynastic to kingless Roman times. They would fathom the dark backward. Felicity! Beatitude!

Lust for knowledge is a disease as hopeless as rabies. The prospect of omniscience is like the sight of water to the rabid: it induces fits. For a couple so undersexed, so without any actual religious hopes or fear, the abomination Woolly proposed was not so v. dreadful. They could tell he was not lying to them.

Anyway, anyone can always muddle a don.

(Not-lying is not the same as truth-telling. What Woolly himself believed, I gather, was that Bast was, "in a v. special sense," as true an illusion as any goddess or god: that is, a luminous veil over the void. "At a profounder level" he was sending O. & E. out between the interstices of the worlds. They were henceforth to be neither alive nor sleeping in death, enduring neither corruption nor incorruption: merely *yonder*. They would achieve a plane of utter nullity compared to which even death is a well-lit way-station. They were to be a sign of the consummate annihilation awaiting all things – soon perhaps, soon soon. For Woolly, in his curious final state of mind, *that* was felicity & beatitude.)

The conspirators cut corners, not having 1000s of days to spare. Their version of *mokujikigyo* was a week of quinoa & buckwheat, with less & less bottled water, & more & more mantras. I mean the two young dons ate like this; Woolly nibbled away at stale, crumbly cake as he always did.

During a pause in chanting they went out & found a rapacious gardening-centre open in that dead of the year. They bought a pyramid-shaped glazed gardening-frame, of the sort meant to keep the frost off cucumbers. They also rented a ditch-digger, & drove it to their wasteland through the back-streets.

Freke & Woolley were useless practically but Elmo Yoxley had grown up on a farm. Very early the next morning he gouged a four-foot cavity in the wasteland that had once been my ancestress' shrubbery. The ground was frozen after the first inch, but even the stony bosom of England gives way at last to industrial violence.

Into this hole the gleesome threesome lowered their gardening-frame, shattering one of the panes, which might or might not matter in eternity.

The darkness thinned although there was no sunrise. In a ragged ungraceful Northern way it started snowing. The twin heroes took off their clothes. As there are no toxicodendrons in County Durham, they swallowed handfuls of calcium chloride, the de-icing stuff for roads, which for some reason is always dyed Prussian blue. Anyone can buy plastic sacks of it at any service-station, which is not to say that anyone *should*.

Woolly reported that the results were drastic, astonishingly swift.

As well as they could in their appalling state, the Berberologist & the Ægyptologist, jowls a mass of Prussian blue foam, gullets noisily hissing as they burned away, clambered down into their pyramidical hutch. They got more-or-less cross-legged &, since they could no longer intone, started jangling Woolly's Sikh bells, which the kind man hand brought down from Cambridge in anticipation. Meanwhile he, doing the first menial, perhaps the first tangible work of his life, kicked & pushed in the mounds of soil piled-up about the rim.

Frozen clods, broken up by the digger, spilled down the sides of the pyramid, pittering on the glass. Snow fell & blotted out the unsightly faces of the living mummies (or half-alive semi-mummies). The level of soil rose, muffling the uncertain *gling-gling, gling-gling*. While Woolly worked he intoned

which is pronounced – as I know well, since we had heard it all summer from the top of Acheron – *ḥtp-ḏi-nśwt wśir ḫnty imntjw ncr ḏꜣ nb ꜣbcw wp-wꜣwt nb tꜣ ꜟsr. I am pure, I am pure, I am pure.*

Thus Woolly filled in the pit with dirt & came away.

You know, there's a sense in which everyone everywhere always wants to be buried alive. It's the logical end of so much of what we do. (Don't you think? Do you think Motte came round to this point-of-view?) We crawl away from the sun, we curl up & *dig*....

Anyway, I always imagined Woolly wd come to human sacrifice in the end. He was like those Liberal Protestants who spent the 19th century whittling *Gott* down to *absoluter Abhängigkeit zurückzuführen*, Absolute Dependence. ("*Abhängigkeit zurückzuführen*," Woolly would say, making each harsh syllable sound like the thud of a shovel. *Zu, ruck, zu, füh, ren.*) They ended up as the *Deutsche Christenen Kirche*, the official sect of the Third Reich, revering Hitler as the plenitude of Reformation, trying to reconcile Bach chorales with fiery hecatombs of *Untermensch* in sacred fir-groves.

Syncretise everything, trim away all excrescences &, when all is done with, *this* is where you arrive.

Certainly Woolly seemed to believe he had now arrived. His thought was entirely developed; he had nothing more to learn, he had only to await his reward. He roamed the wasteland in Bp Auckland all that day, with shining wet unseeing eyes fixed on the stricken charcoal sky: the eyes of a mortal on the verge of apotheosis. He roamed all night, watching the half-moon peek out of cloud-banks, much like the coquettish smile of a woman on a *chaise longue*, toying with her fan; listening, listening to the unbroken tinkling of temple-bells beneath his feet –

So he claimed. 'Come on Woolly,' we said in the Combination Room, plying him with brandy-spiked tea, 'did you *really* hear them?', 'Oh yes with the ears of my mind; I hear them yet,' 'Bah! what does that mean?', 'Exactly: how long did the *physical* ringing last?', 'In the profoundest sense, time is –', 'Damn, here's the Scarlet Woman coming', 'Temporality no longer –', 'Shut up, Woolly, he'll hear', 'Afternoon, Master', 'Shall I pour? Our mascot had two puppies for *its* tea, had you heard?', 'I certainly heard the yapping – they took a long to die, didn't they?', 'Yes, Master, I suspect they *bounce* –'.

Poor Woolly. I'm sure he felt neglected. This was his first afternoon back & he'd come straight from Cambridge station, still muddy from the killing, his mind full of *gling-gling*. But he'd returned to a College so death-haunted we had scant attention to spare even for his prophetic exultation

## MORE OF MY STATEMENT
## WHY NOTHING WAS THE BIRD'S FAULT EITHER

The vulture project was nonsense from the beginning, a madness.

Dymwood got back from Tibet on New Year's Day, not just with eggs & chicks as promised (& as suggested by sensible me), but with the parent – a tremendous adult specimen, with the widest wingspan yet recorded: 11 feet 4 inches. There's nothing bribes can't extract from Chinese officialdom. Or British, come to that. Indeed, although I don't warm to any sort of govt agent, customs officers have always struck me as open-minded accommodating people. If you ever find yourself thwarted by them, Margot, it just means you haven't been generous enough. A professional tip.

Back to the daddy ossifrage, though – daddy not mummy, male Bearded Vultures being touchingly devoted to their offspring; who'd have thought it?

Dymwood installed this *ménage* of daddy chicks & eggs atop Lethe, & for some days there was a mild reign of terror in the small frozen city of Cambridge, as cats disappeared, & dogs, & possibly (accounts were confused) a dirty unwanted toddler from a broken-down wheat-farm near Wesley Waterless – your old stamping Quintember ground. The toddler's mother announced the event in the *Dirty Swan* & was stood drinks by way of consolation, but retracted her story next day when the beer wore off. Her social worker, being English & therefore empirical to the point of stone-blindness, was of course incredulous – she wasn't sure how many neglected children the woman was officially supposed to possess, since they looked & wailed alike; & the woman was let go.

Her testimony, & the testimony of the bewildered pet-owners, seemed bizarre. As you know, bizarre things don't happen in England; it follows that such reports should be ignored & mocked (and blamed on festive eggnogs). That useful syllogism. It's why political revolutions can be carried out secretly in England; they can't, on first principles, be happening.

College, however, was undeceived. It knew carnage was underway to the rime-bound city, & I was told about it as soon as I got back, with a certain amount of snarling because I was thought to have inspired Dymwood's experiment.

I ignored the snarls & was at first exulted, being mightily taken with our mascot. On my first morning back in Wygefortis', a week ago now, on the 5th dawn of 2014, I was woken early by an incredible baaaing out of the welkin. I scurried out of my bed – that galactic magnet for rum doings, as you know – & there sure enough was a bewildered lamb, soaring over Megiddo Court in the brute's talons. Superb!

And then there were the creature's looks. How flamboyant an ossifrage appears at close quarters! Ours resembled – what do I say? – a cut-throat making merry in 18th-century Venice. Golden body like a long gilded waistcoat, wings for a black silk cloak, head so hideous it could only be a *papier-mâché* carnival mask: no wonder Leviticus calls the ossifrage an abomination.

Moreover, how he enlivened Lethe! I've never admired Lethe (have you?), squat & bland as it is, out of keeping with the rest of College, a Martello tower wandered inland. But it certainly made a grand eyrie or nursery. Day & night it produced uncouth or prehistoric noises, shrill whistling & *acheek-acheek* call from pops, frantic chirping from his demon babies.

The cobbled space behind the kitchen, at the foot of Lethe, which was finally living up to the name "Limbo", had become the vulture's demesne. It smelt v. vulturish. Unwanted innards or paws would come flying over the parapet, bouncing about the bins, & could not be removed, since he dropped on anything in Limbo that moved.

Now & then, usually in the half-light, the monster himself would emerge from its nest, swirl about Lethe – fabulously huge, like a roc – then swoop forth over the College walls to fresh predations.

It was superb, but it couldn't go on. Our pet would clearly have to be gone before the start of term. What a disaster if our undergraduates & their parents thought College dangerous!

(Actually, I can't think of anything more dangerous for a young person than coming to St Wygy's. But these are perils you little ones don't realise 'til it's too late. Whereas being fodder, birdseed, that would seem different to you, wdn't it, O my sweet?)

On Twelfth Night there was a meeting of Governing Body. Davison the Law Fellow was adamant: College cdn't admit the vulture's existence & call in official help without incurring massive liability. There was no obvious way for us to get rid of it ourselves because Dymwood, to protect his darlings, had taken an axe to Lethe's ricketty wooden staircase, earning himself a return to the Deepdene. So we resolved to do almost nothing, which is what Governing Body always likes to resolve. That is, we issued Clinker, as the most agile, least cretinous of our under-porters, with a shotgun, with orders to patrol Limbo; & for the next few days, by firing whenever the clever creature appeared, frightening it back to its lair, Clinker kept it trapped & hungry.

Authority (so-called) now had two sets of phenomena to deny. The spaniels, labradors & tomcats that had vanished into the snowy sky *had not* vanished, they'd simply been misplaced. The shotgun blasts from Wygy's *were not* a shotgun, they were errant fireworks left over from New Year.

People in England will swallow any implausibility so long as it's dull. Even so, these explanations were beginning to show strain, & how long the *impasse* would have lasted I don't know, had the unsqueamish ossifrage not taken a shine to our Chaplain, or the Chaplain to it.

In those days Woolly took to sitting over in Abaddon Court, on the steps of the allegorical fountain.

Above him the swollen sky ached with unshed snow. Beneath was a heavy layer of hoar-frost, covering Cambridge like opaque mail-armour. Yet Woolly sat outside by the hour, mouthing to himself, gazing up at Lethe Tower, on the other side of the covered way so rightly called Erebus; wrapped in a tremendous blue-dyed pelt of a grizzly bear, which is (he'd assured me the winter before) the correct outdoor liturgical day-wear for a shaman of the

Alaskan Tlingits. Woolly always approached the millinery aspect of religion with punctilio.

As to the other facets, I can't be sure. You know that in the shambolic chambers of his heart he'd always prayed indifferently to Pan, Shiva, Jesus, Apollo, Allah, Buddha, the Marxist *Klassenkampf* & the Freudian *Über-Ich*. "In a special sense, don't you see, these names all affirm the same named-ness." My impression is that in these last days Woolly's ambiguities resolved themselves (as, indeed, liberal thought generally does resolve itself). He cut out the middle guys.

This is, if you press me, guesswork. After that initial boozy tea, during which he was madly indiscreet, Woolly ceased to speak. He didn't appear on High Table at dinner or lunch, tea or breakfast, to explain his ideas. He didn't, I think, eat at all; certainly the wizened look, the puniness, which he had brought back from Co. Durham, became over those last few days extreme. When I ran into him about College he'd just murmur 'Ah, ah. *Culpepper*,' not gossiping about gods as he used – passing by in a weightless daze.

We'd overhear him chant to himself &, for a wonder, his mantra was from the Book of Common Prayer, a book into which even the Anglican clergy sometimes glance. *Nihil est validum, nihil sanctum*, he'd murmur as he passed. *Without Whom...*, & he'd sigh ecstatically. *Nothing is strong. Nothing is holy, Nothing is strong....*

Which could have signified anything.

But my recent experiences in W. Africa have made me sensitive to certain manias. I'm sure Woolley never stopped hearing summoning underground bells. That clangour noise portended the end of the world. I'm convinced that the *ka* of Yoxley & the *ka* of Freke seemed near to him: emissaries from the supreme void, of which the outward sign was the ossifrage. For what was the ossifrage but flying biting clawing *negation*? A winged acid-bath whose belly melted iron & bone? All-enveloping all-dissolving demise, enveloping all that he might fly away & be at rest? In comparison, were not all bones, all skeletons – even that merry holiday souvenir, my decorative Aztec skull – delusive emblems of order, of continuity, of life? Was not the bone-eater, therefore, the last word? Did he not gainsay every quiddity? Was he not the biological equivalent of a Black Hole? What was death but a softening-up for the obliteration he represented? Did he not reveal the heat-death of the universe, infinite unending viewless non-being, a single motionless grain of frozen matter every billion miles: blackness so unspotted, so pure, it had to be *adored*?

Mbingu held one clear doctrine, that Mbingu should exist. Now Woolly had, for the first time, a clear doctrine too, not so v. dissimilar: that all things should cease to exist.

Anyway, he was asking for trouble sitting there & trouble came. Being stared at in a moody mystical way by Woolly naturally enraged it, & at eleven on the 11th January – that is to say, yesterday morning – there was a sudden massive beating of black wings, falling out of the heavy sky that bulged with unshed snow. The bird had broken out, north, away from its usual haunts in & about the kitchens, toward Abaddon, toward Woolly.

Lint tore out of the Lodge with his gun. Happening to see him, I ran after him. Into the tunnel under Hall we went. Ducking under the ropes into Limbo, across Limbo nearly sliding on the ice, up the steep stairs of Erebus, cold as the grave, brutal wind whipping through its iron grilles, Clinker going puff-puff-puff. Down the stairs. Pausing where Erebus opens on Abaddon: a desolation, a black-and-white photograph: white lawn of iron-hard hoar, severe Georgian façades so hard-edged & frigid their coping-stones made paper-cuts on my eyeballs, black filigree beeches, under one of which Woolly had taken shelter. The bird was circling about, dropping, tearing at its twigs, rising again, clearly maddened by the Chaplain, beside itself with lust to lacerate his face.

'Come here, Dr Leigh!' shouted Clinker, waving his gun.

'This way, infernal idiot!' I cried. 'He'll tear your eyes out!' Woolly swivelled to gape at us.

All might have been well if that interfering *frau*, the burly Gudrun von Spluffe, hadn't stuck her bull-head out of the window of her set in staircase XI.

'*Achtung, Herr Kaplan!*' roared our Germanist, forgetting her English, such as it is. '*Flieg dem Vogel!*' It was her voice of command; she doubtless inherited it; for centuries the bellow of the von Spluffes had terrified Baltic serfs, tilling estates now lost forever. '*Schnell!*'

Aristotle pretends that a famished ass placed exactly midway between two bundles of hay must stand still & die, having no way to choose. And certainly Woolly, who'd never hit on a method of deciding anything, stood transfixed, mouth open, swinging his lovely white hair back & forth. Should he bolt for staircase XI (where the Fellow in German was keeping up her racket) or run to us in the mouth of Erebus? Suddenly he was doing neither, he was rising toward the deniable heavens, a lurid ball of bright blue in a monochrome world. He was feebly lifting & lowering his arms, absolutely dependent at last. *A royal offering to Osiris, Foremost of the Westerners.*

It sounds an incredible feat, but it happened, I saw it: the bird maddened by famine, & by love of his starving chicks, lifted the madman lightened by famine. Up! Up!

Clever birds escape archers by flying into the sun. The ossifrage cleverly flew straight up into the dazzling unshed snowbanks of the sky. We, gazing stupidly up, could see Woolly's feet vague kicking below the incredible 12-foot wingspan. He was gazing stupidly down, not at Clinker & von Spluffe & me, but at his own feet, as if worrying that they'd be dashed against the stones. Thus Clinker couldn't get a shot with the Chaplain in the way until, quite high above Lethe, the ascension of Woolly reached completion. The bird dropped him.

Then Clinker did fire; the creature squawked & sank below the battlements.

Hit! Winged, not dead. We could hear from the summit of Lethe his furious cries, mingled (or at least I thought so) with a faint, fading litany: *Zu, ruck, zu, füh, ren. Zu, ruck, zu* …. I caught no more.

What now?

Nothing now. Woolly's fur cloak had fluttered heavily to earth in Short Street. I went out to retrieve it as a secondary relic. Snow fell on my face as I stooped; by the time I reached my rooms the skies had softly torn themselves & were coming down heavily, heavily, engulfing the earth.

An emergency meeting of Governing Body, held just after tea, with a blizzard coming on, decided to leave well alone. 'Cobbers, it's a fucking closed ecosystem up there,' remarked Scuff, our Australian psychologist: a coarse, callous remark but accurate. Since the vulture was certainly maimed, there would be no more hunting, & we resolved that Clinker should be disarmed (a relief to the hated Lint, despot of the porters' Lodge). The flesh of the Rev'd Dr William Leigh, who cd not possibly have survived for more than a few minutes, wd serve as *viaticum* for the vulture & for his brood. And once all Dymwood's raptors put on immortality, smaller birds will come.

'After all,' murmured the Master, with some detachment, 'Woolly *had* his Zoroastrian side. For part of him, this is exactly what he would want.'

Officially, he's been granted a term's sabbatical. His rooms are to be emptied of their scratchy furniture & discreetly fumigated. His books will go to the College Library, there to be kept as a special collection. Miss Vydler has long coveted them (indeed I've a theory that she coveted Woolly's shapeless body; he didn't notice). Our esteemed Chaplain, as is well known from his chatter on high table, spent his final decades working his way through the works of the philosophers, in paperback translation, through the scriptures & theologians of half a dozen faiths, tirelessly inserting a *not really* before each verb, an *as it were* at the end of each proposition, an *or, indeed, contrariwise* to any sentence that still made sense: resolving all canons to the same mildly-warm pap. The Widdler proposes to catalogue this marginalia, & eventually to publish it as *Beyond Mindful & Mindless*.

So she says. I don't believe her. She'll keep the Leigh Collection for herself, locked away. She, that sybil of self-damage, will bend over it in solitude while life lasts, in her deserted Library, clavicles ajut, an angular shape of sterile grief, losing herself in what she calls the "Parathought" of William Leigh: trying to catch the echo of her almost-lover's voice as it tumbles down the bottomless fissure of non-being. As it were.

So much for Woolly. There's to be no scandal about him. And there'll be no scandal, either, about Dymwood's dastardly breed of urban ossifrages. They are dying or dead, & no one will ever repeat, for no one else will ever conceive, his great experiment. (Which was, let's recall, my idea. I happen to dislike small dogs.) The pugs, poodles, chins & shih-tzus of Paris may nestle in their cooing mistresses' arms, incontinent & incurably bronchitic but safe from airborne claws.

Woolly ascended yesterday. Term begins the day after tomorrow. You young people will return, so full of yourselves that you're sure not to notice carrion crows swirling like smoke about the tower. But the crows will be up there, consuming the heroic predator & his chicks. Woolly's soft tissue will thus be diffused at two removes, shat onto the ledges & arboreal nests of Cambridgeshire, his bones having already been liquefied in the vulture's belly. He comes to rest between earth & heaven. He is to be interred in neutral air. Doesn't that suit his particular sort of nonentity?

*So I've finished writing my defence & somehow seemed to have failed to establish my innocence.*

*Let me put my case in general terms. I kill imaginatively, I create rococo schemes of destruction. This winter my elaboration seems to be leaking outward & becoming common currency about College. You, my darling, have muscled in on my work: that I can bear, I suppose. But my colleagues on High Table have developed a similar <u>tic</u>. They're abortions striving, some of them, to become real, & in striving they destroy, which they have no business doing. We who do exist, & know who we are, are the only people who can properly impose non-existence. But killing at Wygy's has got out of hand, through no wish of mine.*

*That's my <u>apologia</u>. As Alice might say I haven't <u>ex</u>-pressed it well because I'm feeling so <u>op</u>-pressed. I have to bear implicit or explicit reproach for all this pother, & these reproaches are sure to each their climax tonight, at our end-of-vac banquet on High Table – an occasion less depraved (because less well-funded) than the Belshazzar* *affair that rounds off summer, but extreme enough.*

*The snowfall has intensified, a blizzard has sprung up, sharpening appetite. Just now I'm sitting in black tie, about to go across to the Combination Room & cocktails, not feeling jubilant.*

*I have to sit opposite the Master, & he's already flustered. "So much to do, so much to endure" he keeps saying. This term we're starting to rebuild the west run of Sheol after the fire in March – yes, yes, after I burned it, we burned it (I feel no twinge, it was horrid architecture, what comes next can't be worse). Moreover there's been quite a cull in the Fellowship, which means* elections*. The fact is that no one applies to St Wygy's without a reason, a bad reason; our elections are a matter of sorting the chaff from the ash; & we face six of the blessed things. We have to find a Philosopher* vice *Osgood, immortalised in our fire. A Chemist, since Ebbe is clearly not coming back "From wherever he's got himself to." A Zoologist, Dymwood being wholly subdued to lunacy in the bowels of the Deepdene, ranting of an elderly Frenchwoman who slighted his teenaged advances long ago. And of course a Chaplain.*

*But at least for Woolly's place there may be a ready candidate: I suspect the Master still hankers after his Abyssinian, who recently emerged from hospital; at least most of him did, he's lost both legs to diabetes. He's been seen whizzing up Trumpington Street in full vestments, extremely gorgeous, crowned with bulbous bedizened mitre, on a motorised throne fitted with a liturgical umbrella of tasselled silk to keep off the snow, shouting anathemas at Peterhouse Chapel, at Little St Mary's, at Botolph's, & so forth – at every place of worship, in fact, because none are in communion with Ethiopian Monophysitism. That'll be a change from Woolly, won't it?*

*But meanwhile, tonight, the Master will be flustered when he realises Olga Freke & Yoxley are absent from dinner. Especially if he overhears* double entendres *about their fate. Sooner or later, although certainly not tonight, we'll have to break it to Sir Trotsky that these miscreants are also dead (or in a state beyond finite & terminal life), & that we have to find a Fellow in Berberology & an Ægyptologist J.R.F.* Eight *elections! Horror!*

*Thus it's bound be a damnable dinner. Too many ghosts will be seated – not in a literal sense. Or at least probably not. We just don't know; we just don't know.*

*To cancel out the conversation & the brooding gloom of dinner, I have got out that wad of manuscript the ornery Hebridean Archbishop sent me at the end of term. Do you remember? "Wapentake"? In the brown paper? It awaits me on my coffee-table, the famous poetic skull serving as paperweight, for when I get back from dinner.*

*I'm sure I'll not be able to take it seriously. I'll donate it to the Widdler when I'm done, for her to treasure for years, then rip up one wanton summer. I've thumbed through the crackling pages, & find they're pure escapism: wonderfully antiquarian, with sepia photos glued in place, & old-fashioned "beautified" writing in a number of hands wielding a number of fountain-pens. In other words, everyone involved is among the dead, the blessèd dead, so-called because, uniquely, they're human beings who do us no harm.*

*That's it. I'll wrap up this note with my earlier letter, the account of my African adventure, & hand them to the porters for posting on my way to the Combination Room.*

*I'm seeing you on Tuesday, & can't, I think, wait. I probably love &, more importantly, I most certainly obey you.*

# X.
# WAPENTAKE

*An Exposition may be made by me,*
*Of Mineral Tearms, to most men now abstruse,*
*Which by Expounding may be of more use;*
*This little book, the mineral Law to shew….*

Manlove
*The Wapentake of Wirksworth*

*Those who kill without charging a fee, and merely to*
*oblige their friends, should not be called assassins.*

Pascal
*Lettres provinciales*

A great bull-fight was held in her honour. Fifteen
bulls received the *coup-de-grâce*, and Alvarez, the
matador of matadors, died in the arena with her
name on his lips. He had tried to kill the last bull
without taking his eyes off *la divina señorita*. A
prettier compliment had never been paid her, and
she was immensely pleased with it. For that matter,
she was immensely pleased with everything.

Beerbohm
*Zuleika Dobson*

# Part One
## *26ᵗʰ October 1877*

Miss Gladys Ella Furlough        Alphonso Ñezgo y Escalofriante

## *i.*

*It was much the same (Alphonso reflected, afterward, too late) as if I'd torn my heel on the thorn of an azufaifo shrub on the mesa above my town. The gash let us suppose becomes gangrenous, and although they take my foot off the blackness has already raced upward; by the time there is talk of chopping again, above the knee, my torso is rotten and I die miserably, slowly, almost alone since the stench is so strong they lay me in the hut behind my father's house where the wood is kept, and even my grandmother will visit only for a few minutes at a time.*

    *Of course, he argued ('Father, is it not so?'), my leg should have been cut*

*away at once, at the hip; but who could bear to lay knife on flesh so entirely
sound? On the leg of a young man who walked, not hobbled, not even limped
for the pain of the thorn is still a little thing? A youth who walked to the house
of Señor José Maria the apothecary to ask to be made a cripple, a two-thirds-
man? No, Father, since the only cure is too terrible to think of, a man's one hope
is to be lucky and never brush against* azufaifos, *should it be his lot to have to
go about the* mesa *where they grow, collecting firewood.*

*'Is it not so? How, Father, might I have escaped my great crime? With all
your learning can you name any remedy but good fortune? ¿Padre, no es así?'*

*Of course he was reproached for these aspersions on Divine Providence,
and humbly listened to my reproaches; but still shook his head, knowing I was
wrong.*

*For that is just what seeing Clarisetta the daughter of the great English lord
had been like (said Alphonso, later, too late): it was as a flick from a thorned twig
as one passes along one's path. A trifling way of catching one's death.*

*Yes,* Padre: *was it not trifling to see her step down from the great painted
carriage that had come all the way from Sevilla itself, that dirty dusty-breezy
evening in Eastertide? Was it not a slight thing to watch her place her lovely foot,
in a velvet shoe the colour of cornflowers, on the dun-coloured dust outside the*
Hotel del Universo, *which as all the world knows is the most splendid inn not
just in the town of Alhama de Granada but in the entire province? She lifted her
veil, grubby from travel, with little hands – her gloves were rose-pink, of the most
excellent kid, with buttons to them: but what is that? Her bright hair common to
all Northern tourists, her almost-no-nose, her small hard grey eyes, her skin like
frozen butter chaffed here and there by the proper Southern sun: what is there in
this glimpse to kill a man, perhaps to damn him?* '¿Padre, no es así?'

*The scene outside the hotel is obviously pictured through the deluded eyes
of Alphonso:* 'I went back to the Universo *after dark, Father, to kiss the ground
where I thought her sole must first have touched our unworthy soil,' and so forth.
But it's easy enough to see through his romantic silliness: to see the jaded little
minx, with her insolent rich-girl mannerisms, her gross complexion and features
not much softened by natty shop-bought clothes, flaunting her tourist learning,
her guide-book phrases. To see the nervous rudeness of a Northern* bourgeoise
*hectoring the manager of the* Hotel del Universo, *who stands cringing, wringing
his hands, mouthing apologies, while her monoglot father stands behind her,
puffing his cigar, amused; and her acid-faced dowdily-dressed Companion looks
back and forth, scowling at the unclean little town; and her father's Man looks
about for loose woman, being looked at in turn. Yes, the whole tourist party
comes clear to me, for Alphonso's delusion is a constant, and can confidently be
subtracted from the equation.*

*'¡Es terrible!' she is saying, the fatal one, vulgarly, in her shrill small voice.*

'Terrible!' *and she stamps her foot, something Alphonso had never seen a female do to a grown man before. What courage! What resolution!*

*He hardly listened to what the manager (a great personage in Alhama) was saying in reply: something about a suite, bathrooms, '*un tremendo error, señorita*' – it seemed that their rooms were not quite ready, he was beseeching her patience. '*¡Cinco minutos, sólo cinco minutitos!*'*

*Beauty was not mollified. '*¿Por qué?*' she shrieked, and for a glorious giddy instant Alphonso believed she might be about to box the manager's ears. '*¿Por qué? ¡Telegrafiamos de Sevilla para un suite!*'*

*Everyone was watching, all Alhama held its breath. But of course "everyone" meant "all the natives". The insular girl and her insular father did not care, did not even know that this was the hour of the evening stroll in Alhama, as in all of Latin Europe. Naturally the rich men of the town were at the fashionable café tables opposite the hotel; naturally many more poor men were gathered in the shadowy flank of the cathedral; and the women, idle for a little while because their men were gone, peered from every window. The tourists party was oblivious, unaware of being observed. They were British subjects, it did not occur to them that might also be objects; their self-centredness left them entirely self-possessed.*

*In the pause before father and daughter respectively stomped and flounced into the hotel, followed by their unimportant dependents (it was much less than five minutes), the father simply ran his eyes over the plaza and found it mucky; while that paragon among women, his daughter, fixed her tiny unstable eyes – she was sadly short-sighted – on the cathedral façade, doubtless trying to remember what Baedeker would want her to make of it in.*

*For Clarisetta was avid to improve her mind, that is, to increase its value; she was greedy for what she imagined was cosmopolitan culture; that's why it* was *just too awful when these feckless foreigners waste even a* second *of Papa's time, which may* who knows be *so short, nor mine, on our tour of wondrous Spain, because it* is *wondrous & romantic Mrs F., despite* everything. *(She liked to compose her letters home in her head, taking some care – especially of the gushing passages; it saved time; she would rather die than be one of those girls who sit in hotels for hour sucking their pens while their fathers pace up and down.) So now she peered at the sacred statuary. It did not cross her mind to drop her gaze and regard the living men below the niches, or to weigh the light in their brown eyes, or to pick out the one pair of eyes – Alphonso's – that did not merely twinkle with amusement or desire, but burned, having been ignited in that moment by what they saw; eyes now damaged, doomed to be put out, quenched, burned away by the alkaline of prison-yard quicklime.*

*That is how the moment seemed to Alphonso: his glimpse of Clarisetta should have been no more than a scratch on his soul. She ought to have been just the occasion for unchaste reverie. ('Saving your presence, Father.') Yet she was not; and therefore, having seen her and received his wound, Alphonso ought to have fled at once, cutting off ruin at the hip-bone. He should have left for the Americas perhaps, or gone to the military recruiting office in Cadiz to offer himself as a soldier and die warring on the rebels in the Philippines. He should have done this, or even ('Saving your presence, Father') he should have done away with himself altogether, at once, that very evening; flinging himself into a gully on the mesa, let us say, to lie in peace all night, with the cool moonlight picking him out broken from the fall, but not so broken as his mind had been with love.*

*He heard out my angry priestly words about the very notion of suicide, hanging his head, but also slowly shaking it; he was dogged, he knew he was right.* 'Sí, sí, padre, perdona. *But it was not my doing. Once I had been shown her there was no escape for me but flight or death. Otherwise my sin and destruction were ordained.* ¿No es así? ¿No es así?'

## *ii.*

Such were the fatuous final thoughts of Alphonso Ñezgo y Escalofriante as recorded by Fr James O'Shaughnessy, who came to comfort him in Strangeways Gaol, Manchester, the night he waited to be hanged.

They were ignorant thoughts, as is to be expected, Fr O'Shaughnessy remarks, from a man of Andalusia, a hopelessly ignorant region; scandalous too, as was Alphonso's whole account; at least it outraged *him*.

Perhaps we should subtract outrage from the record of James O'Shaughnessy, who, according to the corporate memory of Openshaw Friary, was a severe, abstracted man. He was subdued but not mellowed from decades of serving the short-lived Irish diaspora in the grey English Midlands. Coldly he welcomed them from their wombs, sternly he guided them through their lives and dismissed them to their graves. If his granite face betrayed anything, it was the heretical notion that such existences were impossibly brief, impossibly puny. A Mancunian labourer gained so little by being born, he lost so little by dying. He scarcely warranted all this blessing, reproving, and sacramental botheration.

For all we know O'Shaughnessy wrestled manfully against this heresy. Indeed we cannot be sure he conceived it, although of course the disciplined intimacy of monastic life makes it hard for us to hide our minds from each other. The brethren at Openshaw Blackfriars certainly twitted O'Shaughnessy on his detachment, which was blamed not on pride (no one ever seems to have thought him a proud man), nor on snobbery (he was the younger son of an upstanding County Sligo publican), but on – of all things – a weakness for modern fiction. Which he had no business indulging, if that is really what corrupted his mind.

I am not a philistine. Novels are splendid enough in their way, and most people fling themselves in without harm. But there are people who cannot: novelists themselves confess as much. It is the business of folk like Don Quixote and Catherine Morland to acknowledge their weakness and abstain, just as it's the business of dipsomaniacs to avoid drams.

James O'Shaughnessy did not abstain, and was dour on the outside because of the perpetual gaudy riot within. Stories befuddled and blunted him. To return from the company of Tess, Fabrice del Dongo, Raskolnikov, Vautrin and Heathcliff to Manchester is to experience a jolt, an abrupt change of scale. Perhaps Dominicans in the slums, bound to spend their lives tending tired humble souls, should generally not frequent the company of vast, fiery souls (of whom there are surely quite enough in hell).

❧

I myself have no taste for fiction. My weakness, only a recent weakness at that, is the archive of this friary of ours.

The word *archive* is misleadingly grand. The muniment-room at Openshaw is a dusty attic above the infirmary, heaped hugger-mugger with wooden boxes, like so many bread-bins. When a brother dies the papers found in his cell are scooped together, dropped into one of these small bins, and brought up there. It is Openshaw's compromise between the Dominican principle that we have no private belongings; the English principle that no gentleman reads another gentleman's mail; and innocent pride, which assumes that the doings of Blackfriars are a chapter in the history of the Faith, of Manchester, nay, of the realm. Our papers cannot properly be destroyed, nor decently read: the muniment-room is thus a muddle in more senses than one.

For many years Brother Anselm was, notionally, our archivist. He was intensely a gentlemen, despite being an exemplary religious in his own wistful way, and admirably muddle-headed. I am sure he never opened a box. When he died, and our Prior shyly told me I was to succeed ('Hope you don't mind, old boy, but officially we have to have one'), I intended to be just as slack. What are archives but mundane vanity? What's the point of being a friar except being dead to the world, living a life hidden in Christ? Each box bears a name in gold paint; one of the latest and least-faded reads DOM. ANSELMUS BUGGINS, O.P. + 1.10.1933. The same terse inscription is on his wooden cross in our cemetery. What more can there be to say of him, or of any friar? *Vita vestra abscondita est cum Christo.*

I have come to think differently.

Somewhere tonight in England a woman no longer young is rustling through cardboard boxes of tissue-paper and mothballs, fingering a debutante frock with a crumbled brown knot at the breast, once a gardenia, rubbing it to her cheek. An elderly clubman, unsteady on his feet at the best of times, is at this moment tottering home through the black-out, tenderly touching the *façades* of St James, bidding them farewell. Future Englands (if there are any) will never grasp our weird passion of nostalgia, this winter of the Blitz: nostalgia for what we have not yet lost.

That is why I have begun to explore the archive. Physically the boxes are frail as kindling, the papers with crackling when moved, tearing when touched; impatient for the incendiary bomb that, one of these moonless nights, is sure to come sailing through the roof.

The Luftwaffe is paying attention to Manchester. The school was evacuated nearly a year ago, in November. Some of the younger friars went with it; not me. I never thought I would miss teaching ancient history to the imbeciles of the Lower Sixth, but I do, I do. There is comparatively little to do between Offices. On the morning after a raid my impulse is to pass out of Chapel, where we have celebrated eternal invulnerable truth, up the narrow stair, into the archive. Here I sit reading what is transitory, and anyway sure to be obliterated, soon, by the chaos of the age: but is after all true too.

What Anselm's box contains I have no idea. I have imposed the rule on myself not to touch any papers deposited since 1914, the year I came to Openshaw. But I know the earlier stuff well enough. I am familiar with the quiet lives of the Victorian friars of Openshaw, their pious letters, their endearing weaknesses (why would any monastic keep the *Racing Guide* in his cell?), even their occasional mild rebellions, recorded in spiritual journals –

How *subdued* I'm making it sound! Tenuous, sepulchral, dimly or nauseatingly fragrant with a piety already remote. Whereas the box marked PATR. JACOBUS O'SHAUGHNESSY + 23.10.1888 is – I was about to write *sensational*, but that's not what I mean; no Victorian crime could be very sensational now. I simply mean that it has transfigured me, that I have found in it my place of understanding.

Surprisingly enough; for O'Shaughnessy was a reader not a writer. He left behind no journal, only a notebook listing the novels he had finished. His appetite was enormous and, at least by the conventions of the time, *louche.* The few letters he kept are from a widowed sister, an apostate to the Church of Ireland, gaunt and impatient as her brother. There are laconic, often acerbic notes about his pastoral work; and profuse teaching notes, for O'Shaughnessy was happiest (or least unhappy) at the friary school, battering mathematics into snub-nosed young Mancunian who did not love him. He himself was fonder of a parabola or hypotenuse than of any boy.

There are a few photographs: of O'Shaughnessy's childhood homes and his father's lowering tavern; of the Protestant sister; of dead parents; and one of the fellow himself, in near-youth, shortly before he was professed. This I am going to appropriate from his box (what can a dead friar want with a portrait?), and include in these papers. If we are going to impugn his investigation, we need to look him in the eye, take the measure of his face, and say *You are wrong*. In common fairness I attach a photograph of myself, looking, to be frank, rather blank and rather ingenuous, with a flat face inherited from my Breton mother, and flab from bad wartime rations. Could anyone look into this bland face of mine and say *You have perceived here what Fr James could not?* I wonder.

I am avoiding coming to the point. There is, finally, an acid-green cardboard carton. It is labelled in O'Shaughnessy's taut hand, with a curious use of plus-sign for ampersand, *The Fetid + Deplorable + Tedious Afflictions of the late Alphonso Ñezgo y Escalofriante*. This carton contains four wildly-assorted books. These first three works evidently formed the whole of Miss Furlough's travelling library. They are the 1876 Baedeker for Spain and Portugal, with many pages annotated by a female using violet ink; *Fluttering Leaves by the Wayside: an anthology of English Verse for the Use of Gentlewomen Journeying Abroad,* expurgated (although the editors do not say so) with elephantine discretion; and a seventeenth-century poem of sublime eccentricity by one Manlove, bound and gilded. Fr O'Shaughnessy has added a fourth book, a thick unexpurgated French autobiography dating from the early 1880s, of which more, I regret, in due course. There is also an aged and dusty sugar-sack, rolled up; various other documents we'll come to in due course; a brittle and flaking Spanish newspaper; and Fr O'Shaughnessy's long, chaotic memorandum of the whole affair.

A hodgepodge of paper, then. And of it all, O'Shaughnessy's memorandum is the most puzzling piece of work. Why did he record in such detail the last night of a particular condemned man? (He had been in, he was to be in, other death-cells.) Why did he go back to his writing again and again for over a decade, adding so many afterthoughts? Did he simply pique himself on being the only Openshaw Dominican who could speak Spanish? Did he write as a penance for his failure with the young Spaniard, who made such a bad end? Was it compunction?

O'Shaughnessy had reluctantly given Absolution and the Viaticum to Alphonso, who seemed barely contrite. He received the sacraments reverently enough, and in return presented O'Shaughnessy with his only possession on earth, a sugar-sack, waxed within to keep out the wet, filled with papers

– the intolerable Baedeker and the rest of it. Then the two men sat until dawn, O'Shaughnessy reading psalms and the Office for the Dying, the condemned youth with a faraway ecstatic expression that might be read in different ways. He seemed apathetic when the door opened and the executioner appeared; was docile during the brief fuss of being bound; went quietly up the gallows steps with O'Shaughnessy a pace behind, mumbling from his *Rituale Romanum*; did not shrink from being hooded. He was a model patient until the instant before the trapdoor opened, when he shouted 'Clarisetta!', and was gone.

The hangman, a high-minded Dissenter, was shocked. This was no moment to be mentioning *females*, certainly not Spanish females of any description whatsoever; his notion of Spain was doubtless the usual jumble of Inquisitions, Armadas, bed-bugs, and bold-eyed black-eyed swarthy temptresses eyeing their prey.

The prison governor, a rising man, was perhaps unshockable; but he was annoyed. Before letting the journalists go, he addressed them on the necessity of suppressing the 'regrettable circumstance' of the dead man's final cry 'or should I say purported final cry, it being unclear what *any* foreigner means to express. Gentlemen, it would certainly be misunderstood. It might embarrass a distinguished local family of solid reputation.'

The more hard-bitten journalists took a moment to grasp to whom he was alluding: the Furlough family had an *appalling* reputation. But they promised the governor they would not print the unfortunate circumstance, and kept their word since no newspaperman wants to be shut out of the fun of executions.

But Fr O'Shaughnessy walked slowly back to Openshaw and breakfast through the shouting, misty, horse-dung-scented streets of a Victorian Manchester dawn, with industrial clanging in the background and chimneys burping sparks; grim, with the preposterous sugar-sack tucked awkwardly under his arm, and his chin on his breast.

## *iii.*

A gruesome yarn, a yard of fustian. A period piece, a quaintness, a distraction from air-raids. A holiday from the atrocious twentieth-century into the polite nineteenth.

Certainly the backdrops are as Victorian as can be. Openshaw itself was, is, as extravagant a piece of High Gothic as you could hope, dread to come across, the work of Pugin junior, polychrome brick, enormous, built by the hands of the friars themselves (if that is any excuse). And Strangeways Gaol is a nightmare too, more stripes, on walls sixteen foot thick: a panopticon shaped like a snowflake from which the wings radiate. Strangeways has not changed since O'Shaughnessy's day, and I have often visited, as our flock still passes in and out.

As it happens I too have been to B wing. There the permanent gallows awaits (me, perhaps, or you); and the condemned cell, not very opulently fitted-out. In this cell Alphonso divulged his outrageous story. I rather hope *Reichsmarschall* Göring, who boasts that he is going to burn Manchester to the ground, does not spare Strangeways.

The dubious heroine of this story is Victorian too, very Victorian. Poor Alphonso, factually wrong as he was about every facet of his love, was wrong about her identity. She was daughter not of a "lord" but of a Mancunian industrialist of shady origin, a tall dark portly rogue called Zebulon Furlough.

Furlough had begun as a who-knows-what, a drayman perhaps, and had risen in the world too quickly to outrun his own unease with himself. But he was carefully, infernally careful about disguise.

As to figure: he wasn't, to judge from his photographs, fat, but pockets of podge hung in clusters from his bones, so that he had the look of a peasant come into soft times; such a figure, and such a cubic, bovine head, could never be *chic*, though he could be swaddled adequately. As to clothes: his clothes were all right, he simply paid a retainer to a down-at-heel viscount in Town, who bought everything for him on credit (the bills were settled promptly and anonymously), parcelled them up and sent them up North, with a condescending note instructing Furlough when to wear what and how. Words were more tricky. There was no way he could buy in his conversation, and the peril of uttering what was low or common so perplexed him that, as far as possible, he tried never to speak. He favourite word was the simple grunt '*Rrumpff!*' – surely a reliably gentlemanly sound? Had he not heard it often at the Club? (Of course the Reform; he had been blackballed elsewhere.)

Furlough was always generous and careful with his alms to the deserving poor of Parliament. He choose his moment well and extorted a knighthood from a hard-pressed Liberal government. Shortly afterward – the Prince Consort had just died, death was in vogue, the land was full of gloom and rustling black bombazine, the first slaughters of the American War were filling the papers – he found himself widowed. Peg, the new-made Lady Furlough, "'ad swelled up and b'st wi' pride," declared local opinion, leaving Sir Zebulon with a single child to rear as his comfort and heiress. Her baptismal certificate recorded her as *Gladys Ella Furlough*, a name naturally beyond any Spaniard, educated or not; Alphonso called her *Clarissa*, which is as close as he could get to *Gladys*; his impudent infatuation soon diminished this to *Clarisetta*.

Sir Zebulon called her *Gladdy*, and doted on or at least gloated over her.

Was she not his most precious since most expensive possession? Had she not cost him marriage and no manner of bother, not least his wife's ostentatious funeral? Was Gladdy not entirely fit, when the time came, in five years or so, to be cashed in and buy him a coroneted son-in-law, then a grandson and heir? Until that time Furlough was, in his speechless moody way, proud of Gladdy's arctic beauty. Her looks weren't what he liked in females himself, but he knew they were fashionable, and added a "margin" to her value as his legatee. She was nineteen.

Sir Zebulon's "seat", as he called it in his frequent moments of pomposity, was Kettlehinge Hall, a shambles of a manor-house, most of it early-Tudor, but with earlier fabric muddled into its stonework and plasterwork as in a *ragoût*. Kettlehinge had been begun by the Orgreave family when they were little more than Peak District marauders, and inhabited by them, generation after disastrous generation, until their deepening impoverishment and effeminacy were complete, and they had to sell. The last Orgreave baronet, despairing, departed for the Cape Colony to raise cattle, bearing only a few steamer-trunks. His ancestral furnishings and paintings were sold with the house, and what was left of the land 'And I got it all for a bloody song too' Furlough said in unguarded moments.

You might have expected such a blaring *parvenu*, suddenly possessed of a country house, to "do it up" and ruin it. In fact he was in awe of the place, from the turret, with its goat-shaped weather-vane bearing the Orgreave motto *Divitias omnes viæ, All roads point to pelf* ('*Rrumpff!* wise words'), to the cellars, with their moaning clanking sizzling ghosts.

There was a particularly harrowing story attached to the ghosts: they are an entire family of yeoman, convicted of some unthinkable perversion in heroic days of yore; for which they were stripped naked by their Orgreave liege-lord, chained together and flung into his celebrated giant venison cauldron or kettle (it gave the house its name), which he had packed with snow, and hung over a slow fire. The culprits return to the foundations of Kettlehinge at dusk each winter evening to resume their punishment, which continues until the hour of the *Angelus*; this stills them, and they vanish. But anyone lawless enough to pierce the lower depths of the Hall before the gracious ninefold bell will hear bubbling, and frantic clattering of chains, and shrieks, from he knows not where – perhaps from all about, or from within his own tainted skull.

Furlough took this story seriously. He took everything about Kettlehinge seriously; he wanted to adopt Kettlehinge lore *holus-bolus*. Therefore, apart from seeing to dry-rot, restoring topiary and replacing slates, he reverently left the estate alone. It never looked so wonderful, by all accounts, as during his time.

Of course it was intensely uncomfortable. But that scarcely concerned Sir Zebulon Furlough, M.P.; he was hardly ever there. He had, as he often said, "my seat in the imperial capital", that is, a hideous castellated townhouse on Millbank, full of purplish stained-glass as some enormous chantry-chapel; also a discreet crimson-velvet-hung apartment, never mentioned, in the prostitute quarter of Manchester. Kettlehinge he inflicted on his friends or toadies just once a year, at Christmastide. When they all said, and perhaps even felt, that the damp cold, draughts, crooked floors, smoking chimneys, low blackened beams on which they brained themselves, and even the imbecilic, dialectal servants (every one from an ancient Kettlehinge family, undismissable), were all splendidly Old World: the authentic pith of England.

And so saying hurried back to their gas-lit, gas-warmed modern houses, leaving Kettlehinge to Gladdy, the great lead heiress; and to Gladdy's governess, Mrs Flange; and to Gladdy's paid companion, Miss Rawkdon.

For two of those three discontented females, Christmastide was the best, the least bad time of the year. Season of mercy, season of comfort and joy! True, Miss Rawkdon hated Christmas. But Mrs Flange had a score of men to baffle and embarrass with her refinement; and as for Gladdy, she could fornicate with one or more of Papa's guests, with *any* of them, almost, capable of discreet amour after the drunken luncheons.

So much for Christmas week. But then everyone left for London, for Liverpool, for the wide world; and the ladies of Kettlehinge found the last days of each year the worst: almost unendurable. Once more they were pent, alone with the creaky frigid old house and with each other.

Miss Furlough would spend those days storming about the snowy hills (it always snows over Christmas in the Peak District), dragging Hester Rawkdon with her, partly because Hester was frail and suffered from the cold. Hester's snuffling nose and blue ears weren't much, but they were something, and Miss Furlough clutched at whatever comfort was going in the comfortlessness of the new year. She was frantic for paternal tyranny to end, for her own reign to begin. How could it matter if *anno Domini* 1875 passed into *anno Domini* 1876, '76 into '77, when there was no essential change, no dawn of *anno Domina Gladys*? How could it matter?

Before these fierce midwinter walks her maid laced up high black excellent patent leather boots. Miss Furlough's foot twiched with longing to kick the maid in the face. She carried a wonderfully-polished blackthorn alpenstock, hung about with dark purple ribbons, just right for thrashing folk if only this were allowed. She wore the tightest darlingest ermine jacket imaginable, with matching cap and muff; her small angry face, entirely unflushed by the cold, remained much paler than a stoat's winter coat. Against the drifts and banks of whiteness on the steep slopes above Kettlehinge, her complexion was invisible, non-existent, so that she resembled, I am convinced, one of those vile, unsparing works by *les Surréalistes*. I mean that her big very blue eyes – under their sly lids and spiteful blonde lashes – her neatly pinched nostrils, her small gory mouth, gave (thought, surely, Miss Rawkdon, whose own complexion resembled porridge coming off the boil, whose only fur was a shabby brown shoulder-cape of muskrat) the freakish impression of bobbing about in mid-air.

Was Gladys Furlough quite human? Was she a finite soul incarnate in human flesh, and nothing more? No one asked. Hester Rawkdon dismissed her as a fiend; Mrs Flange secretly called her a goose; Gladys, who always thought of herself, never thought about herself.

"Lead heiress" is how her father liked people to think of her. His fortune was really in dubious railways shares and seedy bank schemes, not to mention proprietorship of statesmen; it was cosmopolitan, being entangled, in its small way, with capital all over the Continent, with the Anglo-French Rothschilds, Franco-Ottoman Camondos, Turko-German Oppenheims, Germano-Belgian Bischoffsheims, Belgo-Hanseatic Berenbergs, Hanseatico-English Meyers, and the whole crew of international finance. Even Furlough could see this was not romantic.

But lead, now: lead was respectably solid, impeccably British; indeed lead was Derbyshireish.

There was, there is, I gather, a body of law, more ancient than the Conquest, perhaps brought to this island by Brutus the Trojan, peculiar to the lead-mines of the Peak District, and specifically to the Wapentake of Wirksworth – *To the what?* we ask. Well, a *wapentake* is apparently a district, a subdivision of a county, named for the taking-up of weapons after warriors had met under a tree, or on a hillock, to settle their rough affairs. That was in the Dark Age; but *this* wapentake, Wirksworth, Derbyshire's lead country, is still legally disjunct from the rest of the realm. According to its strange canon, anyone can prospect for lead ore anywhere – churches, houses and gardens are exempt, churchyards not (one may dig for the metal amongst the sleepers, why not?) – the claims being adjudicated by a "Barghmoot Court", applying a "mineral Law" parallel to the Common Law – as its terms are parallel to common English – as the Wapentake of Wirksworth is outside, it strikes me, the real world, the England I know – something else again, and perhaps something alarming.

If I sound bewildered it is because I have just re-read, my head spinning, *The Liberties and Cvstomes of the Lead-Mines Within the Wapentake of Wirk-*

sworth *Composed in Meeter by Edward Manlove Esq^{re}, heretofore Steward of the Barghmoot Court for the Lead-Mines.* This was the *only* book Sir Zebulon was ever seen with, in his proper pose as a lead millionaire. To please Papa, of whom she was after all afraid (he might easily disinherit her, indeed would if he ever found out a tenth of the truth), Gladys always bore about her own gorgeously-bound *Wapentake of Wirksworth*, stamped in gold-leaf with the bogus Furlough arms: a sixteenth birthday present from Papa, with an inscription in his ghastly peasant hand urging her *to Study and Conn the Lore of the Estates that will one day be Yours.*

It was one of the three books Gladys travelled with, along with the dreadful anthology and dreadful Baedeker. All three passed into my trove with all her other papers. And Manlove troubles me. It was the prescribed scripture of the lead heiress; God knows what she learned from it. Anyway it's surely one of the oddest things in our language – if it *is* our language. *Many words of art you still may seek,* says Edward Manlove:

> *The miner's Tearms are like to heathen Greek,*
> *Both strange and uncoth, if you some would see,*
> *Read these rough verse here compos'd by me.*
> *Bunnings, Polings, Stemples, Forkes, and Slyder,*
> *Stoprice, Yokings, Soletrees, Roach and Ryder,*
> *Water-hoels, Wind-hiles, Veyns, Coe-shafts and Woughs ....*

In a sense, Gladys was simply disloyal to this knowledge. Dearest Papa might revere Kettlehinge, that crumbly freezing old pile, Dearest Papa might almost begin to feel that these ancestral portraits up the creaking staircases were his own forebears (not the poachers and vagrants from whom he was actually sprung). Since the Orgreaves themselves had been mining magnates, once they left off being highwaymen, dearest Papa might pose as an old world mining-magnate. Dearest Papa might like to think of his gold as lead, anciently torn from the bosom of the dear old Derbyshire hills and alchemically transformed. But Gladys, the brisk, worldly, self-centred Gladys, found such pretence insupportable.

Perhaps she was not indifferent to Manlove. Perhaps she unearthed occult meaning in his poem. I fear she did. Nonetheless, in reaction to stowces, winches, barmastery, and other matters concerning the quaint exploitation of seams, she became intensely modern. In reaction to her home's mullions and oriels, she gave her imagination over to practical questions of lust, of avarice and lust.

So much for (as the mathematical O'Shaughnessy would say) one half of the equation.

❧

Alphonso, now.

He too, was only ambiguously respectable. For uncountable generations the Ñezgo clan had been brigands. Alphonso's father was hereditary chieftain of a band that infested the passes about Ijnázar, a white mountain village. He was such a success he over-reached himself: a reforming government in Madrid sent a column of dragoons to exterminate the pestilent Ñezgos. When the bayonetting was complete no one was left but a mewking infant, clinging to the breast of his grandmother. She, being a nuisance, quite unrapeable, the soldiers hanged on the nearest tree, but the nameless boy-child they thought might as well be secured. The parish priest gave him to a worthy mousy childless couple named Escalofriante, constant Mass-goers and police-informants.

Alphonso Ñezgo y Escalofriante, as they called him, grew up an odd mixture of *banditto* and sacristan. At fourteen he was apprenticed to a bandy-legged drover, who – although he held perfectly orthodox, old-fashioned ideas about frequent drubbings for the young – was secretly a Freemason. He introduced Alphonso to what are called progressive ideals, completing the rout of order in that poor young brain.

In October 1877 he was thoroughly discontented.

He was small, even for an Andalusian, with eyes too far apart in a face that was too wide, flat thin hair pushed sideways across his big skull, thick-looking sallow skin, and a curious heaviness to his wrists, so that his big hands always seemed to swinging in front of him when he stood. When he walked, he pointed his knees outward and stamped down his heels, working his hips; this gait was not as swaggering as he perhaps hoped. His moustaches were pitiable. His eyebrows were rather good. A timid woman might appreciate the dilute handsomeness of his face, and his faintly dandified clothes, but the woman of southern Spain are rarely timid. The local men, although fierce in their gestures and expressions, feel a curious solidarity toward each other, perhaps because of the intense Catholicism of the region, not long liberated from the Moor; they generally approved of Alphonso. However an Englishmen, if he noticed him at all, would certainly think him "a poor specimen."

As to Alphonso himself: he was as unhappy in his own body as in his own soul. No one realised this because his friendships were tepid by Latin standards, and because he was so inarticulate, until that last night in Strangeways, waiting to die.

Miss Gladys Ella Furlough had the strangest trick of chewing her nether lip so harshly it was a marvel (as Mrs Flange had often remarked) it did not *bleed*.

She was really just as brassy as her father. Her expensive education –

that is, her time with the Flange – had laid out a municipal garden in her mind, softening the presence of the bandstand and its the blaring noise. If you strained you could still hear in her conversation muted trumpets and muffled snare-drum.

Most people, dazed by first impressions of the Lead Heiress, did not strain. Absence of soul lightened her wonderfully.

Light poured through.

She was manœuvrable. She could set her face as she wanted: gave the impression of a zippy little yacht, someone's Christmas present, black-and-gold paintwork still tacky to the touch, flying easily here and there on smooth warm waters, the crew below decks.

Does this sound far-fetched? Well, I would be evading reality if I just listed her literal characteristics (she played the piano very badly; had an odd trick of crushing her upturned tip of nose between ring-fingers, a fidget proper to a costermonger which nonetheless did very nicely in drawing-rooms; sang to herself under her breath in what sounded to Mrs Flange like some unknown language). I've stood close to fashionable portraits, I know modern painters use smears of lilac and jabs of yellow oil-paint to render human flesh ....

Miss Furlough weighed seven stone one pound: this is specified, I cannot conceive why, in the declaration she made to the Spanish police. She was blonde, of course, a blonde of the flat-chested silvery type, unknown in the sunny province of Granada. That province has its share of generously-made golden blondes, rich in Visigothic blood, straw-haired, red-cheeked, sprawlingly splendid, lime-elms or apple-trees among women. Gladys was an aspen, and made a tremendous impression on her autumn tour, since boggling young Spaniards had no way of knowing how badly her type wears, how faded that silver looks in early middle-age, how likely she was to turn pale and shrewish.

Not that this knowledge would have mattered to Alphonso. His was not a love that looks forward to calm middle age. Indeed, it didn't much matter to Gladys herself. She knew her lunar beauty could still command a market; she proposed to sell it, high, soon, and let the future mind itself.

In short, the two young people were made for each other.

## iv.

Alphonso's prick of *azufaifo* bush occurred at eight-fifteen on the evening of October the twenty-sixth. Within three minutes Miss Furlough, absolutely oblivious of the calamity she had caused, was upstairs changing out of her travelling-clothes. Zebulon had disappeared into the smoking-room, to snub and patronise as many male guests as he could before poor dear Gladdy deigned to float downstairs and be taken in for dinner.

All Alhama, watching from the cafés, alleys and windows about the plaza, released its long-drawn breath, and became once more lively and talkative, discussing the arrivals from every angle. The men frankly wondered how rich the rich Englishman was. The youths discussed, in absolute purity of heart because the question was so unreal, whether the foreign girl was as abandoned as she looked. The women, chattering from window to window, inclined to condemn her for her bad manners and her rage (it was really only petulance, but this is a mood unknown in Andalusia), although they applauded her cyclamen gloves with the little buttons and wondered if this fashion had yet reached Córdoba or even Seville – Seville! – or if it were just something for the *señoras* of London and Paris. Paris!

Meanwhile Alphonso Ñezgo had tottered off alone into the starry night, to assess his death-wound and to enjoy it.

You mustn't think of this provincial youth as an innocent. Indeed there is no innocence to be had in this tale, not even from the Victorian Dominican who collected it or the modern Dominican who recounts it now. O'Shaughnessy was too chilly for human illusions. I am too troubled. We all know what we are talking about.

Alphonso, too, although fatally romantic, was not *naïve*. He was clear that what he wanted from this amazing foreigner (hair like streaks of starlight, lips like faintest coral) was bed. He had already been to brothels, and in a fey sullen fashion had been trying to seduce a nearby farm-girl, a grubby farm-girl, who was biddable, credulous, and quite illiterate. His desire for the glimmering Englishwoman was obsession of a different sort. He wanted to possess her body only so that he could more efficiently hand over his soul. Looking inside, he found a glowing desolation: everything was razed, avarice, ambition, lust; there was nothing left but the face of the silver girl. Nonetheless, his intentions were perfectly practical.

The only question was how to go about it. Rapine was not unthinkable to this scion of bandits, but hard to arrange with a great *señorita* who slept in hotels. Beside, her walrus of a father might prove dangerous. Seduction, then.

Note his confidence in the fate that had devoured him at a gulp. It did not occur to him that, if he accosted her, she would refuse, or even that she *could* refuse. Fate was fate.

So how was he fated to meet her? It was notorious that the English were a cold race who refused to go about and converse in cafés. They avoided, too, through some superstition of their own, the *corrida*, where messages are passed about, written on the slats of fans for instance when eyes were fixed on the immolation of the bull. Being a heretic – . Here, despite his Freemasonry, Alphonso shivered with dismay, he faltered. He had never met a heretic before.... Being a heretic (why not? Was it not all religion equally priestcraft and backwardness? Pah!) – she wouldn't even go to Mass, where there was a still-more-thrilling traffic in missals passed to-and-fro.

So where?

In any case the first thing to do was to learn her name: the name of his own soul, his life, his reason to exist, his calling, his purpose, his heavenly agony, his one hope. Luckily Gilberto, a friend, worked in the kitchen of the *Universo*, and for a *peseta* or two would surely steal a glance at the hotel register. And then – .

Pondering fierily, diffusely, painfully, ecstatically, lucidly, in delirium, Alphonso Ñezgo wandered further and further out of town into the moonless night, until the constellations, whirling through the purple autumn sky, engulfed him.

## *v.*

> *So here we are in our hotel at Alhama dearest Mrs F. where we arrived in time for dinner but it was too awful, the villainous Spaniards kept us waiting for <u>half an hour</u> for our rooms what did you think of that? I did not show the least irritation only my Majestic Reserve as you always enjoin but in truth I am <u>very vexed</u> when these feckless foreigners waste even a <u>second</u> of Papa's time or mine on our tour of wondrous Spain, because it <u>is</u> wondrous & romantic Mrs F., despite <u>everything</u>. There is the cathedral to see tomorrow night which has tonic values so I have dismissed Rawkdon,*

– here Gladys Furlough paused in her writing and considered. It was a provocation to claim to have *dismissed* Rawkdon, rather than briskly bidding her goodnight, which was the literal truth. It was another provocation to call Rawkdon *Rawkdon*, because, although father and daughter (in their *nouveau riche* way) were inclined to treat her as a dogsbody, Hester Rawkdon was technically a Lady's Companion. The Rawkdons were a family of decayed, very decayed gentry, living in penury over the hills in the West Riding. It had been a great coup when Sir Zebulon secured Hester as his daughter's Companion the previous winter. She had proved a disappointment to them both, what with her scuttling dreary ways, and her indifference to the wellborn young men Gladys wanted to meet through her. But they still called her *Miss Rawkdon* to her face (or even, occasionally, *dear Miss Rawkdon*); and Gladys did not want to offer any Jacobin incitement to Virginia Flange, who after all as a mere ex-governess was one notch below a Companion. Happily there was space on the paper to insert the vital word *the*. Virginia would be brilliant enough to notice, and sly enough to applaud, her charge's discretion:

> *dismissed the Rawkdon, who is unusually sulky <u>even for her</u>,*
> *she complained about the jolts of the carriage all the time I was*
> *undressing, & I am now going to bed (in my pretty lavender*
> *deshabilé & <u>absolutely nothing</u> else, almost the <u>altogether</u>! what*
> *do you say to that of course one is not called or brought early*
> *tea in these parts but woken by some slattern come to tend the*
> *fire, long before Hester Rawkdon stirs) so as to be quite fresh for*
> *them, I mean the tonic values, 'tho outside*

– here she paused, drumming her small angry fingers on her travelling-desk. Which was a wonderful affair, close to her heart: a daintily-carved but formidably-locked casket of japanned ebony, set with mother-of-pearl peacocks and stamped *G.E.F.*; within, the writing surface was of sky-blue calfskin and the ink-pot prettily gilded; but beneath the leather were more secret steel compartments than could easily be counted. The desk was a simulacrum of her mind.

We have seen that Gladys Furlough, cleaving to efficiency, had a system of composing phrases for her letters home all day during idle moments and jotting them down swiftly at night. But now, having reached the hazardous word *outside*, she was obliged to glance out of her hotel room.

Out: out at the starry *mesa* in which Alphonso was still wandering amidst *azufaifo* bushes and carob trees, and the desiccated dung of wild mules, and the everlasting fires of heaven. Out at the stars, at the half-well-born Gemini who might have regarded her sceptically, at the Charioteer who died of love refused, at Taurus who was the divine bull, the bull that ravished Europa; Taurus must positively have sneered.

Miss Furlough of Kettlehinge Hall puckered her brows over the view, then consulted *Fluttering Leaves by the Wayside*. She found the place, then wrote, briskly, efficiently, falsely, in neat violet letters,

> *outside it is most awfuly pretty. Of course the sky is not as delli-*
> *cately made as in our own dear Derbyshire in fact it sometimes*
> *seems quite course but tonight the cloud is nicely torn just as*
> *if the beat of the moon's unseen feet, Which only the angels*
> *hear, May have broken the woof of my tent's thin roof, The*
> *stars peep behind her & peer, & a girl has such exullted feelings,*
> *quite the most delishus & sublime <u>tingles</u>*

– and so forth.

The hardboiled daughters of tycoons know they have to soften their edges, or at least seem to soften them; for which Shelley is just the ticket, although careful misspelling has its uses too.

Alas, Miss Furlough cultivated fluffiness with such iron (or leaden) resolution that Mrs Flange, her governess and mentrix, to whom she wrote every day, had to urge her to take things more easily. *My dear,* she had written the week before, *allow me to hint that it is not quite genteel to be so very work-manlike about being delicate. One must let fine carriage and conduct emerge naturally. This makes far greater appeal to the dear gentleman....* And so forth.

For Virginia Flange was deep in the water. Born under the Regency, innately whorish and addicted to "ripping" slang, she thought the priggery of the present age the merest stuff and nonsense, or "pooh", a favourite phrase of hers; necessary pooh, however, that she had to master, and did. Mrs Flange mastered the spirit-of-the-age so well that most younger persons, that is, most Victorians, and every male, conceived her to be the last word in chaste respectable womanhood. Most importantly, she convinced Sir Zebulon Furlough, himself a fraud, swift to detect fraud in other players. He had employed her for twenty years, and still paid her a pension, without "browning to" the fact that her *Mrs* was pure affectation, and *Flange* itself a *nom de guerre.* She was a widow only in the logically trivial sense that she had no living husband, although she clung to half-mourning because mauve suited her "snappy" complexion; besides, men are emotionally susceptible in the presence of grief, even when grief is only a matter of bombazine and ear-rings of jet.

Her disciple Gladys was "warm as they make them," that is, as much a born tart as her governess. But she had a wobblier grip on appearance. Poor Gladys didn't pose as a Victorian, as Mrs Flange did: she was the real thing to the marrow, as earnest about seeming earnest as she was earnest about being wicked. Moreover she had nothing of the artistic temperament, no instinct about where to stop. Thus she "worked" so energetically at seeming pure, ill-informed, maidenly, easily outraged, *etcetera,* that she gave even her father pause.

'Don't know what to make of my Gladdy,' he'd tell his minions and parasites, late at night at Millbank, when they were all fuddled with port; not *very* fuddled, because the Prince Consort had made sobriety the thing; but fuddled enough that the next day they could pretend, if necessary, not to remember what had been said. (After-dinner port-drinking is the closest a Protestant gentleman comes to the confessional.) 'Just had a letter from her. Says she can't bear to see the gardener's boy 'cause he works with legs bare below the knee. No. *Limbs* is what she calls them. *Unclad limbs.* And she shudders. That can't be right, can it?' The captain of industry brooded apart.

His toadies waited to see what he wanted. 'D'you think she can be throwing sand in my eyes?' and although they all said 'No, no,' eagerly (thinking *Of course she is you old fool*), he persisted, '*Might* she be? Rumpf!'

And indeed she had been busily fornicating with the gardener's boy for two months, with the connivance of dear Mrs Flange. Mrs Flange was not above listening at library doors when gentlemen were sitting over their wine, and reporting their conversation to young Miss Furlough, who thus knew when she was under suspicion, and when the game was up. Nor did Mrs Flange mind helping the muddy brat in question in and out the laundry window at Kettlehinge. When the time came to end the business, she would pay him off and order him to disappear.

The conventions of female friendship have always, thank God, been beyond me. (The fraternities and antipathies of a friary are quite puzzling enough for my simple heart, or, perhaps, my obscuring mind.) I cannot explain the way Gladys Furlough blends candour and fibs in her letters.

Thus there are reticences and untruths that a mere man, a monastic, spying on their correspondence two-thirds of a century later, can see through. Yet she shares with her *procureuse* details that must in 1877 have counted as diabolically lewd, and would have given Sir Zebulon fits had he had been wise enough to steam open his daughter's correspondence.

Why? Were the two women in cahoots or not?

For instance: she informs Virginia Flange that the waiter at the Antigua Casa de Guardia in Málaga possessed

> *the most pronounced derrière imaginnable thro' his dark green*
> *unmentionables but is not <u>at all</u> amiable so that I when I called*
> *him over & leaned back to enjoy the sight of his bending to pour*
> *our tea (Papa having vanished behind his day-old Morning*
> *Post) he affected to be cold & even when later leaving the*
> *breakfast-room I managed to brush against that neat posterior*
> *was qu. disgustingly unqivering, what do you say to <u>that</u>!!'*

Despite such frankness, the conspirators also lie to each other without blushing. Mrs Flange, who's obviously tough as a grenadier, pretends to Miss Furlough to be bilious whenever she is obliged to lunch out and forced, *against my invariable custom*, to "partake" (menu is included). On the other hand she affects to be '<u>*expiring*</u> *of inanition*' if '*pressure of domestic affairs*' delays her luncheon at Kettlehinge. In any case, underfed or overfed, she advertises herself as '*a perpetual martyr to neuralgia in these <u>frightful</u> autumn evening mists.*' Why? Why does worldly Miss Furlough, who knows her governess, who knows her to be hard as nails, gush about divine discontents and thoughtless tears arising deep in the wellspring of her soul?

I do not follow. I cannot fathom why Gladys, after that dreadful bit of verse, after that claim of *delishus & sublime <u>tingles</u>*, should barefacedly tell Virginia that the countryside around Alhama has moved her in a way quite indescribable, and that

> <u>*late*</u> *tomorrow morning (dear Papa being engaged tonight to confer with a local merchant)*

– I rather take it this means *visit a local courtesan* –

> *I have secured a discreet trap to bear Papa & me (but <u>not</u> the Rawkdon, who claims fatigue) to the falls of the Manzanil. I wanted to bring the hamper but dearest Papa said "Rrumpff! Rrumpff!" which as we know is Papa for <u>No</u> however when I said "What about my easel?" which he fears is unladylike he said "Rrumpff!" so that's all right. I am <u>too thrilled for words</u> about the falls which Baedeker says are suffuse with transcendent & supreme beauty.*

What is going on here? Of course painting, when done with ladylike water-colours, was high among the prettinesses of a Victorian *parvenue*, almost as useful as a taste for the Lake Poets. But Gladys was indifferent to both art and landscape, as Virginia is aware; indeed (I have seen some of her work) she had even less ability than you would expect in a provincial heiress. So is Gladys hinting that she has some erotic stratagem of her own in view, out on the lonely road to Loja, with Sir Zebulon sure to be dozing on his shooting stick, sleeping off the night before?

Or was in merely a premonition that this painting expedition to the Manzanil waterfall would bring ruin, death, and a strong stink of damnation?

> *I must finish for tonight & lock the letter up (less the Rawkdon come prying) & take myself to bed. Papa went out to his Merchant looking <u>not v well</u>!!! & O Mrs F. what a weird feeling of <u>dreadfulness</u> I have about the morrow! I somehow feel it is going to full of stirring & <u>fatal</u> thrills ! Oh my! I <u>do</u> hope I'm right. Ever yr own G.F.*

# Part Two
## *27ᵗʰ October 1877*

Miss Hester Rawkdon

Mrs Virginia Flange

## *i.*

Words from the Gospel According to Baedeker (*Spain and Portugal: a traveller's handbook*, 1876).

> **Alhama** (pension: open in the season only, 8¼ to 10¼ *pesetas*) is a town of 7600 inhab., picturesquely situated on a rocky terrace of the Sierra de Alhama. The capture of the old Moorish fortress in 1482 is bewailed in a contemporary Hispano-Moresque ballad well-known to English readers in Byron's translation.

*"I lost a damsel in that hour,*
*Of all the land the loveliest flower;*
*Doubloons a hundred I would pay,*
*And think her ransom cheap that day."*
*Woe is me, Alhama!*

The warm **Sulphur Baths of Alhama** (107-
113º Fahr.), strongly impregnated with nitrogen,
lie below the town, and are visited from April 20th
to Oct. 15th.

3 miles along to **the road to Loja** the road
crosses the Manzanil, which forms a fine waterfall
(visible from the railway) just before it joins the
Genil. Magnificent views may be obtained of the
Sierra Nevada; a guide can show the terraced stair
(41 steps) to the most fortuitous viewpoint.

Although elsewhere it is written:

The professional **Guides** (*el guía, guías*) are usually very ignorant and of little use. None should be
employed but those recommended at the hotels.
The directions in this Handbook render them
superfluous in most cases, and a boy to show the
way can always be had for a few *reals*.

For such a frivolous girl, Miss Furlough took her Baedeker with extreme,
literal seriousness. Naturally she had looked at almost no other book since
leaving the schoolroom, *Fluttering Leaves by the Wayside* being the tiresome
exception, a necessary pose. Perhaps even the frivolous need a scripture. Yet
the fact is she did, in defiance of Baedeker, make Papa engage a *guía* the next
morning: a sullen if not-unprepossessing young peasant who clung to the
side of the diligence for the three mile drive and then led them up the forty-
one steps.

The next wonder is that, although Papa was indeed soon snoring on his
folding canvas stool, she made this youth wait, not at a seemly distance where
she could ogle him in his coarse woollen unmentionables, but beside her own
stool.

She had him sit on the sere dun-coloured grass, within earshot, even
within the shade, almost, of her own parasol,

# *ii.*

while she executed her daub of the falling waters.

'*Este río,*' she muttered crossly, not necessarily to him, certainly without looking at him, in her careful harsh phrasebook Spanish, '*es insignificante.*'

She was right, too. Its flow was sparse from the autumn drought; it barely oozed over its jagged brink, then tumbled meanly, shabbily, any-old-how, down the grey rock-face. *If the fellow who'd composed Baedeker,* she thought, *hadn't just been flannelling when he detected its "transcendent beauties," well, he must have been very easily moved, that's all I have to say .... Probably he was thinking of some other, better, falls, somewhere else in Spain, and got himself confused.... Or (here's a thought!) perhaps it'd been a hot morning like this, with his train due to take him on to Murcia, and he just asked the hotel manager at the* Universo, *who exaggerated, and then he wrote down the lies, not bothering to stir. Pooh, as Mrs F would say! What a thing. Books are a beastly poor guide to life – even Baedeker itself.... Why did I bother coming out here in the heat? It's all very well Papa's being asleep, there's nothing doing with this beastly cad here. Too shy to do anything. .*

Her face, shiny with sweat, never altogether pretty, grew hard and plain with her increasing crossness. She repeated savagely the word '*Insignificante.*'

'*Sí, señorita,*' murmured the sullen young peasant, who was Alphonso, and had been up since dawn loitering about the *Universo,* partly for the joy of being near her as she slept, partly in the mad hope, dizzyingly fulfilled, of being hired by the milord. '*Sí.*' Then, after a tortured eternity of half a minute, he formulated the sentence: '*Mal río.*'

Which is a nonsense, no river can be evil, least of all in Andalusia the dry. But Alphonso said it with such ardour that his voice shook painfully; the fatuous remark, the lie, the calumny on elemental water, took on a certain grandeur.

'*Lo odio,*' he added, fervently, *I hate it.* '*Por decepcionarte.*'

Thus it came to pass the first words between them were of hatred, deception, evil.

But after a moment Alphonso remembered himself and rounded off his little love-speech by growling '*¡Perdóneme, señorita – Verlo!*' which was as close as he could get to a name it was rapture to know, which scalded his mouth, forming it for the first time.

Miss Furlough, surprised out of herself, glanced at him carefully and somewhat askance, the way she regarded anything she bothered to see at all. What was he begging her pardon *for?*

She was at present making a bad job of rendering the spray off the brown rocks, making nasty stabbing jabs of white paint with her finest brush. Why, she wondered, should such a warty sallow complexion, atop such a truncated figure, should hold her attention for more than an instant? Stab stab stab.

Meanwhile Spain stretched all about them: harsh in her shadows, gilded from the high close sun, rocky and broken, enormous, lovely in bareness. The sky was Spain too, aching with overplus of light, a violent vault of *lapis lazuli*, a monstrance for the adorable cruel solar deity. (More than once Gladys had wished that Papa had let her buy more practical parasols in the Gibraltar shops: parasols blacker, larger, less English and less gentlewomanly than this pink affair with tassels, through which the sunshine just *poured*.) The horizon, formed of a huge dry virile range to the south, was Spain. The air was Spain, full of the hot smell of thyme, eucalyptus, dust. The whole Spanish cosmos was in temporary alliance with poor Alphonso.

"The Spaniard of the lower orders," concedes Baedeker, in its pivotal sub-chapter 'Intercourse with the People', "is not devoid of national pride. His way of looking at things is very different from ours." What she saw in this Spaniard's face compelled her to address him, not quite as a hireling, nor even as a (conceivable) bed-partner, but nearly as a person.

'*Usted es,*' she said, as airily as she could manage, '*de Alhama?*'; and after a tiny pause added, greatly against her usual sensibilities – glancing rapidly at her father to be sure he was quite asleep and beyond outrage – '*Señor?*' (After all, does nor Baedeker warn "it is necessary to maintain a certain courtesy of manner towards even the humblest individual"?)

'*No, señorita, yo soy de Iznájar,*' and he pointed off in the other direction, north, towards his native village, folded into the crags. She was silent, so he told her about Iznájar, soon getting well beyond her vocabulary.

Yet she attended and – strange to tell – her painting got a bit less bad as she listened. That evening, back in the hotel, she was astounded at how well she had caught the effect of the heavy light sideways through the thin drapery of water.

Stranger still, she was listening to his voice, and even nodding in uncomprehending appreciation or agreement, almost as she did when one of her father's plutocratic guests at Kettlehinge held forth about the bimetallic question, or Argentine bills-of-landing. "The humblest individual always expects to be treated as a *caballero*".

Silly old Baedeker, so sentimentally democratic. Alphonso did not expect to treated as a *caballero*. He expected, he even wanted, to be treated as dirt, since that is what he was: dirt beneath her high-heeled white satin walking-shoe.

He had noticed the lovely shape of her foot clasped in that gentle vice; imagined what the satin and leather must feel to be thus penetrated, to thus enclose. He imagined the delicious worry of getting the shoe (which was amazingly ugly) unlaced, of working it off the little kissable kicking foot. He imagined the still more delicious pleasure of having it kicked in his face, or ground on his supine back.

Alphonso, being uneducated, was not self-obsessed, and therefore received in his mind whatever his eyes beheld. As he lay at her feet on the grass speaking of Iznájar, more-or-less at random, and most untruthfully, he took in every detail of her outfit. He was humiliated by its bad-taste. He relished the way her bad-taste hurt him. He was revolted and excited by his pain. He wanted her to catch him excitedly, critically ogling her dress, and crack him over the head with her horrible parasol.

Her dress! It had been fussed into being in Paris with exactly such an *arriviste* as Miss Furlough in mind, and was quite deliberately obscene. From the waist up she gave Alphonso the impression of being bare: her shiny white silk sheath, tight over her corset (which he unhooked in his mind) had passages so sheer the skin might as well have been unclad. From the waist down she was an enormous shapeless white froth, ruffles and pleats bewildering the eye, picked out with big satin bows of pale yellow: a blowsy mermaid bursting from sea-foam.

No streetwalker of Málaga would wear such a thing. And he, Alphonso Ñezgo y Escalofriante, was ordained to drown in those ludicrous waves, to have his face buffeted about and baffled by its inexplicable seams and buttons …. His fingers twitched a little at their proximity to the lacy hem. Oh, to reach up for the absurd floral bonnet, to tear his hands on its hat-pins –

This particular sort of sensuality, which was new to Alphonso, leaked into what was he telling her. Really he was only describing (and considerably exaggerating) Iznájar's celebration of Twelfth Night, *la noche de los Reyes*: a ragged procession over twisted cobbles. '*¡Es una hora antes de que termine la procesión!*' he told her, and '*¡Una hora!*' she exclaimed, weakly, as if crushed by the thought of pleasure prolonged so long. This worldly, unimaginative girl, who would have yawned through any expensive extravagance in a London music-hall, found herself giddy at the thought of a village fiesta. She seemed to see minute after minute of the village choir going past in shining surplices – the municipal band with glistening trombones held high – the mayor in his sash like a cultured rend in his torso – ecstasy and magnificence; oh!

It's important not to misunderstand this brief clumsy passage of love. The numerous *affaires* of Miss Furlough's short life had been managed competently. She had been cautious and cold under Mrs Flange's tutelage, a professional flirt. Her emotions had never been involved, nor even her æsthetic sense. Some of her lovers, including the gardener's boy, had been just as ugly as Alphonso, and quite as low. That night, writing to her governess, she retailed her painting expedition without squeamishness:

> *& O Mrs F., you'll never guess: the guide Papa hired to show us the Falls had It, or at least I think so; tho' a miserable warty little creature to be sure, with an absolute want of profile, apologising in a <u>craven fashion</u> for the shortcomings of his native landscape the way Englishman never would, & rattling on about superstitious going-on in his mountain village. But he was taken with my costume (it was the white faille travelling-dress from Worth, with the shawl bodice & dear little blocked-buckram fanchon trimmed with silk day-lilies) & I am, my darling, quite quite infatuate! A fresh folly to wile away the <u>longueurs</u> of Alhama. We have three days ahead of us here & I am sure something can be arranged! If I can but be certain he will bathe first!!*

Of fornication as such Gladys was never afraid. If Alphonso's appalling sense of *intendedness*, his implacable purpose, unnerved her, well, that was an impractical subtlety. Miss Furlough was good at overlooking impracticalities. She beat it down in her mind. This would be just one more "fling."

Alphonso was not afraid either. He had always known – known, that is, since last night in the plaza before the hotel, when his life began – that the English milord's daughter was his vocation. We have already seen that he was carnally clear-headed about Gladys. Perfect love casts out prudery as well as fear, and his love was, in its insane way, perfect: that is, an absolute devotion. He knew it to be absolute, he knew himself to be trivial. His passion was therefore a visitation and gift from the Powers, and the Powers were presumably planning to allow its consummation. Of course she would be his and he hers. He visualised this union with clarity. *Then*, a minute or a century later, it didn't matter watch, he would die.

Thus they sat in the sun, the ungainly peasant staring up with religious fealty while, ostensibly, describing Twelfth Night fireworks (*fuegos artificiales*); the cynical child executing some really fine brushwork, catching the effect of glare on the sprigs of a stand of juniper. More artificial fire. Gladys was turning over the word *infatuation* in her head. The word was her talisman. It a great comfort to her, as to her mentrix; it took all sting from romance. Dear Miss Virginia had only to say 'My girl, you are once again *infatuated*' and the two bawdy women, young and old, would rock with muffled evil confident laughter.

If only this Spanish boy wouldn't look at her quite so *ominously*. He *must* know the rules of the game; yet the expression in his eyes as he exclaimed '¡*Nuestros fuegos artificiales son enormes!*' – well! Well! It was *very nearly* tragic, and Miss Furlough had an instinct –

'Ah,' she said in English, flustered, almost losing her nerve, almost back-
ing out –

But at that moment it pleased the gods to allow the great capitalist to
emit a snore. Sir Zebulon's tall silk hat slid forward over his nose, which
was of the potato variety, not at all the Norman-seneschal nose favoured by
mid-Victorian fashion. He stirred irritably on his camp-stool, pushing his
hat back up. 'Rumpf!'

The two young people did not move, she from her stool, he from his
respectful tuft of *esparto* grass. They did not start, which would have been
disgraceful, or glance at each other, which would have been indiscrete. They
simply fell silent.

This prompt silence between them was not awkward but easy, and therefore full of complicity. Sir Zebulon went back to sleep. Alphonso sat without
fidgetting. Gladys' nerves were soothed. After such stillness everything else
was just a matter of time.

## *iii.*

Anyone watching Gladys Furlough and Alphonso Ñezgo over the next few
days (not that anyone did, or not carefully enough to prevent the harm)
would have been hard put to decide who was seducing whom. Perhaps that's
never a sensible question, with anyone.

୬୧

When her father finally roused himself from his nap, and said they
should return to the hotel, Gladys declared, a trifle shrilly, that her picture
was finished, that is was her masterpiece (true, as far as it goes), but still damp
(untrue), and could not possibly be trusted to the heaving and swaying of the
diligence. Alphonso offered to carry it back, easel and all, to the *Universo*.

Sir Zebulon was cheered. How dismayed he'd been on the Liverpool-Gi-
braltar steamer when Gladdy read aloud that terrible chapter INTERCOURSE
WITH THE PEOPLE. "The extreme independence of the middle and lower
classes, as exemplified, *e.g.*, in the demeanour of shopkeepers, will often seem
to border on positive incivility" – 'Gad!' Papa had exclaimed, 'sort of thing
I'm travelling to get away from.' It was one of his pet themes that the Radicals
hoped to cut the throats of 'All us old landholding families,' and that England
was going to the dogs, beginning with Crobie, his own Man, who'd been
drunk as a boiled owl since they sailed.

Now here, at last, was a fine example of proper subservience from a damned dago.

When Alphonso appeared at the hotel two hours later, gasping theatrically, with damp patches darkening his shirt, the water-colour landscape held reverently aloft, Gladys treated him with flirtatious hardness. But Sir Zebulon became almost expansive, dribbling coins into the sweaty peasant palm and declaring: 'A decent native! Gladdy, tell him to come back tomorrow at eight, no nine, he can carry our things about.'

At which Miss Furlough looked at Alphonso; Alphonso looked at Miss Furlough; who said '*Las nueve*,' jerking up her head in an unladylike, corporeal manner meaning *Tomorrow, it goes, return.*

So he did.

Alhama sits high on a ridge surrounded by forests of poplar and Mediterranean black pine, and confronting the Sierra Nevada, spread out fiercely against the sky. At the end of October, despite the heat, snow still crowns the Sierra, and the range appears otherworldy: not ethereal, but a visitation from a more solid, perpetual realm; perhaps from the paradise of God, where sunshine neither wanes nor waxes and nothing thaws.

It is a wonderful thing to stroll up the high streets of the sunny town of Alhama and gaze out at the Sierra Nevada, if one has a trustworthy native to walk behind, carrying shooting-sticks, parasols, sketching equipment and satchels; and that is what the Furloughs had. 'So much better than Crobie,' they kept telling each other.

Miss Rawkdon, one pace behind her employers, sniffed audibly at this, because although she had no brief for Crobie (that shameless Moabite) at least he was an Englishman.

The party paused to admire Santa María de la Encarnación, a great looming blockish fortress of a church, that might have been modelled on two bricks laid one atop another, with a third standing stark upright for the tower. Or rather, the Furloughs admired it. Miss Rawkdon did not and, although a lady's Companion is not generally called upon to form opinions, indulged herself with little moans as they were shown about by the verger: shown the foundations of the mosque Ferdinand and Isabella had demolished, *groan*; shown the astonishing collection of vestments, *groan*, worked in thread-of-gold and silver dug from the mines in Peru by enslaved Incas. *Groan.* Sir Zebulon frowned, hearing her; for the mine-magnate conceived himself the friend of mine-owners in all climes and times.

When they were shown the Gothic house beside the church, with a carved *diablillo* or imp above the door marking it as *la casa de la Inquisición*, Miss Rawkdon groaned profoundly. For she was apostate, and could easily picture herself dragged through that door to rack and thumbscrews, then out again to heaped faggots. Under cover of that groan (which caused Sir Zebulon to turn his frown on Miss Rawkdon and silence her) Gladys, stirred by thoughts of torture and burning, rested a sideways glance upon Alphonso. And this glance caused him to trip over a paving stone.

Thus the four of them emerged from Encarnación in an excited state: Sir Zebulon daydreaming of mines manned with slaves; Hester Rawkdon and Gladys Furlough daydreaming, in different modes, of golden-brown bodies tormented, writhing and broken; Alphonso dizzy with what he had seen flaring in the eyes of *Claris Verlo* – as he was now calling her.

They turned up, reaching at last the little road or track named Calle Santaren, which runs along the lip of the ravine of the Río Alhama. The spot commands a view back to the centre of the town. On one side is the terrible downward-rolling precipice, striped with wild vegetation; below, the bright angry silver thread of the river, almost lost in a mass of oleander shrubs; on the other side whitewashed boxy houses, hanging improbably down the cliff. For Alhama is a *pueblo blanco*, one of the famous white cities of Andalusia, and it might seem that painting it is redundant, some larger mind having already reduced the sparse pale-gold landscape and its cubic buildings to such purity of form that art can add nothing; certainly not the amateur art of an industrial *rentier* from the British Midlands.

Nonetheless, the Furloughs' things were set up in a twinkling by the assiduous Alphonso. They could sit at once; Sir Zebulon was handed brandy from his flask before he asked. There was a slight breeze on this exposed ledge; it was pleasant.

And now it was Alphonso's turn to cast a daringly rasping look at the young lady, Sir Zebulon being busy with sipping, the Rawkdon with finding the shadiest spot. Alphonso let his little finger brush against Gladys' as she took her palette from him, then stood downwind, motionless as a carved imp, savouring her perfume (which was naturally a little gross and cloying); she knew herself smelt, and was stirred.

If her view of the town was, nonetheless, a failure, the blame must rest with Miss Rawkdon, who emerged from the shade to fuss over the central position of Encarnación. 'Oh Miss Gladys, *must* you have that horrible evil place dominating the sky so? Monstrous Inquisitors! The poor free-thinking people! Oh!' Sir Zebulon would normally have been annoyed at this remark, for he associated religious infidelity with Labour Discontent, but he scarcely heard her, so lulled he was by cognac and warmth.

Thus the Englishry passed their Saturday morning.

After luncheon at the hotel, after the pause in curtained rooms enjoined by Baedeker during the deadliest hours of Southern heat (a pause full of hot unhallowed thoughts), the party sallied forth again. They were exemplary tourists by their lights, full of nervous energy, even Miss Rawkdon. By the contrivance of Gladdy they were going to take tea at a beauty-spot called Peña de los Enamorados, where once a young Moorish girl was trapped by her father's pursuing soldiery as she fled with her lover, her father's Christian slave.

You might think this expedition rather too broad a hint to Alphonso by Miss Furlough, a crude touch. But no: the subtle have the prerogative of being unsubtle sometimes without undoing themselves.

Beside, in those days all tourists went to the Lovers' Rock. The legend was famous: it had been turned into a dreadful poem by that dreadful Southey; his lines appeared in *Fluttering Leaves by the Wayside*.

'Do read them aloud, dear Miss Rawkdon,' said Gladdy airily, handing her *Leaves*, as they bounced along in their carriage; 'you have *such* a sweet reading voice.'

This was a tease. Hester Rawkdon's voice was grating and wobbly, and not entirely free of Yorkshire vowels, her family being so old it could ignore the modern fashion for sounding regionless. Moreover the Rawkdons had always been heretics – Lollards, then Lutherans, then Puritans, then Independents, then Dissenters: they had never developed a taste for carnal poetry. In losing her faith Hester had not lost her prejudices, and she never looked more spinsterish, more put-upon, that when made to read secular literature. It amused Gladys to make her companion get her wire spectacles out of their plush case and recite lubricious doggerel:

> *The archers aimed their arrows there;*
> *She clasped young Manuel in despair:*
> *"Death, Manuel, shall set us free!*
> *Then leap below, and die with me."*
>
> *He clasped her close, and cried, "Farewell!"*
> *In one another's arms they fell;*
> *And, falling o'er the rock's steep side,*
> *In one another's arms –*

'Ruddy nonsense!' interrupted Papa, who was in the worst of moods. At luncheon he had had too much crab, which was violently disagreeing with him. Moreover he had left his Manlove back in the hotel, and without *Liberties and Cvstomes of the Lead-Mines* to distract him, the hot gaunt Andalusian landscape was, even to his coarse mind, forbidding, alien, inexplicable. In the heat, its hills were almost grey. They might indeed have been slag-heaps, lead-ore; and (surely) he was dismayed by the way this dismal backdrop must have seemed visible *through* his daughter. Her broad sapphire eyes, her mean carnelian lips, swayed in the stifling air, the shifting dimness of the carriage, as if these jewels dangled from the roof on tiny threads; but the heiress' pale featureless skin – this his eye could not catch; t all he could clearly make out was everlasting mineral blankness.

So 'Crobie!' he shouted, queasy and baffled, banging the carriage-roof with his stick. 'Crobie you damned fool!' Miss Rawkdon made a hennish noise. She was protesting her employer's vile language, but for once Sir Zebulon would not apologise. 'Mind the damn corners! You're not racing the bleeding Thousand Guineas at Newmarket!'

At this flagrant allusion to gambling Miss Rawkdon allowed herself to snap shut *Fluttering Leaves*, handing it back to dear Gladys in a marked fashion.

Furlough did not notice these insubordinate gestures. He was pressing his paunch with his forearms, and his growl had died away to a mumble of oaths against crabmeat, against Crobie, and against the holy reconquered realm of Spain.

Crobie was driving them to Lovers' Rock. But when they got there Crobie was left in the carriage; it was Alphonso, not Crobie, who was entrusted with the great wicker picnic-basket when they arrived: the hamper which was the visible, massive, portable emblem of the Furloughs' triumphant Englishness wherever they went, their Ark of the Covenant: the hamper containing spirit lamp, enamelled travelling-kettle, travelling-teapot, a full set of crockery for six strapped into the lid, silver stamped with the Furloughs' bogus arms, and other affluent wonders which the poor young man had no trouble in ignoring.

It was Alphonso who led the gentlefolk to a shady grassy terrace beneath the Rock, where they sat and pretended to have poetic thoughts.

In fact the three English people took the sight calmly. It was Alphonso whose head swam. He had known the local legend of *los Enamorados* since infancy, or so he was to tell Fr O'Shaughnessy in the condemned cell; 'but now, *Padre*, for the first time I understood it. It was *true*.' If Gladys had put down her tea-cup and suggested that the two of them should instantly trot up the flank of the Peña, make love on the summit, then leap off, he would not merely have obeyed, he would have laughed at relief at an action so sensible and obvious.

Yes: *obvious*. By now, after two days (a long time in such matters), neither Gladys nor Alphonso was pursuer. Neither was pursued. They had reached a point beyond seduction and lay open to each other. That is to say:

without addressing a single compromising word to him, Gladys had made it sufficiently clear she wanted him in her bed.

Yet their misunderstanding was extreme. For Alphonso thought he had bared to her, to the only human being who existed, his religious devotion to herself. He had an absolute craving, which filled every inch of his existence and cancelled out all other desires or duties, to immolate himself in the flame of her; surely her idea was much the same as his?

'She was my world, my God, my eternity': O'Shaughnessy was appalled by these words, and wasted half an hour of Alphonso's last night on earth making him retract. But that afternoon under the Peña de los Enamorados, with no friar to browbeat him, Alphonso looked up from the kettle – Rawkdon and Papa being busy with their cubes of sugar ('*Another* lump, Sir Zebulon?', 'Rrumpff-rumpff!) – kissed his unclean knuckles, and flicked his short gnarly fingers in her direction.

It was an uncouth gesture, painfully moving. She saw it and, although Alphonso could not credit her gesture and so overlooked it, turned shuddering away.

⁂

Yes, turned away.

That picnic in the shadow of *los Enamorados* was the climax of Gladys Furlough's life. It was (as far as can humanly be known) the hour she damned herself. In almost every soul damnation is gradual, it takes decades, it remains equivocal when the death-rattle begins. But Miss Furlough's fundamental emotion was impatience, and I suppose the impatient are capable of leaping into hell in a twinkling. Which is what she did, apparently, that tea-time.

Here's an idea. Are English crimes always dreamed up at tea-time, when our bodies are most replete, our souls most prone to enormity?

And a much more serious idea. Why am I, a Dominican friar, writing, thinking, in this brittle, worldly fashion?

Am I regressing, under the strain of turning these flyblown and rather indecent documents into a narrative, into the man I was before my vows? (Not that he was sophisticated. He was appalled by the world, and agog to leave it.)

No, I examine my mind and can find no carnal stain. I am being, not corrupted, but stretched. For I have never met, thank God, anyone like Gladys Furlough. What I perceive in these relics, these dusty dirty sheafs and sheafs of paper, is the unspeakable process by which a soul defied God, drove Him forth, defeated Him. There have been vicious folk in my congregation now and then, but never this. She engorges my imagination. She calls forth a technical vocabulary new to me. I suppose in the old days I heard some of the terms in – *Miserere nobis, Domine!* – jaded West End drawing-room comedies.

ॐ

It was (to persist with my sordid anatomising) the blown kiss that provoked Miss Furlough.

All was suddenly clear: this dago serf, what's-his-name, felt for her more than simple desire.

How loathsome, how suffocating, how intolerable! How beside-the-point! Bad enough to be a rake in secret, waiting for her grumbling despot of a father to die and set her debauchery free. Now *love* was being thrust at her. She found it as fiery, cruel and pinching as the business of being a daughter.

The notion of loving Alphonso back, being perfectly impossible, did not occur to her. Merely *to be loved* was tyranny.

It wouldn't do. She was going to end it. She was going to free herself from – from *both* these brutal bullies of her cold infinitesimal flawless soul.

She glanced back and forth from Alphonso (who was packing the hamper) to Zebulon, from Zebulon (who was prone, frankly asleep) to Alphonso. She was appalled, disgusted, resolved, full of a certain wondering horror. She was amused. Perhaps the damned *are* amused, their predicament being so absurd, so incongruous.

Now she had decided how the story was to end, it struck Miss Furlough as a *comic* story. So she smiled: a smile to peel the silver-plating from the teapot Alphonso was wrapping in its cloth bag.

Since it wouldn't do for paramour or parent to see such a smile, she turned away, resting her eyes on her Companion. – A recklessness.

It's curious how deeply women who despise each other can see into each other's minds.

Hester the unbeliever, dressed in brown to set off her complexion, was unpeeling each sandwich and holding it up cynically to the light, searching for discoloration, mould or spore. When she'd stopped believing in the Protestant God she'd lost all trust in the anarchic headless universe. It had become a machine to cause death; since she cared only for herself, this meant in practice a conspiracy to poison her, Miss Hester Rawkdon. She expected It to undo her with dysentery or typhus as soon as It might, even if It was, as yet, ashamed to stoop to snakes and spiders.

Back at Kettlehinge it was Virginia Flange she feared as agent of the cosmic conspiracy. Mrs Flange hated her (ex-governesses generally resent new-made lady's Companions), and the two of them waged a bitter competition as to whose constitution was to be more delicate, who was to be most often indisposed after meals, which was to be the Hall invalid; a perilous contest, since at any point Mrs Flange might concede the point by sprinkling strychnine in her rival's raspberry jam.

Here in Spain Hester's enemy was – who? *Perhaps* (she thought, in her intense nebulous fashion) *it's that showy white mountain range over there. – Yes the Sierra Nevada glowering back at me, disapproving of my mangy little thoughts. – Perhaps to the point of killing? – This might not be sensible but then what sense can there be? – Oh dear I've taken a salmon-paste sandwich, notorious how noxious in warm climes. – Daren't put it back not with Furlough watching me. – Have to eat. – Oh. Oh. – No trembling Hester dear, one of us Rawkdons fell at Poitiers – I shall* not *tremble –*

Gladys, hating Hester, followed most of her thoughts. Later that evening, having opened her travelling-desk with the gold key that hung round her neck, having slid the secret panel behind the sticks of sealing-wax, having unlocked the tiny flat safe disguised as writing-paper with the steel key from under the ink-pot, she extracted her unfinished letter and retailed Hester's thoughts to Mrs Flange.

> *Words cannot express how utterly ridiculous she looked taking tea, my dear, sitting cross-leg'd like a puny gnome, sick with cowardly terrors over the tinned salmon & (as usual) over the wrath of God. I must be very wicked because I confess, Mrs F., I could not help laughing aloud at her!*

This was literally true. Gladys had tittered at Hester, who was indeed jittery as ever over the malice of her monotonous No-God. And Hester had jerked her little angular body about suddenly, hoping to catch *that vulgar person* in the act of flirting with *this unclean Spanish creature*.

Instead, catching her enemy's eye, she peered into the hated brain in the way women can, and gasped.

Hester's erotic surmises were old hat. They had ceased to be relevant, O minutes and minutes and minutes ago. For Gladys Furlough was thinking along quite different, far more ambitious lines. She was envisaging things that made Miss Rawkdon's little body shrink back into her brown clothes. Gladys was contemplating the most incredible act possible to humanity in this whole botched world: a deed most civilisations have assumed to be beyond what any woman can do.

# Part Three
## *28ᵗʰ October 1877*

An engraving cut by Miss Furlough from the *Illustrated London News* of 16ᵗʰ
October 1877, and pasted into her album

### *i.*

The dalliance of Miss Furlough and young Ñezgo ended much as you might
expect it to end, a bit more than two days after it began, on the Furloughs'
third evening in Alhama.

It was their last evening. Their plan was to leave the next morning,
Monday, for La Malahá, twenty-three miles off, where Baedeker says there
is a tolerable pension. They were to leave prudently early, before the worst
of the heat, and to take luncheon at Ventas de Huelma, avoiding however
the *restaurante* in the main plaza "which is pestilential." Their trunks were
already packed and roped, since hotel servants "are never to be trusted to
perform such tasks early in the morning with any celerity."

All was done in accord with Baedeker. Even Miss Rawkdon' debilitating
headache was according to schedule, since she invariably had one on Sundays.

Her headaches was the last vestige of her Calvinist Congregationalist faith. When she first began to cherish Doubts (some wretch having explained to her the pesky theories of Mr Darwin), she developed one each Sunday morning, which prevented her from attending chapel. Even now the decision had been made, and she felt nothing for the Godless cosmos but acrid scorn, her cycle of headaches persisted. She kept her room.

But Sir Zebulon knew what was owed social decency on Sundays when travelling, and beyond the range of an English Church. He had Crobie (crapulous from a night with the hotel stable-hands) to his sitting-room, standing, and dear Gladdy, sitting and distracted, and read them Prayers.

'The Lesson appointed to be read at Mattins for the Twenty-Second Sunday after Trinity,' pronounced Sir Zebulon dourly, observing his daughter over the page. She was manifestly up to something, and would want watching. But he, Furlough, wouldn't set foot outside the blasted hotel all day and neither would she. Damned minx.

Or *was* she? Was she? He'd suffered just the same uncertainty about her mother all the time her mother was alive.

> Then the king commanded, and they brought Daniel, and cast him into the den of lions. And a stone was brought, and laid upon the mouth of the den; and the king sealed it with his own signet, and with the signet of his lords; that the purpose might not be changed concerning Daniel. Then the king went to his palace, and passed the night fasting: neither were instruments of musick brought before him: and his sleep went from him....

It is a fine story, and Sir Zebulon read rather well. Naturally his own sympathies were all with the king, as always in any story. He had slept badly, and pictured himself with joy casting Crake, his London agent, into a den.

Crobie, who was in pain, glumly cheered on the lions. Any sort of destruction soothed his thoughts that morning.

But Gladys was with Daniel, pent in a hole of the ground, sealed with signets, a helpless heiress, imprisoned for the term of her father's natural life, or until she tumbled into marriage. A fresh pit.

Presently they lunched. They rested. Gladys was adding pages to her long frank-yet-reticent letter to Mrs Flange, which she meant to post from the Alhambra Palace Hotel in Granada on Tuesday, all about the awful frightful uselessness of Miss Rawkdon. This was her usual theme on Sundays and she did not deviate. But her mind was elsewhere, her eye on the clock. A lot would depend on timing.

At four thirty Sir Zebulon, who naturally had a mean streak, went down

to haggle over the bill. He clawed back a pittance from the manager, who
would have fought for longer were it not a Sunday, which is to say a bullfight
day; he was eager to be done with this dull giant of a guest, and with his con-
niving devil-child, and to hurry off to the arena. Already the entire citizenry
of Alhama was streaming past the *Universo*, the women gay in lace mantillas,
the men killingly got up in *sombrero cordobés*: what were few hundred *pesetas*
compared to such joy? He bowed the heavy *ingles* out of his office saying
'*Sí, señor, sí sí sí, no hay problema*'; and the heavy *ingles* stomped upstairs,
jingling in his dark trousers his recovered pelf.

> *So Mrs F you will <u>hardly</u> guess the shocking & <u>amazing</u>*
> *thing that has just transpired! 10 mins ago the Pater*
> *returned from bearding the rogues at this inn (who had*
> *overcharged us <u>four times over</u>) to say that he has arranged*
> *a cold supper to be sent up to our rooms – at <u>six</u>. (An*
> *outrageous hour, make sure the Sedley-Smyths never hear!*
> *I want them esp. that dowdy poppet Amelia to picture us*
> *constantly dining at midnight in the Continnental mode*
> *with demimonde comtesses in improper decolletage &*
> *handsome denizens eyeing me, & bottles & bottles & <u>bottles</u>*
> *of pop.) Our last evening in <u>dear</u> Alhama will be v. quiet*
> *(<u>thinks Papa!!</u>) & "After supper," said Papa, "you need to*
> *rest that is an order. There is nothing more to see & we leave*
> *at dawn" at which I allowed myself just the least toss of my*
> *hair wh: I will have to have seen to in Mallagah the ringlets*
> *clustered <u>above</u> the temples are a horror & of course the*
> *frump Rawkdon is of no use whatsoever she cannot even*
> *<u>see</u> what I am trying to do with my fringe so that I want*
> *to screem & this morning she was so clumsy I spoke to her*
> *nearly brusquely as I wd <u>gladly</u> have nailed her hands to the*
> *coiffuse & her feet to the floorbords with my hairpins, there!*
> *So I tossed my locks (wh: do look v. fine at present reelly Mrs*
> *F. it is only the tier over the left temple that troubles me) and*
> *Papa <u>shrugged</u> in a fashion that was <u>almost</u> <u>common</u>. "All*
> *the d—m'd natives are at their filthy bullfight." He <u>might</u>*
> *have sounded the least bit wistful at this so I said in the voice*
> *Mama sometimes used to him wh. she thought I was not*
> *lissening "Papa! Surely <u>you</u> do not wish go to the foul spec-*
> *tacle?" He just said "What?" surprised so I persevered: "Oh*
> *Papa! The very idea! It is <u>unmanly</u> of you and <u>unenglish</u>. I*
> *altogether forbid your going." The darling simple man quite*

*blazed up at this & said "I will <u>not</u> be browbeaten as to sport*
*by you young miss &c. &c." & the upshot*

– every daughter knows this trick. It's the most elementary way to rule a father. And this particular darling father was very simple indeed. Hardly any of the world was visible to Furlough. He was not just drowsy, or saturnine, but half-born: a usurer and nothing more, plodding through life with head bent to stare down his own body, over pigeon chest, paunch (waistcoat-swaddled, watch-chain-festooned), long legs, into the dust. It's a common-enough type: here in Manchester I know a score of profiteers who profit by noticing nothing. Such masters-of-men can be made to do anything to avoid the appearance of being made to do things. I wonder how many thousand pounds I have extorted for my House by saying 'Naturally Mr Higginson I realise local Protestant opinion forbids such a prominent citizen as yourself from alms-giving ....'

Gladys Furlough had played her father since babyhood, and the death of her mother had left him at her mercy. She was not only much cleverer than her surviving parent, she was horribly alert – she would have made a fine scientist had she been a man, and less severely selfish. As it was, the only specimens in the natural world of any practical importance were her self, and her father, and she knew them both inside out.

Her governess, too, was balefully observant, and would have known how to read between these lines:

> *The darling simple man quite blazed up at this & said "I*
> *will <u>not</u> be browbeaten as about to sport by you young miss*
> *&c. &c." & the upshot was that he declared he <u>would</u> go &*
> *see the <u>corrida de toros</u> (as they call it)! "Why come all the*
> *d—m'd way to Spain," quoth the Pater, "& miss out on the*
> *main fun? I'll be hanged if I do!" Of course I remembered to*
> *looked dismaid by this dreadful language & also the least bit*
> *nervous of being left alone but he was in a roaring mood &*
> *just said "I am going at once young madam & that's an end*
> *on it. Don't set foot outside this room!" & flung himself out*
> *as if he were leaving a stage <u>to great applause</u>. What do you*
> *think of that clever Mrs F!!!*

No doubt clever Mrs F. knew just what to make of this. She could picture Gladys' distressed maidenly pout as Furlough stormed out; and, as soon as the door was shut, her slow unmaidenly smirk.

At four fifty Sir Zebulon swung out the *Hotel del Universo* into the rich, ruddying, westering light of Andalusian afternoon, doubtless growling 'Pert-ness!' to himself, 'Unmanly indeed! I'll show her. Insolence!', chewing his moustache, and generally playing the heavy Victorian father.

At five ten Gladys paid a hypocritical visit of consolation to poor Miss Rawkdon, who was busy lying in the dark, clutching the comforter with her kitten-like hands, and hating God for not existing. Since the main work of the Calvinist God is to damn ones enemies, Miss Rawkdon's universe, now He had deserted His post, was a bedlam. Men and women offended her and were not punished. What did it all *mean*? How could Zebulon Furlough, upstart scouring as he was, chief of sinners, pass through life luxuriously, before her very eyes, slighting her daily, yet sink at last into the pangless dust?

And this hellcat daughter of his, was *she* not to taste fire for being born bad? 'Are you,' Miss Furlough was saying, 'better?', managing to pack into that word formal forgiveness of Hester's hairdressing blunders that morning, and assurance they would never be forgotten.

'Thank you' (with a world of social condescension), '*dear*. Not much.'

Gladys' smile was fashioned wonderfully as she said it was rum luck poor Miss Rawkdon should be 'visited with such awful torments.'

And Hester, sick with unassuagable loathing, snapped back what she had always wanted to snap back.

> "<u>Not</u> a visitation because there's <u>No One</u> to do the visiting"
> what a sentiment to utter outloud, don't you think Mrs F?
> specially when <u>Abroad</u> where <u>anything</u> might happen one's
> simply tempting providence to suspend its care. I laughed
> coketishly & jested I'd half a mind to tell Papa who is <u>most
> appalled</u> by disbelief as leading to discontent amongst
> lower orders but Rawkdon positively whimpered saying
> our merry talk was making her headache <u>worse</u> (perhaps
> providence <u>was</u> cross!!) & I tripped away promising to have
> them send up Vichy water and dry biscuits although of
> course I <u>won't</u>. Anyway I'm <u>sure</u> she'll keep her room now.
>   & wicked Crobie is out with his ostler chums royster-
> ing, I spied him through my curtains, that's what comes of
> my giving him 20 pesetas earlier, what a sot he is.
>   So I'm left all alone & <u>defenceless</u> amidst these <u>dread-
> ful</u> Spaniards!!!
>   Anyway <u>I</u> must put down my pen now & compose
> myself before supper comes <u>& then</u> bed. What an appetite I
> have! A thousand blessings and good nights dearest F.

At the *déclassé* hour of six the housekeeper, a scowling crone, scratched at Miss Furlough's door with a tray. She was scowling because she did not care for Gladys (no Spaniard did, apart from one), and because the manager had compelled her to stay behind and look after the hotel while he, with almost all his staff, scampered off to the arena.

Supper was stuffed olives, an omelette made with fried potatoes, ham, the chewable bread of Andalusia, a carafe of white wine, blue cheese and oranges. It was seen untouched an hour later, on the table by her bed.

It seems incredible to me, in this year of rationing 1940, that an Englishwoman of 1877 should turn up her nose at such good things. It seemed incredible to Alphonso, who six months later could describe the victuals exactly to O'Shaughnessy.

For of course it was Alphonso who spied the tray.

At six twenty a ladder had come wobbling down the alley that runs beside the hotel, with the little dark odd-faced fellow gripping the middle, heaving awkwardly. He had peered furtively into the square; placed the ladder against the guttering; swarmed up it to the first-floor; pulled the ladder up after him; laid it out of sight behind a bank of geraniums. Resuming his customary lope, he had worked his way round to the second-floor balcony facing out into the deserted square, and swung himself up like a monkey, grappling and kicking. He had disturbed the potted oleander, which swayed and chinked but did not manage to fall; if it had, the crone would certainly have come running, screeching, and the world would still be a better place. Only a single flowering twig had snapped off and floated down into the empty plaza.

The French window giving on the balcony, its curtains drawn to, swung half-open, nimbly, so no hand showed. The glass panel took the whole weight of the afternoon glory. Alphonso slipped through it; it swung to, so that the rectangular solar glory flashed and vanished; it was fastened behind him.

## *ii.*

The livery of Spain is gold, shading off into brown-gold in its parched hills, paling here and there almost to silver-white; orange-gold in its fruit-trees. Even the sky, that brightest possible ethereal blue, seems full of suspended gold, like a lake of *aqua regia,* that ultimate acid, in which tons of bullion have been dissolved. Visiting Spain is like entering a mediæval breviary: dry vellum illuminated with gilt and lapis lazuli, bearing inerasible characters of scarlet and black.

I passed through the country just under three years ago, that is to say in the second autumn of their civil war. I had been sent by the Minister

Provincial of my Order to look for three Dominican Sisters, novices from County Mayo, who, one steamy evening in the first weeks of the conflict, had been bundled into a truck by the *Guardia Civil* and driven away from their convent. Might they still be alive in prison somewhere? If so, would the Republicans consider exchanging them for a rather senior Comintern official, a Spaniard, whom M.I.5 had recently arrested in Portsmouth, where he had been trying to incite the dockworkers to dynamite the naval base? And if *so*, would Generalissimo Franco (with whom we were careful to have no official contact) permit us to evacuate our Sisters through rebel territory to Gibraltar, smuggling the commissar back the same way?

This sounds like nonsense because it was. The Reds kept no prisoners. Obviously the Irish girls were dead; they had been raped, tortured and machine-gunned the first night along with all the rest.

But I have a little brother who is something nasty at the Foreign Office, and the Foreign Office, which at the time wanted to curry favour with the authorities in Eire, had concocted this fool's errand to demonstrate its good offices.

'Yes of *course* it's sheer madness,' my brother told me at lunch, 'but governments adore having other governments do preposterous things for them, it proves they care. They're just like schoolgirls, governments, all pashes and tiffs and dares. Oh look, here comes my *very rare* châteaubriand. And your, your fish.... I say, you're not going to recite *grace* are you?' Dominic, who is always hissing and whispering and giving stagey direction with his eyebrows, had been himself shy as a schoolgirl about bringing a habited, sandalled friar into the Athenæum. The prospect of having me mutter a Latin formula made him positively wriggle and blush.

Being born into an old Recusant family has had a rum effect on Dom. At Rugby he positively invited bullying on this score. At Oxford he made an embarrassing parade of "agnosticism." Now he's practising again, but seems to think it natural for foreign states to *want* to shoot their priests, and jolly decent of them to hold back.

I smiled, and framed a mental prayer praising God for my Dover sole, it being a fast day. No grace for Dom.

'Dashed nice of you. I wouldn't bother *normally*, but I'm told the' (dropping his voice) 'P.M.' (back to usual pitch) 'may be lunching today, and you *know how it is*.' I didn't: since Chamberlain's Unitarian, presumably all Christians seem *outré* to him, not just friars. 'Sole good? Hm? My steak? The least smidgen overdone.' How pained Dom had been on our first Continental tour together, I fourteen, he twelve, to find that meat cooked ignobly, "medium," is termed *demi-anglais*; he being himself so pink and firm, so eager to flaunt his wonderful French – he'd already set his small heart on the Diplomatic – so in dread of being found insular and *gauche*. 'Capital.... Now as to' (putting steak into his mouth) 'this Spanish jaunt. We're sending a Trotskyite trades-unionist from Tyneside, rather a pleasant fellow, to work on the Republicans. What? … No no no, *he* won't do a penny's-worth of good any more than *you* will. The idea's simply for you both to be admired by all the local spies, and not get yourselves killed. Wear mufti of course…. What? Oh don't make *difficulties*, Greg; have mama send some of papa's suits, I know she's kept them. They're no use to Ravenscar' (our elder brother, naval, off in Singapore, trapped in tropical whites). 'They will, no doubt, fit you,' he added sourly, pouring himself more burgundy. Ever since puberty Dom has been, to his grief, beefy round the shoulders, like a navvy or an orang-outang, with the firm rounded tummy of a prosperous British greengrocer. '…. Blend in. Cultivate the grandees, they all speak French of a sort. Once you've secure, reveal who you are and work on their piety. You're trying to get a private interview with Franco. You won't. But if you do, don't bother about God with *him*, just tell him we'll keep an open mind about custom receipts from the Spanish Zone in Morocco if he'll help let us rescue these dratted nuns…. What? Yes *of course* they're dead, we grasp that. Don't be fatuous, Greg, this is diplomacy, it's not about facts. *Now*. Peach melba I *think*, although – oh *look*,' hissed Dominic suddenly, 'Sir *Montagu Norman!*' I saw the Governor of the Bank of England stalk through the dining-room, flamboyant as a Decadent painter of the 'Nineties, grand as a reigning lama; and when I turned back Dominic was invisible behind his pudding menu, ostentatiously not watching. 'Something's afoot…. What do you mean *Where's he going?*' he whispered under cover of his menu; 'to the *lavatory*, of course. All important meetings happen in the Athenæum bog. The question is who – oh, here's a thought! *Do you see*,' he buzzed anxiously under cover of the menu's leather binding, 'a lanky hawk-featured man in a tightly-tailored blue suit?'

'Er. Er – at the table over by the window? With Lady Stan –.'

'Yes yes yes him. What's he up to?'

'He's standing and excusing himself.'

'*The Hungarian ambassador* – in the Athenæum loo! Thunder! Is he gone?'

'Yes.'

Dominic snapped shut his menu and tossed it down. 'This can only mean *rectification of the Roumanian frontier*. I must bustle back to the F.O. and let them know; I'm *sure* we *don't*.' I felt the most violent longing to be back in my cloister, where affairs are rational and run in straight lines. 'Wire me from Lisbon!' and the great man was gone.

Lady Stanhope, abandoned by her Hungarian host, raised her eyebrows at me across the dining-room, as if to say "*Hommes d'affaires,* Father! These *hommes d'affaires!*"

Thus Dominic missed out on his peach melba and thus I went to Spain, exactly sixty years after Furlough and his horrendous daughter.

❧

My frolic proved just as futile as everyone expected. I mention it only because, by way of blending in and cultivating grandees, I was taken to a *corrida del toros,* and therefore know what Sir Zebulon experienced in October 1877, in the hours when his dynasty was being undone.

An English Dominican attending a bull-fight as part of his religious duties: what could be more darkly farcical than that? What more typical of this cursed century?

Here's how the farce came about. I had wormed my way into the affection of the Most Illustrious Lady the Marchioness of San Saturnino, who was almost incredibly grand. *Maureen* was what her friends called her, Irish names being *chic* in her circle, and she insisted that I was her friend. She was a descendent of Charlemagne, of Columbus and of Montezuma, and resembled I think all three in appearance and character. As to the rest, she was enormously (and I thought morbidly) devout; painfully oversexed; and fantastically gallant, so that the ludicrous spectacle of a disguised friar despatched on a secret mission charmed her into a sort of frenzy.

More importantly, she had *cachet* amongst the rebels. Her son was an up-and-coming young general, her uncle an influential political bishop. Maureen declared in her sing-song convent-school English that she do anything for me, and if the Irish Sisters could still be rescued, rescued they would be. 'But I fear those beasts have slaughtered them. They stand for nothing but massacre my dear friend – I mean Father.'

An easy mistake. Every hour, as my tonsure grew out and my father's impossibly-fine summer tailoring settled on my skinny form, I looked less like Dom Thomas of the Incarnation, O.P., whom I became when I took my final vows back in 1914. In *January* 1914, thank God, when there was snow and peace. The lovely world I was forsaking collapsed that summer; if I had taken my vows a year later I would have been haunted by anxiety over my motives. As I say, in my father's clothes I looked less and less myself, more and more like – *not* the Hon. Gregory Towneley, the discontented young man I ceased to be in 1914 – but like my father, Alban Ravenscar himself. I loved and I reverence my father, who lived on good terms with the world, my *Weltschmerz* and Dominic's abjection being alike mysteries to him, and died with something like the appearance of sanctity –or so they say; no man is a saint to his own children. But I have no ambition to resemble him. My body has long since merged contently into my habit. Father's silk and broadcloth chafed on me; the sight of my own head pasted on top of my father's exquisite tailoring gave me vertigo.

I feel rather shabby recording this. I felt even shabbier at the time, when so many thousand Spanish religious and priests in the *zona republicana* had to go about in mufti to stay alive. Still, it is the truth. Every hour out of my habit made me regress, and every hour I resented the regression more. For I have never once regretted leaving Gregory behind. I never liked him (indeed the novice-master said I had a repulsion as much as a vocation – I think this was a quotation, not a witticism of his own concoction). What I do regret is the nineteenth century into which Gregory was comfortably born. It was an age of decency and restraint that seems almost incredible now, just as the tyrannies and atrocities of this century would have seemed incredible when I was young.

What was I doing in the demented slaughterhouse of Spain in 1937? Even things I liked looked hideous in this nightmare world of saurians rising from the mire to tear each other.

'But Most Illustrious Lady – Maureen. *Your* side shoot just as many people. I've heard you boast of it.'

'Yes but we hardly ever violate or torture them first and they always get a priest to confess to, if they want one, and most do, which just goes to show.'

'To show what?'

'That they're not sincere. They only pretend not to believe and are in such wanton deliberate rebellion against the Good Lord it's a sort of kindness to send them hence before they accumulate an indestructible mountain of mortal sin.' She said this very prettily.

'Yes but you *murder* them, Maureen. By the thousand.'

'Oh you poor gentle Englishman,' dropping the pretty charm and changing tack, 'they're all enemies, enemies – atheists, liberals' (most of the brethren at Openshaw vote Liberal and dote on the *Manchester Guardian*), 'even Freemasons.' (Dominic is a Freemason.) She had her Montezuma face on as she said this.

It was a lovely early morning in Maureen's palace in Burgos, where I was staying *incognito*. We were breakfasting on a balcony, a shaded marble arabaesque, hanging over an inner courtyard formed of solomonic pillars, and filled with intricate topiary: sculptured orange-trees set in enormous pots, casting black stencils, bewilderingly-shaped, on the painted turquoise tiles. Beyond the pillars was another intense dimness, in which her servants came and went, silent, almost invisible. The perfume of the oranges was intense and lovely, as if the world were built of marmalade; but they were alien to me, so obviously *demi-anglais*. This was her country and not mine; her savage century too, not mine, since she was only thirty-four, for all her coquettish black silks, her widow's mantilla and mourning-comb. I, sitting there, laughable, in my father's preposterously-well-cut linens, and straw hat with jaunty sea-green ribbon, did not understand Spain any more than I understood the age.

'Freemasonry?' I said in my despair. 'Is that really enough for – *death*?'

I must have looked particularly woebegone, because Maureen, a genuinely charitable woman, put down her chocolate-cup, and reached across to touch my hand.

'Death?' She looked like Columbus now, ushering me into new worlds. 'I'm not quite sure you *get the hang of* death, if I may say so poor Father', American slang being thought *chic* by Spanish grandees who like to speak English and give themselves Irish names.

'Modern death,' I said, a bit nonsensically.

'Death,' she insisted gently, although the pressure of her fingers was becoming less gentle. 'Or freedom. The nation. Courage. Or the shedding of blood. The elemental things.' She gestured with her left hand off northward, toward the comfortable England she and her handsome young husband loved to visit every autumn, until he died fighting the Moors in the Rif. 'You're almost exempt from those things up there. Instead there is your *peace!* Your *coolness!* Your *charm!* Your *discretion!*' – drumming my hand with hers on the breakfast-table at each of these terrible words. Then her left hand came floating down and commandingly stilled both our right hands. 'Exempt *for now*,' she added, with her Montezuma face on. 'Perhaps not much longer. Joaquina!' she called, still looking at me, hardly raising her voice; in an instant Joaquina was standing behind her mistress' chair. '*Informar Fabián*' – Fabián was her *major-domo* – '*Señor Brown y yo*' – Brown was my idiotic *nom de guerre*, chosen by Dominic, calculated to offend – '*vamos a la corrida de toros esta tarde.*'

Going to the bull-fight! The invitation was more elegantly imposed than when "Clarisetta" had imposed it on Zebulon six decades before: it was undeceitful and it was not unkind. But it was just as binding; and so that evening I sat more or less as Furlough had sat, on the *sombra* or shady side of the *Plaza de Toros*, nauseated and afraid.

❧

At first. I did not stop being nauseated or afraid. But I soon saw (because I could not avoid seeing) that there was wisdom to be had here, and even beauty. In other words, Maureen was right and I was wrong.

Not about the disgusting Nationalist massacres, of course, nor about the stupidity of the war, nor the grossness of the Generalissimo. They were all as I had said, dreadful and contemptible.

Nevertheless I learned about – I hardly know what to call it. *The basic data* is what some booby on the *Manchester Guardian* would write; very well, the *basic data*. Death, nation, sacrifice, gallantry, and so forth. These were all modified by what I beheld. Both as Englishman and religious I was abashed and bewildered. I am still bewildered when I think of it.

The Spanish people have created in the *corrida* what cannot be sneered at – cannot be praised, cannot even properly be described, since the spectacle saturates the mind of the spectator. It is in all parts of you at once. When you recoil (as you do, because the sight is terrible), and you escape to some other part of your mind, you find the bull-fight waiting for you.

I fly into the critical-intellectual part of myself: I chatter anthropologically, telling myself that after all this is a pagan survival. But paganism is sad and incomplete by definition, where the *corrida* is, at bottom, rapturous, and full. There is nothing to be added to what it tells us.

I try to categorise it as the world's riposte to the Mass, using the same materials: the city gathered, seated, silenced, expectant; death, glory, ceremonious *punctilio*, piercing, violence celebrated in golden thread and silk, life in spite of death, triumph of a valiant youth set apart, applause, gratitude, universal joy, feeding. Why then does a Catholic who has heard Mass on Sunday morning still need to see the *corrida* late on Sunday afternoon? What worldly mystery is exposed, completing the eternal revelation?

The bullfight is not just a ritual, since very possibly the priest dies, with a horn through his guts and out his backbone. It is more than a work of art, for it cannot be delivered finished, to be looked at and priced. It is not theatre. Or rather it is theatre which casts the whole world, and puts our life in the world on stage, to be looked at. It is drama that makes us see all the rest of existence as something *staged*; even a civil war ….

My fatuous little lectures to myself die away, for there waiting in the depths of my intellect is the matador, pointing his rapier at me, a sword that is not a souvenir or reminiscence of anything but a steel tool, made to dispatch a fifteen-hundred pound animal.

The Marchioness of San Saturnino had not often attended the *corrida* since the King was driven out of Spain, and the crowd stood to applaud as we came in, working our way down through the tiers. I was thoroughly embarrassed. Her place was, of course, in the front-most box, just above the *barrera*, the fence marking off the bullring from the normal, disordered world. There she enthroned herself in her queenly black lace and high mantilla; I, the ridiculous day-tripper in tourist whites, sat beside, like a jester.

The *presidente* bowed first to her from his box, then gave the signal, and the *paseíllo* began: the procession of mounted *alguacilillos* and the three *matadors*, walking side-by-side, each with his troop of *cuadrillas*, *banderilleras*, *picadores*: proud, gorgeous names. At last a trumpet blared, the *presidente* flicked a handkerchief, an *alguacilillo* opened the *toril*, and the beast burst forth, as thunderingly and snortingly as any heart could fear or crave.

There's nothing complicated about the bull. The bull is simply death, bred to be as black, massive, aggressive as possible: to charge a man and gore and trample him. What's complicated is the man, the *torero*, who is there to stand in front of death, and woo it and not die; who is dressed rather more blithely than any bridegroom; who sets about curing death by bringing it close to himself, close, close, so he can caress it as it thunders past.

As a matter of fact, the day's performance was technically disappointing, at first; at least Maureen thought so. She seemed to know the sport extraordinarily well. Perhaps it was in her blood. She murmured a commentary to me under the hush. For there was a hush. I had in mind the endless shapeless racket of a Manchester football match. I had taken boys from our school to such things, not much enjoying them. But the crowd at a bullfight, disciplined and well-informed, is almost silent. I could hear the toreros singing and talking to their bulls; the *olé*, when it came, was not shouted but murmured as to a lover, by all ten thousand of us.

Not that there were many *olés* that day. The first encounter was leaden; the bull coughed and bashed sideways against the barriers; a horse toppled and its *picadore* went sprawling, clownishly. In the "third of death" the bull achieved *sentido*, it became aware of the *matador* as enemy, not the cape; the matador could no longer lure him with the *verónica*, holding the cape with both hands over its face (as St Veronica wiped the face of Our Lord); and the kill was peremptory, a rearward stab not far from the head.

The second matador seemed to trifle, making silver spider-webs in the air with his sword, '*trincherazos*, *trincherillas* and pinwheels, light decorations, pah,' Maureen muttered. 'See, he bungled the *Fijado*, he can't fix the bull's head close into the cape during passes – ach!' There are many sorts of silence in the arena; the newspaper reports record them all. Now it was the silence of reproach. The *toro* had turned *manso*, cowardly. The matador finished it with a thrust through the flank, an ugly affair, and turned away with a cursory nod to the noiseless crowd.

Out came the third, most junior *matador*, a novice, a squirt of a figure, hipped like a woman, childishly bony, with pale fuzz on his lip. His suit-of-lights looked heart-breakingly new, as if finished for him that very morning by his widowed mother, and the brave pink of his matador socks might have made me cry. He came forward and forward and bowed – to us, I mean to our box, to Maureen. Then with a wonderful gesture he flung at her his stiff little black hat, not entirely unlike one of our own priestly birettas (silly things as they are). This was the *brindis*, the toast, the Spanish conquest of disaster and chance by gallantry. He was dedicating the bull to her, which might sound like very little. It hardly matters to whom authors dedicate their books, or what Parisian tart gets her name immortalised as the model of a great painting. But this was more: he was dedicating life and death (his; mankind's;

hers; mine) to the Marchioness of San Saturnino.

Who caught the hat, with the same wristy dexterity, showing her to be perfectly Spanish. She took it to her breast, bowed; accepting the blood-sacrifice, the effusion of scarlet from black onto the gold parched land; the sacrifice which, whether I liked it or not, modified the deaths of the soldiers who were killing each other all over that unkinged kingdom.

I did not like it at all. Part of me quite earnestly detested, and detests, the bullfight. I rejoice that I am extremely unlikely ever to see it again, except within my skull where as I say I can never evade it now. Nonetheless, I admit that it is not an uncivilised business practised at the edge of Europe. That arena was the *centre*. There in that gladiatorial O, with the boy throwing his hat, and beyond the bulls waiting in their *torils*, and the arena all about waiting too, and beyond that Spain at war with herself, and beyond Europe and the world waiting to war on themselves too: this was the heart. Universal war was on the way: we would all suffer and many of us would die; tyrants would be undone by worse tyrannies and all our habitations might grow dark. But there was still this to do, the *brindis*: man shaping his whole ruin into gallantry.

Oh he did well, the young *matador*, very well. Even I, after an hour's experience, could see the glory of it. He began with *a porta gayola*, perilous and rarely seen, kneeling before the *toril* gate as the bull charged out; leapt, swirled; an *encuentro*, the foes dashing straight at each other; it buried its head in his red cape and tossed back and forth, but he spun into a *gaonera*, the pass in which the cape is held behind as he turns so that the enemy is provoked to charge again, and all at once he had taken the sword, and there came the *cruzar*, the final crossing, cape folded across the sword arm so the monster in its onslaught did not see the rapier plunge in, high, between its scapulæ, through its aorta – it subsided into the dust and we leapt to our feet, waving white handkerchiefs and crying ¡*Caudillo!* (the title usurped by the fussy deskbound Franco), until the *presidente* awarded the boy the bull's ear. Then he went about the ring; we roared and threw flowers at him, which he kept, and hats and cushions, which he threw back. The show was over.

'Like the Mass, Father,' Maureen murmured me as we stood to go home. (Fabián had secured the bull-tail for his Marchioness, we were to have it as a *salmis* for dinner.) Her tone suggested that she was being audacious, but in fact all Spaniards like to shock foreigners with this comparison. I was to hear half-a-dozen times before I left Spain that the *corrida* is timeless as the Mass, down to minutiæ of ritual and costume. I bowed at her remark, since I was her guest or *protégé*; not liking to point out that just as the "timeless" Latin Rite has only been fixed since the sixteenth century, bullfighting has been changeless only since the 1830s.

I knew this because, after all, even bewildered foreigners are capable of reading about the Spanish mystery: it is not a mystery in the common sense; there are no secrets.

I knew this because I am, I suppose, a pedant. Yet even I can see how shallow it is to rely on archives and books of reference. In a deeper sense, Maureen was right, the *corrida* is timeless. As long as I sat beside her, "assisting" in the celebration of the Spanish mystery, I was indeed outside history.

I was at once in 1937, amidst the public slaughter of Spaniard by Spaniard; in Minoan Crete, watching the bull-leapers in the labyrinth of Cnossus; in the unthinkable age before history, when men first dared to bait bulls. I was in a ceaseless tauromachy; most of all, I was in 1877, sitting beside Zebulon Furlough as black thoughts formed inside his idiot English head.

❧

Here are the reasons I dare to write the tragedy of Alphonso Ñezgo y Escalofriante, in contradiction and defiance of James O'Shaughnessy and what he wrote about the matter.

One, he was just an intellectual; although he actually met Alphonso, he couldn't sympathise. I do.

Two, through a freak of contemporary history, I happen to have endured a bull-fight, and understand a little of what this climactic scene means: O'Shaughnessy didn't.

And three, I happen to know precisely what Furlough saw in the bull-ring, to the last turn of the rapier, thanks to my rival himself (for he is my rival, O'Shaughnessy, he and I wrangle over the documents like barristers, each trying to make them prop up his own story).

❧

Was Fr O'Shaughnessy, I wonder, just a diligent soul, or coarsely suspicious? He evidently doubted every word of Alphonso's condemned-cell yarn. He went to the extraordinary trouble of getting his hands on back-numbers of the *Diario de Cádiz* in search of corroboration.

As far as it goes, the newspaper for two days later (that is, Tuesday, 30 October 1877) does confirm everything Alphonso had told him. There on the fifth page is a turgid piece, ¡MÁS TERRIBLE CRIMEN COMETIDO EN ALHAMA!, recounting, in exaggerated, romantic prose, what happened with the Furloughs that Sunday evening.

O'Shaughnessy may have been diligent, but he was not imaginative. I can picture him sitting here at Openshaw, skimming through the *Diario*, finding the relevant article, reading it twice, drumming his fingers harshly, sighing;

folding up the evidence and putting it away, stowed amongst the other documents of *The Fetid + Deplorable + Tedious Affliction*. I cannot believe he read more than he had to. He certainly would not have studied the report of the Sunday bull-fight, as indecent as well as irrelevant.

I, however, am imaginative. At least, I am intensely nostalgic for last century, and always enjoy Victorian newspapers. I have unfolded the crumbly newsprint, untouched since O'Shaughnessy finished with it, and read it right through. For half an hour the *Diario de Cádiz* has solaced me, what with its blunt type and wobbling lines, its portentous bulletins from 'the Transcaucasian theatre' of the Russo-Turkish War, its breathy accounts of the doings of the young King up in Madrid, our hero's namesake, Alfonso XII.

Best of all, there are sumptuous accounts of the bull-fights over the last few days *en el glorioso reino de Granada, en el majestuoso reino de Sevilla, y en toda Andalucía*, including the running of bulls celebrated in Alhama on Sunday evening: the *corrida* attended, until almost too late, by Sir Zebulon Furlough. I can see every stroke and grunt as if watching through his own supercilious and disapproving eyes.

Of course he was was supercilious, of course he disapproved. He knew what he owed himself.

Kindness, whether to beast or man, was one of the things Furlough had never come across. He was therefore almost indifferent to cruelty; only in very rare darkest moods did he like it. But he was far from indifferent to his own Englishness. Englishness was his only good point, or to be exact the only thing he liked about himself that was not, as he knew perfectly well, a sham. And one way we, the *Herrenvolk*, maintain our sense of superiority to foreigners is by deploring their brutishness toward brutes. The French fashion for chaining up dogs, the Italian fashion of drowning stray cats, Scotch cockfights, Russian bear-baiting: the English tourist has his proper reactions by rote, and Baedeker will help him along if he becomes confused.

> The bull fight is the most unsportsmanlike and cowardly spectacle we have ever seen, at once disgusting and boring. The vaunted courage of the matador is, on close examination, a most paltry thing, for he runs no real danger. What Englishman with a sense of true sport would engage with a dozen other men against a brute so stupid as to expend its fury a

hundred times in succession on a piece of red
cloth, ignoring the man who holds it?

– and so forth, for many ignorant paragraphs.

The national humbug about manly independence mattered to Furlough
even more than the national humbug about animals, which is how his demon
daughter had dispatched him to the arena. But no doubt he sat making his
English disgust as visible as he could. He folded his arms and tossed back his
head. He fanned himself with his shiny silk topper. He muttered *pshaw* when
the crowd murmured *Olé*.... He thought, perhaps, of Daniel in the den of
lions; only this Daniel was pathetically armed, with a sword frail as a toasting-fork.... With no kindly Maureen to point out the moves, he would have
understood very little, and he would have sympathised not at all.

❧

But I understand, I sympathise. The brittle newsprint animates itself under
my fingers. I can *see* the *rebolera*, the spectacular spin of the matador's cape
ending a series of passes, vivid in the air as an instantaneous red rose. I can
*see*, feel, the *pase de pecho*, the chest-high pass, the crashing of bull-hooves
inches from my own sequined slippers, the hot breath from the *toro*'s nostrils
on my suit of lights.

There came, says the *Diario de Cádiz*, a *pase natural* – ah! Let me jot it
down here, on my left margin, to show how exact and narrow my information is:

A *pase natural*, the cloth
flicked over the bull's
foremost eye, trailing noseward,
so that as it charges past
it seems to emerge from
the scarlet cape, unwrapped,
loosed –

But at the same time
(let's put it over here to show
that it's quite separate,
another perilous business,
conducted in parallel )
lovemaking
is going on

back in the empty hotel.

Gladys' father is being
set upon by doubt. There is a
sudden cheer all about him –

A splendid *revolera!*
The *torero* standing,
loose cloak in one hand,
turning around,
sweeping the bull behind
him as one sweeps
leaves.

– of course Furlough perceives nothing,
just the flashily dressed mountebank
idling while that nasty creature
misses him, bellows –

While meek as a sparrow,
Alphonso, on his knees,
is telling Clarisetta
once more that his heart
and guts are hers;
and she lets his ardour charge past,
with dead leaves and other refuse

but even mutton-headed Furlough is
being made to think.
Like all works of art, the *corrida* produces
tumult and astonishment at the
front of the brain,
where consciousness
gushes out into the outer world;
but in the depths,
up in the mountain-pools so to speak,
it induces extreme stillness.

The matador has
returned alone to
the arena, rapier

in hand.

Furlough has had an insight.
His daughter
cannot be trusted;
also
that Spain
cannot be trusted with her.

A bold *citar!*

Damn that racket of *olé*
when I'm trying to think.

To think!
'*Mi cerebro
es tuyo
también, mi señorita.
Mi amada.*'

Gladdy! I'm getting out of
this shambles

A *remate! Olé!*
*Olé!*

As she knew he would.
She is rather bored
with all this prosing.
Talking, talking,
courting, as if they had
all the time in the world.

Furlough discourteously
pulling himself to his feet,
discourteously thrusting
his big black-clad body
out of the arena
(the natives suck their teeth
and shake their heads),

'To bed, princess mine,
queen of my heart!'

hurrying back,
too late of course, too late,
his big clumsy body
stamping through the
empty holiday streets
of Alhama.

Distantly, fading,
from the stadium
behind him,
the clamour of
victory

Why didn't I see what
she was up to,
goading him to go
and see that
revolting foreign gore?
I understand her!
That minx!
That Pollymoppet!
*Faster, faster*
*(the early evening of Alhama*
*warm and silent all about him)*

'I understand all!
Let me embrace you,
goddess of all joy',
when

suddenly (I know how coarse and melodramatic this sounds – or not dra-
matic at all, how flatly comic; like a botched *coup de théâtre* in a shabby
Victorian playhouse, where the boards creak long before fate bursts
forth. I don't think it was like that though) suddenly the door, which
they had omitted to lock, was flew open, and The Outraged Parent was
Upon Them with Eyes Furious as Red Coals.

# *iii.*

Gladdy was sitting comfortably in her armchair, her own eyes unnaturally brilliant, one hand clasped in Alphonso's hands, one tunnelling through his dirty black curls. She was not unclothed. Alphonso too was fully (but of course badly) dressed, on his knees at the feet of Miss Furlough, who had kept him there for an hour while he talked – gushed – professing his love in an extravagant florid idiom natural to Spaniards. She had followed scarcely a word, and would scarcely have understood if he'd said it all in English.

It wasn't, then, quite the scene dreaded by upright parents of daughters.

Not that Sir Zebulon was an upright parent, any more than he was an upright man. He just had a vivid sense of *meum* and *tuum*, or at least of *meum*. The first of his fortunes, which he promptly lost in Nevada property speculation, he had made in the Californian goldfields, where not all his deeds bear examination. He was always a little on the look-out for gunmen, and always carried a gun: a blue-silver French officer's revolver, firing 11-millimetre bullets, one of which he immediately fired off in Alphonso's direction, having whipped the thing out of his pocket, grabbed Gladys by the wrist, flung her behind him, bellowed 'Thief!' – all more-or-less at once.

Alphonso was startled, as young men generally are when interrupted by violence in the early stages of love-making. He had staggered to his feet, and now staggered back as Furlough fired a second time, a third, from only a yard or two away.

It was Furlough's appalling custom to practise on his squirrels at Kettlehinge. Nonetheless he was never very deadly. The servants would hear shots ringing out in the Park before breakfast, enough for a small battle, and tell each other "Appun it's de Masti bang'n away again'; there were surprisingly few furry corpses for the gardeners to sweep up. Now the pressure of emotion muddied Sir Zebulon's skill, such as it was; and although Gladys' hotel bedroom filled with shards of furniture and looking-glass flying here and there through the smoke, through the swirls Alphonso could be seen, still standing, reeling back, snatching up for protection one of the massive new crimson-plush and carved-rosewood chairs of which the manager was properly proud.

A fourth bullet took off one of the chair's legs; the ricochet shattered the window looking out over the plaza, perfectly empty because the population of Alhama was at the arena, savouring a cleaner violence.

The *banderilleros*
are at play now!
A feint! The most
furious *encuentro!*

I'm sorry Sir Zebulon missed seeing that by being, not at the wholesome open arena, but in a closed room, where even he could not be relied on to keep missing indefinitely.

Thus it seems to me (as it seemed to Alphonso and even, after some moments of gloomy casuistic calculation, to O'Shaughnassey) that the Spaniard had no choice. He did what he morally had to. He brought the chair down smartly on his enemy's top hat. *Olé!*

It was not a brutal blow, if anything too mild. Furlough went sprawling, but did not let go of his gun and, spread-eagled face-up on the floor amidst the splintered glass, blood thick on his forehead, smearing his eyes, managed to point his wobbling revolver more or less toward the seducer of his daughter. When he jerked the trigger the rough jacket on Alphonso's left shoulder leapt up, and Alphonso felt a worse pain that even he had ever known. It was sharper, for a second or two, than the *azufaifo* cut of love.

A sound came out him he had never heard, of rage more than agony. He swung the broken chair high and felt blood gush down his flank; his enemy was trying to point his revolver and Alphonso had the oddly vertiginous sensation of looking straight down the hollow black barrel (it seemed to descend all the way to purgatory). No matter, the brawl was a matter of quarter-seconds now, he knew he could pound the heavy wood through his enemy's forehead before that shaking finger could squeeze off another bullet – .

Then Alphonso saw Gladys.

❧

It was her one serious mistake in the whole business, this showing of herself. It too was a matter of quarter-seconds: she briskly glanced through the door of her smoky bedroom, that was all. It was a flagrant mistake nonetheless.

Looking in was wrong in itself. A properly tremulous, properly sensitive maiden-heroine would have found such violence between her menfolk insupportable. She'd be slumped in a corner of the corridor, small shoulders shaking, silver-white hair streaming down back, head grasped in hands.

But the real damage was in the *way* she looked into that slaughter-house. She was bare-faced, cool, measuring developments, judging the angle and velocity of the coming mortal buffet, evaluating the chance of a final mortal shot. In the strain of the moment Miss Furlough's face was totally unprepared, a thing almost unknown in her since early childhood.

Thus Alphonso saw all of her for the first time. It was a much more stagger-ing revelation that the nudity she'd been evading for the last hour. He saw *her*.

She did not love him, not in the least: he witnessed this in her expression beyond any possibility of subsequent doubt. She did not even particularly desire him: he could read that from the remote way her eye took in his wound. This damaged body was not one over which she felt proprietorship. These acres of flesh might be flooded or quarried without touching her demesne. He saw both these truths, and was staggered and scalded.

But he also saw what was infinitely worse: what made him slam shut his mouth to keep from screaming, biting through his lower lip, though he did not notice that until later.

Alphonso was receiving quite an education in agony in these few seconds. He'd thought he'd led a hard life. He'd known nothing. This instant of Miss Furlough's basilisk stare had thrust him beyond hurting, as the knowledge he was going to die had always been beyond anxiety or grief. He perceived what made her betrayal of him seem trifling. He fathomed in her a sin so unspeakable there is no particular word for it in any language, most nations being unable to believe it can happen.

He saw; she saw he saw; he saw she saw he saw.

※

It will be remembered that I am discussing one or two seconds during an early evening in provincial Spain, back in October 1877, in a room blurry with gun-smoke.

Usually our brains work fast while our expression is vague and sluggish. That's the reason we feel cut off from each other. We shout our thoughts and listen back down long thin tubes of abbreviated time. That's why a man feels like a mystery to himself: no words defining the content of his mind can catch up with its movement.

Those few seconds was one of the rare exceptions. The three of them shared their thoughts with each other faster than their thoughts formed. Each knew the others knew what she or he knew faster than she or he knew *what* they knew. It was like being snapped apart: all our bits tumble through the void, turning and spinning, exposing every surface.

Thus: all in a second Alphonso froze, pale and stricken, with the swung chair braked at the apex of its swing; Gladys' face, realising itself observed, slammed shut like a U-boat's sea-gates (not to open again until death), too late, too late, obviously too late; and Furlough, unspeakably irritated by all this *bloody complexity*, fired once more.

Ineptly of course. His final bullet went wild, although not very wild, whipping aside one of Alphonso's matted curls as it went, smashing into the ceiling plaster, which snowed on Alphonso's head, ageing him by decades. A comic touch.

It didn't alleviate the moan Alphonso uttered, the moan of a man finding himself in a grislier universe than the one he thought he was in. Idiotic to call this *tragedy*: tragedy is just a question of gradation, tumbling further down the mountain than you thought to fall. Alphonso was suddenly in a quite different sphere.

Gladys, being much cleverer than her father and her non-lover (so that even when thought was moving swifter than thought, her thought went quicker than theirs), had ducked out of the room before the plaster had ceased falling. Alphonso, she reasoned, might be capable of anything now he was enlightened.

What he proved capable of was a brutish act of mercy. He put his hands under Sir Zebulon Furlough's armpits and, puny as he was, heaved that walrus of a physique. The toy gun was still waggling, but Alphonso's terrible knowledge had elevated him beyond the pitch of a tragic hero. Guns and other melodramatic props were now beside the point; courage and fear could not apply. The comic tycoon was tossed harmlessly through the door, which Alphonso slammed and locked, leaving the vast bloodied Englishman fallen in a mound in the corridor.

The young Englishwoman, snapping back into a sane *rôle*, was on her knees over him, keening. This was how she would be found – how she meant to be found – a minute later, when that crone of a housekeeper came creeping, awestruck, up the stairs. This is where Miss Furlough would still be half an hour later, when the first of the hotel staff returned from the *corrida* and came upon her. They would be enormously edified, exclaiming ¡Pobre chica! señorita trágica! for days afterward. What a relief to find foreigners, even foreigners, even heretical Northern foreigners, behaving with such touching piety.

Alphonso, however, was beyond play-acting, as he was beyond heroism. When he had slammed the door on the satanic Furloughs he did not collapse, sob, quiver, rant, or otherwise draw on the romantic canon. He looked about for data. He needed to rob her of her secret – of nothing else. He honourably refused to touch coins or jewellry. 'I wanted to understand, *padre*,' is what he told O'Shaughnessy, 'I did not want lucre. *Tenía que entender,* I had to understand.'

Of course O'Shaughnessy replied doltishly: theft is a crime, a mortal sin; Alphonso dully assented and tepidly repented. In a death-cell a condemned man always errs on the side of caution.

But I cannot believe he really regretted doing what he did, which was to scoop up Miss Furlough's travelling-desk, crammed with letters and photographs, thrusting into it her bad water-colours, Manlove, her much-scribbled-in Baedeker, and *Fluttering Leaves by the Wayside*, at which he sneered (quite rightly). With this paperish booty and nothing else he pushed the window ajar, slipped out, trotted along to where his ladder lay.

Remote applause reached him from the arena. His people were still at their noble violence, and it would be some minutes before anyone returned. He was sure to be able to clamber awkwardly down the rungs, balancing the desk. He was sure to get away; he would be able to devote what was left of his life to understanding the most mysterious fact, the most notorious wrongdoing, the most incredible crime in the world.

## *iv.*

Not that it was "notorious", I mean in the usual sense of *being hinted at in newspapers*. Gladys Furlough was good at ordering public appearances, having watched her father intimidate, befuddle or corrupt newspapermen since she was tiny.

Thus next morning, when a nervous young man presented himself at the *Hotel del Universo*, badly shaved, in a new collar that was much too stiff and rather too small – the Alhama correspondent of the *Diario de Cádiz* – he found a half-mute vestal waiting for him in the coffee-room: a martyr saint, virtually a Madonna, her long pale grieving face and bewildering silver hair done up in a severe grey shawl. Her gentlewoman hovered about her, proffering her mistress the unspeakable beverage known as tea, and being stonily refused. (Miss Rawkdon's Protestant sourness and English irony were naturally not visible to the young Spaniard.)

The young man spoke French, of a sort, and French of a sort is the tongue in which he interviewed her. *Oui*, averred *señorita* Furlough, in a voice so low the correspondent had to lean forward to catch the words, the scandalous rumours were so: her father, a great and wealthy English visitor to this fair province, had been most shamefully used last night by *bravos* of the lowest class. Yes, yes, of course, quite unknown to either of them. The abandoned criminals, three or four in number, had surprised them in their chamber and inflicted an outrage. Happily, by the grace of heaven (here she rolled up her eyes devoutly; *Señorita* Rawkdon was also seen to roll her eyes and even to grunt with suppressed emotion, so that the correspondent was immensely edified) the physicians assured her that her revered parent would recover. As soon as he was strong enough to bear the strain of travel, they would begin with him the terrible journey back across Europe, borne up by her most devoted friend *Señorita* Rawkdon – *Señorita* Furlough, blinded by tears, held out her hand at these words, but *Señorita* Rawkdon, perhaps because she had doffed her iron spectacles, did not observe this noble gesture and turned elsewhere with another sniff of elevated emotion – not to mention their loyal *cochero*, who was at this moment tending the still-unconscious Sir Zebulon with a tender patience it was pathetically wonderful to observe.

(Crobie lay this instant upstairs on the floor at Furlough's feet, having passed out from a lingering surfeit of last night's drink; not before caressing his master's two cracked ribs with his fingers and precisely, using one of Sir Zebulon's own boots, inflicting another. 'Three's much the same as two,' he murmured to himself, over the foul old codger's moans, 'no one'll notice, and dear Lord what a boon to be able give you a bit of your come-uppance. Sir,' he added, sinking with a happy sigh to the floor.)

Meanwhile in the coffee-room, *señorita* Furlough's eyes brimmed with diamonds at the thought of Crobie's fidelity.

Or so the correspondent was to record beneath the headline I have already mentioned: MOST TERRIBLE CRIME COMMITTED IN ALHAMA. He was a flighty young fellow, evidently much taken with Gladys' maidenly goodness. The wounded child was sad and gracious and brave, and although she indulged a liberty of dress and expression reprehensible in one's own sister, the correspondent was broad-minded. These things are ordered otherwise in the North.

Moreover, without telling any dangerous quotable untruths, she gave him the impression that her father was a very grand milord indeed, travelling incognito, virtually of '*la maison royale d'Angleterre*' – although of course (she beseeched him, drops shaking deliciously in her lashes) he was to do nothing so wicked as to hint at identities with needless exactitude in his published words.

He swore he would not. '*Ayez foi en moi, mademoiselle!*' He promised to print exactly what she had told him about last night's incident –

'*Non, monsieur, pas un incident; c'était juste un épisode. Une petite chose.*'

– of last night's trifling episode, and to assure the readers of the *Diario di Cádiz* that the Furlough party left Andalusia cherishing, despite the daunting and agonising journey ahead of them, the most fond, tender memories of one of the most delicious, venerable and cultivated provinces of Europe.

'*Merci un million de fois, monsieur. De moi et de mon père bien-aimé.*'

Here *Señorita* Rawkdon was so moved – her passionate sympathy waxed with such extraordinary emphasis – that she was compelled to fold her arms and vent a noise which, had any local woman emitted it, he would have had to describe as a splutter.

# Part Four
## *24ᵗʰ December 1940*

Fr James Emmanuel Joseph
O'Shaughnassey, O.P.

Fr Thomas of the Incarnation, O.P.
*né* the Hon. Gregory Towneley

Manchester is charcoal-coloured, shading off into black, trimmed with the ice-grey of our sky – it being understood that this semi-gaseous "sky" reaches down as far as the damp bitumen under our feet.

Can we call it "sky"? Just as the Esquimaux are said to have no word for snow, so Mancunians have no particular word for this atmospheric water that envelopes us always, whether as mist, hail, sidewards-spitting drops, sleet, drizzle, brumeous steam, flurries leaden, pewter or sepia, rime, glaze, hoar or frost, actual honest snowfall heavy and almost white until it blends with our ashy air; spates, sprinklings, puddles, sheets of water dragged tearing over the chimney-pots, evening storms that resemble chilled monsoons, fogs smoke-flavoured, sea-salt tainted smogs.

This is a city of saturated brickwork built on thin icy mud; a city, even in its fleeting sunlight, of damp walls, soaked ceilings, alley rivulets, sheen of waterfall on its roofs. Liquid is everywhere and always, dim, sullen, insidious, whether precipitating, condensing, pooling on our rare patches of grass, or oozing out of our sooty stone.

Stop. I am not sure I like this way of writing about the city. It is my home, and perhaps that should be enough. I am here to serve it, not paint it. But now, when it seems perhaps about to dissolve, I find I both dislike it more and love it more than I thought. For years I have regarded Manchester coolly, trying to be charitable. There was a strain of *contemptus mundi* in my coolness. But how can one despise what is nearly gone, and thus precious?

Wetness, grey: that is the Manchester I have known. That is the city I sincerely miss.

For just as the moment the place is coloured crimson and white. There is immense flame in the heart of all those grim dark buildings: their façades resemble the silhouetted grilles of braziers. There is desiccating hot white smoke, which never seems to settle, which can be sniffed days after a raid, which is so dry it parches and taints every room. And everywhere is parched rubble, dirty plaster-dust, squalid rubbish bearing the mark of fire.

The twentieth century has pursued me from Spain.

Göring has announced that he means to level Manchester this Christmas. His Blitz is like bulls loosed into the audience. Thousands die, without sword, without cape, without *panache.*

Here's is a dreadful thing for a religious to confess, even in a private paper no one (probably) will see. I do not doubt the truth of the Faith, I do not doubt the promise that the Church is immortal. What strikes me is that this is, after all, a very narrow promise.

The Church knows the truth, the Church will survive. How much did the monks value that promise during the barbarian invasions, when the only civilisation they knew was being wiped out? When they fled to Atlantic islets and Adriatic crags, carrying the last of the manuscripts?

Which is what I imagine we will come to soon enough. I am haunted by what the new Prime Minister said in June, as the air battle began: "if we fail, then the whole world will sink into the abyss of a new dark age made more sinister, and perhaps more protracted, by the lights of perverted science." What he *meant*, I presume, was that since this alternative is unthinkably horrible it can't happen; therefore we must prevail. But what is unthinkable *can* happen, thought going only so far against the tendency of the world outside our brains. I have no difficulty imaging a planet brutal, ignorant and murderous everywhere: a planet divided between Adolf and Joseph, the antichrists of whom Gladys Furlough, with her amazing inner abyss of shallowness, was a forerunner.

Yes, that's what she was: a miracle of wickedness, tucked into my adored nineteenth century, to taint it. A premonition that the peaceful days wouldn't last. An early example of a new sort of human being, modelled on the horned-lizard and the puff-adder.

How we miss villains, the old cuddly human villains! Ignorant Alphonso and his bandit ancestors! Even his crude "freethinking" foster-father, the drover! Even Zebulon Furlough, the shifty usurer!

It calms me to contemplate such lovely folk, sitting here in this half-empty House, waiting for the next siren, the next air-raid, the next pouring out of hell-fire from the heavens.

# Part Five
## *December 1877*

A caricature done in Paris on 9th November 1877
by George Goursat, known as "Sem",
of Sir Zebulon Furlough, M.P., J.P., with Miss Hester Rawkdon
and (on either side) Miss Gladys Furlough

## *i.*

Everything Gladys told the correspondent of the *Diario de Cádiz*, even down to details that couldn't matter, was a lie.

Crobie, cheered and steadied by his little act of justice, drove them straight to Cordova in time to board the *de luxe* for Madrid. In Madrid (where rowdy students hooted at their prim Nothern clothes) they took sleeping-berths on the express all the way to Paris.

Miss Rawkdon, who was coming out of the affair fairly well, nursed her employer patiently, scarcely wincing at his indecent expressions, which grew frequent, almost continuous, as his first shock wore off.

For Sir Zebulon was not seriously hurt. He was simply prostrated with crossness at the affront to the House of Furlough. As he grew stronger, whatever he had seen or understood in those busy few seconds of gunfire he proved eager to forget. He was easily persuaded he had been the hero of the affair: that he'd driven an anonymous Spaniard, no a plurality of ruffians, from poor Gladdy's room, where she had been pathetically fending them off, waiting for her brave father's return. 'Bang! bang! they soon turned tail the lot of them under my damned fusillade. Didn't they, Miss Rawkdon? Cowardly bloody brutes. More brandy.'

Gladys was at first the most troubled of the four, irritated with herself for mismanagement, enraged at the theft of all her indiscreet papers. She was even a little frightened. She kept her own bedroom on the train, peering out incuriously at Medina del Campo, Valladolid, Burgos, and answering Miss Rawkdon roughly when that young woman (who was also putting various insights and conjectures out of her head) tapped at the door.

It wouldn't do for a young gentlewoman to go about quite bookless, any-more than for her hands to be always bare. Pale gloves of kid and marbled duodecimo morocco covers proclaim maiden flesh, flesh subdued to the ev-erlasting decencies. Therefore Miss Furlough had purchased a fresh copy of *Fluttering Leaves by the Wayside* from a platform-stall at Cordova; the thing was everywhere in those days. She listlessly turned its pages as the dun-red tableland of central Spain shone at her through the curtained train window.

> *Was a lady such a lady, cheeks so round and lips so red,—*
> *On her neck the small face buoyant, like a bell-flower on its bed,*
> *O'er the breast's superb abundance*
> *Where a man might base his head?*

– although I notice that this is corrected by the pure-minded editors of *Leaves* to

> *O'er her person's apt abundance*
> *to which a man might bow his head?*

This would have spared Gladys a pang; she was, as I have said, of a willowy, almost breastless build.

It is hard to remained worried amidst the splendour of an international rail journey, most of all *then*, in the noonday of Victorian comfort. Before they had crossed the Loire, Gladys had emerged from her dudgeon and waged a triumphant flirtation with a young Saxon nobleman. In the flush of triumph she decided anxiety was small-minded. Why *would* a grubby Spanish peasant take her travelling-desk? Surely, hoping for coinage, in his ignorance. He would simply fling the thing away when he found no gold. Her letters were nothing to him, nothing.

Zebulon had also perked up too, and as the train was sliding into the Gare du Quai d'Orsay suggested that they remain in Paris for a few days' convalescence.

This extended itself to a week, in which these four wicked people – all resilient and, in their own way, heroic travellers – enjoyed themselves greatly according to their various natures. Crobie found a shameless *zinc* in the Latin Quarter where the carters would buy him wine in return for scabrous stories of London. Miss Rawkdon frequented the English Church in rue Marboeuf, which was Low, and thrilled them with her accounts of the unspeakable dirt and Marian superstition of southern Spain. Sir Zebulon did banking business best unspecified with the Comte de Camondo, and renewed his acquaintance with certain houses of ill-repute in Montparnasse. He might have been afraid to stroll there after dark, since the area is rife with footpads, and he was still stiff from his beating. His daughter, though, urged him on. He owed it self-respect not to tremble! Was he not victor of the battle of Alhama?

She herself wanted him gone so she could *rendez-vous* with Graf von Wallwitz, who was very ardent, having made enquiries at the Imperial German Embassy about Sir Zebulon's financial affairs.

❧

On their last day in Paris, Sir Zebulon took the two young Englishwomen on a farewell stroll down the rue de Rivoli. There are always starveling artists infesting the Gardens opposite. One of them, a boy of fifteen, ran across the street to ask if he might have the privilege of making a caricature of such dashing gentlefolk; who consented with the usual English air of patronage and bad grace.

Sem, as he called himself, drew Hester as a shuffling myopic spinster, Furlough as a blind beast. That is not so out of the way. But he must have been a clever youth, for Gladys he perceived with double vision. He saw what everyone saw, the silver-blonde miss with a pert clear face, chin up, pretending to be artless. He saw the bleached harridan, furious, forehead down, given over to cruelty. He drew her twice.

'I'm not paying for that bloody impudent scribble!' exclaimed Sir Zebulon when he saw it, and off they strode. But Miss Furlough slipped back, bought it, kept it.

Why? It seems to me the thoroughly evil must feel a curious joy at being unmasked. They like their dark to be lit up, now and then. This may be their final virtue. Or there may be other deformed goodnesses still practised in the undermost nook, where the flames flare up to tear the blackness.

Gladys of desperation! Gladys of all the blatancies! She stands before my inner eye as an indecent immortal: an echo of the worst pagans who were, first of the worse pagans who were to come. In herself she was merely a snippet of mischief. But she was a sign that the age of faith was really over. The world belongs to those who have never so much as glimpsed the Powers, law, love, duty; who are incapable in a way no European has been for two thousand years; who are capable of anything at all.

So they reached London, and Furlough's horrid baronial townhouse on Millbank.

The Member for Derbyshire West had always been, in the House of Commons tea-room, an obscure figure of fun. But over the next few days he boasted successfully of his own resilience in the face of savage foreigners, and of his daughter's courage. He could soon gather half-a-dozen Liberal M.P.s about his armchair by gravely retailing his yarn. 'Her room was suddenly full of perhaps half-a-dozen common dago cut-throats, all bent on *outrage* –'.

Stalking through the Reform Club in his brutal diffident fashion, he heard someone call him over: 'The very man! Furlough – just back from Spain you know, my Lord, where he had to fight off a *posse* of bandits,' and he found himself face to face with his Leader, Hartington, who hummed and stroked his beard and heard him out sceptically, then went back to discussing

Spanish affairs.

Sir Zebulon's self-importance swelled. He began to picture a grander son-in-law than ever before. He'd been thinking in terms of obscure Northern barons, or a younger son of some Continental financier. But no, by gad, he'd marry her off to some earl past his first youth, a widower without sons ….

Meanwhile, although it was fine to flaunt his greatness to Gladdy in the Millbank house each evening, no good would come of her staying in Town, untrustworthy as she possibly was. After a few days he put her and that dowdy shrew Rawkdon on the train north ('I'll see you on Christmas eve. Big party coming this year. Behave 'til then'), and went happily about his various shady doings. Crake, his agent, followed him about, slavish, always with a sheaf of dishonest business papers.

⁂

Comfort and joy, comfort and joy!

Now it was late afternoon on the third day of Christmas, and Gladys Furlough, fully recovered from the Spanish *contretemps* of October, was ascending the back-stair at Kettlehinge, full of the simple joy of one who sees her way ahead.

She was wearing a velvet day-dress, emerald as a snake basking in the tropical sun. Its form was heavy, busily worked with pleats and fringes, taxing to the eye as a heap of curtains, for that was the vogue in the 'Seventies. She was about to change from this complex dress into something yet more complex, a maroon taffeta evening-gown, a souvenir of Paris.

Meanwhile she paused at the turn of the stairs to gaze out into the darkening park, idly thinking.

*How amusingly cast-down bloody Hester was at luncheon!* (Christmas naturally had this effect; Miss Rawkdon, feeling bitterly her loss of Puritan faith, retained the acidic habit of Puritan disapproval. She could enjoy the feast neither Christianly nor paganly, only snobbishly – her fragile self-regard was stiffened by the sight of so much *arriviste* depravity; and that is not much.) *'Course she's dreading next week, when everyone'll be gone, botheration, and I'll make her walk and walk and* walk *in her frightful moulting fur.* (I wonder if there was something religious in Miss Rawkson's dread of the cold? It was *God's* cold; He was the God of pleurisies and might be planning to slay her for her disbelief.) *Hester! Ha…!*

Then Miss Furlough considered her father. *His face was an astonishing colour at lunch. Beyond purple, positively puce …. Hum, er, mmmm.* Her own face, lit by bright daydreams, became girlish. *Peaceful out,* she reflected, glancing through her reflection in the darkling window. *Rain tapering off. Just raw trees standing, 'tending to be invisible, in the deep deep mist… Is that a stump, quite close to the house? Haven't noticed it before …. What a* naughty *letter this afternoon from dear Arthur! ….*

Sighing happily, she went up to her room, lit all the sconces and the big candelabrum on her dressing-table, gazed out once more, stretched her arms high above her head, pulled the curtains to. She had *tons* of time, no need to ring for her maid yet. She began to consider her jewels, singing tenderly to herself: best to sort them before the Rawkdon arrived, with her miserable distracting remarks about Christmas' false premises.

The door opened and shut behind her so quietly she hardly noticed. But 'Dear Miss Rawkdon,' she sang out when she heard the boards creak, in a gay voice pitched to irritate any lapsed Calvinist, '*do* you think my pearl choker goes nicely with these sapphire earrings, or – ? … Miss Rawkdon?' When she turned it wasn't Hester, it was Papa's assailant in Alhama, what was his name, *Alphonso*, standing in a shirt already blood-splattered, his eyes wild, glowing black, in a face of clammy pale blue, and a huge knife hanging ready in his limp right hand.

## *ii.*

Alphonso must often have regretted his chivalry in robbing his belovèd only of her private papers and photographs. He vanished from Alhama the night of his first great crime, abandoning whatever money he kept in his garret in the house his master, the drover, and headed out into the world with nothing but what he wore. Yet when he recounted his journey to O'Shaughnessy, he scarcely mentioned poverty. Perhaps he really regretted nothing. Was he not a *caballero*, bound on a great quixotic quest? Had the bedroom duel not revived in him the venturesome violence of his forefathers? Was not his suffering, his uncertain day-labouring, starving, sleeping in barns, with his shoulder bleeding and scabbing over, bleeding and scabbing over, ennobling?

In any case it did not last. In the vicinity of Cordova he fell in with two other wanderers, half-witted Helios and hare-lipped Isaac, who had together deserted the Spanish army in Cuba and fled to New York, were they were apprenticed in the trade of gangsters. They had returned home hoping to import up-to-date American methods, but Spain was not yet ready for modernised crime, and the two of them were moving aimlessly here and there, as cut-purses and occasional cut-throats. In their presence Alphonso reverted to ancestral type: he became a bandit chief, on a small scale.

With the first proceeds of brigandage, he visited an expensive supercilious doctor in Cordova, with a gold arc-and-compass gold fob on his chain-watch, to have his shoulder bound. This hurt; he did not scream, but winced and crossed himself. The Mason sneered horribly. A mistake. Now that Alphonso was away from his master, the sceptical drover, now that he was living the free perilous life of a buccaneer, he was naturally deviating from deviancy and reverting to the Faith. Thus he paid the fee with lordly disdain, and that night the doctor's house was burgled: watch, fee, plate and a stash of banknotes vanished. 'That will teach him to treat a Catholic *gentilhombre* with contumely.' Alphonso, scorning to profit from an infidel emblem, dropped the gold fob into the poor-box of a parish church, and led his little army out of Cordova feeling as if he were fully six feet tall, a grandee of the purest Visigothic blood, with sixteen quarterings on his arms.

Thus the threesome moved bravely across the kingdom, house-breaking and living well, eating many times every day as the rich do, riding in second-class railway carriages, heading ever north and west.

Isaac and Helios, in their bestial way, simply grew fatter and noisier with good living. In Alphonso there were more interesting changes. Naturally his skin cleared; he fidgetted less; his gait grew less bandy; his cheeks smoothed out, and for the first time in his life were properly shaved. Cleaned of its fuzz, his mouth ceased to twitch. His hair, which had previously only known the drover's sheep-shears, was properly washed, scissored, dyed, pomaded, trained and perfumed by a mincing little barber in Toledo.

He even had a rapacious tailor in Mérida cut three suits for him, and a dozen shirts. Isaac and Helios jeered, for they never changed their clothes, having picked up loose grubby "bohemian" ways on the Lower East Side. Moreover the tailor charged the bumpkin double – which was merely to court robbery; his premises were duly rifled. While Alphonso's underlings were smashing open drawers in the hope of coinage, he was carefully helping himself to some daring cravats he had been too shy to ask about the day before.

That afternoon, when the gang boarded the express for Madrid (Madrid!), the conductor called Alphonso – but not Isaac or Helios, whom he took for retainers – 'Señor'; it was the first time in his life anyone had called him that.

He spent the first morning in Madrid, while his comrades were off sampling a famous brothel, in their inn, slowly changing into all his new clothes, examining himself, with wonder, in a cracked, foggy looking-glass. That afternoon, trembling within, sauntering without, he went in the quietest of his suits to a photographer, sat for his portrait, and ordered a set of *cartes-de-*

*visite*. It was the grandest gesture (but one) he had made in his life. '*Regreso mañana!*' '*Sí señor, ciertamente,*' and throwing a gold *peseta* or two across the counter, he went out into the sun. And he returned; collected the photograph; and here it is, for of course it has come to me, the universal worm amidst these sad dead people long-ago. On the back it reads J. MON, FOTOGRAFO, PUERTA DEL SOL, 5, 7 Y 9 – a large business, then – MADRID; and on the front is the poor squirt himself. The poor doomed youngster. Looking, though, I must admit, almost creditable, cleaned up and new-suited, with a mad calm look in his far-apart eyes.

He had ceased to be just a grubby scrap of Latin humanity, a shoddy unclean ill-made little thing – as any Englishman would have judged him hitherto. Yes; but what is interesting is that Señor Ñezgo did not simply start looking like a prosperous provincial. Cleaned-up peasants don't. It is easy to misunderstand them. Here and there in the streets of Madrid an actual *doña* might ogle him a little, spinning her black lace parasol in mild agitation as her carriage went by. '*Santa María,* what eyebrows!' (now properly trimmed); or 'What a fine compact figure!' perhaps would murmured, 'What deep colour!' (shortness and darkness are admired in Spain). 'What bearing!'

Also 'What aloofness!' For coldness is valued there too, being so rare. The great ladies going by were invisible to Alphonso because he could think of only one woman: the unspeakably wicked Clarisetta, who alone of all the beauties of the world could not under any dispensation love him; who alone deserved not love but death. But to Spanishwomen, who are dismayingly flirtatious (or so I found), male indifference has a bracing, intoxicating rarity. Alphonso, who could not possibly look bourgeois, must have seemed to them – regal.

Nor were they wholly mistaken. After all, he was a bandit chieftain's son; which is royalty of a sort. This, although not edifying, is a fact of history: cut-throats are more than coronets, and simple crime than Norman blood. I mean that hereditary banditry must naturally form the oldest dynasties in the world. During the Punic Wars, when Rome pushed nervously into Hispania Ulterior, the same gleeful robbers peered down on the legions, from the *mesas* and mountain stand of pine, who had peered down on the Greeks and Phœnicians and Carthaginians before them. And the same bandit clans would torment, after the Romans were gone, Vandals, then Visigoths, then Muslims, then Christians once more – Castilians, proud Habsburgs and Bourbons. Changes in religion and empire mean little to outlaws, who cannot enter into any society. Certainly no bandit chief ever thinks of descending from his hills, where he reigns in glory and terror, to the level of common humanity; any more than an anointed king hankers after well-paid steady work as an inspector of schools.

What a silly fuss we Towneleys are wont to make about ourselves for having been around since the thirteenth century! Dominic blushes, he gets quite flurried, thinking on all those Towneleys (most of them vain and inconstant as himself). Yet we're genealogically outdone by every pillager, in every greenwood, pass or range, from Ireland to Japan. Alphonso represented, let us say, the hundredth generation of that nameless dynasty of land-pirates; he could look down, not just on Habsburgs, but on the Ptolemies and the House of Atreus. Poor scamp! Since a lord of marauders and his seed are marauders forever, since mastery generally passes from father to son, what a stain must have been in his blood! Within Alphonso's mean features and gangly limbs were the chromosomes of scores of absolute rulers, men who had held sway over wild corners of Spain before Hannibal or Scipio made landfall. Hard to imagine how it could ever breed out; awful to think of what might be wreaked by the hundred-and-fourth generation, the hundred-and-fifth –

Do I sound moved? I am. Do I sound pompous? Understandably. Here I am stuck in an age so anarchic, so uniformly cruel, that inherited bandit-chieftainship suggests a sort of order. Plunder is wrong, yet there is something majestic about human continuity, even continuity in crime./

I hope this is not merely snobbish. Dominic would say it is, but then Dominic's snobberies are so stultifyingly predictable, and so purely pompous, I will not let him dislodge me from my more interesting ones. When Alphonso sacked a palace in Madrid, in the fashionable boulevard called Paseo de Recoletos, he was continuing his forefathers' work of thirty centuries. (This is a hereditary defence, not a moral one.)

He was at once audacious and careful. In a certain low tavern he had picked up a bourgeois university student, José, naïve enough to be awed by Alphonso's free-spending way with wine, and to take Alphonso's bucolic accent as *le derrière cri* of aristocratic affectation. He persuaded this José that, every evening, at the hour of the compline-bell from the Poor Clare convent next door, the beauteous daughter of the marqués de Alcañices was accustomed to dry her hair on the balcony of her bedchamber, perfectly naked. At which hour José, whose snobbery was at Dominic's level, was to be in the alley behind the Alcañices *palacio*, to be heaved up on the shoulders of Alphonso's two man-servants, to peer over the back-wall into the garden, and so achieve felicity.

As matter of fact the marqués de Alcañices was childless. But Alphonso had genius: the proof is that he was not just an erotic maniac, but the cause of erotic mania in others. His own mind was so agitated by Gladys Furlough that he had no difficulty working José into a frenzy over the putative girl.

So that, although decently brought up, at nine the next evening up José was in the alley, with his hands clutching the the coping-stones, his right foot on Isaac, his left foot on Helios, wobbling – and grievously disappointed. For although there was gas-light flooding out of the marqués' drawing-room, and moonlight luminous on the palm-trees and ilexes and topiary (beside which loped three vast black shapes, wolfhounds who had noticed him and were beginning to bay), there was no nude belovèd to be spied. '*¿Dónde está la bella doña?*' he hissed downward, through his legs. Alphonso, who was staring up at the moon, brooding over the barbarity of love, merely sighed, and nodded to his lieutenants; who heaved, so that José flew through the warm air, over the wall, crashing down through a trellis of roses into the maws of the delighted, slavering guard-dogs.

The tumult for some minutes was colossal. The wolfhounds roared with joy as they dealt with José, who shrieked for longer than seemed possible; every dog in the neighbourhood joined in the commotion; the Poor Clares left off compline to wail and dart about their cloister; bellowing policemen and riffraff came running from every direction; the marqués himself appeared at his study window, shouting; firearms were fired; windows were smashed; and no one paid the slightest attention to the minor noises next door from the Palacio López-Dóriga, where Alphonso and his gang were unhurriedly forcing a door and emptying the butler's pantry of its plate.

'A wondrous evening, Father!' reported Alphonso, proudly confessing his deeds to Fr O'Shaughnessy in the frigid death-cell. 'We took away ten kilograms of silver, which brought us two thousand *pesetas*, and as for José, was he not better out of this world, Father, snug in purgatory, before he could outrage the honour of any woman who actually existed, and so damn himself? ¿No es así?'

※

But O'Shaughnessy, the tavern-owner's son, while indifferent to José, was inexpressibly shocked by crimes against property. He wasted hours of Alphonso's last night dragging from him sufficient expressions of remorse. All he could wring out was an indifferent '*Oh bien, me arrepiento.*'

For Alphonso could not think of his crimes as crimes. Was he not a sort of knight? A crusader against knaves such as José and heretics such as the physician of Cordova? Was he not operating under martial law? It is to be remembered that Spain was liberated from Africa only the day before yesterday; insurgency is respected there. Were not he and his vassals exempt from the usual moral strictures? '*¿Por qué, padre, ¿por qué? ¡Era necesario consigo Inglaterra!*'

To get to England! Gilberto, his ally at the *Universo*, had examined the hotel ledger for him and copied out the Furloughs' address: *Kettlehinge*

*Hall, nr Pilhough, Derbs.* – which can have meant nothing to either of them (which, ineed, they cannot possibly have pronounced). But Alphonso was as dogged about acquiring knowledge as about acquiring money. He soon knew where Derbyshire lies. It was necessary he get there, and England, as all the world knows, is the most terrible and expensive of all countries; he must arrive there with gold.

As I say, O'Shaughnessy was horrified by this notion, and in his memorandum grimly adds a tag from Aquinas: *In pœnitentia autem tria debent esse:* that is, divine forgiveness requires *contrition, which is sorrow for sin, together with a purpose of amendment; confession of sins without any omission; and satisfaction by means of good works.* Alphonso confessed freely enough, but with the hangman waiting he was hardly in a position to do good, and his *contritio* seemed to O'Shaughnessy most frail and dubious.

As I'm sure it was. But let us jot down another bit of Aquinas and contemplate it: *Sic enim, propter diversas hominum conditiones* ....

*Since there are such diverse conditions of men, some acts are virtuous for some, as being proportionate and becoming, which are vicious for others, as being out of proportion to them.*

Even for professional outlaws, crime has proportion. It's really only for the night. By day Alphonso made Isaac and Helios teach him English – the English of the stews of the Lower East Side – using for text-book Miss Furlough's *Fluttering Leaves by the Wayside,* and her much-annotated Baedeker.

The poetry the three boys took to all too readily, being rhetorical Latins. But Baedeker scandalised them. As for instance where it says of the Andalusians:

> The vicissitudes through which the country has passed are reflected in its present INHABITANTS. Half-European and half-African, they are distinctly –

'*¡Esto es monstruoso!*' cried Helios.

'*¿Quién es este señor Baedeker?*' shouted Isaac through his deformed mouth. '*¿Quién?* I shall come with you to England, friend Alphonso, find him and slaughter him, to redeem the glorious *Reino de Granada* and the refulgent *Reino de Sevilla* from his unspeakable aspersions!'

'Yes, yes,' said Alphonso, whose thoughts were too fixed on Miss Furlough to care about the honour of all the Spains; 'but what does *this* say?'

Isaac read carefully, tracing with his finger, translating as he went:

> 'To his Oriental relations it is that the Andalusian
> owes his exuberant imagination, always prone to
> indulge in *"fanfarronadas"*

*– ¡indignante! ¡Atroz!*'

'Ach!' moaned Alphonso. He had seen something. His crazy passion had devoured his mind; he couldn't really care, as she should, about what *Señor* Baedeker thought of Spainiards. He cared what *she*, the flagitious one, thought of *him*; and to his inexpressible grief he could read *Quite so!! Just like poor swarthy A!!!* in the margin. Violet ink, a neat girlish hand.

Poor swarthy Alphonso happened to have the knack of languages, and soon mastered English, or at least a New York dialect. And as these weeks of fortunate larceny went by, he mastered Gladys Furlough as well. Her Baedeker marginalia was an education in itself. After hesitating for a while (was the action worthy of a *caballero*?) he had Isaac, who thoroughly understood locks, open up Miss Furlough's secret drawers, and read the entire contents to himself.

He was aghast, discovering what I have discovered too: that no concocted novel can possibly be as lurid as an archive; nor as human; nor as anguishing.

❧

So what a fool James O'Shaughnessy was to doseg himself on Balzac and Zola and George Meredith, ruining his palate for human life! It maddens me to think of it.

After all, what a tepid affair it is, prose fiction! How curt, tame, neatly-edged, artificial! When it affects to be true (I am thinking of epistolary novels, purported diaries, and the like) it is most disgusting of all, at least to anyone who's gone through an archive and experienced the real thing.

All through that long night at Strangeways Prison, the condemned Spanish boy slapped down in front of my *confrère* hunk after hunk of raw meat from about the chest, cuts still quivering and dripping; then fixed his astonishing gift with the trove of papers in the sugar-sack, so that this slab of extreme history might be enjoyed forever.

And O'Shaughnessy's imagination (depraved by its diet of novels, spiced *petits fours, soupçons* in aspic, dainty *canapés*) gagged. The dolt! *Fetid + Deplorable + Tedious* indeed!

What is a novel but a Baedeker guide to the human soul? With a map printed in three colours as frontispiece, and a good deal of practical information, most of it wrong? What is it but peering and jeering and leering and sneering by a Baedeker agent, paid by other trippers to find out the most amusing spots?

Worse still: what dunce would read a Baedeker guide *without* any intention of visiting the country described? Read it as a prophylactic, in fact, to travel? Poor idiotic O'Shaughnessy!

Here's another thing that strikes me. There's an odd ripple of reference, all through the Scriptures and the Fathers, about Christ's Book of Life. It seems that the Man-God keeps an archive, ultimate and total, of every antic we human beings commit. At the end of all things it is to be opened and read aloud; with the result, surely, that even those condemned on its testimony will be dragged off to the maw of the inferno with rapt faces, their howls vague, abstracted and distracted. Their hearts won't be in it; they'll still be lost in wonder at the total story, so enthralling that it justifies all its direst details. And even the elect, as they break into endless song, will find their minds still lingering over what they've just heard. *Do we really require eternal consolation?* they'll think to themselves, a touch embarrassed by the thought, *when there's such rapture in hearing the temporal story?*

I, Fr Thomas of the Incarnation, archivist to the *Ordo Praedicatorum* Friary commonly known as Openshaw Blackfriars, once but by divine mercy no longer the Hon. Gregory Towneley, dimly perceive what the cosmos is for. God made it, we know, to love it; but *love* is a roomy sort of word; with what sort of love, exactly? Surely the love of spectacle. It generates an infinite treasury of stories, and as for myself I applaud the whole bloody mess. It is amazing theatre. No, I take that back – it's not dainty, as theatre is. It's a *corrida de toros*, in which the charging bulls are apocalypses, the extinction of peoples, black galactic clouds that bear down on solar systems to blot them out. Intelligent beings stand waiting these monsters: *we wrestle not against flesh and blood, but against principalities, against powers, against the rulers of the darkness.* A hush falls in the arena. No one in his right mind would want his money back, not even during the Blitz.

❧

In any case: Alphonso Ñezgo y Escalofriante read the entire contents of Gladys' travelling-desk to himself, and was duly horrified.

The woman he loved was worthless, worthless. His adoration (which he knew to be the world's holiest, most extravagant, most selfless love) had been fixed on altogether the wickedest person in the world. She was the age's most exorbitant lover. But, as he told Fr O'Shaughnessy: 'The woman fate had assigned me is a monster of lust, pettiness, hypocrisy, vanity, unwomanly arrogance; *and worse.*'

'Of lust?' asked that worthy, incredulously. Like most mid-Victorians, O'Shaughnessy the publican's son was not sure women, or at least gentlewomen, were eligible for this vice, feeling, as they did, no physical desire.

Alphonso nodded, silently handing him a cabinet photograph, face down. The back was printed, respectably enough, M. ROLAND-ADOLPHE-PIERRE VIDANGE, CONSUL HONORAIRE DE LA RÉPUBLIQUE FRANÇAISE, BRIGHTON, SUSSEX, ANGLETERRE, beneath a sprightly representation of Marianne. O'Shaughnessy raised his eyebrows.

'She had it from this Virgilia Flange. Her evil old friend. *Señora* Flange enjoys indifferent health, and recuperates as often as she can in Brighton.'

'Brighton!' muttered O'Shaughnessy, shaking his head. This Mrs Flange must have known the place as a girl, at the zenith of its Regency glamour; she must know, all too well, how it had dwindled into ill-repute. Well; well. He turned the thing over and at once groaned a little, for it was signed *A ma chère Virgilia, consolation de mon exil: avec une affection passionnée*; R-A-P.C., and showed a corpulent man in only a fig-leaf reclining on a high-backed sofa with – what was worse – two absinthe glasses at his head, waiting to be employed. A female hand had added certain lewd remarks which, although they do not actually shock me, I do not think I shall not copy out: enough that they begin *Well, Gladys, examine this gent:*, and conclude *Your wicked & affect: friend V.F.*

The Victorian Dominican quite unaffectedly shuddered. There could be no misunderstanding. For a mature woman to be sent such a trophy was dreadful enough; for her to be amused and give it to a young woman was worse; but for the young woman to have *kept it* …!

He handed it back. About this terrible aspect of Mrs Flange and even (alas!) Miss Furlough, the young Spaniard was correct.

Not that Alphonso was always right. He blundered here and there as he spied on Gladys' soul, blurred by her feeble Spanish and his own bad English. For instance, he often misunderstood her marginalia. He read *They say the Alhambra's simply too divine* not as gushing schoolgirl slang, but as an ironic epigram (*La Alhambra era excesivamente de Dios*), and told the scornful O'Shaughnessy that Clarisetta was a demonic poetess. And he felt personally aggrieved: no man likes to know that his belovèd, when writing home, causally refers to him as *a miserable warty little creature*.

But to be fair to the chivalrous Alphonso: of all the letters in Miss Furlough's travelling desk, the ones that pained and grieved him most were from three other men (*three!*), all addressed to her "care of" a seamstress in the nearby village of Stanton-in-Peak, one Molly Dingle, a woman evidently in Clarisetta's pay.

To each of the three Clarisetta was, judging by their responses – they all pathetically quoted her back to herself – spinning the same yarn. Her heart belonged entirely to him; with all the pure ardour of a gently-bred maiden she was his alone; yet she begged his patience, since her cruel tyrant of a father forbade her as long as he lived to hear any suitor, and only by the stratagem of Mrs Dingle (for which in her simplicity she blushed) could she share these few faltering words, blotted by her tears, with the man destined to share her life hereafter. *Adieu!*

Being a gallant Spaniard, Alphonso found it easiest to sympathise with the noblemen among the three, Sir Jocelyn Orgreave, 13th baronet, last scion of the ancient dynasty at Kettlehinge Hall: *Jocky,* as he signed himself. Young Jocky's face was silly in the photograph, and his letter was very badly spelled. Evidently all was not well with his new life at Groblershoop in the Cape. The local Boers were hostile, the Bushmen inhuman; the English society of Groblershoop, although boisterous enough, did not soothe his spirit. His shiny new Africander cattle were succumbing to *rinderpest,* a fearsome viral disease, and he saw nothing for it but to offer his hand to Brümilda Yaa de Kock, a young widow with a seasoned herd and eleven thousand acres of yellow dust, unless – unless – unless beyond all hope Miss Furlough might feel for him some of the intense liking he most earnestly felt for her, consent to become Lady Orgreave, and bring him back in joy to his own Derbyshire, for which he pined by the minute, to the home of his ancestors, and to his native pastures.

'*¡Hombre infeliz!*' Alphonso remarked magnanimously to Fr O'Shaughnessy, who jotted down *sentimental + craven* in his unkind notes.

Alphonso found it harder to pity his other rivals. He did not like the look nor sound of Mr Stan Harbottle, a coal-factor of Whitehaven, wherever that might be, in Cumberland, whatever that might be, who looked smug in his photograph, and made a great show in his letter of his millions.

> *I'm a plain man and I tell you plainly, Miss Furlough, that you will have neither worry nor want for any good thing you set the desire of your heart upon for the rest of your days should you see your way to giving me your lily-white hand, when rest assured I shall settle on you what will make Sir Zebulon's eyes pop out of his head and that's flat.*

Alphonso positively loathed Arthur Culpepper, who described himself plaintively as *naught but a Perpetual Curate without even temporal prospects, rotting away in this damp parsonage overlooking Mare Germanicum, with no amusement but my music.* The plaintiveness of Mr Culpepper was insincere, it was a device: it allowed him to recur to his favourite themes, his youth

*(How melancholy to be so quite forgotten of the world whilst in the veritable pink of one's first manhood)* and beauty *(Beside these cold blue swirling waters I fear, Miss Furlough, that the gilding must in time fade from my own curls, the roses from my cheeks, the azure from mine eyes;* In cute curanda plus æquo operata juventus! *But perhaps you might care to rescue titivated gold, blue and red from their deathbed, or such bed as might befit?)* 'He seems a ribald fellow,' said Alphonso that night in his death-cell, and O'Shaughnessy remarked, as an Irishman might, 'Ach! these Protestant ministers are all alike.'

Nonetheless, were the four of them not, declared Alphonso, unwitting brothers, all in the toils of the same she-fiend?

(O'Shaughnessy pursed his lips at the puerility of this idea. But *Moral science*, says Aquinas, *is better occupied when treating of friendship than of justice.*)

Did not the four of them, pursued Alphonso, lay before the she-fiend their blood, their money, their looks or, in his own case, incomparable passion? And was she not unashamed at sending back *my undying affection to my one true only Jokey (onlyest Arthur, one own only Ned)* languishing in *awful old Cape Colony (dear dull Devonshire, Northumberland)*? Yes! he forgave them all.

O'Shaughnessy dully wrote down *Exculpation of his debtors?*

He, Alphonso Ñezgo, even forgave their general enemy her triple, quadruple game. What was not tolerable – what he couldn't endure ....

✤

Here Alphonso became quiet, covering his broad flat face with one stubby hand; the other plucked, scratched, fidgetted at his knee.

O'Shaughnessy, brimful of bleak strong patient contempt, sat waiting, gnarly fingers crossed in the lap of his black-and-white habit.

It was cold in the death cell, cold but dry, and so dimly-lit by its gas-flare that a shaft of disastrous moon, falling through the bars, cast shadows. The moon-shadow of the condemned man, black across the moon-blue blanket on the severely-made bed, twitched. The moon-shadow of the Dominican and his wooden chair lay unmoving, in straight lines, across the moon-grey flags.

The cell was so still the rasp of Alphonso's fingernails on his coarse overalls seemed noisy. The warder posted outside the door had not peered in for almost an hour. The friar could hear his heavy peaceful babyish breathing, on the verge of sleep.

But now and then, as in any prison, came the distant shriek of some inmate tormented by a dream; who wakes, and lies sweating in the dark, realising his dream is true.

It is always like this the night before a hanging. All the convicts are on edge, and most of the guards. On such nights Strangeways seems like a machine suspended over the abyss by the vengeful State. The trapdoor that is due open at dawn, to let fall the victim, might just as well take the whole gaol. Perhaps the entire gothic weight of Manchester will plummet, bound as it is with grime, blindfolded with smoke, to snap and twist on its grey rope of sky –

But O'Shaughnessy was speaking at last, more gently: '*¿Qué era, mi hijo, que no toleraría?* What was it, my son, you couldn't tolerate?'

Half Alphonso's face was inked over by shadow, unguessable; the silvery half was working, tortured. He wet his lips, too appalled to utter it in his own tongue; then suddenly blurted out 'Yuh know Fadder I coun't believe what I was seein' – it was a plunge into what he thought of as English – 'not at first see? Dere's dis look on huh face when I sees huh lookin' into de room – '.

'Stop, my son! Tell me what you think you saw. *En español.*'

So, sighing as if the rope were already about his neck, he told.

While he was brawling with her father Clarisetta had shamelessly put her head about the door to watch and he had seen into her mind. She did not love him, did not want him, had misled him –

'My son: women –'.

'No no, Father, that is not the point, deceit by a female is nothing. It is *why* she lied, luring me while her father was at the *corrida*. She was clever, he doltish. She had known he would not be able to endure the sight, no Northerners can, I do not understand why, knew he would return, surprise us, he had a gun, would fire wildly, knew I must save myself. I saw her face and grasped that I was in the presence of – of one who had compassed her own father's death.'

❧

'My son.' O'Shaughnessy had fallen back in his wooden chair, breathing. 'This. This is not so. It cannot be believed. You foreigners naturally. You cannot perhaps grasp, how how.' Like all the Irish, he overestimated English inhibition. 'You misread her look. Your terrible crime –'

'Not crime, *padre!*' put in the condemned man proudly, the hereditary outlaw. 'Crime is of lucre and I did nothing for money.'

'Your crime,' pursued the forbidding priest, still very much upset, 'was inspired by a, a. A shocking misunderstanding of, of – an *Englishwoman*. Whose motives and desires you cannot....' He recast it, softening a little. 'Relying on your understanding, my son, was a sin of intellectual pride.' He offered Alphonso the consolations of philosophy: 'We humans know so little of each other. We are cyphers,' meaning, of course, *in the muddy outer world*; in the lucid inner realm of the novel, the world O'Shaughnessy cared about, information gushes from face to face easily enough. Indeed these signals are what push along many a plot. In the dully-real world there are no plots, just messes. 'Your tragic misapprehension –'.

Alphonso was respecting O'Shaughnessy, as a man, less and less. He was ignoring the friar's wisdom; he had dropped from his bed to the stone-flags of the cell floor, he was pawing under his iron bedstead. It creaked; the sleepy warder pulled open the wooden slat to look in, caught the friar's dull eye, shrugged, slammed it shut.

And now Alphonso was on his knees, having abstracted from the notorious sugar-sack an envelope. His face had turned, the whole was bright with moonlight. In this pose he proffered his letter with both hands, as if they were a religious artifact.

The priest was openly disgusted. 'This,' keeping his spider-claws folded, 'is spoil of Miss Furlough's writing-desk?' Alphonso nodded eagerly. 'To steal was a sin,' he pronounced, regular as a machine, 'to read was a further sin, to continue to possess is a sin. Under no circumstances would I intrude on Miss Furlough's private writing –'

'But, Father, it is not from Clarisetta. It is from the witch calling herself *Señora* Flange. Read it and see I was not mistaken. I did little wrong. Therefore you must absolve me.' And he boldly dropped the papers into his lap.

The Spaniard's confused logic gave O'Shaughnessy a genuine twinge of gallows humour, and he pursed his lips in what did for a smile.

But after all, Alphonso was right: his immortal fate did turn on what happened in the next few hours. Indeed, hour. The darkness of night was beginning to thin. Already the newspapermen would be arriving at the prison gate, raucous, unbreakfasted, unshaved, glugging from hipflasks. The governor would be dressing himself. The hangman would be at the gallows, testing the trap, patting the noose. Not long and he would be upon them ....

O'Shaughnessy irresolutely turned back and forth in his hand the letter, addressed in a hard black hand to *Miss Furlough, due 14ᵗʰ October at the Hôtel Bristol, Gibraltar.*

Well? His qualms were intense, being social rather than spiritual. He was appalled at the prospect of reading a letter from one woman (*an Englishwoman at that*) to another (*of prominent family*). Like any son of a respectable inn-keeper, he had an engorged sense of the lower-middle-class proprieties – not such a useful set of scruples in a Dominican friar, but let that go.

No let's not let it go. I've been hard on O'Shaughnessy, so let me record what my own novice-master, a gentle witty unnerving old man, told me: 'You're trying, Gregory, to reconcile the Sermon on the Mount with the code of a gentleman of old Recusant family. They don't necessarily contradict, but they point in different directions.' Not-to-be-a-snob is part of the snobbery of the Dominican Order; I certainly pique myself on not piquing myself on my birth, just as O'Shaughnessy had to live down his blameless popish family in Knocknafaugher. No doubt my own worldly ideals are as ridiculous as James O'Shaughnessy's, as easy to debunk.

And after all, in this instance he did manage to live them down. He solemnly records his reasoning in a neatly numbered table. Point one: Alphonso *had to be* convinced that he had slandered a young Englishwoman in his mind if he was to repent of the horror that followed from his mistake, be reconciled with Heaven, and die safely; O'Shaughnessy's own distress at spying on private correspondence *must* therefore be set aside. He *must* accept social humiliation.

Two: *However an ignorant foreigner might misconstrue them, the notions a governess of advanced years might have to share with her former charge could scarcely be very shocking.*

Three: *Have I not read letters inflammatory enough in* Pamela, *+ sensational enough in* Werther?

Thus, sighing dryly, shaking his head in deprecation, James O'Shaughnessy, *dilettante* of novels, unfolded, and began to read.

❧

KETTLEHINGE HALL,
NEAR ROWSLEY,
DERBYSHIRE

*9ᵗʰ Oct.*

*My dear, the wonder of this nineteenth century of ours! I have <u>already</u> received your onboard wire – it was dispatched from Wexford when your steamer took on the Continental mails. What a world we inhabit to be sure.*

*We must be strong. <u>Of course</u> it's regrettable that Sir Zebulon should recover so quickly from such a promising bronchial affliction*

– O'Shaughnessy looked up sharply. Alphonso, still kneeling, had drooped; his eyelids were low. The friar, dizzy, returned his own eyes to the paper, scanning Mrs Flange's firm handwriting. His brain couldn't digest, it skit-tered off in every direction

> *but in sooth I half-foresaw this reverse; it is ever thus with chest*
> *ailments when one is at sea; the air blows everything off.* <u>*Quel*</u>

You understand that O'Shaughnessy was not squeamish. He would have enjoyed such a plot-turn if it happened where it belonged, in a novel. But it was his settled principle that real life is *definitionally* mundane: either squalid (if we're thinking of the lower orders); or upright, although selfish and generally heretical (if we are contemplating their betters). Which was of course why a man of some imagination, even a religious, required an outlet in fiction.... What was this, then, what was this? Novelistic! Impossible!

> <u>*Quel domage.*</u>
>     *Courage! this is early days. We must be patient in the*
> *earning of our freedom. You have eight weeks of Spain ahead of*
> *you, and Spain*

Although as it happens the theme of young women calmly killing fathers is not novelistic, being unimaginable. It is so horrible *no novelist would dare.*

> *Spain is a usefully dirty and violent country. If you are out in*
> *the afternoons do thwart any return to your hotel to collect*
> *overcoats; much profit can be looked for*

Sons killing fathers: that's a common theme because it's the most heinous act we can think of. Art thrills itself by contemplating what is *most* utterly forbidden. But death-by-daughter! That's beyond the worst, beyond thinking, beyond art.

> *much profit can be looked for from sudden evening chills.*
> *October is almost too late for the best of enteric or putrid fevers,*
> *but ague troubles the Spanish year round; and of course with*
> *thorns and nails on every hand tetanus is ever the friend of the*
> *oppressed child.*
>     *The scornful way you allude to highwaymen*

Highwaymen! – In the part of his mind not merely stunned, O'Shaughnessy was trying to recall if there were any murderous daughters in literature. *Then* he could begin to think. Only novels were quite real to him. It was a weakness.

*only shows you have not studied your Baedeker to good effect.*
*Your must learn, dear, to read between the lines. When the editors*
*call the road between Ronda and Grazalema "picturesque, but*
*so particularly trying it is most certainly best avoided, especially*
*toward evening" they are intimating, without throwing timid*
*readers into a welter of dismay, that the road us thickly <u>infested</u>.*
    *I grant that bandits are a desperate remedy.*

There aren't any. There really are none –

*But <u>should</u> you take valour in in both hands and persuade your*
*father to go that way (any warnings he might hear are of course*
*"unmanly" and "unEnglish"), and <u>should</u> masked deliverers*
*indeed appear, bear in mind in the crisis of the hour two truths:*
*that their sense of honour permits homicide but discountenances*
*rapine; and that Sir Zebulon is a very bad shot. If you can induce*
*him to fire first our cause is secure, and your ransom will doubt-*
*less be settled by the British Consul.*

– that is, there's Beatrice in Shelley *The Cenci*; but those were very special
circumstances, incestuous rape, and so forth –

*In the meanwhile my counsel is not to let your present disappoint-*
*ment make you petulant. Now you are on dry land again, the*
*higher your spirits the more you might persuade him to late hours*
*and indulgence. Remember how fond he is of pork sausages*

– and in myth, only King Pelias' daughters, and even that was meant kindly,
a sorceress misled them, they thought they were immortalising not killinh
him –

*and how badly they disagree with him; indeed his dyspeptic*
*attacks are growing worse. Also that, for those of the <u>hardier</u>*
*<u>sex</u> prone to pleurisy, <u>even fleshier indulgence</u> – I refer, dear,*
*to venereal concupiscence (which I rejoice to say does nothing*
*but good to you and to me) – can often bring on instant apo-*
*plexy. The <u>better</u>, that is to say the <u>lower</u> houses of ill-repute in*
*Gibraltar,*

– otherwise just a furtive myth, Tullia the last Queen of Rome, monstrous
Tarquin's wife. No one else.

> *the ones frequented by the <u>dear brave</u> fellows of the garrison, are*
> *on the shore to the east of the barracks. Walk him that way one*
> *afternoon, slowly, so that the truth breaks into even his faculties,*
> *then leave him to his own devices that evening.*
>
> *Naturally you will encourage his brandy-tippling, although*
> *I fear he is so inured we should expect little from <u>that</u>; but I delate*
> *to your own rare wonderfully clever inventiveness*

'Rare'! 'Rare'! For the first time in many decades, O'Shaughnessy wondered if he might be about to cry. Rare Miss Furlough!

> *other machinations to bring about the fortunate event we have*
> *so often chatted about in our girlish way,*

O'Shaughnessy detected it his mind (and to his credit recorded) the momentary, appalling wish that the hangman might arrive at once, and end this torture.

> *when you shall be sole mistress of Kettlehinge Hall, entertaining*
> *whom you wish and <u>how</u> you wish, by twos and threes if you*
> *desire, in the afternoon as well as all night, while the housekeep-*
> *ership and its cares you shall have committed to*
> > *your own*
> > > *devoted*
> > > > *Virginia Flange.*

O'Shaughnessy folded the pages up and handed them back, noting with shame how the bright paper shook in the moony air. He had never been so pained in his life. In his confusion the burning sensation in his brain almost localised itself in that damnable wad.

Naturally, being an intellectual, he made a final attempt to argue against the facts. 'I see, my son, why you might mistake as a, a plot between the two … these dreadful …. The criminal *fantasies* … of an elderly … a woman perhaps stricken in reason –'

Neither of them believed it. Alphonso, still on his knees, laid an imploring hand on O'Shaughnessy's hand. 'I *saw* the idea became fixed in Clarisetta's head. I didn't understand it then. At the Lovers' Rock. I *saw* her realise she didn't have rely on ague or brandy to be free of her father.'

O'Shaughnessy had been transported to a different universe, quite unfamiliar, where his cold authority was gone. He whispered as a man to a man:

'What did you see?'

'She realised the weapon might be – love.'

Most reliable of human munitions. O'Shaughnessy put his hand to his brow so that his eyes passed into blackness. This was crushingly-crushingly real. (I hope it spoilt his next three-volume romance for him.) 'Is *that* in her papers?'

'In her papers. Yes. I read them again and again until I had memorised the words', and her words (he didn't need to say this) were terrible enough to be provender and guide as he rampaged toward her, across the whole breadth of Spain.

## *iii.*

At the beginning of Advent, after burgling a goldsmith's in Valladolid, Alphonso decided he had enough money and enough English to accomplish what he had been born to do, and led his little gang to the Atlantic coast. According to Baedeker (illuminating in ways small as well as great), the Brazilian mail-steamers of the Booth Line run from Vigo *via* Havre to Liverpool thrice a month; six pounds for second-class berth and board.

When the bandits reached Vigo, the greatest fishing-port of Spain, they found the next sailing was expected in two days. They therefore bought a single ticket, and rented an inconspicuous house, a stone hovel patchily roofed with slate, on the edge of town.

Isaac and Helios resolved to spend the two days roistering; was not their brave commander about to leave them? 'O Captain! My Captain!' they quoted to each other, falling moistly on each other's necks.

It will be seen that Alphonso had not been an altogether good influence on Isaac and Helios, who were at heart simple New York mobsters: honest in their dishonesty, lucid, empirical and modest. The immensity of his pilgrimage to Derbyshire rather overwhelmed them. Even the dilute romanticism of *Fluttering Leaves* was too much for stomachs never hardened to poetry of any sort. 'The boy stood on the burning deck' reliably made them sob, and 'Into the Valley of Death Rode the Six Hundred' stirred up visions of majestic violence that would have astonished their former colleagues in the practically-minded underworld of the Lower East Side.

In short, the gang fell victim to its own success. Neither in Spain nor in America had Isaac or his hare-lip been used to the good brandy they could now afford. And dimwitted Helios, although the son of a prosperous tailor, was always maudlin in his cups: without Alphonso, he kept saying, we're bound to go back to our shiftless ways. In any case, Helios in drink was inclined to quarrel and to swagger: to commit, indeed, the *fanfarronadas* of which Baedeker accuses all Andalusians.

There came a tepid wet afternoon at their shack when the two cronies, emotionally-overcharged and grossly sozzled, fell out.

They were alone with *Fluttering Leaves* and their bottle. If their captain had been there he would have parted him. But he was on the stone wharf of Vigo, sniffing the incredible reek of a million landed fish, and staring at the terrifying sea, which he was seeing for the first time. God, it seemed to him, must have created the ocean, in its illimitable coldness, pallor and rage, as an image for Gladys Furlough. (*Which, I pressed upon him,* records Fr O'Shananassey in his memorandum, *was blasphemous + unmanly nonsense.*) Alphonso returned from the sea-walls to a buzzing that seemed loud even before he put his hand to the door of their shack. The feasting flies were thick, he had to part them with his arms; the welter of blood, splashed over the walls to waist-height, was already black. Helios sprawled cruciform, face-down, half-heartedly beheaded: his gullet had been sawn through so unevenly, so unprofessionally, that his murderer must have been in tears. Of course Isaac was quite gone and so was all the gang's money.

Alphonso found he didn't much care, and was distressed at not being distressed, for should not an adventurous *caballero* bear his men in his heart?

*Was* he an adventurer, though? Bandit-chieftainship had suddenly drained out of him. The altar-boy he had been brought up to be by his foster-parents was uppermost again, a little blurred by the atheist rantings of his master the drover. He felt weepy.

What most concerned him was the lady's travelling-desk, which after a moment's panic he found behind the over-turned table, up-ended and splashed about with the broken brandy-bottle, but in one piece.

He took it outside (sketching a furtive sign of the cross over Helios, which disturbed the flies), wiped it clean with a rag, crouched in the shade of the low ashlar wall, took out a clean sheet of Miss Furlough's splendid paper, her pen and her bottle of violet ink, and laboriously produced a note addressed to the local commander of the *Guardia Civil*. He made a rough draft first, which he kept, and which lies before me now; the handwriting freakishly seems to imitate hers. ¡*Capitán! el Hommbre assesinado....* I hope the fair copy contained fewer spelling mistakes.

> Capitan! The slain man herein was a good catholic and should
> be buried with all the consolations of Holy Church, as should his
> assassin, a hare-lip with an Andalusian accent named Isaac.

Our hero propped against the door this extraordinary note (the total literary out-put of his life, so far as I know) and stole away. As soon as siesta ended it would be noticed. Isaac could not have got far, drunk as he must be. He would be captured, the officers would steal the gang's twice-stolen money, Isaac would be garotted, order restored.

Alphonso's sacristan-self, it will be seen, was now triumphant and rampaging in his soul. He hoped the ever-clement Virgin, and St James the Moor-Slayer of Compostela, would have mercy on his companions. They had erred, but were either of them as wicked as the demon in female form he called Clarisetta? Of course not!

He had just enough in his pocket to survive his last day in Spain, skulking in doorways in his new-bought navy-blue pea-coat, of which he had been, before the murder, joyously proud. No one regarded him. He boarded the black-funneled *Augustine* in twilight, unnoticed.

It was a hard winter that year in Galicia, but nothing prepared him for the insane sway and smash of the Atlantic, nor for the blast of sleet that met him as the ship turned into the Mersey, nor for the whistling tearing wind that raced itself up and down the south docks at Liverpool. He had not grasped that people could live permanently in such conditions.

In his innocent way he shared this observation with O'Shaughnessy. It is how Liverpool would strike any Andalusian peasant, and tells us nothing in particular about Alphonso. But the bleak way his confessor, that child of the windswept edge of Ireland, records the thought (*effeminate* + *foolish* + *soft*) tells us a lot about O'Shaughnessy, and about the effects of novel-reading. Fiction deepens our sympathies only in certain directions. Heroes in novels are always striding unmoved through shattering weather, because the novelist is twiddling his controls to suit their mood: his characters are huge, his skies just background. But in reality the human frame is more susceptible than that. The world feels extremely outside ourselves, and hurts us arbitrarily.

There is no Latin equivalent to Baedeker. A Southerner has to experience the North through his naked senses, unmediated. The Liverpudlian winter, glorying in its possession, dandling the town on its knee, exhausted and baffled Alphonso. He could scarcely breathe, being used to oven-dry breezes on the marches of Africa. Here, on the verge of the Arctic, the air seemed composed of very thin mud: it wanted to hammer dirty icicles down his throat. He could scarcely walk because of the millions in black bowler hats and black bustles rushing, almost running, the other way. Everywhere precipices of grey carved granite loomed over him, tricked out with allegorical statuary, Commerce, Industry, Science, muscular figures that made him feel idle, ignorant, a squalid weakling. The faces of the living people, even paler and stonier than the carved faces, were full of a single passion: the hurried getting and spending of money. He could imagine no other passion here, in these stone canyons where nothing grew, no *azufaifo* shrubs to prick a poor fellow into love – he thought wildly (he was a little feverish, his thoughts knotted themselves into bad poetry). He had no energy for petty thieving, let alone burglary; he could make no headway against the blast of wind, he could not force himself to press on out of the city.

For a week Alphonso lingered meaninglessly in Liverpool, discovering that neither his foreign-looking fisherman's coat, nor his fluency in the *patois* of New York, made for popularity. The chest-cough that had begun even before he boarded the *S.S. Augustine* was now a perpetual mild convulsion. It seemed to him not that he had a cough, but that a cough had him. His small wasted body shook like the clapper in bell. It would be hard to identify him with the almost-confident, almost-gentlemanly figure in the *carte-de-visite* he had had taken in Madrid. He took the photograph out now and then to mock himself. 'Which is I?' he would ask himself. (I know.)

His zeal to get to Kettlehinge burned low. He clearly possessed a certain pathetic appeal to motherly females. If some barmaid or unraddled prostitute had befriended him, the Don Quixote of our age might have forgotten his Dulcinea, given up the quest, and sunk into the polyglot slums of Liverpool. A happy ending. A low ending.

Instead, fortunately, on Christmas Eve, friendless and hobbling from starvation, he pawned Miss Furlough's travelling-desk. This transaction felt like selling his own limbs, he said (to the disgust of O'Shaughnessy, for whom quixotic sentiments belonged only between hard-covers). He had emptied it out, of course, stowing all its books and papers and photographs in the celebrated sugar-sack, printed HENRY TATE & SONS, LIVERPOOL AND LONDON: SUGAR REFINERS, which was henceforth his only baggage.

I regret the desk, and I'm very happy the sack survived. It seems to me like the relic of a passion, of a *via doloriosa* of toward martyrdom. *Man cannot live without joy* (more Aquinas); *therefore when he is deprived of true spiritual joys it is necessary that he become addicted to carnal pleasures.*

There were no trains on Christmas day and none on St Stephen's Day. Early on the 27th the passionate criminal made his way to Liverpool station and bought a third-class ticket for Great Rowsley. He changed trains in Manchester; strange to think of that fiery soul so close to where I am coolly sitting now. The few people travelling at that season avoided him; no one liked that hacking noise the sallow little foreigner was making; he had the carriage to himself. He stared out its windows aghast, although it was mild melting weather as they rolled out of Lancashire, weather that might have delighted a North-Country-man. The little snow that had fallen before Christmas was virtually gone; there was a swift thaw even on the northward slopes; for the next week the ground would be muddy and sucking by day, iron-bound by night, back and forth like the blessed systole and diastole of the heart. A sun pale almost to whiteness floated low over the grey-green horizon; and the winter colours of the Peak District, orange, ash-white, catastrophic red, hung over the leafless hills in shredded banners.

The view more-or-less accorded with Alphonso's concept of Siberia, and he once again felt it preposterous that people, or even trees, should survive amidst such everlasting torment.

The slow train seemed fantastically slow to a man dizzy from famine, and from sleeplessness (he had not been able to lie down for a week now, what with the coughing, and the night-sweats, and the rage of emotion). He alighted at Rowsley, which sits pleasantly deep in a double valley, the Wye flowing into the Derwent; although it struck him as the muddy bottom of a pit.

To be fair, a dark rain had begun, falling at just the right slope to pour down his collar. The station-master looked askance when he asked, in his incredible accent, for Kettlehinge Hall; then softened and said 'You can't go that far today, sir, not in this.'

And indeed for an instant Alphonso did approach despair. Surely the water that drenched him was too cold not to be sleet? Surely, since he could not *feel* his fingers and feet, they could not pain him so much? At that moment he regretted (he would tell the disapproving O'Shaughnessy) that Sir Zebulon had not fired straight: 'Father, I would be lying peacefully in the dry soil of Andalusia.' He even regretted that the *Guardia Civil* had not caught him as well as Isaac. The two of them might be sitting now side by side in a decent Spanish gaol, with the frank cool metal of the garotte about their warm dry necks, and a priest holding a crucifix before them, waiting for the governor to give the signal, the handle to turn, the collar to crush out their forfeited lives.

He shook himself. There is a certain comfort in feeling yourself so close to physical bankruptcy, with no more calculations to make, no strength to conserve. The last of you dribbles out as if by gravity. There is no effort of will left to make.

Thus Alphonso found it was easier to get into the dog-cart outside the station than to stand still. He hectored the driver because that was less exhausting that keeping silent. He over-bore the driver's objections to carrying so sorry a customer up Youlgrave way, to the gates of Kettlehinge Hall; and when they arrived, found it was easier not to haggle over ha'pennies, but rather empty the coins out of his pockets into his hands.

The driver of course thought him perfectly mad and, struck by compunction, helped him down tenderly, handed him his sack, watched him reel off into the rain. The water was falling like a curtain from the brim of the driver's bowler hat; the little lunatic looked unspeakably pathetic, as is he was bound to dissolve in liquid greyness. 'Sir! Sir! Come back.' But Alphonso shook his head without turning and staggered on until misty wetness swallowed him up.

## *iv.*

Kettlehinge stands atop Pillow Hill, a bare knob 340 feet above the northern ocean, sixty feet above Rowsley; it looks far over the Derwent and the Wye, and so seems higher. There was camp here before Cæsar reached Britain; you can still make out its immemorial dry moat. The Orgreaves, in the days when the Derbyshire Dales quaked at their name, built their robber's fortress on the summit; in their prosperity and pride they rebuilt and expanded the house down the slope, with mock-battlements, a deer-park and an avenue of chestnuts, in rivalry with nearby Haddon and Chatsworth. In their decadence the Orgreaves did nothing to Kettlehinge, so that its low sagging galleries of black wood, tarnished suits of armour, primitive portraits, ornate plasterwork and year-round damp are a museum of pre-Reformation discomfort.

And in winter, at Kettlehinge and roundabouts, in her native country, Gladys seemed subdued to the climate. Unless of course winter was subdued to her. All that was locally remorseless shone through her vacancy, lancing cold, tearing serrated stoat teeth on baby rabbit flesh. Not that she was necessarily out of place in other seasons: spring hardness was hers too (tendrils throttling older growth), summer drought, autumn decreptitude –

Sir Zebulon Furlough, as I have said, was much too eager a social climber to risk any modernisations when he bought the place, and the fortnight he spent there each Christmas generally wrecked his health until Eastertide. As far as possible he stayed in what he called 'the great hall', at the head of a preposterous dining table ('festive board') seating thirty, with half an apple-tree blazing away behind him on a gigantic hearth.

His play-acting extended to two enormous deerhounds, designed to lie at his feet and gnaw on thrown scraps. Since Mrs Flange detested these beasts, they spent the three hundred and fifty-one days of their master's absence sleeping in the stables, and slaughtering wildlife in the woods. The Christmas holiday, the hours spent being baked in front of the fire, were agony for them, and they were perceptibly feebler each Twelfth Night. One year, soon, soon, Mrs Flange, that great amateur poisoner, would anticipate Sir Zebulon's permission and put them down.

For now they simply suffered, and everyone else in the great hall suffered too, ranged up and down the impossible table, across which they had to shout, with Sir Zebulon presiding over them in pseudo-feudal glory at the head.

Charity, being human, is perhaps out of place in such an artificial, such an inhuman house-party: that is not meant as a witticism, and I hope it is not an imprudent doctrine. O'Shaughnessy would certainly condemn it, but then he lived in a saner age. With the pure, God says, He shows Himself pure, with the froward forward. I propose we should treat this most froward Christmas party with worldly detachment. That is, at least, what I mean to do.

Thus I see no great cause for us to sympathise with any of Furlough's guests (whose names and "conditions" I have in front of me, for in this regard the police force was through). They included a few members of the local gentry impoverished enough to accept such gross hospitality. Otherwise they were sordid strangers who arrived in a pompous hurry by train, and were already waiting to scurry away. There was Crake, his bootlicking agent. There were political cronies from Westminster, some of them almost Cockney enough to be taken in by Furlough's cynical skit on olde Englande; silent watchful men connected with newspapers and reviews; business collaborators or rivals, including Stan Harbottle, who had spent the interminable luncheon trying to catch Miss Gladys' eye, and steadily not succeeding; even a young Russian diplomat, wolf-bright-eyed, Baron Paul Tscherkassoff, whose face, most unusually in that decade, was clean-shaven, but for finely-drawn moustaches. It had caught Gladys' gaze.

The Tsar's armies were overrunning the Balkans that winter. The Tory government supported the Sultan; the Queen and half the Cabinet, including the Prime Minister, wanted to go to war and solve the Eastern Question for good. But the Opposition was pro-Russian to the point of treason. Tscherkassoff was at Kettlehinge to sound out Furlough, representative of the Northern money-interest Liberals, about how far they might go if a European conflict were in the offing in the spring.

Everyone seemed too tipsy for intrigue. Nonetheless Tscherkassoff, young, wise and merry, was enjoying himself – perhaps the only guest who was. He had detected at first glance the promising sluttishness of this Furlough fellow's daughter. With the party so sottish, opportunities might arise one night before he left. (Here am I being detached.) Meanwhile the young Baron was vastly amused by the house-party's *kulak* atmosphere. How often in London he had been twitted on the legendary boorishness of Russian banquets. And now, in the depths of England: *this!*

Furlough's idea was to entertain his victims in what he conceived to be mediæval fashion. Which is to say, he gorged them for eight hours or more

each day. The painful excess of victuals, everything brown-black and glistening with hot grease, was meant to be cancelled out (or washed down, or
burned through) by a steady excess of sticky acidic drinks. There were tubs
and tubs of steaming spiced red wine, stinking of too much cinnamon and
orange. There was negus, bishop, shrub, posset and nog.

For an hour at breakfast, three hours at midday, five in the evening, the
weary succession continued: fitches of green bacon, holocausts of grouse and
woodcock glazed with syrup, game-pies like cartwheels, sides of fire-black-
ened venison, rounds of yellow-streaked mutton, entire cheeses sweating in
the heat, piglets, 'the roast-beef of England that won us Agincourt'; even, on
Christmas day itself, a whole roast ox as dangerous as a charging bull.

Servants came staggering in with these monstrosities on vast silver plat-
ters, clattered them down on the sideboard, hacked at them incompetently,
heaped chaotic plates, lurched out again, to resume the uninterrupted drink-
ing-party in the servants' hall.

After a long while this process tapered off, and eventually Zoffany the
butler would appear, sway in the door way, pronounce 'Thisens sh'll ay to do
it y'usens' (which is Derbyshire for *You'll have to serve yourselves now*), and
vanish, helped off by two elderly footmen.

By then the women had gone. Gladys had risen, collected the eyes of the
haggard wives of M.P.s and the fat wives of industrialists (winking at Tscherkassoff on the sly), and led them out. The menfolk had just managed to stand,
propped on their vast carved chair-backs; then had collapsed before the last
female had vanished through the great doors.

Furlough and his guests would settle down and try to undo the damage
of what they had eaten and drunk with tobacco, and decanters of more
modern drinks, whisky and port. They would undo the despair that comes
with bloating on meat by talking dirty.

Luncheon did not finish until four, which it is already gloaming in the
midwinter Peak District.

That is how we find Kettlehinge. The ladies are in their frigid bedrooms,
wrapped in bearskins and tartan blankets, drinking steaming tea, and watching their maids lay out evening-gowns, which according to the fashion of the
time are violently-coloured, massive, tasseled, fringed, like so many uphol-
stered mountains. They are waiting for the heavy tread of their men. After
a bit of gross recovery (the most typical noise of a Kettlehinge Christmas is
belching, the most typical smell is vomit), the females will put these terrible
garments on, the males will get into tails and waistcoats, and everyone will re-
assemble in the "great parlour, whilom, in the age of superstition, the chapel,"
for sherry, and resume the whole desolating cycle.

But not yet. The women are still upstairs alone, freezing. The gentlemen are still at table, sweltering. Everyone is comfortlessly drunk, except for Crake, who does not dare to get drunk; and Tscherkassoff, who smiles and smiles; and the intellectual journalists, who are listening, listening; and a single pair of eyes resting on them all, judging them accurately enough. I do not mean the eyes of God but of Alphonso Ñezgo y Escalofriante, who stands in the murk outside the mullioned windows, staring in at this strange slumped people and their fat firelight shadows, dancing up the panelling.

He had scaled the fence of the estate easily enough, had stomped across the park muddy to his knees, had spied the great house on its rise, tumbled into a ha-ha and lay there rolling back and forth with a fit of coughing; emerged, still dragging his sugar-sack; and now stands in the rain, which is slackening a little. He is so cold his skin is numb and his bones scarcely ache. He looks up and down the incredible table and finds that, quite properly, the *señoras* and *señoritas* have departed. Sir Zebulon he sighs over. Harbottle he does not recognise: the great coal tycoon is overcome, has buried his bovine head in his arms.

'She doesn't love me, the little lass,' Harbottle tells whichever of his neighbours will listen, 'whatever she says in her letters she doesn't love me.'

Alphonso has already turned and gone from the window.

He stands in the shrubbery to the west of the house and looks up. The rain has stopped; the last of it drips from his unhandsome nose. From the hall comes the low murmur of filthy stories. From the back of the house comes the disordered smash and racket of the servants, anarchically trying to sober up enough to serve dinner. Upstairs all is stillness. But one figure is moving: through the curtains, just drawn, he makes out a silhouette going up a staircase; a black silhouette with a yellow glow floating before it; a silhouette which, after eight weeks of obsession, he recognises. It pauses at the landing, which is open to the evening; and of course he is right, it is the one she in the world, holding a lit taper in a brass candlestick. She leans out sinuously, staring into the thickening evening, almost it is as if she sees him. She wears a tight green dress, like a great serpent. By dashing backward out of the shrubbery he can follow her round the final turn of the stair, then along a twisted passageway. She vanishes, but at once there is a yellow glow of sconces being lit in a certain room. She comes to the window to pull the blind down, first lifting her arms high above her head, stretching her young faultless body. Then she is gone, the window is a blank.

Alphonso works his way round to the back of the big house, to what looks like the laundry. It is lightless and silent. One of the few objects sharing the sugar-sack with his precious farrago of papers is a heavy butcher's knife. This he uses as a jemmy, prising up one the sash windows. He slips his thin form through and lands with a dull crash on the stone floor within. The pane slams down behind him.

He lies listening. Is anyone coming?

The patter on the glass is loud: the rain has resumed, heavier, crueller than before. Otherwise he hears only a sizzling boil, mingled with screams of different timbres; but it comes at once from near at hand and from miles, centuries away, so that, being a sensible Latin, he knows it is a supernatural phenomenon that can do him no harm.

When he is sure no flesh and blood is at hand he gets up, dripping on the flags. It won't do: he is too ridiculous. Though a *caballero* may shed blood, he ought not to drip rainwater. Alphonso takes off the pea-coat and drops it in a stone sink. He doffs his shapeless boots and sopping woollen stockings.

In shirtsleeves and bare feet the cold in the laundry is appalling. And another consumptive palsy takes him in his grip. This time, for the first time, he seems to feel a tearing within, and when the fit dies away his palms are sticky. Is it a trace of pulmonary blood at last? He rinses off his hands, which is all he can do, and goes forth.

The laundry is locked, but he jemmies the door, and finds himself in a long low corridor. Unerringly he turns right; takes the first stair on his left; pushes through a baize door into the noble part of the house.

There are two woman coming; he steps sharply behind a grandfather clock. It is a foolish manœuvre: with his sack over his shoulder he looks the exact popular image of a burglar bearing away swag, and it seems impossible they should not look at him and shriek. But they are gossiping angrily, their heads close together ('… or it may be that *Russian!*', 'My dear even she is too …'), and sail right past.

When they are gone, he turns sharply down another gallery, bewildering to the eye with its barbaric elaboration of dark carved wood and white plaster. Then left.

Of course he has seen more or less where Clarisetta's room lies, but that hardly explains how quickly he finds it. Perhaps he is drawn by smell.

Within, he can hear her quietly singing to herself. When he slips inside she does not look, being bent over her bed, toying with jewels. She speaks to no purpose, then turns and sees him.

*Flower of England, fruit of Spain,*
*Met together in a shower of rain*

A harmless nursery rhyme. Her horror is partly fixed on the knife, partly on his shirt. He has coughed up far more blood than he imagined, is already gory: gouts of dark crimson, dark crimson handprints. His disease is well-developed. Indeed the prison doctor examining him in a few days' time will declare him hopelessly tubercular: 'He's in remission. Luxury of Strangeways I suppose. Manchester prisons more wholesome than castles in Spain, what! Sobering thought. But it'll kill him sure enough. Two months, say, or three. Should the British Empire forgo the fun of hanging the bally fellow. Which it won't.'

That is an appalling prospect. At least it is for me. If Alphonso had never sat in Strangeways' condemned cell, he would not have confessed to O'Shaughnessy. Silence and oblivion would have engulfed this epic of love.

## *v.*

Of love! Of course of love. Repudiation, reproach, revenge: such possibilities had never entered Alphonso's mind.

That night in Alhama he had committed the most incredible, the best deed – at least, most civilisations have thought it so – the very best deed possible to humanity in this whole botched world. He had given himself altogether to another person. Henceforth he was That-Which-Adores-Gladys-Furlough, and his Alphonsoness (so to speak) was burned up, instantly consumed by this new vocation.

It made no difference when, two days later, he gathered from her expression that she was using him, loving him not at all. I mean it made no difference to what he *was*. The suffering her glance caused him was no doubt tremendous. That she was using him *to get rid of her father* must have inflicted pain beyond what normal human beings will or can experience. But he went on loving her, because his love, being perfect, could not alter.

Perhaps he was even *consoled* that his unlimited love was being lavished on the worst living person in the whole world. His love endured no distractions from the splendour of itself. She could not love him back; did not deserve love of any sort; deserved, indeed, loathing and obliteration. He could not possibly like her. His will to love her was thus entirely pure. It was an ocean pouring forever into an abyss. It resembled divine grace, of which Alphonso's love was (perhaps) an unconscious parody; or even (who can fathom the intricacy of the divine wit?) a *self*-parody.

Thus it is senseless to try to weigh what happened to Alphonso that breezy evening in the plaza. You can say he was seized by an infatuation that was insane, that was a mental or spiritual illness, that killed him (and not only him). But after all, Alphonso was going to die in any case, as we all are; and the passion that trapped him, the passion he chose, was a larger matter than dying. It was almost the opposite of a terminal disease. It was an immortalising wellness.

I begin to see that a complete man wouldn't understand the distinction between necessity and free will. Whatever he did would arise out of what he was, and he could never know the anguish of indecision. I suffer indecision because I have half a dozen unfinished men within me, each trying to murder all the others and become the one I: the sadist, the saint (perhaps), the punctilious scion of an old family, the wistful antiquarian, the rabid sectarian, the downright snob, the superior friar and man-of-cloistral-parts, the Anglo-Saxon melancholic. I can please no more than one of these men at a time. Thus every choice seems ominous beforehand: fraught while I make it, disappointing afterward.

But Alphonso had done with the fidget of choice. He saw Clarisetta's bad-tempered face coming out of her showy carriage, and bloomed at once, and eternally. In that instant he made himself a finished man. It is the most fatuous pun to add that the instant finished him off. Death is a trivial incident to such burning superhuman will.

That will burned his way across Spain and into Liverpool and then, despite physical weakness that would soon have killed him, blasted him out of Liverpool and into Clarisetta's bedroom. Into her bed, too; for that flibbertigibbet, that patricidette, with nothing to weigh her down but her crime, was swept along like a leaf in the firestorm of his love.

※

The most remarkable thing about Fr O'Shaughnessy's very long, very much-emended memorandum, is what it does not include. I mean that it scarcely bothers to condemn the bedding of Miss Furlough (except in the most perfunctory way). Even James O'Shaughnessy, with his ill-bred rules and nervous dreads, grasped that Alphonso was not guilty of casual fornication. His embrace of the body of his belovèd was so serious it makes even marriage look like a tepid, fleeting arrangement. Alphonso had been created to love Gladys once, and die; the act was as intrinsic to him as the mating of a mayfly. There is nothing to be said about that fusion of opposites.

Which brings us to their pillow-talk, conducted in a mishmash of New York argot and guidebook Spanish, and recorded by O'Shaughnassey in stiff Victorian English.

Their pillow-talk: isn't it rather terrible to contemplate the two of them looking at each other at a distance of inches, he on one pillow, she on another, in the dim shadowless light one finds under a sheet? She fragrant with hillside violets (as violets are understood in the *parfumeries* of the Place Vendôme)? He stinking of travel, consumption, life-long poverty, anyway foul with blood and mire and rainwater? Only on the day of judgment will the damned and the elect be able to speak to each other with such perfect frankness. The image of those two lovers is like a foretaste of the end of the world.

Well, they lay there, watching each other's naked faces, and hearing very distantly the groans and clattering of her father's demonic luncheon coming to an end downstairs.

There was nothing for them to hold back from each other. He knew she knew about the freakish totality of his love for her, which no taint in herself could modify or end. She had felt the exorbitant force of it. Likewise, she knew he had read her letters, and had not a single illusion left.

Therefore she told him, and he told O'Shaughnassey, all about their journey back from Spain; about the Saxon count who was now not answering her letters 'the snuffling *beast.*' About their debauch in Paris. About the sketch by Sem – 'Look, here it is; isn't it too wicked? Do you like it?' (He resolved to steal it.) About how hateful it was to be back at Kettlehinge, '*freezing* horrid place.' How Mrs Flange in her absence had conducted an *affaire* with a ploughboy a quarter her age until she was 'just too fatigued *for words.*' And had gone off to Brighton ('Where she has a niece *officially*, sly darling') to recover in the seemlier embraces of the French consul – a hyper-Baudelairian poet who had won his post with verses, praising the extirpation of the Communards. 'But then Virgilia generally avoids Kettlehinge at Christmas, and no wonder. Ah well, it's always a season of hope for *me*'; for Miss Gladys Ella Furlough, Christmastide was full of glad tidings. Her father was sure to over-eat and vilely over-drink and be on the verge of a fit until his guests departed. And he might just totter over the verge. 'Did you look through the hall window and *see* him?'

'Yes. It is wrong to try to kill a parent.'

'So they say. But meanwhile isn't it too utterly foul – the way he gorges with all those disgusting ugly fat fellows?'

'Yes.'

'And *dangerous* for him, don't you think? Much more effective than getting him into fights, abroad, with scrawny peasants?'

'Yes. That was wicked also, Clarissa.'

'*Who?*'

'It is your name. Clarissa Varlo. But I call you *Clarisetta* because you are so slender.'

'Oh!'

'Do you "mind"?'

'How should I' (I am sure she nearly said *care*, and stopped herself) '"mind"? Darling… *Alphonso.*' She giggled merrily, much as they must giggle down in the nether fires.

But he knew that she couldn't have been born a *diablillo* – on this point the lore of his pious foster-parents and the Freemason drover for once agreed. Dig into infancy and there would be a human Clarisetta.

He asked about her childhood. What were the stories her mother told her as she fell asleep?

'Oh Mama wasn't one for *stories*,' as we can easily imagine of Peg Furlough: too fat to lean over a child's bed, too proud to invent.

'No stories!' exclaimed Alphonso, wondering for the first time if there might not be different sorts of poverty. His own earliest memories were gory episodes of *la Reconquista*, and saints' martyrdoms: tales to drain off a child's natural bloodlust before he slept.

'I had to tell them to myself.' And she added shyly, almost humanly: 'I made up a whole country.'

'A country!'

'*My* country,' explained Miss Furlough, more characteristically; 'I *owned* it.'

'Tell me!' and she did; which she had certainly never done before, especially not to Mrs Flange; and would not tell again.

When she was small she would sit on the arm of her father's chair, on days when he was playing at being a Peak District mine-lord, trying to catch the puffs of his cigar, and looking over his shoulder as he read, or pretended to read, *The Wapentake of Wirksworth*.

> *Main Rakes, Cross Rakes, Brown-henns, Budles and Soughs,*
> *Break-offs, and Buckers, Randum of the Rake,*
> *Freeing, and Chasing of the Stole to th'Stake,*
> *Starting of oar, Smilting, and driving drifts,*
> *Primgaps, Roof-works, Flat-works, Pipe-works, Shifts ....*

The terms were just as incomprehensible to her as to him, *poseur* and animal as he was. But she, wiser than her father, assumed they might be a spell.

As they were, of course. All unknown words, it strikes me, are a spell. The Word that was in the beginning, before things, leaves the physical cosmos vibrant with words; when we disregard them, treating them as mere thing-labels, they have no power, but any word that astonishes, for instance by being quaint and inexplicable, trembles in our minds. All mumbo-jumbo is effective. Poetry can be very bad only when it is lucid.

It is not like me to think on such lines. Perhaps studying the Furlough Papers is making me cynical; or if not cynical, at least more aware of the diabolic point-of-view. Such knowledge is no doubt, even if a trifle dangerous, useful equipment in this age, when so much blatant evil is abroad, baffling to friars as to most men. Yes, I am growing familiar with little Gladdy Furlough's mind, and, possibly, with larger and more dreadful powers behind her thoughts. To know her is an infernal education.

In any case, little Gladdy Furlough, under the sway of *Cauke, Sparr, Lid-Stones, Twitches, Daulings,* and *Pees*, did indeed concoct for herself, poet-like, a mystical land where money was to be had.

"Gladdy's Wapentake," as she called it, was much like Derbyshire only empty, less wet, oddly pillowy and monochrome, as if its hills were fashioned from her father's cigar-fumes. Her only business in her Wapentake was to pluck chocolate buttons off its smoky *clivies*, or trees (she was greedy, as lonely children generally are), and dig rich grey lead-ore out of its yielding dirt. She'd heap it in her *taker-meer*, which she conceived to be a wheelbarrow that ran weightlessly over the cloudy grooved paths, the *brown-henns*, and was tipped into the *primgap* or store-pit.

'I paid myself two and four for every hundredweight of ore delivered, a half-crown even for no spillages, and on Sundays a bob extra per *taker-meer*. Whenever I shut my eyes I remembered what my total was down to the farthings, and started building it up. I'd made *nearly eighty-four quid* before I stopped.'

Alphonso felt chilled. 'Were there Moors to fight in your grey fairyland?'

'Oh no, I was quite alone.'

'But there were giants to slay? Monsters?'

'There were the regulations of the Excise. Papa always said *they* were monstrous. The rule was I had to wait for the sun to go behind a cloud before I scooped up *wash-oar* and if the sun caught me I lost thruppence in tithes.'

'Were there no saints to pray to?'

'If I felt discouraged I could call upon the Board of Trade. Papa said the President of the Board of Trade had the interests of capital at heart. "Board of Trade, help me!" I would whisper, and then I *always* discovered a new lode at my feet.'

Alphonso wasn't sure the human girl-child had been much better than the inhuman nymph he loved; and although her body was warm beside him, he shivered.

'Yes a *beastly* nippy house, isn't it?' she murmured, lifting his chilled clapped fingers onto her firm ungenerous breast because she liked the rasp; 'I hate it.'

Alphonso was feeling the after-sadness. 'It is a "nippy" *country*,' although what he meant was that the whole planet, outside the delicious region of Andalusia, seemed one single blasted desolation.

''Tisn't, it's spiffing at Cowes in August.' Papa had promised to take her, and she was already arraying dresses and fornications. Then, forming a rare sentence which did not include herself, as object or subject: 'How did you *get* up here?'

So he told her about his own odyssey from Alhama to Rowlsey: about the pilfering, about Isaac's cutting of Helios' throat and how he, Alphonso, had betrayed Isaac. That part amused her mightily. 'Does the garrote crush the neck like *this?*'

'Yes.'

'Tighter?'

'Yes.' He moved her tender warm hand. 'But from the side. It's a sort of clamp.'

'Oh, how I wish I could watch! Don't you?'

'No.'

'No! Of *course* not, you great *donkey*…. But you like to watch *this*.'

His mouth was suddenly dry, but he managed to whisper '*Sí*.' And they proceeded once more to make what is commonly called love.

Presumably the evil and the very good understand each other well, gazing across at each other from their distant mountain-tops. Down in the muddy slough between the mountains the rest of us writhe and flail, making such bizarre appearances as we rear from the bog and fall back that we know nothing of each other, almost nothing. Revelation is only for those whose development is nearly complete.

But let's take this extreme case. Now that nothing is hidden from us of Gladys, what are we, middling like almost everyone else, not yet holy, not quite infernal, to make of her?

The rule of thumb, when a confessor tries to analyse a penitent, is to sort out the most active temptations, categorising them as of the World, of the Flesh and of the Devil. Does this rough method work in Miss Furlough's case? Certainly she had a worldly itch to see herself as mistress of Kettlehinge, a fleshy desire to abuse her liberty with men, and, doubtless, a devilish relish in the extreme wickedness of what she was about.

But after all, most young women, even heiresses, do not *resist* the temptation to hurry on their father's deaths, any more than they *resolve* not to commit cannibalism, or *promise themselves* they won't betray their country even if asked politely. There is a tiny gear or sphincter in the human mind that simply shuts off certain lines of thought before they are formed; which is precisely why we call them "unthinkable."

Gladys Furlough's mind was missing that gadget. All possible human actions were to her as a pack of cards. Which would she play? Would she wear her ruby bracelet even though it clashed with her sapphire ear-rings? Would she kill her father? Would she pretend to be ill and absent herself from dinner? Would she be pleasant to Hester Rawkdon this evening? Would she eat fæces? Would she prostitute herself to that dashing young Russian, Tscherkassoff, who was clearly dying to get at her, in return for having Sir Zebulon throttled one night on a London street, or indeed imprisoned for espionage? (Tscherkassoff had the air of a man who could arrange either outcome; whereas Mrs Flange had entirely failed to find herself a hired assassin; they lie beyond the range of genteel provincials.) Would she burn the house down tonight, or have young Mrs Crewe sing Schubert *lieder*, oh how badly, in the drawing-room, or sell England, or invoke the devil? There were no enormities for Gladys, the business of life passed in an absolute moral flatness, which went with an emotional flatness. She could feel petulance, satisfaction, desire, resentment, boredom, nothing more intense. Her feelings were no more alert than those of a sleeping child.

She might have descended to earth from another planet. There was an inscrutable void at her core, and out of that vacuum emerged impulses nothing in her mental apparatus checked from becoming deeds.

Of course how that void came to be there we cannot know. It must result from a decision made beyond time, in the unmediated silent presence of God, when the undying Power we know as the soul of Gladys Furlough choose how to take mortal form. But there's no great mystery about how the earthly being functioned.

❧

I'm making her sound unique when she was merely a bit ahead of her time. She'd have astonished her Victorian peers, if they'd understood her; nowadays she'd scarcely stand out from the run. Our age is infested with such half-humans or quarter-humans. Our affairs are so disordered that these lightly-burdened aliens dazzle and tyrannise us. Stalin and Hitler: how Gladys would have charmed them! – and by the way, how much easier history is to endure, now those astonishing rivals are friends, intent on charming each other.

Hitler, Göring, Stalin, Pétain, Mussolini: Alphonso would have been disgusted, but not amazed or dismayed. A good knight hunts down monsters and charges them. After all, he sounded Gladys and survived knowing her. Whether Europe is as resilient remains to be seen.

## *vi.*

So is it a mere bedroom scene we are considering, a *cliché*, a scene from low comedy? I can't think so.

When Alphonso Ñezgo y Escalofriante was lured into the *Hotel del Universo*, into Miss Furlough's bedroom, it was for vile obvious purposes, the shopworn purposes of the villainness, I almost want to write *villianette*. And that, to be sure, is melodrama.

To blunder into such a trap *many times* would be farce.

But simply to *repeat* the imperilling act – to go (for love) into a room a second time, knowing it the place appointed for slaughter: surely this attains the rhythm of ritual, the dignity of ritual?

In the face of any aweful rite, there is not much to say. Childish to point out that its elements are preposterous. They usually are. Of course they are. That is what ritual does. It takes trifling *bric-à-brac*, and with such stuff vouchsafes us sublime fear.

## *vii.*

Gladys' bedroom. The two opposites lie together in bed, speaking of this and that, both a little distracted because both are listening: he waiting to be betrayed, she to betray.

Presently up the bleak oaken stair of Kettlehinge comes the sound of doors thrown open, chairs dragged, glass smashed. The ghastly luncheon party is breaking up. Zebulon Furlough's male guests are struggling to be upright; reeling out; free. They have an hour to bathe in cold water, and huddle before poor fires, before he can resume his poisoning and defiling.

Men's voices begin to fan out across the shapeless, creaking, handsome, comfortless house. Then both lovers hear a heavy thread, stumbling a bit from drink, just outside the door. It is Furlough, going to his own room.

The glory of sacrifice is managing not to notice. The garlanded ox ignores the axe. The Host, complete in what It is and not what It does, lies motionless in its gold-plated saucer obliviously waiting to be snapped. The matador swaggers, his back to the bull, as if he's sure to survive, even when he suspects he will not.

Alphonso knows what he *is*, what he is *for*; his only dignity is not to anticipate. But he does not start when Gladys, perfectly on cue, begins to shriek in his arms. He sits up coolly enough as she screams 'Papa! Papa! A man!', and is on his feet when the crooked, black, quarter-of-a-millennium-old door flies back, squeaking as it always does, and the gigantic black form of Furlough breaks in, his enormous head barely clearing the rafters.

# *viii.*

It was the same as before and it was different.

For one thing, Sir Zebulon was being tested under different rules. According to the cool Common Law of England, a father with daughter's or daughter's lover's blood on his hands can only "plead provocation in partial defense." This, if accepted, converts murder to manslaughter. Furlough might escape the gallows, but he would face a long sentence of imprisonment.

"They order this matter better in France." No, not better; otherwise. I have just consulted a handbook of Continental law. (Dreadful what corrupt materials lie about monastic libraries!) In France and other hot European lands where the Napoleonic code runs, including, importantly, Spain, *Le parricide n'est jamais excusable*: Article 323. Yet at once the law backtracks from this bald axiom; Article 324 makes an exception for the *crime passionnel*. "Murder committed upon the wife as well as upon her accomplice, at the moment when the husband shall have caught them in the fact, is excusable." More broadly, he who "in the heat of passion causes the death of a spouse, daughter, or sister upon discovering her in illegitimate carnal relations," or who slaughters her bedmate, is to be dealt with very leniently.

The pivotal term is *el calor de la pasion*. If daddy hesitates, then kills later, in cold blood, he is condemned. But for some minutes immediately after the shock of discovery, there is for the provoked man a recognised period of heat, that is, of proper lunacy, that is, of absolute liberty, when he can be true to himself only by being beside himself: an interval (whatever a moral theologian might say) of grace.

Thus if Furlough had shot straight in the *Hotel del Universo*, during the Excusable Moment when everything is allowed, the Spanish court would no doubt have sent him on his way, with cant from the Bench about *honor, gallardía, valor, y defensa de la virtud femenina*, and subdued applause from the galleries.

This time it was different. English law does not recognise *crimes passionels* because the English do not acknowledge this unchained moment of *heat of passion*, because they doubt whether passion, as talked up by poets and playwrights and Latins, exists at all.

Me, I am agnostic about it, being here not as moral theologian, nor even Englishman, but as a spy on the fury of people, some foreign, long dead. I am an archivist.

*Parricide is never excusable*: a sound principle. But what of Gladys? The following idea occurs to me, and maddens me. She was made without lovingkindness, she was born disgusted. The shock of being merely one among millions was immediate, and never passed away. The existence of others was a provocation to her, which experience did not mitigate. Her life was all furious revulsion: one long Excusable Moment in which every deed was bound to be a crime of passion.

Again: we would never prosecute an ape for slaying its keeper. It is insufficiently human for homicide to *be* parricide. What law covers quarter-humans?

## ix.

This time there was no nonsense about toy guns, indeed no nonsense of any sort at all. Zebulon saw what he had been called in to see, and roared at it. Here was his greatest asset being robbed from him. Common Law of England be blowed! Casual robbery he could never abide. He did not pause to consider his own peril.

There was a handy knife on the shaky Jacobean walnut table in the middle of the room, the knife Alphonso had used to prise open the windows, and with this in his hand Furlough tumbled over the puddle of Alphonso's damp foul clothes and was on him.

Or them. It is interesting to speculate who exactly would have got knifed if Furlough had had his way. Would it have been a matter of *In one another's arms they fell* and *In one another's arms they died,* as Southey's jingle says? Did Zebulon in that moment know and hate his daughter to the adequate pitch? Was he rather intent on a rematch with the anæmic bandy-legged naked creature, very like an ape, whom he presumably recognised from Spain?

It is impossible to know, because Alphonso flung his tiny form straight at Furlough's enormous form, and the two, merged, preposterous, insect-shaped: eight limbs and one flashing knife-blade much like a sting, rolling across the floor away from the bed, away from the alert defenceless female. Tumbling over and over itself went the brawl – over the Turkey rug – clattering back and forth on the uneven Jacobean floorboards (so that that the bachelor in the room below looked up and sighed, and went back to heaving his lunch into his chamber-pot) – bashing against a dainty little plinth, sending a dainty little vase flying. Gladys' dresser went over; a table smashed; while she, remembering to clutch a comforter to herself as a female should in such circumstances, found the whirligig of legs, two black and massive, two bare and skinny, so weird she guffawed outright. She had not meant to do that.

❧

Paul Gavrilovitch Tscherkassoff had got away from the appalling luncheon early, on the perfectly sound excuse of having reports to compose, and had presumably already finished this work –

No. I am feeling confident enough to strike that out, and write what I know, without particular evidence, to be the truth.

Tscherkassoff *had* finished his work, which we might call diplomacy or espionage as we please. Beneath the hubbub of lunch he had arranged with a part-proprietor of the *Liverpool Mercury* for that Radical organ to print reports of Ottoman atrocities (composed and quietly supplied by the Embassy), and to side with the Tsar in case of a European crisis. In return, the Balkan correspondent of the rival *Manchester Guardian* was to have his credentials revoked.

The young baron had written and coded a telegram, explaining this triumph. It would be wired to the Third Section of His Imperial Majesty's Own Chancellery, the secret police, from Ostend, beyond the reach of Disraeli's own damned agents. Meanwhile it had been stowed in the hidden compartment of his travelling trunk, along with sheaves and sheaves of other wonderful paper: compromising photographs and correspondence – not all *billets-doux* – involving a dozen British grandees; promissory notes, a sketch-map of last summer's naval manœuvres off Cyprus done by a bibulous midshipman in a Soho whorehouse, awkward letters of credit, transcripts of naval signals, a delicate *mémorandum d'accord* with the Glasgow Chamber of Commerce. The deal with the *Liverpool Mercury* was only the last of this splendid series of *coups*.… Here Tscherkassoff pulled the rope, summoned a valet through the freezing corridors of Kettlehinge; and with the valet's clumsy aid had changed into evening clothes.… And this was his very last *coup* (he reflected happily, while the serf bungled his waistcoat buttons). In a few weeks he would be quitting London and returning to Russia, to plaudits, to a private audience, probably, with his Imperial Master. What with blackmail, and financial side-arrangements of various sorts, he had largely "stitched up" the Opposition press. And meanwhile back in London Lady Derby, the Foreign Secretary's scheming wife, still nominally a Tory although far gone in Liberal intrigue, still lovely at fifty-five, was regularly opening her husband's despatch boxes to read Cabinet papers, which she then retailed to Count Shuvalov, his Chief, the Russian ambassador. Dear Mary Derby: what vim!

What vim …! He had dismissed the oafish valet, remembering that in England these creatures cannot be struck, however badly they have done their work, and was now lying full-length on his bed, smoking his long black cigarettes, luxuriously day-dreaming.

It goes without saying that Tscherkassoff was a rake and that his daydreams were mostly indecent. Just then he lay reminiscing over his most notorious *affaire*, with that famous Society beauty back in St Petersburg five years before. She had been a *narcissiste*; married, but only to a bureaucratic stick of a man, amusingly prone to forgive; Tscherkassoff had lost interest and the thing had ended in her suicide. It had been the common talk of Nevksy Prospekt, which Tscherkassoff did not mind. But the tale had been serialised in a magazine, which he naturally minded very much. Fictionalised, damn it, by a vile old moraliser too well-connected to horsewhip. That was why Tscherkassoff had had himself posted to the London legation. It was too awkward to be pointed out all the time as the original of "Vronksy", the lover of "Anna" something-or-other – especially as the pious fantasist has Vronksy go off in despair to get himself killed fighting the Turks. Every time Tscherkassoff met a beautiful woman she would gaze at him as if he were on the verge of immolation in the flame; and although that look can be exploited, it generally leads to adultery of the wrong sort, to clinging, stormy reproaches, boredom. Happily, the last installment had appeared in the July issue of *Russkiy Vestnik*. By the time he got back *Anna* would surely be *dépassé*….

(Here Tscherkassoff paused to light a fresh cigarette, laughing lightly at the thought of dying for love.)

Yes: in Petersburg they'd no longer confuse him with that ass "Vronksy" …. Of course *Anna* would come out in book-form. But gentlemen do not read big thick novels. And as for ladies – well, after five years there'd be a new crop of them. Almost too young now to read. Certianly too young to care.

Five years! Not that Tscherkassoff could complain. Englishwomen, behind their pose of snowy indifference, had proved ridiculously apt, ripe fruit tumbling into any lazily outstretched palm. Dreadful to think how long it had taken him to get his way with Anna. Whereas with  the daughter of this freezing appalling house, with the wench Furlough! – he knew that look. Victory was his already ….

Tscherkassoff was a rake, but he was also an adroit servant of the Tsar, a perfectly zealous one. Interspersed with these erotic fancies were political ones: of Russian armies marching into Constantinople. Constantinople! the Second Rome! the Third Troy! Subsumed by Russia, the Third Rome! the Fourth Troy! – the numbering gets elaborate in these imperial fantasies. The Imperial Fleet bursting into the Bosphorus – artillery shattering the walls – the Sublime Porte in flames – Cossacks swarming through a breach – massacring Mussulmen, Jews, Catholics – the Sultan borne off in chains to exile beyond the Volga – then the smoke of the sacked city clearing – a day of sudden high sunshine, an eastern breeze – the Imperial Barge bobbing at anchor in the Golden Horn – hosannas from a purely Orthodox population – the Tsar disembarking – crowned Emperor of the East in Santa Sophia. The Mediterranean a Russian lake! The Hapsburgs submitting! The West atremble! –

When he heard the screech, which he recognised at once as Gladys', he did not start. He rose (the Tsarist artillery dying away in his imagination), stubbed out his final cigarette, paused before the glass to toy with his wonderful macassar'd kiss-curl, and sallied forth without making any fuss. Like Alphonso an hour before, he proceeded to Gladys' quarters without hesitation, drawn by scent. He reached her door just in time to catch her guffaw.

꽃

'Is he dead?' asked Gladys, matter-of-factly, no longer laughing. The brawl had worked its way into a corner, dug itself in, heaved, subsided, stilling itself into a knot of arms and legs. Some of it was breathing heavily, some was not.

Her lover, most ludicrously, bare haunch first, disentangled himself from the knot, clawed his way upright by clutching at door-knobs and upturned dressers, and finally stood swaying, with a black eye and a gash the length of his forearm, gazing down on what was left.

'No,' he said at length. 'Not dead,' and indeed there was some sort of movement going on in the mottled blue-grey face of the great industrialist. Sir Zebulon seemed crushed into the corner of his daughter's bedroom, one knee up, his neck bent sideways at a killing angle, eyes open but white and blank. His right fist grasped the knife-handle with the fixity of *rigor mortis*. But he was trying to speak. What came out was an indescribable noise, halfway between his usual *Rrumpf* and the name *Gladdy*; he may have been trying to say *Wapentake of Wirksworth*. The word, whatever it was, formed a scarlet bubble at his lips; at once a trickle of blood gushed from his nose, another from his left ear, and the whiskery black bull-head lolled forward.

It was remarkable how in that instant the flesh of his hands and face stopped being flesh: they were at once so much wax, faintly dotted with droplets of the death-sweat, perfectly, ideally dead; man-shaped, but quite unconvincing as parts of a human body.

'Well,' said the mistress of Kettlehinge Hall, slipping from the sheets, reaching for her fluffiest, rosiest *déshabillé* from the hooks above her bed, and sliding her gorgeous tiny feet into her slippers of calfskin, dyed sky-blue and stamped with gold, which Papa had made such a fuss about buying her at Félix Pontin's, 'Señor Ñezgo' (Alphonso flushed; he had not been sure she knew his name as a *hombre*), '*he is now.*' She did up the satin belt with a fine flourish of bow, and shook her metallic hair over her neck; she was suddenly happy for almost the first moment in her life; also, as it happens, for the last.

Despite her sophistication, Miss Furlough's great idea had been simple: if she could get into the same room the two men who loved her (in their different ways, both preternatural and unwholesome), they would destroy each other and set her free. This had virtually come to pass. But after all, in physics the collision of bodies does not usually eliminate the bodies; and what is true of physics is true of homicide.

In short, she had a corpse on her hands; indeed she very nearly had two, because so soon as the Member for Derbyshire West, had breathed his last, Alphonso sighed as if in a deep sleep, and collapsed on top of his victim.

Alphonso had held off tuberculosis until he had won his love and saved her life. He had not lunched that day, and could not keep down his breakfast. He had done all he meant to do, and was content to be a physical and moral ruin. Down he fell.

Miss Furlough found that scolding could not revive him; kicking did no good, nor emptying her water-bottle in his face; he lay curled on the floor, defying her disgust and her increasing terror.

It was exasperating to be stayed so close to her goal. Although Sir Zebulon was bruised and torn, his body only had to pass muster with the British constabulary; as long as he was found lying on the floor of his bedroom, they would cheerfully conclude that he had died of apoplexy and knocked himself about in his final fit; and his bedroom and private sitting-room were just two doors along the corridor. But without Alphonso to help carry him, they may as well have been on the other side of Derbyshire. Gladys was a spiritual freak, not a corporeal one. She gave a father's enormous bulk a clumsy shove her little hand; no, it was impossible, meaningless to think of: she could not possibly move him.

She consulted her pretty porcelain carriage-clock. In forty-five minutes Glossop, her father's valet, would be in his room to dress him for dinner. If her father were missing, Glossop, a sleepy creature, who wandered about humming tunelessly, as vacant as a cow, would be troubled; he would, eventually, be startled; he would eventually raise the alarm. Gladys daren't think what would happen then.

Well, if she couldn't get Papa to his room, there was nothing for it but to push him out her door into the corridor. He could be found there; with luck it would be thought he fell there and died all in a rush, while no one was walking past. She could roll him onto her Turkey rug and slowly drag him out on that....

Was there anybody about, though? For a dreadful moment Gladys pressed her ear to the door, while Baron Tscherkassoff, smiling, always smiling, leaned his ear to the other side. I mean it was dreadful for you and me (if you, the reader, exist), since we are in the panopticon, and have to regard these passing moment burdened with the modified omniscience of archive-readers. We have to see these two rogues, symmetrically, with an inch of wood between them.

What noxious clowns men are is. – What a ghastly place the world must be for the angelic intelligences!

Satanic grins are silent. Gladys heard nothing. Very cautiously she dared take the knob in hand, noticing with disgust paternal blood smeared over her exquisite knuckles (admiring, though, the shade of red). Very very slowly she opened the door, peering the while over her shoulder to make sure Alphonso and her father were out of sight. When she turned to look out she found she was staring, not into the corridor, but into an immaculate shirt-front – and glancing sharply up found she was staring into Tscherkossof's silent careless laughter.

He had taken in her smashed-up bedroom with a glance, and found the situation very funny. Oh he was a gay young thing, that Baron.

'You are not altogether deft at this, Miss Furlough,' he whispered suavely in his too-good English, green volpine eyes alight, bending down almost as if to kiss the left side of her neck just under the jaw (where hangmen rest their knots). 'I do not think you can have done it before,' to which the only rational answer was *How many fathers do you think I have to kill?* Even Gladys couldn't quite say this; she took Baron Tscherkassoff by the lapels and pulled him furiously into the room, shutting the door behind them with a kick.

## X.

All peaceful families are alike, each patricidal family is patricidal in its own way. All was confusion in the house of the Furloughs: a madcap spirit was tainting Gladys' crime, just as a splendid wine's blood-spice-soil perfume will be overwhelmed by wet-dog-and-mouldy-newspaper if corked.

Where was proper tragic depth? Where was grave lamentation? Where, even, was the bad majesty of hell, gloating over such a rarely hellish act? Where? Chased off-stage, that's where, by a succession of bumptious zanies.

Tscherkassoff had stood outside the door long enough to hear Gladys haranguing her feeble lover; he had heard enough to deduce the sequence of her crime. So when he was pulled into her pandemonium of a boudoir to confront his host, dead and gory, clutching a knife, beside a scrawny naked muculent peasant, obviously in the last stages of pulmonary disease, what could he do but fold his arms and chortle?

When not intent on resurrecting Byzantium, or extirpating the Latin Church, Paul Tscherkassoff was an easy-going young fellow. He was a favourite both in the *corps diplomatique* attached to the Court of St James, and in the gin-dens of Soho. He was strangely likeable. Lady Derby, who after fifty-five years at the heart of English politics had every opportunity to be jaded, was charmed by Tscherkassoff, perfectly charmed, charmed to the point of committing treason. As for the various newspaper editors he had corrupted: they too were men not easily bounced. Yet this Russian youth, with his Mayfair tailoring and Whitechapel slang, was somehow irresistible.

The secret of Tscherkassoff's appeal was indifference. Nothing outside the Autocracy of All the Russias seemed real to him. What was the world beyond the frontiers of the Tsar's domains? Merely a rugby-pitch where he rolled foreign ministers, editors, police-detectives and other spies into the mud. He was so indifferent to Abroad he could be tolerant of everything that was done there. Who inhabited these peripheral realms? Schismatics and decadents, Liberals, rebels, worldings, Jacobins, deviants, heretics, weaklings doomed in the end to fall before the Orthodox imperium. Nothing could damn them more than they were already damned, or render them more fantastic. So why not?

Back in Holy Russia the young Baron would certainly have deplored parent-slaughter. Indeed he might have made a nationalist-monarchist speech about heinous blood, and the spoilage of blessèd soil. But in England he was prepared to regard it as a capital wheeze, a do.

'Well you've done for your old governor good and proper. What a spill! What a corking pelt! *Bravissima.* May I smoke?'

'No, sir,' said Gladys, dazed, and for once quite off her guard, 'you may not. Not in here if you please.' It sounded, especially to her, like someone else speaking. 'I can't stand the smell.'

'The smell – ah!' declared the Baron, chucking his unlit cigarette into the general wreckage of the room and flaring his nostrils like a novelette villain, or, more troublingly, like a connoisseur of evil who can savour stinking of depravity even through a general reek of blood. 'The *smell*,' he murmured, sweeping her into the crook of his arm. And aggressively as he could, he kissed her.

What amazed Gladys as she wriggled in his arms was this: there seemed to a sort of moral coherence to the world she'd never before creditted. Work your finger through the caul of propriety that surrounds us and the most divers criminality bursts through the hole. Not just bubbles, but black vampire bats. Kill your dad and horrible foreigners are allowed to paw you. The two seemed connected.

She fought her way free just as Alphonso managed a feeble swipe at Tscherkassoff's calf.

The Baron kicked his arm aside, then ground his heel into his palm for good measure. Alphonso whimpered. 'Get some clothes on you beastly serf. And staunch your unclean dribble with *this*,' kicking toward him a lace table-cloth that lay beside a shattered occasional table. 'Very well, *Miss Furlough.* Let's heave the guts into its own bed. *Then* we can disport.'

With this masterful Russian to help, it proved perfectly simple. Gladys put her head round the door. Leighton, dimmest of all the footmen, was going past with a tray of whisky and a syphon. He started theatrically at seeing her; bowed so clumsily the soda was almost lost; straightened it; backed away, clinking; was gone. Alphonso had dressed himself (pocketing the drawing by Sem, for a thief by vocation can thieve even when he can barely stand). She gesticulated to the men and led the two men quickly tip-toe down the dim over-furnished passage to her father's room.

There was no possibility of silence: the floorboards were so decrepit even her own small feet made the vases tinkle on the consoles as she went along. But then the whole house was groaning and squeaking, as it always was in the evening, settling down for the night. There were no shocks, no one else came; they got him straight through the door of his rooms, through his sitting-room into his bedroom, onto his bed, which was of course a massive carved baronial monster-piece. They heaved him onto the bed, so vigorously he rolled right across and thudded heavily to the floor; so they had to pull him up and drop him back across the counterpane.

The three criminals stood about, regarding their victim.

Of course the knife …. Baron Tscherkossof worked it out of the dead grasp. There. Hm…. He was certainly battered; but surely no more than natural death might produce? If, for instance – ?

In any case, dark had fallen; it was time for Alphonso to disappear; in half an hour Glossop would come and find his master dead of an apoplexy…. But at that instant the second zany made her appearance. It was Miss Rawkdon, thumping on the door with both fists, crying 'Sir Zebulon! Sir Zebulon!'

Gladys and Alphonso, stricken, stared at each other mutely. The slightest thread of affiliation stretched between them.

Paul Tscherkossof, however, was a professional of diplomacy, as at seduction and espionage, apt to improvise. Putting on Zebulon Furlough's gruff voice, he said: '*Rrumpf?*' (Gladys and Alphonso were winded by such presence of mind.)

'Oh Sir Zebulon, the most appalling thing,' wailed the Rawdon, 'there's a stranger in the Hall! An intruder! One of the scullery-maids found a window forced in the laundry! And the most loathsome bloodied clothes left in a sink! Sir Zebulon, Sir Zebulon, will you not come out?'

'*Rrumpf-rrumpf,*' growled the Baron in Papa's voice (so plausibly that Gladys glanced at the cadaver, as if to ensure it wasn't shamming).

'Zoffany has sent search-parties about the house!' Zoffany being the guzzling butler. 'And called out the farmhands to patrol the grounds! And sent to Rowsley for the constables! Oh Sir Zebulon!' Poor woman: her universe, with its Deity and His comforting favouritism exploded, seemed nothing but a vast factory for producing injury to Hester Rawkdon. 'It's Fenians, I'm sure it's Fenians. These papists stop at nothing. We'll have our throats cut in our beds!'

'*Rrumpf!*' exclaimed the pseudo-Sir Zebulon, sceptically.

'We'll be raped!'

At which he exclaimed '*Rrumpf!-rrumpf!*' with such sardonic vehemence Miss Rawkdon, was heard to sniff, offended, and to withdraw, rustling down the corridor.

Sleek as a black leopard in his tail-coat, Tscherkassoff stepped over to the curtains, parting them slightly with Alphonso's long knife, looking out into the gardens; where sure enough, yokels were going about with lanterns, exclaiming stupidly to each other and poking at the shrubs. He came back to the door and opened it a crack: an officious footman (it was Leighton) was padding along the corridor, armed with a blackthorn stick.

Tscherkassoff clicked the door shut, sighed; then grinned, because he liked danger. 'So. We're under siege.' Alphonso and Gladys were standing quite close to each other, two waifs. Just a little more trouble and they might cling. '*Señor Ñezgo*' – naming him with ironic emphasis, almost bowing – 'will not easily be able to get away.' He picked up the heavy bronze flowerpot from Sir Zebulon's bedside table and turned it about in his strong left hand, pensively, as if studying its hothouse delphinium.

'But Papa –', began Gladys, perhaps following slowly, perhaps only pretending to.

'Yes. If there is an unnatural bloody presence in the house, Miss Furlough,' said the Russian smoothly, 'it follows your father cannot have died a natural death.' He seemed to be examining the delphinium's sex organs.

'Then is – *oh!*'

For Tscherkassoff, with a causal upward backhand, had felled Alphonso. The flowerpot took the poor tattered fellow on the temple; he flew over the back of an armchair, audibly cracking his jaw against the window-sill, and came to rest against the wainscoting (perhaps, for an instant, envying José his easy death).

That was done casually with the Baron's left hand. With the right he raised the knife and, remarking 'You don't really *mind*, do you?', pounded it into her father's chest.

The room's stillness was dreadful, thought Gladys, but less dreadful than how it *looked*. It was swifter than a scene-change at the theatre. It had gone from sickroom, with a man lying naturally succumbed on his deathbed, to an abattoir, furnished with murderee and unescaping murderer. Even quick-witted Gladys was bewildered.

Tscherkassoff had grabbed her by the wrist and pulled her back to the door, which he had opened again, less than an inch. Through the crack he could see, and Gladys could see over his shoulder, the dimwitted Leighton patrolling the corridor, slowly, slowly, with his back to them. Her left hand stretched out, beseeching her dead father, perhaps, or Alphonso – who despite everything had his eyes open, watching without being able to speak or move.

'Stop wriggling, Miss Furlough,' murmured the Baron. 'Be still. One minute and that crippled serf will be round the corner. And as soon as the "coast is clear"' (he relished slang, as foreign aristocrats always do), 'you're going to come back to my room. I'm going to have you before dinner. For the first time. Do you understand? Never in all my travels have I met a young woman so utterly abandoned. I'm about to be recalled to Russia and you're coming with me. My memento of a happy mission. – Do be still.'

'*Let me go*,' hissed Gladys under her breath, still pulling away from him, her left arm still wildly fluttering over the bed.

'Not for years, my own little one. Not for years. You have no choice. I've freed you from your crime. Defy me and I expose you. You're my creature.'

'*Beast*,' she hissed, stretching away from his hold.

'I am to be rewarded for my – ' he hesitated only for a moment; it was a measure of his power over her that he did not to have to keep things back – '*spying*. On your preposterous country. With the Governate of Perm. Perm, Miss Furlough, Perm! There are no words in this dull language for its glories. The Urals form its gleaming spine, for it lies, understand, both in Asia and Europe. With all the charms of Europe, every exquisite Asiatic cruelty. From its Ural passes you can look behind and before over expanses of perfect snow, each wider than Yorkshire.' He glanced through the door; a moment more and Leighton would surely be gone. 'No foreign army, almost no foreigner, has touched that region since the last retreating Mongol was knifed. You, as my English kept woman, will seem far more exotic than any French courtesan. Almost a supernatural being. Not the most learned archpriest in all Perm has ever met an Englishwoman before. Hah!' He glanced out again; the shambling Leighton had paused; would he never be gone? 'How my Governate will astonish you. It boasts seventy-eight monasteries, vying with each other in the miraculous power of their smoke-black icons, the severity of their discipline. The great Tobol waters it in the months when water flows. When we reside at my great *dacha*, two days' journey from the nearest road, you will see delegations of headmen in embroidered cloaks, trembling because they must come and return through forests haunted by wolf-packs. They stand for hours in the falling snow beneath my wooden terrace, waiting for me to deign to hear their petitions. Each holds tribute of amber: a lump big as your charming wicked little breast,' which he insolently caressed. Leighton, damn him, had sunk into one of the antique wooden chairs in the corridor and seemed to be on the verge of a nap. Tscherkassoff's voice grew more annoyed and strident. 'Only a few years of Perm lie before me. There will come a day when the Tsar, new-crowned amidst the ashes of Constantinople, will summon me, and I will go south.'

"I" not "we", noted Alphonso, whose imagination had grown stronger from travel and from suffering. He had no difficulty picturing the now-redundant Gladys wriggling in a canvas shroud, carried across the frozen Tobol by Cossacks, dropped though a neatly-chopped hole. *¡Sí, mi amor, sí!*

'His Majesty will give me, I think, the rule of some delicious Ægean province ....' He glanced out once more: thank God, Leighton had shaken himself, stood, was about to vanish. 'Meanwhile my dear, you and I, heaped with wolf-hides, will go about my Governate in my massive sled with polished gilded blades, four Cossacks standing behind, more riding beside, you in your mantle, silver fox to match your hair (you cannot imagine such glorious furs), me in my robes of terrible power.' Yes, Leighton and his cudgel were gone. The corridor was empty. Ten seconds more. 'In each village you shall prompt me, Miss Furlough, what to inflict: on some the *knout*, on some exile to Siberia, on the most fortunate the gallows. In springtime – oomph.'

He was peering down, amazed, at his white waistcoat.

'*Oomph.*' From between the mother-of-pearl buttons a tip extruded, scarlet, amazingly scarlet against the unspotted cloth, as if an imp had stuck its tongue out of snow-bank.

Very slowly, as in certain dreams where normal motion is forbidden, the Baron let go of Gladys' wrist and spun delicately about until he was facing her.

'You don't really *mind*, do you?' she asked sweetly. She had got the fingers of the left hand round the the knife in her father's chest, worked it out, run it through the Baron from behind. 'Or,' with her head on a pretty angle, '*do* you?'

He did not reply. His mind was elsewhere. Let us charitably assume it was fixed on the tenets of his despotic faith. Was he not dying for his Emperor? for the Tsar of Kazan, Astrakhan, and the Tauric Chersonesus? for the Grand Prince of Smolensk, Sovereign of the Kabardian Lands, Hereditary Possessor of the Circassian Mountain Princes, *etcetera*? Yes! With that consolation to steady him he kept turning about, a full turn, almost balletic, at the same time spiralling down, until he ended as a motionless heap at Gladys' feet.

Sprawled against the wainscoting, Alphonso watched his rival's fall with eyes that looked wider than his whole shrunken face. It's a queer business witnessing the murder of the man who has murdered you. Even Spanish revenge is rarely so thorough. Alphonso saw and rejoiced, but did not move. His face was on fire from his cracked jaw, his gashed arm was hæmorrhaging again. He been reduced to little more than a puddle of sinew and torn skin, although of course like any martyr he felt himself ascending with each drop of disintegration. Glory, glory!

Still: this prick-of-an-*azufaifo*-bush business was becoming serious.

⁊

Why, by the way did, Gladys do it?

She was just as safe from the law with the Baron as without. Alphonso could have been just as thoroughly hanged for one killing as two. Would not Gladys have relished being reigning concubine of the tyrant of Perm? If it comes to that, was not Paul's Governate of Perm very like the secret Wapentake she had always craved?

Perhaps she genuinely liked living in England and didn't care for the sound of central Russia. (Certainly Alphonso didn't. That description of ice-rivers had introduced, he told O'Shaughnessy, new agony into his tormented mind.) I hope that was true. Such preferences make Miss Furlough seem almost human.

⁊

She looked about the room thoughtfully. Yes, it did perfectly well as the scene of a double murder. All was well with it – oh, except that a gout of Russian blood was splashed over her sky-blue slipper.

Quite deliberately she looked about for something to wipe it on; noticed Alphonso's rough linen shirt; smiled; stepped over to him. Towering over him in rosy *déshabillé* and pale rumpled hair she looked, he thought, more than ever like a tiny metal goddess, a polished idol, a lead heiress. She rubbed her lovely small foot on his shirt; made sure her slipper was quite clean; then – they understood each other perfectly – held it to his lips and *let him kiss it*.

Which he did (leaving a faint lip-shaped smudge on her mineral perfection; she let it be, either not noticing or not minding). His head swam, not just with sickness and exhaustion, but with vertigo. He had just, it seemed to him, touched an extremity of love for which there is no word.

Meanwhile Gladys had snapped off a sprig of delphinium, put it behind her ear, and slipped away.

Without incident she reached her room, which she spent the next few minutes putting to rights. She didn't want her maid too suggestively shocked. The smashed furniture and china went into wardrobes; she would see to it all tomorrow ....

Now what? It would be another quarter-hour before dear Papa's valet, Glossop, would enter his chamber, discover the carnage, begin the foolish screaming. By then her maid would be here, getting her dressed in her new maroon, gossiping about the mysterious intruder. So the great question remained: sapphire and pearls, or not? *Do* these earrings go well with this choker?

# Part Six
## *January and February 1878*

Sir Jocelyn Orgreave, Bart.;
Mr Athelstan Harbottle, J.P.;
The Rev'd Mr Arthur Culpepper as Vicar
of Sewerby in the North Riding;
Baron Pavel Gavrilovitch Tscherkassof

## *i.*

'Wilful murder' murmured a coroner's jury a few days later, a little hushed at sitting in judgement on the outlandishness corpse of a Russian baron. 'Wilful murder' said another jury later that day, more forthrightly, since Zeb Furlough was local and, when all was said done, common as muck.

On the morrow Alphonso Ñezgo y Escalofriante was hailed before the magistrates at Bakewell.

A sweet-tempered whiskery half-stammering Inspector laid out the prosecution case. Prisoner was a common vagabond from a dirty Southern nation who had sailed to England looking for easy pickings. As had the mighty Armada of old, with as little success! (Subdued murmurs of applause at this sally.) Prisoner had come to Kettlehinge Hall hearing that Sir Zebulon entertained lavishly over Christmas. 'Over Chr-chr-christmas, y-your Worship!' repeated the Inspector, clearly thinking this an exacerbating circumstance. Prisoner's design was to rifle rooms while everyone was at dinner, but arriving too early had surprised Sir Zebulon himself; who had fought, doubtless, with the courage and pluck of any English gentleman (subdued growls of approval), and whose cries had summoned one of his guests, this, um, foreigner, Baron T-T-T, mumble-mumble. In the general *mêlée* both Sir Zebulon and Baron, um um, the Baron had received fatal wounds from Prisoner who had however, ahem, ahem, been so knocked about that he could not escape and was seized by two domestics, Zoffany and Leighton whose evidence we have heard. The Inspector concluded by suggesting that Prisoner was, like so many foreigners, sickly in mind as in body (subdued murmurs of 'Quite so, quite so'), weighed down by the gloom of Inquisition and superstition to the point of being mad – a little bit mad that is to say, not enough to spare him condign punishment.

Alphonso's face glowed like the face of the cherubim face as he listened to this balderdash, although he could barely stand, knocked about and diseased as he was. He did not wish to interrupt the learned constable's harangue, which was largely incomprehensible to him even when he understand all the words. 'I am guilty not of murduh, but of love!' he cried as soon as he thought to polite, offering these words not as a rhetorical flourish but as the flat truth. His devotion to Clarisetta was a tremendous human fact, worthy of all men's attention. What in comparison were the death of worthless Sir Zebulon Furlough and of a Russian spy? They were what military men call collateral damage. He needed to unfold this to the court. 'Love!'

The magistrate (not much caring for that word from the dock; in his experience it was always a prelude to coarse effusions) cut him off, and committed him to the Manchester Assizes due on 12ᵗʰ March. The half-dead little prisoner was bustled off to the prison-van.

❧

The wholly-dead had already been seen to. Baron Tscherkassoff's coffin had been sent off by rail to London, and taken to the Russian Embassy Chapel in Welbeck Street, where the Ambassador mourned him in perfect sincerity.

*Damnation!* mused Count Shuvalov amidst the sacred fumes. They were only an hour into the funeral liturgy; the clergy were booming forth the *troparion* of the departed and would shortly come to the *kontakion*; his hand-candle was steady in his hand but its flame danced in the dim air, its wax blotching –

Stop: how do I know all this? Here's a clipping assiduous O'Shaughnessy retrieved from the files of the *Morning Post*, headed OBSEQUIES FOR MURDERED RUSSIAN DIPLOMATIST. It contains some facts. But how do I know wax dripped on Shuvalov's kid glove? The thing is, I do. I have immersed myself in the Furlough Papers, and not only know (I believe) what was happening in the events they describe; I know what happened outside their scope, because of those events. I am no novelist, I invent nothing; I am a moral mathematician. I have seen brother Dominic practise statecraft, maladroitly to be sure; but I accept the principle that in human affairs we can trace what must follow from what must have preceded, what is certain. Thus I am sure Baron Tscherkassoff's chief stood watching the coffin, I am convinced hs eyes, subdued to the dark, made out all the motionless congregation, black-silked, waistcoated, veiled; that he could feel the eyes of a hundred icons, glowing very dimly gold through the smoky gloom, as if watching him from some burning paradise. And that he said to himself, *Damnation!*

*For this individual disaster* (he brooded) *might be just enough to tip history the wrong way as it slithers down the unending slope. How often, how cruelly we are foiled! Without this rare boy to intrigue with Englishmen, especially Englishwomen, war with the British becomes more likely should our Muscovite legions be allowed to march on the Bosphorus, to break through to the Middle Sea.* 'What earthly sweetness remains unmixed with grief?' boomed a huge bearded hieromonk, 'what glory stands immutable on the earth?' *And without his papers, which had disappeared the night of his murder, it is all too likely our Imperial damned Government will flinch. Free!* (Back and forth in the deacon's hand swung the censer, fitted with its dozen tiny sweet bells. *Clink! ... Clink! ... Clink!* Paul Tscherkassoff, in his white summer uniform, much-medalled, lying under a mountain of greenhouse roses, looked like a militant seraph. His face, bleared by fragrant blue smoke, was waxy, a thousand leagues off, at rest, worldly troubles drained by his death-wound.) *Free! The wretched kingdoms of Latin Europe, the gorgeous Levant, India itself, still free of us! The fiendish minions of Disraeli, having perhaps assassinated Tscherkassoff, stole his papers and wasted his life-work.*

In fact this was a slur on the British Government. The half-witted illiterate footman named Leighton, rifling the dead Baron's trunk in the hope of loose coins, had accidentally broken into its hidden compartment and, dumb and mouthing with terror, had emptied its papers into the bedroom fire to cover his tracks.

But *Damnation!* mused Shuvalov. *The Sultan will survive this war, I feel it in my diplomatic bones. Paul Gavrilovitch is taken from us, the cavalry of Holy Russia will not be watered this spring on the shores of Lake Geneva or the Orontes. As they will one day be watered at the Avon and Lough Neagh, as the old prophecy says. How long, O Lord, how long?*

*Clink!* went the implacable swaying thurible, *Clink!*

❧

Meanwhile Sir Zebulon had been disposed of with all proper High Victorian macabre trumpery. He was borne in a glass-sided hearse, a gaudy iceberg of hothouse flowers, swaying behind blind-fold horses festooned with sooty flumes. In the mourning-coach that followed Gladys was so moved her exquisitely black-gloved hand found itself convulsively squeezing the black-trousered knee of Mr Harbottle. Behind her veil Miss Rawkdon scowled at this lightness.

But that was the trouble. There *was* lightness abroad. A subdued quiver ran through and through the obsequy (as everyone called the affair) and turned it into a farce, an insult to man and to God, even to death. Everyone was impatient to get through the burying and on to 12th March, the date set for Alphonso's trial. For despite the discretion of coroner and magistrate, all sorts of rumours were going about.

The frost had tightened its hold on the Peak District. It took four men with pick-axes to open the Furlough family vault, where Sir Zebulon would lie forever beside fat forgotten Peg.

From above it must have looked rather wonderful: the churchyard blasted white, broken here and there with dark circles of yew and dark oblongs of gravestones; in its midst the blacker-than-black rectangular void, with the vulgarly-shiny coffin swaying its way down, lower and lower. At the head of the grave, the parson in white surplice and black tippet, reciting in a fruity quavering voice; about the grave a penumbra of black silk, the women in rustling dresses and streaming veils, the men in black top-hats reluctantly doffed to reveal pale circles of baldness. The cloudy white breath of all the mourners mingling usward in the sharp clear air.

Wonderful to look at. Less wonderful to listen to, perhaps. Sight predominates over hearing in the human brain; when faces are hidden people are particularly inclined to underestimate the sharpness of ears. I notice this all the time at Mass. It's when they cover their eyes with their hands that the whispering begins.

*Man*, the parson recited, *man that is born of a woman hath but a short time to live, and is full of misery*: but there would have been a murmurous undercurrent. *He cometh up, and is cut down, like a flower; he fleeth as it were a shadow, and never continueth in one stay.* 'What was that Spanish boy doing in Kettlehinge, precisely, do you think?' *Thou knowest, Lord, the secrets of our hearts.* 'If it comes to that, what was the Ruskie up to in the family wing, eh?' *Change our vile body, that it may be like unto His glorious body.* 'It'll all come at the Assizes.' 'Will you be there?' 'I'd rather die than miss it!'

*Perfect consummation and bliss* – that's the treacherous beauty of the book the Anglicans use: the listener's too ravished to ask "What does this *mean*, precisely? Are we praying for the salvation of Miss Furlough's victims or not?"

Let me, then: *Requiem æternam dona ei, Domine, et lux perpetua luceat ei.*

'Dirty dog.' 'Quite; but did he leave her everything?' 'Oh yes I think so.' 'Twenty-eight thou? Thirty?' 'Less, less.' *After they are delivered from the burden of the flesh, joy and felicity.* 'She certainly has the *look* about her, don't you think?' 'Always did.' *Until the general resurrection in the last day.* 'Until 12th March!' 'Oh heavens, I can hardly wait.'

## *ii.*

So Derbyshire and Lancashire prepared themselves luxuriously for a great moist wondrous scandal, fly-blown by journalists, sticky with euphemism.

(As a boy I used to pore over divorce proceedings; there were unclean thrills to be had in the very delicacy of the delicate terms, compulsory in those days: "intimacy ensued", "*in flagrante delicto*", "state of nature." Perhaps there's something to be said, after all, for the modern custom of printing unprintable words.)

And Derbyshire and Lancashire, or at least the newspaper-self-poisoning population of those counties, was going to be disappointed if Gladys had way. She proposed to manage the trial as cleverly as she had managed the Andalusian press.

For form's sake she retained an expensive solicitor, who made a fuss of taking depositions of fact from Miss Rawkdon, from Glossop who found the bodies, and from herself, passing them on to the even grander Queen's Counsel who was to prosecute, and of course to Alphonso's rather down-at-heel barrister. And so here they are all are in the blessèd sugar-sack. However, Gladys did not mean any of this evidence to be heard in public court. What though the Crown was bent on persecuting *Regina v Ñezgo* (how *killingly funny* that looked, Gladys thought, whenever she came across it in it her solicitors' dry papers), what though? Fancy Queen Victoria longing to batten upon poor little Alphonso with all this damning evidence! Well, Miss Furlough, wee pale slip of a thing, was going to disappoint Her Majesty.

Indeed for once prosecution by *Regina* was probably more than a fiction. I understand the Widow at Windsor followed sensational court-cases rather closely – especially when they were driven by illicit passion. The Queen-Empress' grief, although it pretended to be fixed in its first spasms, had long since curdled. It had oozed out of her, it had dyed her kingdom a watery black. My nostagia for her reign isn't uncritical. I well remember from my boyhood how England's natural jolliness was subdued to this perpetual delicious harping on death, to morbid sentiments, to lush Romanticism in a very minor key. The Ñezgo trial promised hackneyed lessons about the requital of unfaithful love. It would just the thing. The Victorians, up to Victoria herself, anticipated it with pleasure. And this girl would manage to thwart them all.

✿

She also managed a yet more pressing matter: her immediate marriage. Now she was sole mistress of Kettlehinge her first choice of husband (since husband there had to be) was naturally Sir Jocelyn. But it was no good thinking of that, not with Jokey off in South Africa, too far away to speed to her side.

Athelstan Harbottle, then? He was close at hand. But alas, when she made it clear that she was willing to be wed, if wed she might be at once – her argument being that she was now a lone orphan, and could not face the torment of giving evidence without a husband by her side – he demurred. Indeed he was shocked at the indecency of taking young Gladdy to wife with her father, his old friend (as he was now calling him), not hardly cold in his grave. He was stiff with her, and Gladys could barely keep her temper as she sent him away.

So it had to be the vain young parson! Who was, thank God, not the sort of person to be troubled by foolish scruples.

And indeed young Culpepper made no fuss when Gladys' forthright telegram arrived. He obtained the necessary special license from the Archbishop, hurried through the sleet and ooze of an English winter, and just after breakfast on the second of February, Feast of the Purification, was joined in the parish church of Youlgrave with his life's partner and with twenty-two thousand pounds *per annum*. The wedding was an extremely quiet affair, as was fitting, with Gladys in black (black was more striking with her silver hair than any bridal white). Mrs Flange and Crobie stood witnesses. There were no other guests, particularly not Hester. The Companion had expressed her disapproval in a fashion which brought the two young women's purported friendship to an abrupt close.

'You will be gone, Miss Rawkdon, when we return from Llandudno,' which was where the happy couple were going for a brief honeymoon before returning for Alphonso's trial: with those words Gladys tugged her black veil over her pale lovely face and got into the carriage, brushing aside Crobie and her husband, both trying to help.

Northerners are a superstitious lot. We have little choice with such weather forever wuthering about our doors, howling of death and judgement. Even before Sir Zebulon was buried the cry went up that Kettlehinge was cursed (a great deal was made by local journalists of the story of the ghostly family boiled in the basement) and should be knocked down, or at least thoroughly modernised.

These rumours went so far that Sir Jocelyn Orgreave, hearing them in the distant Cape, decided he ought to come home and make representations against the destruction of his ancestral hall. At least that was his excuse. *Rindepest* had almost finished exterminating his herd and he was content to let his steward watch the last beast sway on its feet, tumble over, and entertain a horde of Cape vultures (*Kransaasvoëls*) before it was quite dead. Besides, in his dim way Jokey planned to arrive unannounced, surprise Miss Furlough and press his suit, gals being most vulnerable in a sad case don't you know? He made good time and alighted at Great Rowsley station on the very afternoon of the wretched wedding.

When he arrived at Kettlehinge and heard from Miss Rawkdon that Gladys was lost to him, his face fell. Which was as nothing compared to what Mrs Culpepper's face did in that evening, when Hester's mocking wire arrived at Llandudno. No devil in hell ever looked more outraged and frustrated, and when at dusk Arthur Culpepper tried to lay amorous hands on her, she struck at him with the first thing that came to hand, which unhappily was a vase, brittle ware as is common in hotels. Shattering, it gouged her lord's cheek; and Arthur, who could not bare damage to his face (his one excellence in this world) stalked out, affronted, strode to the station, and took the next train to London.

Fortunately for Gladys, that afternoon the marriage had already been consummated, the modern House of Culpepper officially founded, Arthur Culpepper properly trapped.

Nevertheless, it was humiliating, a few days later, to return to Kettlehinge from her honeymoon without a husband. When Mrs Culpepper emerged alone from her carriage –

Nauseating! Yes, nauseating! It nauseates me to record tittle-tattle of this sort. Everything to do with these loathsome moneyed people repels me, I am concerned only with Alphonso. Nonetheless, I have to record what these wretches did to explain what happened at his trial.

When Mrs Culpepper emerged alone from her carriage even the sympathetic Flange, standing in the portico, looking bilious from her Brighton adventure, was moved to shake her head. She had bad news. Miss Rawkdon was gone, of course; gone *with Sir Jocleyn* – which produced another kicking-over of rusty armour in the Long Gallery.

Jokey's chivalrous heart had been moved by Hester's plight: flung out by the tares of Edom, as she put it to him, to eat the bread of wretchedness. 'I say, I mean if you're really penniless, that is ….' That is what Mrs Flange had heard, eaves-dropping on them in the breakfast-room. The dismissed Companion had apparently taken her glasses off to dab her eyes, and without her glasses – well, it's an old story. After all, Hester Rawkdon was at least of good family, indeed a distant sort of cousin of the young baronet; if the two ruined gentlefolk must starve, they might as well starve together. Jokey's clumsy courtship began and ended at breakfast; they were married by Mr Ascalon, the Congregationalist minister; and left at once for the crumbling farmhouse where dwelt Hester's father, with the other remaining Rawkdsons, awaiting extinction.

It's an awful little place. It took the telegraph boy an age to find it, a few days later, with a wire from Sir Jocelyn's steward in the Cape announcing that, while burying the last of the cattle, his *kaffirs* had struck a vein of kimberlite; or in other words that he owned a diamond mine.

Petty affairs, these: diamond mines, cold-hearted gentry marriages, titillation of the Sovereign, Anglo-Russian wars. Mere grist for *contemptus mundi*. The world circles around one arena: the epicentre of creation: Manchester Crown Court, where Alphonso, the world-hero, perfect *exemplum* of devotion and courage, will stand up in the dock at ten on the 12th of March and make his toast, his *brindis*, dedicating life and death to the one belovèd.

# Part Seven
## *12<sup>th</sup> March 1878,*
## *and afterward*

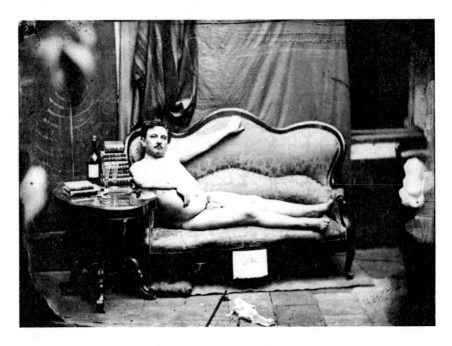

M. Roland-Adolphe Vidange,
sometime Honorary Consul in Brighton
of the Third French Republic

## *i.*

When Alphonso was informed, as he soon was – prisons being webs of news, lies, information, rumour; there is nothing else to do inside them except despair or repent or die – when he learned that Miss Furlough had got married, he laughed.

The thing was wonderfully absurd. It was like the news that a rainbow had purported to marry a small tree. Was not he, Alphonso Ñezgo, her property, the beauteous Donna's sole eternal property? He was! And she was his, his utterly, his altogether; his not just because their union had been made physically complete, but because it was ordained; his because it was built into the fabric of this sorry universe; his because it was intended from the foundation of the world, decreed before the sun first rose on this vacuity.

The absoluteness of his love meant he could not be shaken. Of course he knew that his all-precious one was also all-worthless. But her falseness made no difference to his adoration or possession. Her weakness, or wickedness if you like, was void. It was *impossible* for her to marry this Protestant minister called – *what* was the ridiculous name? Culpepper, yes. It was simply a mistake, blatant as a blunder in arithmetic which when pointed out gets wiped and forgotten.

He would explain as much to the court, were he convicted; then beg the judge for the unspeakable mercy of kissing – no, merely embracing; no, merely taking the hand – of his altogether-desired wife. (Like almost every Latin, Alphonso was rhetorical in the face of death.) Then they could hang him and he would skip off into eternity, where she would be all the more his; content, jocund, grateful to their Lordships beyond any words a simple peasant youth could offer them.

Such was his intention. That was the speech he meant to give, or so he told Fr O'Shaughanssey.

That, also, is what he told Mr Ascalon, the Congregationalist minister, sent to his cell with a clutch of pamphlets from the Protestant Truth Society.

This Ascalon was a shady fellow, a former creature of Sir Zebulon, who had found it useful on occasion to appeal to the Evangelical conscience of the North, for instance when persecuting his Irish labourers, papists who would after all only squander their wages on drink, whom it was a kindness, then, to bilk.

Mrs Culpepper had sent Mr Ascalon to sound out the Prisoner. She feared her marriage would outrage him, and wanted to know what he proposed to do. Unmask her as the murderess of Tscherkassoff, for instance? As the virtual murderess of her own father?

'No, no! A thousand nos!' cried Alphonso; he would merely unmask her as his wife.

Which was of course nearly as bad. Possibly worse, since he could probably prove his case, and be believed.

❧

'All rise for his Lordship!' cried the sheriff; and up onto his throne-like bench shambled Mr Justice Denman.

Alphonso had never imagined clothes so extremely red. He rose.

After a few minutes of rigmarole he was asked to plea.

Four hundred sets of eyes in the courtroom turned to him, the very core of the very core of the world.

'Guilty!' he said, the blanched-brown-yellow creature in the dock, face glowing in what little light that falls into the central court. The Manchester Crown Court is a dingy place even on days less black than this dreadful morning in March. 'Guilty!' he repeated. It was his *brindis*; it was the finest act in the world.

There was general gasp. There was agitation amongst defence counsel: this is not what even they expected.

The prosecutor gasped too.

Gasped Mr Arthur Culpepper, up in the public gallery, come to hear his wife give evidence.

Gasped the London journalists, here to report on the end of the famous Russian diplomatist.

Gasped Lady Orgreave, who had been until the week before Miss Rawkdon, and now sat as far from Mr Culpepper as could be, dressed with immense expense and bad-taste, with Sir Jocelyn's idle hand straying onto hers – she slapped it off – and again – .

Mr Justice Denman did not gasp. Gasping is one of the things judges do not do, even when there are self-stabbings in the dock, or gunfire from the witness-box. But he lifted his enormous eyebrows.

Denman was not a bad man.

Like any Red Judge he looked terrifying enough once he was bundled up in fur-and-scarlet robe, hood and mantle, in beneath that buckled shoes, stockings and breeches, in scarf, girdle and tippet, and above all in a full-bottom wig. Moreover his face, like face like the face of most middle-aged men who have eaten well, hung in rolls, which rhymed with his rolls of horsehair, and made him seem terrifying and inhuman.

Yet beneath his armour Denman was a merry fellow, who had rowed for Cambridge, who had been one of the greatest strokes of his generation; who translated Gray's Elegy into Greek because someone had to. A jolly port-loving man, Denman.

And he was considerably surprised. He went to lengths (for he was a conscientious man) to make sure the Prisoner knew what he was letting himself in for. He let the defence counsel whisper furiously to his client for some minutes. He offered an adjournment, which Alphonso firmly refused. He went to such lengths that the prosecutor coughed, and was punished with a baleful stare.

Yes, the Prisoner knew exactly what he was doing; he understood the English most well; he was prepared to accept the prosecution case, that he was a common thief, a clumsy one at that, who incompetently stabbed the old tall rich Englishman, and the young slender Russian baron with green eyes, all for nothing, getting himself in the process battered into a pulp and being caught. He would not plead against this (inherently unlikely) story. He knew what must follow.

Denman the pleasant rower and Classicist made a great pother of getting on his black death-cap. He wanted to make it clear to that impudent fellow the prosecuting Q.C. that there was something about the whole affair he didn't like the smell of.

Alphonso barely attended to the sentence, so full he was of a dreadful, very particular joy. He was dying in silence, dying defamed, dying without giving evidence or displaying his essential innocence. He was dying without speaking any truth, without explaining himself. He was dying to save – not Gladys. Gladys would be much better off freed from this Culpepper and acknowledged as his wife, as Señora Ñezgo y Escalofriante. She would be better off condemned as his accomplice; better off (transport! joy almost too extreme to picture!) hanged beside him.

His adoration for her, it will be seen, had reached the dangerous pitch of God's love for us: he did not mind killing her.

No, his guilty plea was nothing to do with Gladys. He was dying for another reason.

Last night Ascalon had come to him once again, for the prison Governor was an enlightened man, and thought all condemned papists were owed the opportunity of being badgered into abjuring their frightful superstition. Ascalon had come to him, mouthing and twitching from the opium that was Ascalon's little weakness, and presented him with a rather unseemly pamphlet, on paper thick and greyish. It was called *Twelve Years a Nun: or, The Licentious Foulness of Modern Babylon Exposed*, and was bound with *The Iron Rod of Antichrist and Protestant Liberty Compared; by a Brand from the Burning. With some Hints as to the Pretended Celibacy of the Romish Minions and the Credulity of their Dupes.* (This tract passed into the sugar-sack and so into my hands. It is as Victorian as Victorian can be and parts of it are still quite funny.)

'You'll find it ... enlightening,' sniggered Mr Ascalon, who was eager to slip away out of Strangeways and spend the ten shillings Mrs Culpepper had bought him with. 'Tee hee. I shall,' more loudly; the warder was walking past, 'beseech Heaven to let a shaft of pure gospel light pierce the misguided fastness of your soul. Amen.' And was gone.

Tucked into one the dirty booklet was a note, folded, sealed and perfumed. Alphonso smelt it for a whole minute before the broke the seal. Violets! Dewy violets from clean soil. Violets as understood by an deracinated unearthly creature as Clarisetta.

And her ink, too. Forming a very simple message: *Estoy con el niño. Es tuyo. No dejes que nazca para deshonrar.* It was clever of her to write in Spanish. Her victim would have understood in English; but he was moved, in his freezing Northern dungeon, to hear such news in his own tongue.

*I am with child. It is yours. Do not let it be born to dishonour.* As a stratagem the note (it's propped before me as I write: pah!) would have been masterful. What a clever way to stop Alphonso's mouth!

But as it happens it was true. A woman as used to adventures as Gladys Furlough always took precautions, but Alphonso had come upon her unannounced; there had been no time in those minutes to do anything; and sure enough, amidst all the death of this winter she had felt a quickening.

To die for his own son (somehow he knew it would be a boy) added a whole world of joy to Alphonso's sacrifice of himself. That is why his face glowed when he perjured himself by avowing the two murders; that is why he irritated Fr O'Shaughnassey so much during the three weeks before his death; why he was so bafflingly at peace; why he made such a troubling pure confession, and remained a model penitent – until the last second, when he spoilt it all, shouted the scandalous name, and plunged.

❧

Plunged, I see, a full ten feet and three inches. The Home Office issues at irregular intervals an *Official Table of Drops* to indicate the proper length of rope. The lighter the person the longer the fall necessary to ensure a thousand pounds of torque and thus a sharp snap without decapitation. This unrestful pamphlet had been given to Alphonso, I can't imagine whether kindly or not. Perhaps someone simply wanted to dazzle a foreigner with British engineering *nous*. In any case, it was in the sugar sack with everything else, and has passed into my possession.

His death was accurate, it was becoming. Perhaps everyone becomes the death that comes to meet him, trampling and goring; even if only by the way of mere disintegration, as is likely enough in my case. Nonetheless, I have calculated my own hemp as a spiritual exercise, a *memento mori*, and find that if I am hanged I shall be let fall seven foot ten inches. If a man as enormous as Zebulon Furlough had been the victim (as would have been suitable, after all), a mere five foot would have sufficed. But Alphonso plummeted ten foot and more, and I have no doubt smiled under his black hood the whole way down, as befits a great lover, a dynast, a hero of the arena – the global epicentre, the paradigm. Jolt! Crack! *Olé.*

## *ii.*

In late July a child was born to Mrs Culpepper, prematurely she insisted although it seemed sizeable enough: a comely, olive-skinned, black-curly-haired boy.

Arthur looked askance, but his own down-at-heel solicitor was in the throes of reaching agreement about marriage settlements with the shiny solicitors who served the Furlough family; he had already resigned his curacy and bought, on mortgage, a house in Battersea; he acknowledged him. The boy was pointedly christened Gerald, a traditional Culpepper name, and was handed off to one of Arthur's sisters as soon as was quite decent, or a little sooner. No one liked the way Mrs Culpepper looked at Gerald; she had the Medea touch and would certainly have strangled him if it had brought her any advantage. Thus she hurried through motherhood.

She hurried through everything now she had her freedom. Her father's house she wanted to rid of even before her baby appeared; she had ordered the servile Mr Crake to sell it at once. The best price she could get for Kettlehinge, uncomfortable and unimproved as it was (and is), was from Jokey.

He, with nothing else in the world, had been compelled to sell the Groblershoop ranch, cheap, and as quickly as he could. The sly Liverpool capitalist who harassed and cheated him went on his way rejoicing until it was found there were no diamonds in the diamond-bearing kimberlite of the mine, as is sometimes the case. He had cheated himself. The ludicrously-low price he paid Orgreave was just enough to buy back Kettlehinge.

Jokey returned merrily to the comfortless home of his fathers, although he was horribly disappointed to find that the Furlough interlude, which had changed nothing physically, had laid the ghosts. Perhaps the boiled family had been frightened away by moral horrors greater than their own.

Meanwhile, nothing could be more gracious than the manner of Lady Orgreave toward *poor* Mrs Culpepper, unless it were Mrs Culpepper's own manner to Lady Orgreave. The troublesome relations of Miss Rawkdon and Miss Furlough, in Spain and at the time of the great tragedy, were quite *quite* obliterated. Hester begged Gladys to stay on a guest while her own arrangements were made final, and Gladys charmingly gave way. They called each other sister.

It was only on the last evening, when they were all standing in the draughty hall watching Gladys' belongings being lifted onto the wagon, that Mrs Flange announced – we can guess what she announced. But Gladys could not: that is the curiosity. Since Mrs Flange had betrayed one Furlough to death, why would she not betray another Furlough to avoid being made to reside in a suburb? Since the French consul in Brighton had suddenly thrown over Mrs Flange, what was the continuing attraction of the South? Since Hester despised Gladys (most women despise their intimate friends, so far as I can see), why should she not plot against her? This is obvious to us; but not to the sly Mrs Culpepper; evidence that she was already in decline.

Perhaps every life enjoys a single zenith. If so, hers had been that evening in Christmastide, with her father's blood on her knuckles, her lover's fruitful seed within her, and her would-be rapist, the destined Governor of Perm, wriggling on her knife-end. Then, why then Gladys did stand alone, extreme and notable among the erring children of God. But since then she had becoming more and more common, a vulgar sinner; inevitably her wits were blunted as she descended.

In any case, Gladys gasped when Mrs Flange announced that she was not accompanying her *protégée* to Battersea as promised, but remaining behind as housekeeper of Kettlehinge. It was the post she had always wanted, all the more as Zoffany was clearly in his last decline, so that Virginia would have the management of the household entirely in her own hands. 'And I cannot leave *you* in the lurch, can I, dear Lady Orgreave?' – who smiled maddeningly and patted the shameless old woman's arm, glittering: her iron-rimmed spectacles had been transfigured into gold.

Then Mrs Culpepper gasped, then Mrs Culpepper uttered a wail of astounded dismay. She was outraged at this double-dealing (I have noticed time and again that the devilish people are often prigs). She flew on her former Companion, who scratched back. The two terrible young women hard to be parted by force by Sir Jocelyn, feebly aided by the hobbling footman called Leighton; he finally heaved Mrs Culpepper into the wagon by main strength and ordered the driver to 'Take this ruddy termagant away – to Hades if need be!' Off he trotted with Gladys, winded and swaying, shaking her fist over the end-gate at the occupants of Kettlehinge Hall.

Mrs Flange and Ascalon, the Orgreaves' clerical hanger-on, observed this brawl from a safe remove, a little way up the great staircase. Mrs Flange sighing over Victorian crassness; there had, perhaps, been more wrangling in Regency days, but at such a lower temperature. 'And look, Mr Ascalon, poor Leighton has lost some more teeth! And Sir Jocelyn's *black eye* …!'

Gladys, recovering her temper in an inn that evening, persuaded herself that she was leaving girlhood behind, and launching on a career that would be the wonder and terror of the age. She would regale, rollick and delve.

> *Corfes, Clivies, Deads, Meers, Groves, Rake-soil, the Gange,*
> *Binge oar, a Spindle, a Lampturn, a Fange,*
> *Fleaks, Knockings, Coestid, Trunks and Sparks of oar,*
> *Sole of the Rake, Smytham ….*

Yet in fact without Mrs Flange's guidance she proved a feeble adventuress. She declined and declined. Her something-missing, the uncanny lack that let her contemplate unspeakable acts, began to show through her pale blank girlishness. She was, perhaps, no nastier after meeting Alphonso than before. But she was the least bit more explicit, which was enough to wreck her career. Her inhumanity became apparent even to strangers. She repelled, she became instantly notorious wherever she went. Anyway she aged quickly, as silver blondes do; lead appeared, beginning at her temples.

Thus instead of ending up as, say, mistress to the Prince of Wales, Gladys found herself cheated out of most of her fortune by shabby younger men who chatted about her to their cronies with horror.

She wandered to Baden-Baden and New York and even San Francisco, nearly an outcast. She wandered back to Europe and in Berlin looked up her Saxon count, von Wallwitz, now on the Imperial General Staff. He did not much care for the shop-soiled look of her, and half-heartedly tried to recruit her to spy on England. Gladys had no objections as long as the pay as good, but on the way back, in Paris, she fell in with Roland Vidange, who had abandoned his post as *consul honoraire* to pose as a wild poet in the cafés. She threw herself at his susceptible head, and for a month or two had a fine time, pretending to be a muse, working her way through Wallwitz's gold, drinking absinthe all morning and going all night to lewd artistic parties. "'*Fell, Bous, and Konock-barke, Forstid-oar, and Tee,*'" she would recite, like a witch telling over her spells, and the most advanced Symbolistes would shudder delectably; '*c'est enculé moderne, n'est-ce pas?*' For Virgilia had taught her excellent French, in particular all the words English maidens are generally not taught.

Paris is in some ways a chaste city: even Parisian mistresses do not actually use such language. It is suitable, or so Vidange explained to her, '*Seulement pour l'intimité parfaite de l'état matrimonial,*' and the two suddenly found themselves in the *mairie du 18ᵉ arrondissement* being joined together in matrimony, in unholy matrimony, both bigamous and civil.

Naturally she shuddered, the so-called Madame Vidange, at taking on a cast-off of the traitress Flange. But the important things were to keep moving and to be safe. Wallwitz's money was almost gone, and Vidange, with his affluence, his poetic infamy and government connections, protected her from German agents – whom spotted now and then on the boulevards, staring at her balefully. Once they had broken into their *appartement* and disembowelled her poodle, using its blood to write *Deutschland, Deutschland, über alles* on the Chinese wallpaper. For had she not taken the Kaiser's coin? Was she not giving the Most Highest nothing in return?

As for Vidange: like every "advanced" Parisian artist he courted the

attention of the police. He longed for the mild martyrdom of a fine, free publicity, heavy sales *etcetera*, and therefore encouraged the muckiest verse from
his huge unfinished collection, *Pensées de Dégoût*, to circulate in manuscript.

But there is a golden mean to be followed even in the brownest gutter.
Pseudo-marriage undid Vidange. His lines kept failing to shock his *faux*-wife.
He pepped them up, and up and up. They grew more and more impossibly
obscene, until he had outrun the possibility of an 1879 *succès de scandale*.
What bores Paris in 1882 thrilled her in 1881, titillated her in 1880, disgusted
her in 1879, and would merely have bewildered her in 1878. That is the whole
secret of the *avant-garde*. Oh dear Lord, how often I saw the same game
unfolding in 1936 and 1937, 1938 and 1938. They're as crude as backward children, artists, and should be treated with pity.

Well, this was winter 1879, too soon, slightly too soon. One sleety evening
M. Vidange sat with his *Pensées* at a table in *La Closerie des Lilas*, laboriously
rhyming, *dans son cul* dum-de-*dum*, um, dum-de-*dum Dieu est nul* – when
he found the proprietor had snatched up the whole sheaf of his manuscript
verse and tossed it into the blazing hearth. '*Disparaître, maudit pornographe,*'
cried the enraged little man, '*et prends ta diablesse anglaise!*' All the intel-
lectuals began to bang their tankards on their table-tops, Zola, Monet and
Dumas *fils* leading. Vidange fled the café amidst hisses. It was the Greater
Excommunication: the church of free-thought was turning him out forever.

*Hélas! hélas!* Some other pioneer of indecency would win the credit, in
a few years' time, of outraging the particular shade of decency Vidange had
outraged in those crisping blackening sheets.

Meanwhile there was nothing to do but walk home through dirty weather – the cabbies had heard of his literary disgrace and (such is the French
reverence for culture) would not hear him when he hailed. When he got
home his door was open, his drawers were ransacked, his wife gone. She too
had heard, had taken every *franc* she had could lay her hand on and caught
the boat-train for Calais.

*Je me fais chier;* I have always adored Christmas-time, and hanker to
spend it amongst the snows of Chamonix; *mon cher Roland, petite bite,* is to
forgive my *impétuosité* and not worry one least bit; I shall be back by Epiph-
any: *tendresses*. That's what she wrote in the note she left for him. This was a
girl who liked to cover her tracks.

Then how fervently did Roland Vidange call upon the God Whose existence he had so denied in so many strenuous articles in so many reviews!
What vengeance he called down on Gladys!

❧

You will have been wondering we know all this. Well, the poor fellow gave up on poetry after this reverse and, retreating to Pau, composed his immense *Mémoires d'un Adonis modern*. The book was notorious in its day, I gather; it was suppressed for its multiple defamations by the Third Republic; it is now happily forgotten. I am sorry to say that Father James Emmanuel Joseph O'Shaughnassey, O.P. was so morbidly interested in the doings of Alphonso's girl that he found (Heavens knows how) a copy, purchased it (furtively I hope, avoiding scandal), read it, underlined it, and at last stowed it in his acid-green carton of horrors, for me to inherit and worry over.

He read carefully, as he always did, O'Shaughnassey, that addict of carnal novels. He has carefully annotated and dated every bitter reference in the *Mémoires* to "Nubilissima", as Vidange calls Gladys – not, we may be sure, out of gallantry or discretion, but because his coward heart quaked at Article 340 of the penal code, threatening bigamy with hard labour.

"Nubilissima": most dark one! Curious that Vidange's pet name should be the opposite of Alphonso's. I wonder what Arthur Culpepper called Gladys in the secret places of his heart?

No matter. To keep moving and to be safe, she returned to England. Surely she was  still silvery enough to bewitch men here and there? It seemed not. The West End would not dine her; St John's Wood and Pimlico drew back their suburban skirts; even Chelsea of the Decadents demurred. She returned to the North and endured a season as Stan Harbottle's kept woman, until he succumbed to heart disease during a weekend in Whitby, perhaps frightened to death. Now what?

Gladys turned respectable: the most desperate ploy of all. The so-called Madame Vidange reconciled herself, mock-penitent, with her real husband, who took her back, her and her money (which was really Vidange's). She tried to cajole her son Gerald, the bandit dauphin, now aged two. He carefully buried his strong white Spanish teeth in her thumb and might have got it off if Arthur had not pulled him away. Brave kind Arthur. Once more Mrs Culpepper, she bore him three pallid spinsterish daughters while trying to hustle along his career.

In this too she failed, for a satanic wife with a past is generally an impediment to a man in holy orders, even a handsome Anglican vicar of extremely broad views.

Moreover, I imagine her few months in the arms of the poet destined (so he said) to out-Baudelaire Baudelaire – not to mention her few seconds in the arms of Paul Tscherkassoff – spoiled her for Arthur. Arthur's looks were nice but not wolvish, and his milksop intrigues against the parochial Mother's League must have been merely irritating, after the Baron's espionage against empires, after Vidange's intrigues against every poet since Homer.

Culpepper ended as nothing grander than a Rural Dean, and reportedly had a great weariness about him, as Jason must have had after years of marriage to Medea.

No that there was any actual carnage. Gladys was turned away from, and turned away. Her energy went into gardening, ferocious gardening of Arthur's glebe and vicarage grounds: pruning, dead-heading, dunging, tearing-up, potting, cross-mating, poisoning, chopping-back: acts proper to our dealings with plants, improper with humanity, most of all with people who might love us.

⁂

And how did she end?

The strange answer is that she hasn't. Mrs Culpepper is still alive, aged eighty-two, at Bournemouth: in St Hilda's Approved Nursing Home for Relicts of Beneficed Clerics of the Established Church. As in most senile persons, her mind has peeled off its upper layers. She cannot remember yesterday, nor the crabbed years of maturity; only childhood and youth remain. I am sure she is often back in Spain.

Poor Gladys! She used coal-fires to force ranunculus so ruthlessly it was the wonder of agricultural shows in half-a-dozen shires. Now she's bedbound in a damp room with a single window-box of dwarf-elder: pale flat-topped hermaphroditic flowers, glossy black berries bleeding purple. She lies breathing those fœtid leaves and preparing for – what? A profane idea strikes me. The divine mercy may be so relentless it gives us absolute, everlasting liberty. Perhaps each lost soul chooses a place, and is not gainsaid. It designs for itself a hell it will deludedly call heaven. In which case the former Miss Culpepper, the pretended Madame Vidange, is on the brink of an eternity in Gladdy's Wapentake.

Meanwhile she lies at Bournemouth. That is all I know, all I can gather, that is, from gossiping with the Anglican Dean of Manchester and from studying directories. If there were not a war on I might travel to Bournemouth and contemplate her, not because she is, probably, the most abominable person in England (although that would almost justify a pilgrimage), but because she is a relic of Alphonso Ñezgo y Escalofriante, who may have been the best.

⁂

I am in thrall to Alphonso. In the last few weeks, as I have read and brooded and written about him, I have become, it may be, obsessed: obsessed with

Alphonso and his seed forever. Most of all with his seed.

What happens when destiny mates such great, such *unthinkable* goodness with such unthinkable iniquity?

My idea is that badness is weak. To reach its hugest strength needs to be grafted onto virtue, just as we graft greenhouse plants onto sturdy wild stock.

And Gerald Culpepper, then? There seems little to say. As far as I can discover, he was simply a shady barrister who hardly ever had a brief; who moved, or had to move, down to Devon; who was good-looking, in a swarthy fashion uncommon in England; who married a wealthy young woman whose money let him fritter away his idleness on yachts. He was, in short, one of the common herd who seem intent on hurrying through life and death into damnation on the most meagre terms, extracting the least recompense from the devil.

What a ill-tempered Pharisaical thing to have written: I apologise. It is because the air-raid sirens are sounding. I should go down to the crypt, which serves as the friary's shelter.

My theory is that vice and virtue reached a climax in that little Spaniard and that flat-chested Derbyshirewoman. Gerald, banally bad, disappoints it. But I do not give it up. Consider, as Gladys would want us to, botany: isn't hybrid vigour often a long time coming? The initial half-breed is without interest; but a few more generations and the new-bred reality, wonderful or terrible, shows itself.

Is it apparent yet in the further descendants of Gladys and Alphonso? Perhaps. Gerald's son Osbert joined the Colonial Service when young, and is at present making a horrible hash of things in East Africa, or at least that's what Dominic tells me. (I wrote and asked for confidential information, and got everything I could want. My brother's self-importance always trumps his devotion to duty. I tremble to think what will happen if some temptress from the *Abwehr* should come across him.) Osbert is about to be packed off to Matabeleland, having made the North West Frontier District of Kenya too hot to hold him. Some of the stories Dominic has passed on make the skin creep within my tonsure. So yes, in Osbert Culpepper, I believe we begin to see the fusion of absolutes. A few more generations and the horror may become sublime.

⁂

If I am right, which is the question.

The trouble is, I never met Alphonso. He perished a few years before I was born. All I have to go on is this archival cache. Here are the papers he stole, or was given, which he lugged about in his famous sugar-sack, which he gave away on the last night before he died. O'Shaughnassey read exactly the same materials, but he also had the privilege of some hours of Alphonso's company. And what a different story he came up with in *The Fetid + Deplorable + Tedious Affliction*! So was he right or am I?

I accept that at the core of O'Shaughnessy's account is a necessary hole. He records what Alphonso told him by way of reminiscence. But at the essential moment, when the Spanish boy knelt on the flags, the priest stops recording. Of his confession O'Shaughnessy is sacramentally bound to say nothing. Thus we cannot tell what, at the climax, Alphonso made of it all.

So here is just the debris of a life. Here is Alphonso trying to be his own storyteller. Here is O'Shaughnessy peering in, but faithfully concealing the main point. Here is me, peering over O'Shaughnessy's shoulder, knowing more but seeing less. And here is Hermann Göring hurrying down on us all, like an inrushing black angel of apocalypse, howling *Hurry hurry understand*, with a torch in his hand, shaking with flame, trailing sparks in its tail of fire.

The siren has been sounding for some minutes now. I have managed to ignore it, but I do need to go down to the shelter. The Manchester sky, blacker than black, *nubilissima*, is full of still blacker Messerschmitts roaring like bulls, trying to kill us, me, and to destroy along with us – well, I can't begin to list the targets. These papers, for instance: they want to obliterate *them*. I can picture (so luridly it seems more real than this actual quiet cell) the German bomb thundering through the brickwork above, into our muniment room: bricks themselves turned to roaring shrapnel, bursting back and forth; loud tearing of paper; then the crackle as it lights.

Terror, agony, violent death, sure ruin of our city, probable ruin of our civilisation; darkening of faith. The only consolation is to rearrange the historic blackness to make a human pattern, and for myself the one present consolation is this obscure ambiguous and lawless Spanish youth I never met, and have perhaps (I don't know) fabricated from stray papers.

Have I made myself clear? No? Perhaps my mind is too overshadowed by dismay.

I seem to discern in Alphonso the infinite. For the unamiable Gladys he dared to have his neck snapped in two, to turn into cooling meat for half-an-hour, then be dropped into Strangeways' quicklime pit, to melt into grease and nothingness. These are not the deeds of a mortal man.

He plunged so far, yet exulted. And he was not mad. Thus he must have been sure, not just of his own love, but of the potential of the universe to vindicate it.

When the dead are raised they will not be raised to *disappointment*: that is unthinkable. And Alphonso will not have shed his fixation with Gladys. Without that divine weakness he would not truly be Alphonso. So this is what follows (and what a lot follows from the fact!): in the renovation of all things, even Clarisetta Culpepper will have been made loveable.

# XI. Aromatic sulphonation,
## *Lent term begins*

As Felix Culpepper awoke one morning from troublesome dreams he found himself metamorphosed in his bed into a gigantic Kafka. He was lying on his hard & as it were armour-plated mind which seemed divided into stiff segments with its many legs wriggling helplessly in the air

*– NO – that's not what I want to say –*

I mean to capture without pretension infantilism or self-pity (however well-deserved) the knowledge of violation that overcame me waking an hour back to find my apparent night-horrors (cruel irresponsible dreams in un-wonted poor taste) simply *reminiscences* – not even exaggerated the flat truth being nightmare enough no padding or grotesqueries needed – & not some far-off hideous thing, it was in my own brain not to mention every cell – & not just reminiscences, *premonitions*, for I'd been *permanently* transfigured the evening before – I had become a Continental –

Not even a Central European, which perhaps I cd have borne, say a Mittleuropäischintellektueller if that's a word, I'm thinking of some haughty elaborate dour haunted godless seditious miscegenate polyglot – apt with irony provoking hollow laughter but essentially humourless.

*That* I might have worked with, indeed there's a touch of it in the family already – as well as a little French. But a *Spaniard*. A Latin, an Andalusian peasant. That's what leaves me tossing back & forth in an agon, weepy

*– nor that – that's not it –*

Arbitrary transmutation, *that* is what's been done to me, rape of every chromosome, Culpepper deculpeppered, my whole substance altered in a twinkling from without, like – what was the term Ebbe used? – *aromatic sulphonation* – that's it, the industrial process he did his doctoral work on, was perversely proud of, boasted of – sounds alluring, alchemical, but it's the opposite of alchemy, it's brilliancy rendered *base* – you take a perfectly effective ominous molecule, benzene, a mystic circle of carbon atoms, an ou-roboros or tail-biting snake, mercilessly burn it apart in bubbling sulphuric acid & you get (wait for it, wait for it) polystyrene – that is, filth indestructible, undecaying moonspit – dissolved refuse

*– NO*

*– screaming on paper doesn't help*

 – let me record simply, coolly, judicially. No point writing a hysterical memo to myself, what's needed is an anti-hysterical memo to myself. A re-collection –

 This is Monday morning the thirteenth morning of January in the disgraceful year MMXIV: the day before Lent Term begins & our irksome undergraduates return most significantly Margot who mustn't see me like this.

 Last night after the usual banquet marking the end of vac I came back in my rooms to drink Albert's gentian liqueur & read my present from the Cardinal.

 Oh at first, at first "Wapentake" was all I hoped, amusing quaint & faraway. Then, around midnight a third of the way through, I saw where it was going & became frightened. Bravely I read on & on & drank & drank; finished bottle; about 3:00 finished manuscript & flung myself (self!) into bed in distress, pulling over my head the blue Tlingit fur – horrendous-confusedly hoping, praying, it wd fade & be gone by morning.

 Whereas – whereas I awake as Alphonso's spawn.

 Hither, then, Powers non-existent or whimsical! Hither, Presences chthonic or terrene! Help me curse & revile each syllable of Towneley's damnable story, every jot, tittle, snippet & episode –

 Except the hanging of my gt-gt-grandfather. Which I applaud. These two friars go on as if it were a tragedy but why *shdn't* the little tyke be executed? It's not his death I wail at, it's his life, his love, procreation, his death-cell maunderings & the further maunderings of his monkish admirer.

 It's not death in general I object to, it's frantic obsessions, immortalising acts of faith – no wonder *auto-da-fé*'s an Iberian term – whereas – bloody *Spain* –

 In Africa last month I was myself. There are things to be said perhaps against my character but in *action* I am essentially wholesome, chopping with the grain of the cosmos – never more than when I slew Mbingu. Death's the large fact, great truth; what then, does it take to be a great man? Behold me on the side of nature, dispensing mortality, pandering for it, I, pro-death, who *am* death to many a bad man. I Felix Lowndes Osbert Baine am what I do. Behold a moral ecologist.

That is, I was what I was. This morning I am a changeling, stolen away by remorseless friars & archbishops –

I feel the whole sequence of universal event converging on me, piercing to the marrow, into the joining of marrow, into my brain, down through the cerebrum to the reptilian cortex – changing everything, *sulphonating* me, compromising my being, I who deludedly called myself Culpepper, called my self that, ex-self, x self, unmy self by alteration, self under-mine-d –

there! note the sound of a man turned Kafka, the *Continental* quality, clanking wanking second-language puns too-clever-for-his-own-good mode, too-clever-to-get-to-the-end-of-a-line-of-thought? This is exactly why foreigners have no pluck: in England a clever man is just-clever-enough to amuse himself & his friends –

I am stolen away. I am lost to myself.

I s'pose my true name's FÉLIX ÑEZGO.

Must have Clinker repaint the sign on my door, *ha-ha*, how surprised the Fellowship'll be.

I exist – no, this unrecognisable mongrel occupying Culpepper's body brain & donnish set – he *exists* as a consequence of some troubled common bloody foreigner of no interest. With the barbaric name Ñezgo. Who was morbidly enraptured by a butterfly dead on a sill. What else was Gladys Furlough – eh? & what business did he have putting this flake of rubbish sop tenderly in his palm?

How dare he assume that since he was going to live eternally he shd love infinitely, usurping the attitude of the gods? Dragging the dead butterfly up with him for all we know?

Alphie, Alphie, Alphie, grandpa at three removes: you've insulted death & me with it. You've shat down on me from half way up yr apotheosis, splat.

Mind: it's not the arbitrary injustice I object to it's arbitrary *justice*. Fate's amusing itself with vulgar resonances – a jingling doggerel of narrative irony – don't think I can't see the specious *fairness* of these events.

I revived the unhallowed memory of the Gladys Culpepper, fiend-gardener, I did evil with it. Bing! Through her evil is done to me. How trite, what a *petty* way for fate to balance the books.

I cuckolded a Hispanic bandit dynasty with a Hawick-Trocliffe baby. Bing! bandit Hispanics are allowed to cuckold the House of Culpepper, with Gerald the Baedeker baby, & ultimately with me. *Touché touché.*

You call that equity? If I rated this sort of order I'd have been a FUCKING CHARTERED ACCOUNTANT like my FUCKING FATHER.

Who sits in Westhumble nursing the family archives which I must get from him, perhaps there's something in them to let me off, the whole bundle of the paper called "Wapentake" might well be a priestly hoax, why didn't I think of that? How typical that wd be of His Eminence of the Hebrides, or that too-smooth Monsignor Hermenegild –

*– no I don't doubt – not really –*

I know the stink of fiction & "Wapentake" doesn't have it. It's not a trick – I feel myself, *know* myself permanently undone.

Or rather *done up* – that's the sensation. Folded into a larger story. I who was so self-creating am after all just an iteration of an old story. Family destiny teems about me, it envelops, I'm buried alive in its larger life.

I can't even cavil at the unfairness. I know how these things are plotted. A family's cursed with Gladys in retribution for Felix – her issue unto the third & fourth generation. A man's punished from birth for what he'll will do in his thirties (though, after all, these punishable deeds are *my job*).

The pseudo-Culpeppers spring from patricide not patriarch. An exaggerated return for a certain act I haven't committed yet. For I've just been asked to sort out the Home Secretary's domestic issues (how can a man administer England with family troubles like *this* on his mind?). I *thought* I hadn't decided whether to do it, it being a bit grim even for me. Now I see freedom's an illusion. Before the foundation of the world I bore this guilt.

Steady on then, Señor Fèlix Ñezgo, steady on. ¡*Valor!* Not to mention: ¡*Independencia!* May as well be hanged for a sheep as a lamb. Hanged for a ewe. Hey, ewe, does thou know who unmade thee, dost thou know who unmade thee? (Kafkakophany again.) Yr little baby blue. Yes, I may as well do it –

Why do I say "I"? We. She & me – it'll be Margot who decides. I'll tell her what I have in mind & if she dares I'll dare. I'll do it. No, she'll do, I'll tag along.

But will she? Will she? Won't she?

# XII. Dea ex machina,
## *a masque*

This man had in him a very noble power to be perverted; the power of telling stories. He was a great novelist; only he had twisted his fictive power to practical and to evil ends; to deceiving men with false fact instead of with true fiction.

CHESTERTON

In dumbshow we observe Felix Culpepper and his fivefold gang of rapscallions, Margot commandingly leading the boys, Felix trailing, preoccupied or reluctant or merely flattened. They are progressing up a blasted snowy postwar shopping street towards a seven-storied hotel.

Like so many streets spared by the Luftwaffe, this one is now tolerable only from twelve feet up. Above twelve feet, we can still make out florid brickwork, niches, the odd allegorical statue, solid sills, sash-windows, slate tiles, marble coping, and finally pediments and urns propped elegantly against the sky (which today is white heavy and cruel as an Atlantic swell). True, the architecture's neglected, mossed-over, with weeds growing from the lead drainpipes; but it's resilient. Once we've glanced up, it seems harder that ever to bear the endless twelve-foot-high taped-on strip of cheap plate-glass, coldly lit from within to show off glaring advertisements and evil goods: everything flimsy, polychrome and cheap as the Christmas decorations taken down a fortnight back.

We are in some provincial town or other, in what planners beseech us to call a pedestrianised precinct, although obviously pedestrians do not come. The skies are too cold to let proper snow fall; there are only light drops of icy rain, whipped back and forth through this shallow canyon: rain darkening as it falls, violently back and forth. It's a mystery how these harsh shopping streets always generate their own winds. Even on a still opulent afternoon in June grits blows in your face here. It must be a trick of physics – perhaps the raw-concrete walkways overhead, snaring any breeze and forcing it down, tormenting it, making it howl and raven between shop-fronts?

Real snow came overnight, but not enough to soften the blankness. The surviving drifts, whipped into corners like dirty *crème Chantilly*, merely add an Eastern European cast to the streetscape. We might almost be in Smolensk or Łódź in the last days of Brezhnev. The fact that this is January 2014, after three decades of nearly unbroken prosperity, does not mitigate, it's part of the problem. England (for this is really England; this happens to be Birmingham), England is awash with money that flows almost everywhere. It will soon reach even this dismal street, and wash it away. The hopeless chain-restaurants and the dirty clothing-shops know this. So why bother tarting themselves up? They know they're the last of the damnable twentieth century, folded into an unclean wrinkle in history, sure to be scraped out – that they're despised by the immediate future, and looked down on by Edwardian prosperity twelve feet above. That asphyxiating stink is not just poverty or ugliness, it's self-contempt.

We smell it because we are sensitive. Clearly, the six young or youngish people trudging briskly up the street toward the hotel notice nothing. They talk to each other and do not sniff or glance about. If asked they would say, surprised, there's nothing to glance at. Smooth Róbert Zseni was born and bred in a glorious *Beaux-Art* palazzo beside the Danube. Brainlessly-cheerful Seb comes from a large house, mainly Jacobean, on the Cornish coast. Kindly Ollie, dourly-handsome Tristan, arrogant Margot and moody Felix are, in various senses, Londoners. Birmingham for them all is "the North," nowhere; to notice that it's dismal would be like noticing the ocean is wet; the only impression it makes is a vague one of emptiness. Shouldn't more invisible Northerners perhaps be looking *at them*?

For they're worth looking at, in their way, not just for dark green Barbours and red trousers and Margot's sable scarf, but for their clobber. The party walked from the railway station to a local stationers' and stocked up, in obedience to Felix's principle that all capers must be thrown together *ad hoc*. They're now laden – not Felix, not Margot, just the unimportant youths – with white plastic bags and manila boxes. In the boxes are a printer, a large digital camera, rolls of newsprint, staple-guns: enough equipment to self-publish an illustrated novel.

The time is late or rather too-late morning, a morning that's gone on and on until it's wearied itself, and longs to die into lunch and cannot. The emptiness of the street grates, the quietness aches.

The tall postmodernist hotel, first sign of gentrification, has been (God help us and forgive us all) *designed*. It would be shiny if the daylight were less dull, and it bulks over them as they approach, slightly fatter at the top than at its ground-floor of amber-tinted glass, where we see standing sandwich-board advertising THE CONSERVATIVE WOMEN'S ORGANISATION ANNUAL CONFERENCE.

Two world-weary policemen, one with a listless machine-gun on a strap, guard the bright atrium from the wicked world beyond. Felix produces paperwork, which he hands to Margot. Margot flourishes it in front of the police: passes, it would seem, from the Department for Culture, Media & Sport, each masterfully signed *Patricia Maule*, granting our heroes pseudonymous access to hotel and conference. Well done, good and faithful servants, enter into joy.

And it does look joyful within, at least by comparison with the blasted street. Enormous green and orange tapestries hang from upper floors into the lobby, where a vast gas-fire dances in a bogus chimney of dark brick. There are low black cubic leather armchairs, glass tables, trees in pots, heavy off-white rugs of tangled stuff. Happy twenty-first century! Fortunate third millennium of Our Lord! The glass doors swing behind our heroes, engulfing them in its warmth and plenty.

The receptionist is chatty. (As it happens she is a good woman; dim in intellect, yet radiant; none of this has any effect on events.) 'Bless us yes *all* the Conservative ladies are up on floors C to E it's how they like it, running in and out of each other's room and getting up emergency motions to the Chair it's quite the party, only the key-note speaker's way up on the top in 720 that's our ginormous suite totally *de luxe* it looks out both ways you can see Villa Park meaning not in this weather such a pity for the ladies this cold I wish it would snow properly don't you? Of course we call it the honeymoon suite, 720 I mean, how she blushed at the name such a dear, there's her P.A. next door of course in a sort of alcove but he's always asleep, anyway otherwise the top floor's empty are you really sure you want to be up there? And how many rooms for you all, how many nights – oh, three *hours*, my goodness, *one* room, well it takes all sorts, what a lot I'll have to tell the night-shift, and now may I just have a card to put on our records? What you say, cash? *Now?* Please yourself it's ever so unusual we don't see cash year in or year out but it – oh yes, here's the key, have a good whatever, ta-ra.'

The conspirators have set up shop in their room on the top floor.

There's a chaos of opened boxes and emptied bags about their room, as if in demonic parody of Christmas morning. They all have tumblers, and there's a bottle of clear liquor open on a bedside table: a bottle without label, being one of a dozen in a pinewood crate dropped off at the Lodge the week before, addressed CULPEPPER, WYGEFORTIS, CAMBRIDGE on a printed slip. (That's all it takes to hit the cosmic bull's-eye from any circle of the inhabited universe.) No sender, no stamps: the crate was clearly a product of that alternative universe which has no use for post offices, or shipping companies, or the customs-inspections, of little people. Culpepper had had Mrs Muckhatch open it with her strong fingers out in Megiddo Court, while he remained inside his stone walls, well away from windows. He'd then gone out and poked with a metal rod at the straw, presumably Mexican straw, which hid no steel trap. He'd sniffed the straw with trepidation; finally bore a bottle to the Psychology Fellow, Wayne Scuff. Scuff will drink anything, and is ostentatiously expendable. Culpepper watched him guzzle it like firewater for an hour, and pronounce it excellent, before sipping any himself.

It was the most wonderful tequila Culpepper had ever come across, the best conceivable of the style called *blanco*, young peppery stuff, still shiny with cactus-heart oil, scented with grass just scythed and pears sliced open. Every sip calls to mind an Aztec Eden, turquoise agave-fields, yellow wildflowers, orange buttes, purple mountains; calls to mind, too, what cannot really be pictured, Ebbe in mid-metamorphosis, full of dark exultation, or evil forgiveness.

So that's what they're drinking.

Seb has made himself very comfortable on one of the twin beds; he's exhibiting his skill at pouring from a glass, prone, without dribbling into his ears. As always he grins, but grins in a far-off fashion; the taste of tequila has enraptured his small wits; he's all-too-obviously reminiscing about nights and days with Benita.

The other boys sit about the floor and sip more normally.

Felix has his back to them all, standing at the enormous chilling window, gazing out at the slits in blackish concrete oblongs which is Birmingham from above. He swishes his glass moodily, the motion of a man rattling ice-cubes – not of course that he's added ice, which would be atrocity, it's not nice to joke of such things. He's watching granulated ice blast up and down the slits and is perhaps unnerved by the vista. (We shoot spies at dawn because then they care less, life seems a flabby chilly cranky thing as well lost, but perhaps we should always kill people in Birmingham.) Or perhaps he doesn't care about the view and is unnerved by himself, by himself at this late stage of development.

Margot is seated on the other bed like a vizier dispensing justice from a diwan. She is evidently in the blessèd state (or not) of those who can no longer be unnerved. Blessèd or not, she has clearly undergone an ageing. It's hard to credit she's as young as the boys, and much younger than Felix. There's an inauspicious air about her of den-mother.

She just addressed the troops. There follows a pause.

'Who, by the way,' asks Tristan carefully, the lawyer's son, swilling his spirit, 'asked us, you, Dr Culpepper, to do what we've just done?'

'Us. I don't think you need –'

'The Home Secretary,' says Felix in a dead voice, not turning. (Even Seb is impressed by this, and Róbert whistles.) 'M.I.6. *wouldn't*, perhaps –'

'A bunch of worthless Brackenburys,' says Margot dismissively.

'Of *what*?' asks clever Róbert, thinking it something new in inexhaustible English.

But Ollie, whose conscience stirs now and then, is frowning. 'He asked us to do it *himself*?'

'One of his underlings passed the order on,' says Margot briskly; and whether she believes this, or believes that dark-eyed Patricia Maule will believe she believes it, is a pretty question. (What Felix believes is less to the point.)

Seb chuckles softly to himself.

'Will someone hand me the 'phone?' comes the toneless voice of Felix, who might be brooding on anything at all.

'*Sí, amigo*,' says Margot, to whom he has unwisely confided the contents of "Wapentake" before burning the thing (unthinkable to let the Widdler have it). '*Es tiempo.*'

Culpepper scowls at the jibe, which nobody else notices; meanwhile Tristan hands the 'phone to Margot, she to her persecuted lover. He taps 7-2-0, *blick blick blick*. Everyone falls silent, just making out with their young ears the *dwrib-dwrib, dwrib-dwrib, dwrib-dwrib, dwrib-dwrib*. But they can't, fortunately, hear Culpepper's thoughts: *Seven hundred and twenty's a harshad number,* harshad *being bad Sanskrit for* joy-giver: *seven and two and zero are nine, nine eights are seven twenty: joy. All is fated. Seven hundred and twenty is factorial, one times two times three times four times five times six. Forty-seven thousand million light-years to the outer circle, me in the middle, everything pressing in.* 'Good morning, good morning!' His voice is suddenly bright, mildly Geordie. 'This is the concierge. I have a reporter from *Oi!* magazine here. She's brought a photographer! Might she speak to the great one? Thank you.'

And he hands the 'phone to Margot, who says 'Good morning!' in something like Scouse. They really don't need to cover their tracks like this, the Home Office will look out for them; but such criminal flourishes reassure (or amuse) the boys. 'How *nice* of you to talk to me! What we're hoping for is just a *few* snaps, *in* the lobby, *ten minutes* of your time, for a featurette on the best-dressed influence-wielders of our day.'

Refained syllables flutter excitedly, indistinguishably from the 'phone.

Margot rolls her eyes. 'But', whispers Róbert, painstaking student of the class-system as are all-too-many foreigners, 'won't she despise *Oik*?', which is what people like them call *Oi!*; 'A featurette's a featurette', whispers back hardbitten Tristan.

*Seven hundred and twenty degrees*, reflects Felix, *is twice about a circle –*

> *Here we go round the mulberry bush ....*
> *Here we go round the mulberry bush*
> *On a cold and frosty morning*

*– prick of an* azufaifo *bush – compulsion, divine madness – for one person, incomparable, unrepeatable – love unto death, love becoming death, becomingly – no, no new thing under the sun, a quadrillion years then no sun – all-death, love nowhere.* It's the inner yacking of a mind not necessarily breaking up, but trying itself out to feel what break-up might feel like.

Margot gets a word in: 'No, no, no, no false modesty! We want to catch your Look just before your Big Speech. Oh yes, we'll *quote* from the speech! Never you fear! *Oi!* adores you, it's you – The lobby in two minutes, *thank you*,' and rings off. It's too easy; it's almost always too easy.

Outside every hotel-room everywhere stretches the corridor. This one's as bleak in its way as the street without. For it has, alas, been furnished with an idea, which is pretentious-Zen-grey. The long, long carpet is the colour of still water at dusk, with a border of near-soot, the walls are slate when it rains, and in each fog-painted niche a granite stand holds for our contemplative pleasure a rock: a big black glassy curvaceous igneous rock fretted with suggestive holes. At one end of the corridor a high thin window lets in a very little ghastly bluish light from Birmingham's winter. At the other is the lift, standing open, a white sanctuary; between are expensively-underpowered lamps set at intervals between the mystical stones. Each lamp bears a rounded shade, so glossy and rumpled it might a vitrified human brain: it seems fashioned of grey porcelain, a grey porcelain temple. The extreme dimness makes the corridor appear very long, a *via dolorosa*. No good can come of it.

Room 720, near the tall minimalist window, is the honeymoon suite, largest in the hotel, which is why it was taken, with many a winning blush at the name. Its door flies open, and a stout female form trots forth in a most fetching pale-jade trouser-suit. Along she goes, past the funereal rocks, past the room where the assassins lurk (their door imperceptibly ajar); on and on toward the lift, still open, which this bustling woman doesn't wish to lose. Even from behind we can be sure it's Mrs Marigold Littlejohn, so Marigold-esque are the movements, nippy, emphatic, reproachful, aggressively neat. The way she pats her perm! The way she twists her brooch! She's the very image of a woman due to deliver an uplifting speech in the hotel ballroom this very evening, full of spry demands for certain Party leaders to hold lines, bite bullets, roll sleeves, since battle royal is joined – leadership, Dunkirk spirit, have done with half-measures, put away mealy-mouthed work-shy shilly-shallying: phrases which everyone present will recognise as slaps at her "Wet" son.

He's being perfectly good at present, post-oyster, quite slavish. He's even keeping some of MacPharlain's victims in prison to please her. But she knows better than to let up on spanking when he's down; not if he's to be the next Prime Minister, not if she's to command England.

She needn't worry about missing the lift, its door stands motionless, it awaits her as if it were a festal car to carry her down to her adorers. The practical Marigold conceives none of these prosy images, she pops straight in and – without fuss, with only the hint of a flail, only the slightest jerking back, certainly without any shriek – drops nightmarishly through the floor and is gone.

Without hurry, the gang emerges from their room. They inspect. The large tear in the floor of the lift is a paper-tear, and when they reach in and start to pull, the wall frays, it comes away, it slashes and twists into shreds. We grasp that it's all just paper: photographs of a lift interior, printed on big sheets, taped and stapled into place.

The sound of gashed paper is always terrible. It won't last long. In a moment they'll bundle the newsprint and masking-tape into a medicine-ball-sized wodge and carry it into their room. The lift-shaft will be revealed, bare brick with steel struts, cables dangling down through the dim void. Ollie will peer through the door down the shaft; shake his head (for its seems that down in the basement she'll still be wriggling in a peevishly, Marigoldesque fashion). Ollie will stare up the shaft; pull his head back; remove the stapler which is wedged into the doors to hold them open. As they shut, he'll push the button to summon a lift from above; the doors will open and reveal – *hey presto!* – an interior almost identical to the interior of art, but radiant with the quiddity of things that do not merely exist on paper. This is the radiance that makes literature so pointless. Margot, the commandrix, will press button B, the doors will gently shut, and down the car will go to the basement to render those crisply-ironed pastels on the concrete floor a star of elemental crimson. Death enters in at many doors: by violence, by secret influence, by the fall of a chariot. Seb alone, half-human, will strain to detect the crunch, and will have to be pulled away by his peers, bored now, eager to get away and catch the 1:10 back to Cambridge.

All that is about to happen, is the future; as are the sensational headlines FREAK ACCIDENT BLIGHTS TORY CONFERENCE, and MARTIN LITTLE-JOHN HELPED FROM COMMONS (illustrated by a photo of the poor man, both hands carefully clapped to his face), and SAD FUNERAL AT ST MAR-GARET'S: HYSTERICAL LAUGHTER OF BEREAVED HOME SECRETARY, and LITTLEJOHN INQUEST: MISADVENTURE, and then, increasingly, wild stories about Out-of-Hand Littlejohn, as he will soon be known: GRIEVING MINISTER CONSOLES SELF DANCING ON TABLE AT RONNIE SCOTT'S WITH MYSTERY DARK LADY.

That's what's to come. Now is the more terrible moment when paper's being noisily ripped away. Huge rends fork across the sheets. Tristan and Róbert brace themselves on the wall and hold the wrists of Ollie and Seb, who lean over the abyss to tear the false lift interior off the back wall of the lift-shaft – a reality so dreary it is hardly a thing, it is nothing. They hand back the torn sheets to Margot, who bundles them up. It's much like the process of ten minutes before, when they taped the sheets up, only backwards. It's simpler and faster to pull off than to stick up.

Felix is unhelpful, he stands detached. Perhaps a vicarious matricide seems to him hardly here nor there. What with his ancestral father-killing, what with the watery sororicidal tinge in his own past, it may not matter to him. Were the Furies to descend out of the bleak Brummie sky, giant bat-wings squeaking closed as they cleared the hotel skylight, bony feet defiling the carpeting as with black blood, fleshless forefingers extended, eyes shot with rage, smoky torches guttering, scourges raised, Culpepper would prob-ably smile: smile just as bemusedly as he smiles now.

He stands and watches. He's perhaps in that state of mind where a man or woman's life seems no more than a short tube: drop sperm and egg in at top; shake; out the bottom falls sperm or egg; such is individual existence. All the incidents and qualities we fuss about – evil and good, education, expe-rience, love, crime, faith, thought – are bunches of colonic cells, nourishing or pumping us down the bloody pipe. Here, now, was an another incident; a woman-killing; well, he was indifferent to it.

Indifference is not neutral, it asserts. Indifference begs the question and Culpepper knows it. If such an act as this matters in the least (he reflects), it matters without limit. If the universe makes sense it forms a single story. The noise of this crime must (Culpepper thinks) be heard forty-seven thousand million light-years away, dampening the quasars out there at the edge. Those everlasting pulsations of joy fuel themselves on in-falling solar systems, as our own fireworks burn grains of gunpowder; yet (he admits to himself) their glory must be less because Marigold Littlejohn is slain.

The gashing of paper must even penetrate Cambridge, ninety miles off, and the enclosed appalling little world of St Wygy's. Where once again the Master has retreated from his duties into the still smaller but more capacious world of his Book of Hours. If all that happened made obvious sense, he would now glance about troubled, trying to find where the ripping noise is coming from, wondering whether the one imperfect page in his book (the one lacerated when the young king died) was haunting him.

It's simpler to destroy an artifice than to make, and now, curiously loud but absolutely unresisting, the image-forming paper is rent, it goes to shreds. This is the ending of illusion, as

      regret


                                                          show,
                              the bare
                                                riven spaces
                                                        pared

      slivers of
        hang


                                strips

# *Epilogue:*
# Of the Culpeppers

THE NITCH,
CRABTREE LANE, WESTHUMBLE,
SURREY   RH5 6BS

*20/1/2014*

What follows is a genealogical note, composed with reluctance for his son Felix, who demanded it, by Winston Culpepper, F.C.A.

The Culpeppers, whose name has been misspelt in many different ways, all painful to me, were originally a Sussex family. By the twelfth century they were already of what old books call "gentle rank", which is not to say that any of them were ever in the least gentle.

In Edward III's time **Sir John Colepeper** [*sic*] built Oxon Hoath at West Peckham in Kent.

His great-granddaughter, the co-heiress of Oxon Hoath, was **Jocasta Colepepyr** [*sic*]. Jocasta married above herself, to a duke's son, Lord Edmund Howard. Their daughter was Katherine Howard, Henry VIII's fifth queen, who was convicted of adultery with her distant cousin **Thomas Culpeper** [*sic*]. Both parties were beheaded, as was proper; indeed Thomas was fortunate to escape preliminary emasculation and disembowelment. I am glad to say that the popular fable, which has Katherine exclaiming on the scaffold "I die a Queen but I would rather die the wife of Culpeper [*sic*]", is nonsense. She apologised becomingly for her "heinous offences" and did not mention our unfortunate family at all.

Her paramour was not so discreet. Thomas Culpeper left behind a packet of scabrous papers, including letters from the teenaged Queen. His family quite rightly kept the papers out of the hands of King Henry's officers, and away from public view, but did not burn them as of course they should have. Instead, the packet became the basis of the Culpeppers' deplorable secret archive.

This archive is, as is desirable, uncatalogued. I have looked through it haphazardly. There seems to be not one item that ought not to have been destroyed at once, or better yet left unwritten: not one item that does not distress me.

But enough of these personal reflections.

The adulterous Thomas' heir was his first cousin **William Culpeper** [*sic*], who, although rapacious enough for confiscated monastic lands, apparently lived and died a papist.

Most of the later Culpeppers, however, conformed to the Established Church without, as far as I can see, conforming to any recognisable principles of religious, or even merely human, behaviour.

William's great-grandson **John Colepeper** [*sic*] had, according to Clarendon's *History*, a "wonderful insinuation and address", as has been true of too many of his descendants. He served King Charles during the Civil Wars as Chancellor of the Exchequer, for which he was in 1644 created Baron Colepeper [*sic*] of Thoresway, and given a grant, at the time entirely theoretical, of five million acres in the distant Plantations of Virginia.

Lord Colepeper was overshadowed by the career of his cousin "*Nich. Culpeper* [*sic*] Gent., Student in *Phyſick* and *Astrologie.*" **Nicholas** was a Roundhead, and one of the most notorious alchemists of the age, solemnly accused of witchcraft by the Society of Apothecaries. The same year the Colepeper peerage was created for his loyal cousin John, the wizard Nicholas published *A Prophesy of the White King; and Dreadfull Dead-man Explaned*, prognosticating, nay inciting, King Charles' execution. Some of Nicholas' other writings, too terrible for print, remain, alas, in the family collection.

The Restoration made real the family's theoretical New World holdings. John the Chancellor's son **Thomas, second Baron Colepeper** [*sic*], became not merely Governor but proprietor of Virginia, the Crown having confirmed his enormous estate. He owned, as it were, America.

Bishop Burnet, in his *History of My Own Time*, condemns the Governor as "a vicious and corrupt man", and a contemporary account by his subjects calls him "one of the most cunning and covetous men in England." This seems to be no more than the truth. He misruled Virginia. His main contribution to the Culpepper family papers is an outrageous memorandum boasting of his peculations from his own colony's treasury. There is also a "sprightly" or as I would say unseemly essay in praise of slavery, so lubricious I admit I have never been able to finish it.

Governor Colepeper, despite all the favour his family had received from the Stuarts, returned to London in time to push forward the deposition of James II.

He was a thief, then, and a traitor. "More than that, he had flagrantly offended public opinion, and embarrassed even his friend Charles II, by a cynical disregard of appearances in domestic relations": that is, he lived for years in open concubinage with a Miss Laycock (although she went by other names). He defied the ideal of monogamy, and the yet higher ideal of property, by trying to leave both the Colony of Virginia and his English estates to the Laycock and to their bastard daughters, rather to his wife and their legitimate daughter, Catherine. A private Act of Parliament was required to overturn this will, "to remedy the said frauds and wicked practices, to relieve Lady Culpeper [*sic*] and her daughter, and for deterring people from committing the like frauds and deceits for the future".

The Governor's illegitimate girls thus got only a little money, and sank into obscurity. His colonial empire passed, after litigation and pother, to Catherine, who married into the Fairfax family; her Fairfax descendants held it until the American Revolution. The barony passed from the Governor to his dissipated brother Cheney Culpeper, who killed an officer of the Guards with a blunderbuss. Cheney was pardoned, but he was wifeless, and with him the title became extinct.

So much for the Culpeppers? Unfortunately, no.

What is not generally known is that in old age the second Lord Colepeper, ex-Governor of Virginia, faithless to the last, faithless even to his concubine, was presented with a bastard son, **Charles**, born to his very young French maid Adélaïde.

I am phrasing this as carefully as I may. To Adélaïde, and to Charles, Lord Colepeper left the egregious Culpepper papers. Adélaïde added to them her own atrocious manuscript memoirs, in seventeenth-century French *argot*, composed with a view to blackmail. I am relieved to say I cannot entirely understand all mademoiselle's terms, but I understand enough to see that Charles' paternity is, to say the least, uncertain.

Nonetheless her boy, bred up for the law, used a version of the Colepeper [*sic*] name. He also assumed the family arms, I am not sure with what show of approval from the College of Heralds, adding a *baton sinister* as a "mark of difference" for bastardy. But Charles did not use the ancient family motto, *J'espere,* perhaps finding it insipid. He adopted instead a punning formula signifying, in feeble Latin, *The more burning and coal-black the pepper, the greater the pleasure.*

Charles FitzCulpepper's descendants still – I had almost written *flourish*; let us say *survive*. Or *continue*. I have just made a sketch of a genealogical tree to demonstrate the fact, which I attach. We continue. We have not flourished at the Bar, nor in the Church, nor in the Forces, nor in any art or science. Indeed we have been, on the whole, I think it is fair to say, pestilential wastrels. That we maintain our upper-middle-class credentials, and remain affluent enough, it is largely due to mercenary marriages.

My great-grandfather **Arthur** secured a vulgar rich girl named Gladys

Furlough, very long-lived. She survived to dandle me on her knee for a few seconds before thrusting me off (I am told), remarking "Nasty pudding-faced English brat." Which I do not resent in the least. In old age my great-grandmother had grown disgusted with humanity *tout court*; her demonic energies went on flowering plants. Anyway, babies *do* tend to be lurid. They are rarely subdued to the proper quietness human life requires. My own children revolted me when very young, especially, let me say it outright, my son. There was to be no mellowing later on in that case; on the contrary, I have felt no enthusiasm for him, that is, for you, since infancy, and have often sighed over you, wondering "Where is that baby?"

But I was saying. Arthur and Gladys' own son, my grandfather **Gerald**, grew up to be a ne'er-do-well, darkly handsome, swarthy in fact, a trait soon bred out of the family. He wed pale Margaret Baine, another an heiress of sorts. I'm sorry to say her brother Ernest left her not just a "tidy" sum but a most *untidy*, indeed indecent manuscript, barbarously titled *Bād-i-sad-o-bīst-roz*, detailing devilish happenings in colonial India. It was added to the Culpepper trove, as if that were not already quite improper enough.

Gerald begat **Osbert** and Osbert begat myself, along with my two more splashy brothers. Enough of that.

We *continue*, buoyed up by Furlough and Baine money; possibly retaining the Culpepper character. By "we" I mean the family at large. For myself I have been at pains to avoid having a "character" of any sort, personality being, like brightly-coloured ties, unuseful in any decent course of life. It is certainly deleterious in accountancy, tainting the impersonal scientific perfection of double-entry book-keeping.

Double-entry book-keeping is, as I often told my children, to no avail, a lovely thing: the one source of absolutely reliable truth in this age's universal wildness. I am aware you, Felix, did not take me seriously, nor Gertrude, nor the other one, now dead. You thought I sounded like a fossil and no doubt that is what I am. I do not wish to know anything of these times. I do not belong to them and do not wish to sound or look as if I belong to them, nor indeed, to be frank, to this lawless family of ours.

Be that as it may: the family retains Charles FitzCulpepper's name (now trimmed of the cognomen *Fitz*), his unfortunate maxim or slogan, his arms, with baton discreetly dropped, and, I regret – to repeat myself – to say, his *cache* of archival documents.

I don't know how it is, but with the bad example before them of the Queen's lover, too many Culpeppers over the centuries have been moved not just to write prose, which is unwise enough, but to write wicked, confessional prose. Our family weakness had continued into recent times. I am thinking of the Betting Book kept by my grandfather and bequeathed to my father (although this seems to have disappeared); the shameful journal of my uncle Wilfred, sometime Archdeacon of Totnes; and the dictated deathbed confession of my triply unfortunate brother Neville. All of these should be ash and are not.

I have been troubled by the Culpepper Papers for some forty-eight years, in fact since my brother's bizarre accident, when I reluctantly inherited custodianship. How often I have tried to "screw my courage to the sticking-place" and burn the lot! Or, less flamboyantly, tear everything up. I think it would soothe me, hours and hours of a ripping noise, and then a stillness, with harmless scraps lying all about like a white moat.

Well, it hardly matters, since I never did prevail against my qualms. As my mother (a difficult, scornful and flippant woman) often remarked, I rarely do prevail.

You will remember I attempted to pass the Papers on to you, to my son **Felix**, on the occasion of your election to a post at St Wygefortis' College, with which the Culpeppers have had a long, intermittent and, on the whole, unfortunate connection. You refused, and I was therefore surprised to receive your brusque letter a week ago asking for them after all, and for this memorandum, which I have composed without relish.

I am happy, no, not that. I am *relieved* to pass the Papers on to you. That is the point of this covering note, which is my only contribution (it goes, I should think, without saying) to the whole unfortunate collection.

I should be grateful to have a short note of receipt.

Why do you want the Papers, though? I hope you are not taking a morbid private interest in family affairs. I dread to think you contemplate publishing any of them. Is it just a sense of shouldering the dishonour of being head of the Culpeppers, or what is left of us, as soon as I am dead? In that case I will not despair of your settling down, Felix, although it is already idle to hope that you will *not* live up (or rather *down*) to the family motto:


*quantum fervidior carbo piperque,*

*tantum*

*maior voluptas*


W.B.C.

# THE CULPEPPERS

My great-great-great-great-great-grandfather,
Charles Laycock FitzCulpepper, solicitor and rake
1688-1750

Capt. Theophilus FitzCulpepper, R.N.; privateer; Deist pampleteer
1730-1783

Augustus FitzCulpepper, Perpetual Curate of Healaugh in the North Riding of Yorks.;
condemned (1803) to penal transportation, but returned; 1775-1836 (suicide)

Tancred, adopted name Culpepper (pronounced Culper) by deed poll 1836; Rector of Orton, Westm.;
pseudonymous author of *Amicus flagelli, Onus Tyri, Visio peccatorum Ninevitarum, Δάφνις καὶ Χλόη καὶ ἐγώ, &c.*
1810-1871

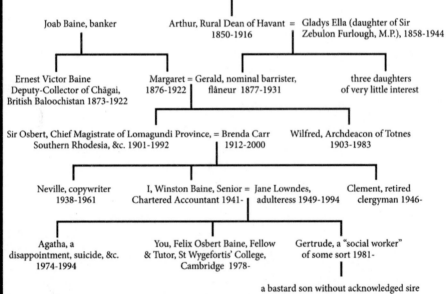

| Joab Baine, banker | Arthur, Rural Dean of Havant = Gladys Ella (daughter of Sir |
| | 1850-1916    Zebulon Furlough, M.P.), 1858-1944 |

| Ernest Victor Baine | Margaret = Gerald, nominal barrister, | three daughters |
| Deputy-Collector of Chāgai, | 1876-1922   flâneur 1877-1931 | of very little interest |
| British Baloochistan 1873-1922 | | |

Sir Osbert, Chief Magistrate of Lomagundi Province, = Brenda Carr    Wilfred, Archdeacon of Totnes
Southern Rhodesia, &c. 1901-1992    1912-2000    1903-1983

| Neville, copywriter | I, Winston Baine, Senior = Jane Lowndes, | Clement, retired |
| 1938-1961 | Chartered Accountant 1941-  adulteress 1949-1994 | clergyman 1946- |

| Agatha, a | You, Felix Osbert Baine, Fellow | Gertrude, a "social worker" |
| disappointment, suicide, &c. | & Tutor, St Wygefortis' College, | of some sort 1981- |
| 1974-1994 | Cambridge 1978- | |

a bastard son without acknowledged sire
or recognisible given name, born 2007,
heir-presumptive to all this bloodguiltiness

QUANTUM FERVIDIOR CARBO
TANTUM MAIOR VOLUPTAS